A GRAPHIC NOVEL FROM
The LAND *of* STORIES

GOLDILOCKS

WANTED DEAD OR ALIVE

CHRIS COLFER

illustrated by
JON PROCTOR

L B

Little, Brown and Company
New York Boston

About This Book
This book was edited by Alvina Ling and designed by Christina Quintero and Ching N. Chan.
The production was supervised by Virginia Lawther, and the production editor was Jen Graham.
The text was set in CCComicrazy, and the display type is Bulmer MT Std.

Lettering by Maria Caritas, Dwi Febri Novita, Dies Caya of Caravan Studio.

Little, Brown and Company
Hachette Book Group
1290 Avenue of the Americas, New York, NY 10104
Visit us at LBYR.com

First Edition: June 2021

Little, Brown and Company is a division of Hachette Book Group, Inc.
The Little, Brown name and logo are trademarks of Hachette Book Group, Inc.

The publisher is not responsible for websites (or their content) that are not owned by the publisher.

Library of Congress Cataloging-in-Publication Data

Names: Colfer, Chris, 1990– author. | Proctor, Jon, illustrator. | Weber, Lisa K., illustrator.

Title: Goldilocks: wanted dead or alive / Chris Colfer; illustrations by Jon Proctor [and] Lisa K. Weber.

Description: First edition. | New York: Little, Brown and Company, 2021. | Series: Land of stories | Summary: When King Charming and his brothers set out to purge the Dwarf Forests of outlaws and rule it themselves, they must face the most feared outlaw, Goldilocks—and then, their wives.

Identifiers: LCCN 2020008478 | ISBN 9780316355933 (hardcover) | ISBN 9780316355957 (paperback) | ISBN 9780316355926 (ebook) | ISBN 9780316355971 (ebook other)

Subjects: CYAC: Kings, queens, rulers, etc.—Fiction. | Robbers and outlaws—Fiction. | Brothers—Fiction. | Characters in literature—Fiction.

Classification: LCC PZ7.C677474 Gol 2021 | DDC [Fic]—dc23

LC record available at https://lccn.loc.gov/2020008478

ISBNs: 978-0-316-35593-3 (hardcover), 978-0-316-35595-7 (pbk.),
978-0-316-35592-6 (ebook), 978-0-316-42706-7 (ebook), 978-0-316-42707-4 (ebook)

PRINTED IN CHINA

APS

Hardcover: 10 9 8 7 6 5 4 3 2 1

Paperback: 10 9 8 7 6 5 4 3 2 1

To Pam,
for being a hero to so many.
Thank you for helping
me fight my battles.

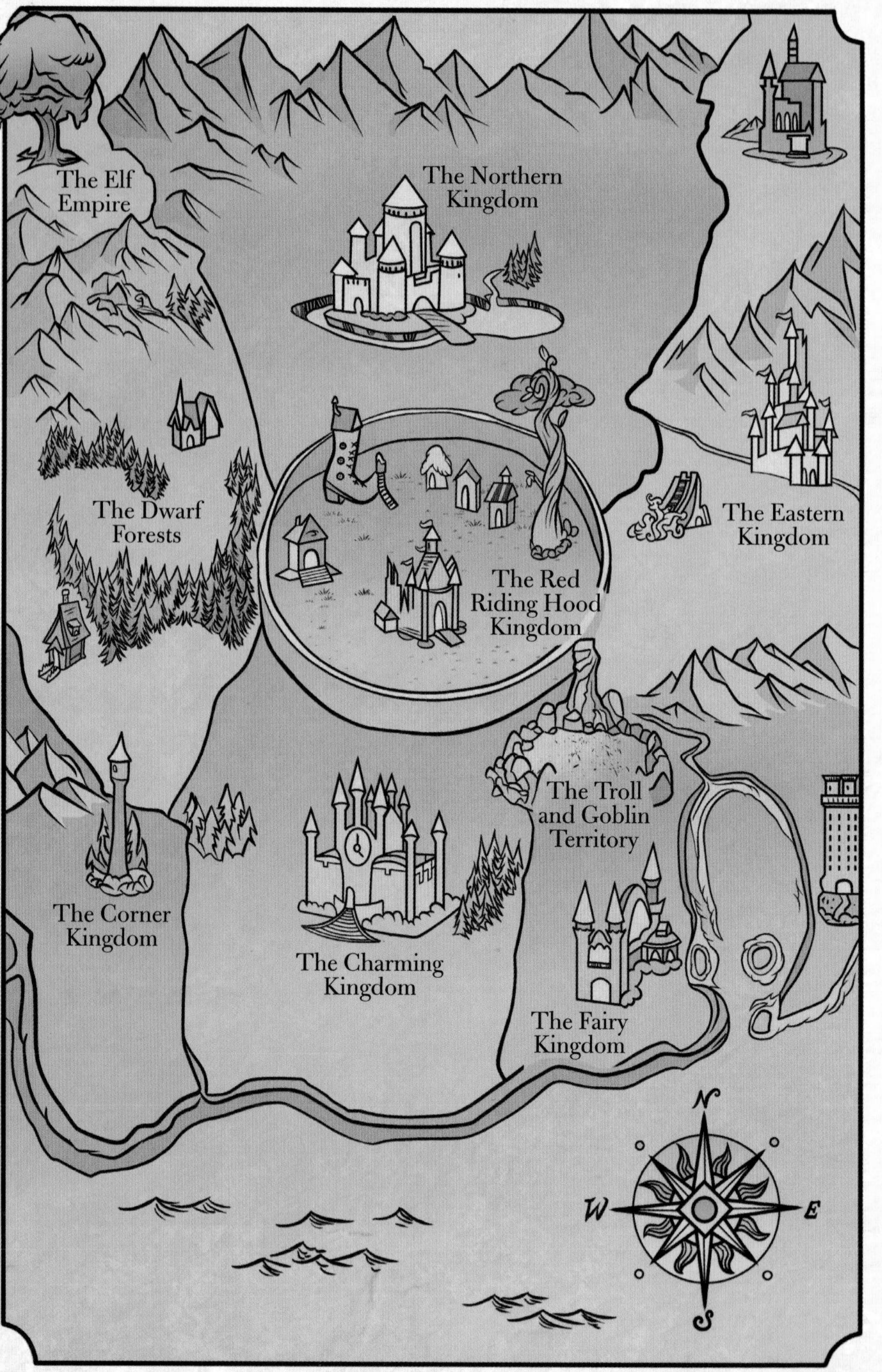
The Elf Empire
The Northern Kingdom
The Dwarf Forests
The Eastern Kingdom
The Red Riding Hood Kingdom
The Troll and Goblin Territory
The Corner Kingdom
The Charming Kingdom
The Fairy Kingdom
N
W
E
S

The kingdoms of the fairy-tale world are enjoying a much-needed period of peace. After the imprisonment of her evil stepmother, Snow White inherited her father's throne and was crowned queen of the Northern Kingdom. In the Eastern Kingdom, Queen Sleeping Beauty and her people have finally awoken from the terrible one-hundred-year sleeping curse. In the south, the Charming Kingdom has been in a constant state of celebration since King Chance Charming married his beloved consort, Queen Cinderella.

In the southwest, Queen Rapunzel established the Corner Kingdom after inheriting land from the witch who infamously imprisoned her in a tower. The Red Riding Hood Kingdom was founded by a large farming community that successfully separated from the Northern Kingdom. They elected Red Riding Hood as their queen, and her first royal act was naming the nation after herself.

The Fairy Godmother and her Fairy Council oversee the majestic Fairy Kingdom in the southeast. Together, the fairies and the kingdoms of man have created the Happily Ever After Assembly—a coalition that maintains peace and prosperity throughout the land.

While the humans and fairies are united in diplomacy, not all territories in the fairy-tale world have been invited to their union. After centuries of rambunctious behavior, the troll and goblin populations have been confined to the Troll and Goblin Territory deep underground in the east. The elves live in the secluded Elf Empire in the northwest. The majority of the west is occupied by the Dwarf Forests, where criminals are allowed to roam free from laws and convictions.

Despite the vast range of people and creatures living in the fairy-tale world, there is nothing threatening the harmony between borders in any way…

Yet.

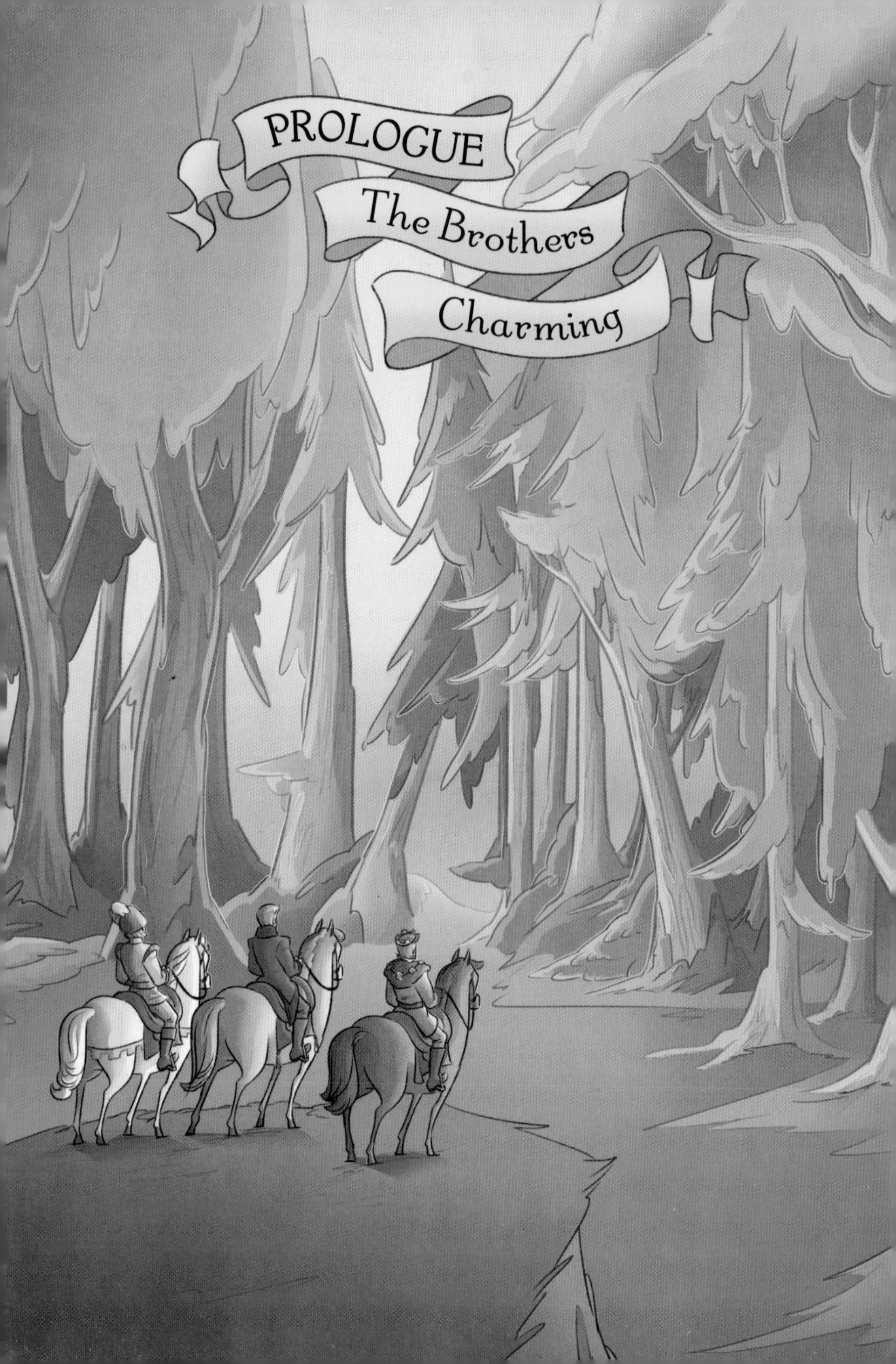
PROLOGUE
The Brothers
Charming

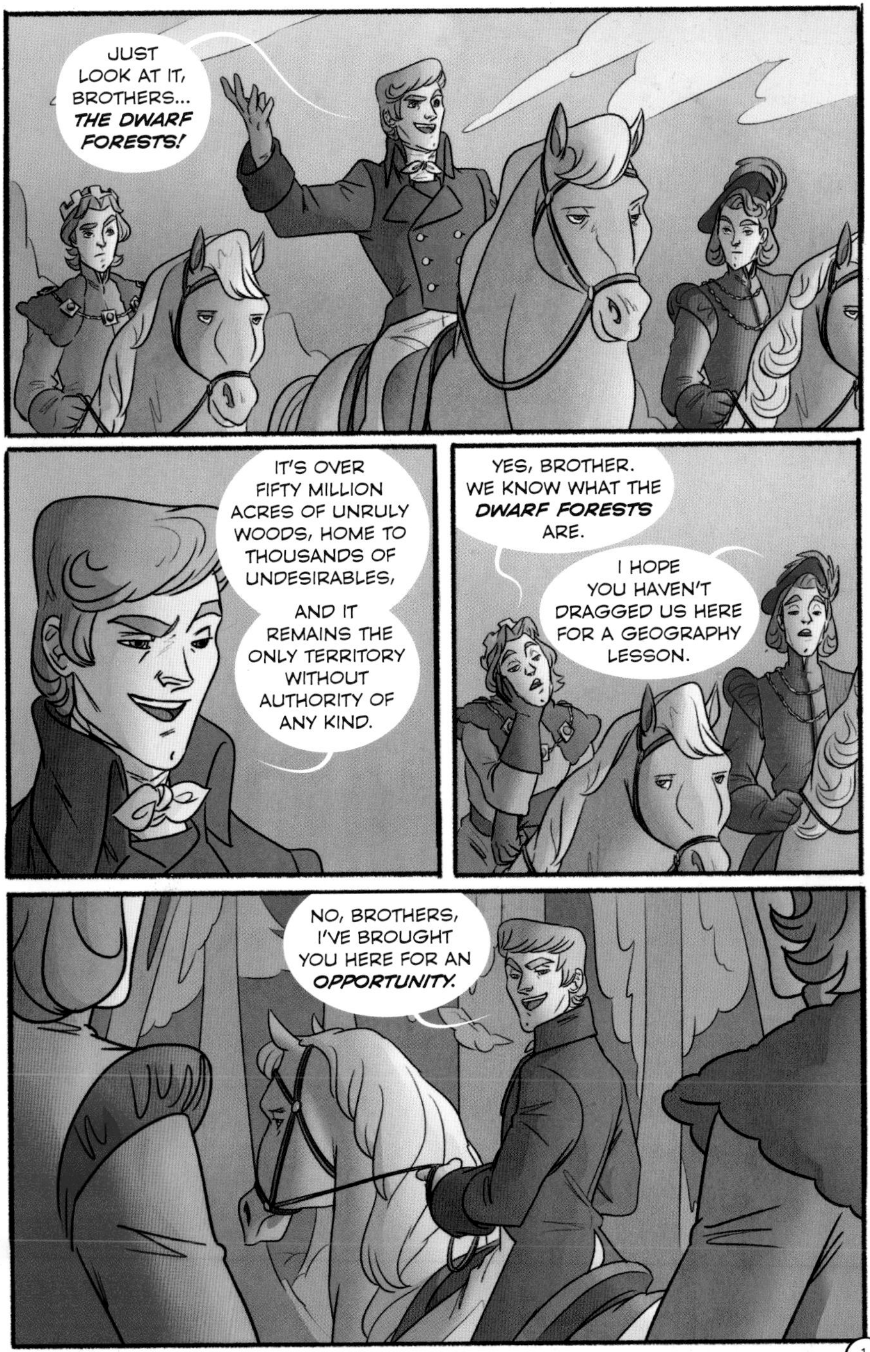
JUST LOOK AT IT, BROTHERS... *THE DWARF FORESTS!*
IT'S OVER FIFTY MILLION ACRES OF UNRULY WOODS, HOME TO THOUSANDS OF UNDESIRABLES,
AND IT REMAINS THE ONLY TERRITORY WITHOUT AUTHORITY OF ANY KIND.
YES, BROTHER. WE KNOW WHAT THE *DWARF FORESTS* ARE.
I HOPE YOU HAVEN'T DRAGGED US HERE FOR A GEOGRAPHY LESSON.
NO, BROTHERS, I'VE BROUGHT YOU HERE FOR AN *OPPORTUNITY.*

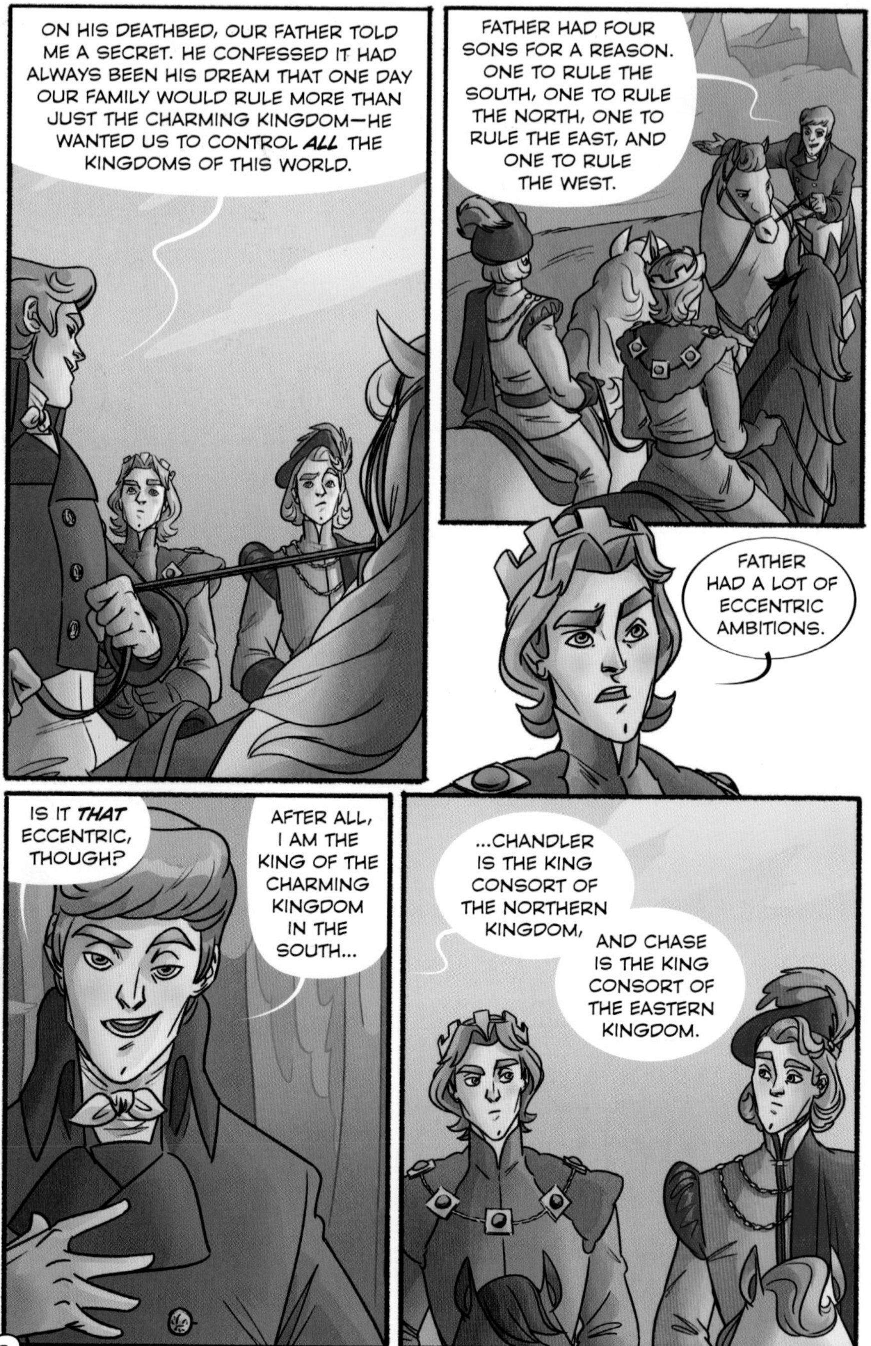
ON HIS DEATHBED, OUR FATHER TOLD ME A SECRET. HE CONFESSED IT HAD ALWAYS BEEN HIS DREAM THAT ONE DAY OUR FAMILY WOULD RULE MORE THAN JUST THE CHARMING KINGDOM—HE WANTED US TO CONTROL ***ALL*** THE KINGDOMS OF THIS WORLD.
FATHER HAD FOUR SONS FOR A REASON. ONE TO RULE THE SOUTH, ONE TO RULE THE NORTH, ONE TO RULE THE EAST, AND ONE TO RULE THE WEST.
FATHER HAD A LOT OF ECCENTRIC AMBITIONS.
IS IT ***THAT*** ECCENTRIC, THOUGH?
AFTER ALL, I AM THE KING OF THE CHARMING KINGDOM IN THE SOUTH...
...CHANDLER IS THE KING CONSORT OF THE NORTHERN KINGDOM,
AND CHASE IS THE KING CONSORT OF THE EASTERN KINGDOM.

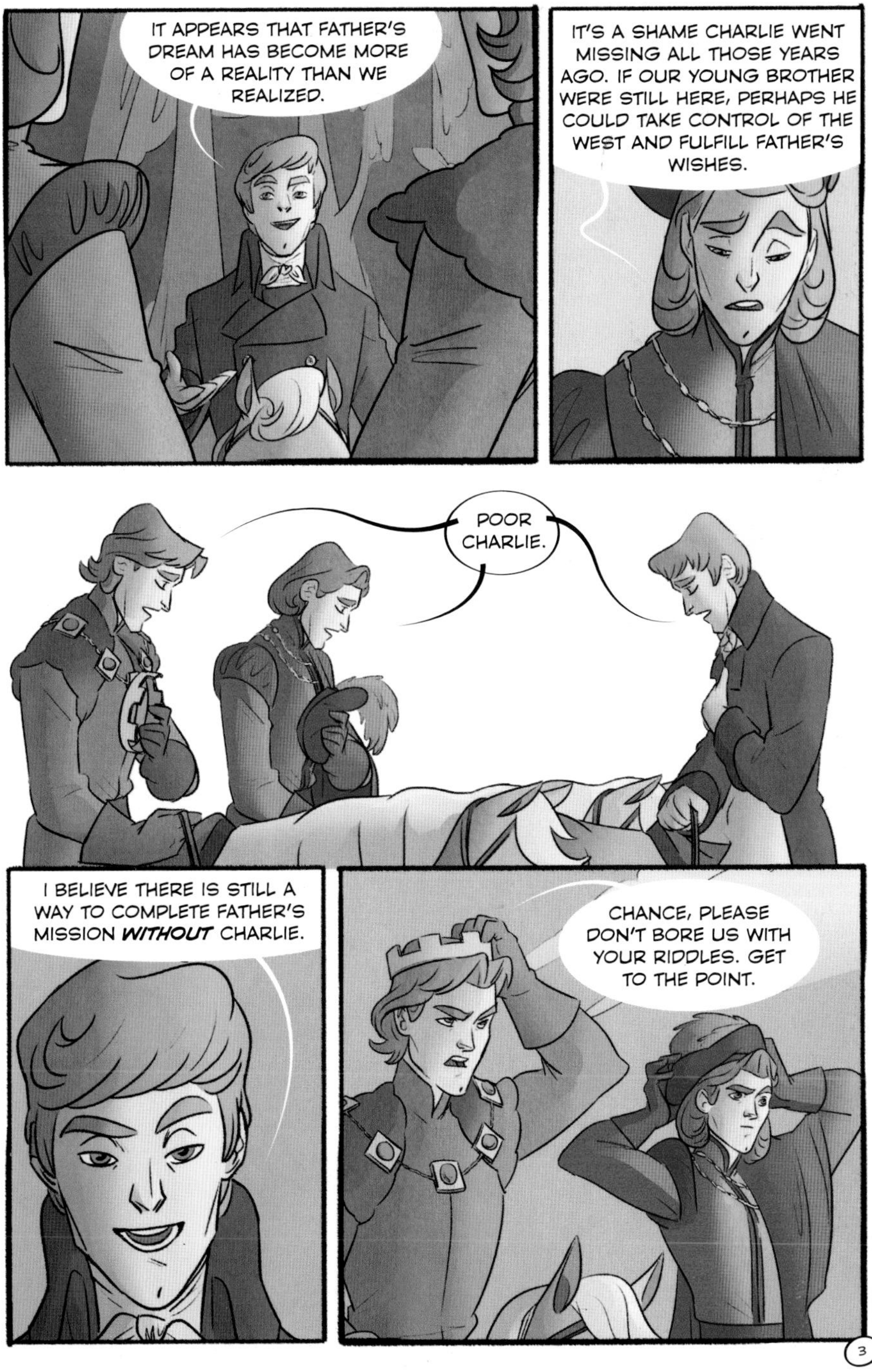
IT APPEARS THAT FATHER'S DREAM HAS BECOME MORE OF A REALITY THAN WE REALIZED.
IT'S A SHAME CHARLIE WENT MISSING ALL THOSE YEARS AGO. IF OUR YOUNG BROTHER WERE STILL HERE, PERHAPS HE COULD TAKE CONTROL OF THE WEST AND FULFILL FATHER'S WISHES.
POOR CHARLIE.
I BELIEVE THERE IS STILL A WAY TO COMPLETE FATHER'S MISSION ***WITHOUT*** CHARLIE.
CHANCE, PLEASE DON'T BORE US WITH YOUR RIDDLES. GET TO THE POINT.

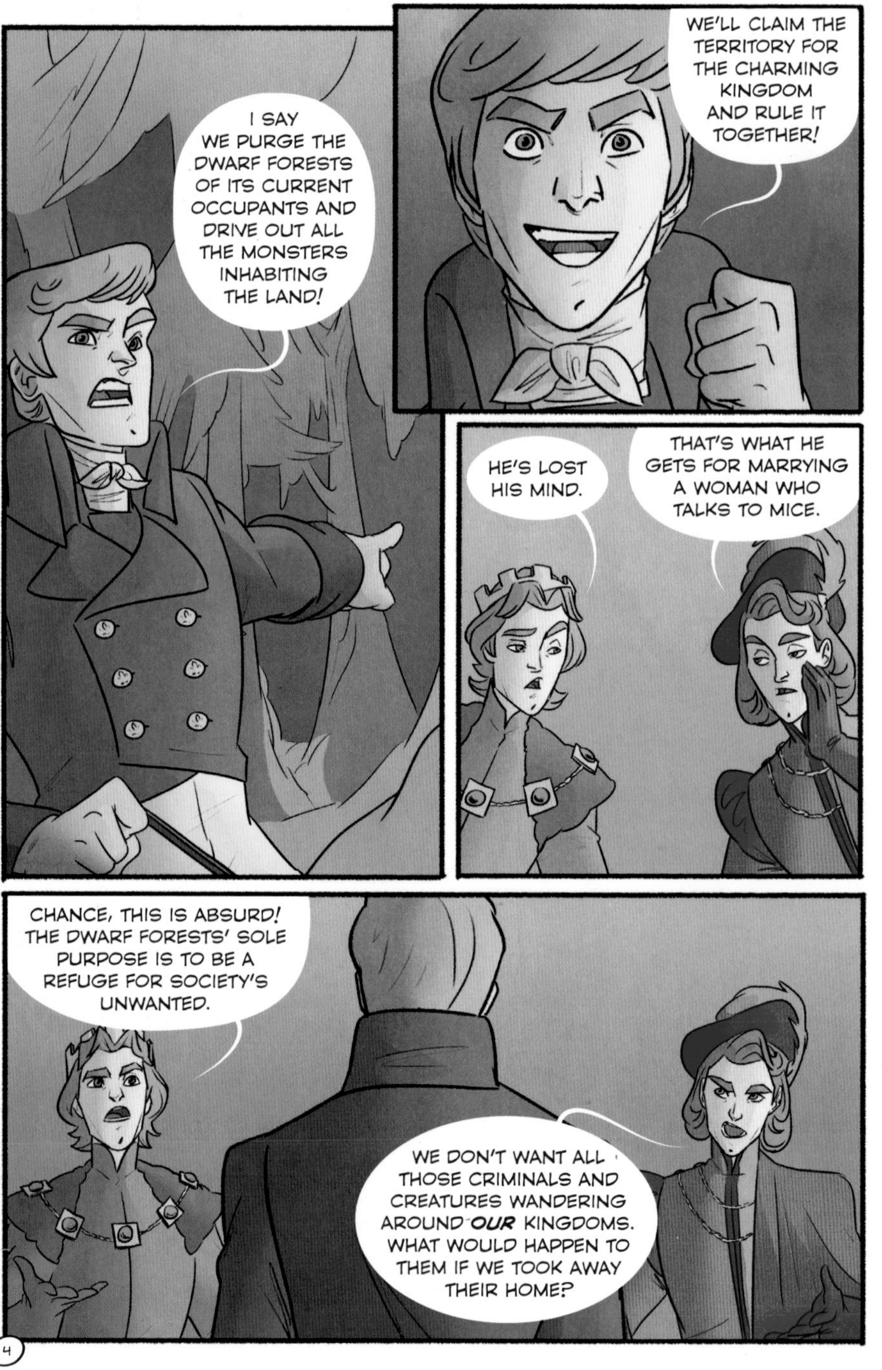
I SAY WE PURGE THE DWARF FORESTS OF ITS CURRENT OCCUPANTS AND DRIVE OUT ALL THE MONSTERS INHABITING THE LAND!
WE'LL CLAIM THE TERRITORY FOR THE CHARMING KINGDOM AND RULE IT TOGETHER!
HE'S LOST HIS MIND.
THAT'S WHAT HE GETS FOR MARRYING A WOMAN WHO TALKS TO MICE.
CHANCE, THIS IS ABSURD! THE DWARF FORESTS' SOLE PURPOSE IS TO BE A REFUGE FOR SOCIETY'S UNWANTED.
WE DON'T WANT ALL THOSE CRIMINALS AND CREATURES WANDERING AROUND OUR KINGDOMS. WHAT WOULD HAPPEN TO THEM IF WE TOOK AWAY THEIR HOME?

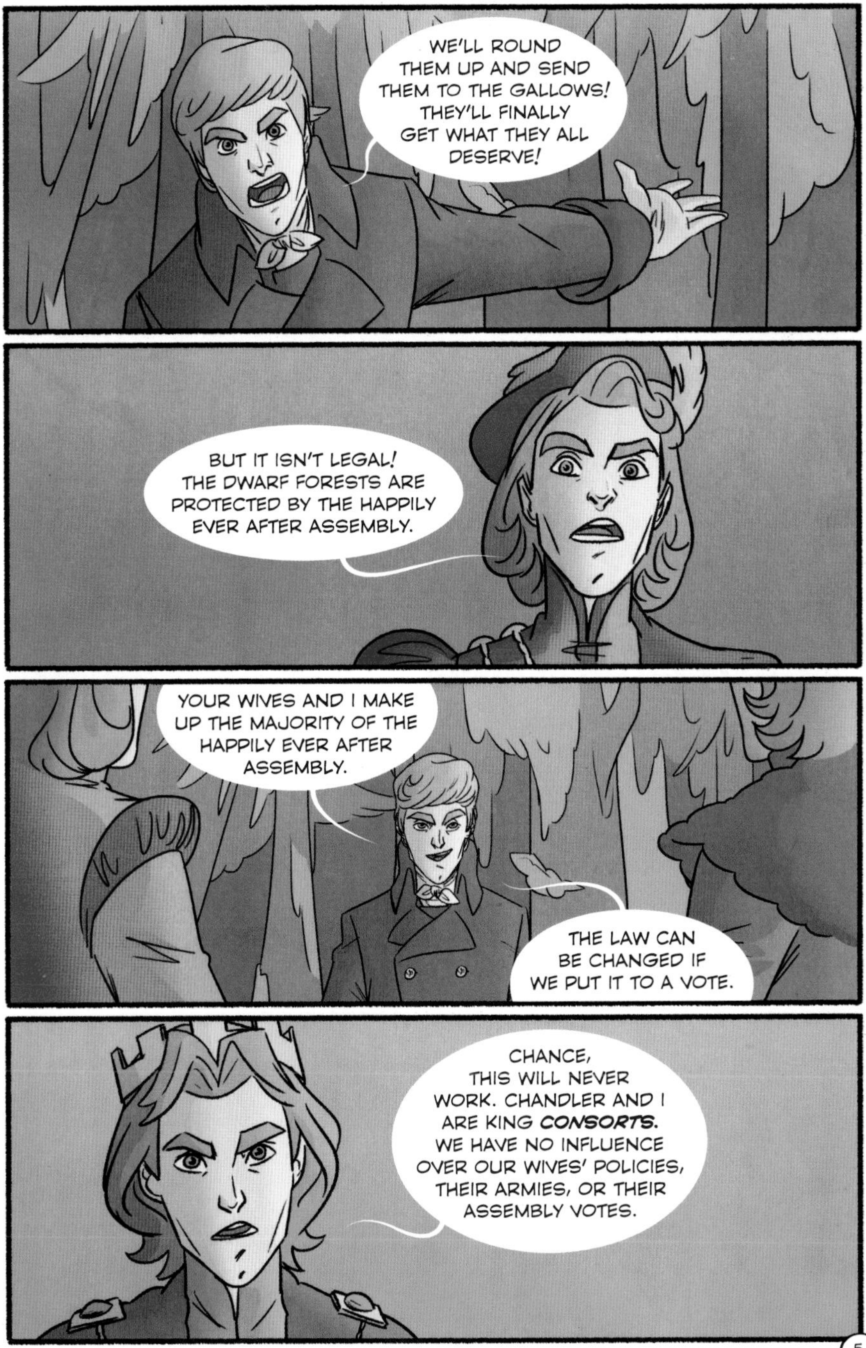
WE'LL ROUND THEM UP AND SEND THEM TO THE GALLOWS! THEY'LL FINALLY GET WHAT THEY ALL DESERVE!
BUT IT ISN'T LEGAL! THE DWARF FORESTS ARE PROTECTED BY THE HAPPILY EVER AFTER ASSEMBLY.
YOUR WIVES AND I MAKE UP THE MAJORITY OF THE HAPPILY EVER AFTER ASSEMBLY.
THE LAW CAN BE CHANGED IF WE PUT IT TO A VOTE.
CHANCE, THIS WILL NEVER WORK. CHANDLER AND I ARE KING ***CONSORTS.*** WE HAVE NO INFLUENCE OVER OUR WIVES' POLICIES, THEIR ARMIES, OR THEIR ASSEMBLY VOTES.

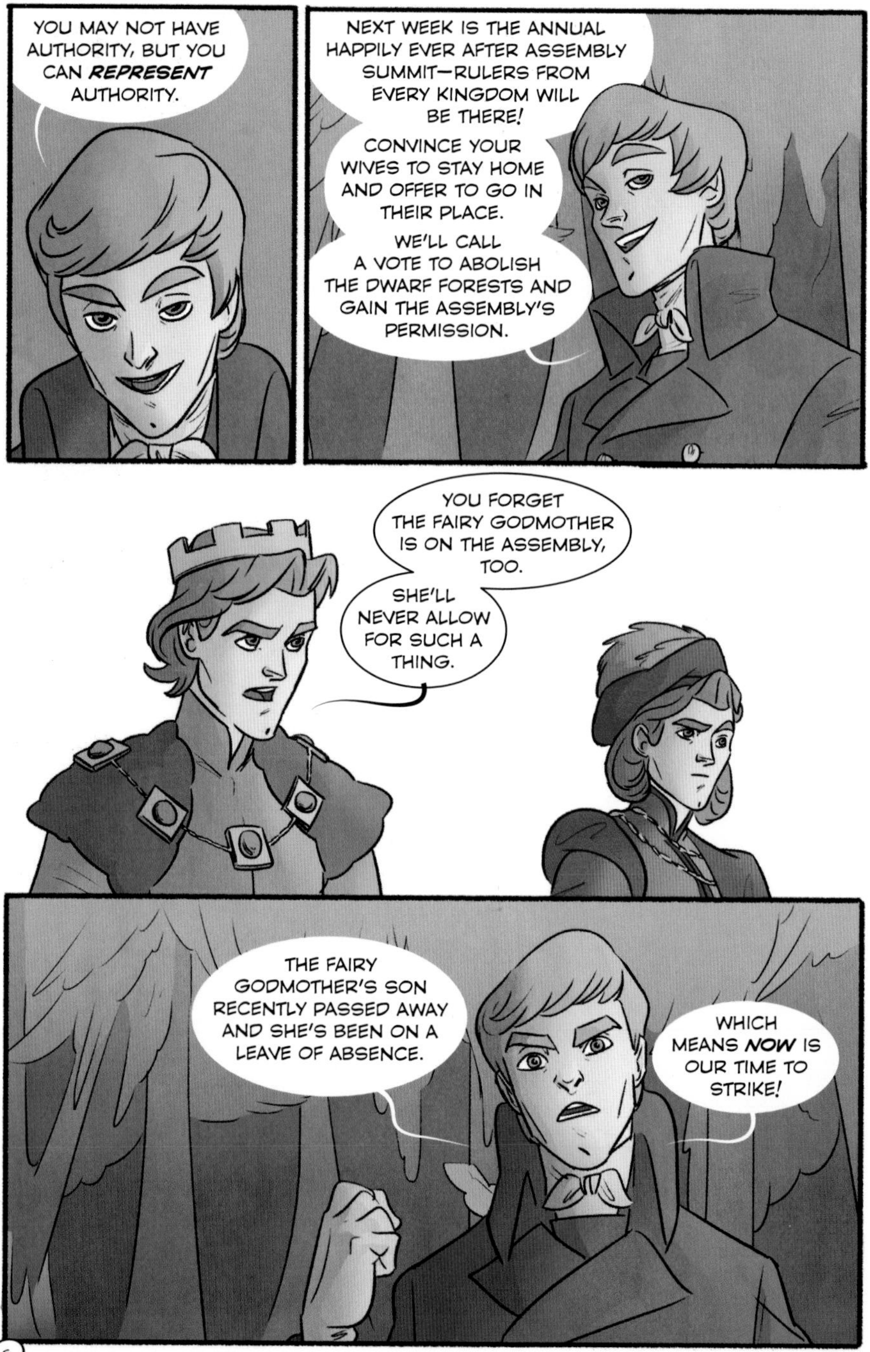
YOU MAY NOT HAVE AUTHORITY, BUT YOU CAN *REPRESENT* AUTHORITY.
NEXT WEEK IS THE ANNUAL HAPPILY EVER AFTER ASSEMBLY SUMMIT—RULERS FROM EVERY KINGDOM WILL BE THERE!
CONVINCE YOUR WIVES TO STAY HOME AND OFFER TO GO IN THEIR PLACE.
WE'LL CALL A VOTE TO ABOLISH THE DWARF FORESTS AND GAIN THE ASSEMBLY'S PERMISSION.
YOU FORGET THE FAIRY GODMOTHER IS ON THE ASSEMBLY, TOO.
SHE'LL NEVER ALLOW FOR SUCH A THING.
THE FAIRY GODMOTHER'S SON RECENTLY PASSED AWAY AND SHE'S BEEN ON A LEAVE OF ABSENCE.
WHICH MEANS *NOW* IS OUR TIME TO STRIKE!

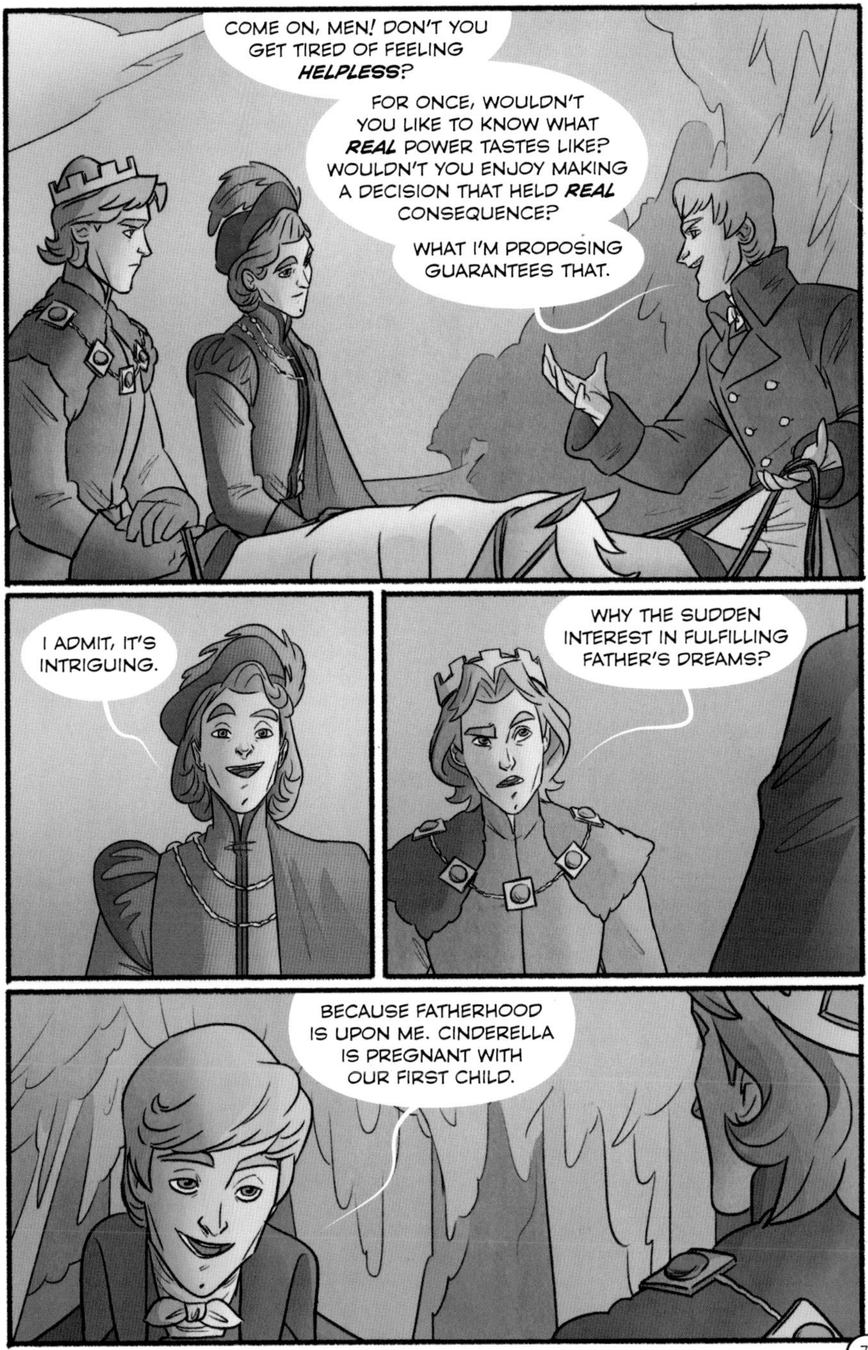
COME ON, MEN! DON'T YOU GET TIRED OF FEELING *HELPLESS*?
FOR ONCE, WOULDN'T YOU LIKE TO KNOW WHAT *REAL* POWER TASTES LIKE? WOULDN'T YOU ENJOY MAKING A DECISION THAT HELD *REAL* CONSEQUENCE?
WHAT I'M PROPOSING GUARANTEES THAT.
I ADMIT, IT'S INTRIGUING.
WHY THE SUDDEN INTEREST IN FULFILLING FATHER'S DREAMS?
BECAUSE FATHERHOOD IS UPON ME. CINDERELLA IS PREGNANT WITH OUR FIRST CHILD.

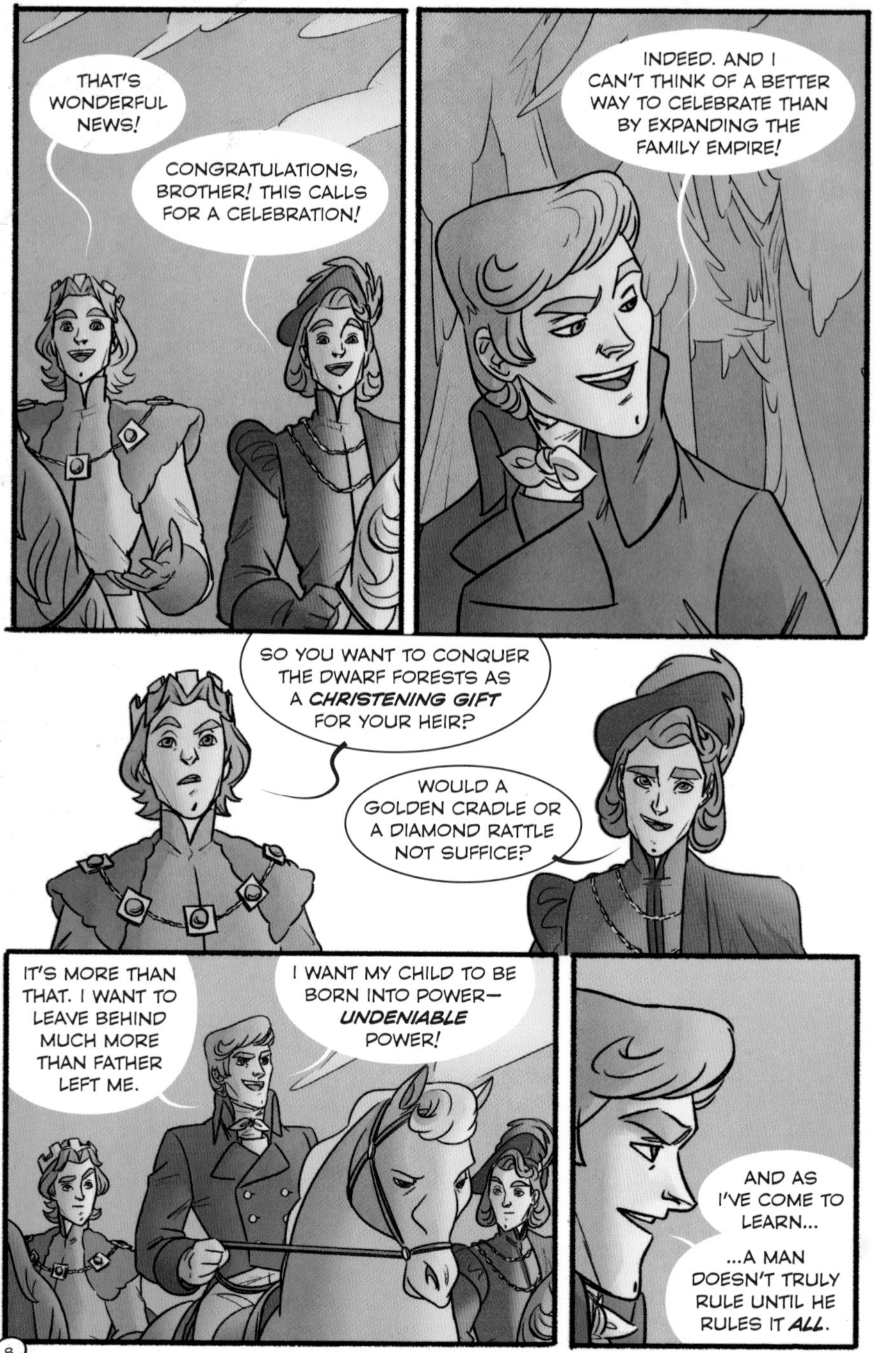

THAT'S WONDERFUL NEWS!
CONGRATULATIONS, BROTHER! THIS CALLS FOR A CELEBRATION!
INDEED. AND I CAN'T THINK OF A BETTER WAY TO CELEBRATE THAN BY EXPANDING THE FAMILY EMPIRE!
SO YOU WANT TO CONQUER THE DWARF FORESTS AS A ***CHRISTENING GIFT*** FOR YOUR HEIR?
WOULD A GOLDEN CRADLE OR A DIAMOND RATTLE NOT SUFFICE?
IT'S MORE THAN THAT. I WANT TO LEAVE BEHIND MUCH MORE THAN FATHER LEFT ME.
I WANT MY CHILD TO BE BORN INTO POWER—***UNDENIABLE*** POWER!
AND AS I'VE COME TO LEARN...
...A MAN DOESN'T TRULY RULE UNTIL HE RULES IT ***ALL***.

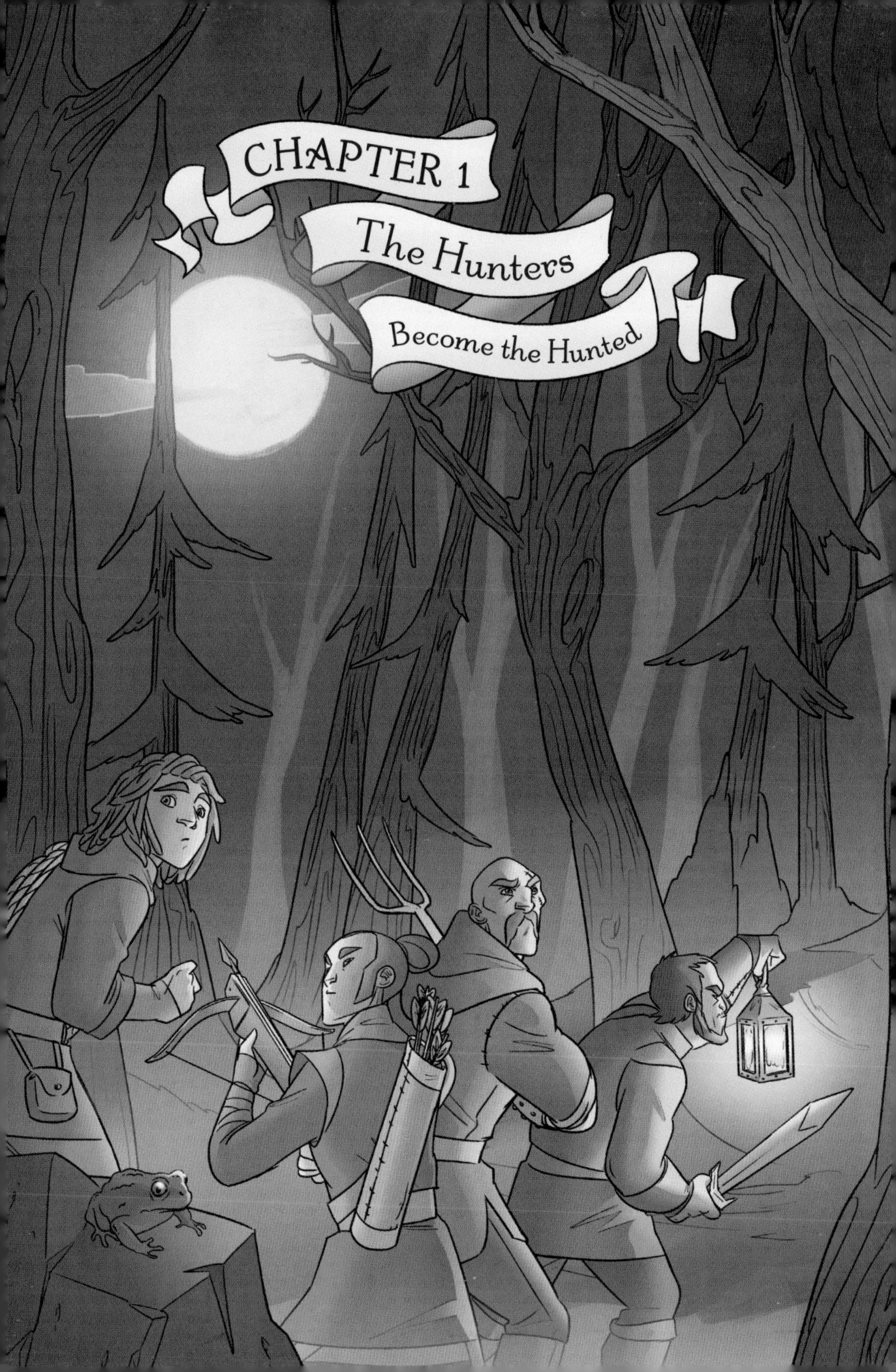
CHAPTER 1
The Hunters
Become the Hunted

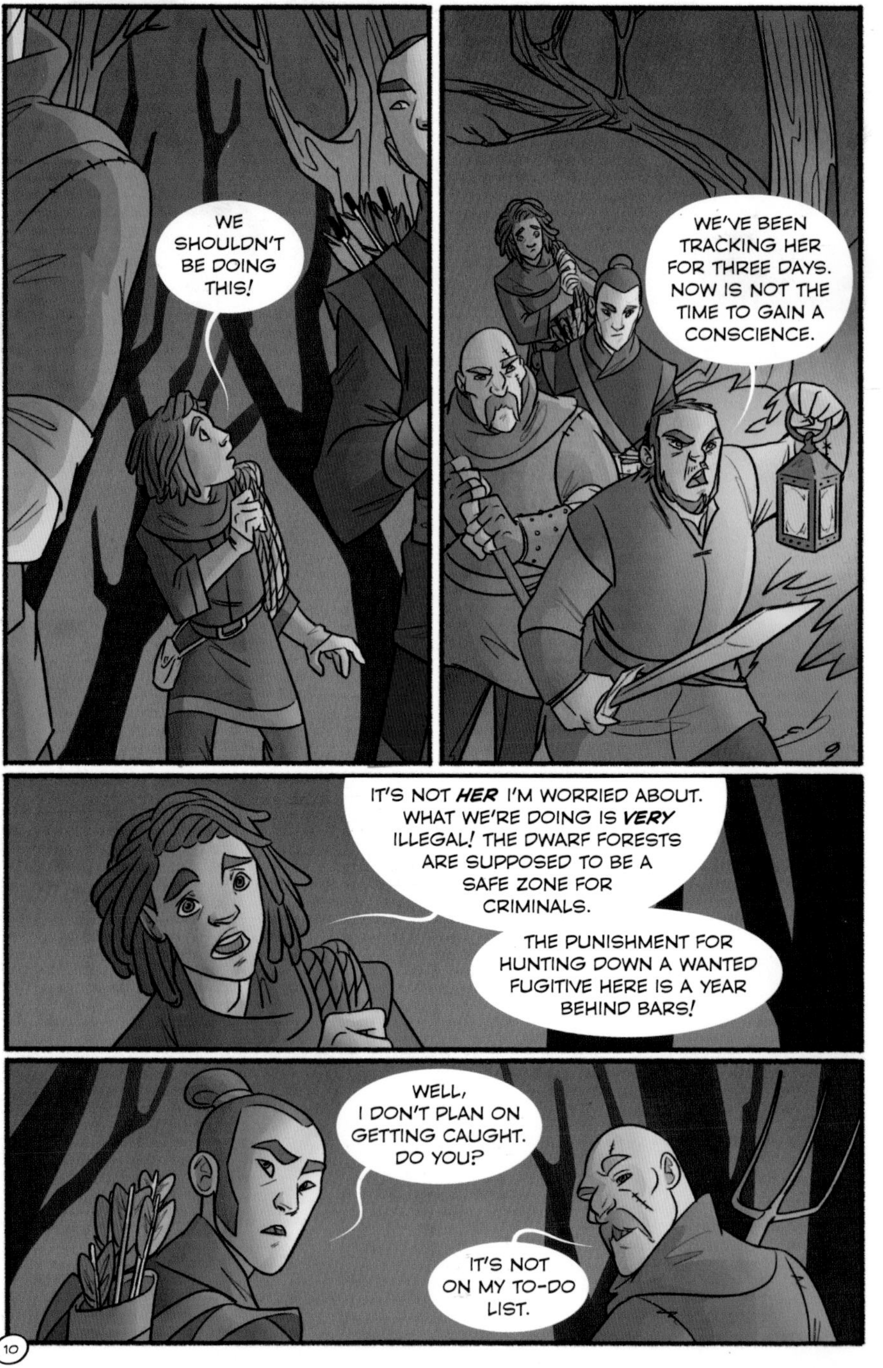
WE SHOULDN'T BE DOING THIS!
WE'VE BEEN TRACKING HER FOR THREE DAYS. NOW IS NOT THE TIME TO GAIN A CONSCIENCE.
IT'S NOT ***HER*** I'M WORRIED ABOUT. WHAT WE'RE DOING IS ***VERY*** ILLEGAL! THE DWARF FORESTS ARE SUPPOSED TO BE A SAFE ZONE FOR CRIMINALS.
THE PUNISHMENT FOR HUNTING DOWN A WANTED FUGITIVE HERE IS A YEAR BEHIND BARS!
WELL, I DON'T PLAN ON GETTING CAUGHT. DO YOU?
IT'S NOT ON MY TO-DO LIST.

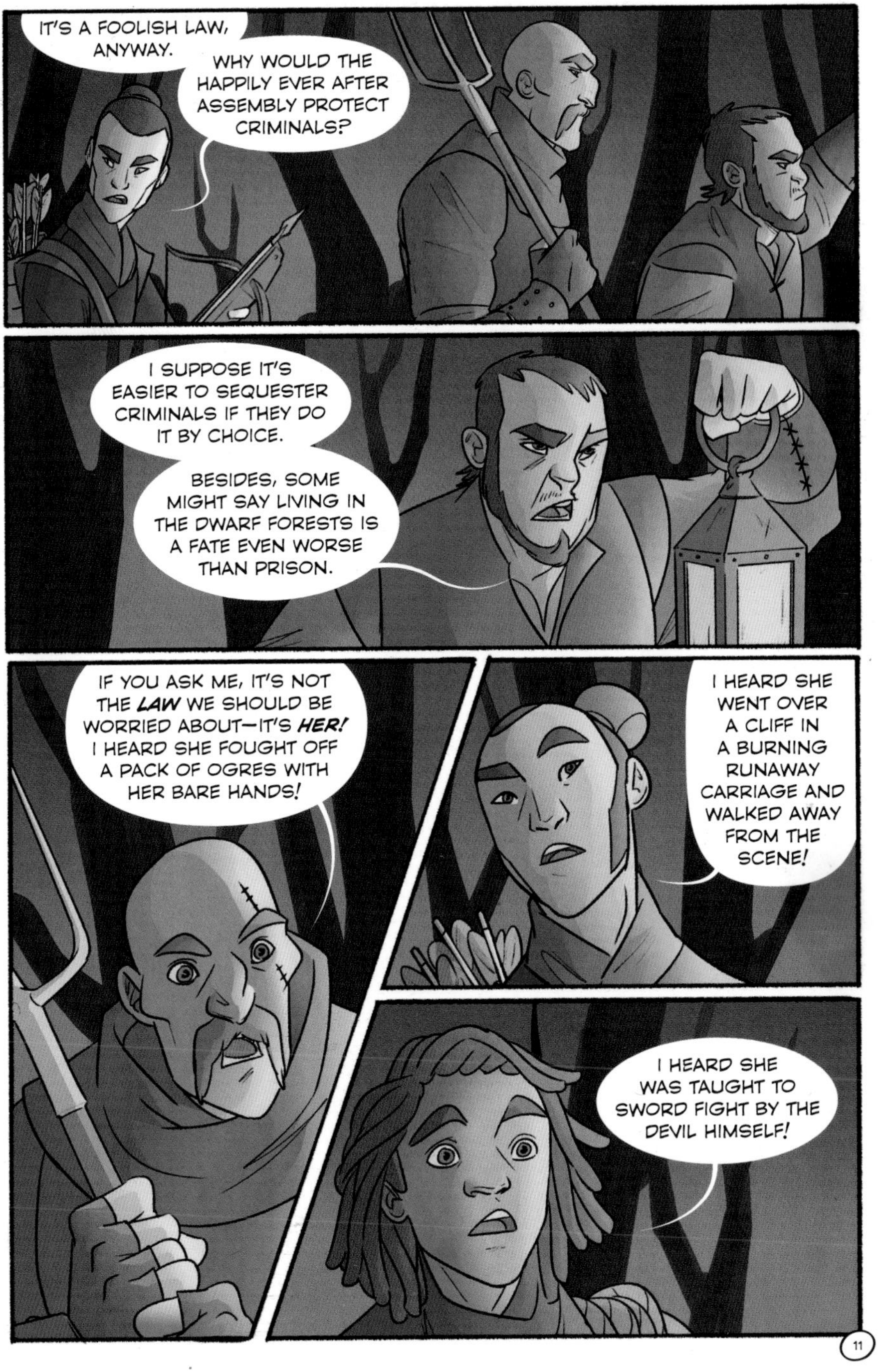
IT'S A FOOLISH LAW, ANYWAY.
WHY WOULD THE HAPPILY EVER AFTER ASSEMBLY PROTECT CRIMINALS?
I SUPPOSE IT'S EASIER TO SEQUESTER CRIMINALS IF THEY DO IT BY CHOICE.
BESIDES, SOME MIGHT SAY LIVING IN THE DWARF FORESTS IS A FATE EVEN WORSE THAN PRISON.
IF YOU ASK ME, IT'S NOT THE *LAW* WE SHOULD BE WORRIED ABOUT—IT'S *HER!* I HEARD SHE FOUGHT OFF A PACK OF OGRES WITH HER BARE HANDS!
I HEARD SHE WENT OVER A CLIFF IN A BURNING RUNAWAY CARRIAGE AND WALKED AWAY FROM THE SCENE!
I HEARD SHE WAS TAUGHT TO SWORD FIGHT BY THE DEVIL HIMSELF!

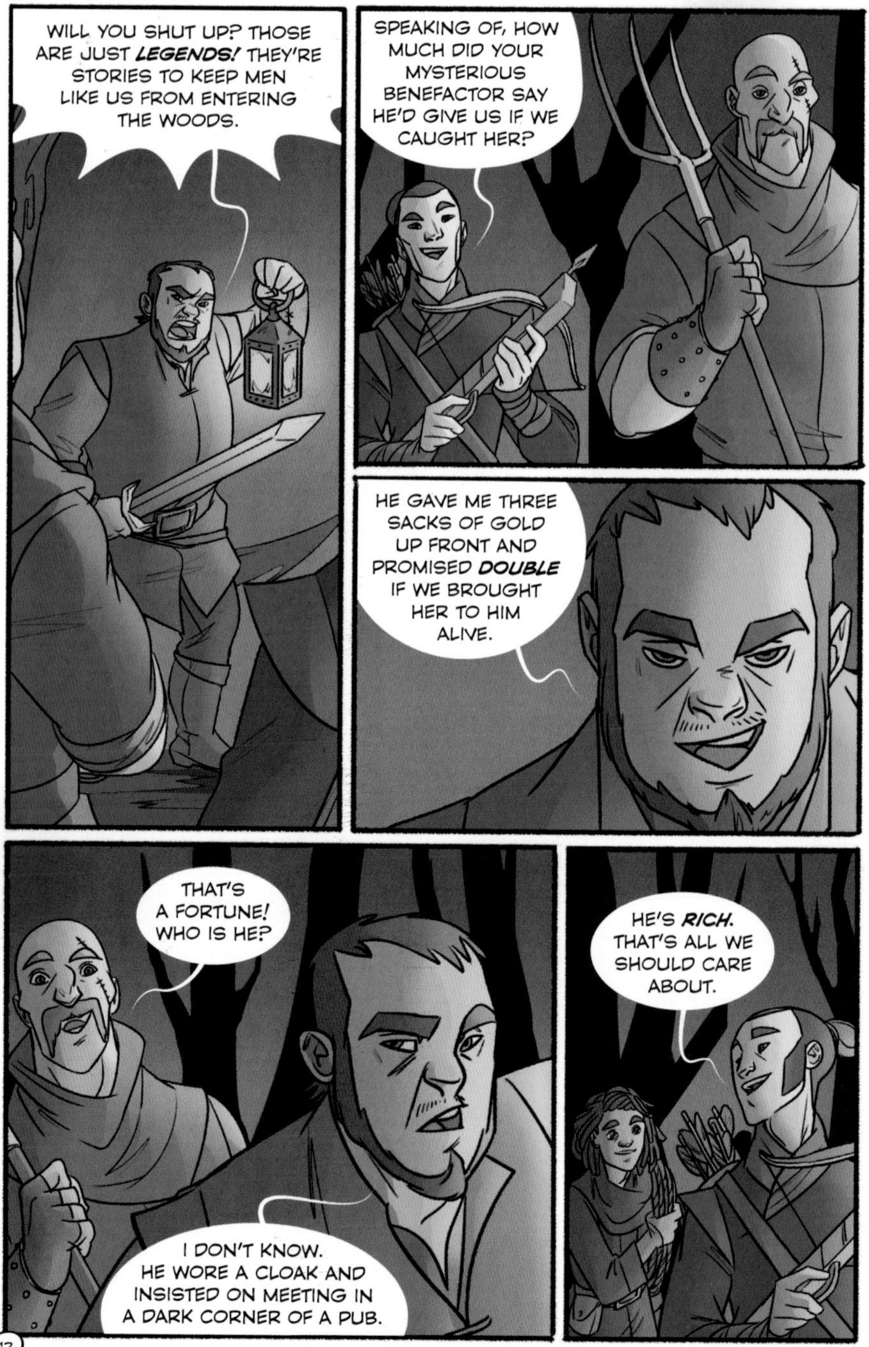
WILL YOU SHUT UP? THOSE ARE JUST LEGENDS! THEY'RE STORIES TO KEEP MEN LIKE US FROM ENTERING THE WOODS.
SPEAKING OF, HOW MUCH DID YOUR MYSTERIOUS BENEFACTOR SAY HE'D GIVE US IF WE CAUGHT HER?
HE GAVE ME THREE SACKS OF GOLD UP FRONT AND PROMISED DOUBLE IF WE BROUGHT HER TO HIM ALIVE.
THAT'S A FORTUNE! WHO IS HE?
I DON'T KNOW. HE WORE A CLOAK AND INSISTED ON MEETING IN A DARK CORNER OF A PUB.
HE'S RICH. THAT'S ALL WE SHOULD CARE ABOUT.

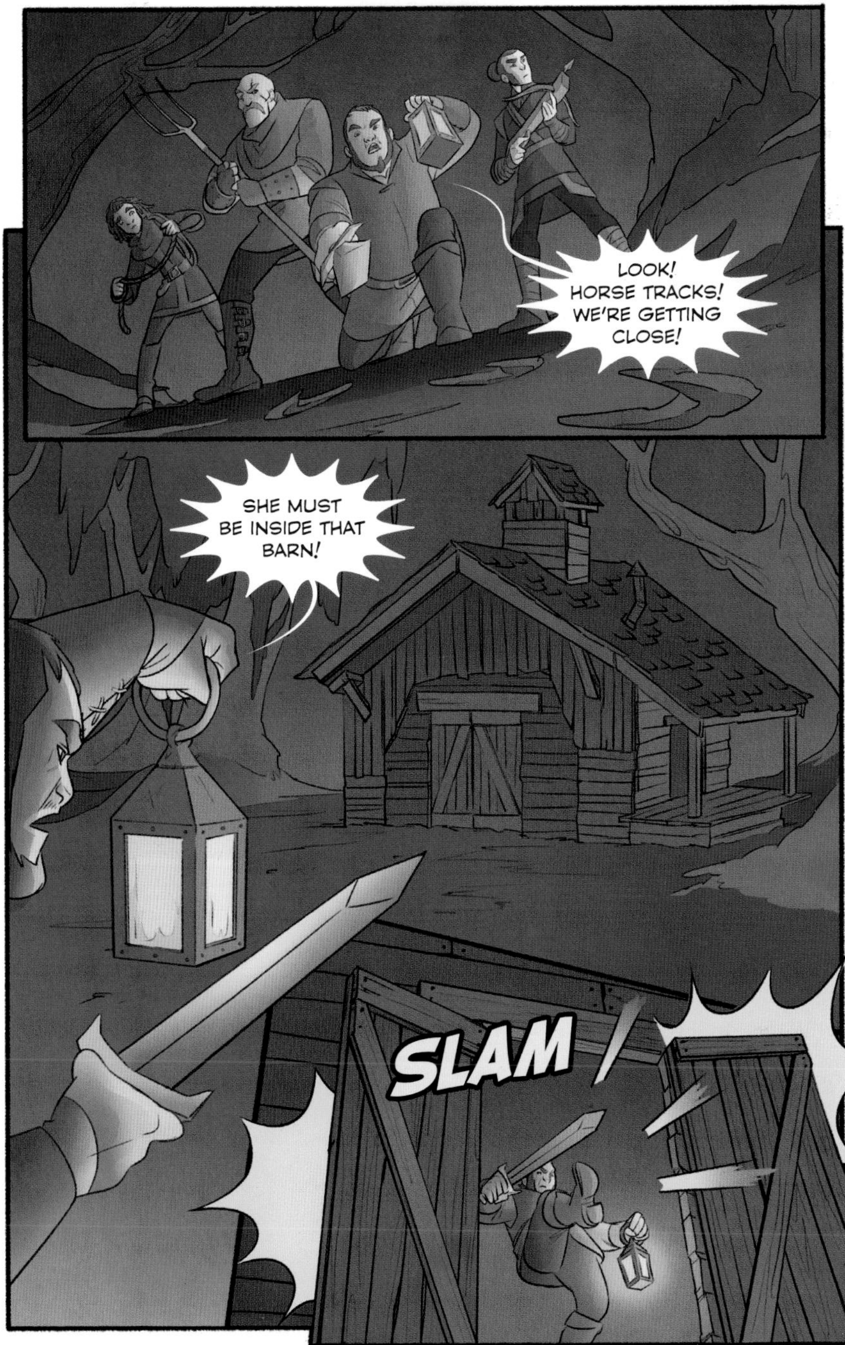
LOOK! HORSE TRACKS! WE'RE GETTING CLOSE!
SHE MUST BE INSIDE THAT BARN!
SLAM

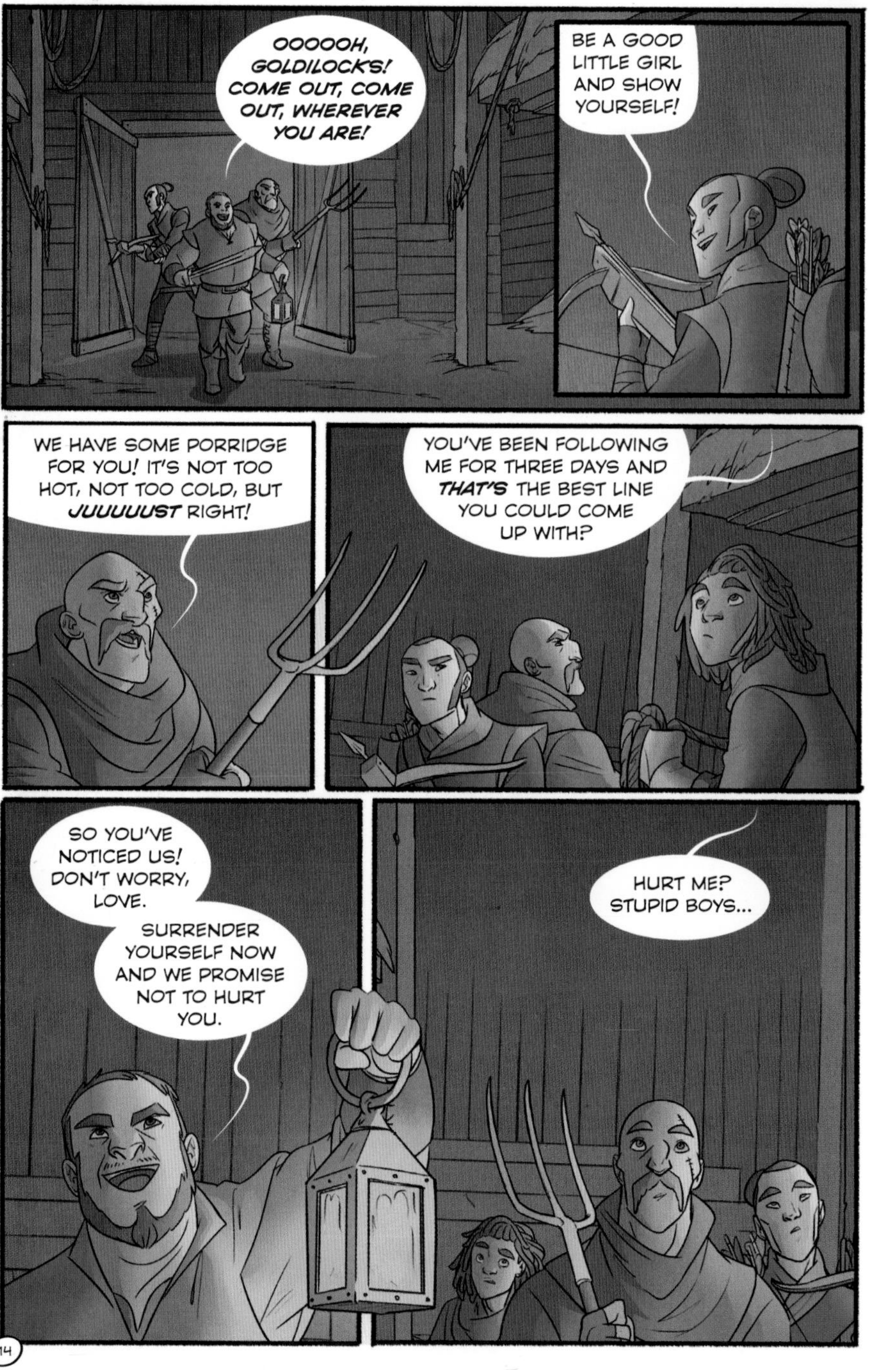
OOOOOH, GOLDILOCKS! COME OUT, COME OUT, WHEREVER YOU ARE!
BE A GOOD LITTLE GIRL AND SHOW YOURSELF!
WE HAVE SOME PORRIDGE FOR YOU! IT'S NOT TOO HOT, NOT TOO COLD, BUT JUUUUUST RIGHT!
YOU'VE BEEN FOLLOWING ME FOR THREE DAYS AND THAT'S THE BEST LINE YOU COULD COME UP WITH?
SO YOU'VE NOTICED US! DON'T WORRY, LOVE.
SURRENDER YOURSELF NOW AND WE PROMISE NOT TO HURT YOU.
HURT ME? STUPID BOYS...

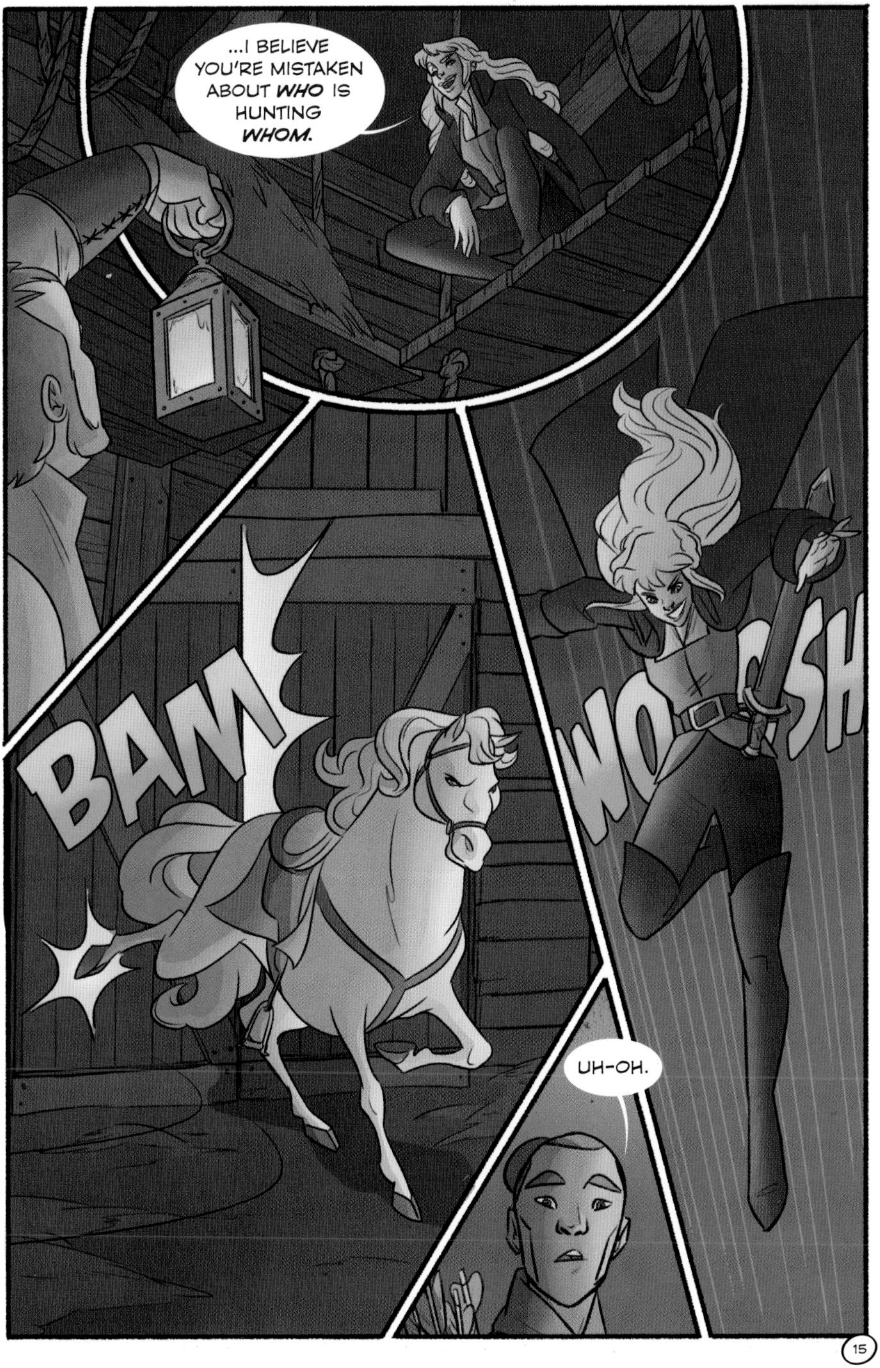
...I BELIEVE YOU'RE MISTAKEN ABOUT *WHO* IS HUNTING *WHOM.*
BAM
UH-OH.

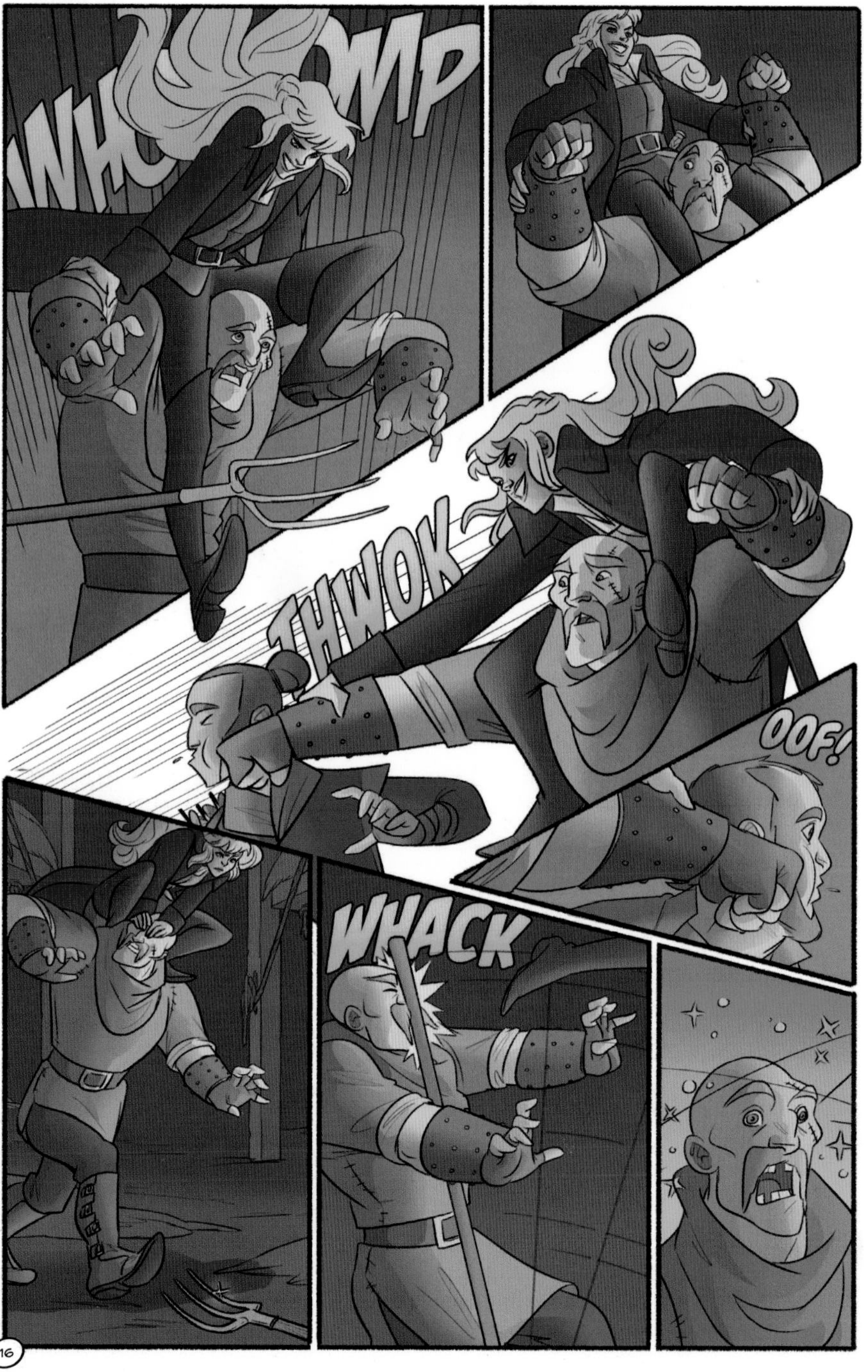
THWOK
OOF!
WHACK

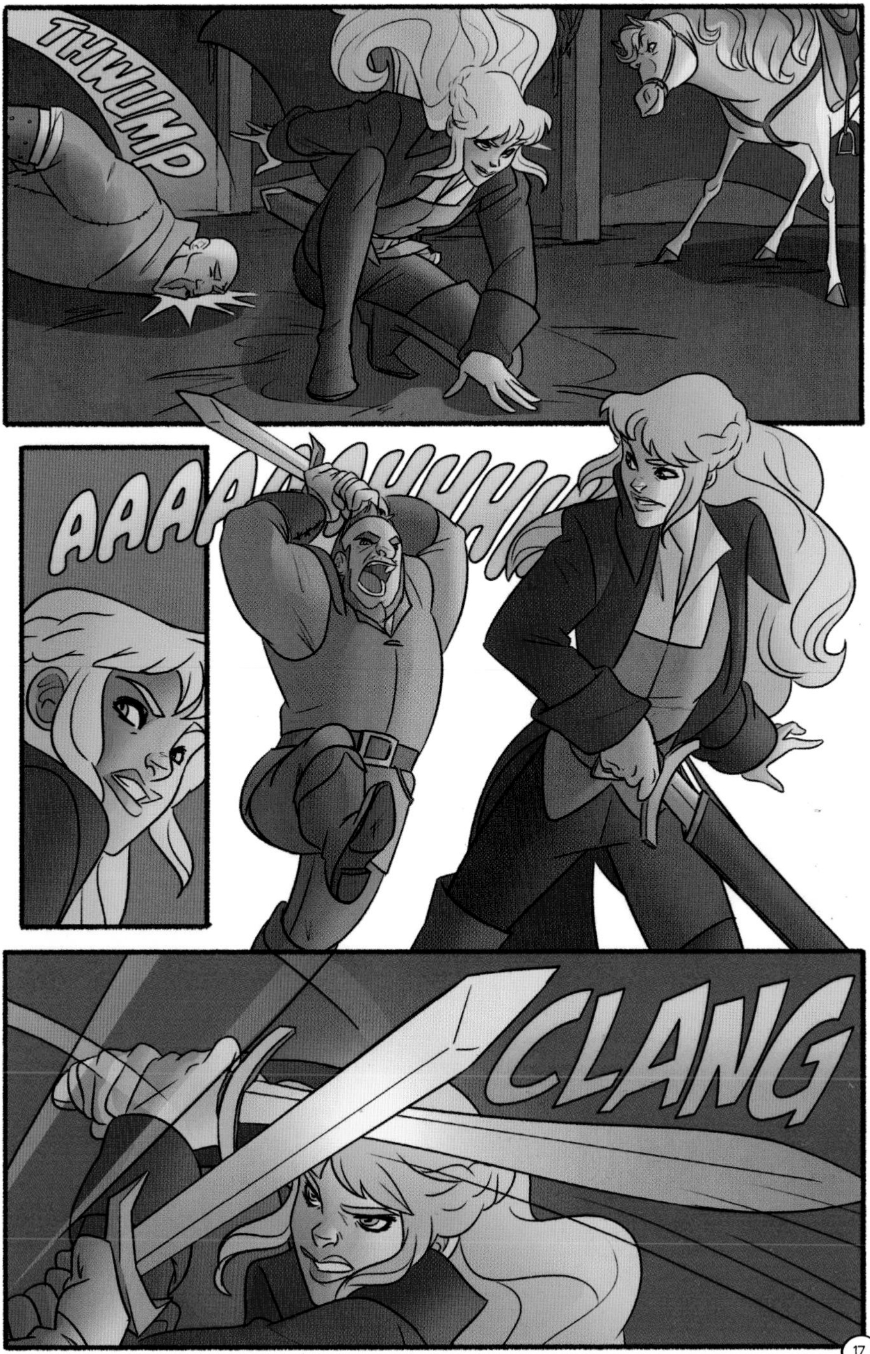
THWUMP
AAAA
CLANG

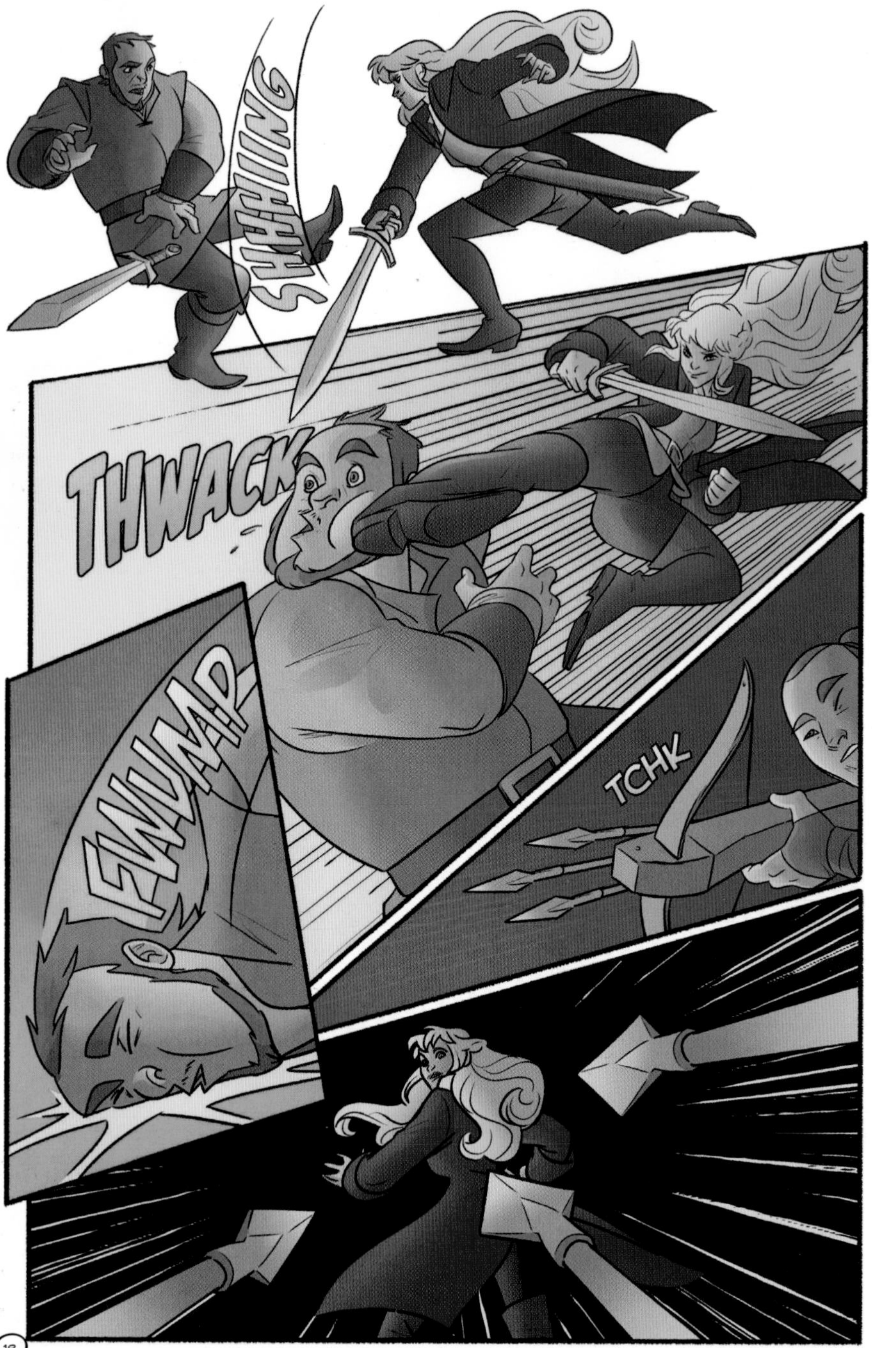
SHHHING
THWACK
FWUMP
TCHK

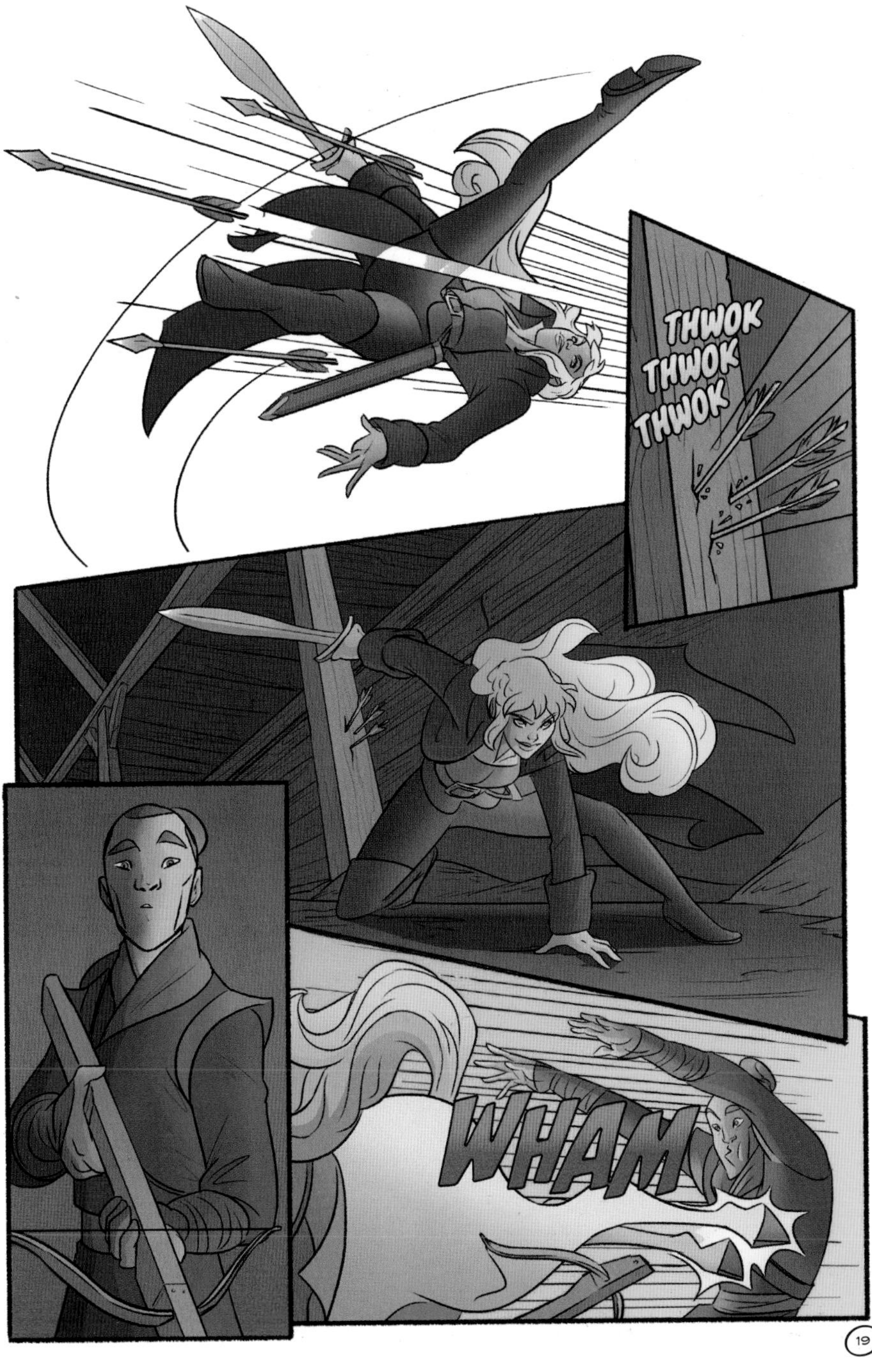
THWOK
THWOK
THWOK
WHAM

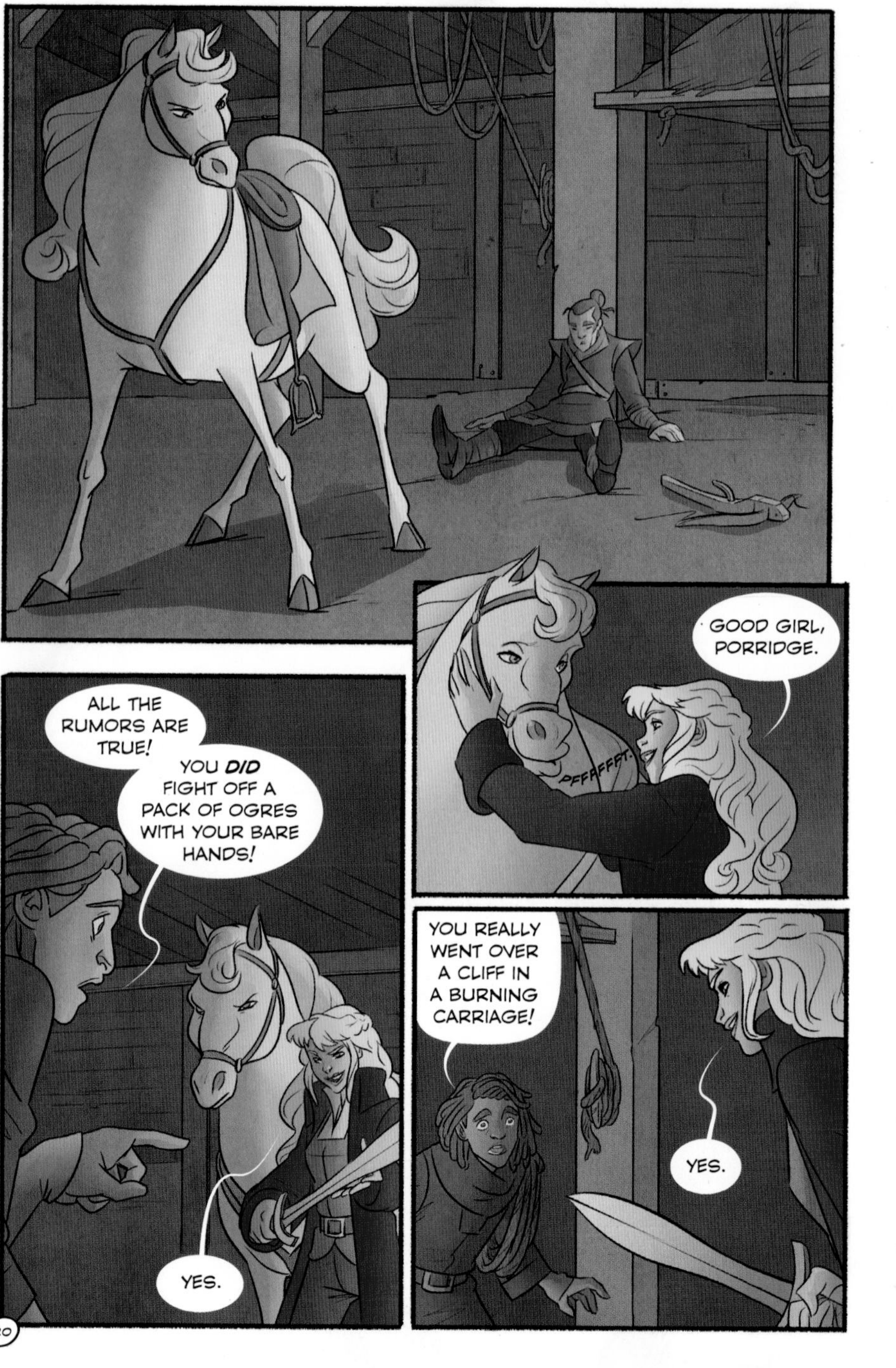
GOOD GIRL, PORRIDGE.
PFFFFFFT.
ALL THE RUMORS ARE TRUE!
YOU *DID* FIGHT OFF A PACK OF OGRES WITH YOUR BARE HANDS!
YES.
YOU REALLY WENT OVER A CLIFF IN A BURNING CARRIAGE!
YES.

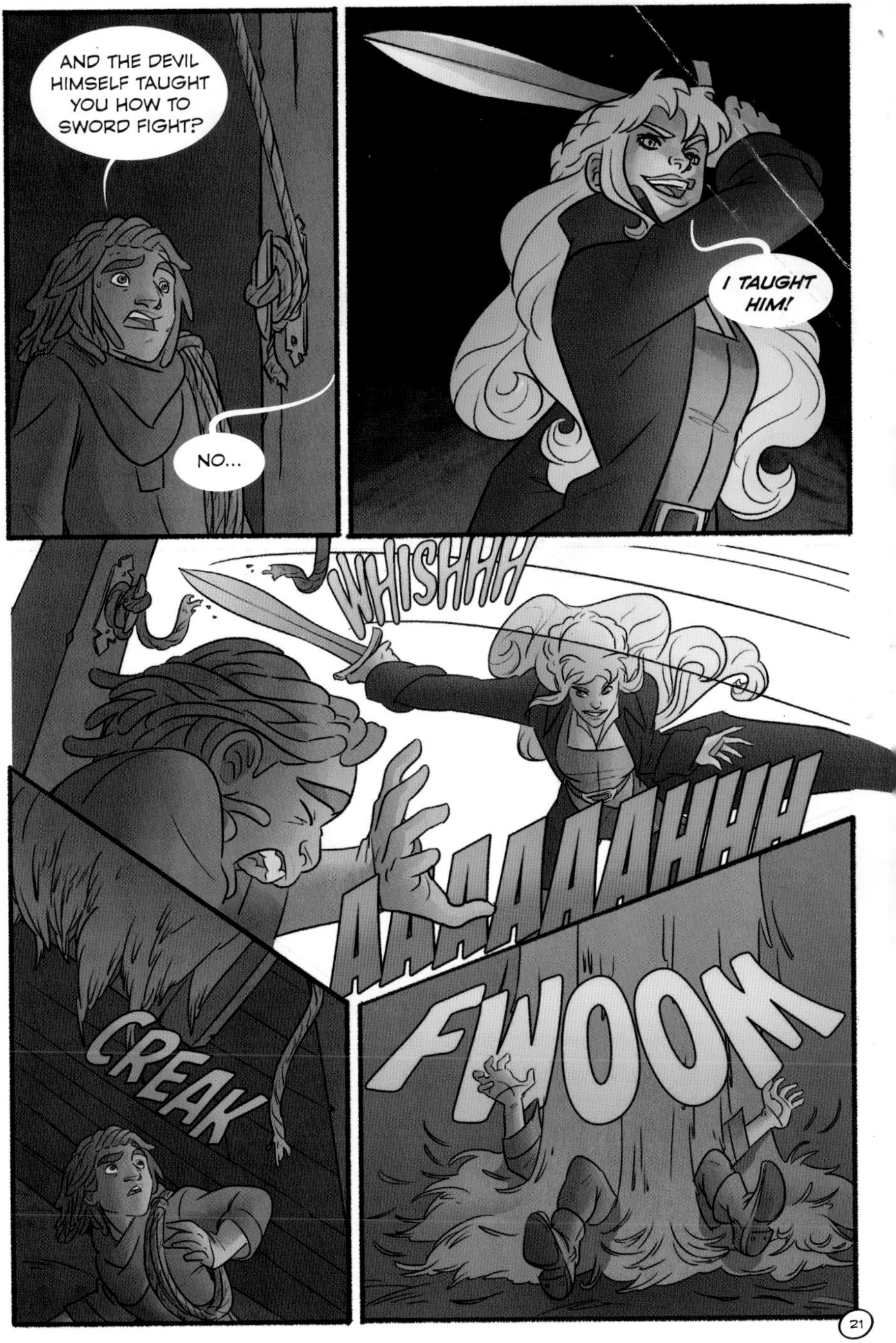

AND THE DEVIL HIMSELF TAUGHT YOU HOW TO SWORD FIGHT?
NO...
I TAUGHT HIM!
WHISHHH
AAAAAAHHH
CREAK
FWOOM

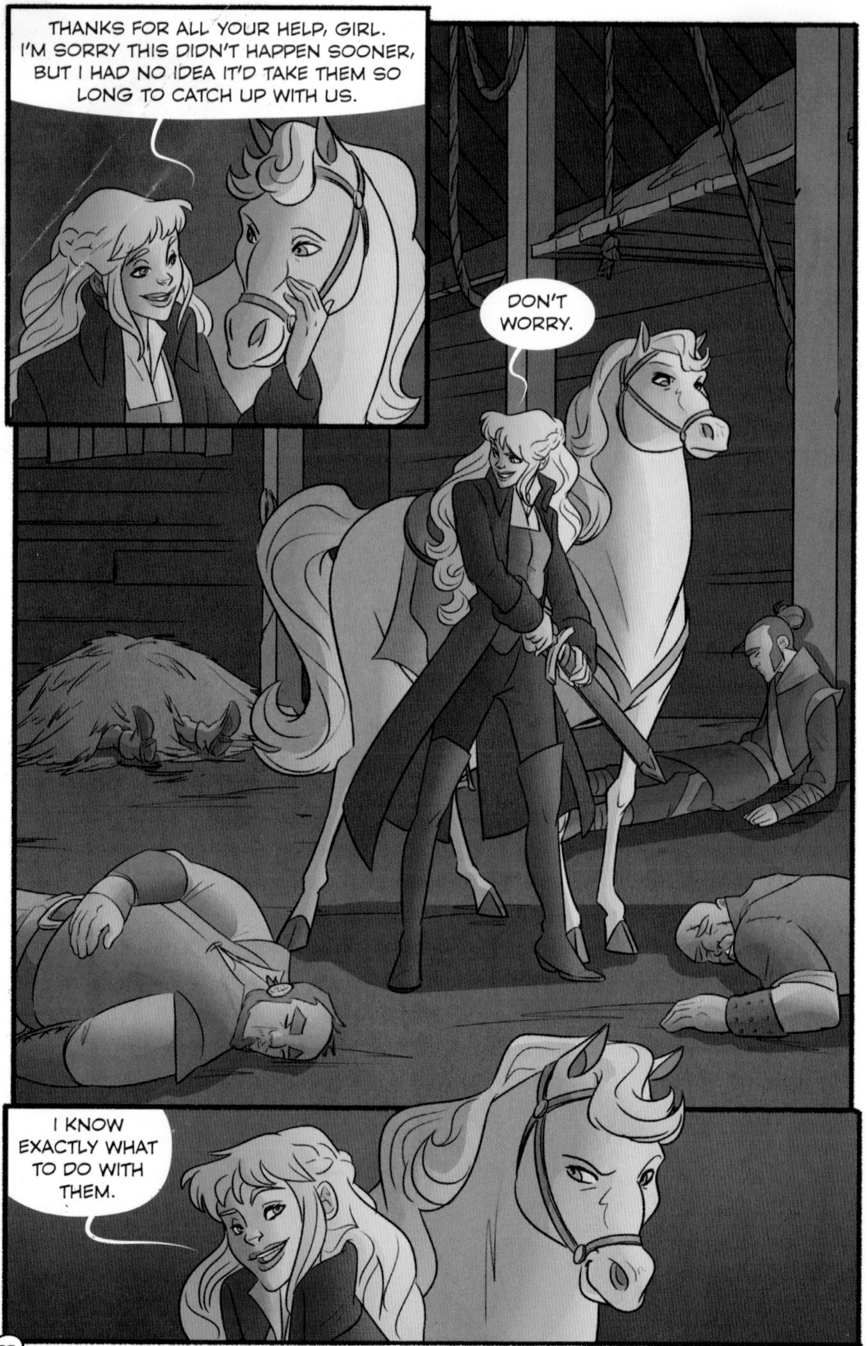
THANKS FOR ALL YOUR HELP, GIRL. I'M SORRY THIS DIDN'T HAPPEN SOONER, BUT I HAD NO IDEA IT'D TAKE THEM SO LONG TO CATCH UP WITH US.
DON'T WORRY.
I KNOW EXACTLY WHAT TO DO WITH THEM.

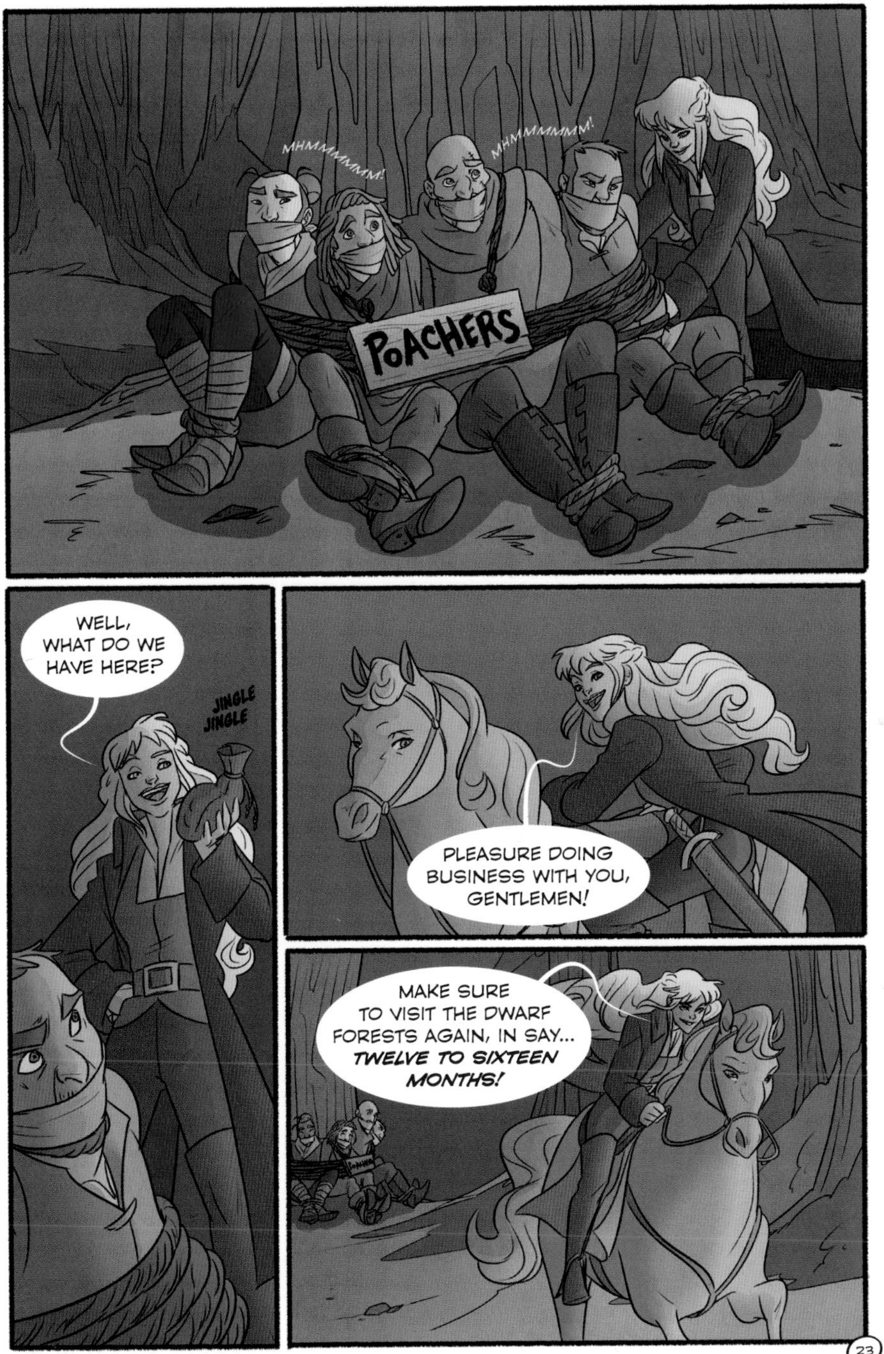
MHMMMMMMM!
MHMMMMMMM!
POACHERS
WELL, WHAT DO WE HAVE HERE?
JINGLE JINGLE
PLEASURE DOING BUSINESS WITH YOU, GENTLEMEN!
MAKE SURE TO VISIT THE DWARF FORESTS AGAIN, IN SAY... *TWELVE TO SIXTEEN MONTHS!*

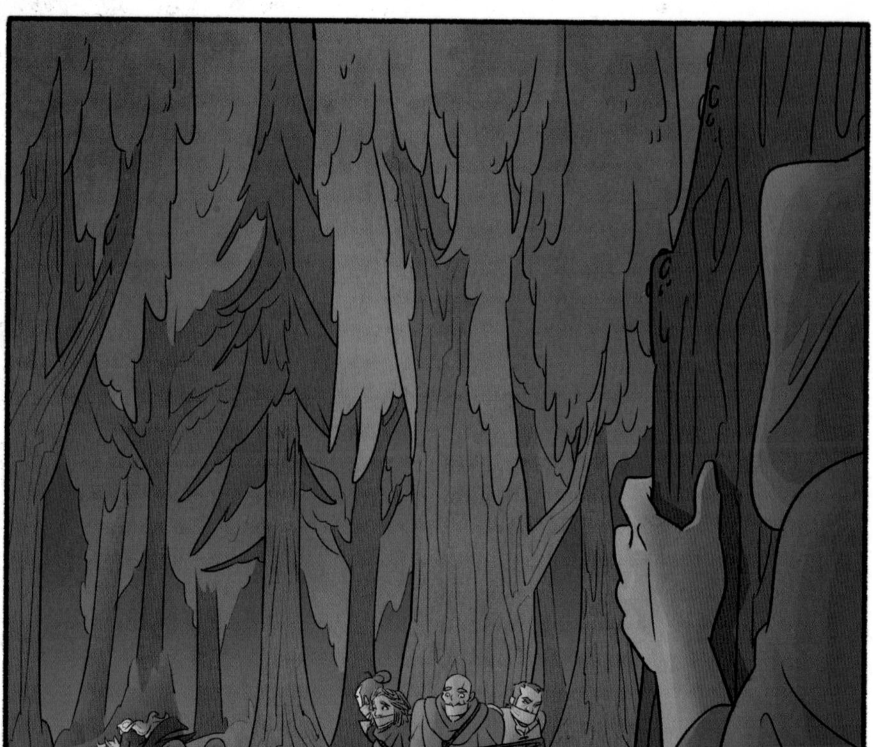
POACHERS

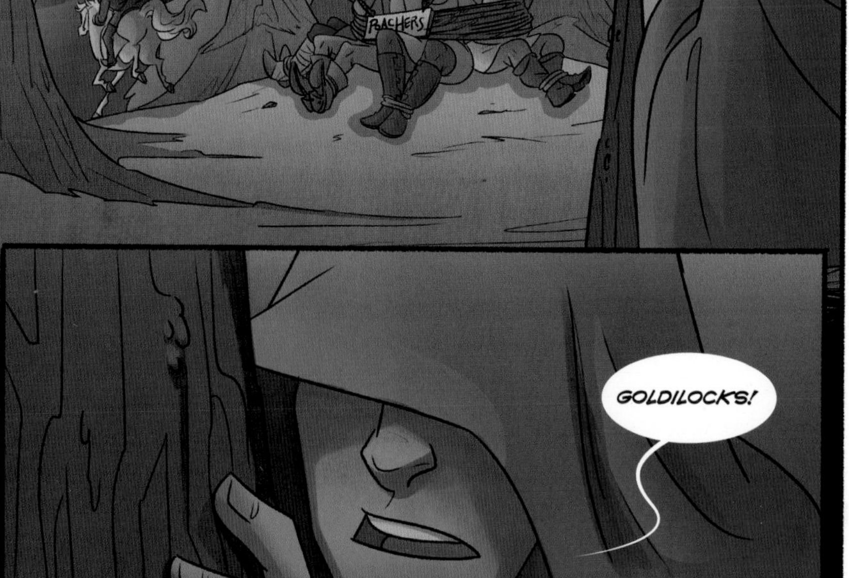
GOLDILOCKS!

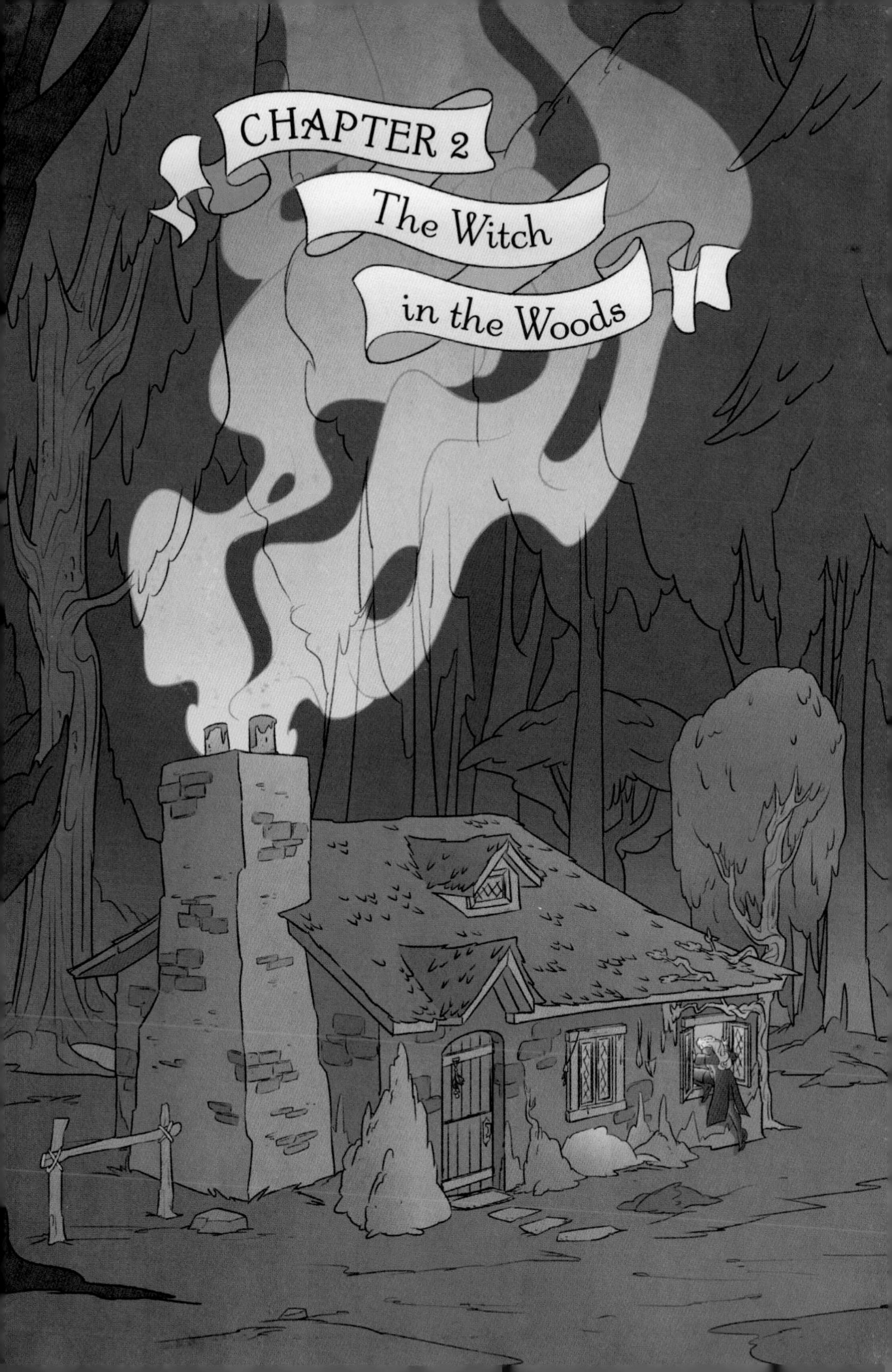
CHAPTER 2
The Witch
in the Woods

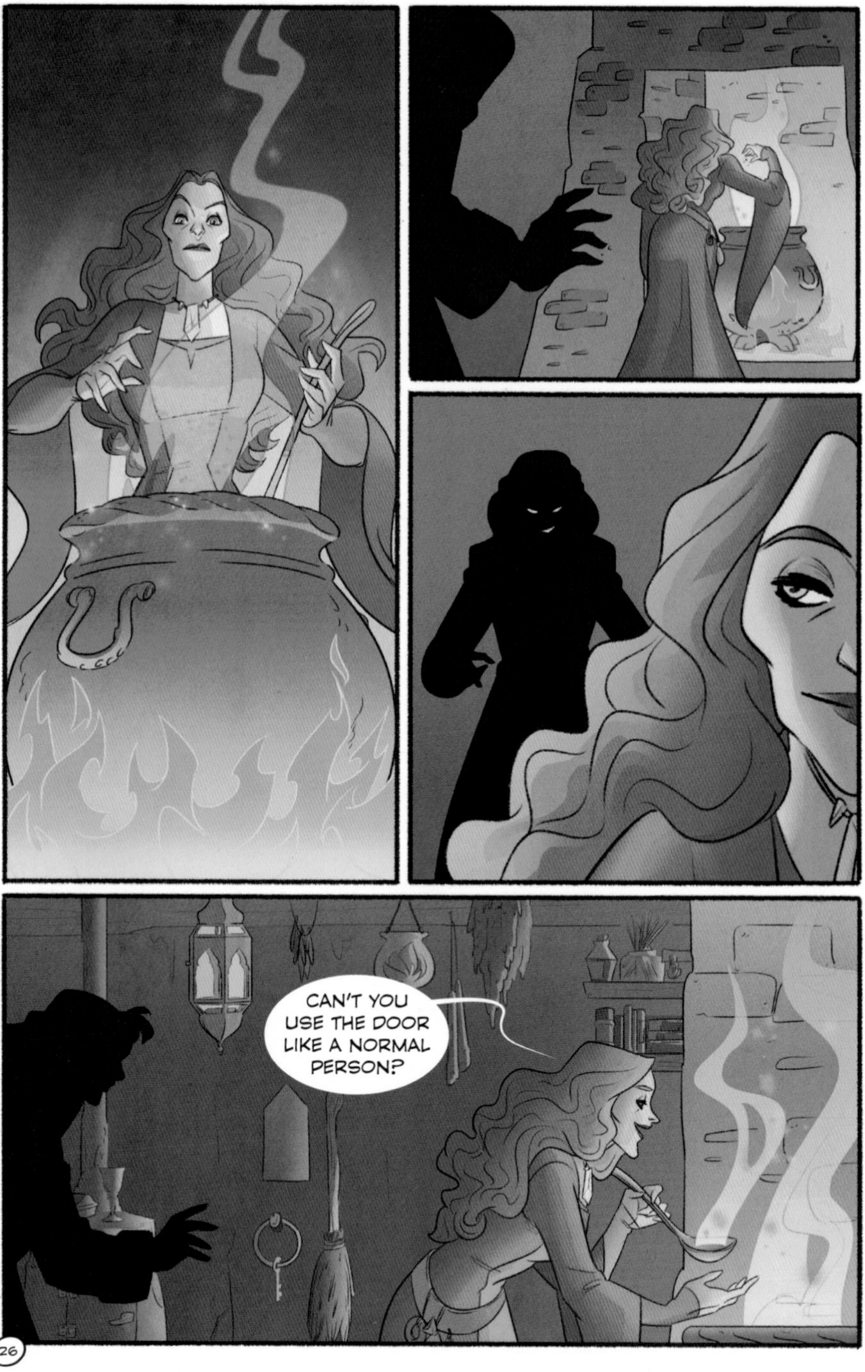
CAN'T YOU USE THE DOOR LIKE A NORMAL PERSON?

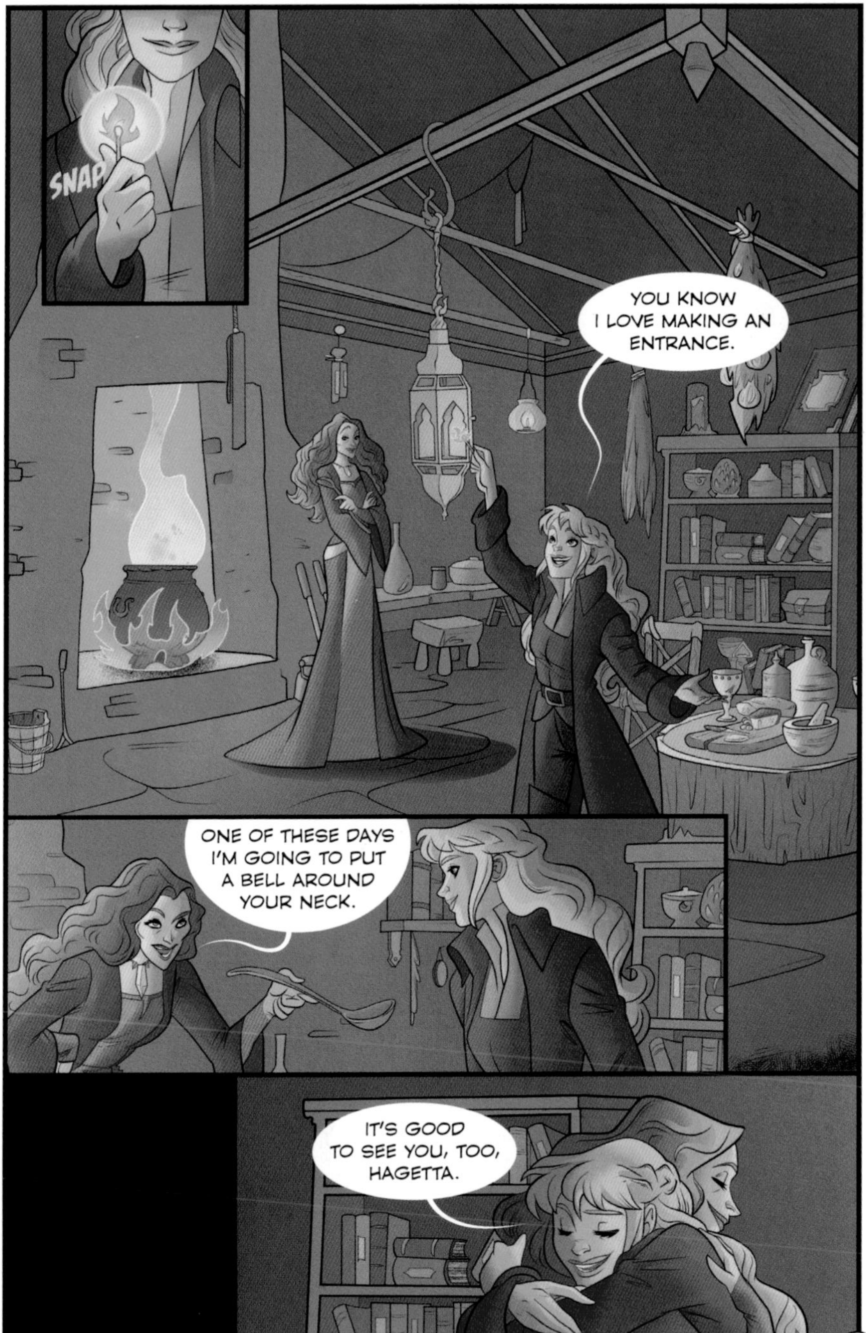
SNAP
YOU KNOW I LOVE MAKING AN ENTRANCE.
ONE OF THESE DAYS I'M GOING TO PUT A BELL AROUND YOUR NECK.
IT'S GOOD TO SEE YOU, TOO, HAGETTA.

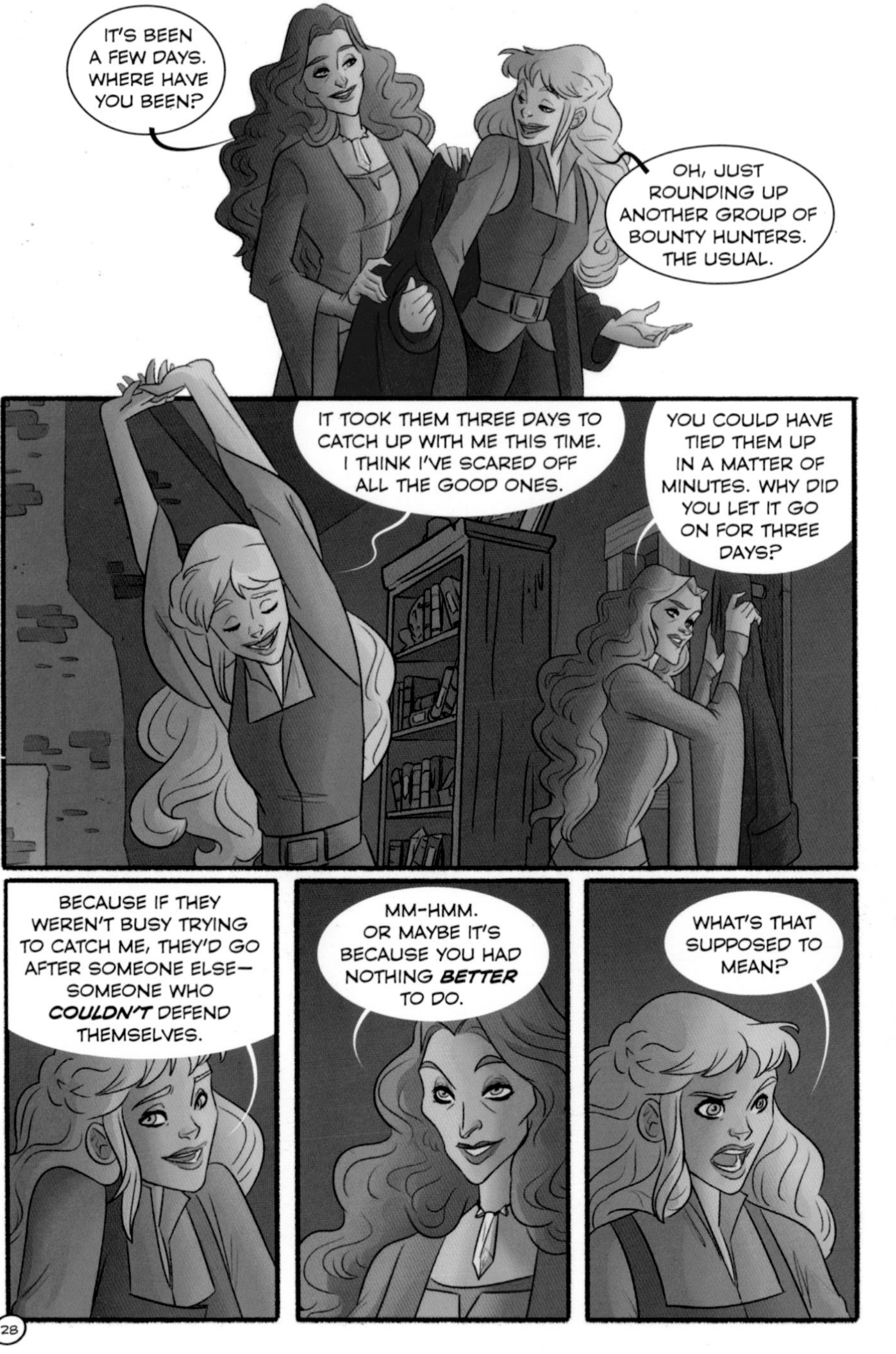
IT'S BEEN A FEW DAYS. WHERE HAVE YOU BEEN?
OH, JUST ROUNDING UP ANOTHER GROUP OF BOUNTY HUNTERS. THE USUAL.
IT TOOK THEM THREE DAYS TO CATCH UP WITH ME THIS TIME. I THINK I'VE SCARED OFF ALL THE GOOD ONES.
YOU COULD HAVE TIED THEM UP IN A MATTER OF MINUTES. WHY DID YOU LET IT GO ON FOR THREE DAYS?
BECAUSE IF THEY WEREN'T BUSY TRYING TO CATCH ME, THEY'D GO AFTER SOMEONE ELSE—SOMEONE WHO ***COULDN'T*** DEFEND THEMSELVES.
MM-HMM. OR MAYBE IT'S BECAUSE YOU HAD NOTHING ***BETTER*** TO DO.
WHAT'S THAT SUPPOSED TO MEAN?

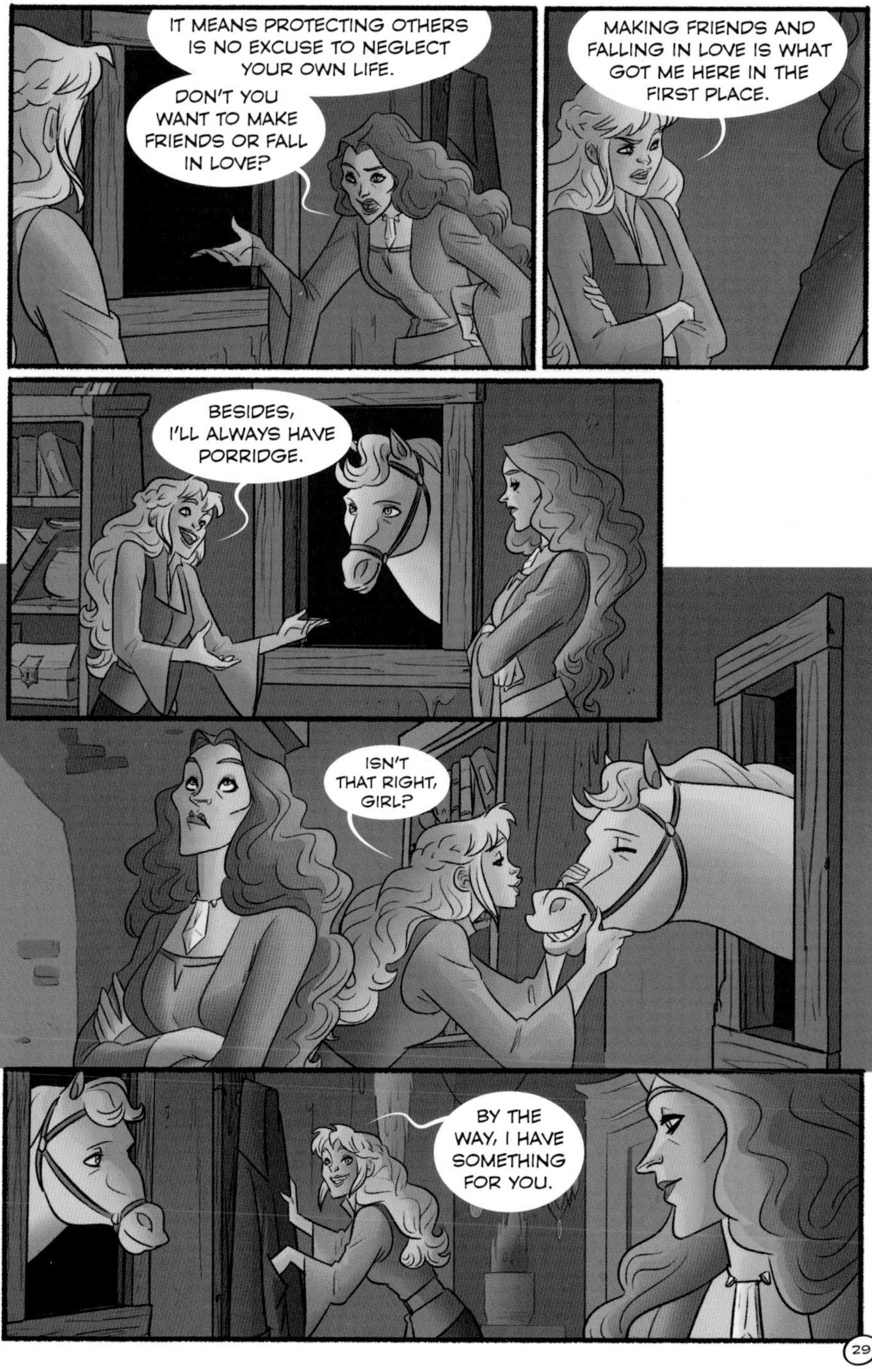
IT MEANS PROTECTING OTHERS IS NO EXCUSE TO NEGLECT YOUR OWN LIFE.
DON'T YOU WANT TO MAKE FRIENDS OR FALL IN LOVE?
MAKING FRIENDS AND FALLING IN LOVE IS WHAT GOT ME HERE IN THE FIRST PLACE.
BESIDES, I'LL ALWAYS HAVE PORRIDGE.
ISN'T THAT RIGHT, GIRL?
BY THE WAY, I HAVE SOMETHING FOR YOU.

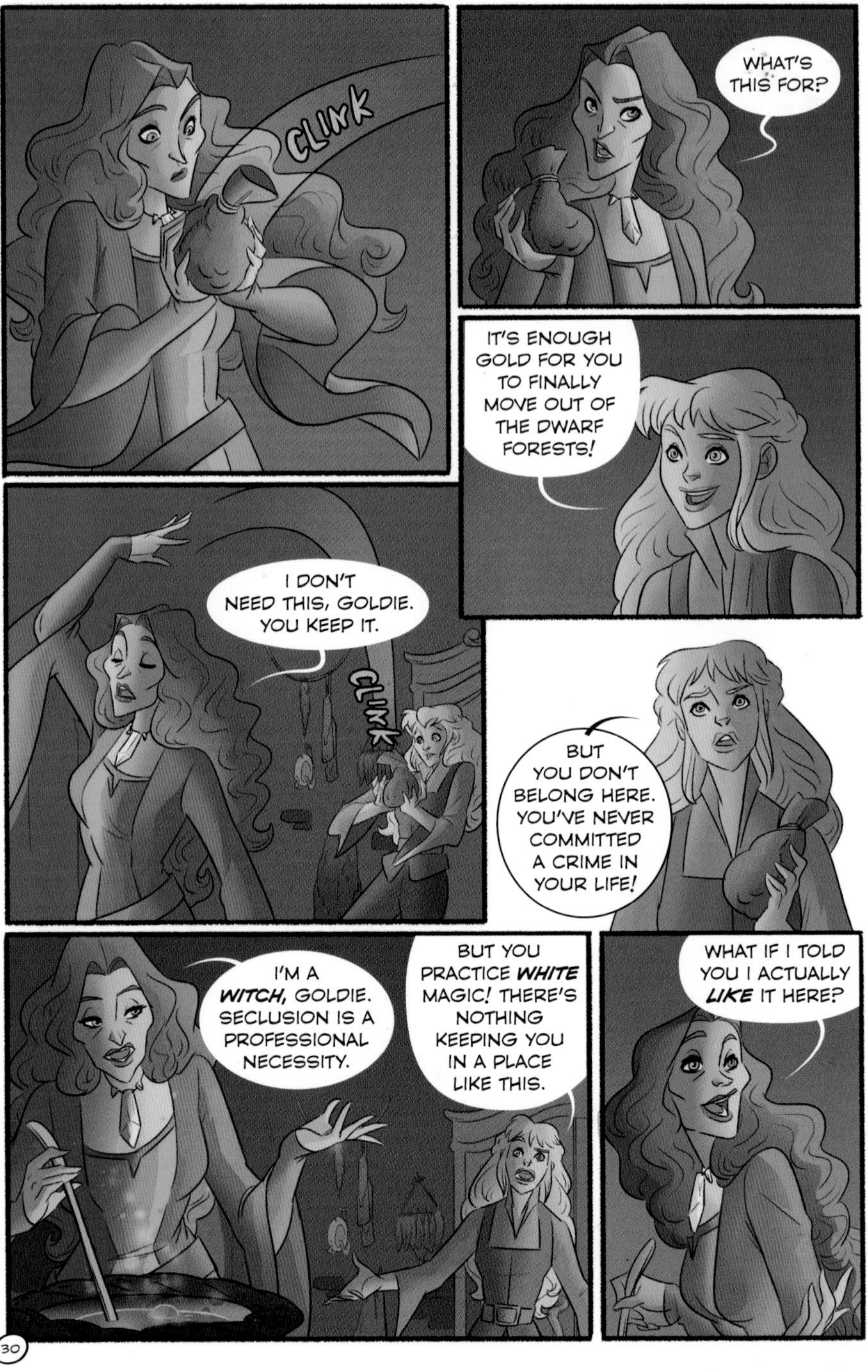
CLINK
WHAT'S THIS FOR?
IT'S ENOUGH GOLD FOR YOU TO FINALLY MOVE OUT OF THE DWARF FORESTS!
I DON'T NEED THIS, GOLDIE. YOU KEEP IT.
CLINK
BUT YOU DON'T BELONG HERE. YOU'VE NEVER COMMITTED A CRIME IN YOUR LIFE!
I'M A *WITCH*, GOLDIE. SECLUSION IS A PROFESSIONAL NECESSITY.
BUT YOU PRACTICE *WHITE* MAGIC! THERE'S NOTHING KEEPING YOU IN A PLACE LIKE THIS.
WHAT IF I TOLD YOU I ACTUALLY *LIKE* IT HERE?

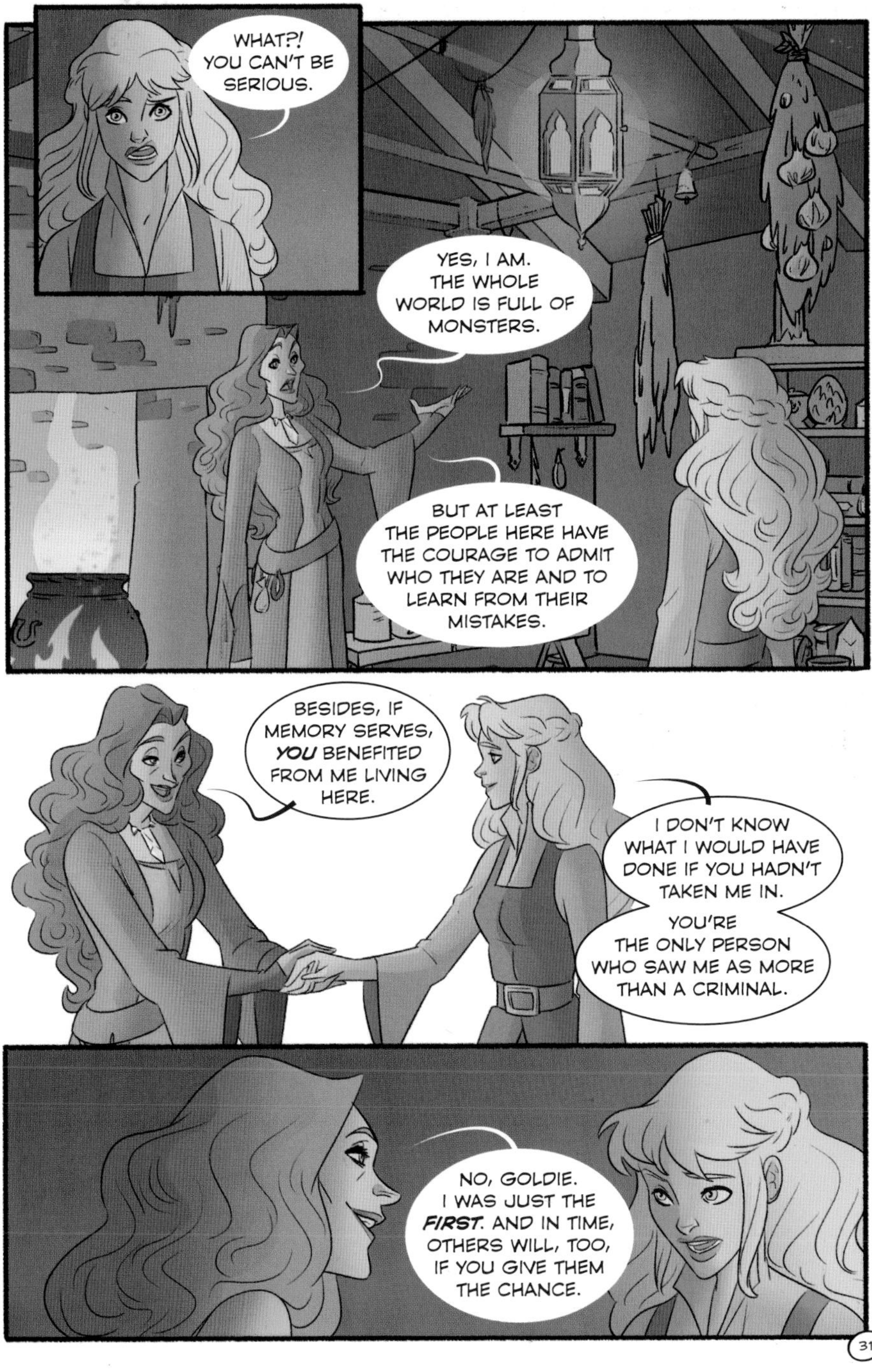
WHAT?! YOU CAN'T BE SERIOUS.
YES, I AM. THE WHOLE WORLD IS FULL OF MONSTERS.
BUT AT LEAST THE PEOPLE HERE HAVE THE COURAGE TO ADMIT WHO THEY ARE AND TO LEARN FROM THEIR MISTAKES.
BESIDES, IF MEMORY SERVES, ***YOU*** BENEFITED FROM ME LIVING HERE.
I DON'T KNOW WHAT I WOULD HAVE DONE IF YOU HADN'T TAKEN ME IN.
YOU'RE THE ONLY PERSON WHO SAW ME AS MORE THAN A CRIMINAL.
NO, GOLDIE. I WAS JUST THE ***FIRST***. AND IN TIME, OTHERS WILL, TOO, IF YOU GIVE THEM THE CHANCE.

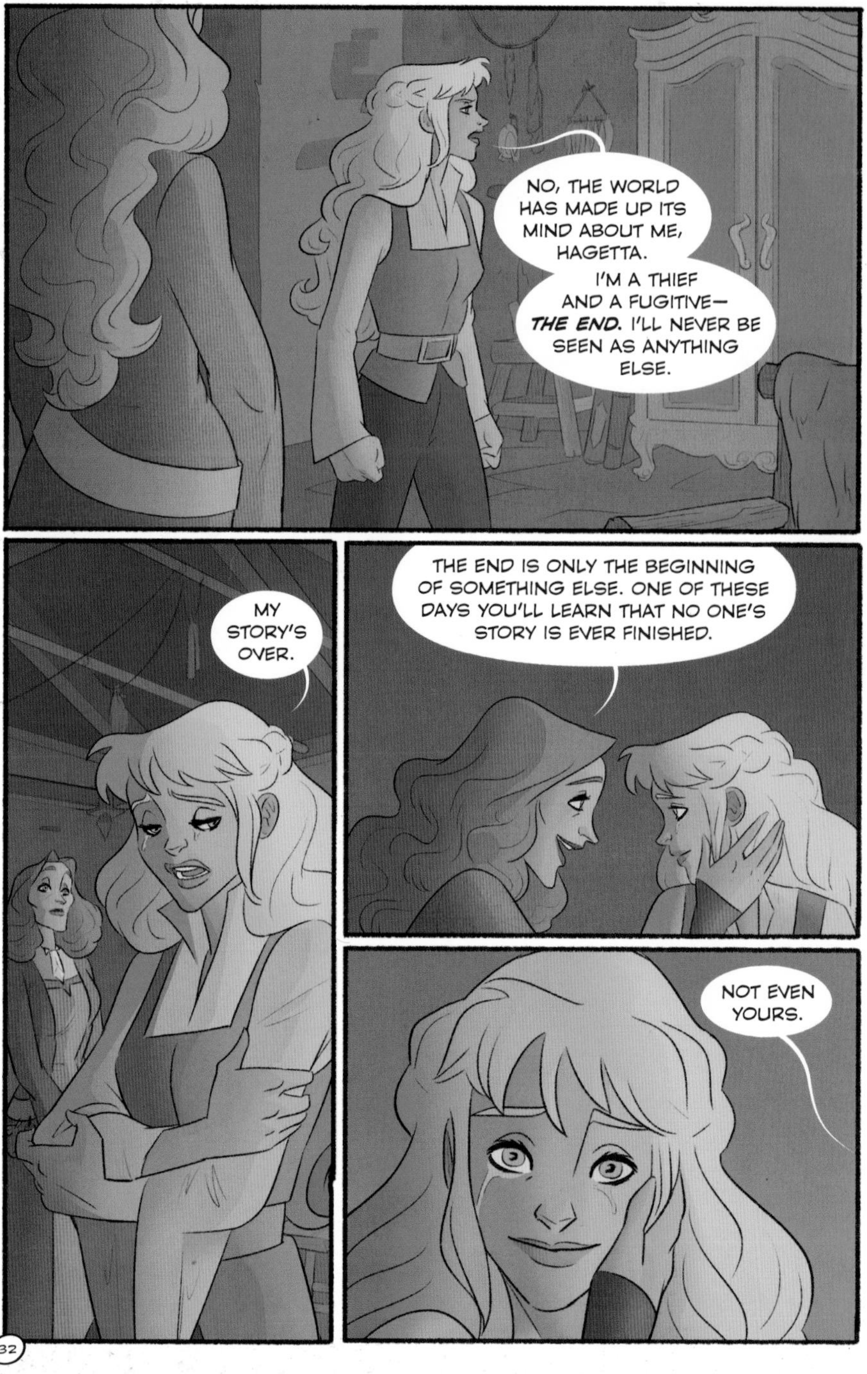
NO, THE WORLD HAS MADE UP ITS MIND ABOUT ME, HAGETTA.
I'M A THIEF AND A FUGITIVE— ***THE END.*** I'LL NEVER BE SEEN AS ANYTHING ELSE.
MY STORY'S OVER.
THE END IS ONLY THE BEGINNING OF SOMETHING ELSE. ONE OF THESE DAYS YOU'LL LEARN THAT NO ONE'S STORY IS EVER FINISHED.
NOT EVEN YOURS.

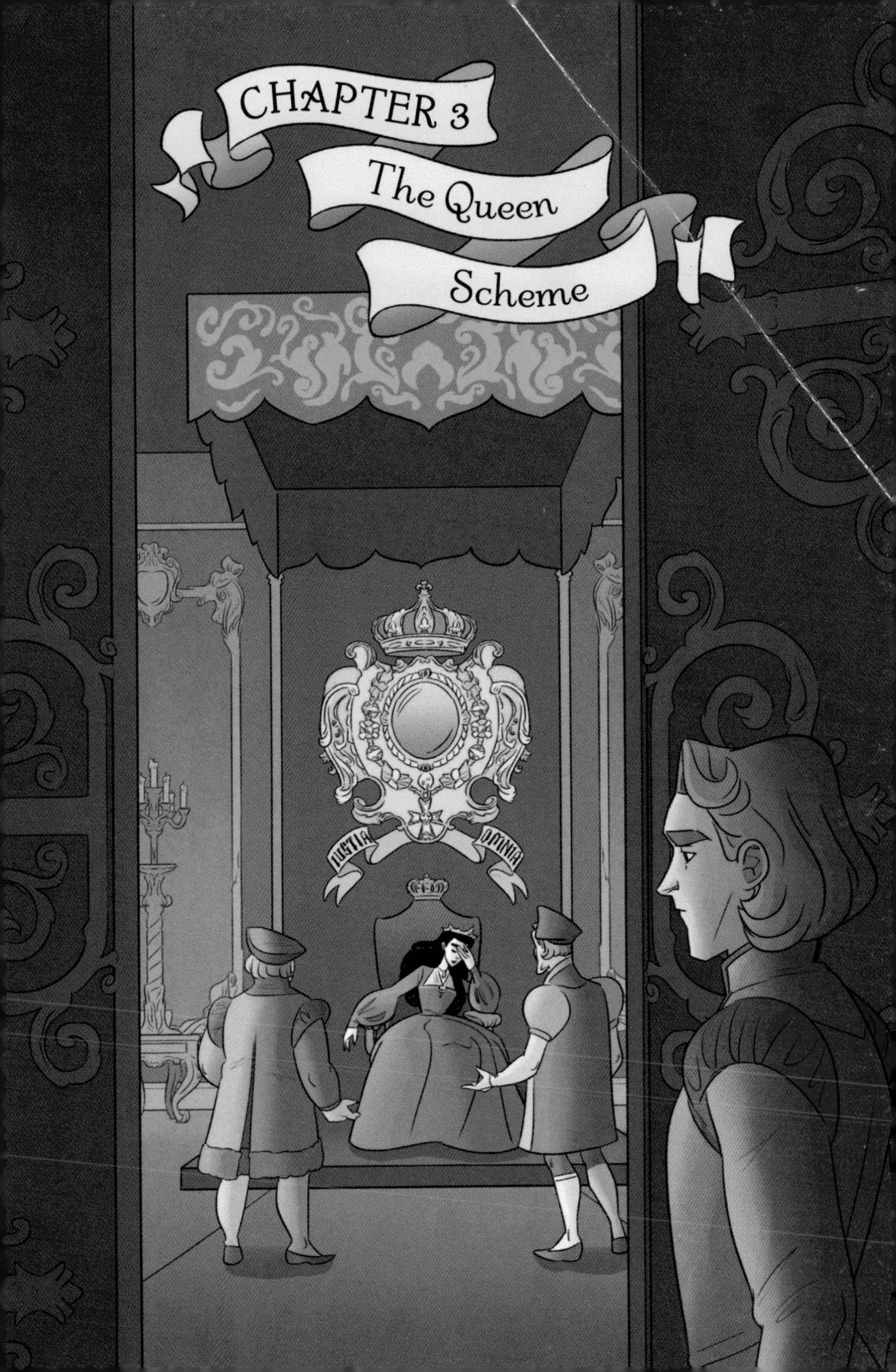
CHAPTER 3
The Queen Scheme
IUSTIA
OMNIA

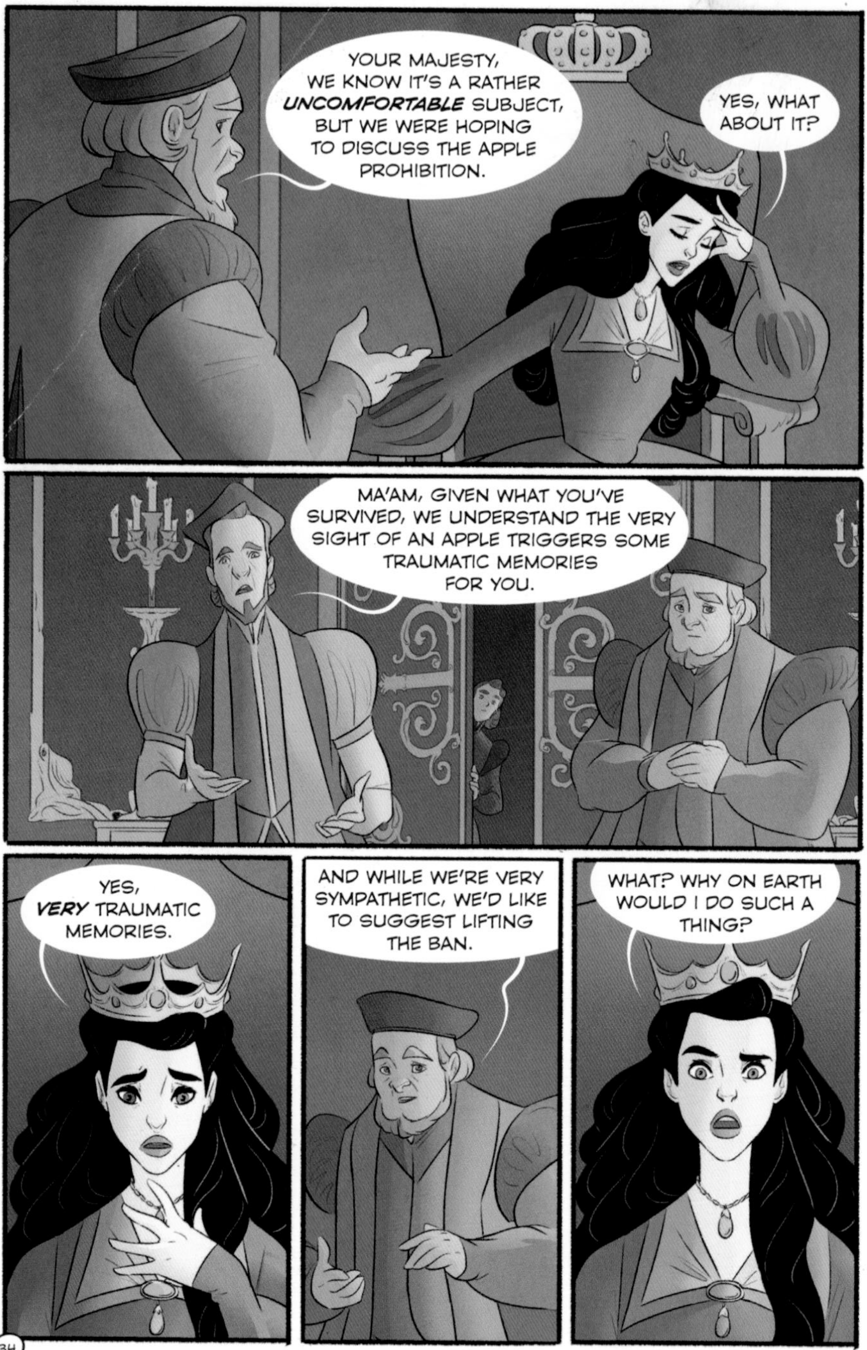
YOUR MAJESTY, WE KNOW IT'S A RATHER ***UNCOMFORTABLE*** SUBJECT, BUT WE WERE HOPING TO DISCUSS THE APPLE PROHIBITION.
YES, WHAT ABOUT IT?
MA'AM, GIVEN WHAT YOU'VE SURVIVED, WE UNDERSTAND THE VERY SIGHT OF AN APPLE TRIGGERS SOME TRAUMATIC MEMORIES FOR YOU.
YES, ***VERY*** TRAUMATIC MEMORIES.
AND WHILE WE'RE VERY SYMPATHETIC, WE'D LIKE TO SUGGEST LIFTING THE BAN.
WHAT? WHY ON EARTH WOULD I DO SUCH A THING?

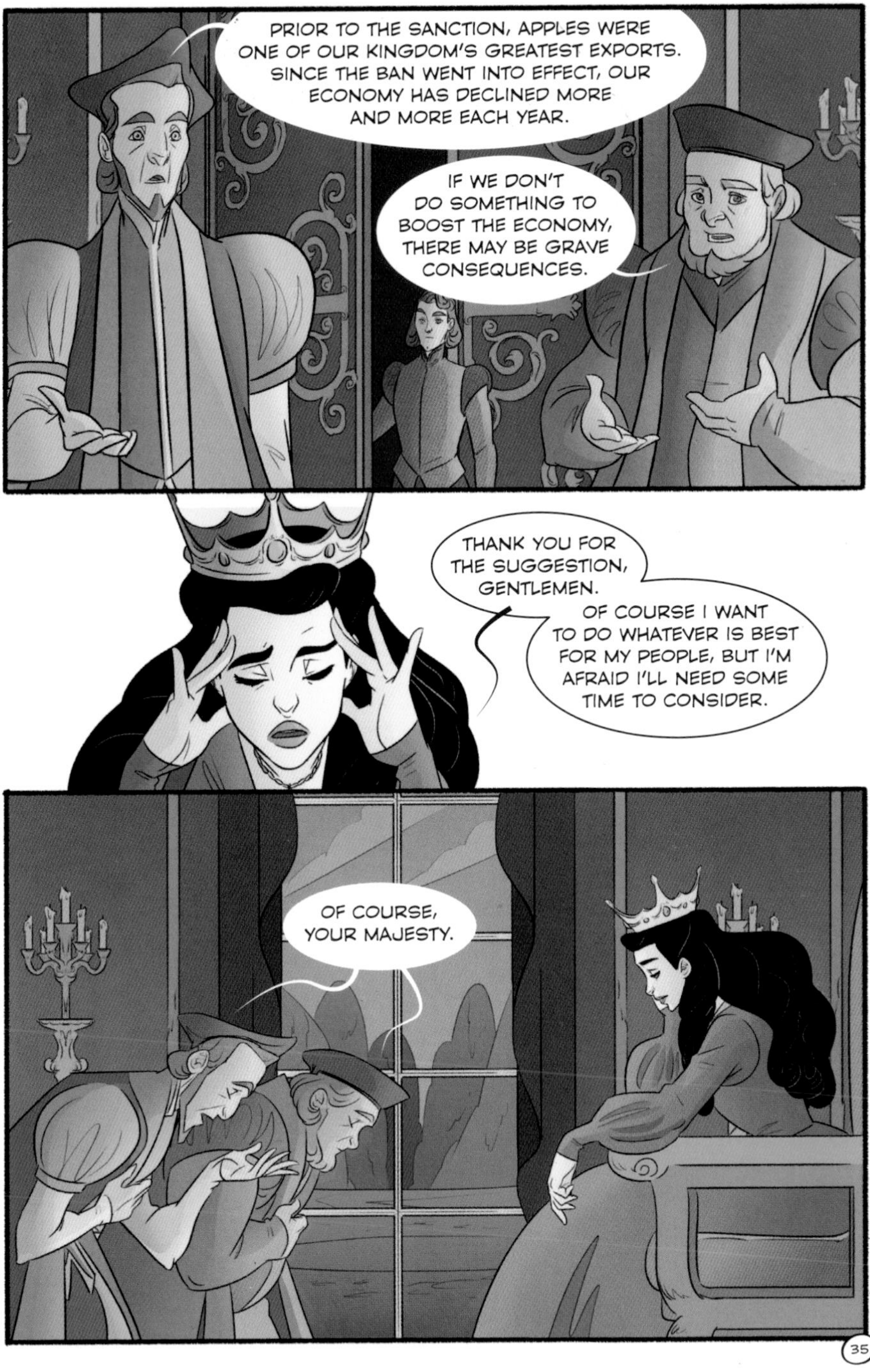
PRIOR TO THE SANCTION, APPLES WERE ONE OF OUR KINGDOM'S GREATEST EXPORTS. SINCE THE BAN WENT INTO EFFECT, OUR ECONOMY HAS DECLINED MORE AND MORE EACH YEAR.
IF WE DON'T DO SOMETHING TO BOOST THE ECONOMY, THERE MAY BE GRAVE CONSEQUENCES.
THANK YOU FOR THE SUGGESTION, GENTLEMEN.
OF COURSE I WANT TO DO WHATEVER IS BEST FOR MY PEOPLE, BUT I'M AFRAID I'LL NEED SOME TIME TO CONSIDER.
OF COURSE, YOUR MAJESTY.

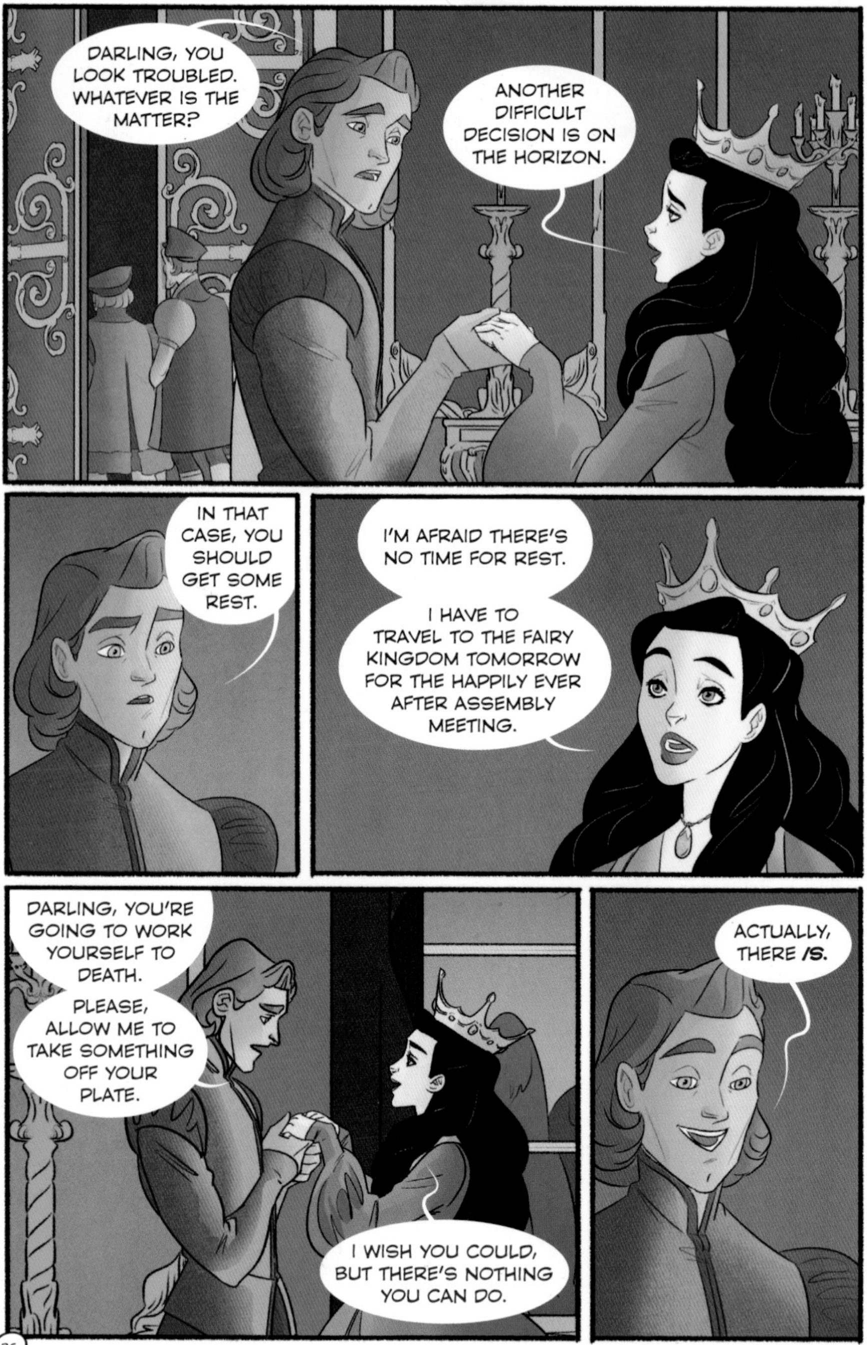
DARLING, YOU LOOK TROUBLED. WHATEVER IS THE MATTER?
ANOTHER DIFFICULT DECISION IS ON THE HORIZON.
IN THAT CASE, YOU SHOULD GET SOME REST.
I'M AFRAID THERE'S NO TIME FOR REST.
I HAVE TO TRAVEL TO THE FAIRY KINGDOM TOMORROW FOR THE HAPPILY EVER AFTER ASSEMBLY MEETING.
DARLING, YOU'RE GOING TO WORK YOURSELF TO DEATH.
PLEASE, ALLOW ME TO TAKE SOMETHING OFF YOUR PLATE.
I WISH YOU COULD, BUT THERE'S NOTHING YOU CAN DO.
ACTUALLY, THERE ***IS***.

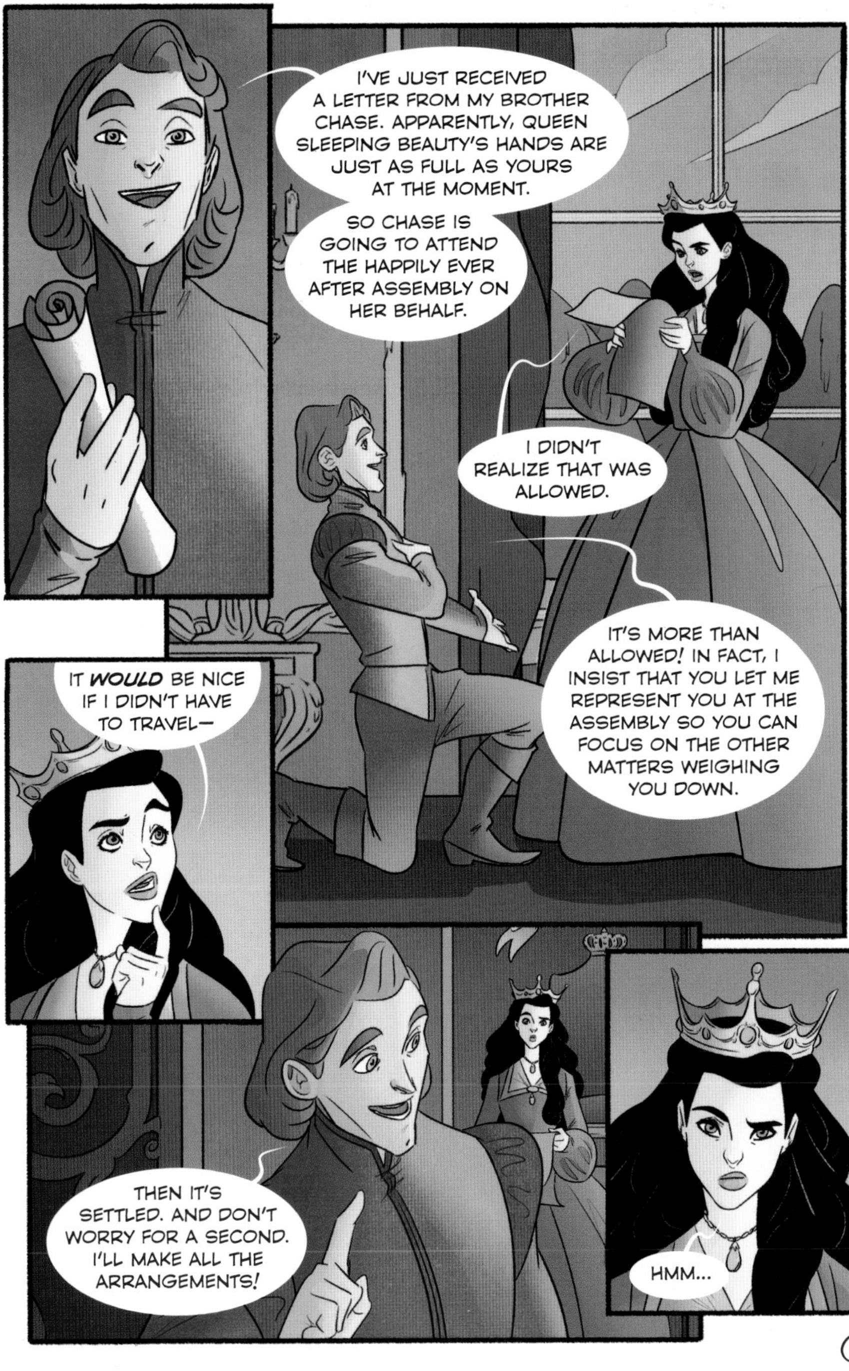
I'VE JUST RECEIVED A LETTER FROM MY BROTHER CHASE. APPARENTLY, QUEEN SLEEPING BEAUTY'S HANDS ARE JUST AS FULL AS YOURS AT THE MOMENT.
SO CHASE IS GOING TO ATTEND THE HAPPILY EVER AFTER ASSEMBLY ON HER BEHALF.
I DIDN'T REALIZE THAT WAS ALLOWED.
IT'S MORE THAN ALLOWED! IN FACT, I INSIST THAT YOU LET ME REPRESENT YOU AT THE ASSEMBLY SO YOU CAN FOCUS ON THE OTHER MATTERS WEIGHING YOU DOWN.
IT **WOULD** BE NICE IF I DIDN'T HAVE TO TRAVEL—
THEN IT'S SETTLED. AND DON'T WORRY FOR A SECOND. I'LL MAKE ALL THE ARRANGEMENTS!
HMM...

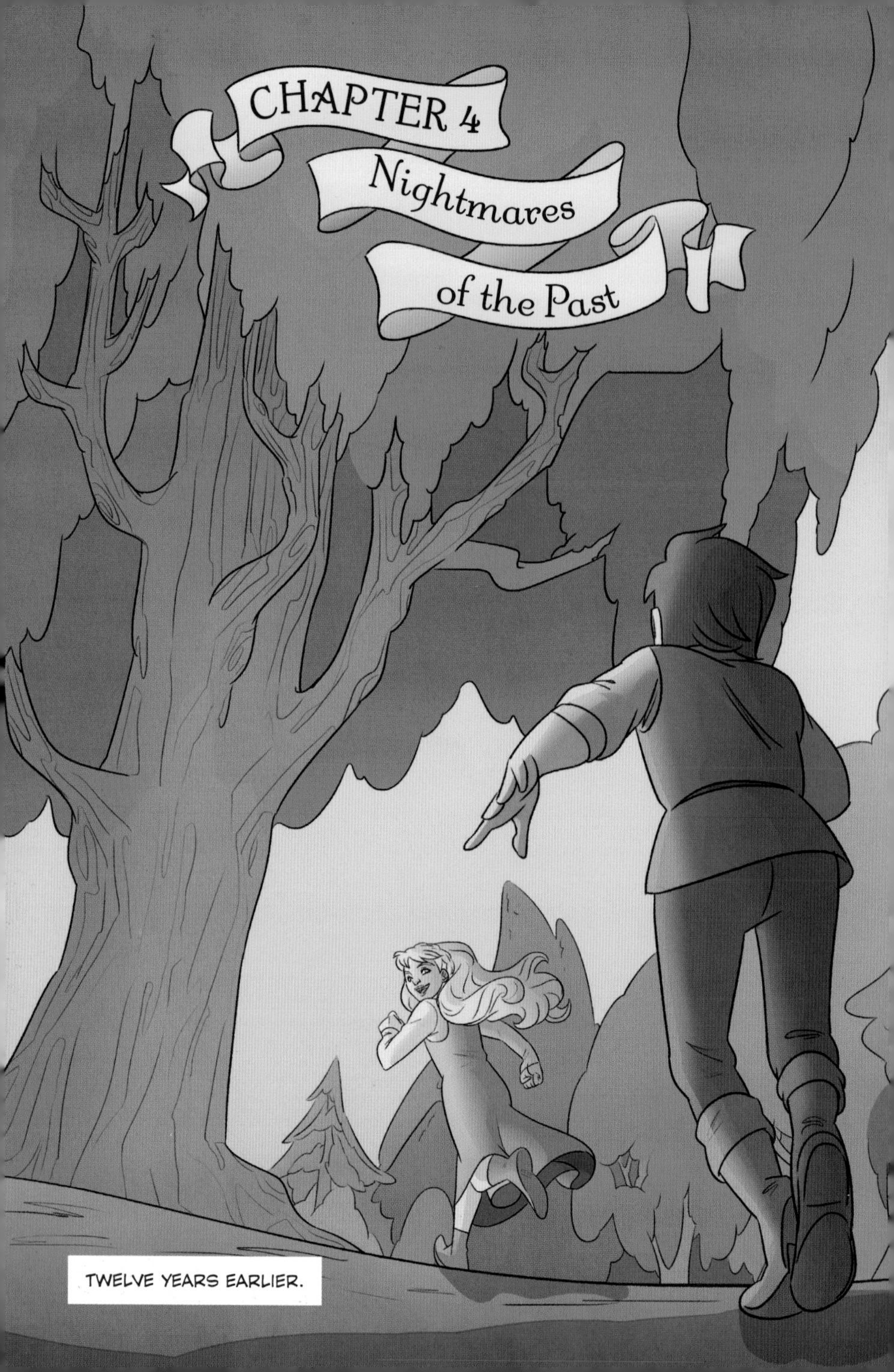
CHAPTER 4
Nightmares
of the Past
TWELVE YEARS EARLIER.

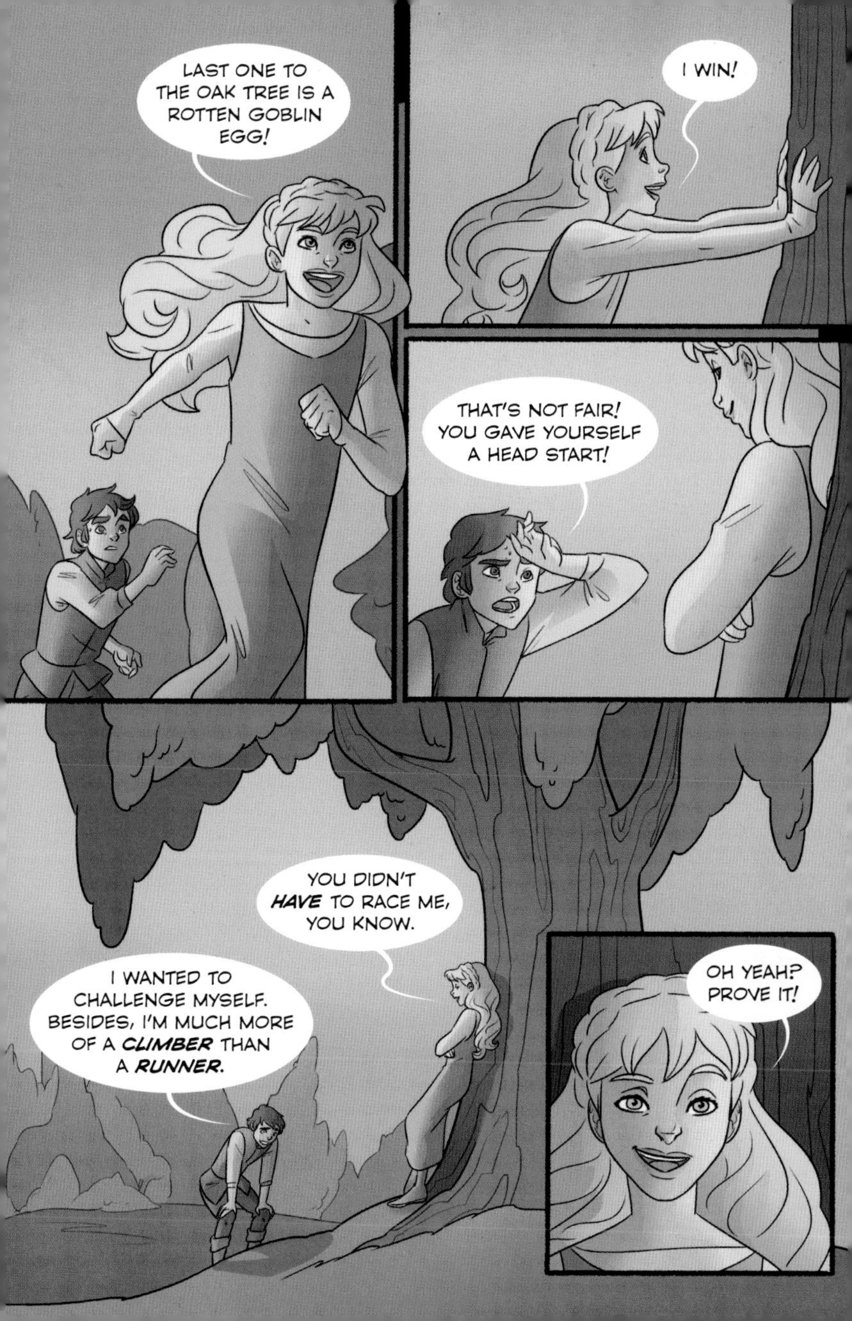
LAST ONE TO THE OAK TREE IS A ROTTEN GOBLIN EGG!
I WIN!
THAT'S NOT FAIR! YOU GAVE YOURSELF A HEAD START!
YOU DIDN'T **HAVE** TO RACE ME, YOU KNOW.
I WANTED TO CHALLENGE MYSELF. BESIDES, I'M MUCH MORE OF A **CLIMBER** THAN A **RUNNER**.
OH YEAH? PROVE IT!

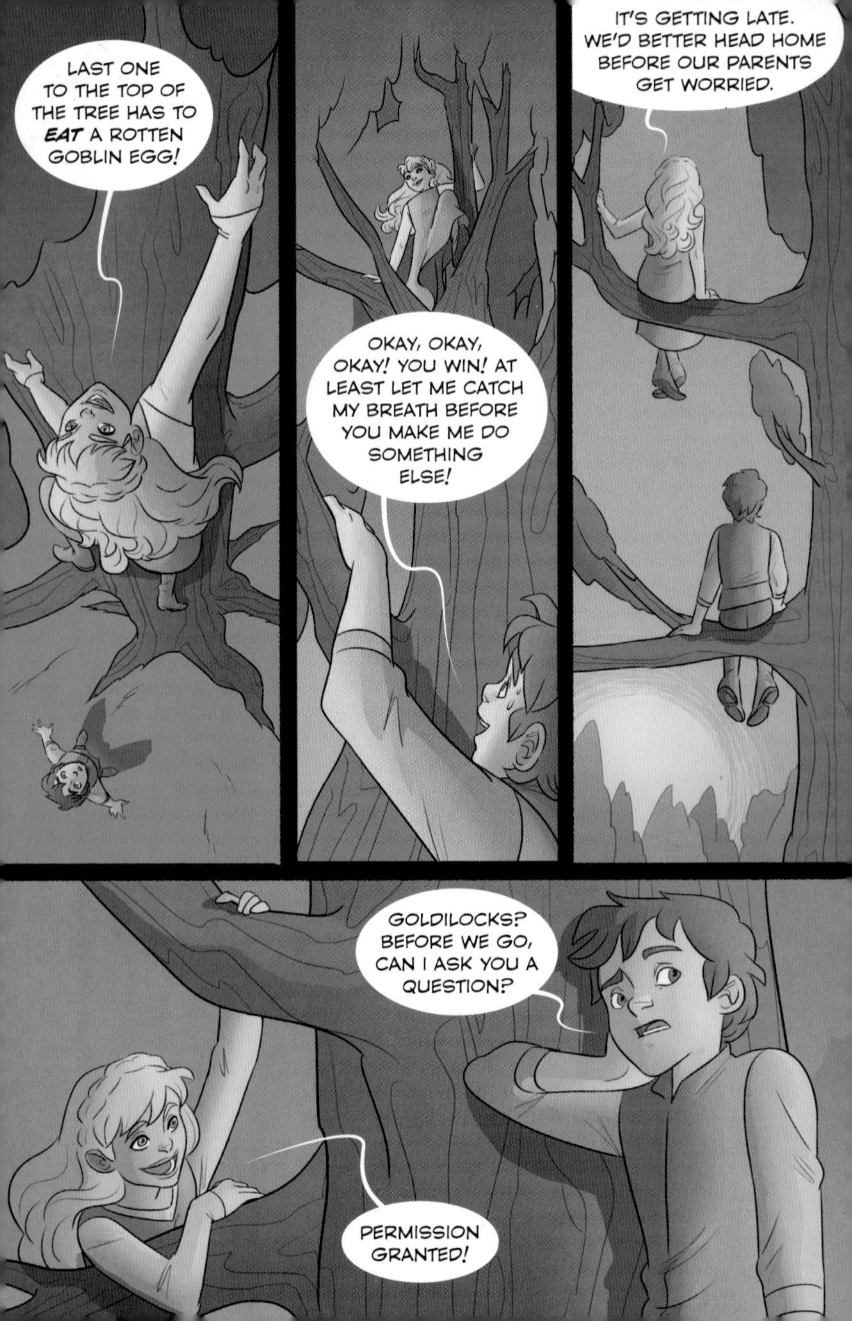

LAST ONE TO THE TOP OF THE TREE HAS TO *EAT* A ROTTEN GOBLIN EGG!
OKAY, OKAY, OKAY! YOU WIN! AT LEAST LET ME CATCH MY BREATH BEFORE YOU MAKE ME DO SOMETHING ELSE!
IT'S GETTING LATE. WE'D BETTER HEAD HOME BEFORE OUR PARENTS GET WORRIED.
GOLDILOCKS? BEFORE WE GO, CAN I ASK YOU A QUESTION?
PERMISSION GRANTED!

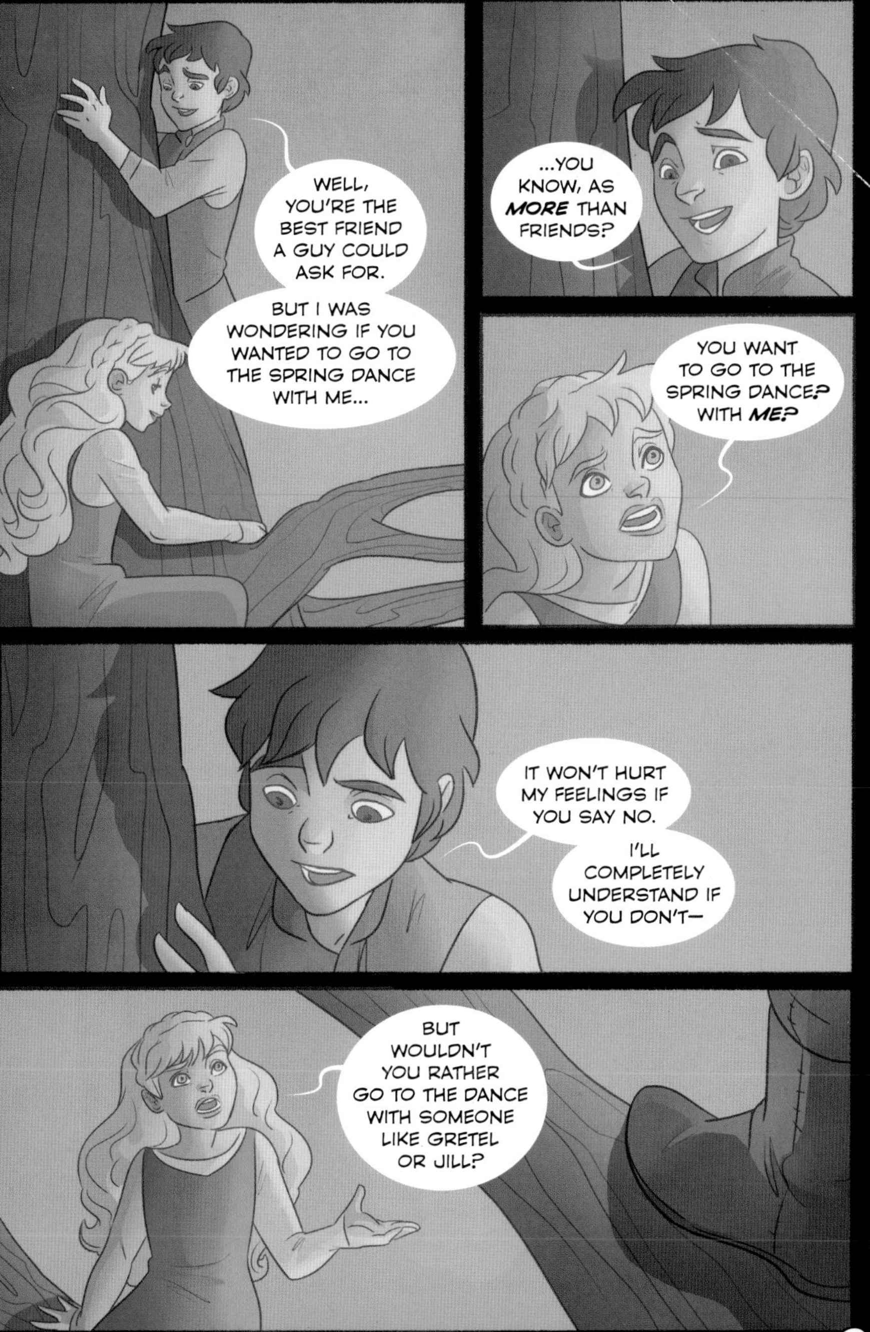
WELL, YOU'RE THE BEST FRIEND A GUY COULD ASK FOR.
BUT I WAS WONDERING IF YOU WANTED TO GO TO THE SPRING DANCE WITH ME...
...YOU KNOW, AS *MORE* THAN FRIENDS?
YOU WANT TO GO TO THE SPRING DANCE? WITH *ME?*
IT WON'T HURT MY FEELINGS IF YOU SAY NO.
I'LL COMPLETELY UNDERSTAND IF YOU DON'T—
BUT WOULDN'T YOU RATHER GO TO THE DANCE WITH SOMEONE LIKE GRETEL OR JILL?

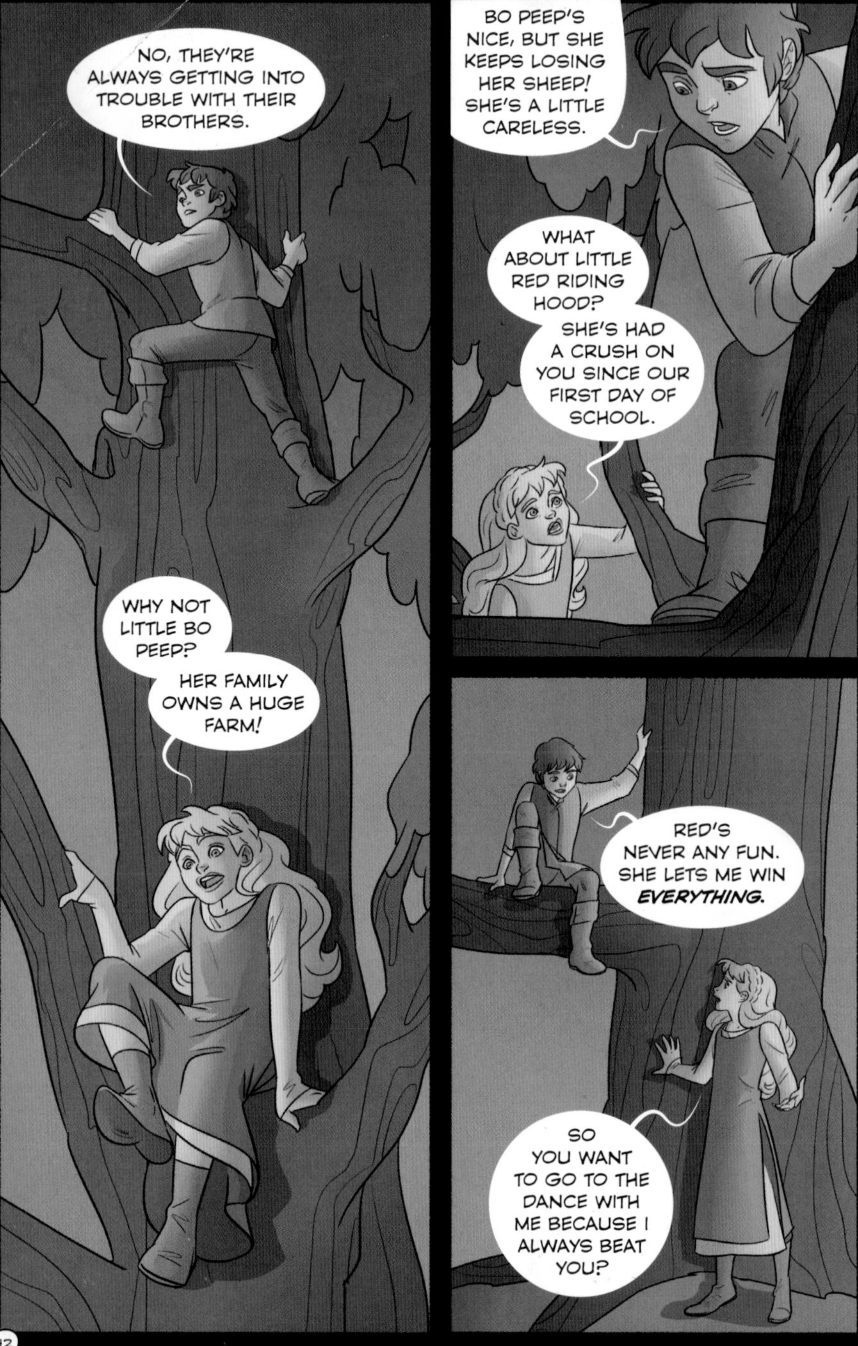

NO, THEY'RE ALWAYS GETTING INTO TROUBLE WITH THEIR BROTHERS.
BO PEEP'S NICE, BUT SHE KEEPS LOSING HER SHEEP! SHE'S A LITTLE CARELESS.
WHAT ABOUT LITTLE RED RIDING HOOD?
SHE'S HAD A CRUSH ON YOU SINCE OUR FIRST DAY OF SCHOOL.
WHY NOT LITTLE BO PEEP?
HER FAMILY OWNS A HUGE FARM!
RED'S NEVER ANY FUN. SHE LETS ME WIN *EVERYTHING.*
SO YOU WANT TO GO TO THE DANCE WITH ME BECAUSE I ALWAYS BEAT YOU?

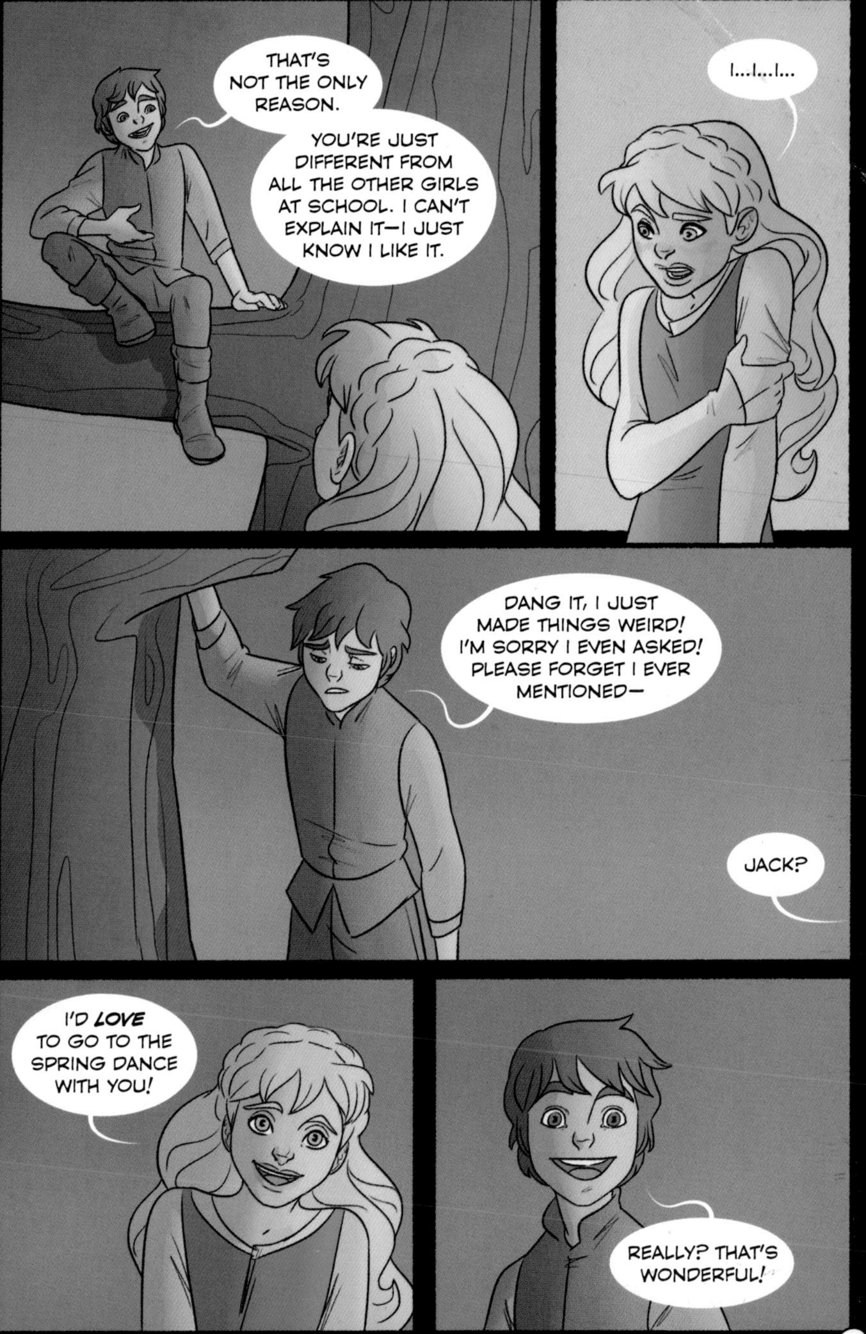
THAT'S NOT THE ONLY REASON.
YOU'RE JUST DIFFERENT FROM ALL THE OTHER GIRLS AT SCHOOL. I CAN'T EXPLAIN IT—I JUST KNOW I LIKE IT.
I...I...I...
DANG IT, I JUST MADE THINGS WEIRD! I'M SORRY I EVEN ASKED! PLEASE FORGET I EVER MENTIONED—
JACK?
I'D ***LOVE*** TO GO TO THE SPRING DANCE WITH YOU!
REALLY? THAT'S WONDERFUL!

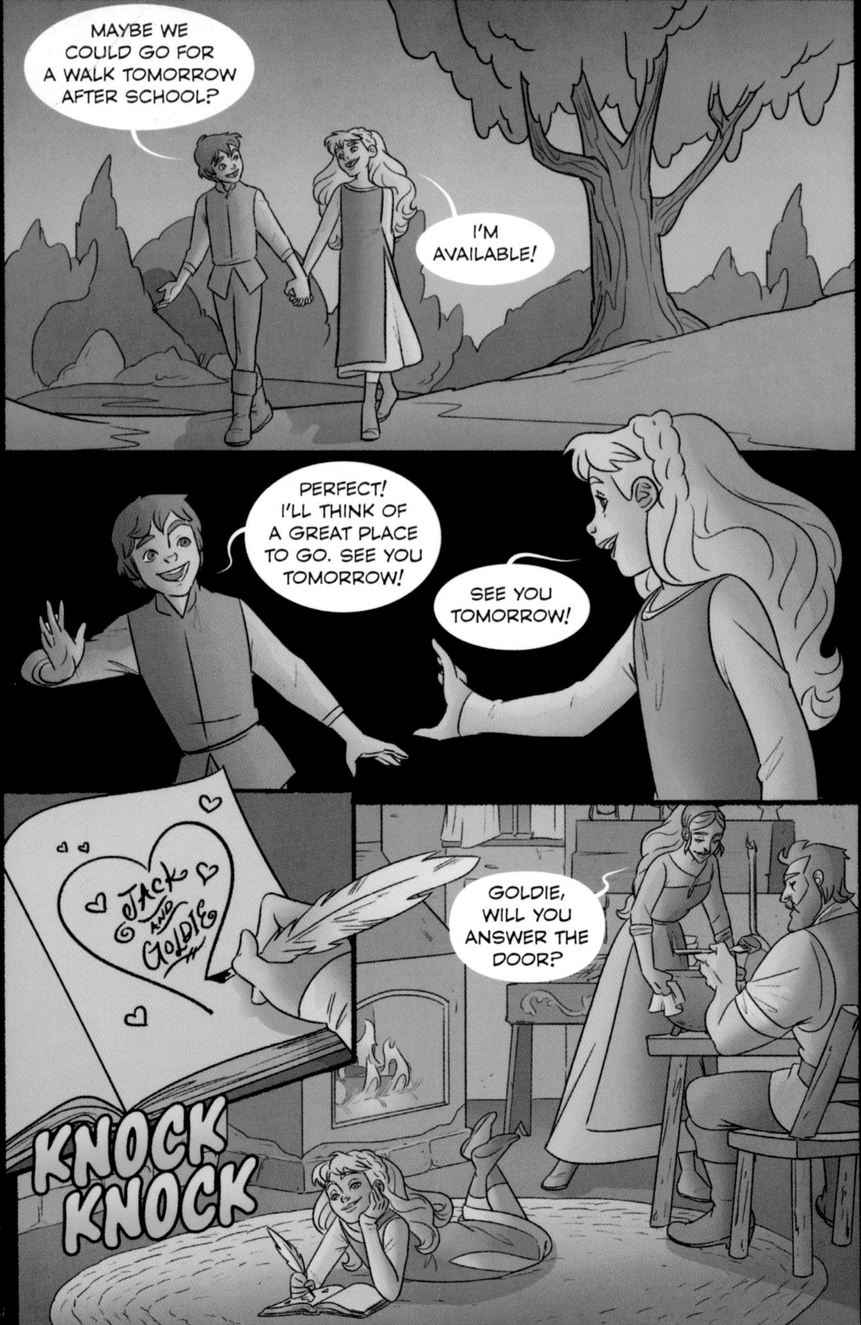
MAYBE WE COULD GO FOR A WALK TOMORROW AFTER SCHOOL?
I'M AVAILABLE!
PERFECT! I'LL THINK OF A GREAT PLACE TO GO. SEE YOU TOMORROW!
SEE YOU TOMORROW!
JACK AND GOLDIE
GOLDIE, WILL YOU ANSWER THE DOOR?
KNOCK KNOCK

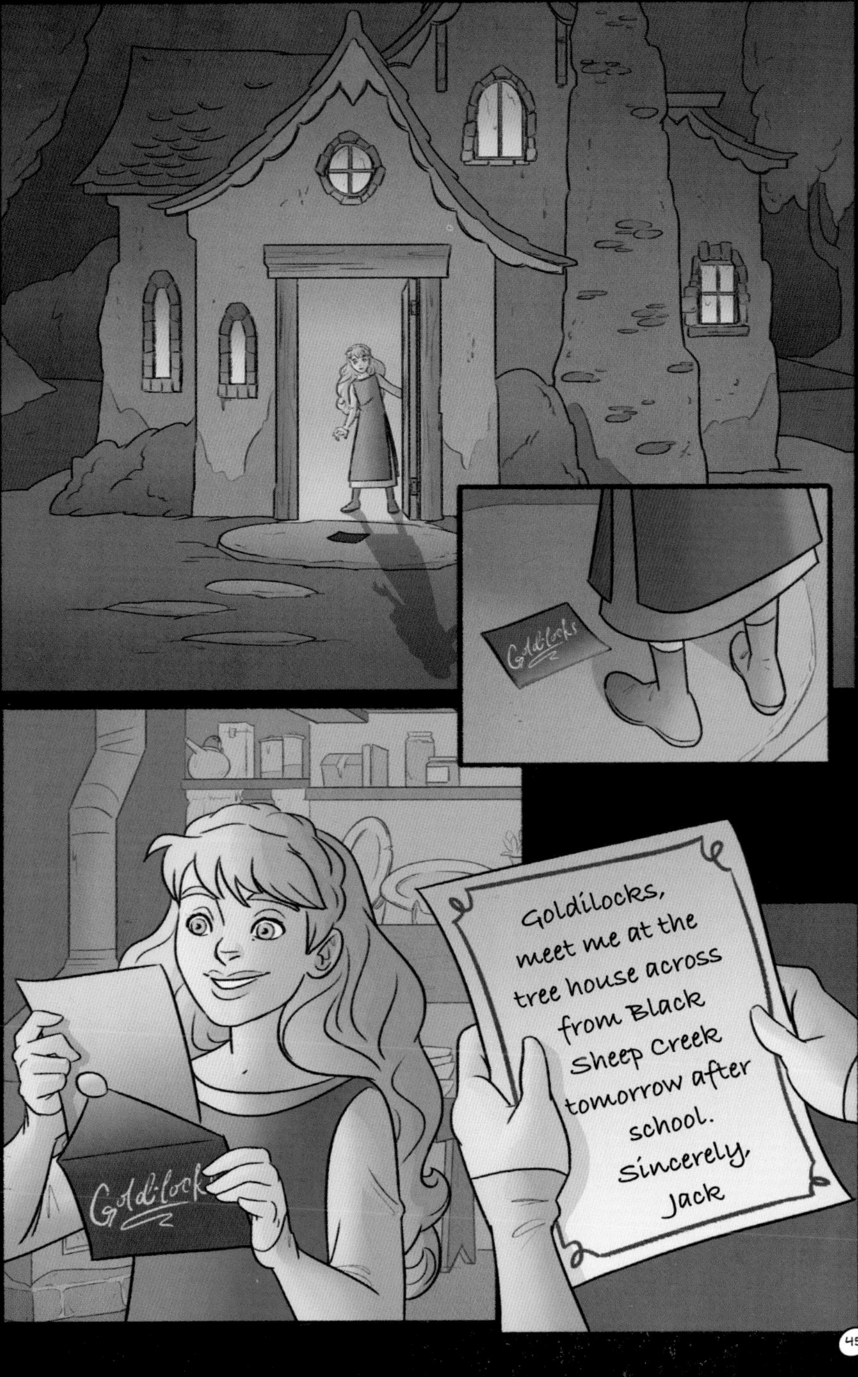
Goldilocks
Goldilocks,
meet me at the
tree house across
from Black
Sheep Creek
tomorrow after
school.
Sincerely,
Jack

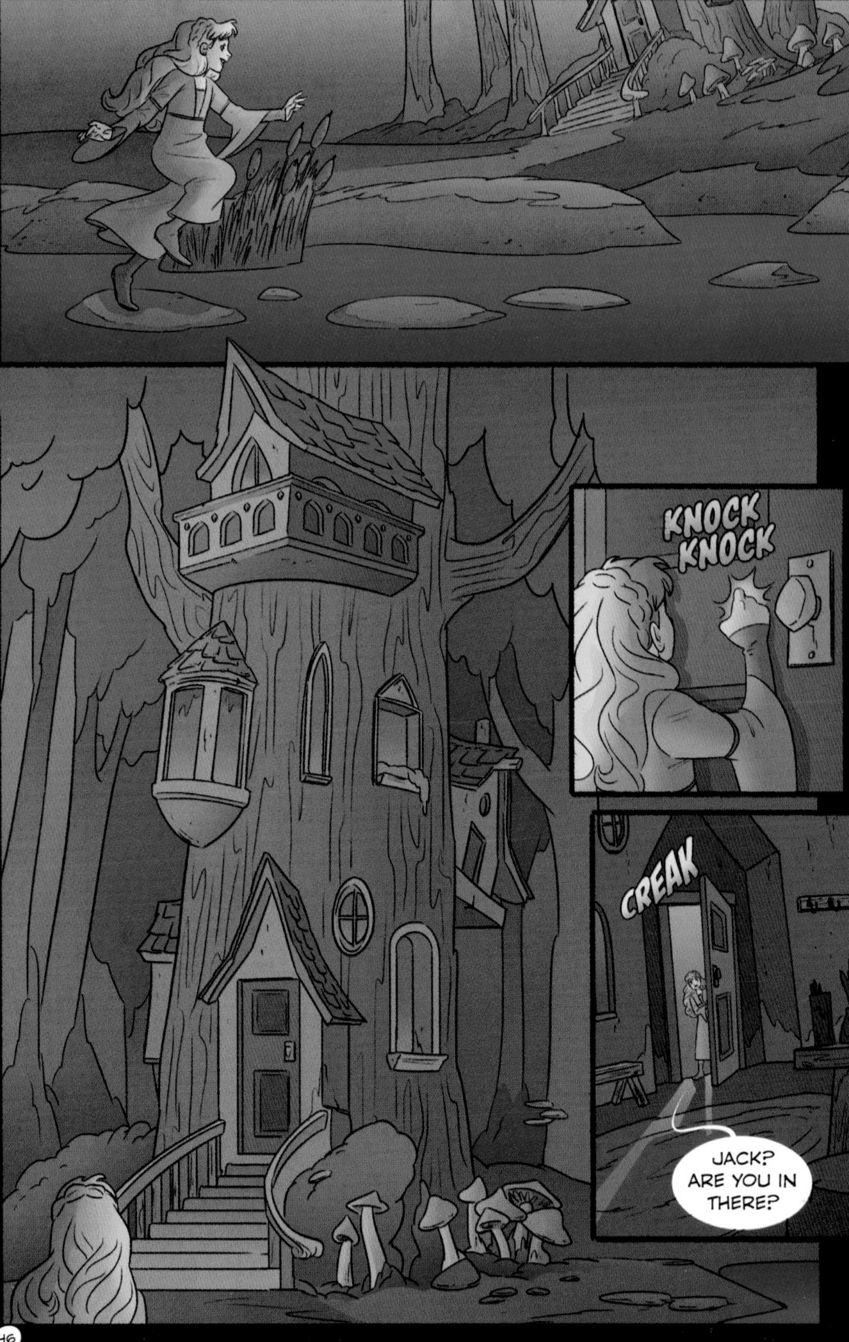
KNOCK
KNOCK
CREAK
JACK? ARE YOU IN THERE?

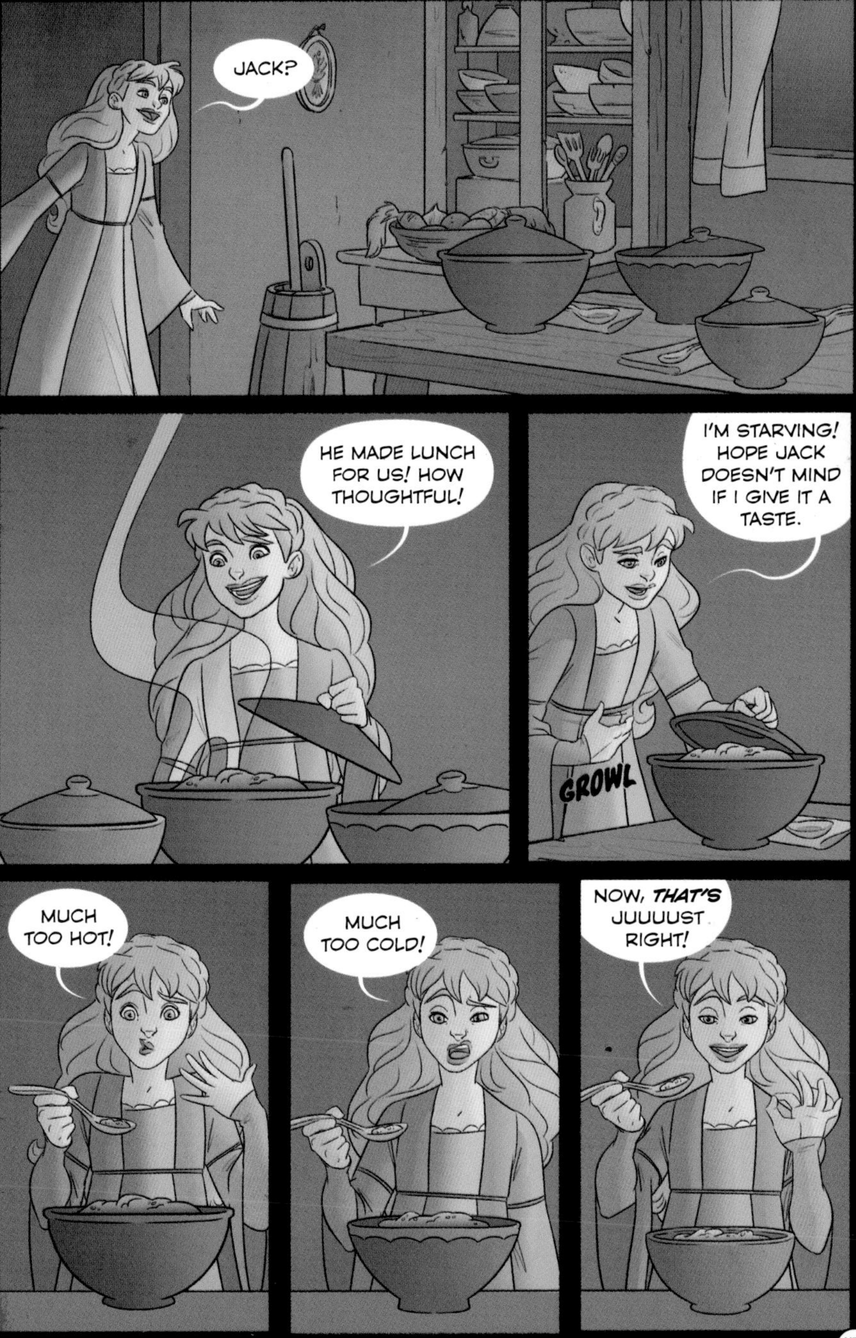
JACK?
HE MADE LUNCH FOR US! HOW THOUGHTFUL!
I'M STARVING! HOPE JACK DOESN'T MIND IF I GIVE IT A TASTE.
GROWL
MUCH TOO HOT!
MUCH TOO COLD!
NOW, *THAT'S* JUUUUST RIGHT!

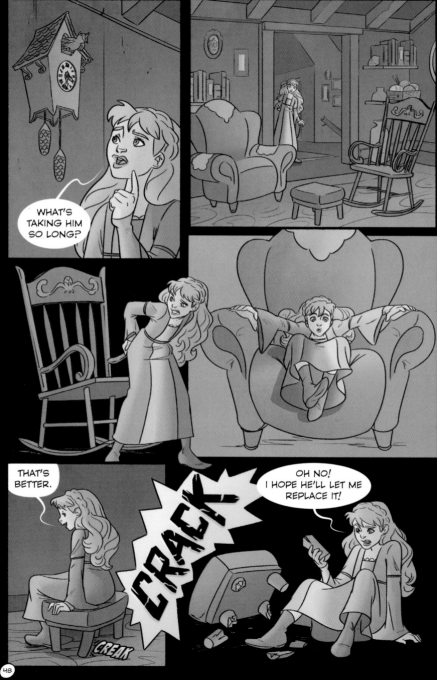

WHAT'S TAKING HIM SO LONG?

THAT'S BETTER.

CRACK!

CREAK

OH NO! I HOPE HE'LL LET ME REPLACE IT!

48

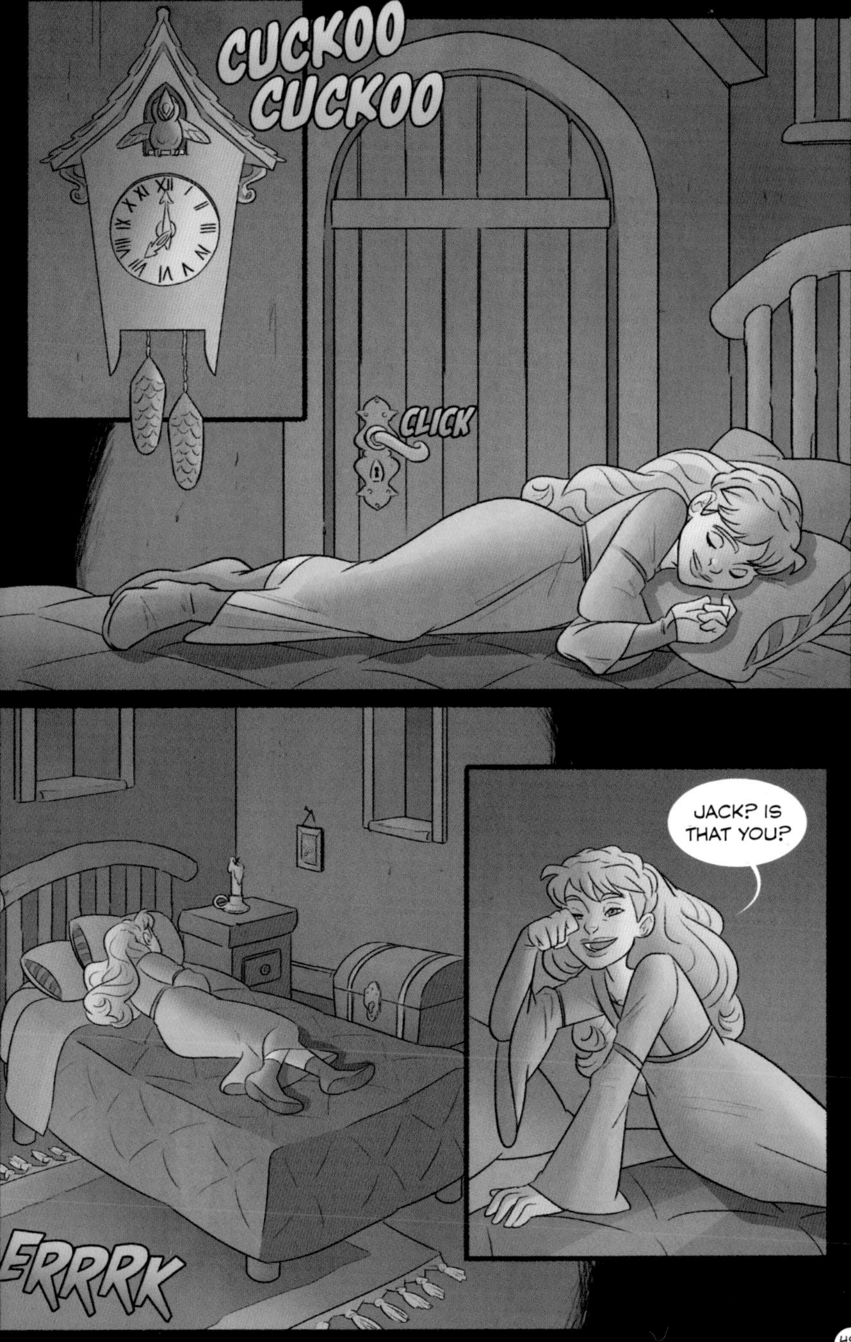
CUCKOO
CUCKOO
CLICK
ERRRK
JACK? IS THAT YOU?

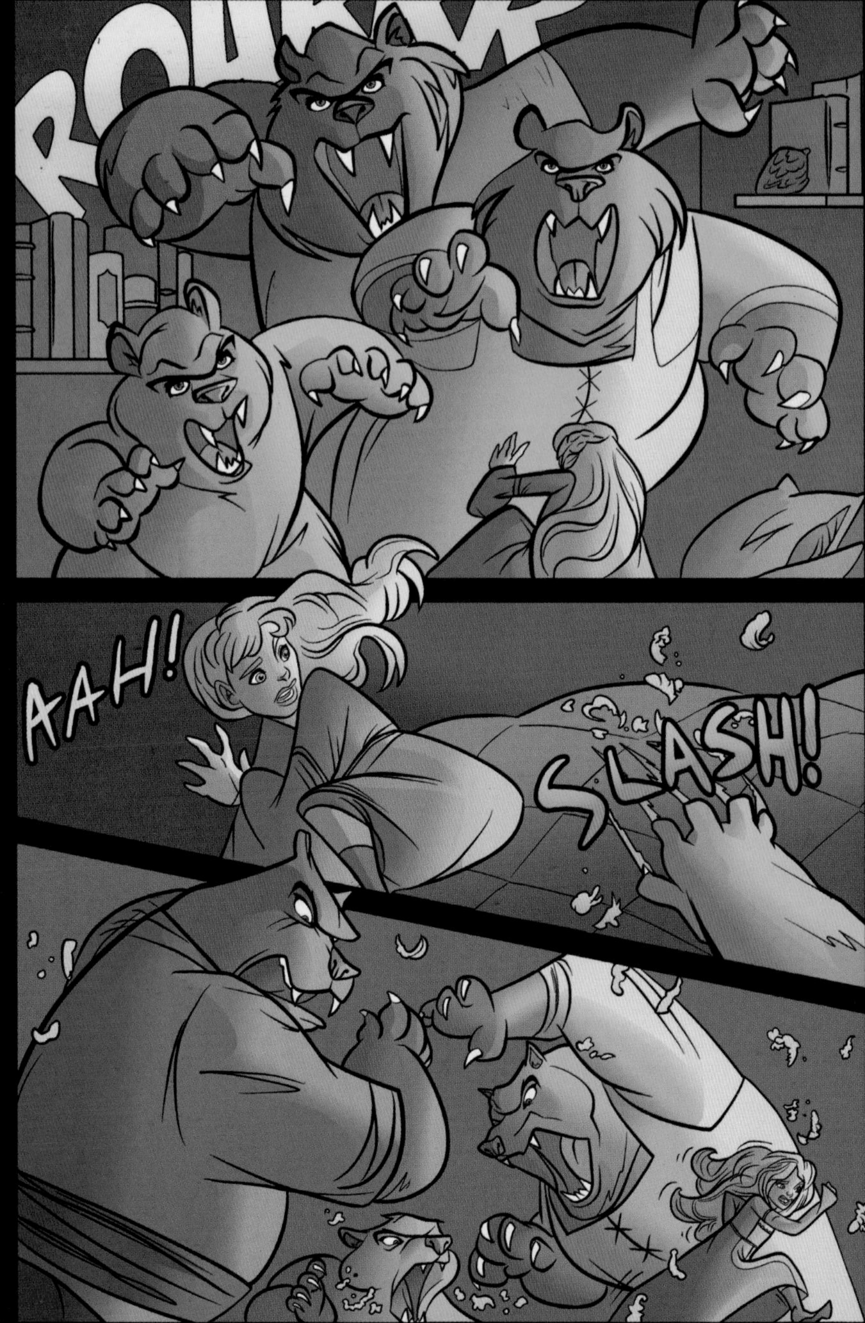
AAH!
SLASH!

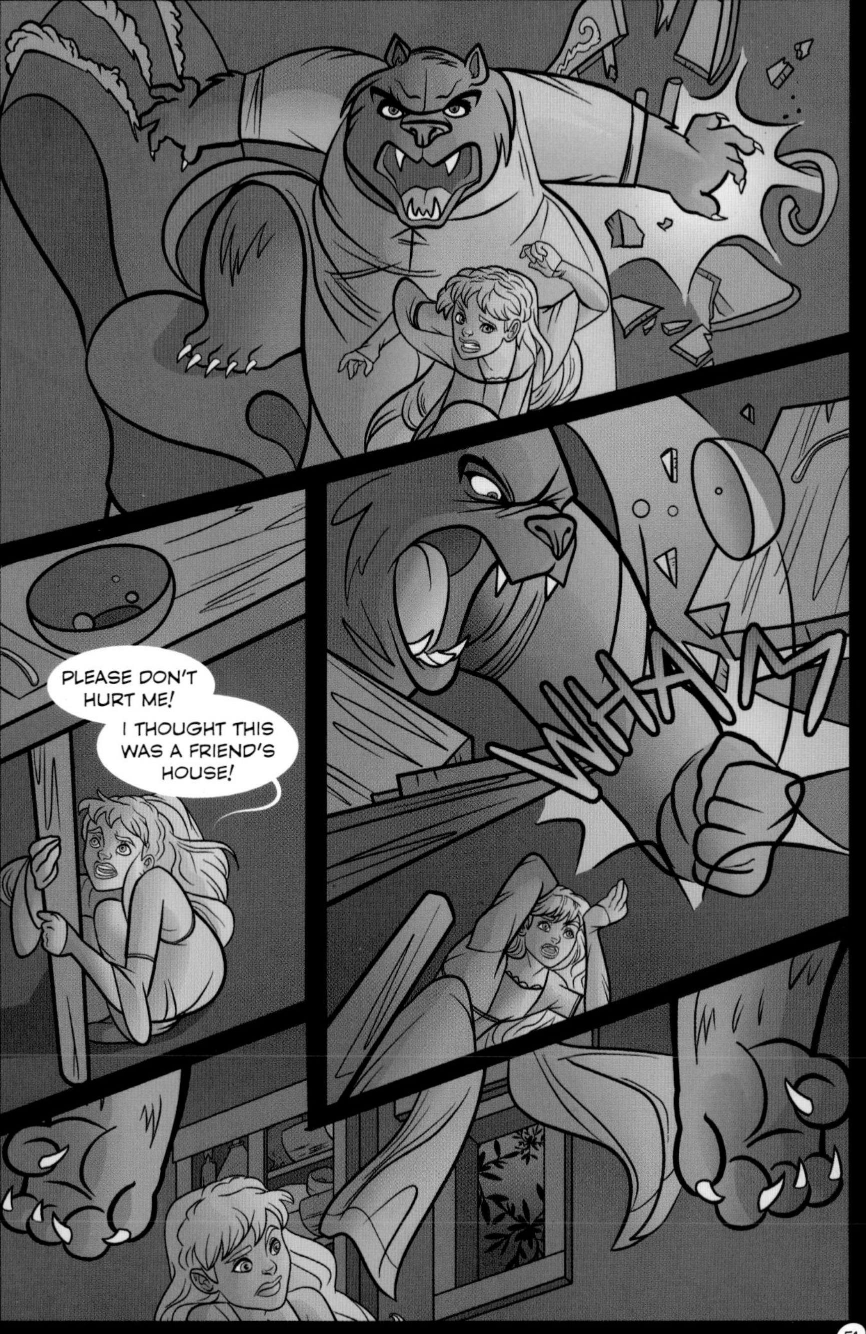
PLEASE DON'T HURT ME!
I THOUGHT THIS WAS A FRIEND'S HOUSE!
WHAM

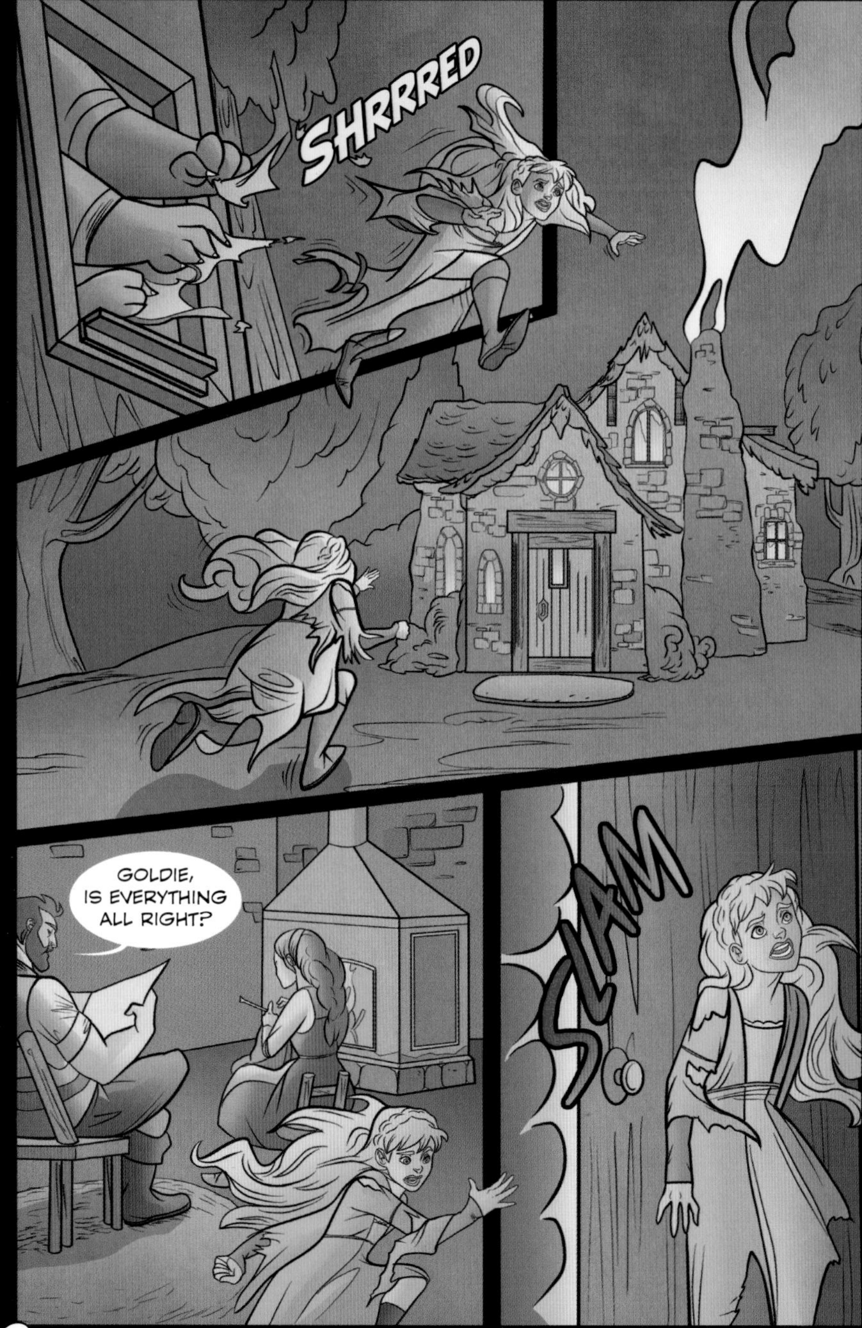
SHRRRED
GOLDIE, IS EVERYTHING ALL RIGHT?
SLAM

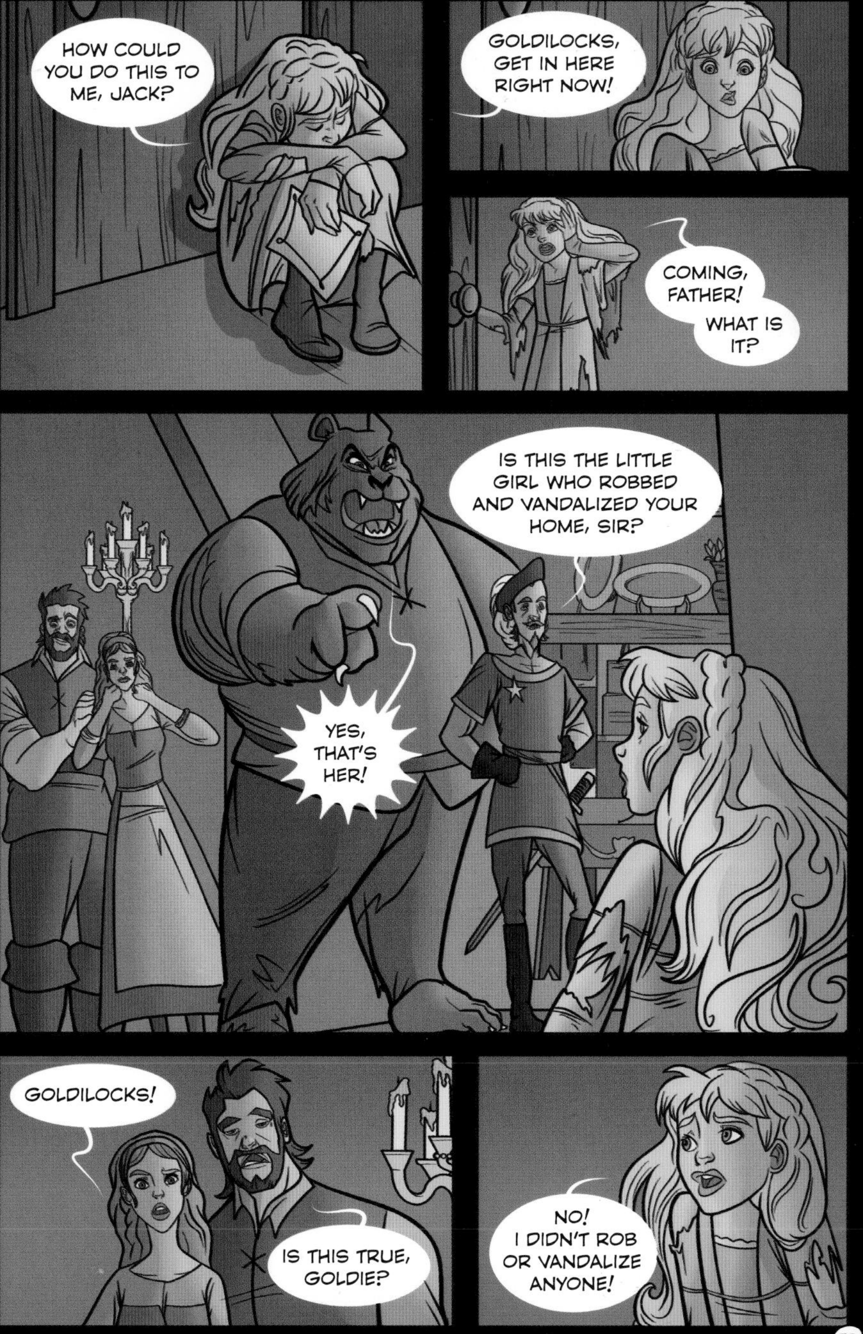
HOW COULD YOU DO THIS TO ME, JACK?
GOLDILOCKS, GET IN HERE RIGHT NOW!
COMING, FATHER!
WHAT IS IT?
IS THIS THE LITTLE GIRL WHO ROBBED AND VANDALIZED YOUR HOME, SIR?
YES, THAT'S HER!
GOLDILOCKS!
IS THIS TRUE, GOLDIE?
NO! I DIDN'T ROB OR VANDALIZE ANYONE!

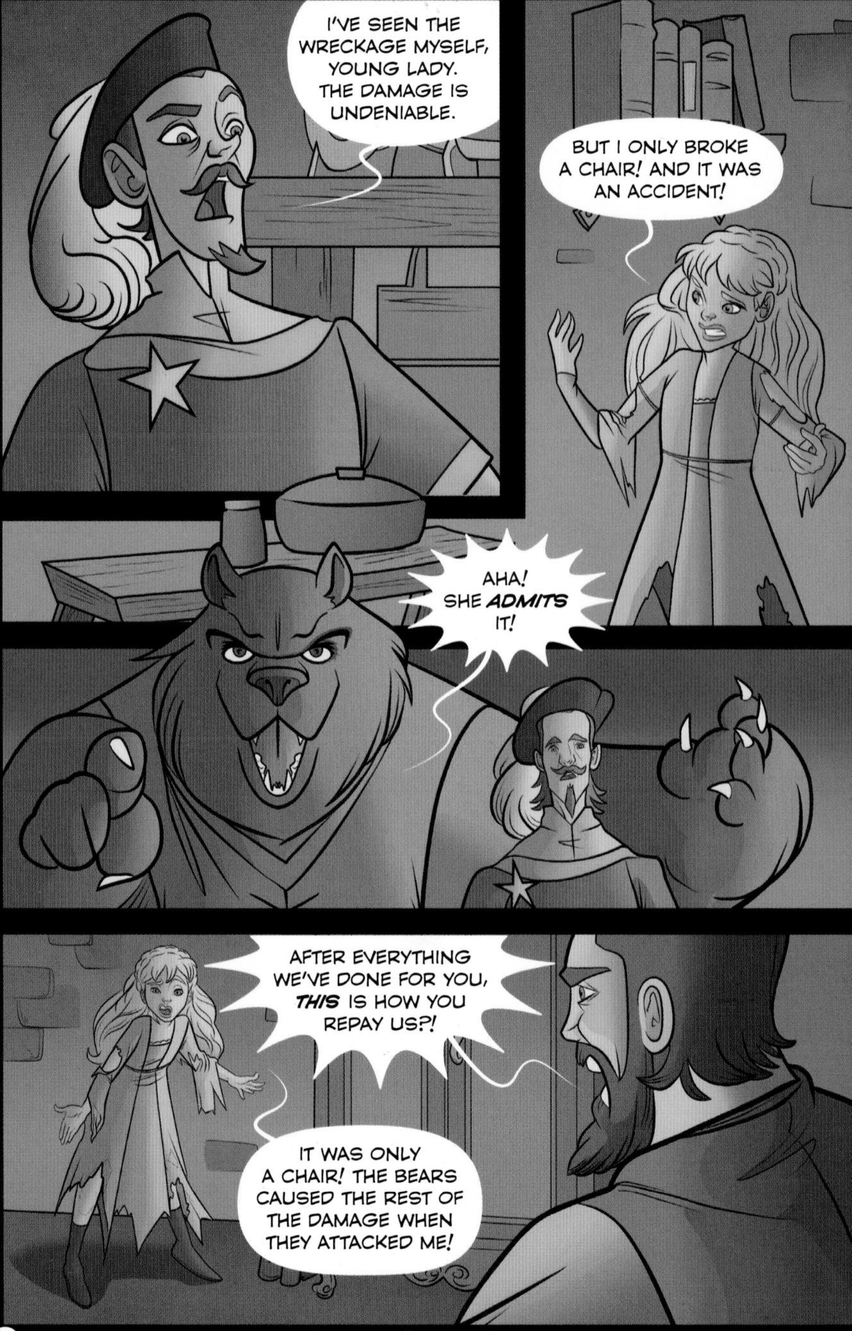
I'VE SEEN THE WRECKAGE MYSELF, YOUNG LADY. THE DAMAGE IS UNDENIABLE.
BUT I ONLY BROKE A CHAIR! AND IT WAS AN ACCIDENT!
AHA! SHE **ADMITS** IT!
AFTER EVERYTHING WE'VE DONE FOR YOU, **THIS** IS HOW YOU REPAY US?!
IT WAS ONLY A CHAIR! THE BEARS CAUSED THE REST OF THE DAMAGE WHEN THEY ATTACKED ME!

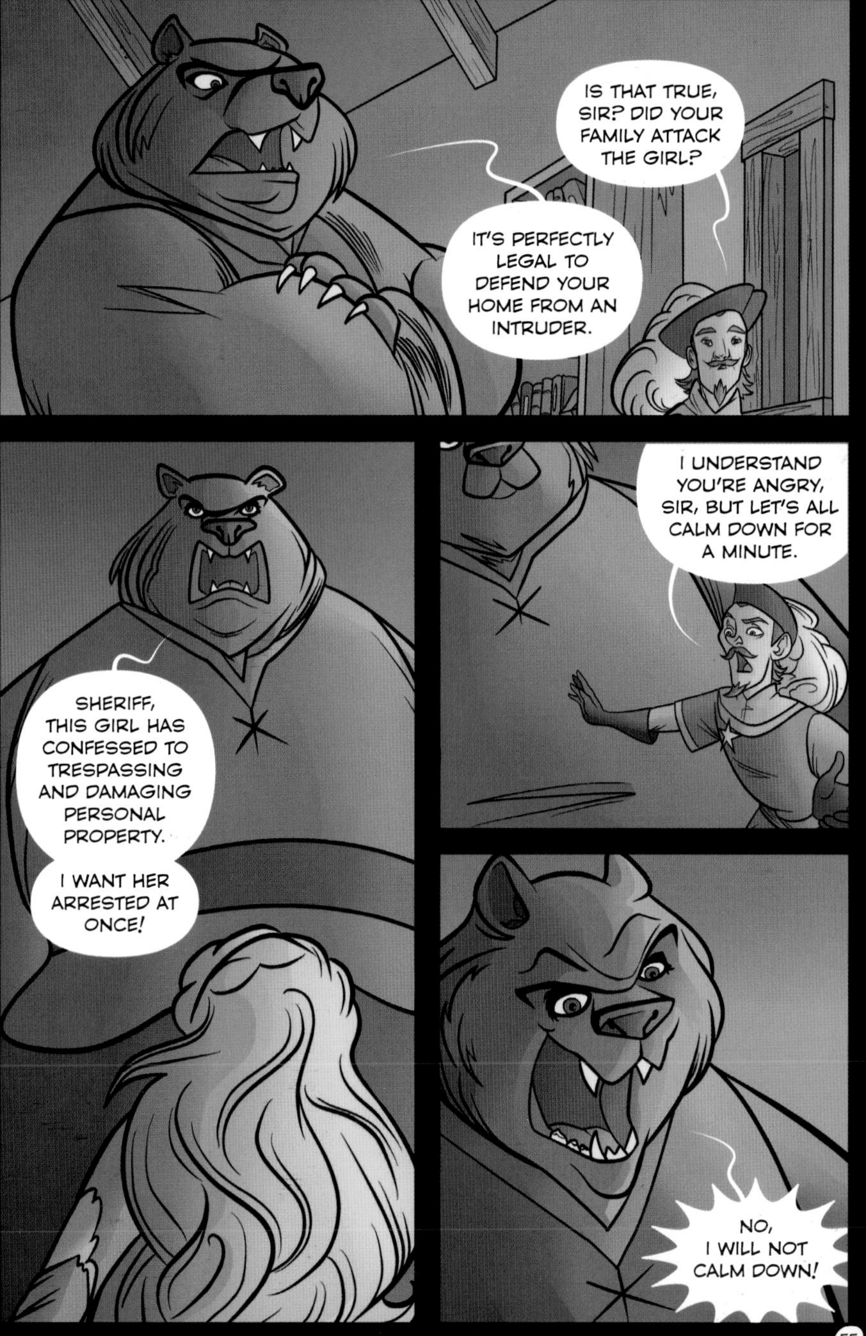
IS THAT TRUE, SIR? DID YOUR FAMILY ATTACK THE GIRL?
IT'S PERFECTLY LEGAL TO DEFEND YOUR HOME FROM AN INTRUDER.
SHERIFF, THIS GIRL HAS CONFESSED TO TRESPASSING AND DAMAGING PERSONAL PROPERTY.
I WANT HER ARRESTED AT ONCE!
I UNDERSTAND YOU'RE ANGRY, SIR, BUT LET'S ALL CALM DOWN FOR A MINUTE.
NO, I WILL NOT CALM DOWN!

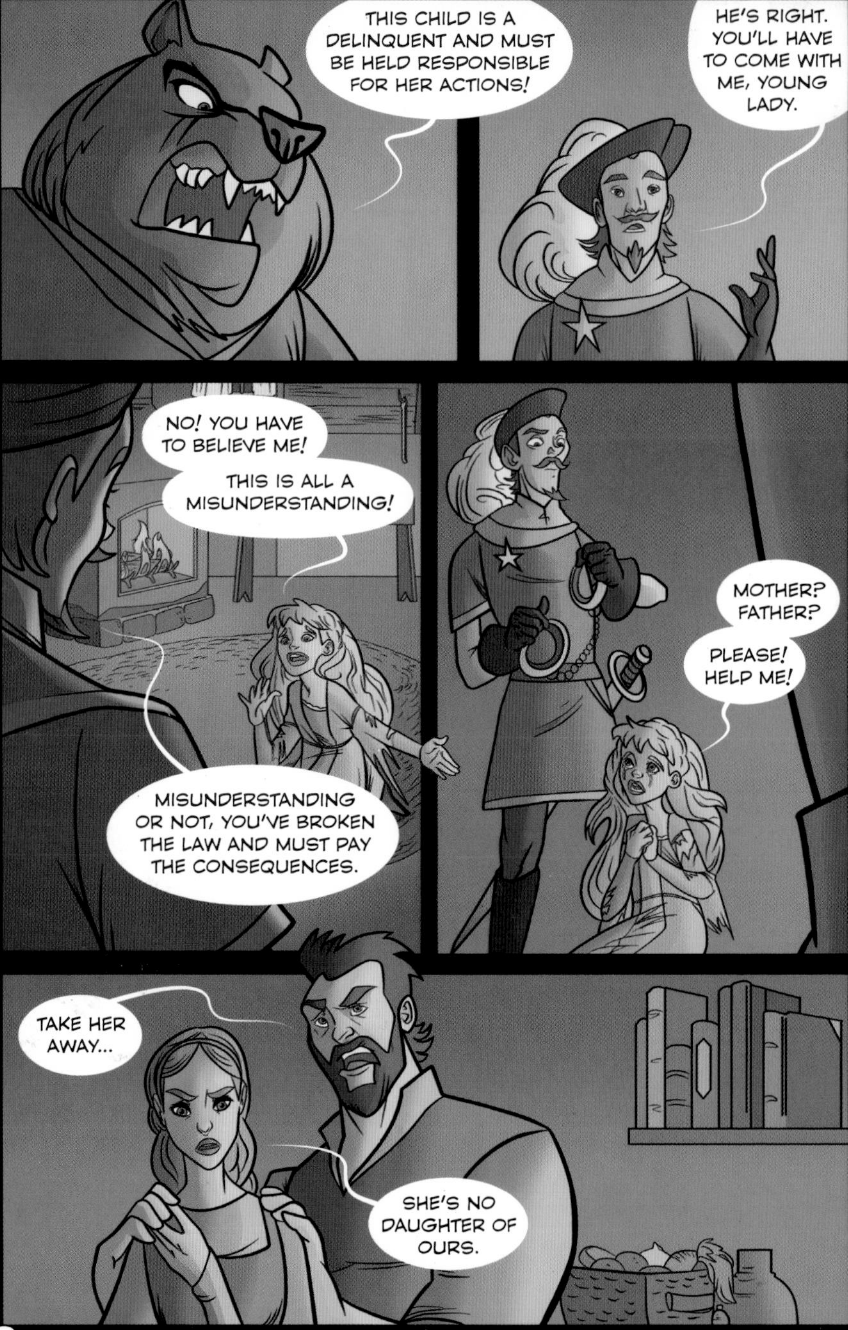
THIS CHILD IS A DELINQUENT AND MUST BE HELD RESPONSIBLE FOR HER ACTIONS!
HE'S RIGHT. YOU'LL HAVE TO COME WITH ME, YOUNG LADY.
NO! YOU HAVE TO BELIEVE ME!
THIS IS ALL A MISUNDERSTANDING!
MISUNDERSTANDING OR NOT, YOU'VE BROKEN THE LAW AND MUST PAY THE CONSEQUENCES.
MOTHER? FATHER?
PLEASE! HELP ME!
TAKE HER AWAY...
SHE'S NO DAUGHTER OF OURS.

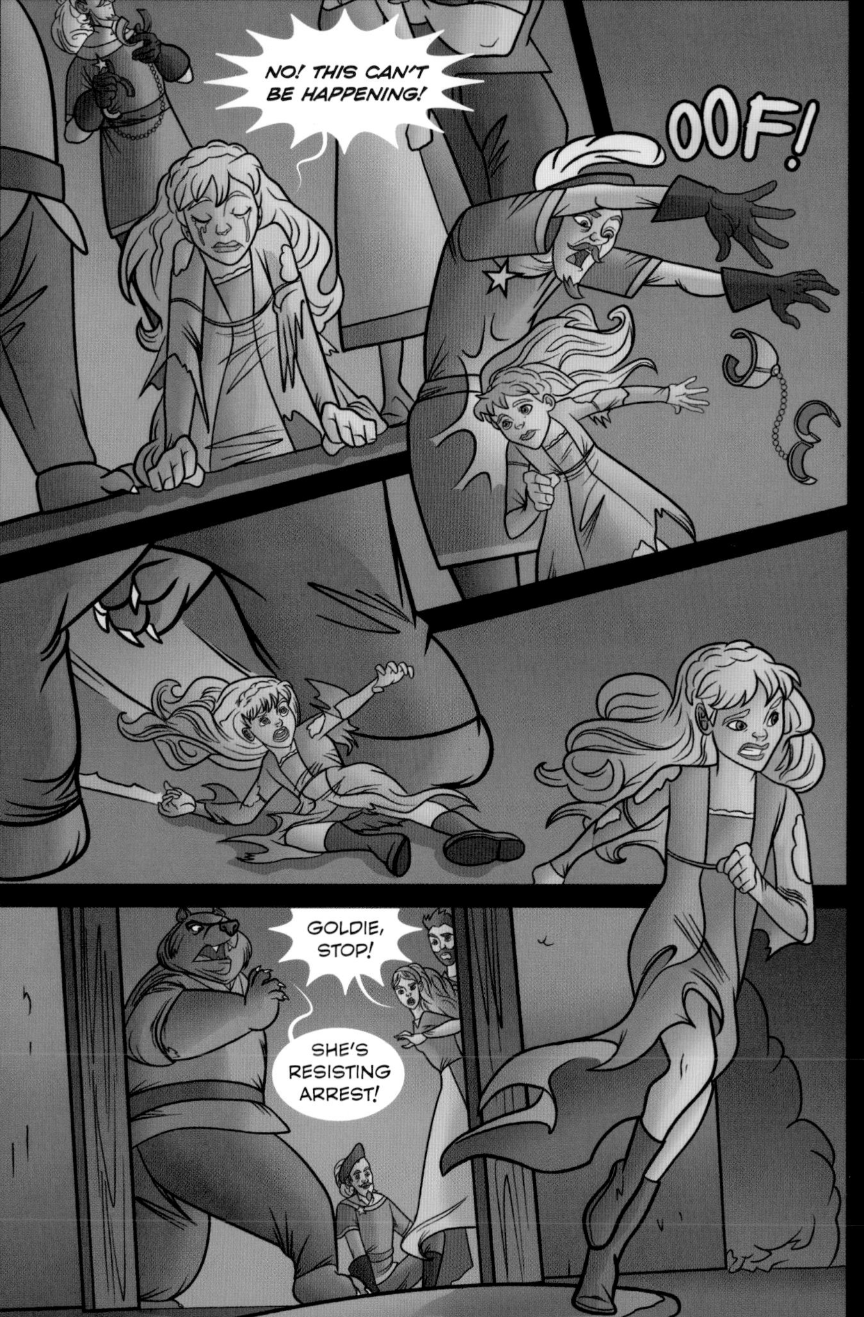
NO! THIS CAN'T BE HAPPENING!
OOF!
GOLDIE, STOP!
SHE'S RESISTING ARREST!

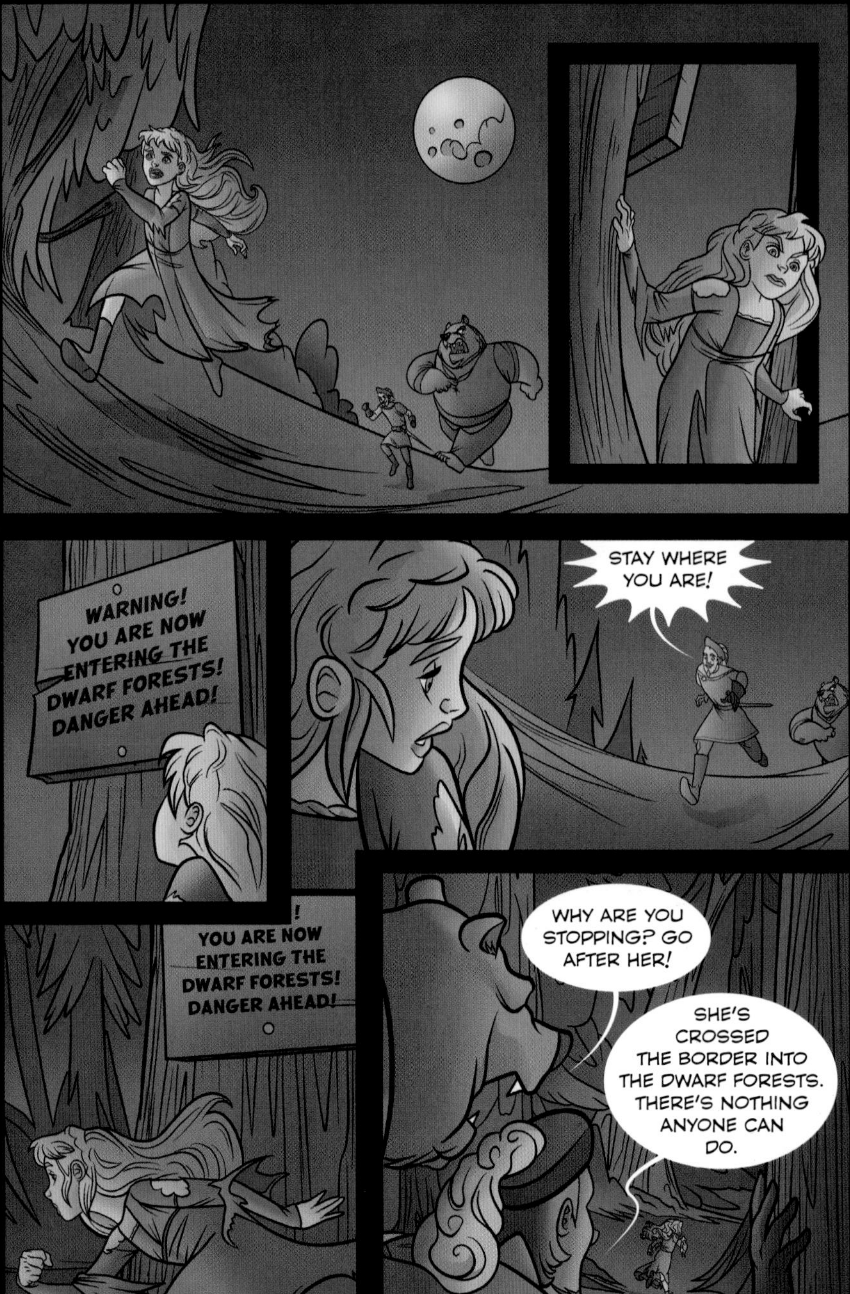
WARNING!
YOU ARE NOW ENTERING THE DWARF FORESTS! DANGER AHEAD!
STAY WHERE YOU ARE!
YOU ARE NOW ENTERING THE DWARF FORESTS! DANGER AHEAD!
WHY ARE YOU STOPPING? GO AFTER HER!
SHE'S CROSSED THE BORDER INTO THE DWARF FORESTS. THERE'S NOTHING ANYONE CAN DO.

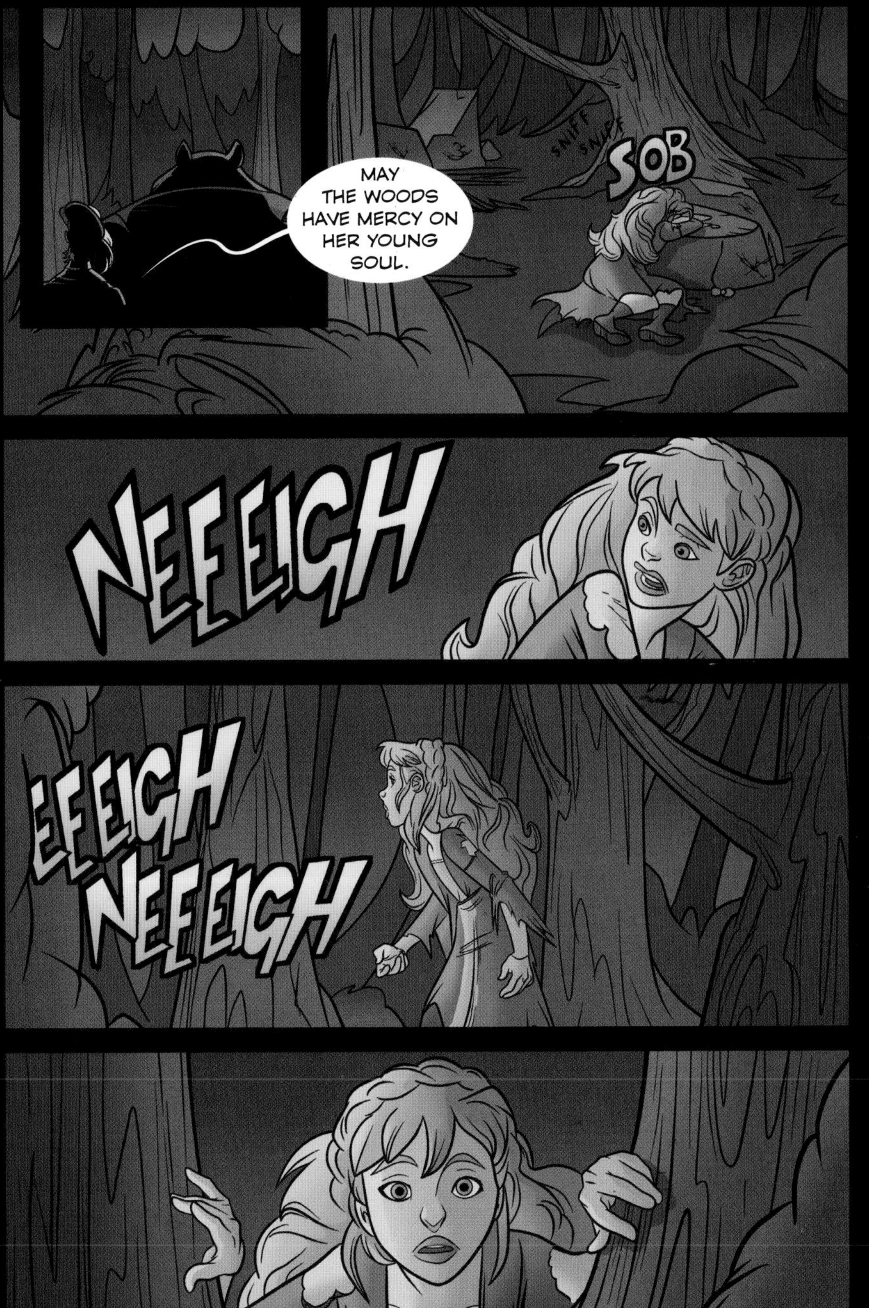
MAY THE WOODS HAVE MERCY ON HER YOUNG SOUL.
SNIFF SNIFF
SOB
NEE EIGH
EE EIGH
NEE EIGH

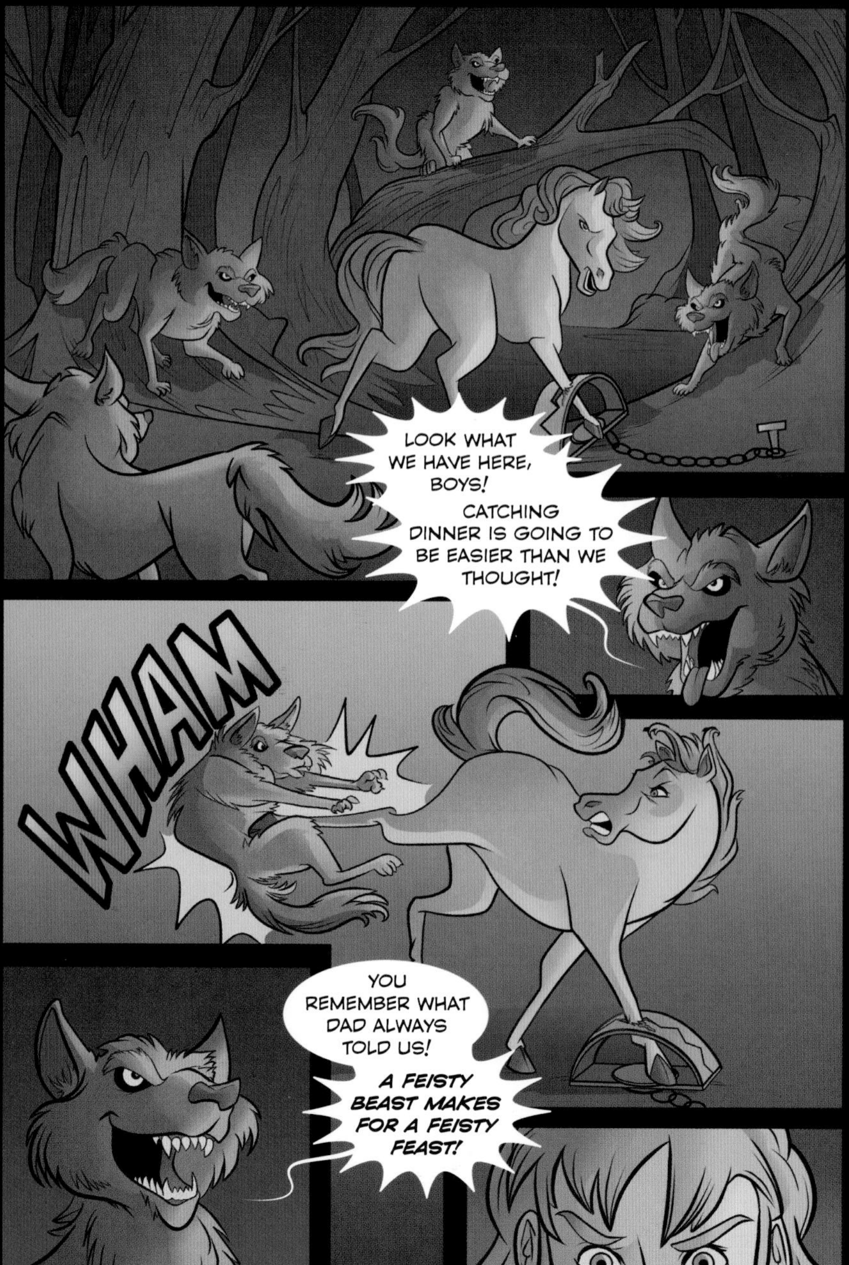
LOOK WHAT WE HAVE HERE, BOYS!
CATCHING DINNER IS GOING TO BE EASIER THAN WE THOUGHT!
WHAM
YOU REMEMBER WHAT DAD ALWAYS TOLD US!
A FEISTY BEAST MAKES FOR A FEISTY FEAST!

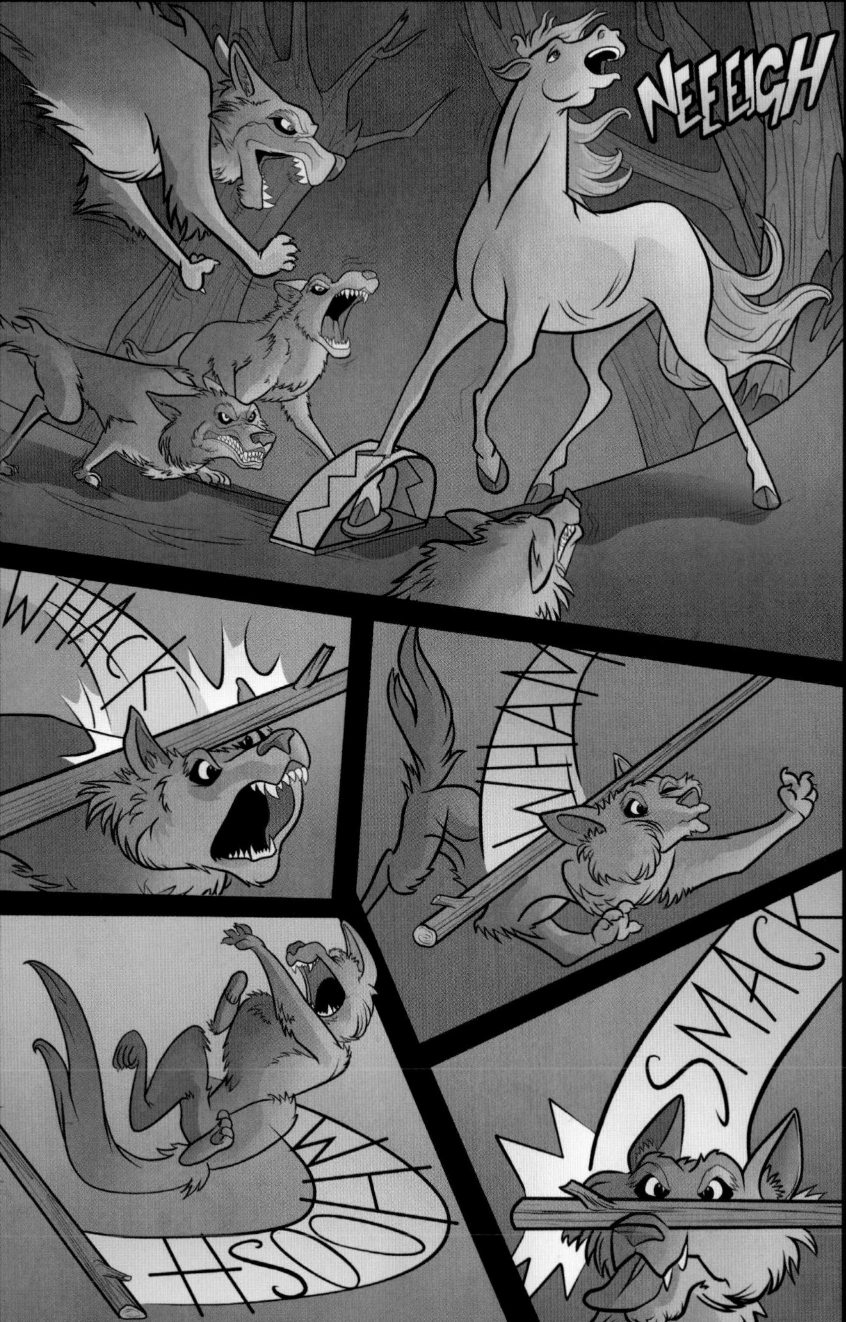
NEEEIGH
WHACK
WHAM
SMACK
WHOOSH

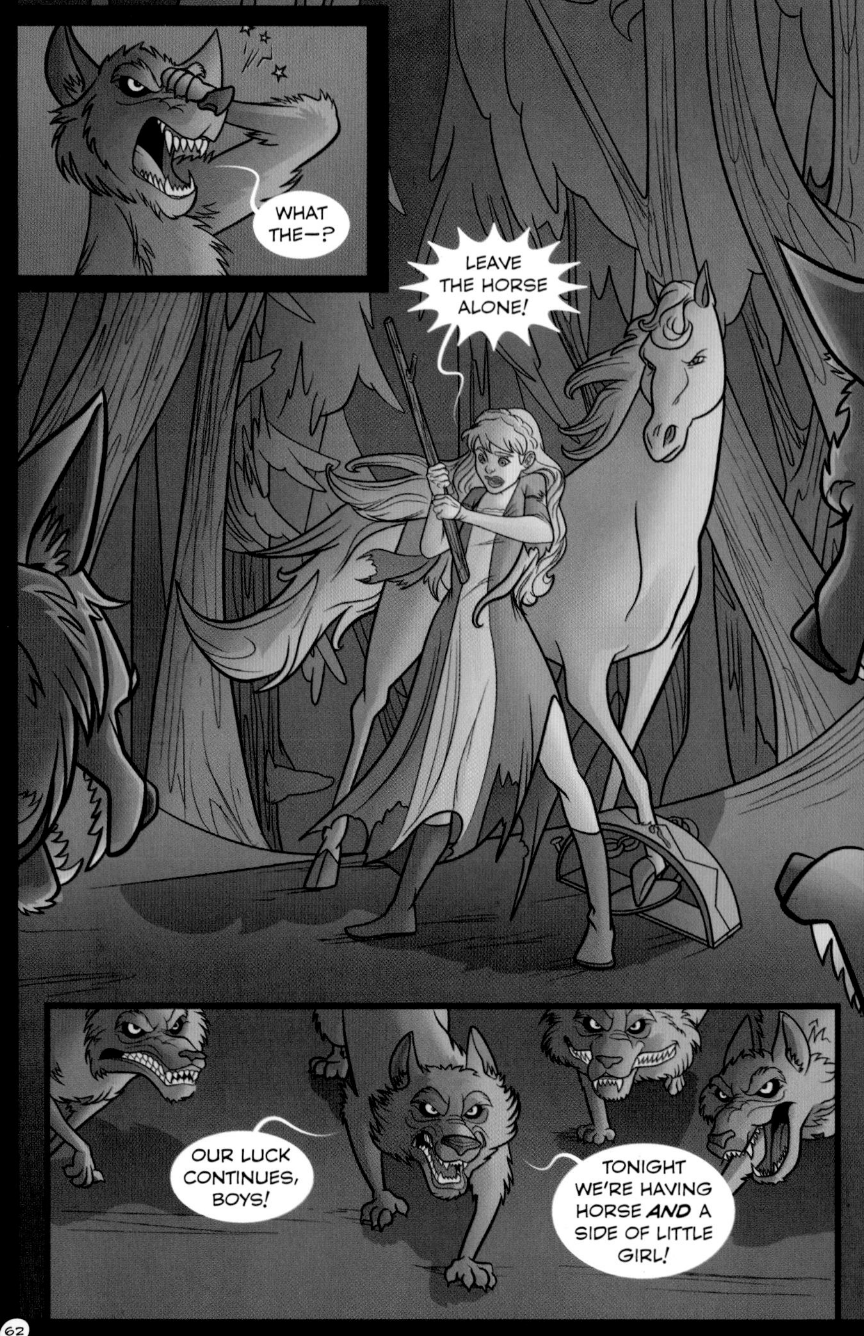
WHAT THE—?
LEAVE THE HORSE ALONE!
OUR LUCK CONTINUES, BOYS!
TONIGHT WE'RE HAVING HORSE ***AND*** A SIDE OF LITTLE GIRL!

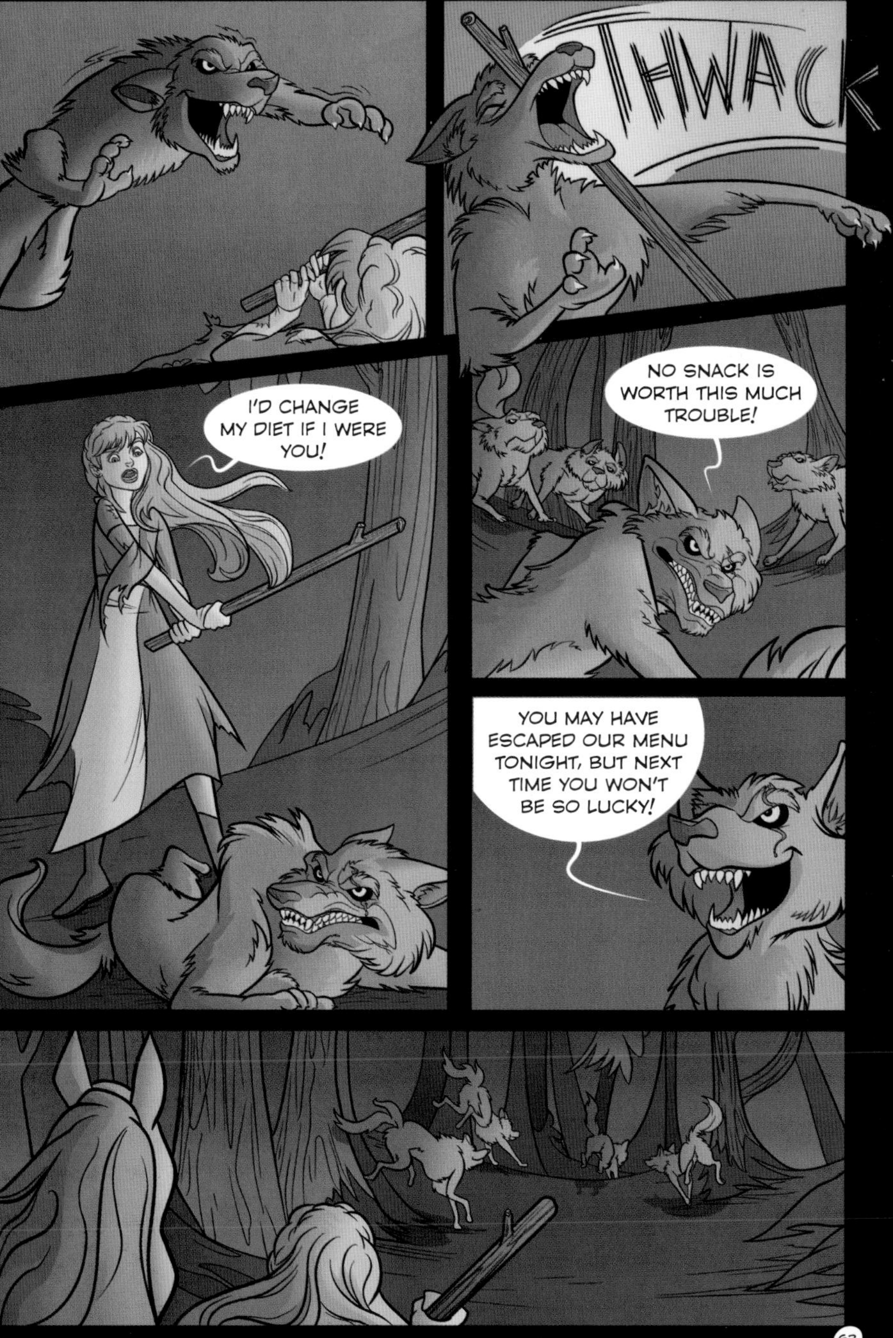
THWACK
I'D CHANGE MY DIET IF I WERE YOU!
NO SNACK IS WORTH THIS MUCH TROUBLE!
YOU MAY HAVE ESCAPED OUR MENU TONIGHT, BUT NEXT TIME YOU WON'T BE SO LUCKY!

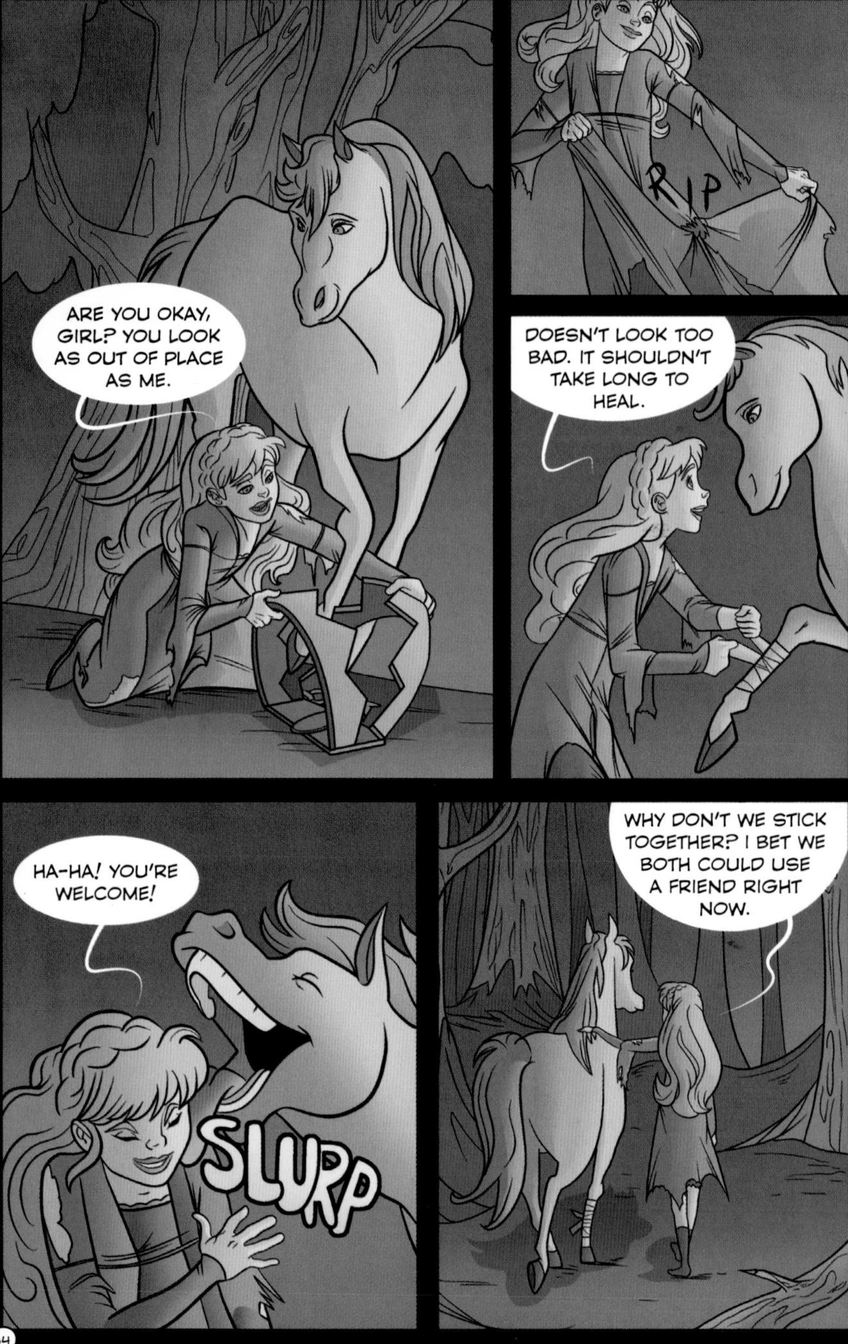
ARE YOU OKAY, GIRL? YOU LOOK AS OUT OF PLACE AS ME.
RIP
DOESN'T LOOK TOO BAD. IT SHOULDN'T TAKE LONG TO HEAL.
HA-HA! YOU'RE WELCOME!
SLURP
WHY DON'T WE STICK TOGETHER? I BET WE BOTH COULD USE A FRIEND RIGHT NOW.

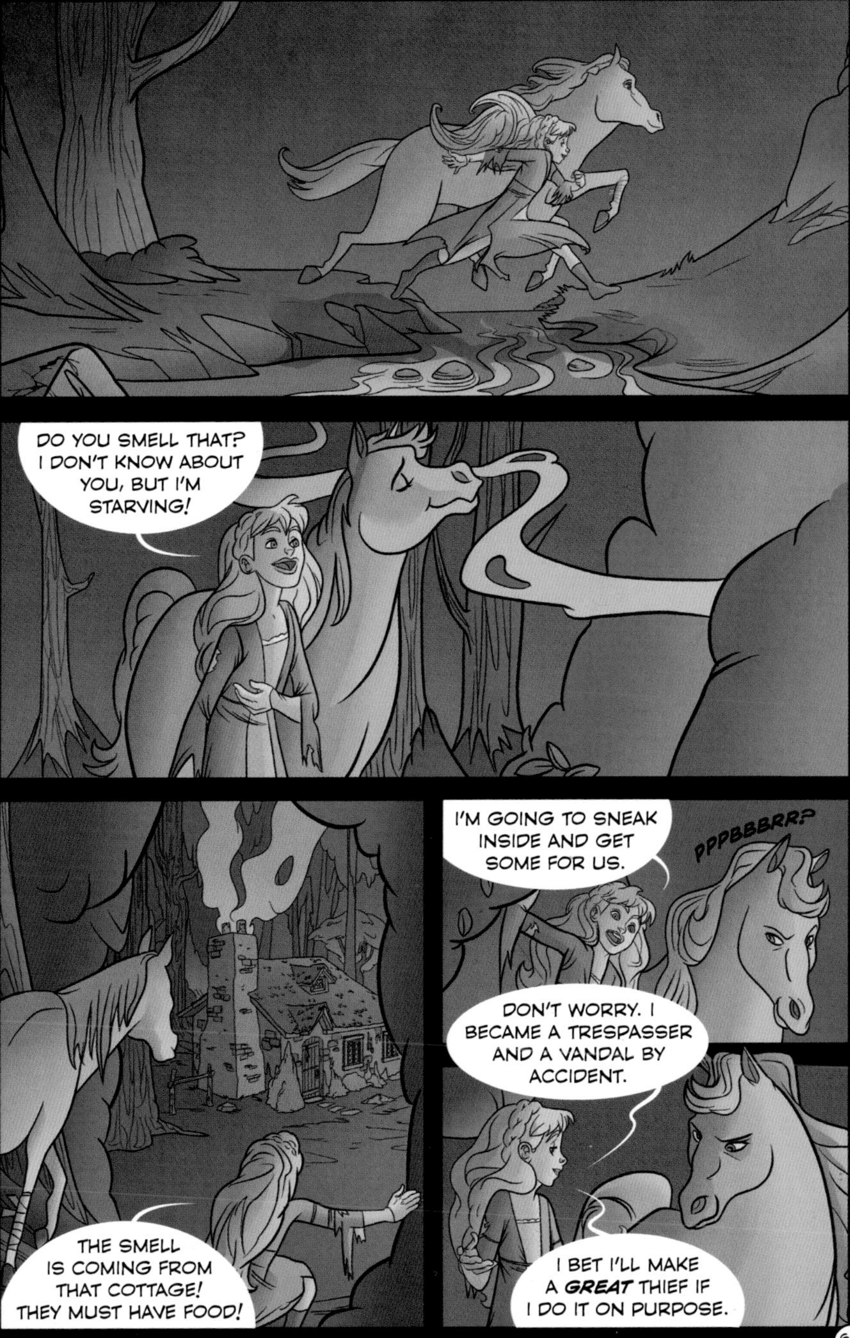
DO YOU SMELL THAT? I DON'T KNOW ABOUT YOU, BUT I'M STARVING!
THE SMELL IS COMING FROM THAT COTTAGE! THEY MUST HAVE FOOD!
I'M GOING TO SNEAK INSIDE AND GET SOME FOR US.
PPPBBBRR?
DON'T WORRY. I BECAME A TRESPASSER AND A VANDAL BY ACCIDENT.
I BET I'LL MAKE A ***GREAT*** THIEF IF I DO IT ON PURPOSE.

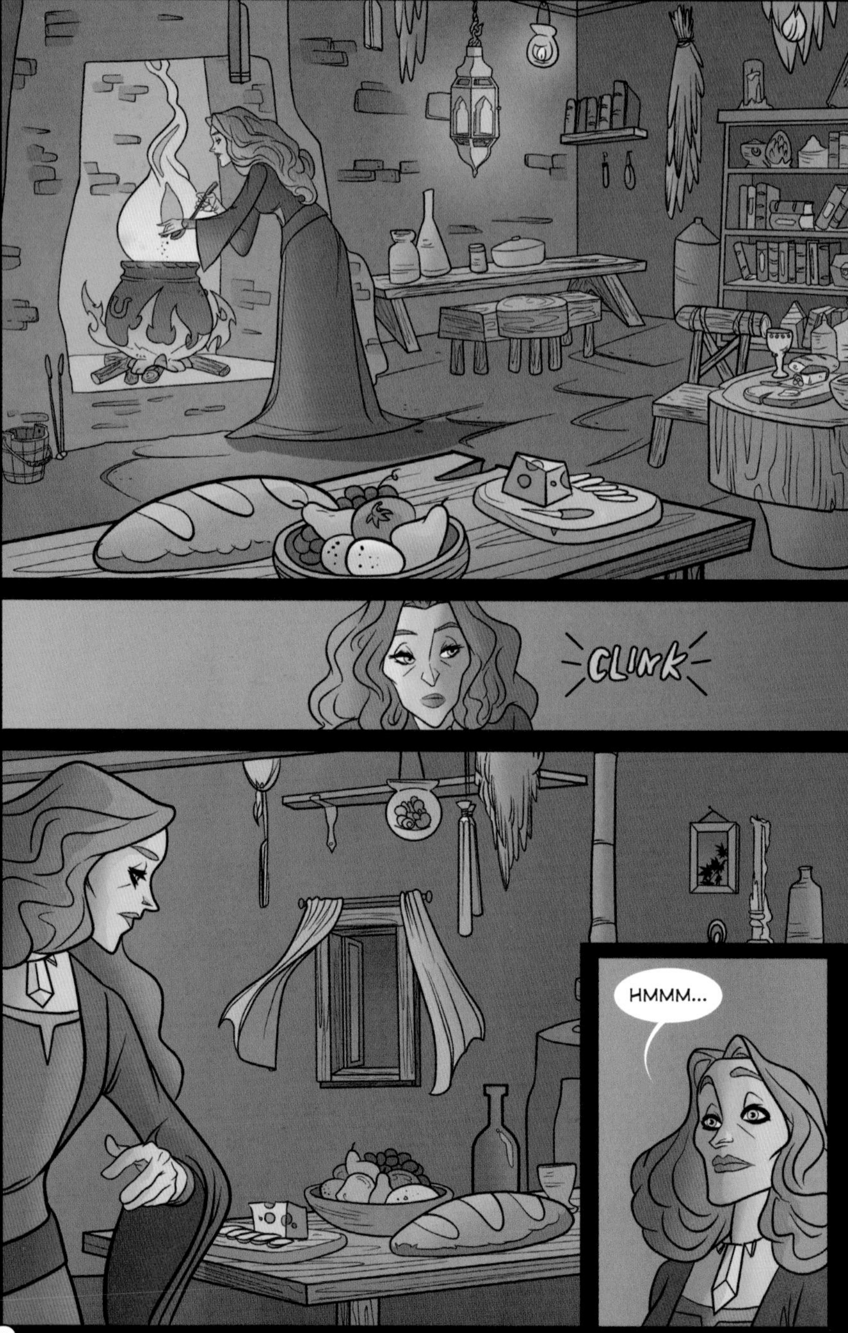
CLINK
HMMM...

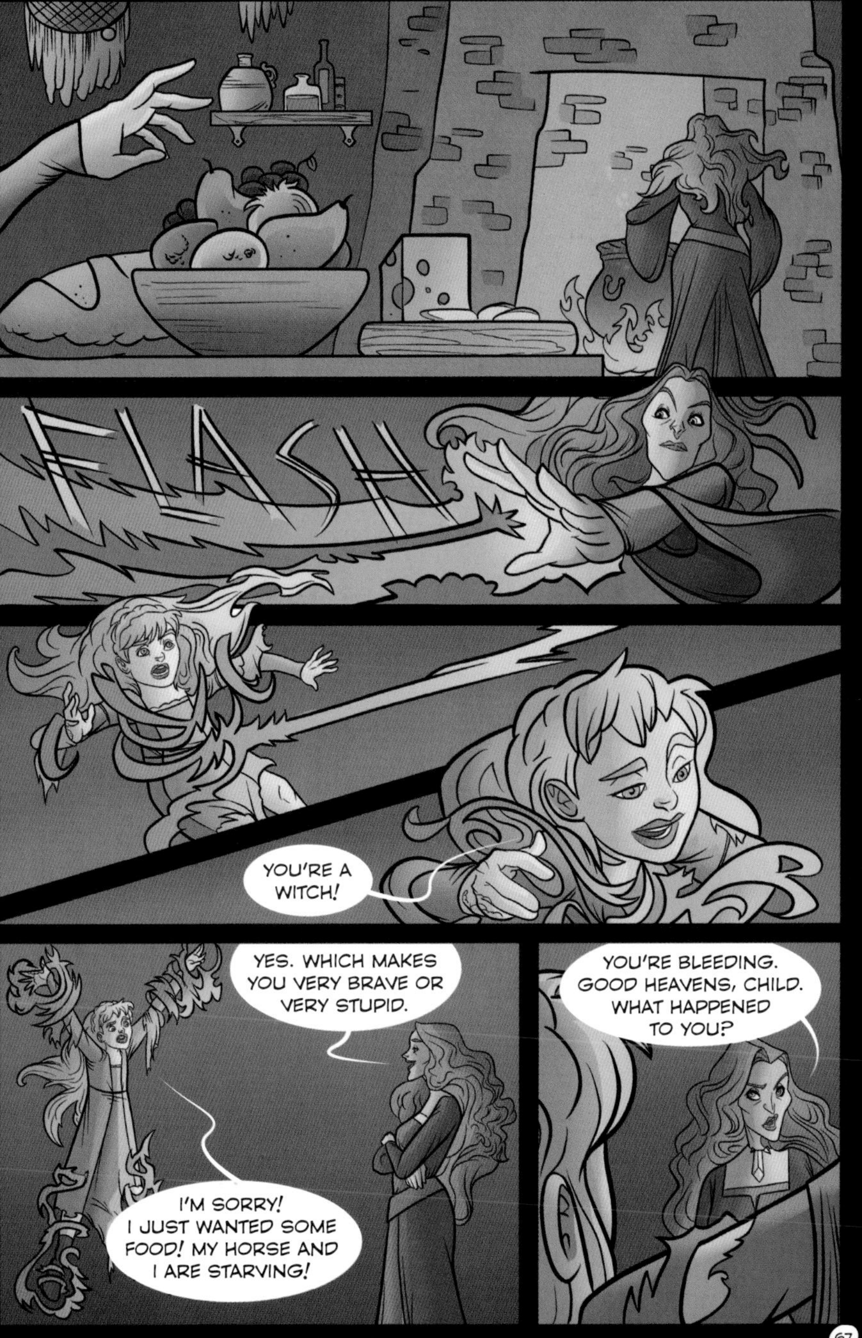
FLASH
YOU'RE A WITCH!
YES. WHICH MAKES YOU VERY BRAVE OR VERY STUPID.
I'M SORRY! I JUST WANTED SOME FOOD! MY HORSE AND I ARE STARVING!
YOU'RE BLEEDING. GOOD HEAVENS, CHILD. WHAT HAPPENED TO YOU?

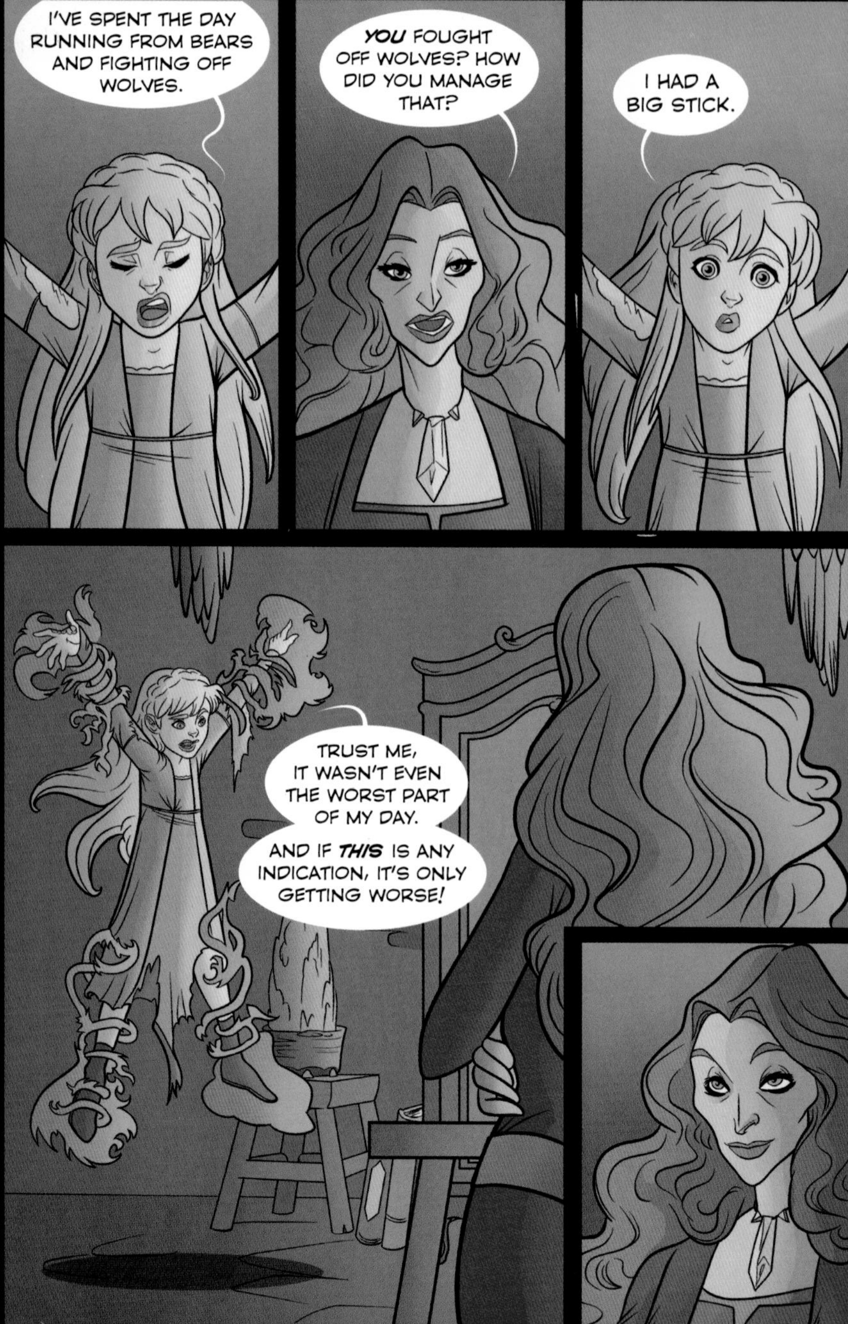
I'VE SPENT THE DAY RUNNING FROM BEARS AND FIGHTING OFF WOLVES.
YOU FOUGHT OFF WOLVES? HOW DID YOU MANAGE THAT?
I HAD A BIG STICK.
TRUST ME, IT WASN'T EVEN THE WORST PART OF MY DAY.
AND IF *THIS* IS ANY INDICATION, IT'S ONLY GETTING WORSE!

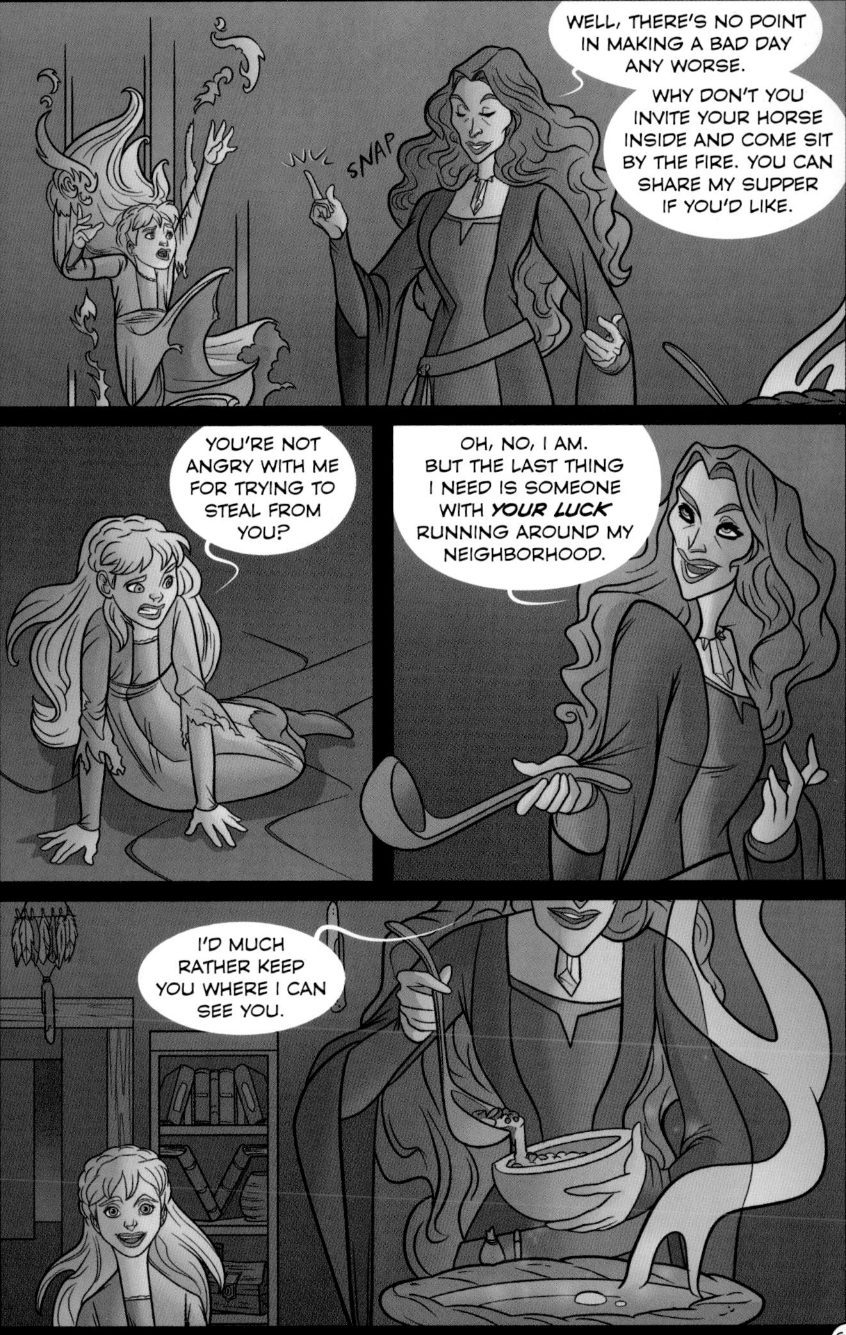

SNAP
WELL, THERE'S NO POINT IN MAKING A BAD DAY ANY WORSE.
WHY DON'T YOU INVITE YOUR HORSE INSIDE AND COME SIT BY THE FIRE. YOU CAN SHARE MY SUPPER IF YOU'D LIKE.
YOU'RE NOT ANGRY WITH ME FOR TRYING TO STEAL FROM YOU?
OH, NO, I AM. BUT THE LAST THING I NEED IS SOMEONE WITH YOUR LUCK RUNNING AROUND MY NEIGHBORHOOD.
I'D MUCH RATHER KEEP YOU WHERE I CAN SEE YOU.

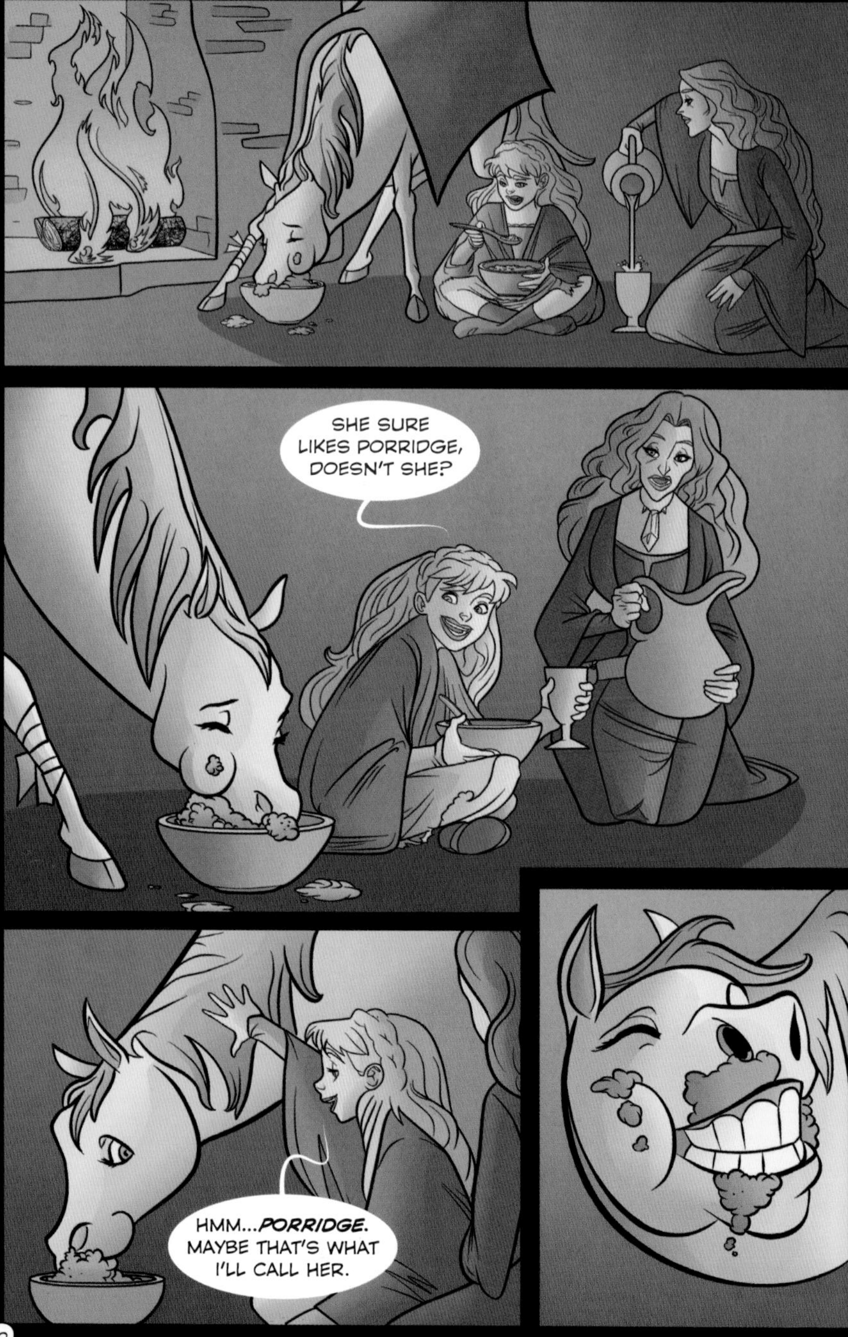
SHE SURE LIKES PORRIDGE, DOESN'T SHE?
HMM...*PORRIDGE.* MAYBE THAT'S WHAT I'LL CALL HER.

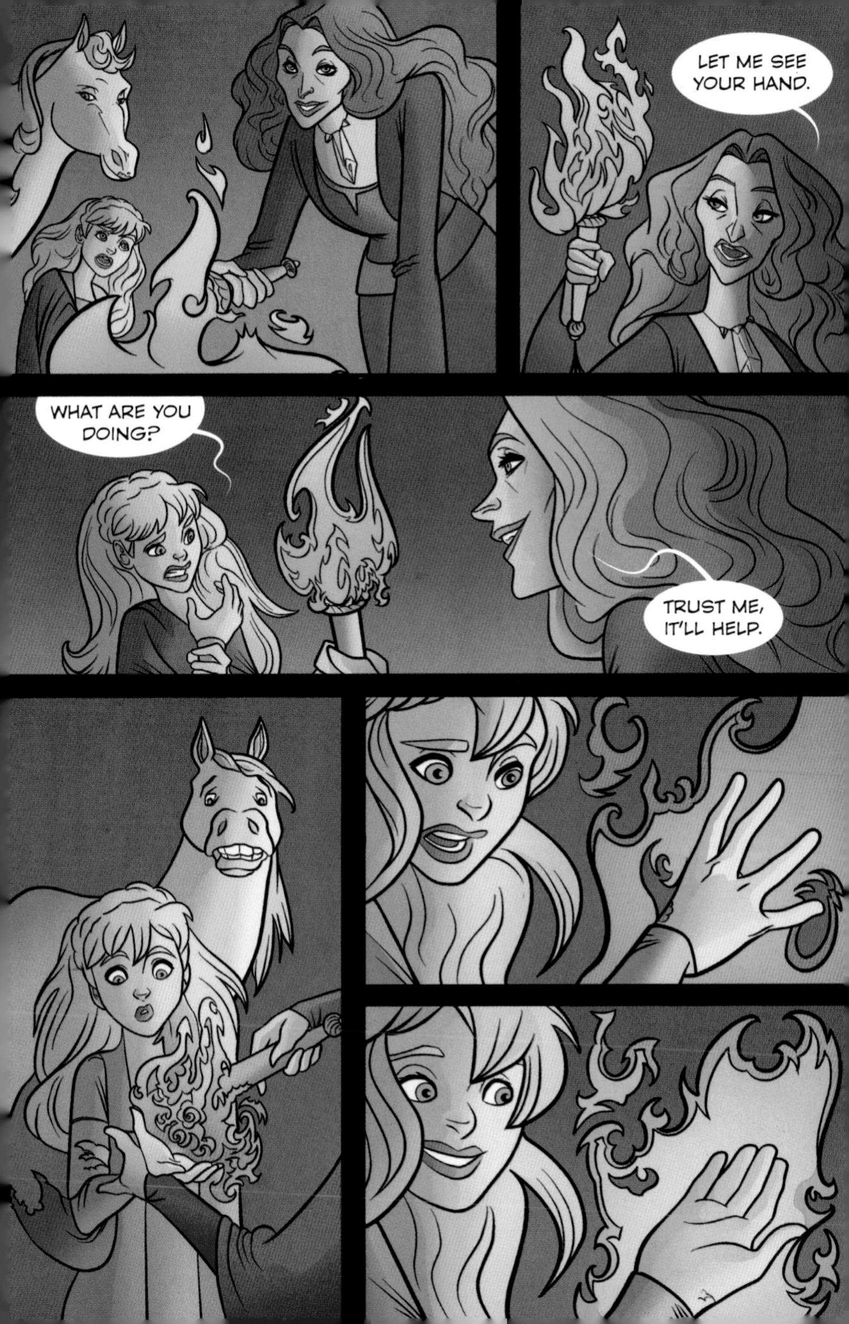
LET ME SEE YOUR HAND.
WHAT ARE YOU DOING?
TRUST ME, IT'LL HELP.

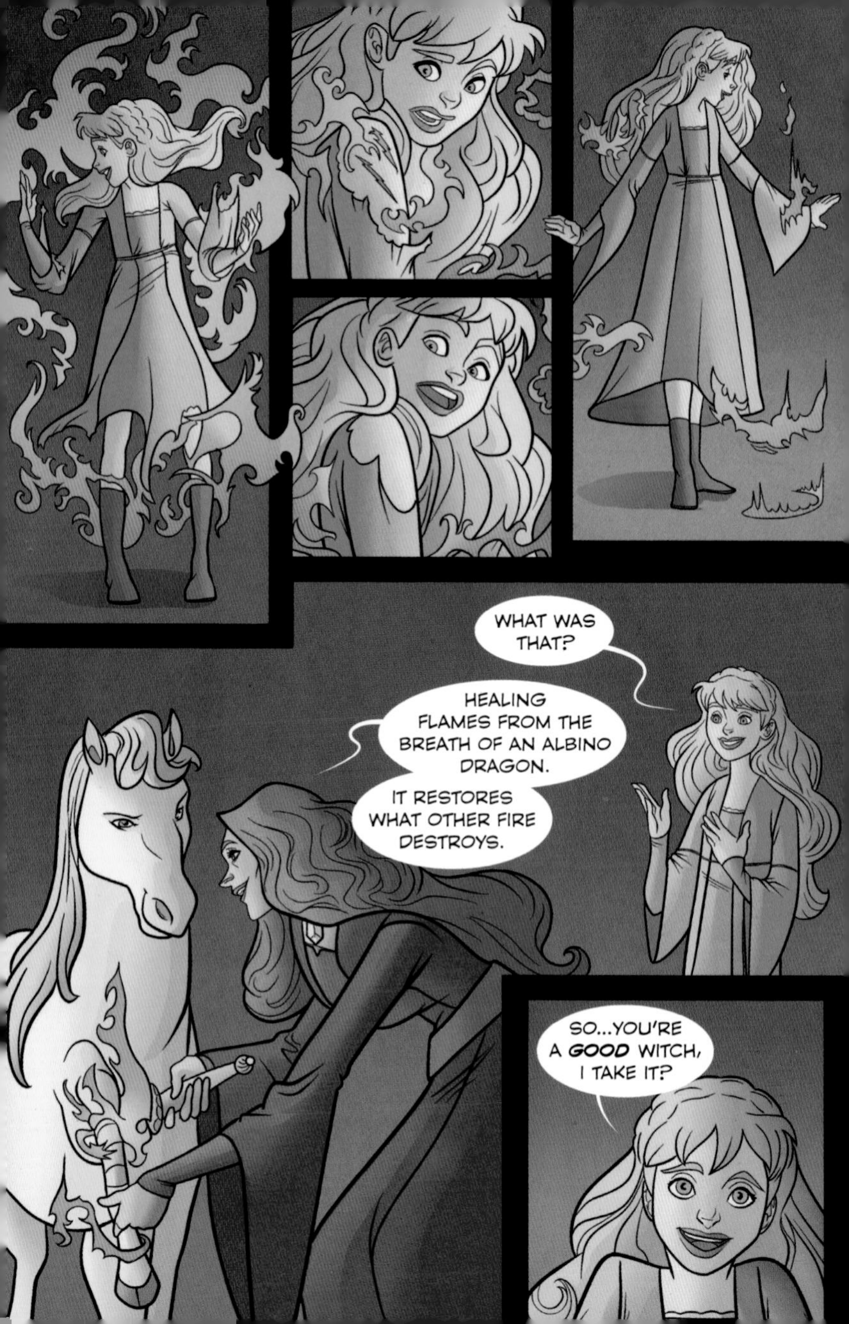
WHAT WAS THAT?
HEALING FLAMES FROM THE BREATH OF AN ALBINO DRAGON.
IT RESTORES WHAT OTHER FIRE DESTROYS.
SO...YOU'RE A *GOOD* WITCH, I TAKE IT?

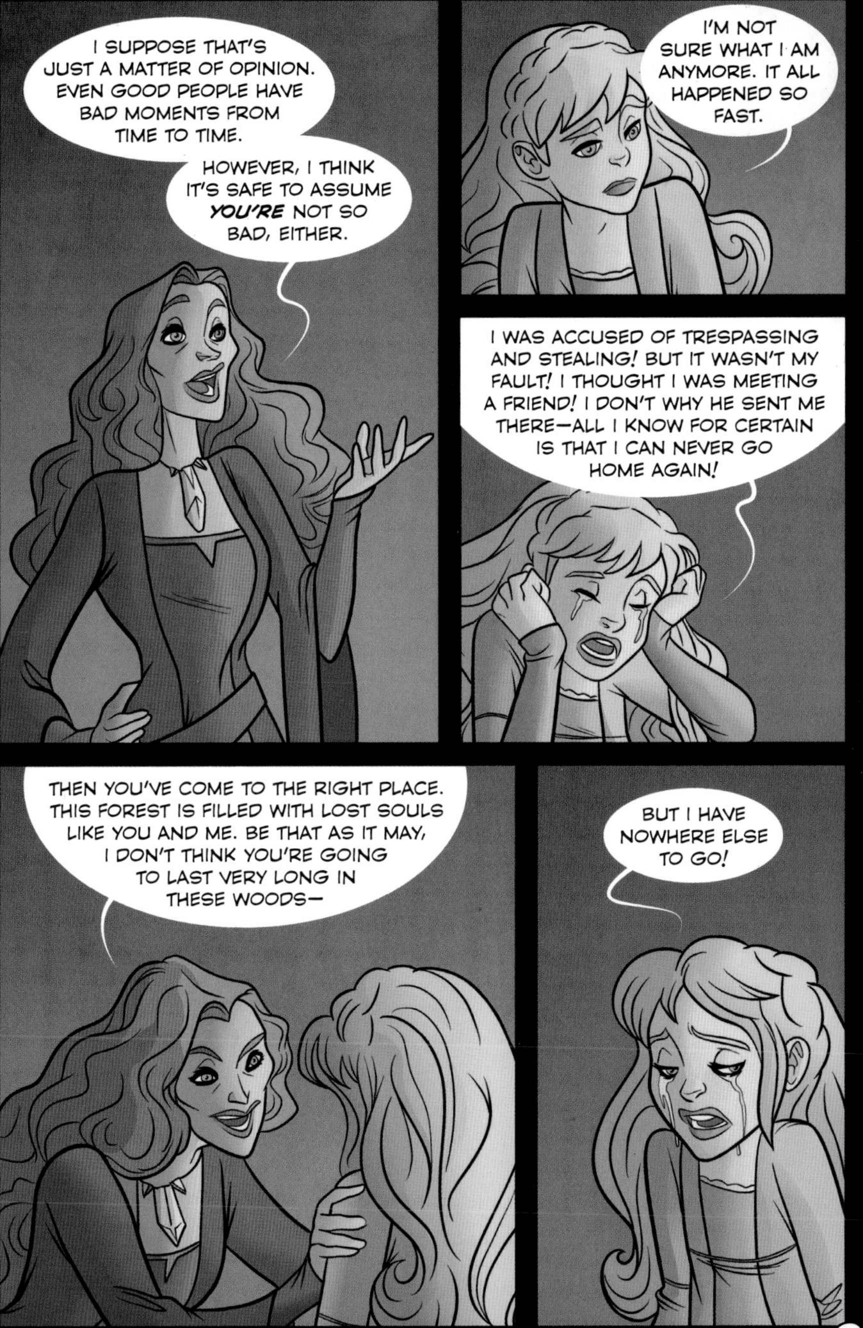
I SUPPOSE THAT'S JUST A MATTER OF OPINION. EVEN GOOD PEOPLE HAVE BAD MOMENTS FROM TIME TO TIME.
HOWEVER, I THINK IT'S SAFE TO ASSUME ***YOU'RE*** NOT SO BAD, EITHER.
I'M NOT SURE WHAT I AM ANYMORE. IT ALL HAPPENED SO FAST.
I WAS ACCUSED OF TRESPASSING AND STEALING! BUT IT WASN'T MY FAULT! I THOUGHT I WAS MEETING A FRIEND! I DON'T WHY HE SENT ME THERE—ALL I KNOW FOR CERTAIN IS THAT I CAN NEVER GO HOME AGAIN!
THEN YOU'VE COME TO THE RIGHT PLACE. THIS FOREST IS FILLED WITH LOST SOULS LIKE YOU AND ME. BE THAT AS IT MAY, I DON'T THINK YOU'RE GOING TO LAST VERY LONG IN THESE WOODS—
BUT I HAVE NOWHERE ELSE TO GO!

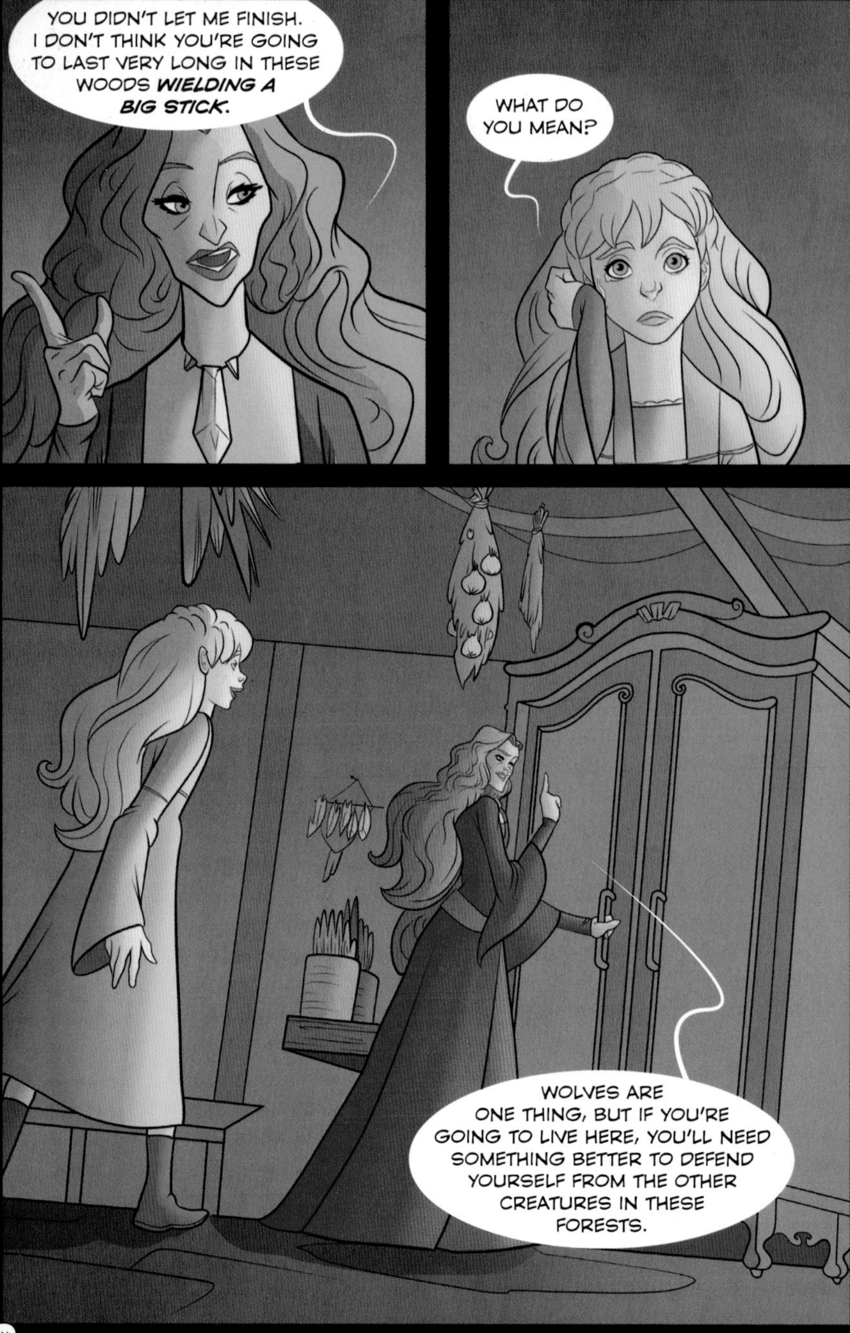
YOU DIDN'T LET ME FINISH. I DON'T THINK YOU'RE GOING TO LAST VERY LONG IN THESE WOODS ***WIELDING A BIG STICK***.
WHAT DO YOU MEAN?
WOLVES ARE ONE THING, BUT IF YOU'RE GOING TO LIVE HERE, YOU'LL NEED SOMETHING BETTER TO DEFEND YOURSELF FROM THE OTHER CREATURES IN THESE FORESTS.

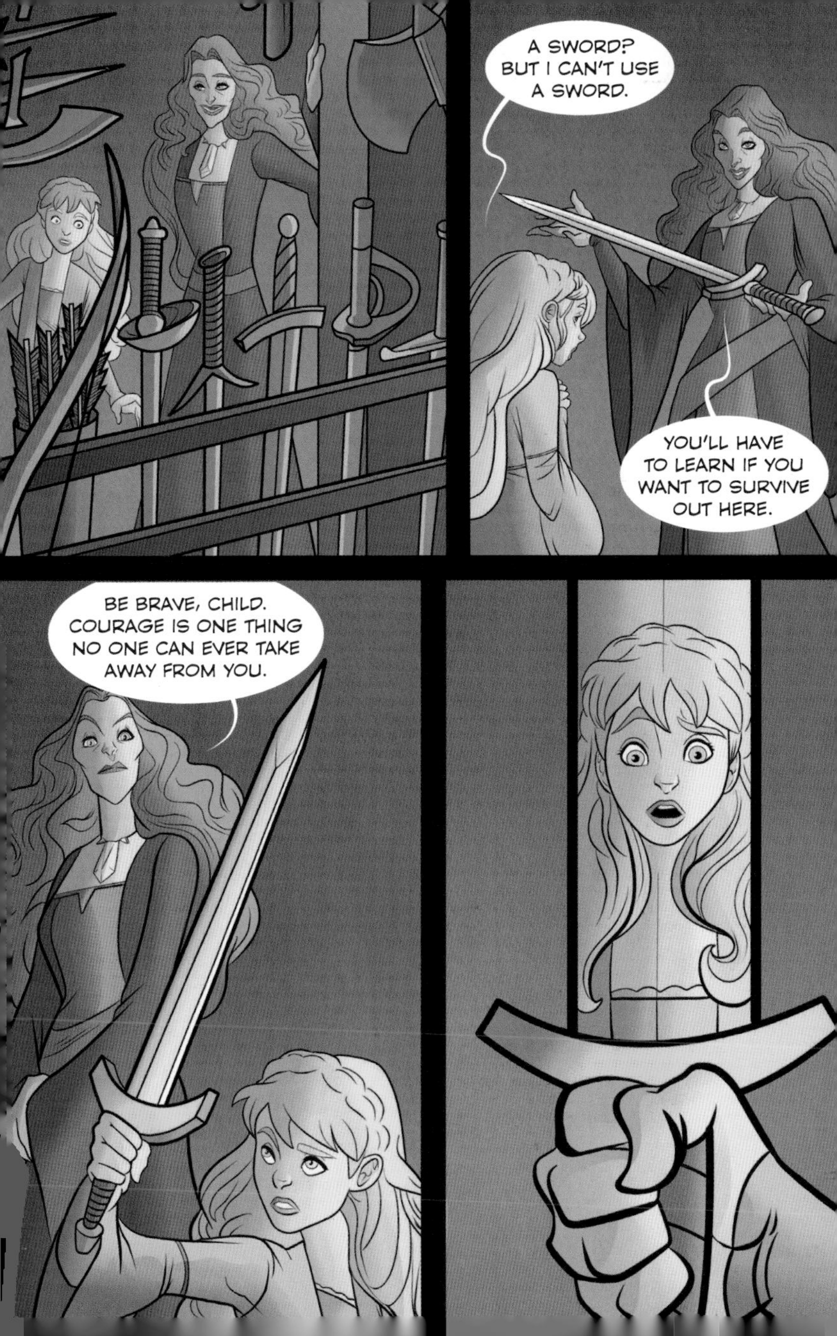
A SWORD? BUT I CAN'T USE A SWORD.
YOU'LL HAVE TO LEARN IF YOU WANT TO SURVIVE OUT HERE.
BE BRAVE, CHILD. COURAGE IS ONE THING NO ONE CAN EVER TAKE AWAY FROM YOU.

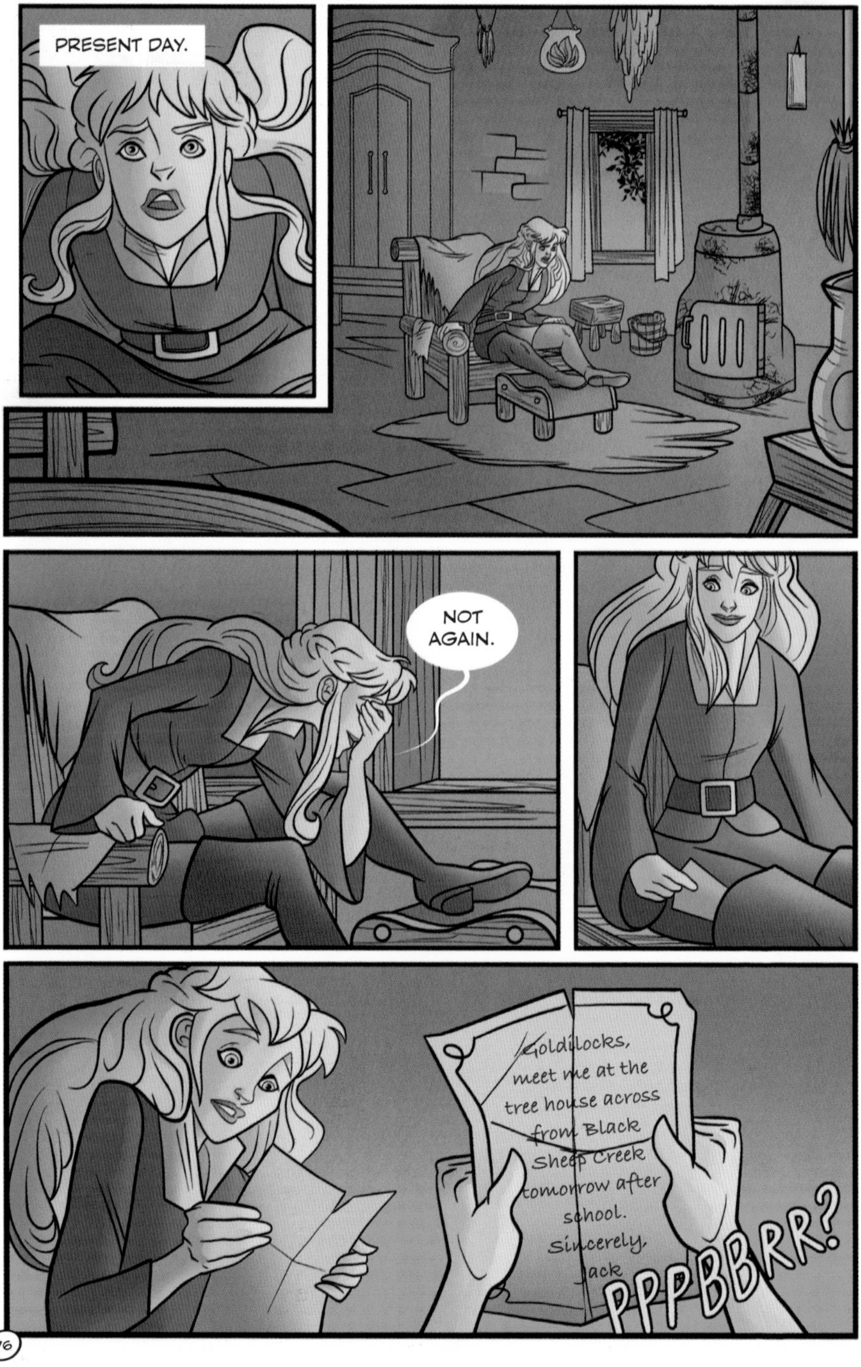
PRESENT DAY.
NOT AGAIN.
Goldilocks, meet me at the tree house across from Black Sheep Creek tomorrow after school. Sincerely, Jack
PPPBBRR?

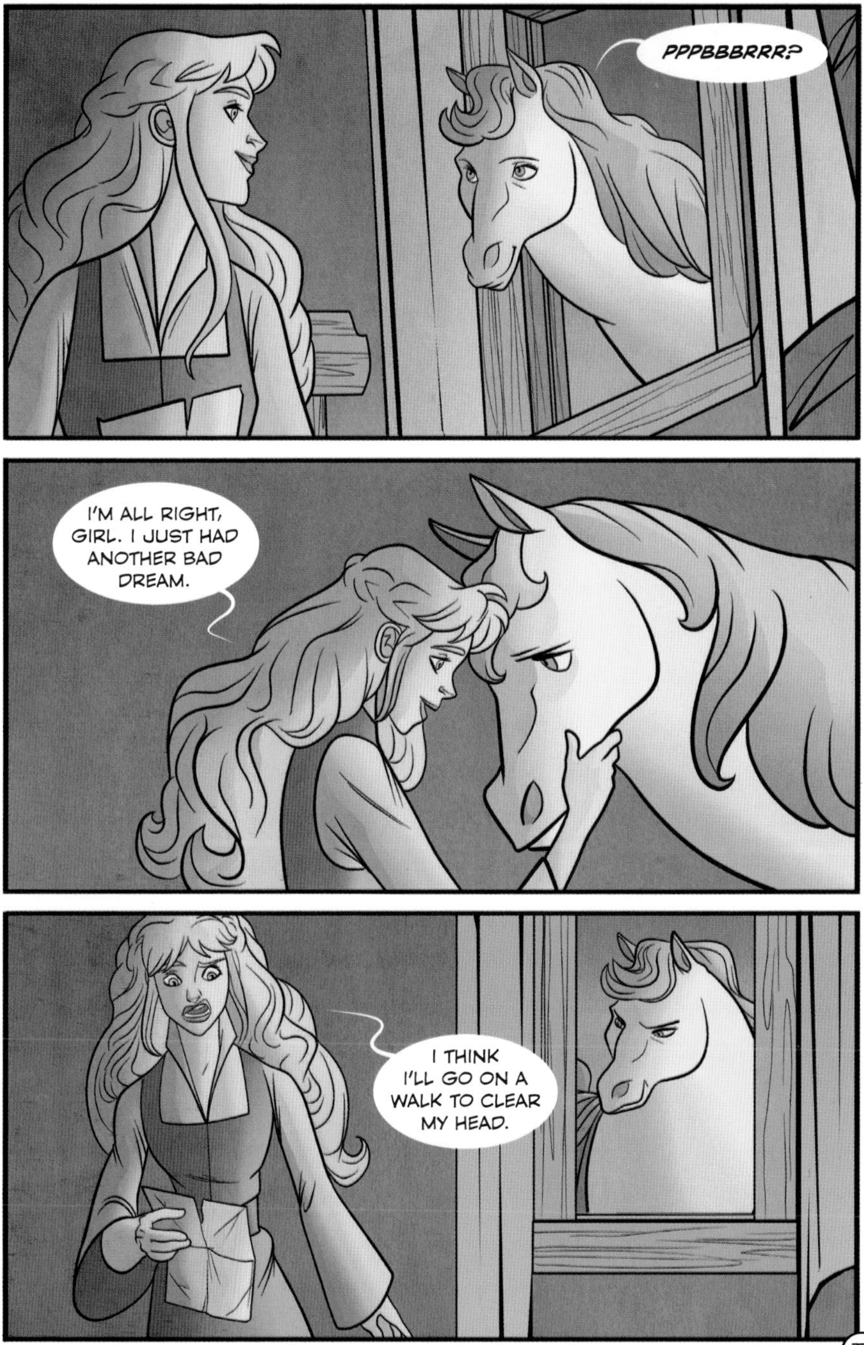
PPPBBBRRR?
I'M ALL RIGHT, GIRL. I JUST HAD ANOTHER BAD DREAM.
I THINK I'LL GO ON A WALK TO CLEAR MY HEAD.

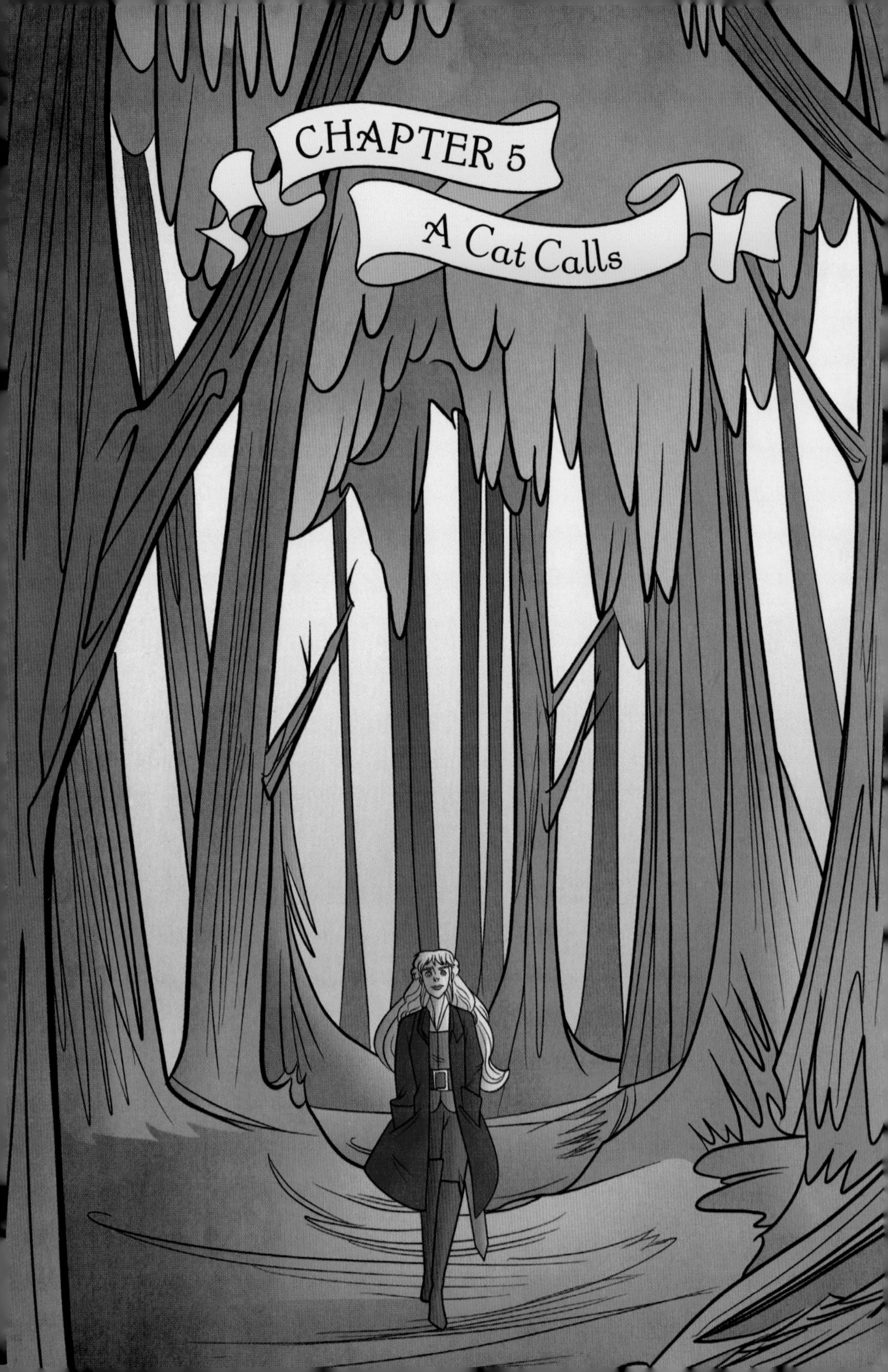
CHAPTER 5
A Cat Calls

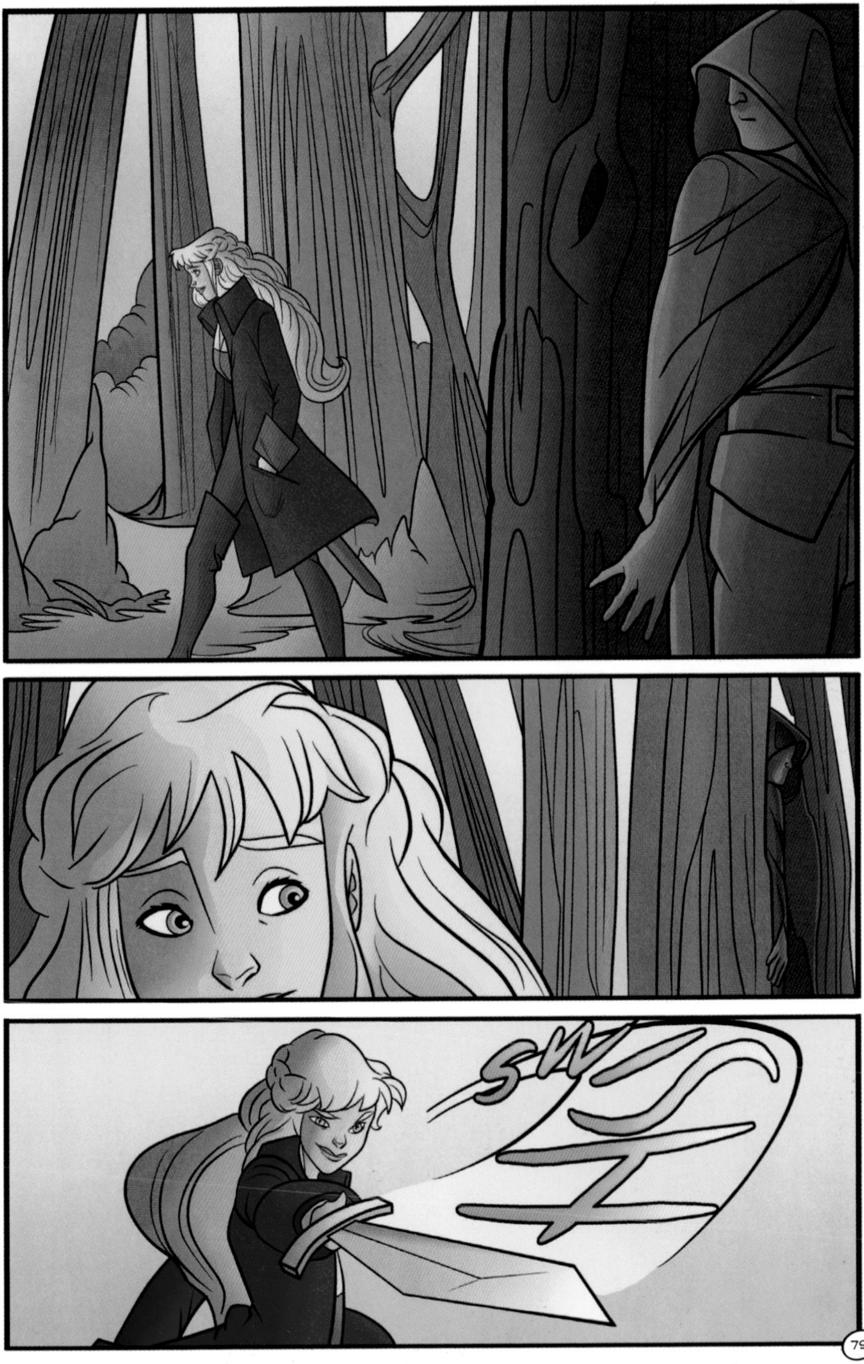
SWISH

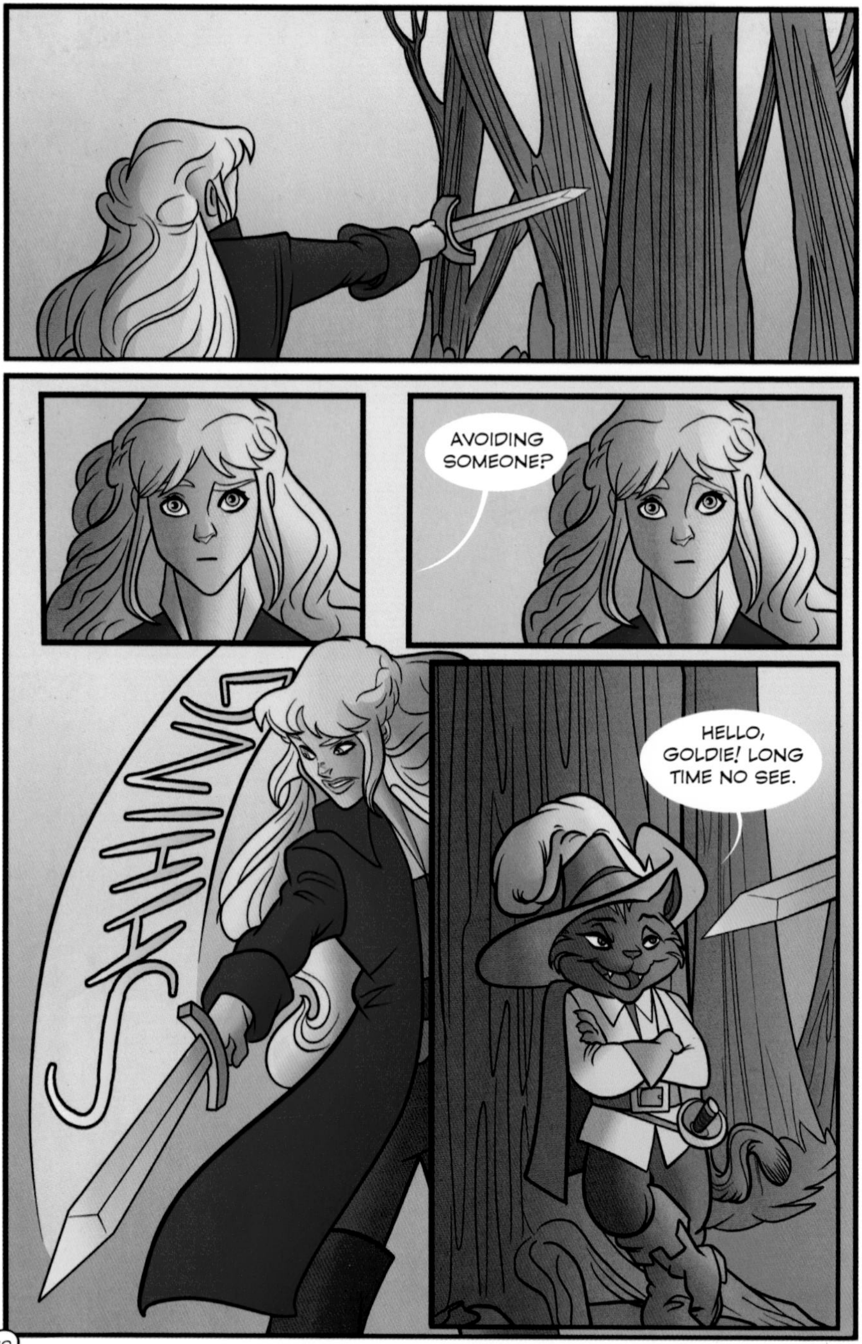
AVOIDING SOMEONE?
SHHING
HELLO, GOLDIE! LONG TIME NO SEE.

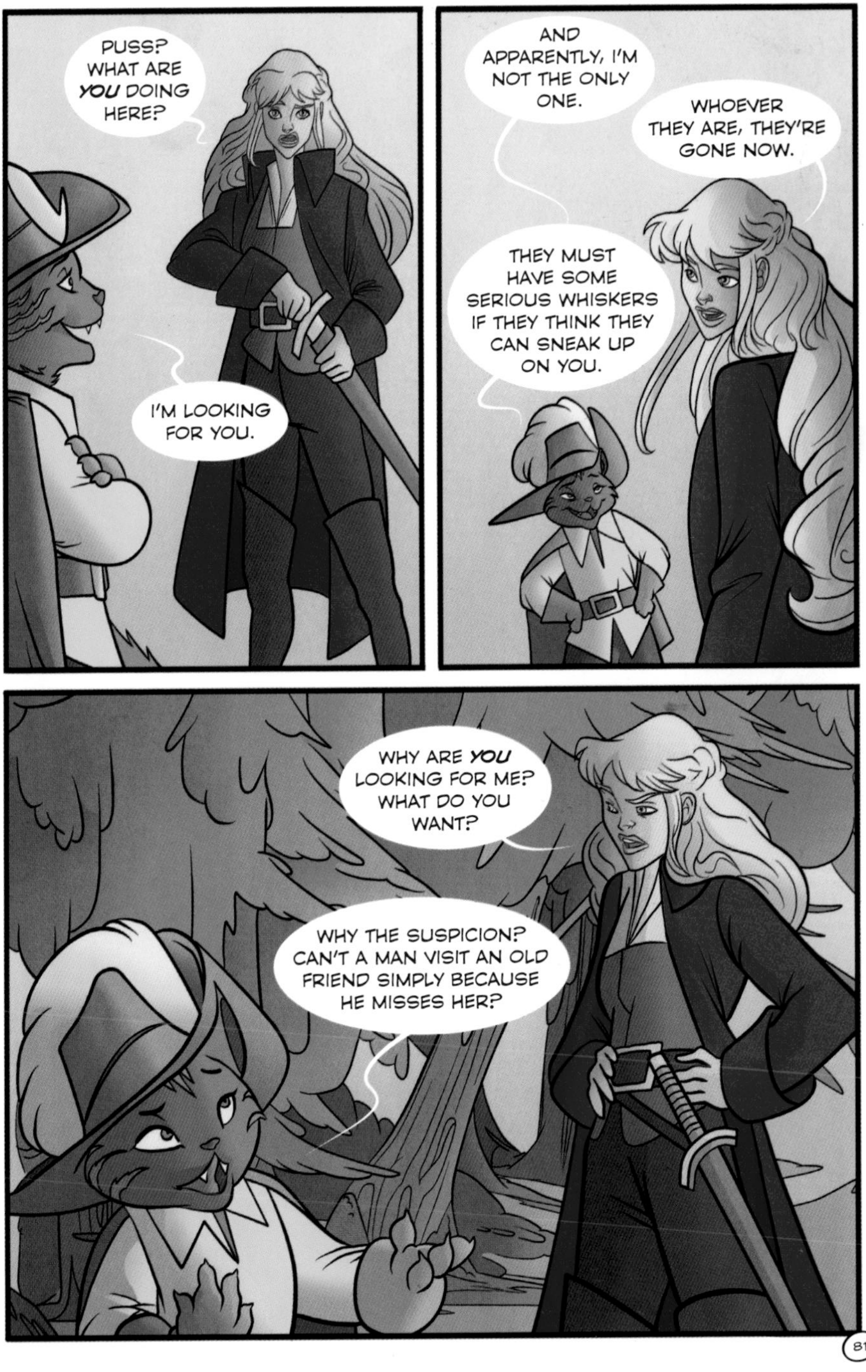
PUSS? WHAT ARE *YOU* DOING HERE?
I'M LOOKING FOR YOU.
AND APPARENTLY, I'M NOT THE ONLY ONE.
WHOEVER THEY ARE, THEY'RE GONE NOW.
THEY MUST HAVE SOME SERIOUS WHISKERS IF THEY THINK THEY CAN SNEAK UP ON YOU.
WHY ARE *YOU* LOOKING FOR ME? WHAT DO YOU WANT?
WHY THE SUSPICION? CAN'T A MAN VISIT AN OLD FRIEND SIMPLY BECAUSE HE MISSES HER?

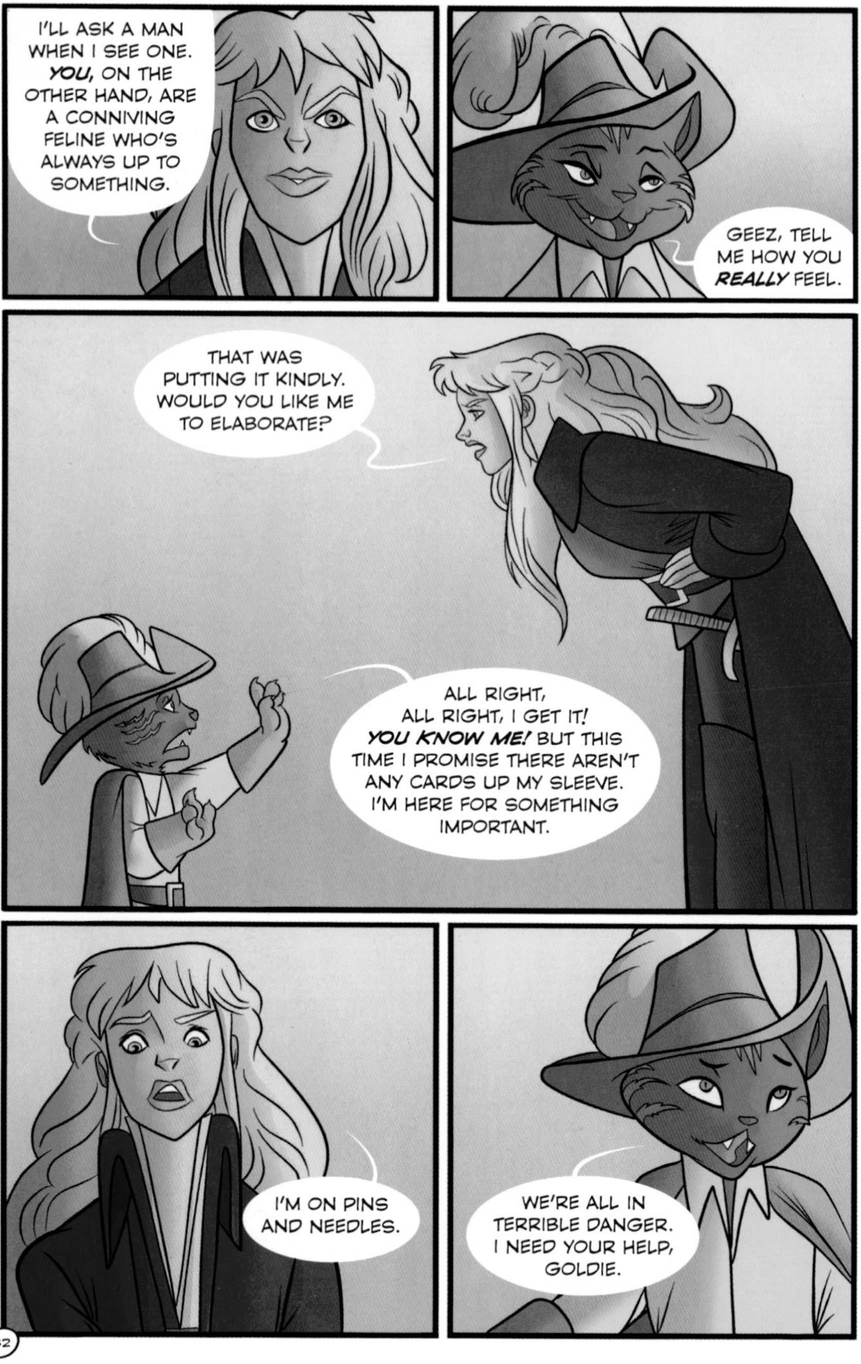
I'LL ASK A MAN WHEN I SEE ONE. ***YOU,*** ON THE OTHER HAND, ARE A CONNIVING FELINE WHO'S ALWAYS UP TO SOMETHING.
GEEZ, TELL ME HOW YOU ***REALLY*** FEEL.
THAT WAS PUTTING IT KINDLY. WOULD YOU LIKE ME TO ELABORATE?
ALL RIGHT, ALL RIGHT, I GET IT! ***YOU KNOW ME!*** BUT THIS TIME I PROMISE THERE AREN'T ANY CARDS UP MY SLEEVE. I'M HERE FOR SOMETHING IMPORTANT.
I'M ON PINS AND NEEDLES.
WE'RE ALL IN TERRIBLE DANGER. I NEED YOUR HELP, GOLDIE.

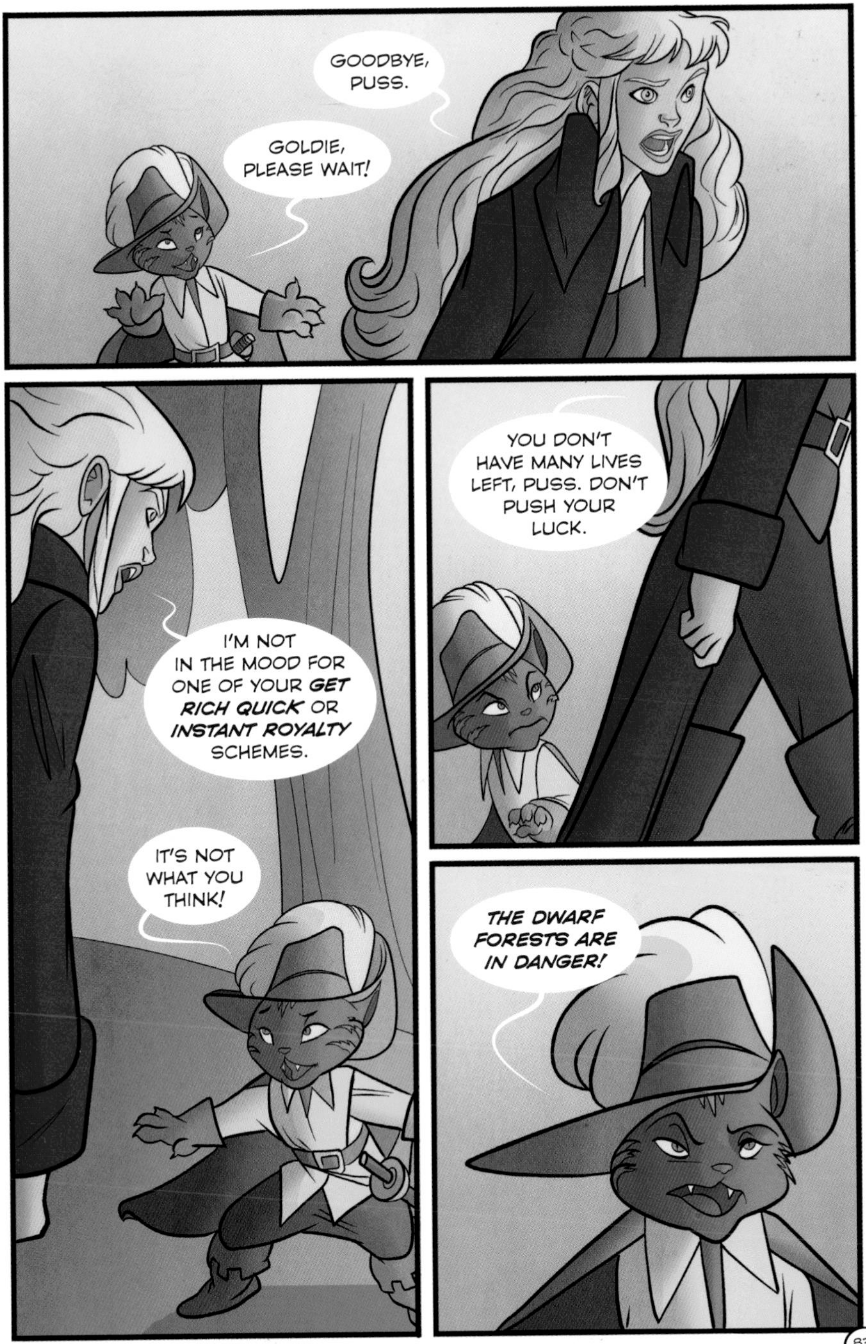
GOODBYE, PUSS.
GOLDIE, PLEASE WAIT!
I'M NOT IN THE MOOD FOR ONE OF YOUR ***GET RICH QUICK*** OR ***INSTANT ROYALTY*** SCHEMES.
IT'S NOT WHAT YOU THINK!
YOU DON'T HAVE MANY LIVES LEFT, PUSS. DON'T PUSH YOUR LUCK.
THE DWARF FORESTS ARE IN DANGER!

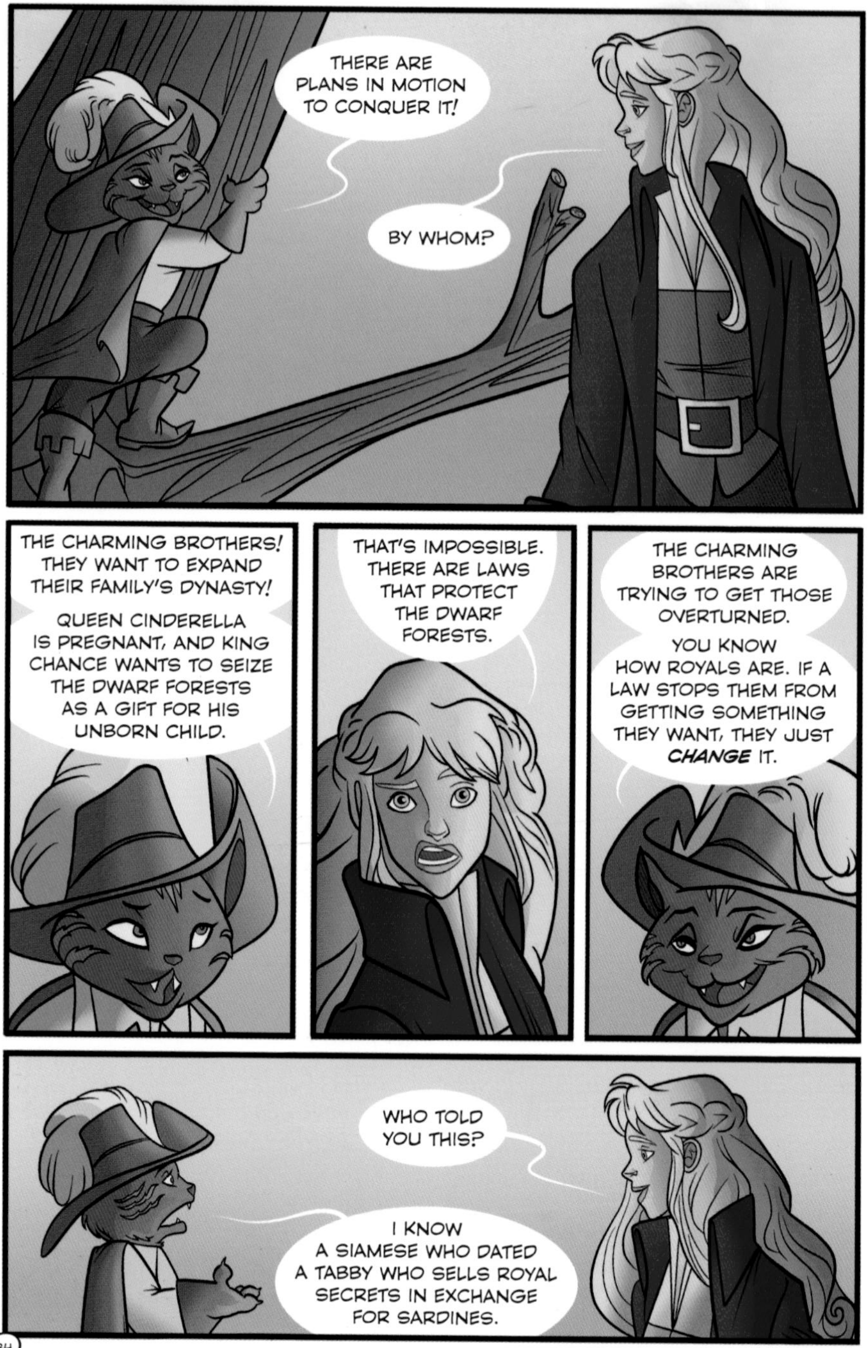

THERE ARE PLANS IN MOTION TO CONQUER IT!
BY WHOM?
THE CHARMING BROTHERS! THEY WANT TO EXPAND THEIR FAMILY'S DYNASTY!
QUEEN CINDERELLA IS PREGNANT, AND KING CHANCE WANTS TO SEIZE THE DWARF FORESTS AS A GIFT FOR HIS UNBORN CHILD.
THAT'S IMPOSSIBLE. THERE ARE LAWS THAT PROTECT THE DWARF FORESTS.
THE CHARMING BROTHERS ARE TRYING TO GET THOSE OVERTURNED.
YOU KNOW HOW ROYALS ARE. IF A LAW STOPS THEM FROM GETTING SOMETHING THEY WANT, THEY JUST *CHANGE* IT.
WHO TOLD YOU THIS?
I KNOW A SIAMESE WHO DATED A TABBY WHO SELLS ROYAL SECRETS IN EXCHANGE FOR SARDINES.

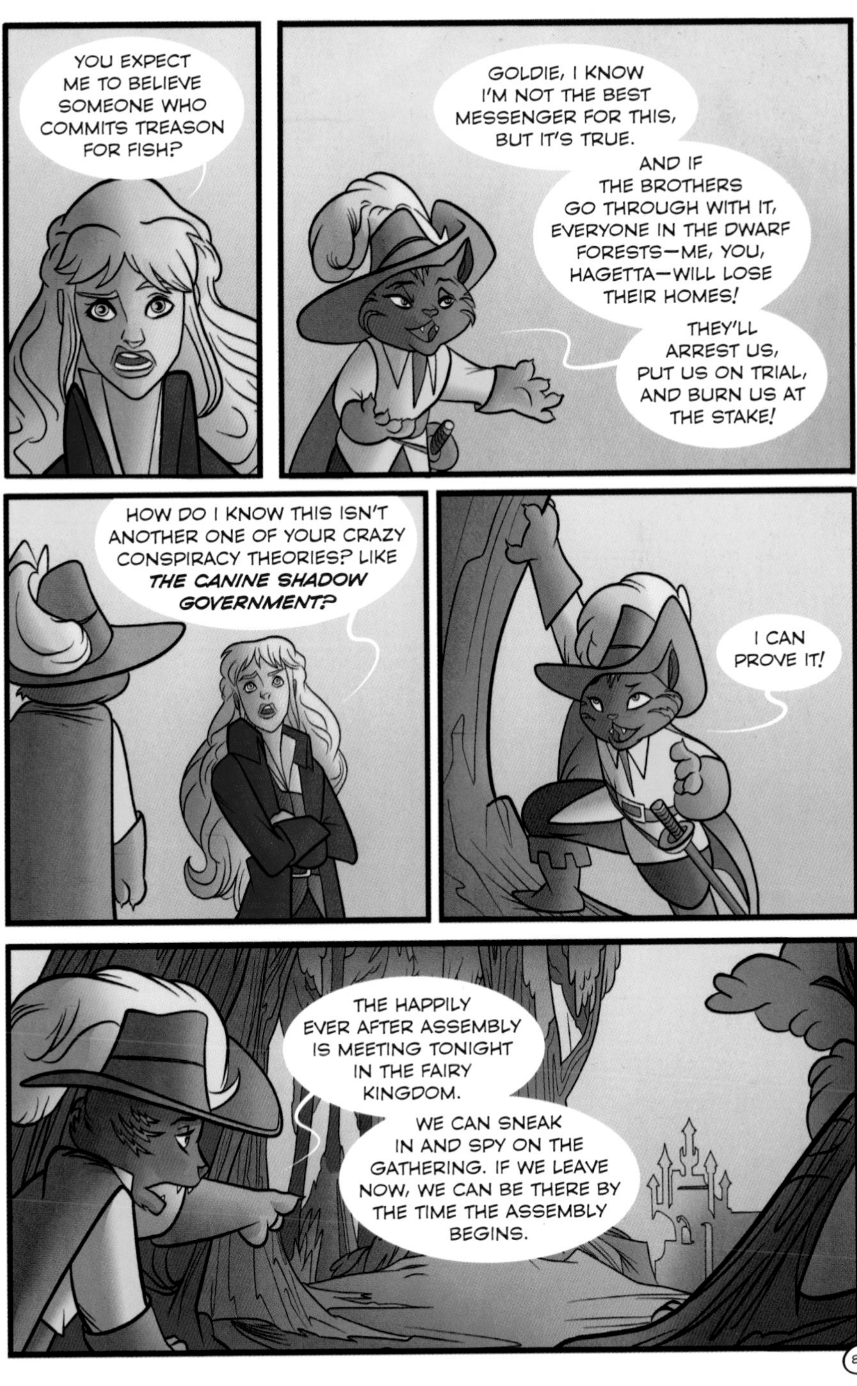

YOU EXPECT ME TO BELIEVE SOMEONE WHO COMMITS TREASON FOR FISH?
GOLDIE, I KNOW I'M NOT THE BEST MESSENGER FOR THIS, BUT IT'S TRUE.
AND IF THE BROTHERS GO THROUGH WITH IT, EVERYONE IN THE DWARF FORESTS—ME, YOU, HAGETTA—WILL LOSE THEIR HOMES!
THEY'LL ARREST US, PUT US ON TRIAL, AND BURN US AT THE STAKE!
HOW DO I KNOW THIS ISN'T ANOTHER ONE OF YOUR CRAZY CONSPIRACY THEORIES? LIKE *THE CANINE SHADOW GOVERNMENT?*
I CAN PROVE IT!
THE HAPPILY EVER AFTER ASSEMBLY IS MEETING TONIGHT IN THE FAIRY KINGDOM.
WE CAN SNEAK IN AND SPY ON THE GATHERING. IF WE LEAVE NOW, WE CAN BE THERE BY THE TIME THE ASSEMBLY BEGINS.

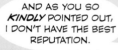

PLEASE, GOLDIE! IF THE CHARMING BROTHERS GET APPROVAL FROM THE ASSEMBLY, WE WON'T HAVE MUCH TIME TO WARN THE OTHERS.

AND AS YOU SO *KINDLY* POINTED OUT, I DON'T HAVE THE BEST REPUTATION.

IF THE FORESTS ARE IN DANGER, PEOPLE WILL NEED SOMEONE THEY TRUST TO SOUND THE ALARM. THEY'LL NEED SOMEONE LIKE *YOU*.

FINE. BUT IF THIS IS A WASTE OF MY TIME, YOU WON'T HAVE LEGS TO FILL THOSE BOOTS ANYMORE!

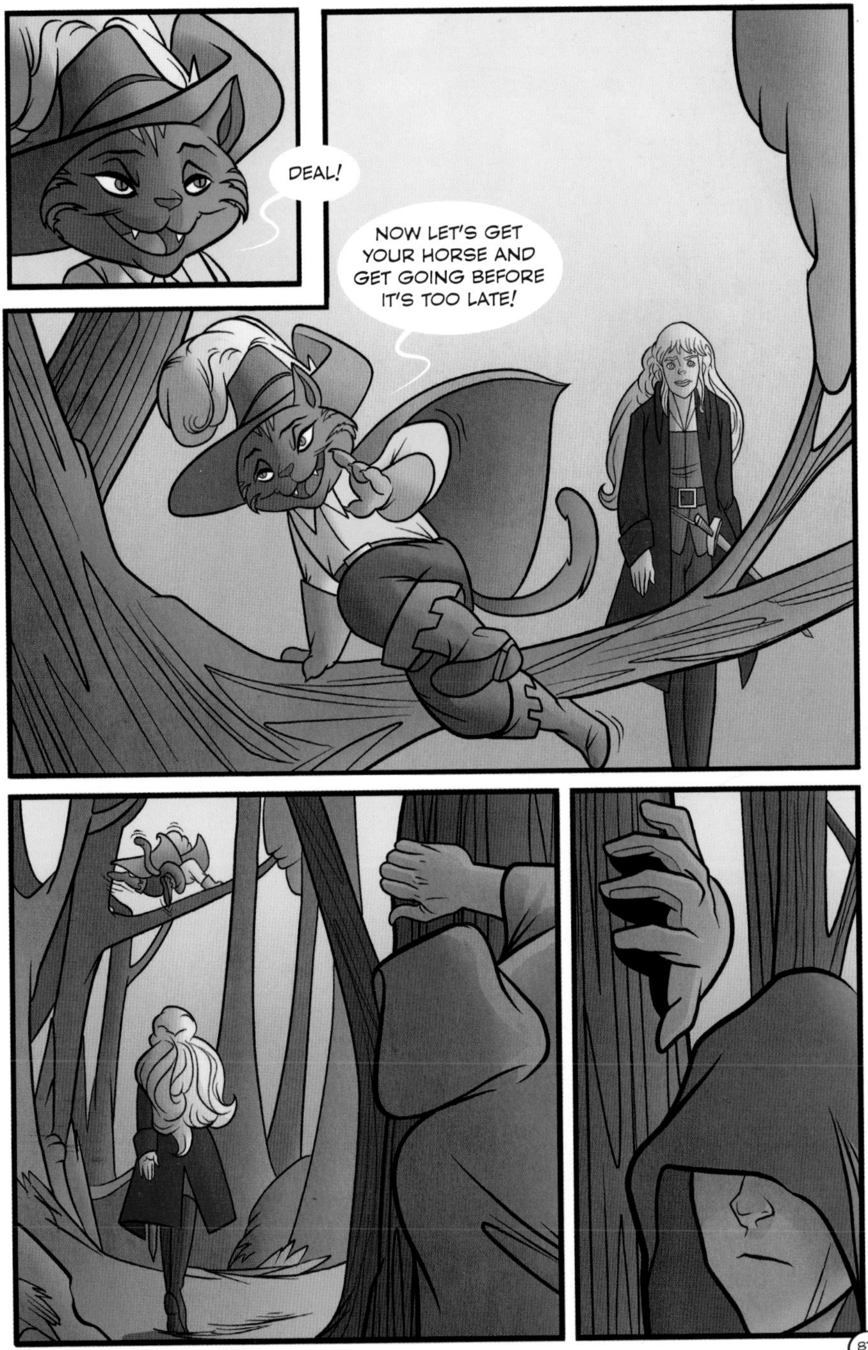
DEAL!
NOW LET'S GET YOUR HORSE AND GET GOING BEFORE IT'S TOO LATE!

CHAPTER 6
The Assembly

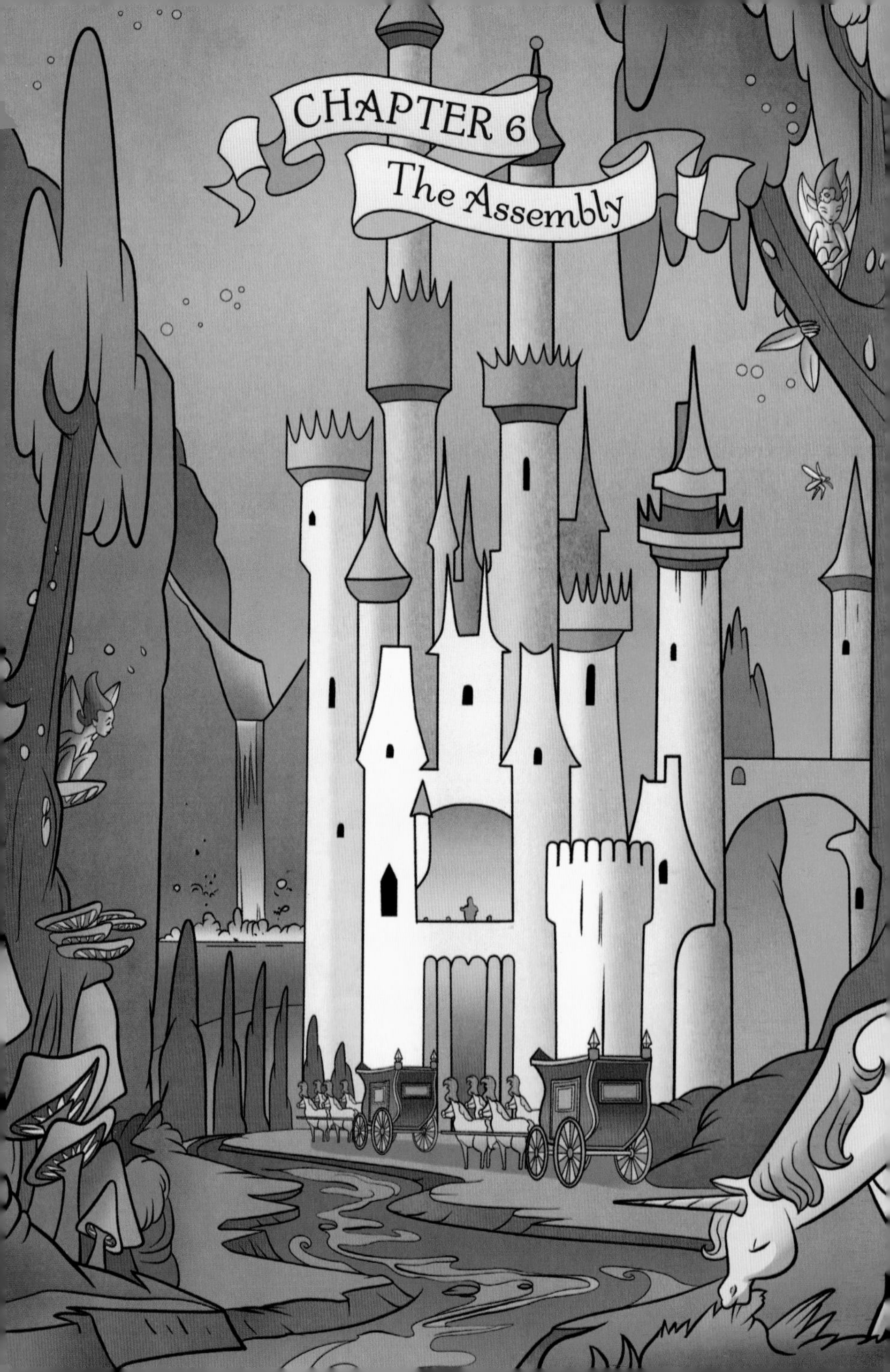

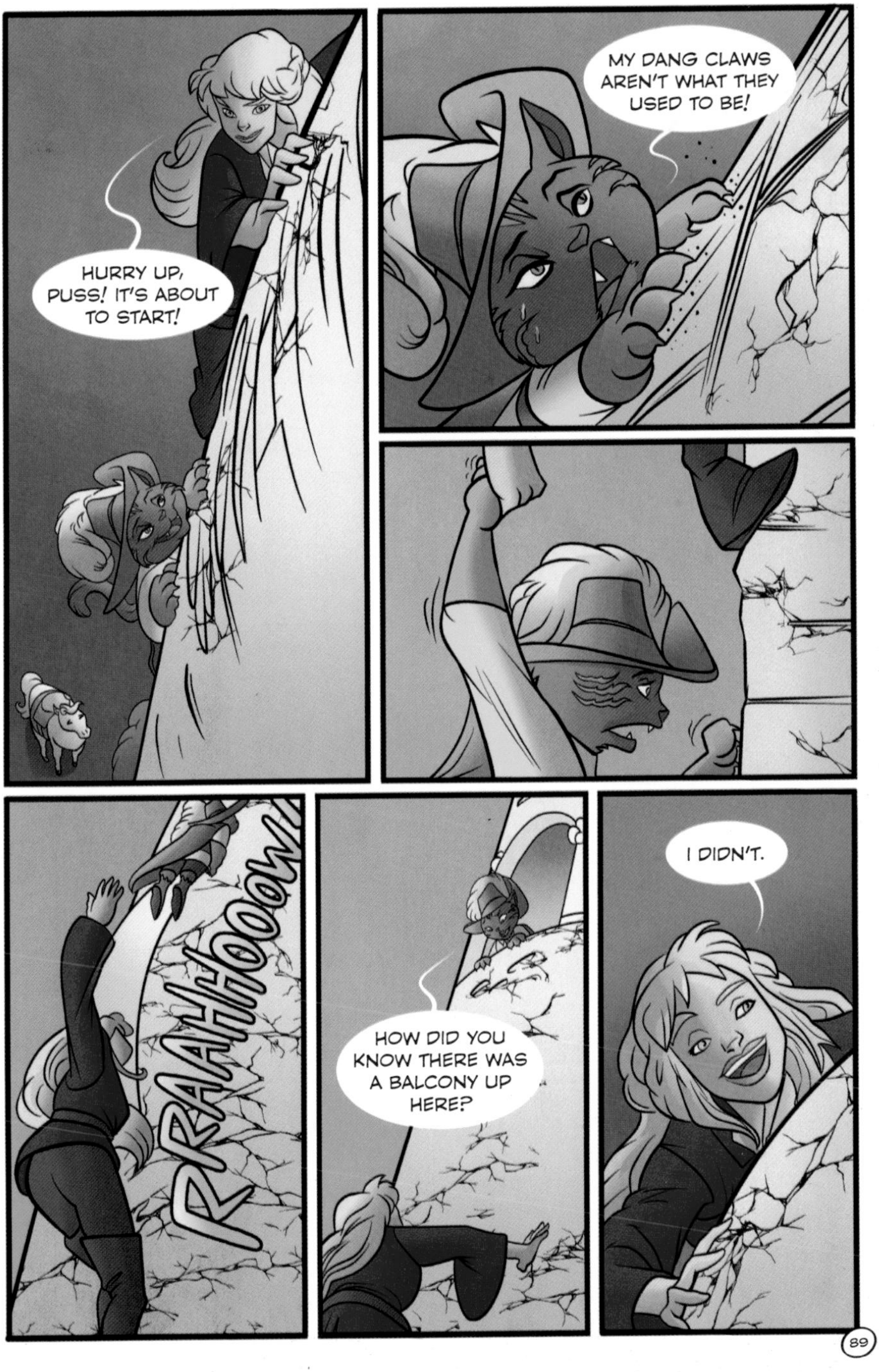
HURRY UP, PUSS! IT'S ABOUT TO START!
MY DANG CLAWS AREN'T WHAT THEY USED TO BE!
RRAAHHooow!!
HOW DID YOU KNOW THERE WAS A BALCONY UP HERE?
I DIDN'T.

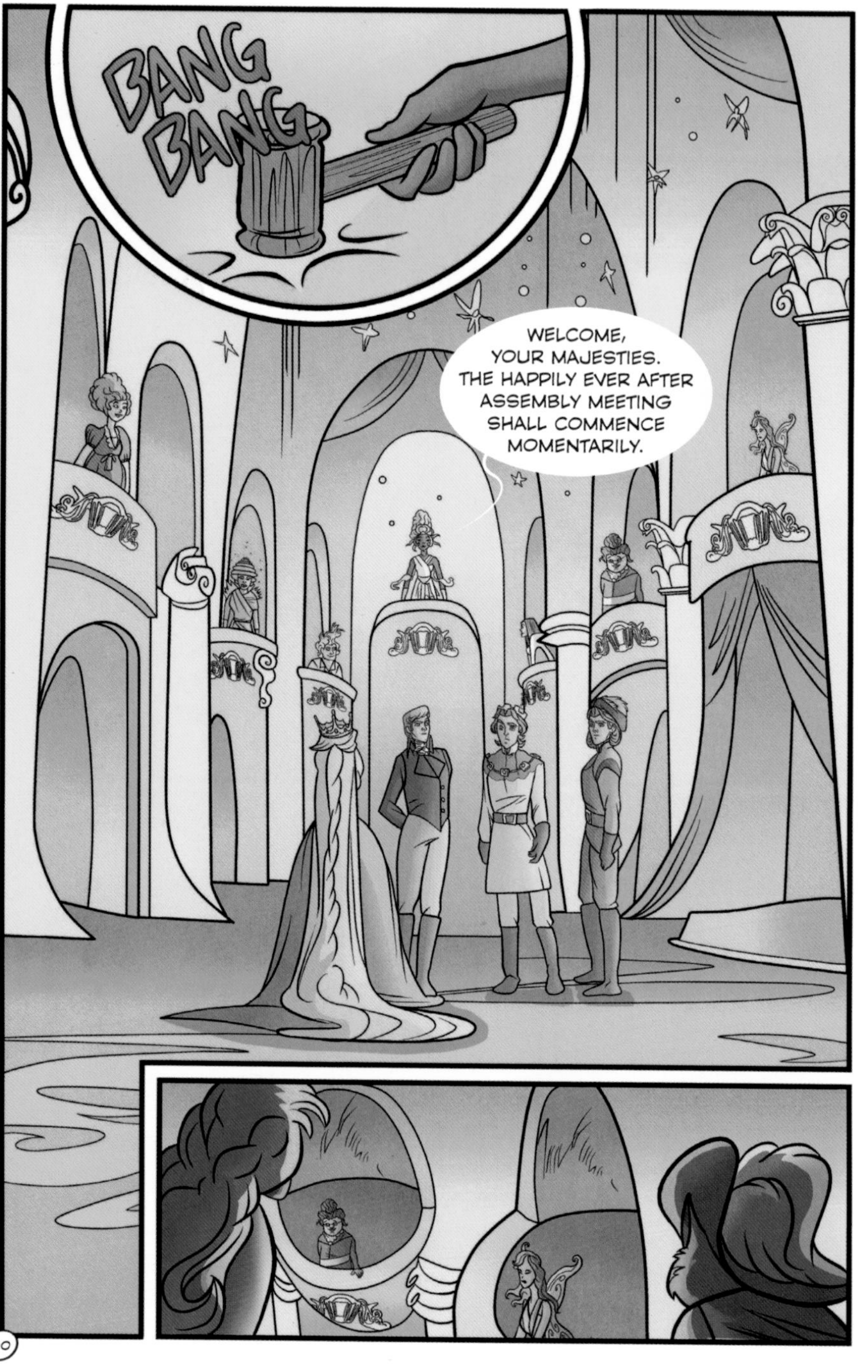
BANG
BANG
WELCOME, YOUR MAJESTIES. THE HAPPILY EVER AFTER ASSEMBLY MEETING SHALL COMMENCE MOMENTARILY.

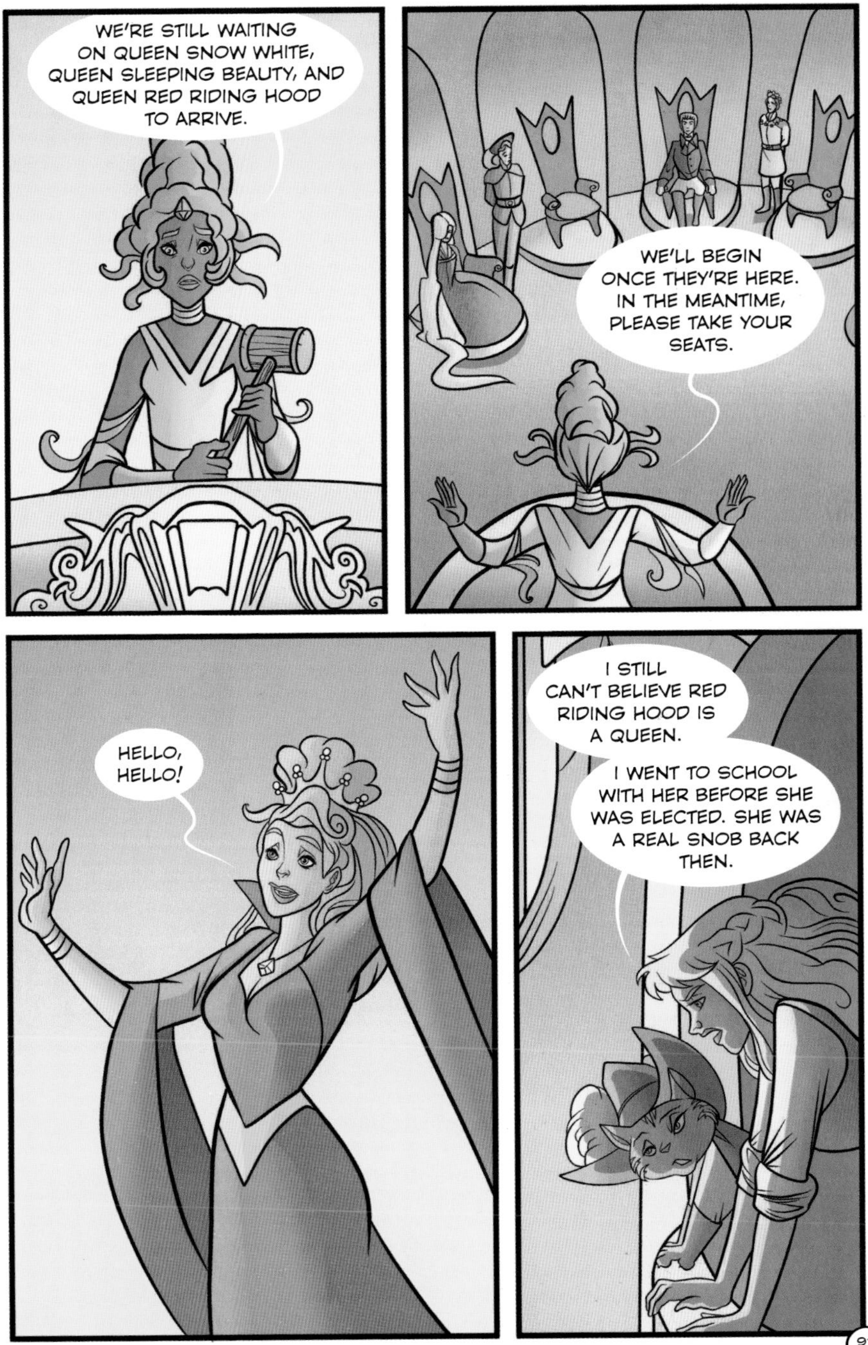
WE'RE STILL WAITING ON QUEEN SNOW WHITE, QUEEN SLEEPING BEAUTY, AND QUEEN RED RIDING HOOD TO ARRIVE.
WE'LL BEGIN ONCE THEY'RE HERE. IN THE MEANTIME, PLEASE TAKE YOUR SEATS.
HELLO, HELLO!
I STILL CAN'T BELIEVE RED RIDING HOOD IS A QUEEN.
I WENT TO SCHOOL WITH HER BEFORE SHE WAS ELECTED. SHE WAS A REAL SNOB BACK THEN.

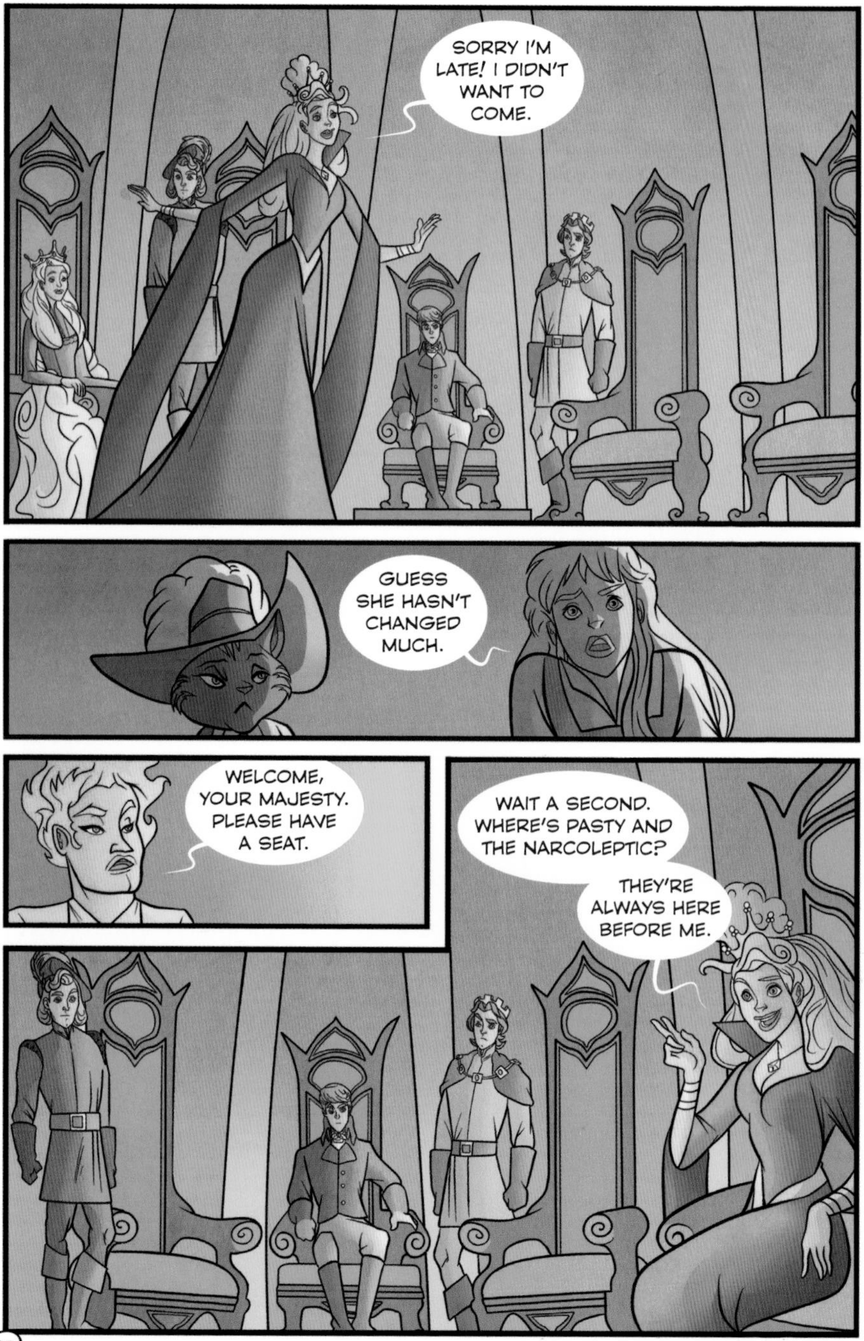
SORRY I'M LATE! I DIDN'T WANT TO COME.
GUESS SHE HASN'T CHANGED MUCH.
WELCOME, YOUR MAJESTY. PLEASE HAVE A SEAT.
WAIT A SECOND. WHERE'S PASTY AND THE NARCOLEPTIC?
THEY'RE ALWAYS HERE BEFORE ME.

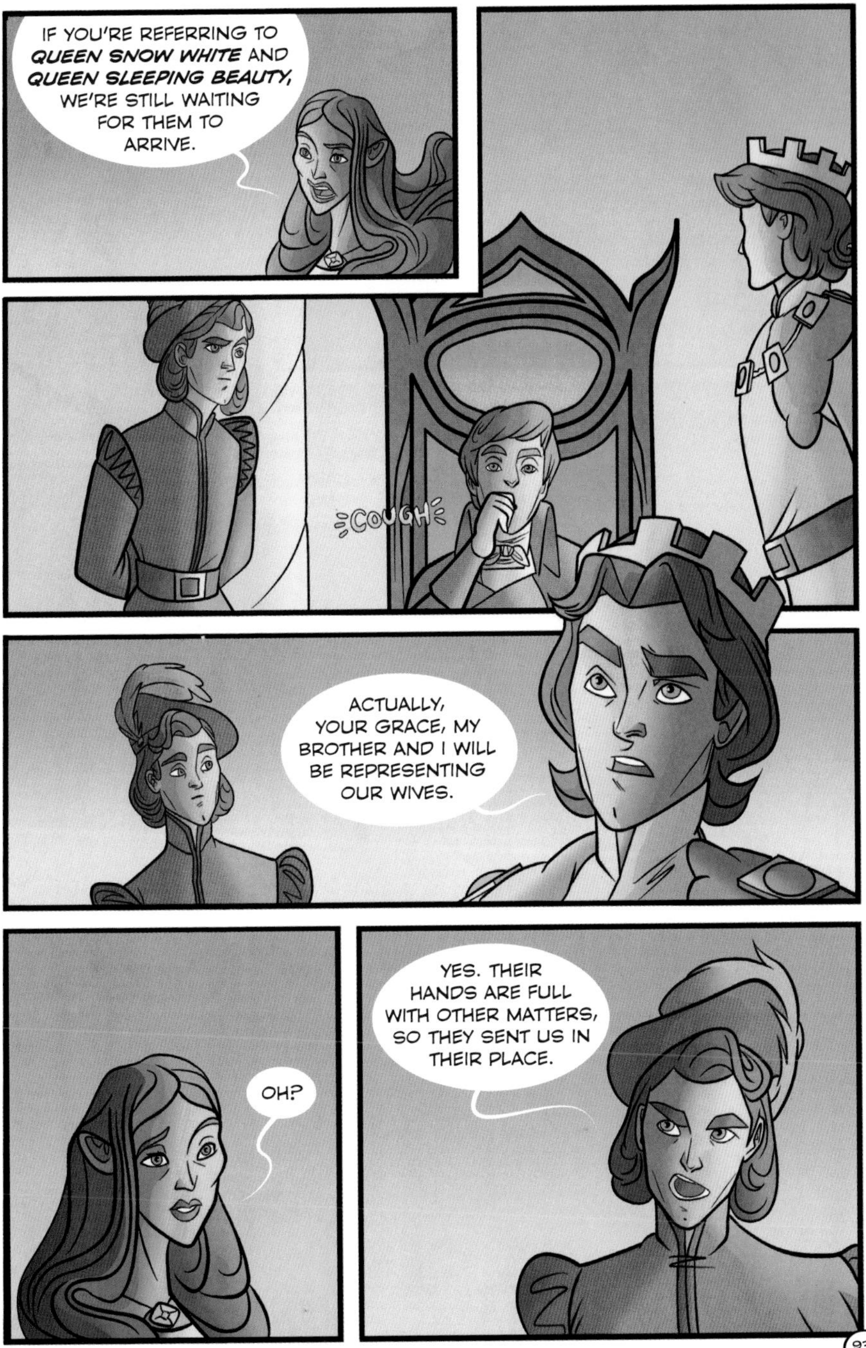
IF YOU'RE REFERRING TO QUEEN SNOW WHITE AND QUEEN SLEEPING BEAUTY, WE'RE STILL WAITING FOR THEM TO ARRIVE.
COUGH
ACTUALLY, YOUR GRACE, MY BROTHER AND I WILL BE REPRESENTING OUR WIVES.
OH?
YES. THEIR HANDS ARE FULL WITH OTHER MATTERS, SO THEY SENT US IN THEIR PLACE.

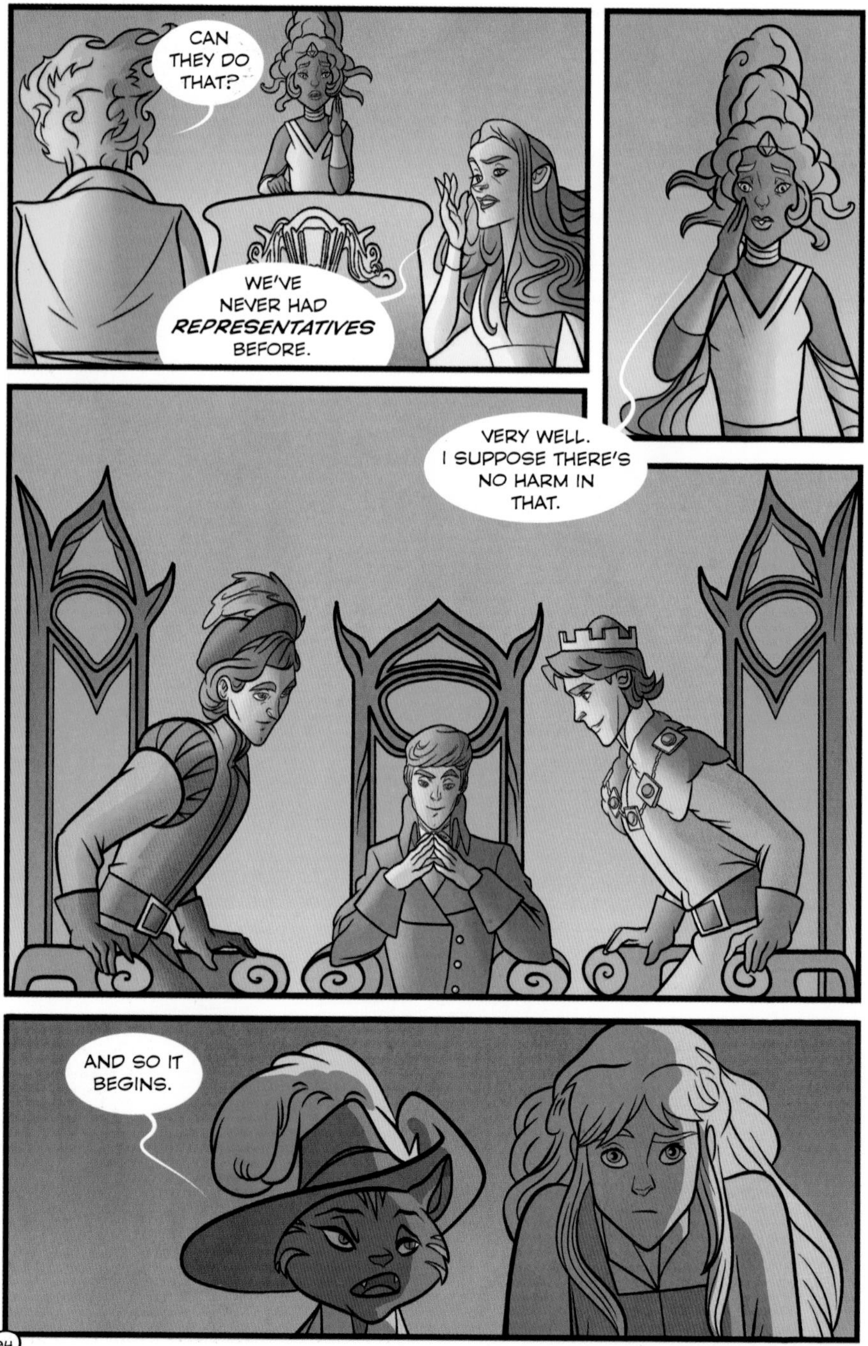
CAN THEY DO THAT?
WE'VE NEVER HAD *REPRESENTATIVES* BEFORE.
VERY WELL. I SUPPOSE THERE'S NO HARM IN THAT.
AND SO IT BEGINS.

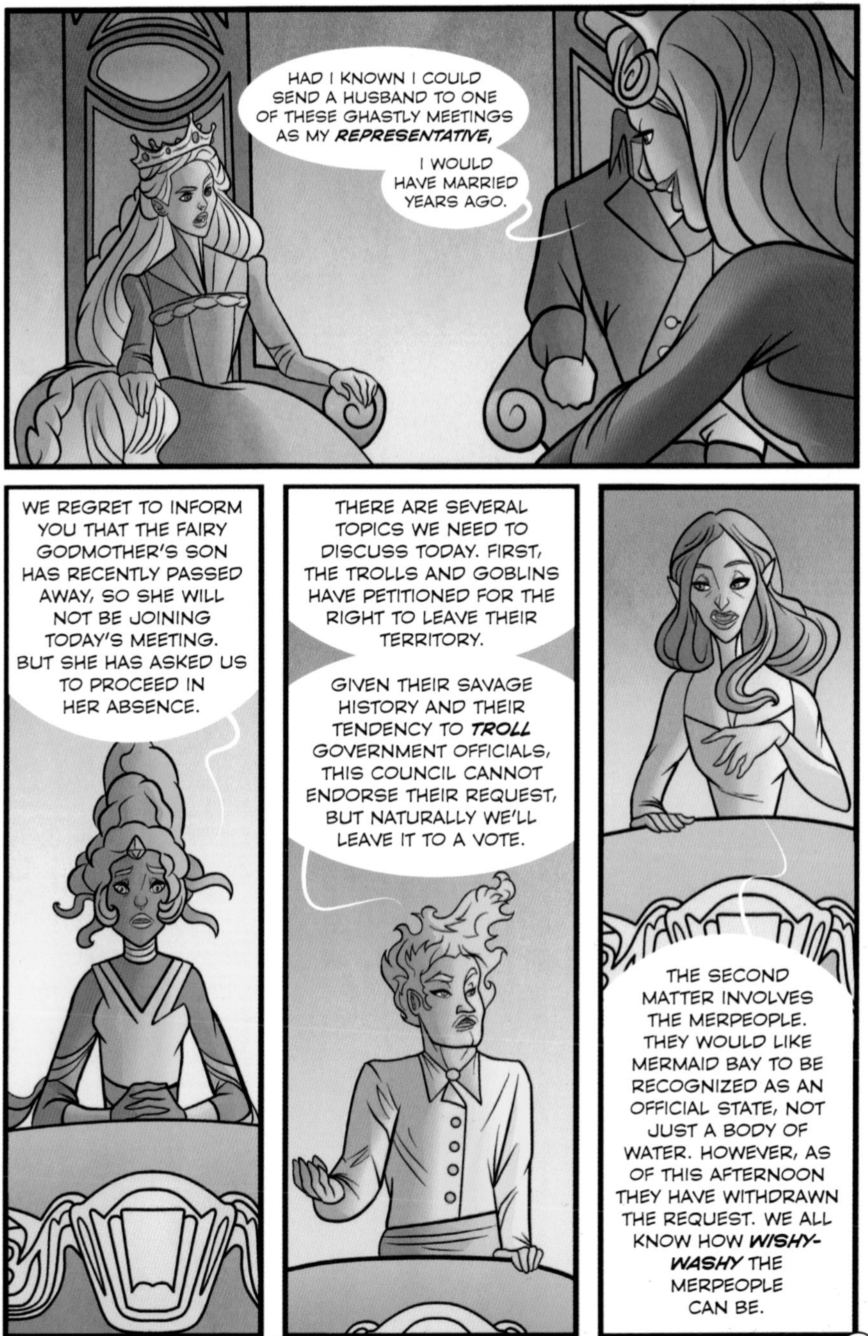
HAD I KNOWN I COULD SEND A HUSBAND TO ONE OF THESE GHASTLY MEETINGS AS MY *REPRESENTATIVE,*
I WOULD HAVE MARRIED YEARS AGO.
WE REGRET TO INFORM YOU THAT THE FAIRY GODMOTHER'S SON HAS RECENTLY PASSED AWAY, SO SHE WILL NOT BE JOINING TODAY'S MEETING. BUT SHE HAS ASKED US TO PROCEED IN HER ABSENCE.
THERE ARE SEVERAL TOPICS WE NEED TO DISCUSS TODAY. FIRST, THE TROLLS AND GOBLINS HAVE PETITIONED FOR THE RIGHT TO LEAVE THEIR TERRITORY.
GIVEN THEIR SAVAGE HISTORY AND THEIR TENDENCY TO *TROLL* GOVERNMENT OFFICIALS, THIS COUNCIL CANNOT ENDORSE THEIR REQUEST, BUT NATURALLY WE'LL LEAVE IT TO A VOTE.
THE SECOND MATTER INVOLVES THE MERPEOPLE. THEY WOULD LIKE MERMAID BAY TO BE RECOGNIZED AS AN OFFICIAL STATE, NOT JUST A BODY OF WATER. HOWEVER, AS OF THIS AFTERNOON THEY HAVE WITHDRAWN THE REQUEST. WE ALL KNOW HOW *WISHY-WASHY* THE MERPEOPLE CAN BE.

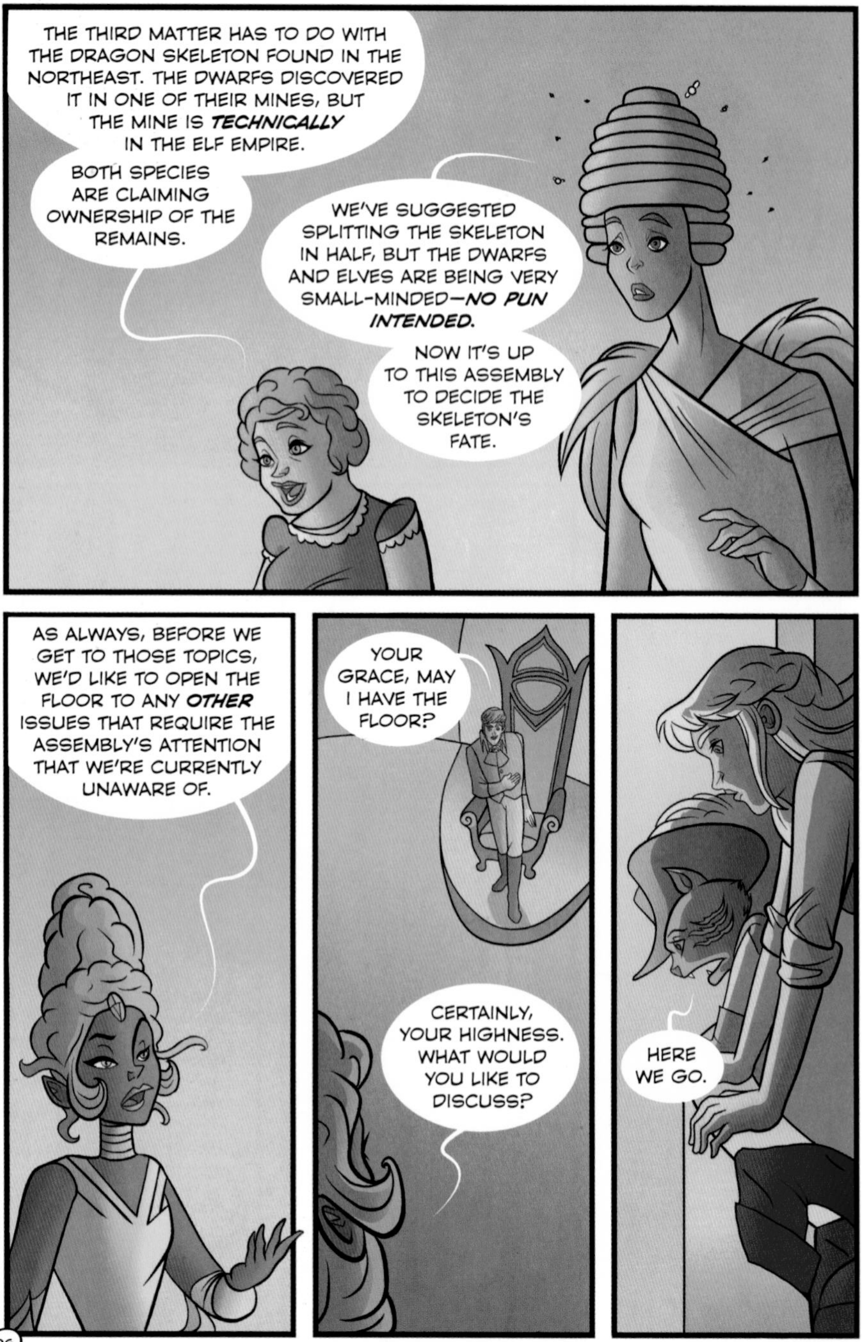
THE THIRD MATTER HAS TO DO WITH THE DRAGON SKELETON FOUND IN THE NORTHEAST. THE DWARFS DISCOVERED IT IN ONE OF THEIR MINES, BUT THE MINE IS ***TECHNICALLY*** IN THE ELF EMPIRE.
BOTH SPECIES ARE CLAIMING OWNERSHIP OF THE REMAINS.
WE'VE SUGGESTED SPLITTING THE SKELETON IN HALF, BUT THE DWARFS AND ELVES ARE BEING VERY SMALL-MINDED—***NO PUN INTENDED.***
NOW IT'S UP TO THIS ASSEMBLY TO DECIDE THE SKELETON'S FATE.
AS ALWAYS, BEFORE WE GET TO THOSE TOPICS, WE'D LIKE TO OPEN THE FLOOR TO ANY ***OTHER*** ISSUES THAT REQUIRE THE ASSEMBLY'S ATTENTION THAT WE'RE CURRENTLY UNAWARE OF.
YOUR GRACE, MAY I HAVE THE FLOOR?
CERTAINLY, YOUR HIGHNESS. WHAT WOULD YOU LIKE TO DISCUSS?
HERE WE GO.

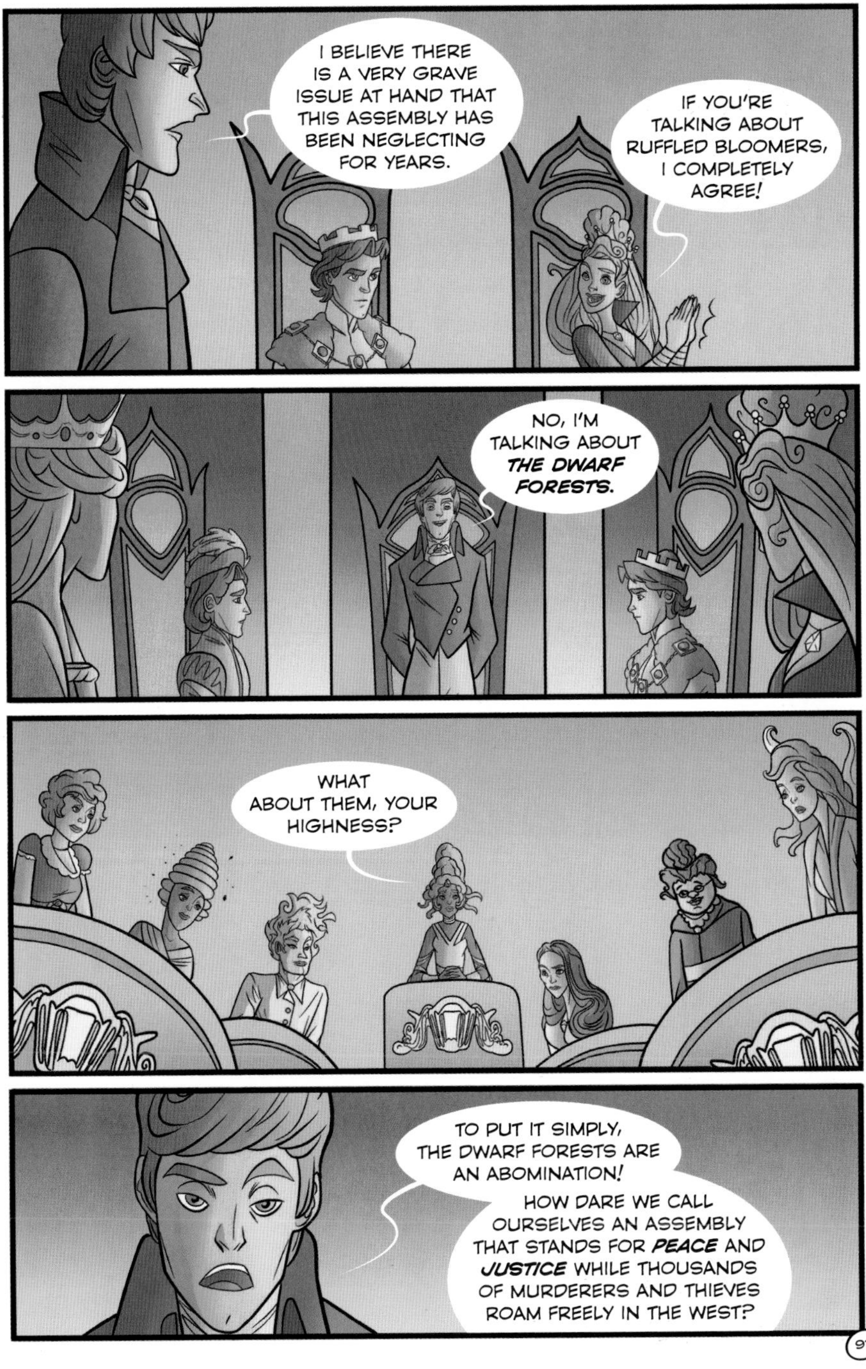
I BELIEVE THERE IS A VERY GRAVE ISSUE AT HAND THAT THIS ASSEMBLY HAS BEEN NEGLECTING FOR YEARS.
IF YOU'RE TALKING ABOUT RUFFLED BLOOMERS, I COMPLETELY AGREE!
NO, I'M TALKING ABOUT *THE DWARF FORESTS.*
WHAT ABOUT THEM, YOUR HIGHNESS?
TO PUT IT SIMPLY, THE DWARF FORESTS ARE AN ABOMINATION!
HOW DARE WE CALL OURSELVES AN ASSEMBLY THAT STANDS FOR *PEACE* AND *JUSTICE* WHILE THOUSANDS OF MURDERERS AND THIEVES ROAM FREELY IN THE WEST?

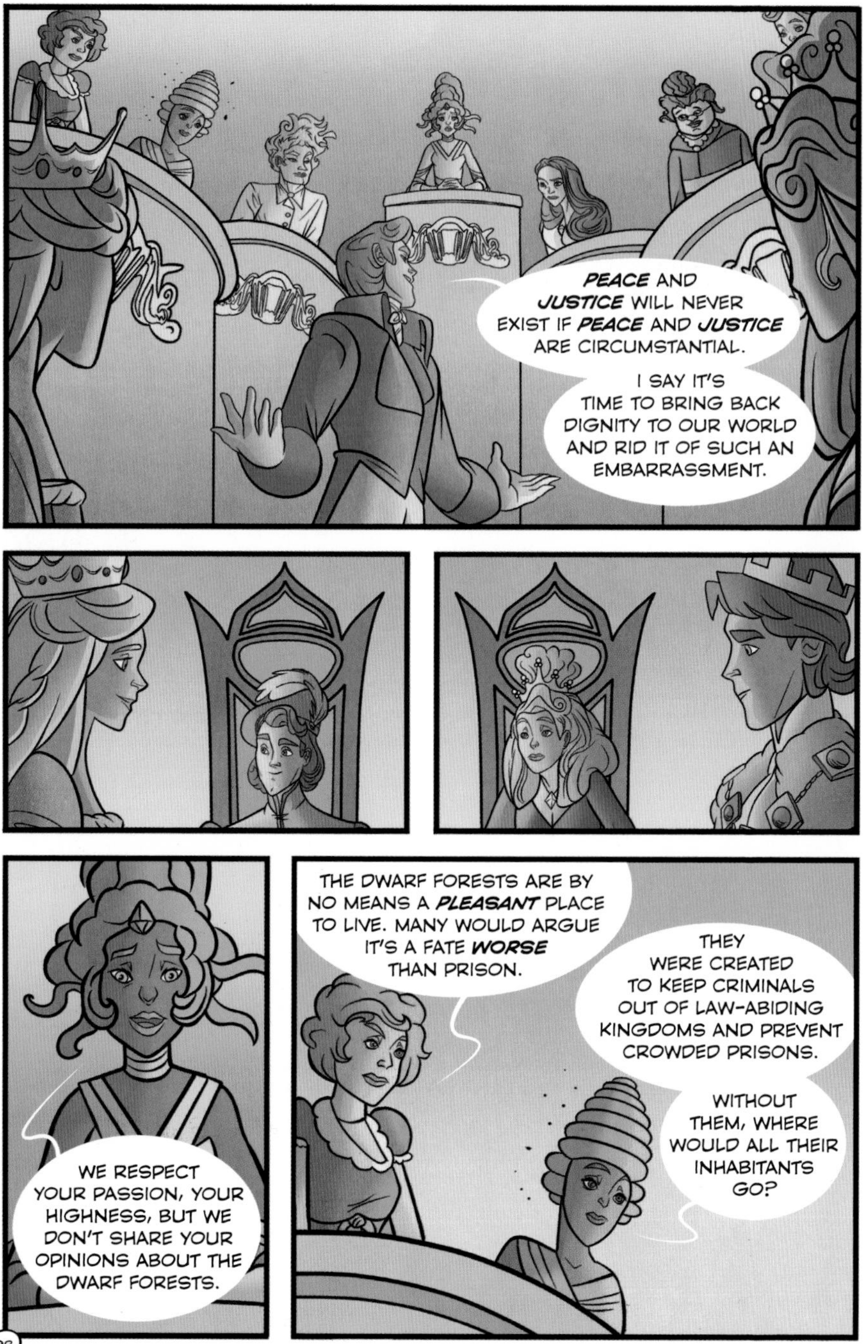
PEACE AND JUSTICE WILL NEVER EXIST IF PEACE AND JUSTICE ARE CIRCUMSTANTIAL.
I SAY IT'S TIME TO BRING BACK DIGNITY TO OUR WORLD AND RID IT OF SUCH AN EMBARRASSMENT.
WE RESPECT YOUR PASSION, YOUR HIGHNESS, BUT WE DON'T SHARE YOUR OPINIONS ABOUT THE DWARF FORESTS.
THE DWARF FORESTS ARE BY NO MEANS A PLEASANT PLACE TO LIVE. MANY WOULD ARGUE IT'S A FATE WORSE THAN PRISON.
THEY WERE CREATED TO KEEP CRIMINALS OUT OF LAW-ABIDING KINGDOMS AND PREVENT CROWDED PRISONS.
WITHOUT THEM, WHERE WOULD ALL THEIR INHABITANTS GO?

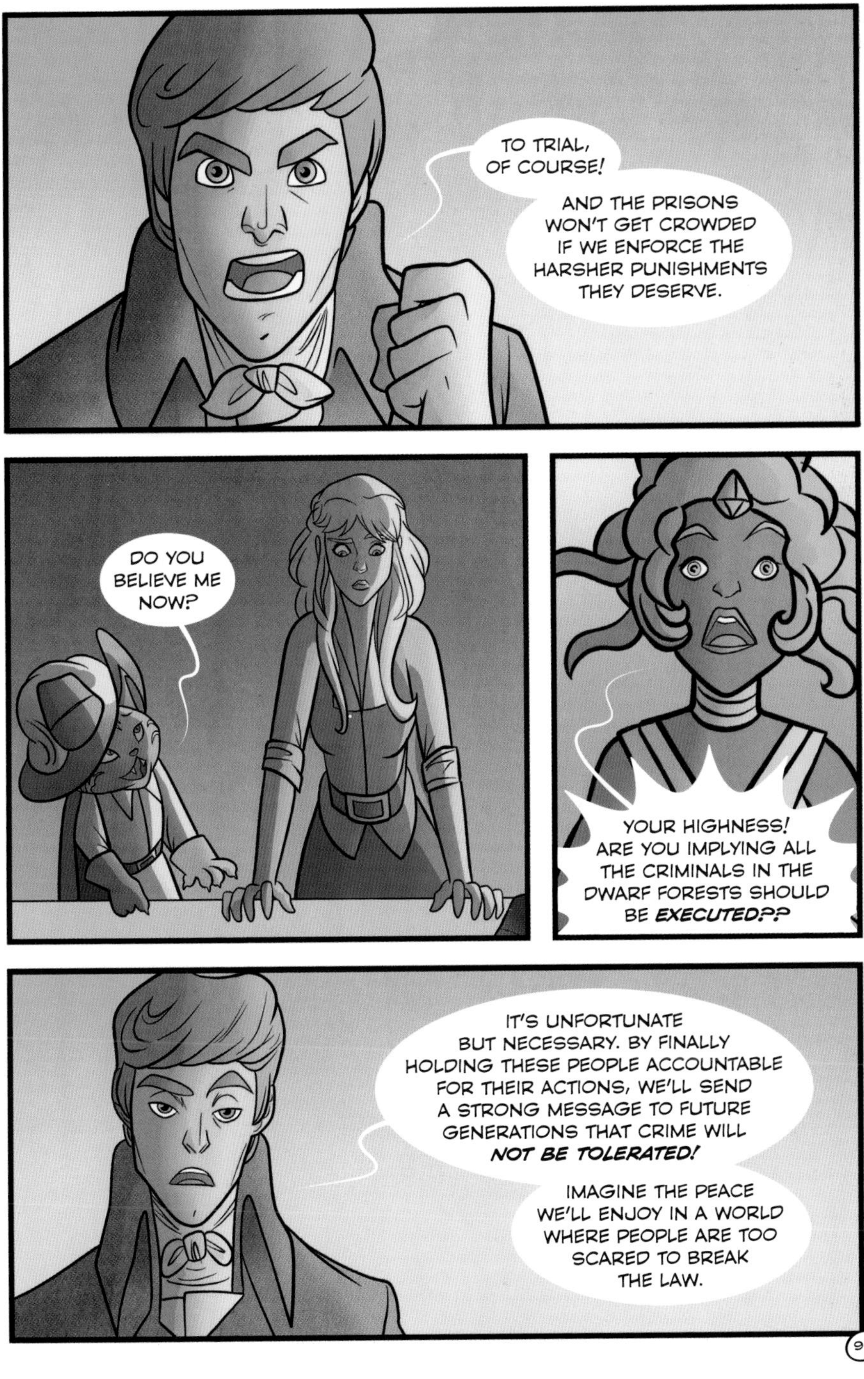
TO TRIAL, OF COURSE!
AND THE PRISONS WON'T GET CROWDED IF WE ENFORCE THE HARSHER PUNISHMENTS THEY DESERVE.
DO YOU BELIEVE ME NOW?
YOUR HIGHNESS! ARE YOU IMPLYING ALL THE CRIMINALS IN THE DWARF FORESTS SHOULD BE ***EXECUTED?!?***
IT'S UNFORTUNATE BUT NECESSARY. BY FINALLY HOLDING THESE PEOPLE ACCOUNTABLE FOR THEIR ACTIONS, WE'LL SEND A STRONG MESSAGE TO FUTURE GENERATIONS THAT CRIME WILL ***NOT BE TOLERATED!***
IMAGINE THE PEACE WE'LL ENJOY IN A WORLD WHERE PEOPLE ARE TOO SCARED TO BREAK THE LAW.

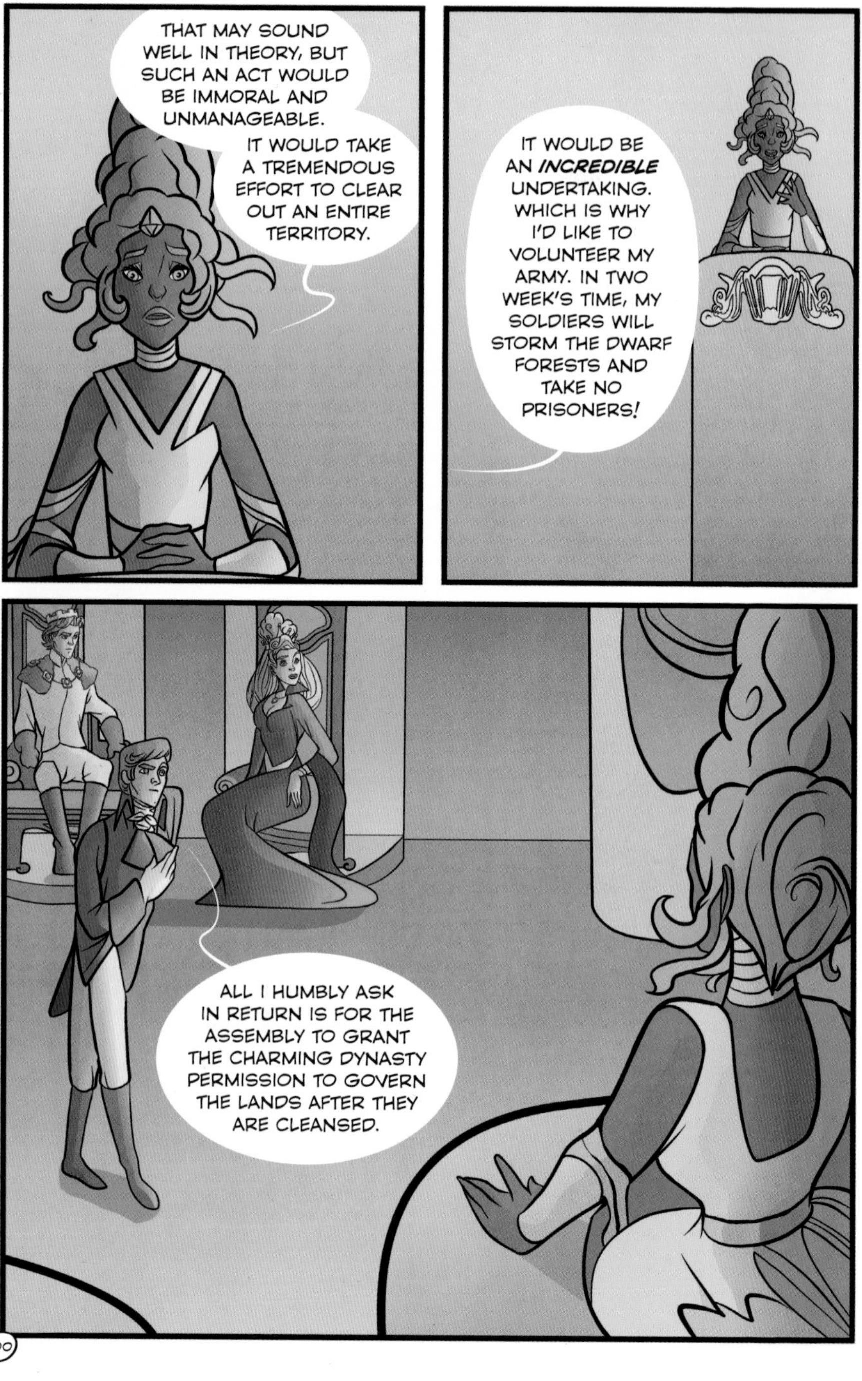

THAT MAY SOUND WELL IN THEORY, BUT SUCH AN ACT WOULD BE IMMORAL AND UNMANAGEABLE.
IT WOULD TAKE A TREMENDOUS EFFORT TO CLEAR OUT AN ENTIRE TERRITORY.
IT WOULD BE AN *INCREDIBLE* UNDERTAKING. WHICH IS WHY I'D LIKE TO VOLUNTEER MY ARMY. IN TWO WEEK'S TIME, MY SOLDIERS WILL STORM THE DWARF FORESTS AND TAKE NO PRISONERS!
ALL I HUMBLY ASK IN RETURN IS FOR THE ASSEMBLY TO GRANT THE CHARMING DYNASTY PERMISSION TO GOVERN THE LANDS AFTER THEY ARE CLEANSED.

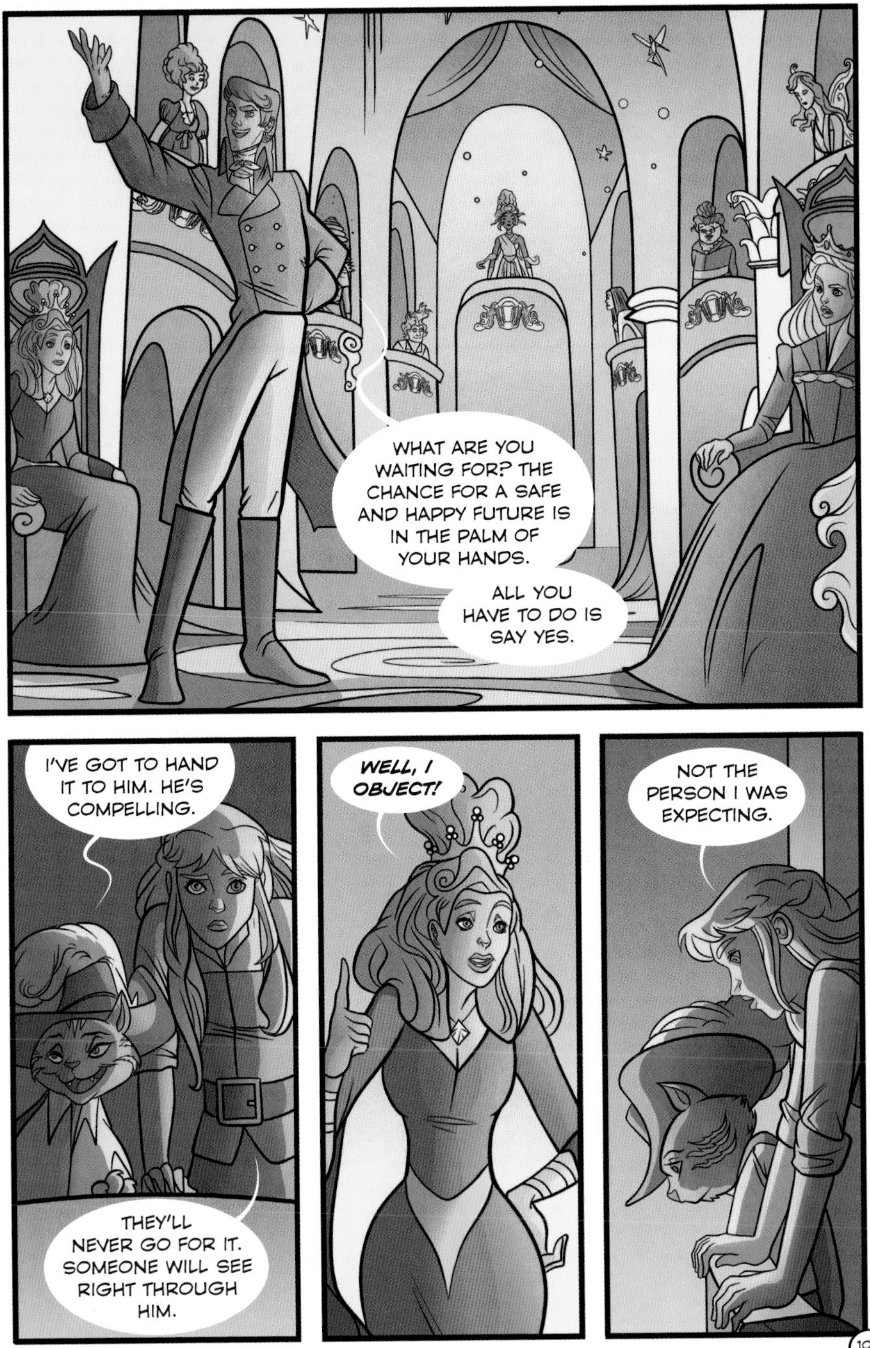
WHAT ARE YOU WAITING FOR? THE CHANCE FOR A SAFE AND HAPPY FUTURE IS IN THE PALM OF YOUR HANDS.
ALL YOU HAVE TO DO IS SAY YES.
I'VE GOT TO HAND IT TO HIM. HE'S COMPELLING.
THEY'LL NEVER GO FOR IT. SOMEONE WILL SEE RIGHT THROUGH HIM.
WELL, I OBJECT!
NOT THE PERSON I WAS EXPECTING.

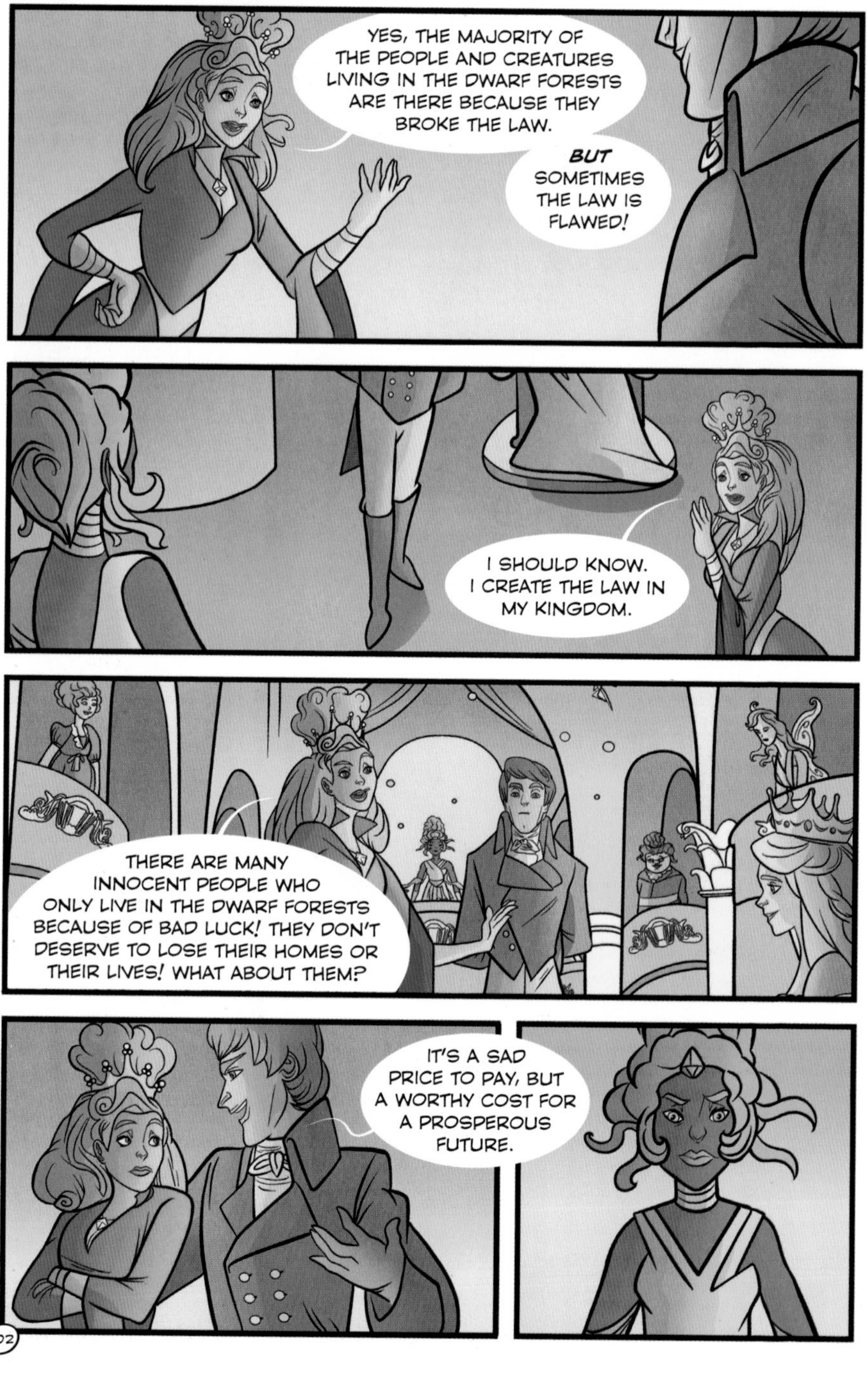
YES, THE MAJORITY OF THE PEOPLE AND CREATURES LIVING IN THE DWARF FORESTS ARE THERE BECAUSE THEY BROKE THE LAW.
BUT SOMETIMES THE LAW IS FLAWED!
I SHOULD KNOW. I CREATE THE LAW IN MY KINGDOM.
THERE ARE MANY INNOCENT PEOPLE WHO ONLY LIVE IN THE DWARF FORESTS BECAUSE OF BAD LUCK! THEY DON'T DESERVE TO LOSE THEIR HOMES OR THEIR LIVES! WHAT ABOUT THEM?
IT'S A SAD PRICE TO PAY, BUT A WORTHY COST FOR A PROSPEROUS FUTURE.

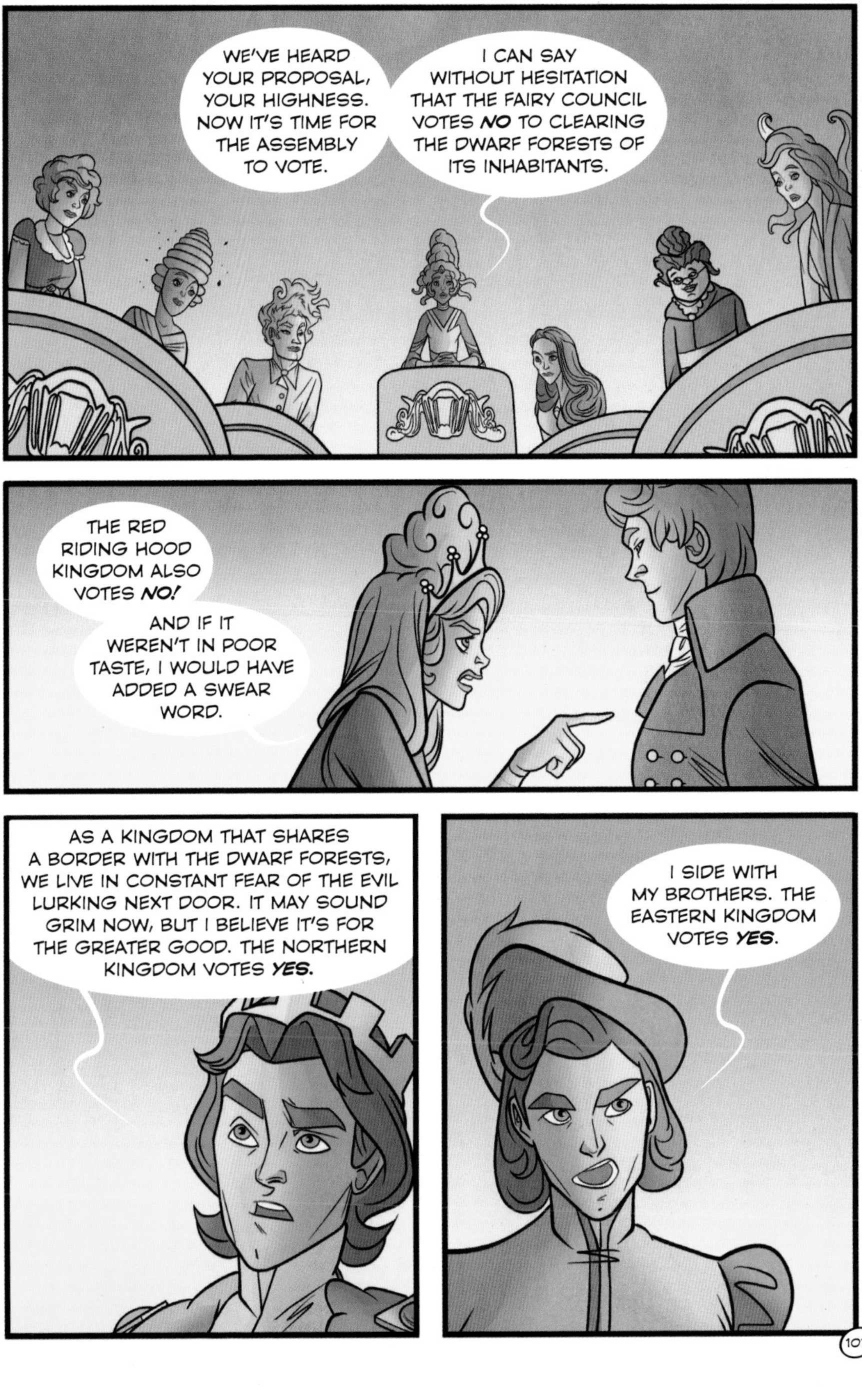
WE'VE HEARD YOUR PROPOSAL, YOUR HIGHNESS. NOW IT'S TIME FOR THE ASSEMBLY TO VOTE.
I CAN SAY WITHOUT HESITATION THAT THE FAIRY COUNCIL VOTES *NO* TO CLEARING THE DWARF FORESTS OF ITS INHABITANTS.
THE RED RIDING HOOD KINGDOM ALSO VOTES *NO!*
AND IF IT WEREN'T IN POOR TASTE, I WOULD HAVE ADDED A SWEAR WORD.
AS A KINGDOM THAT SHARES A BORDER WITH THE DWARF FORESTS, WE LIVE IN CONSTANT FEAR OF THE EVIL LURKING NEXT DOOR. IT MAY SOUND GRIM NOW, BUT I BELIEVE IT'S FOR THE GREATER GOOD. THE NORTHERN KINGDOM VOTES *YES*.
I SIDE WITH MY BROTHERS. THE EASTERN KINGDOM VOTES *YES*.

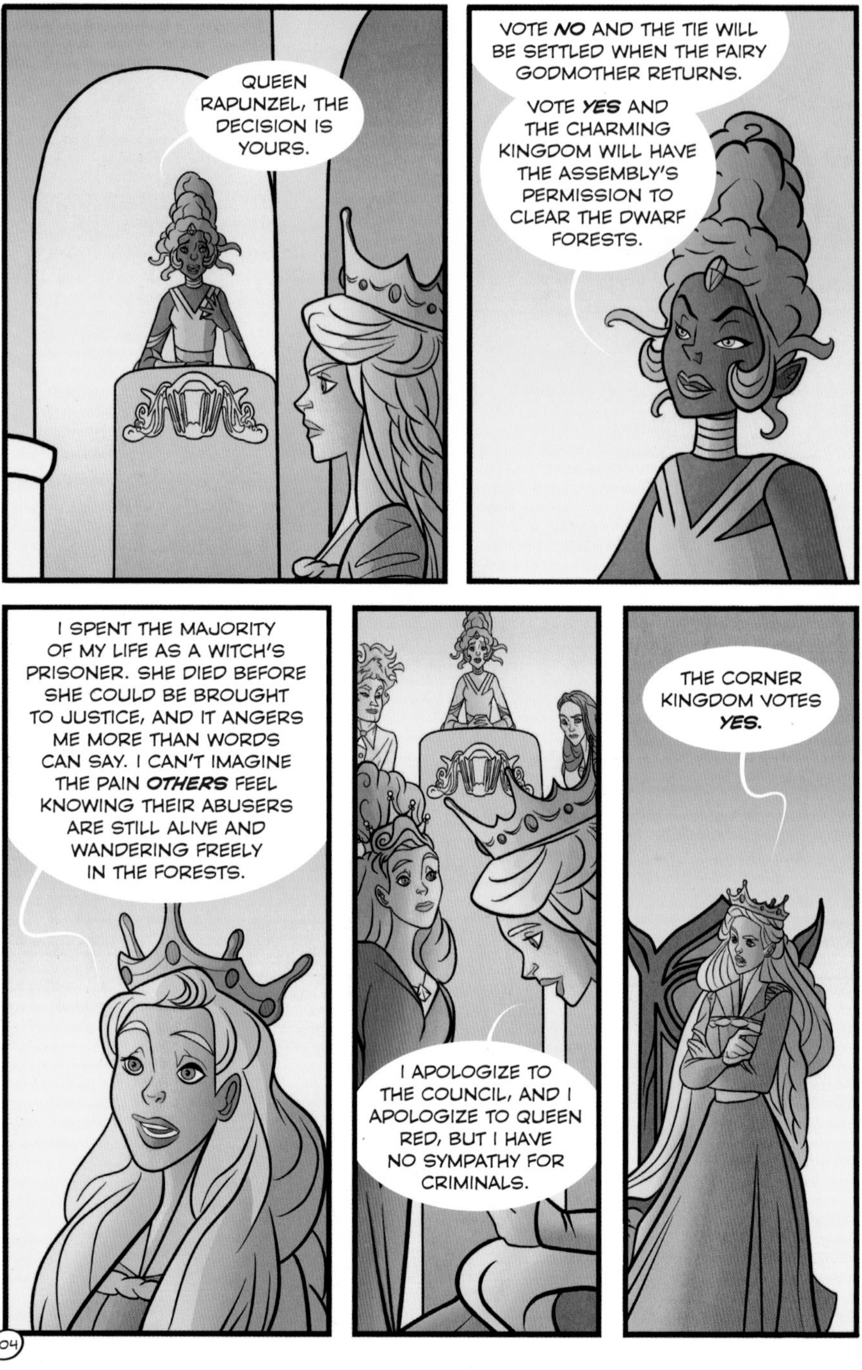
QUEEN RAPUNZEL, THE DECISION IS YOURS.
VOTE NO AND THE TIE WILL BE SETTLED WHEN THE FAIRY GODMOTHER RETURNS.
VOTE YES AND THE CHARMING KINGDOM WILL HAVE THE ASSEMBLY'S PERMISSION TO CLEAR THE DWARF FORESTS.
I SPENT THE MAJORITY OF MY LIFE AS A WITCH'S PRISONER. SHE DIED BEFORE SHE COULD BE BROUGHT TO JUSTICE, AND IT ANGERS ME MORE THAN WORDS CAN SAY. I CAN'T IMAGINE THE PAIN OTHERS FEEL KNOWING THEIR ABUSERS ARE STILL ALIVE AND WANDERING FREELY IN THE FORESTS.
I APOLOGIZE TO THE COUNCIL, AND I APOLOGIZE TO QUEEN RED, BUT I HAVE NO SYMPATHY FOR CRIMINALS.
THE CORNER KINGDOM VOTES YES.

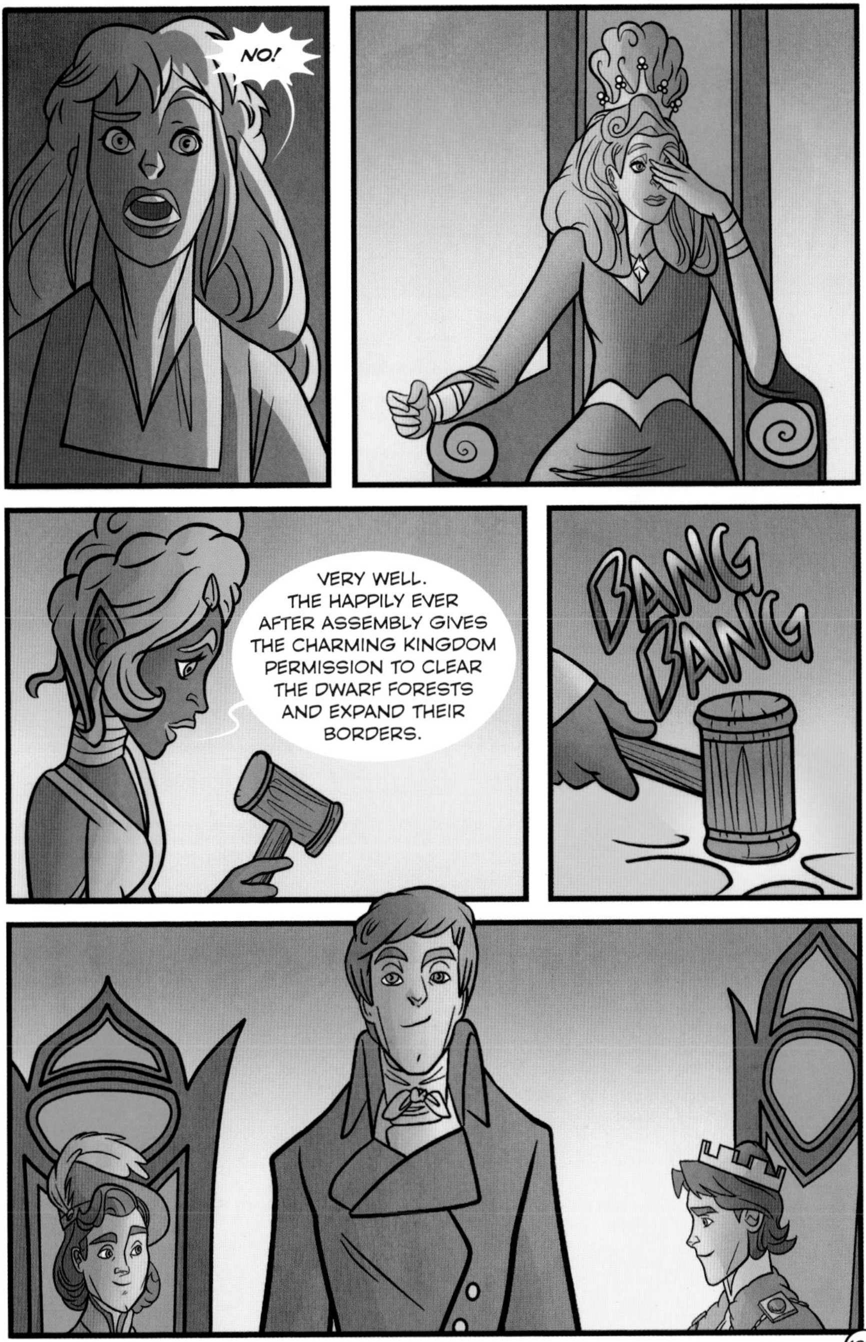
NO!
VERY WELL. THE HAPPILY EVER AFTER ASSEMBLY GIVES THE CHARMING KINGDOM PERMISSION TO CLEAR THE DWARF FORESTS AND EXPAND THEIR BORDERS.
BANG BANG

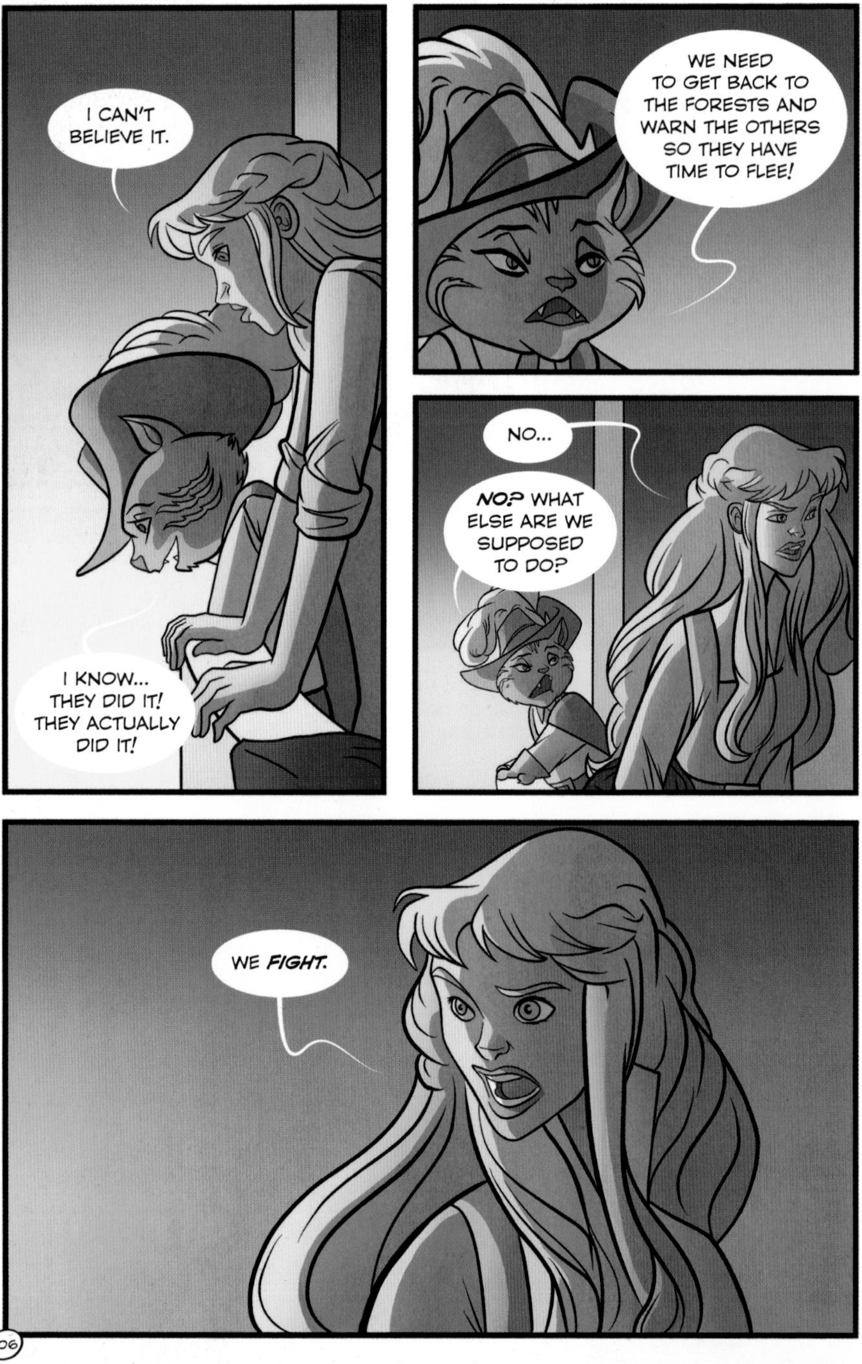
I CAN'T BELIEVE IT.
I KNOW... THEY DID IT! THEY ACTUALLY DID IT!
WE NEED TO GET BACK TO THE FORESTS AND WARN THE OTHERS SO THEY HAVE TIME TO FLEE!
NO...
NO? WHAT ELSE ARE WE SUPPOSED TO DO?
WE FIGHT.

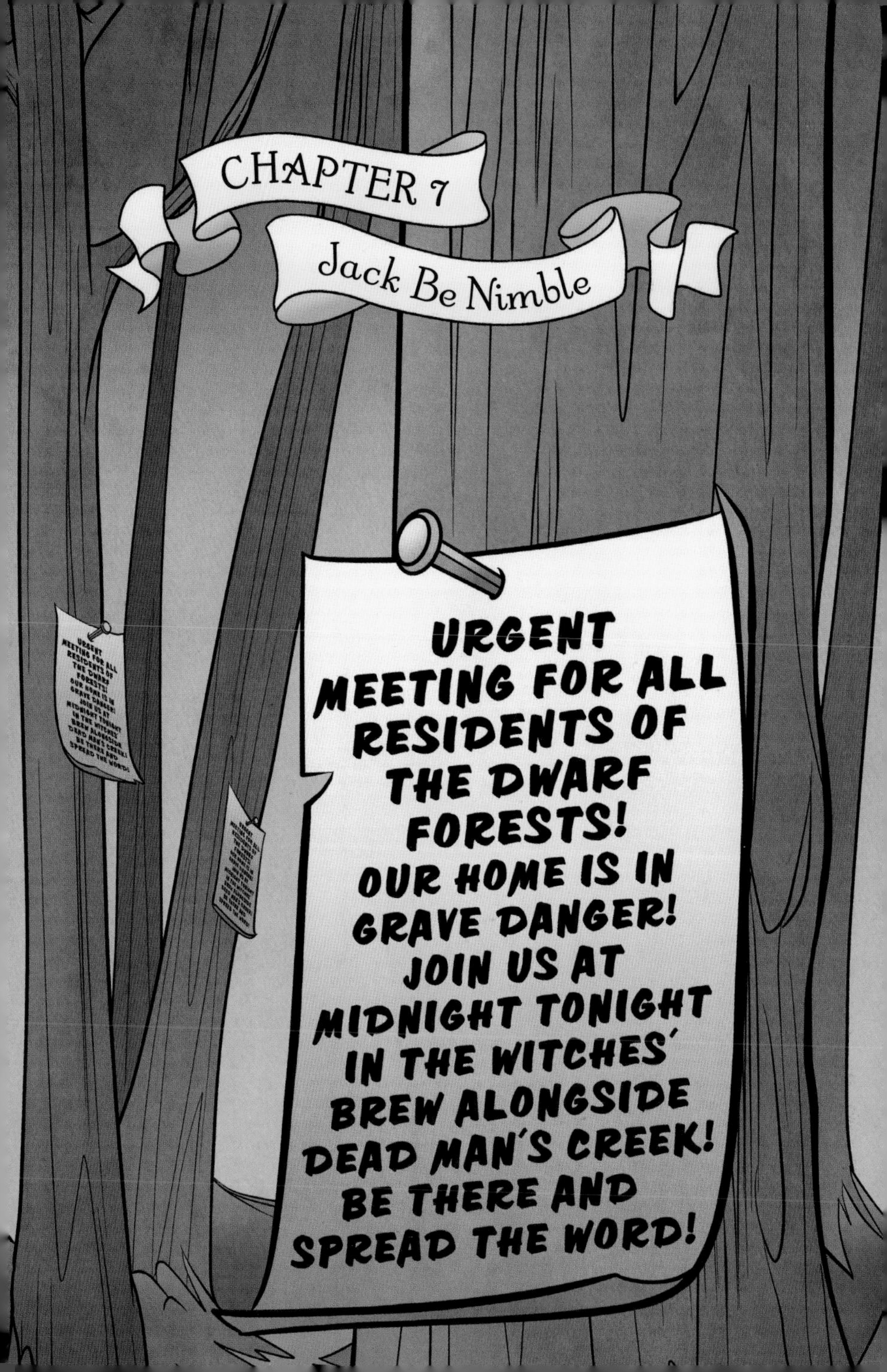
CHAPTER 7
Jack Be Nimble
URGENT
MEETING FOR ALL
RESIDENTS OF
THE DWARF
FORESTS!
OUR HOME IS IN
GRAVE DANGER!
JOIN US AT
MIDNIGHT TONIGHT
IN THE WITCHES'
BREW ALONGSIDE
DEAD MAN'S CREEK!
BE THERE AND
SPREAD THE WORD!

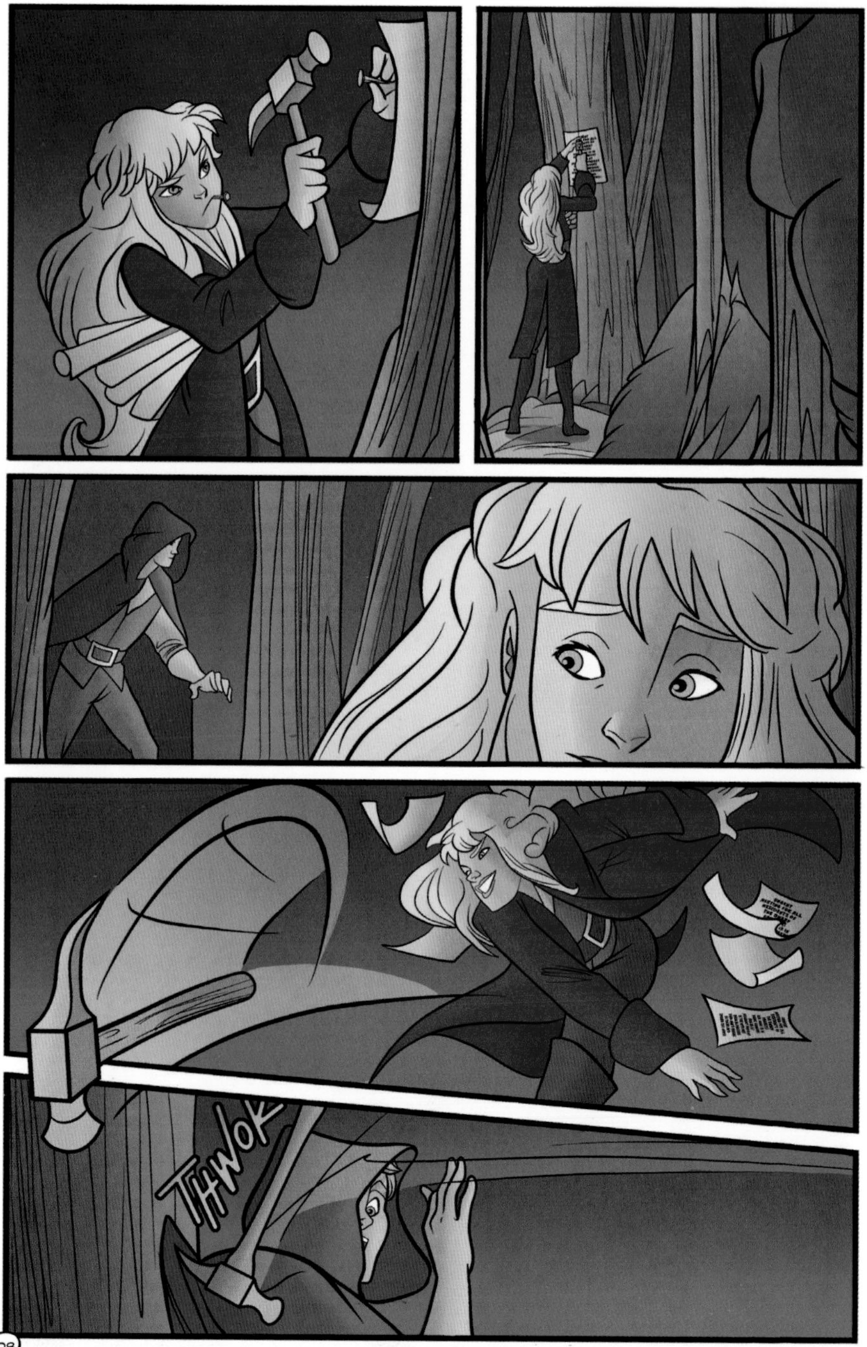
THWOK

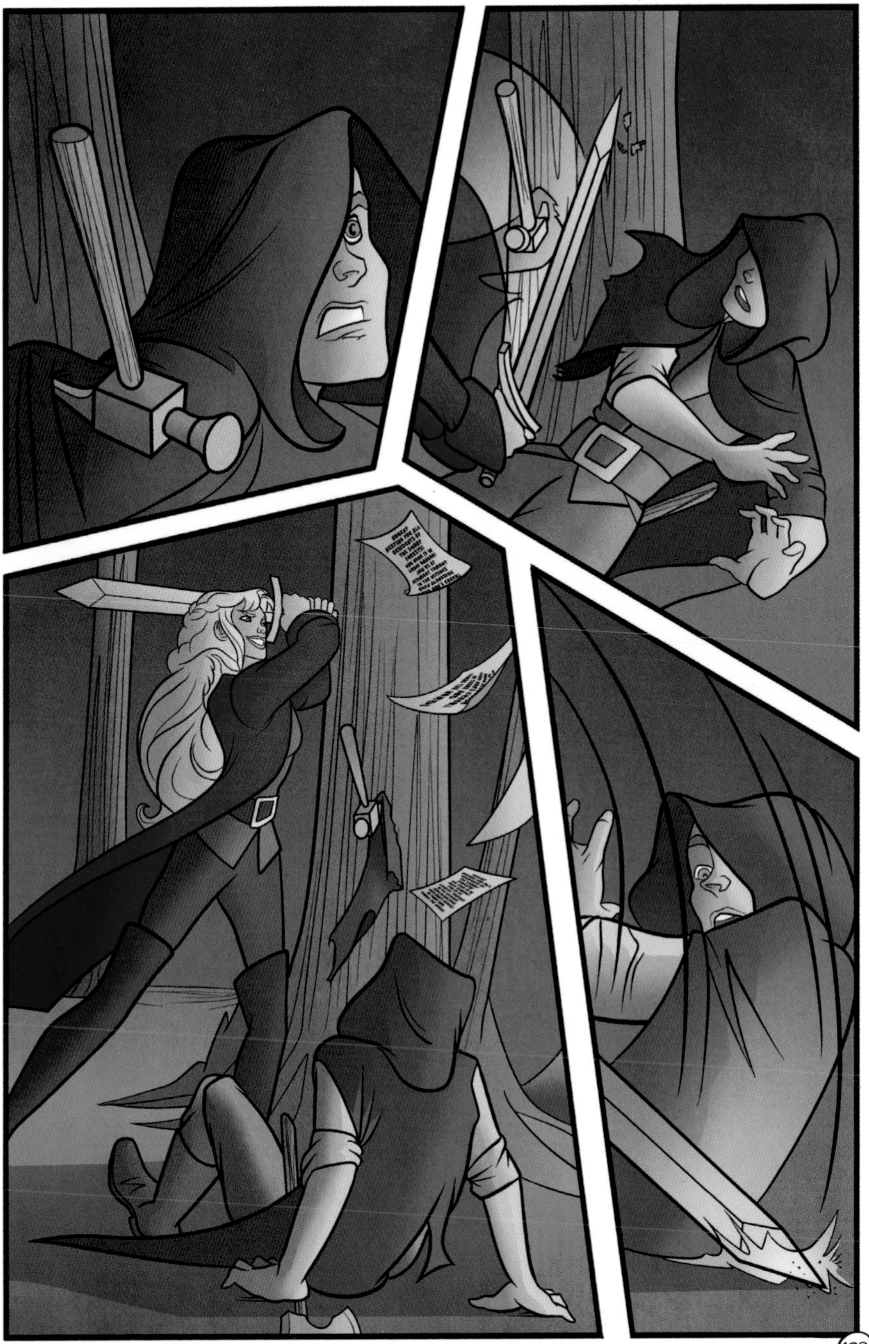
URGENT

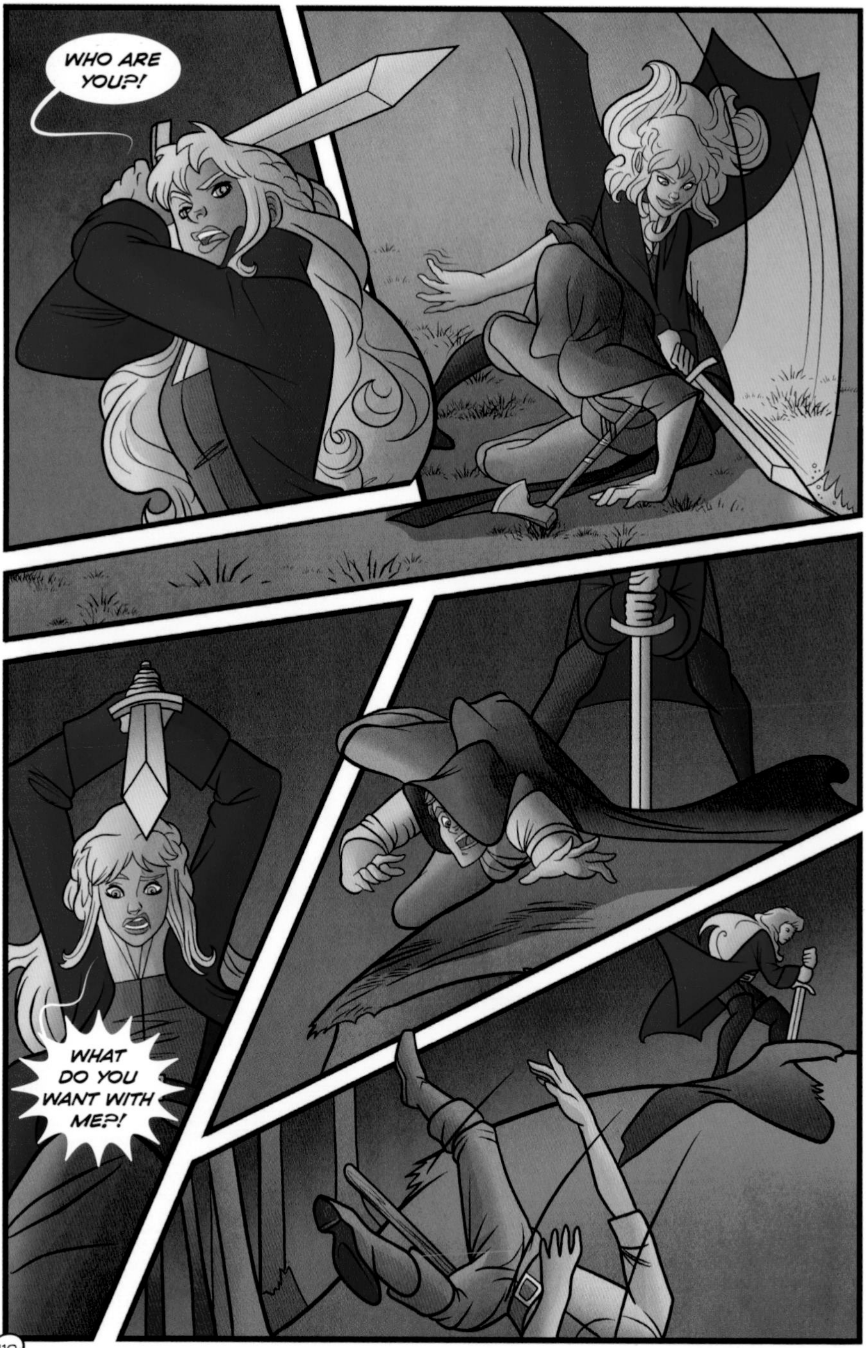
WHO ARE YOU?!
WHAT DO YOU WANT WITH ME?!

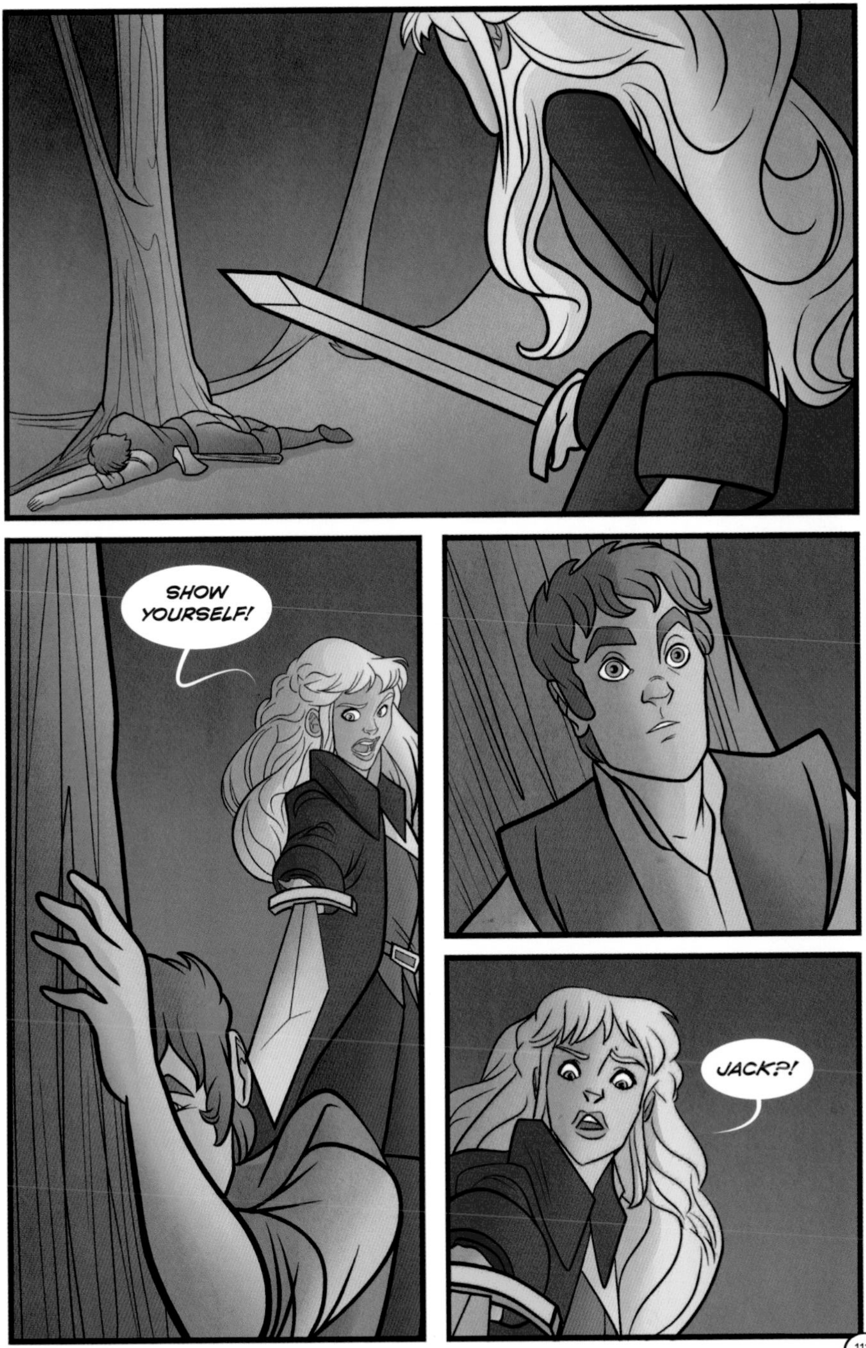
SHOW YOURSELF!
JACK?!

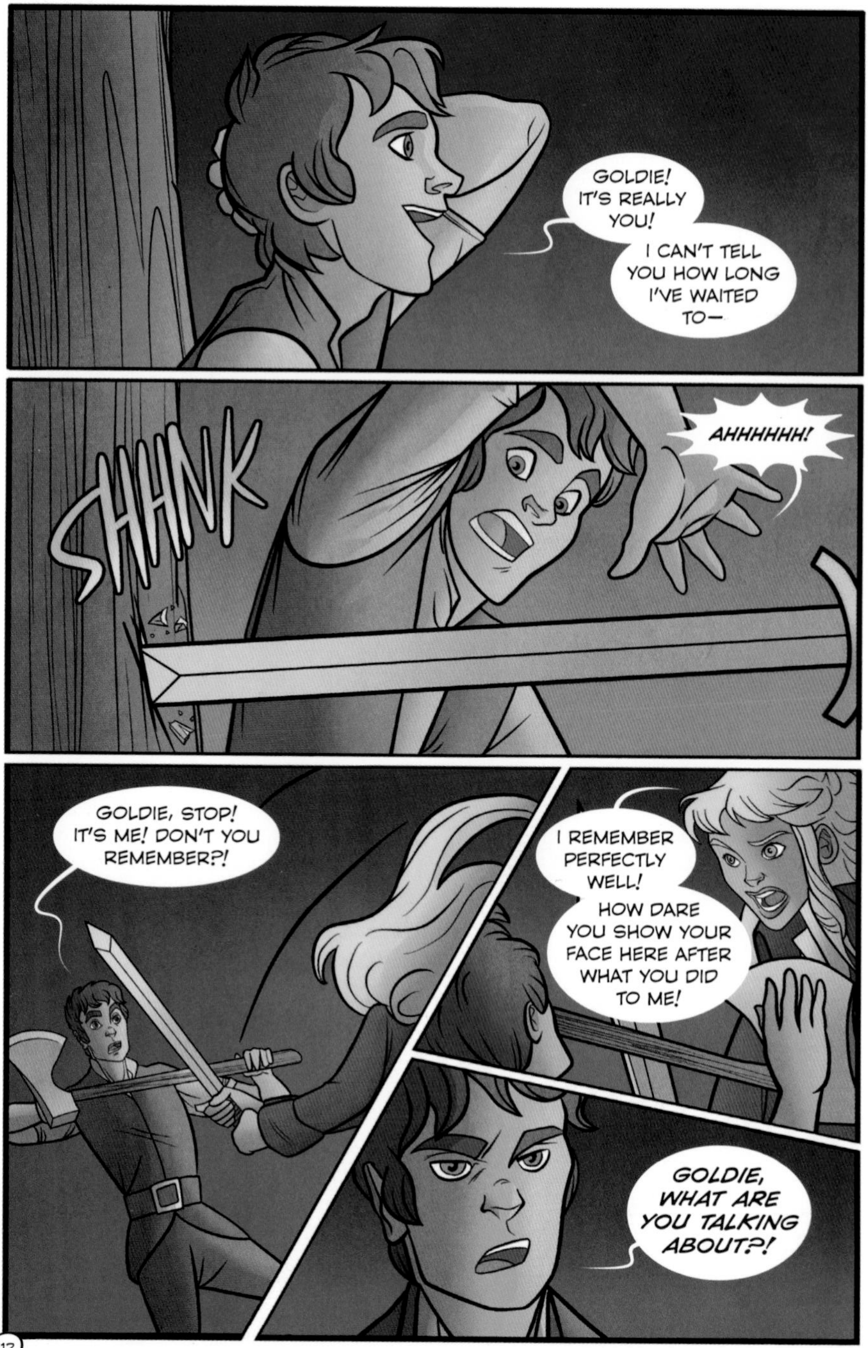
GOLDIE! IT'S REALLY YOU!
I CAN'T TELL YOU HOW LONG I'VE WAITED TO—
SHHNK
AHHHHHH!
GOLDIE, STOP! IT'S ME! DON'T YOU REMEMBER?!
I REMEMBER PERFECTLY WELL!
HOW DARE YOU SHOW YOUR FACE HERE AFTER WHAT YOU DID TO ME!
GOLDIE, WHAT ARE YOU TALKING ABOUT?!

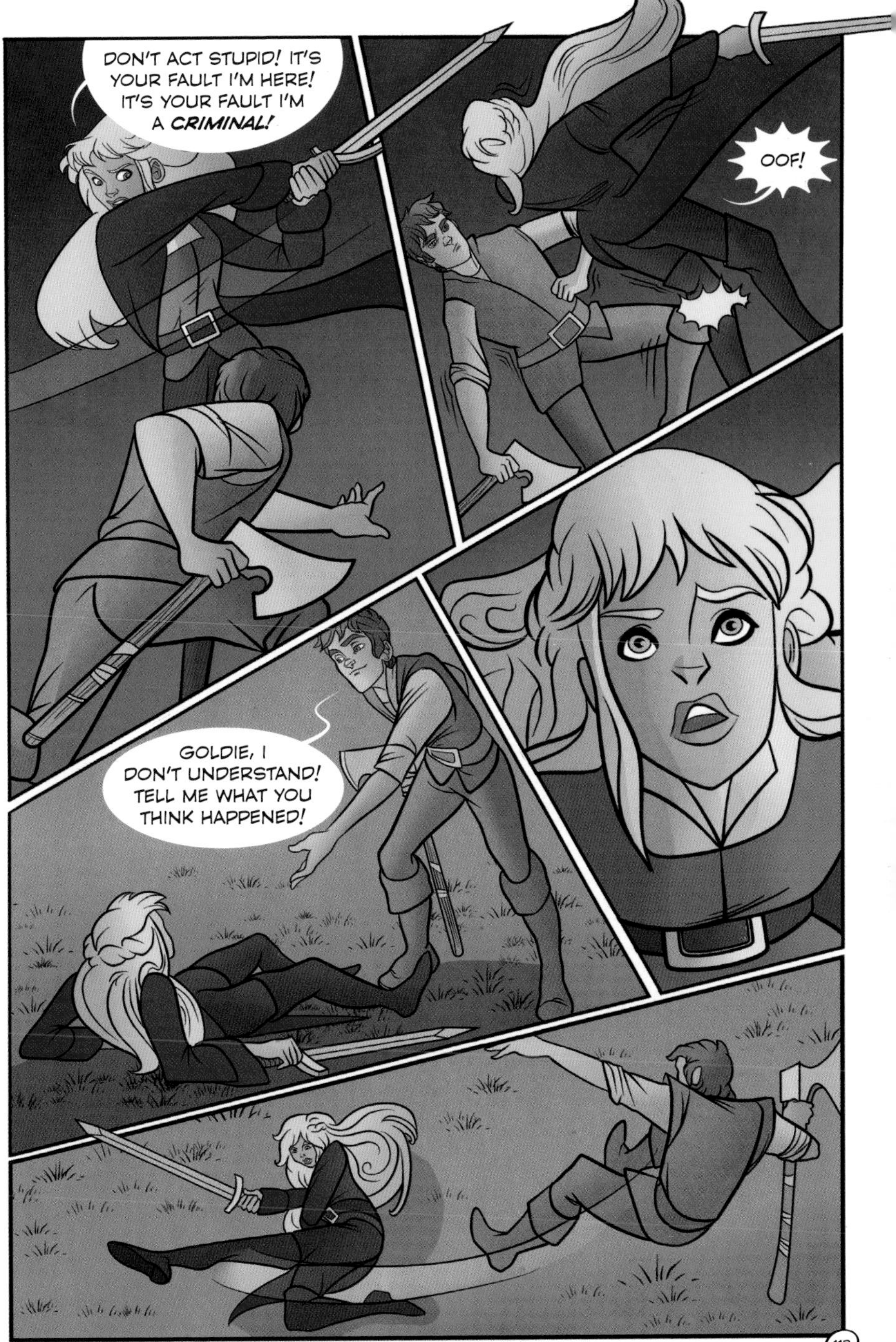
DON'T ACT STUPID! IT'S YOUR FAULT I'M HERE! IT'S YOUR FAULT I'M A CRIMINAL!
OOF!
GOLDIE, I DON'T UNDERSTAND! TELL ME WHAT YOU THINK HAPPENED!

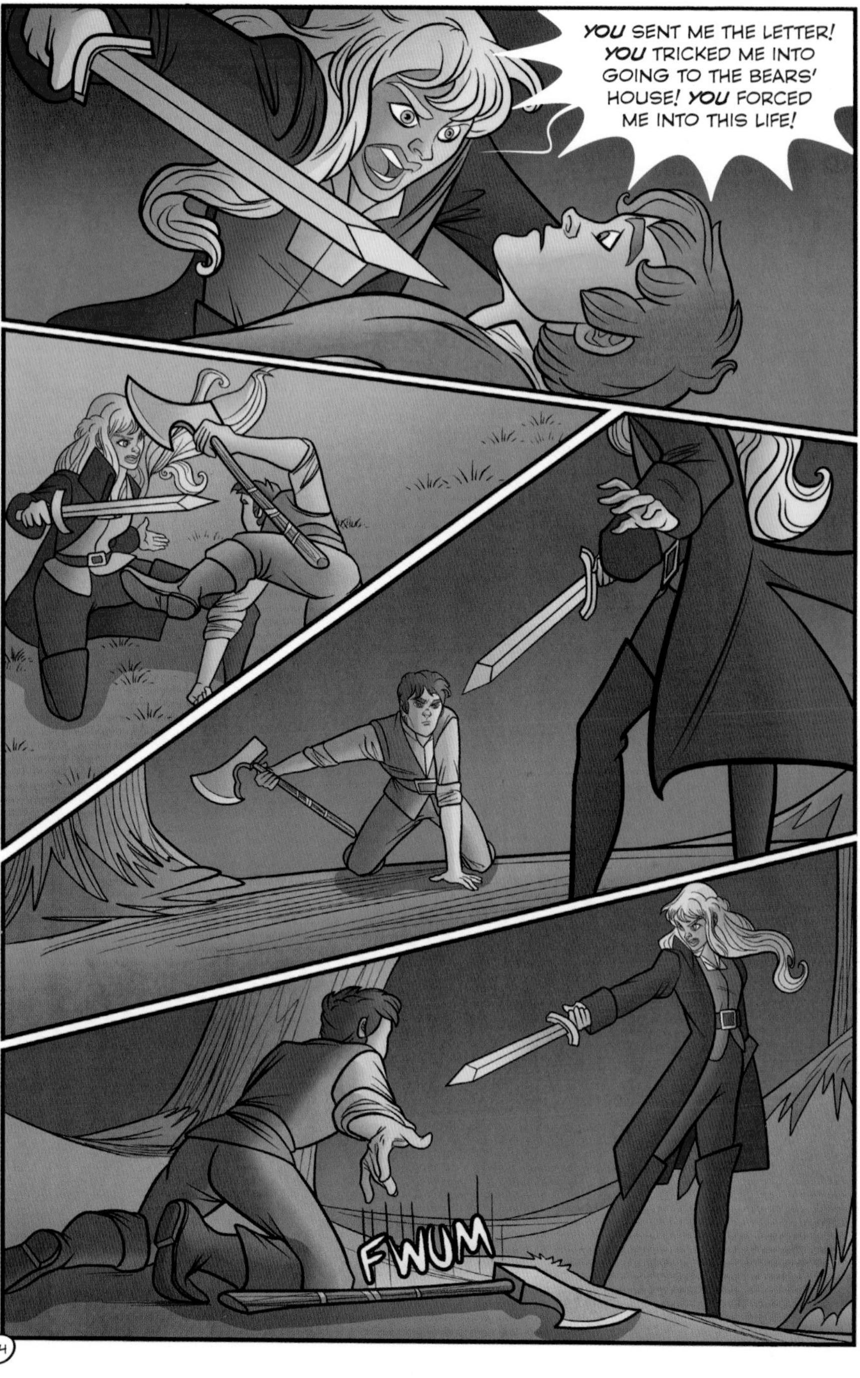
YOU SENT ME THE LETTER! YOU TRICKED ME INTO GOING TO THE BEARS' HOUSE! YOU FORCED ME INTO THIS LIFE!
FWUM

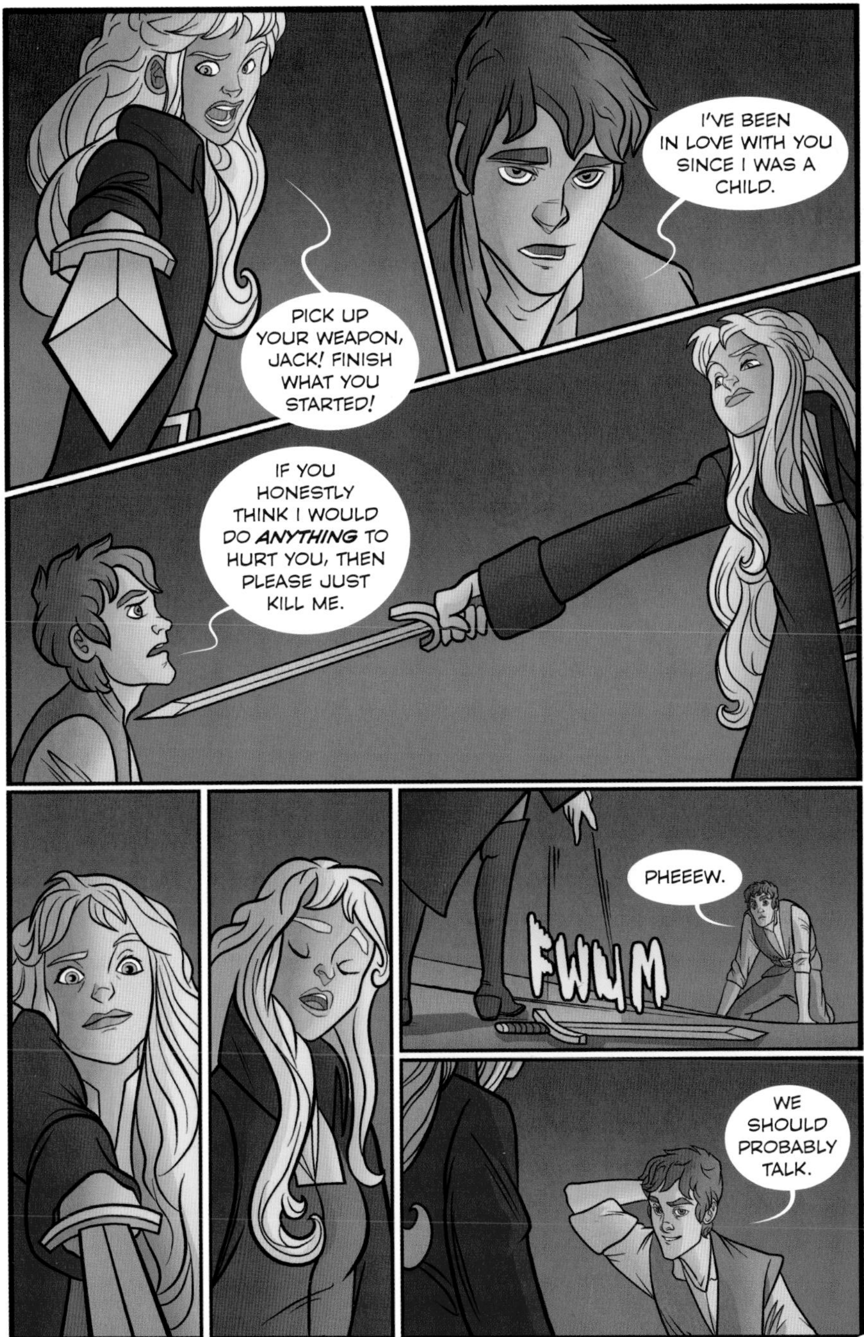
PICK UP YOUR WEAPON, JACK! FINISH WHAT YOU STARTED!
I'VE BEEN IN LOVE WITH YOU SINCE I WAS A CHILD.
IF YOU HONESTLY THINK I WOULD DO *ANYTHING* TO HURT YOU, THEN PLEASE JUST KILL ME.
FWUM
PHEEEW.
WE SHOULD PROBABLY TALK.

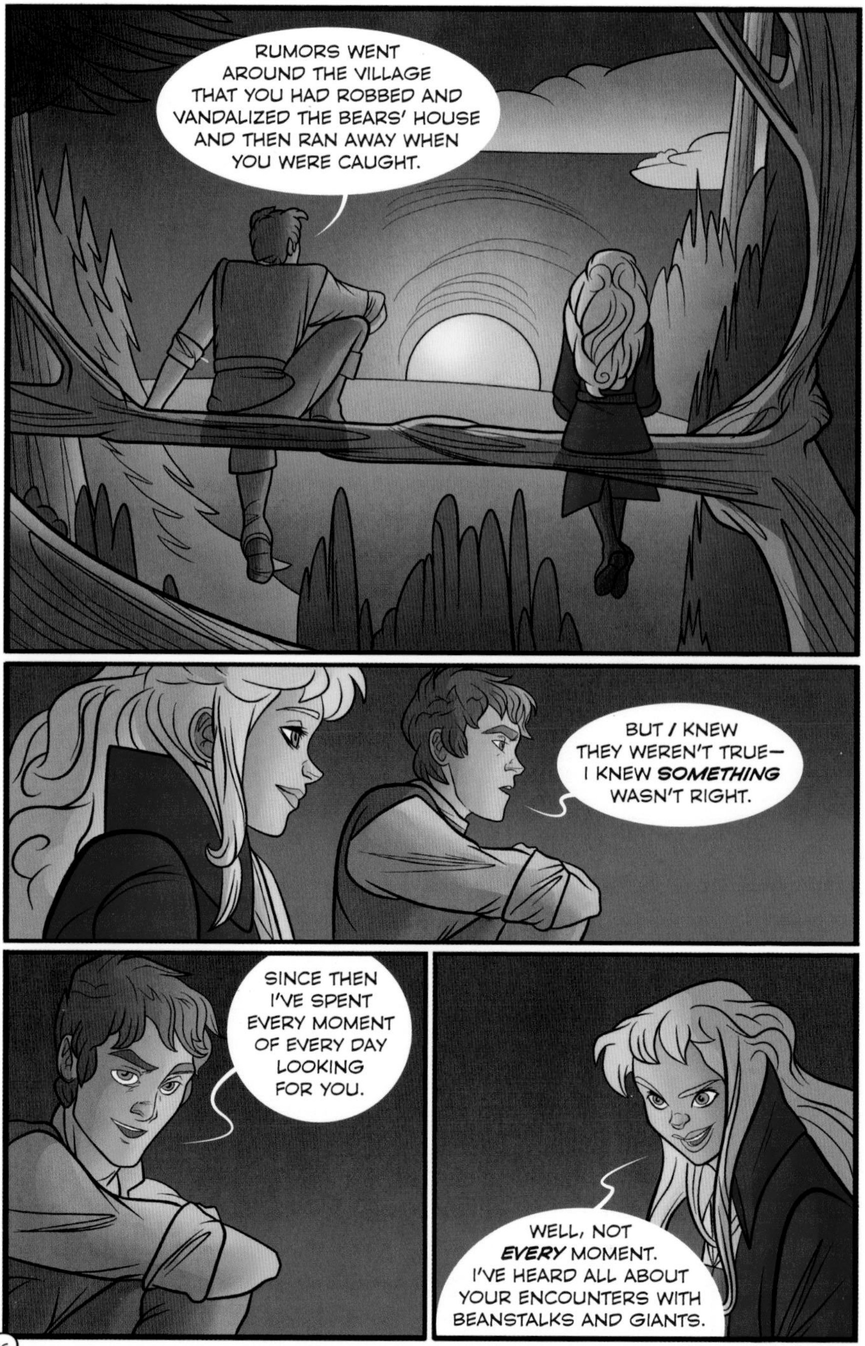
RUMORS WENT AROUND THE VILLAGE THAT YOU HAD ROBBED AND VANDALIZED THE BEARS' HOUSE AND THEN RAN AWAY WHEN YOU WERE CAUGHT.
BUT *I* KNEW THEY WEREN'T TRUE— I KNEW ***SOMETHING*** WASN'T RIGHT.
SINCE THEN I'VE SPENT EVERY MOMENT OF EVERY DAY LOOKING FOR YOU.
WELL, NOT ***EVERY*** MOMENT. I'VE HEARD ALL ABOUT YOUR ENCOUNTERS WITH BEANSTALKS AND GIANTS.

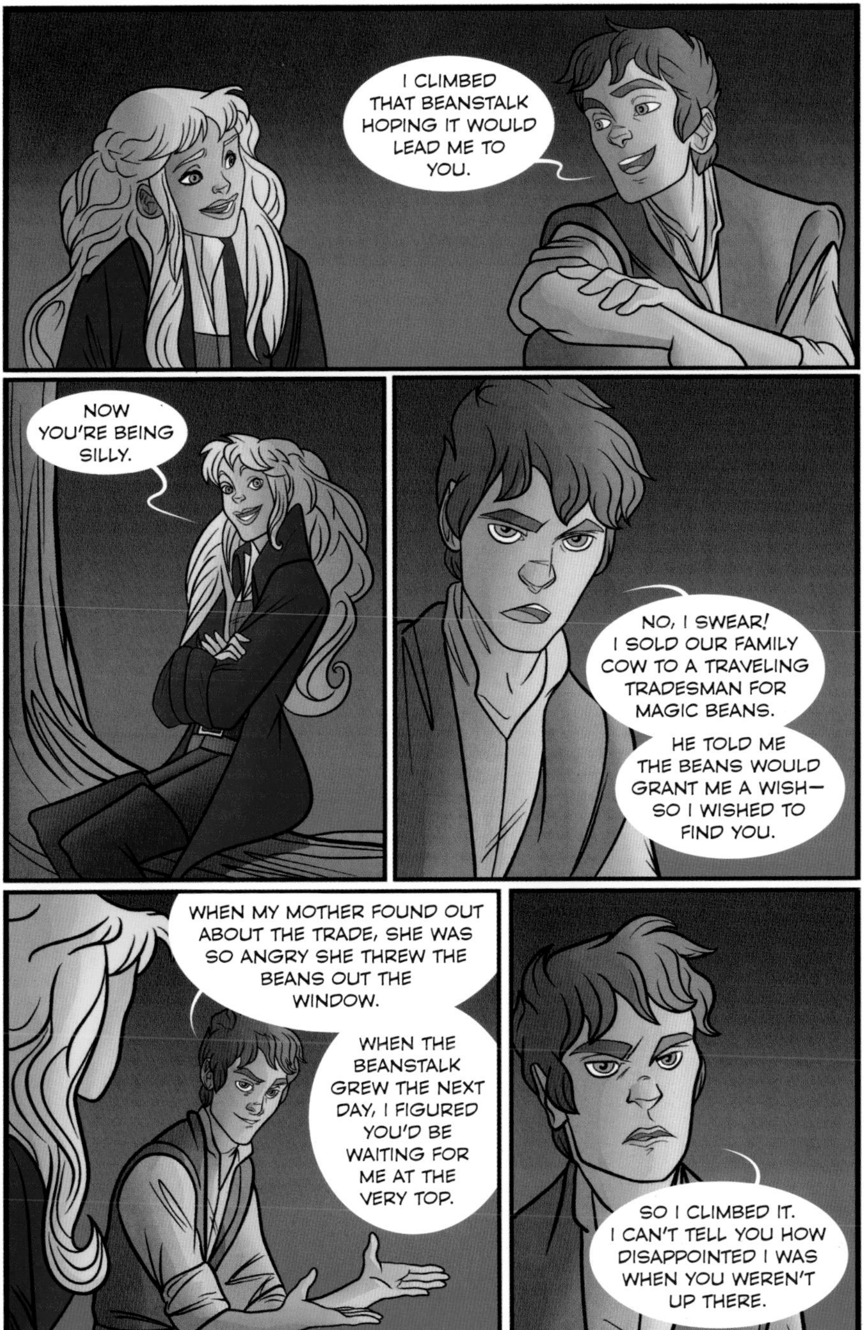
I CLIMBED THAT BEANSTALK HOPING IT WOULD LEAD ME TO YOU.
NOW YOU'RE BEING SILLY.
NO, I SWEAR! I SOLD OUR FAMILY COW TO A TRAVELING TRADESMAN FOR MAGIC BEANS.
HE TOLD ME THE BEANS WOULD GRANT ME A WISH— SO I WISHED TO FIND YOU.
WHEN MY MOTHER FOUND OUT ABOUT THE TRADE, SHE WAS SO ANGRY SHE THREW THE BEANS OUT THE WINDOW.
WHEN THE BEANSTALK GREW THE NEXT DAY, I FIGURED YOU'D BE WAITING FOR ME AT THE VERY TOP.
SO I CLIMBED IT. I CAN'T TELL YOU HOW DISAPPOINTED I WAS WHEN YOU WEREN'T UP THERE.

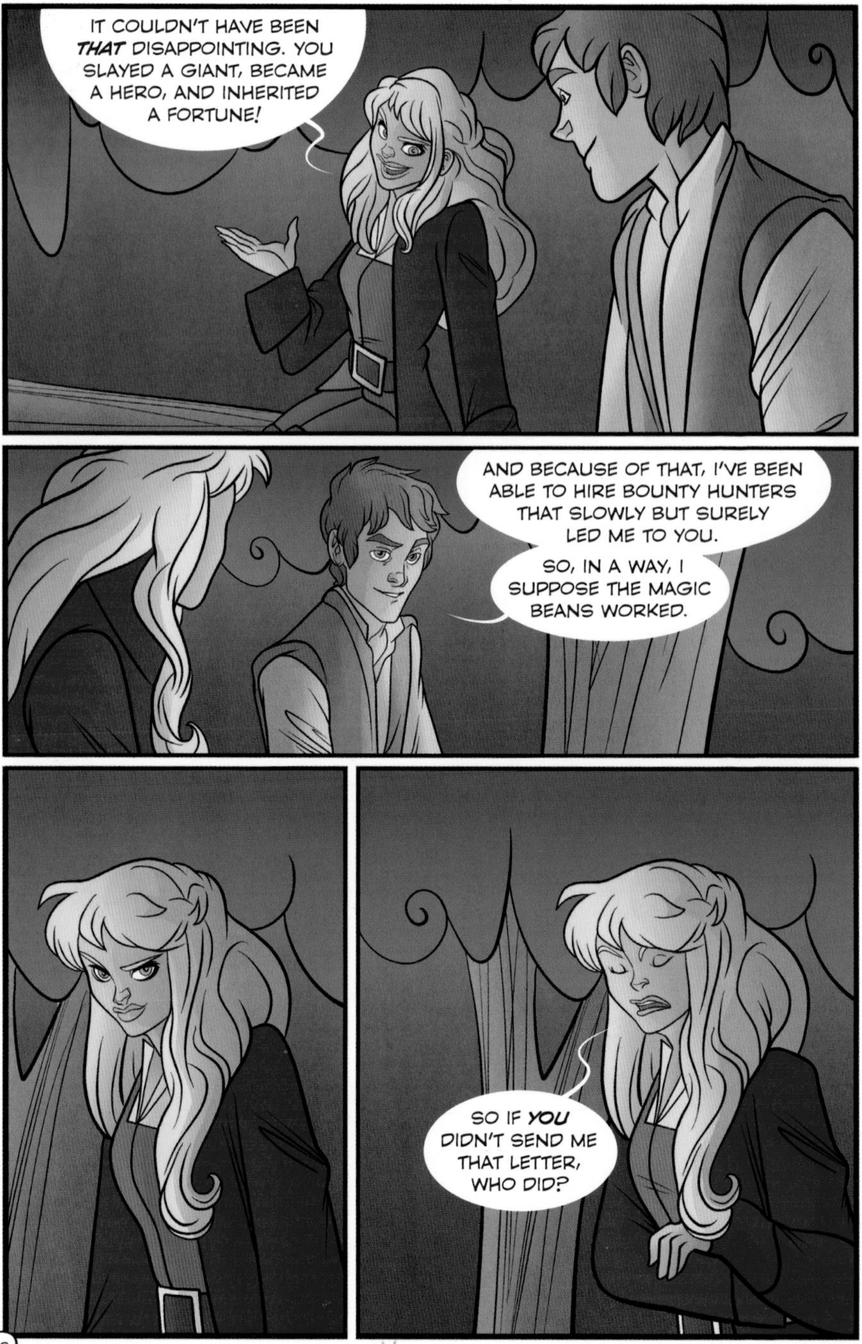
IT COULDN'T HAVE BEEN *THAT* DISAPPOINTING. YOU SLAYED A GIANT, BECAME A HERO, AND INHERITED A FORTUNE!
AND BECAUSE OF THAT, I'VE BEEN ABLE TO HIRE BOUNTY HUNTERS THAT SLOWLY BUT SURELY LED ME TO YOU.
SO, IN A WAY, I SUPPOSE THE MAGIC BEANS WORKED.
SO IF *YOU* DIDN'T SEND ME THAT LETTER, WHO DID?

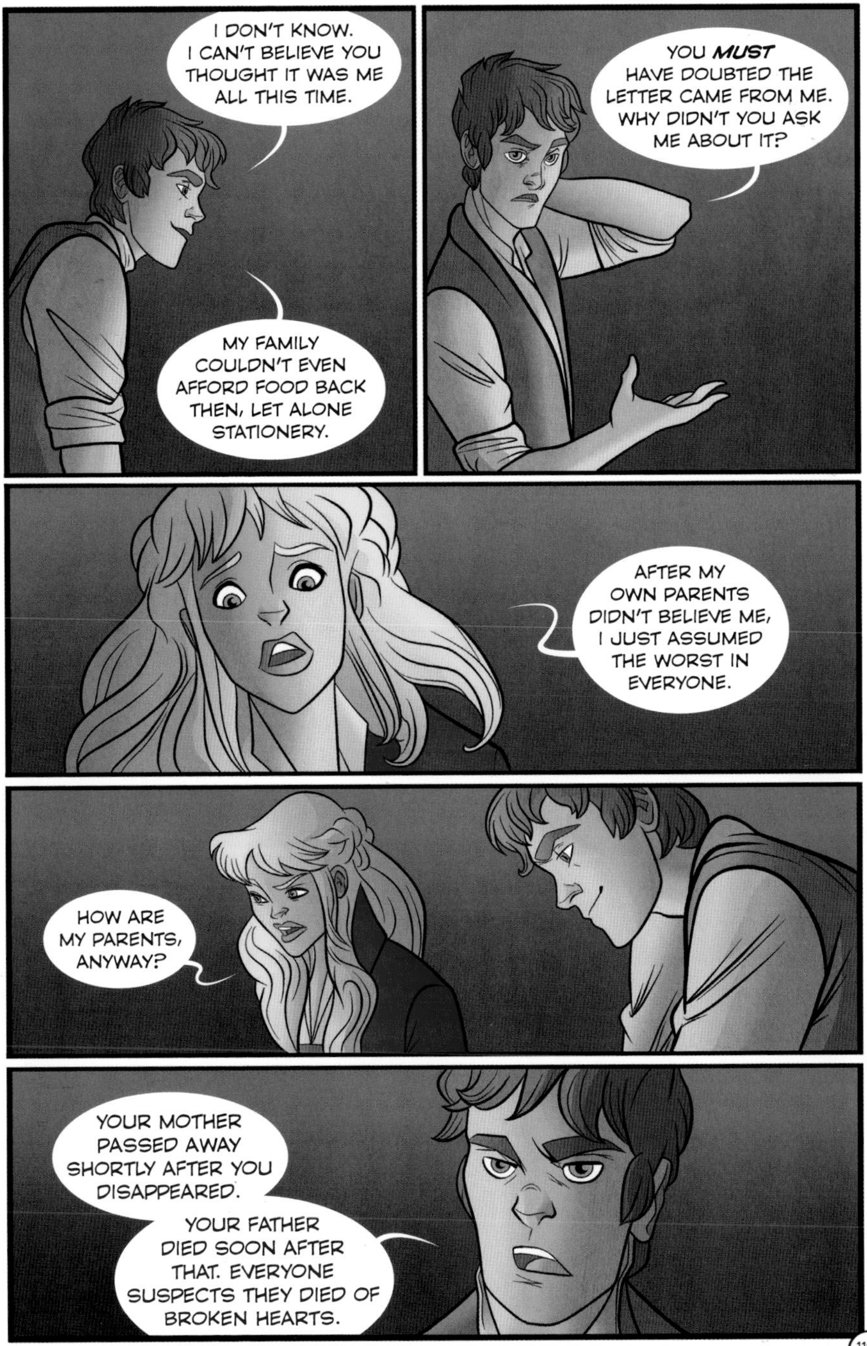
I DON'T KNOW. I CAN'T BELIEVE YOU THOUGHT IT WAS ME ALL THIS TIME.
MY FAMILY COULDN'T EVEN AFFORD FOOD BACK THEN, LET ALONE STATIONERY.
YOU *MUST* HAVE DOUBTED THE LETTER CAME FROM ME. WHY DIDN'T YOU ASK ME ABOUT IT?
AFTER MY OWN PARENTS DIDN'T BELIEVE ME, I JUST ASSUMED THE WORST IN EVERYONE.
HOW ARE MY PARENTS, ANYWAY?
YOUR MOTHER PASSED AWAY SHORTLY AFTER YOU DISAPPEARED.
YOUR FATHER DIED SOON AFTER THAT. EVERYONE SUSPECTS THEY DIED OF BROKEN HEARTS.

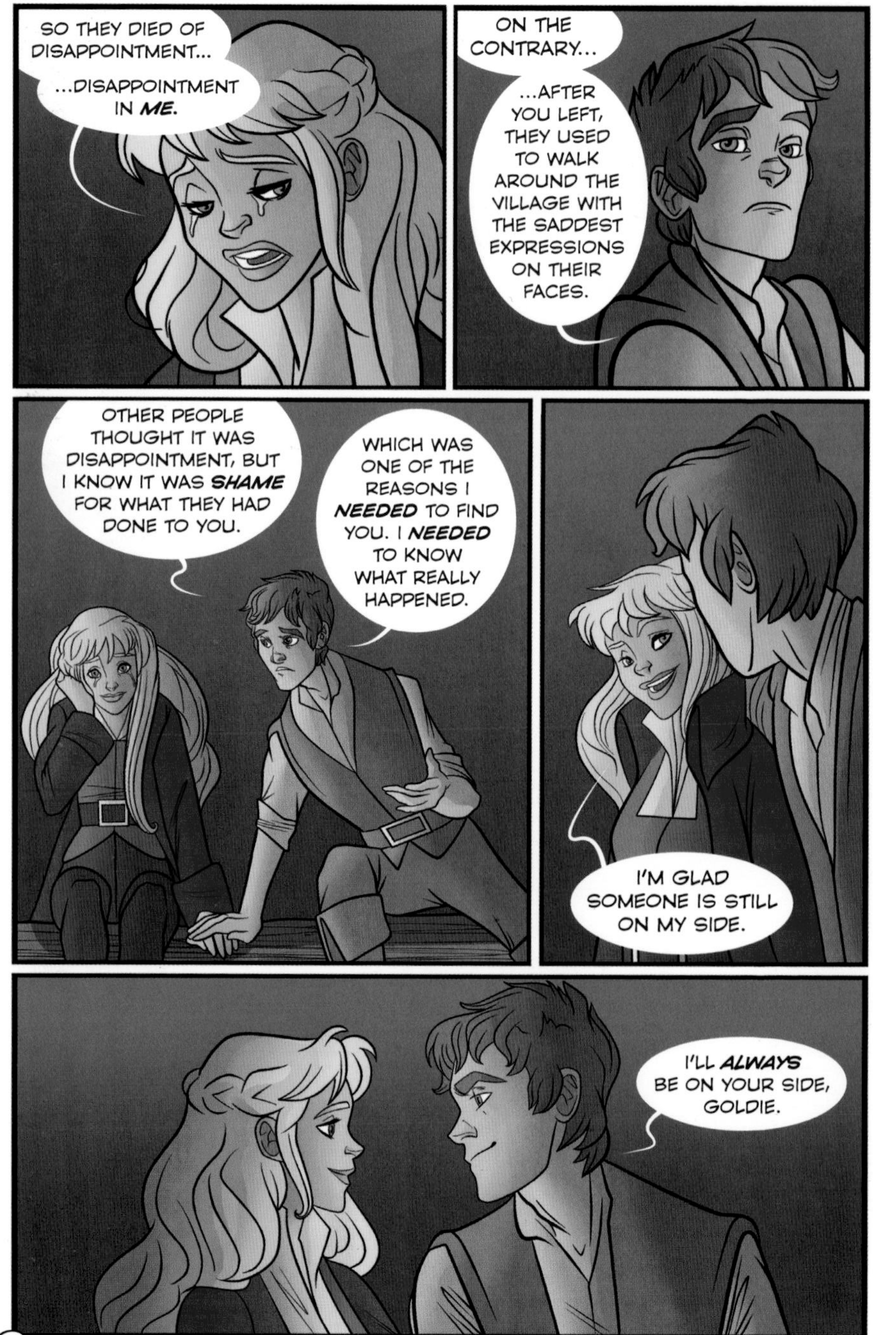
SO THEY DIED OF DISAPPOINTMENT...
...DISAPPOINTMENT IN ME.
ON THE CONTRARY...
...AFTER YOU LEFT, THEY USED TO WALK AROUND THE VILLAGE WITH THE SADDEST EXPRESSIONS ON THEIR FACES.
OTHER PEOPLE THOUGHT IT WAS DISAPPOINTMENT, BUT I KNOW IT WAS SHAME FOR WHAT THEY HAD DONE TO YOU.
WHICH WAS ONE OF THE REASONS I NEEDED TO FIND YOU. I NEEDED TO KNOW WHAT REALLY HAPPENED.
I'M GLAD SOMEONE IS STILL ON MY SIDE.
I'LL ALWAYS BE ON YOUR SIDE, GOLDIE.

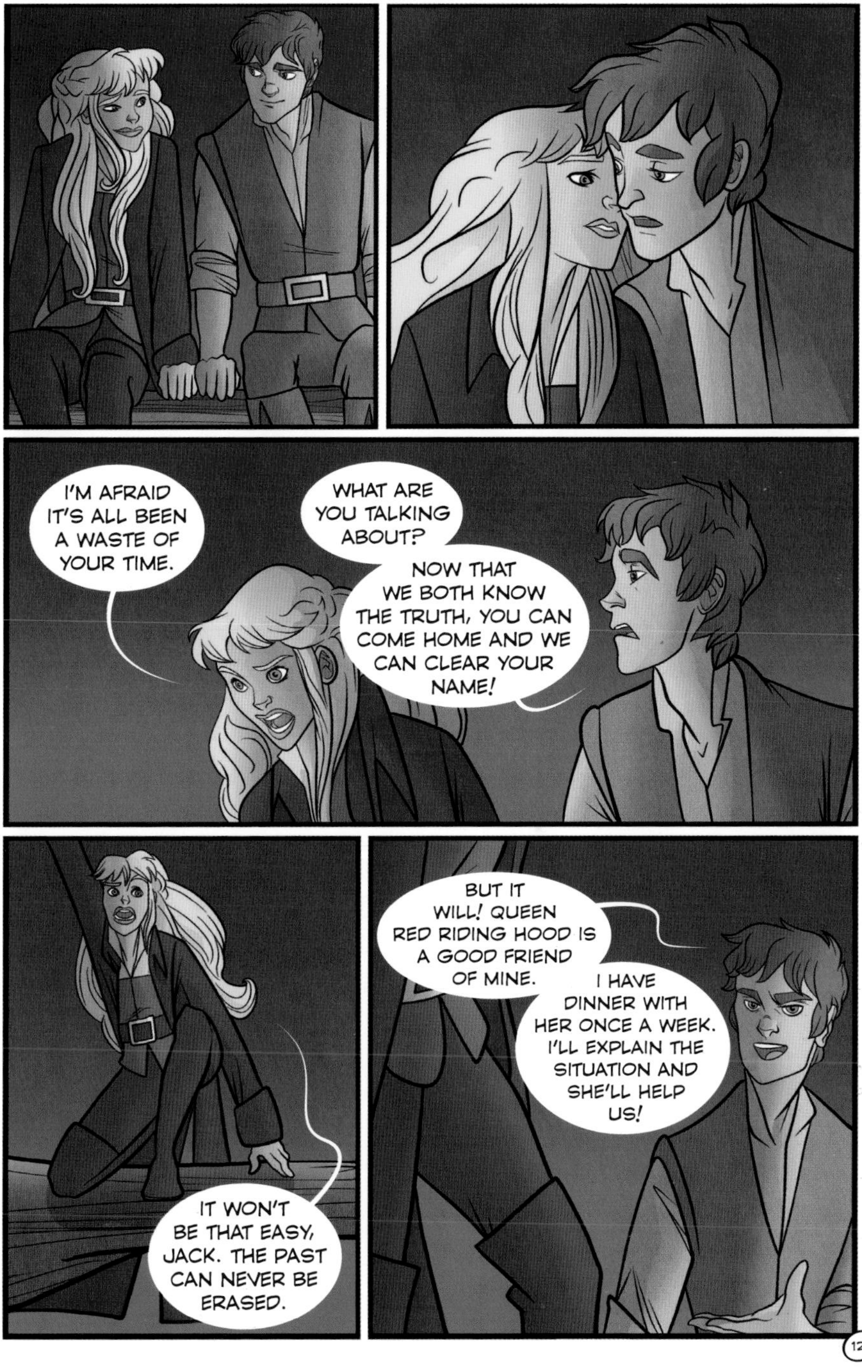
I'M AFRAID IT'S ALL BEEN A WASTE OF YOUR TIME.
WHAT ARE YOU TALKING ABOUT?
NOW THAT WE BOTH KNOW THE TRUTH, YOU CAN COME HOME AND WE CAN CLEAR YOUR NAME!
IT WON'T BE THAT EASY, JACK. THE PAST CAN NEVER BE ERASED.
BUT IT WILL! QUEEN RED RIDING HOOD IS A GOOD FRIEND OF MINE.
I HAVE DINNER WITH HER ONCE A WEEK. I'LL EXPLAIN THE SITUATION AND SHE'LL HELP US!

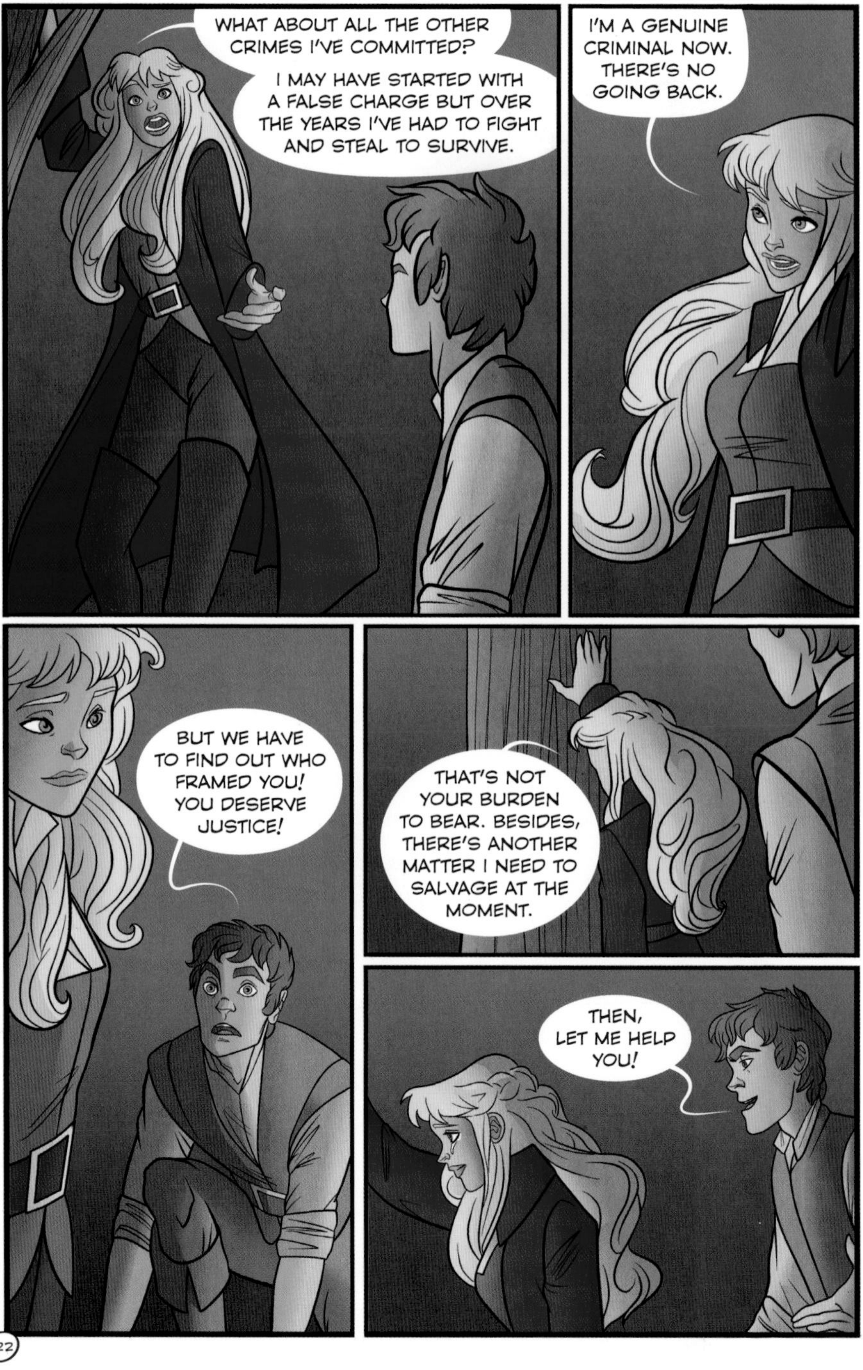
WHAT ABOUT ALL THE OTHER CRIMES I'VE COMMITTED?
I MAY HAVE STARTED WITH A FALSE CHARGE BUT OVER THE YEARS I'VE HAD TO FIGHT AND STEAL TO SURVIVE.
I'M A GENUINE CRIMINAL NOW. THERE'S NO GOING BACK.
BUT WE HAVE TO FIND OUT WHO FRAMED YOU! YOU DESERVE JUSTICE!
THAT'S NOT YOUR BURDEN TO BEAR. BESIDES, THERE'S ANOTHER MATTER I NEED TO SALVAGE AT THE MOMENT.
THEN, LET ME HELP YOU!

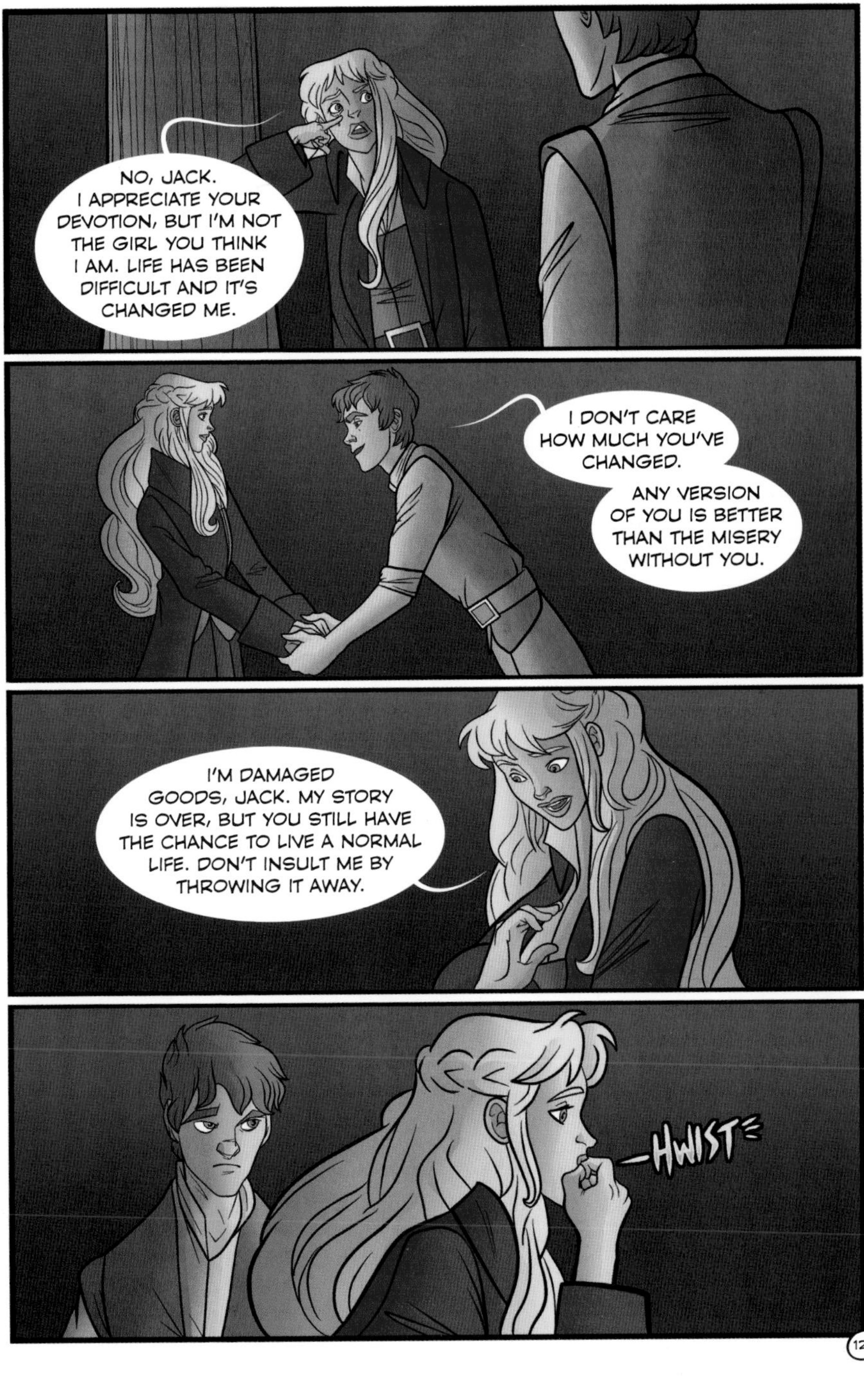
NO, JACK. I APPRECIATE YOUR DEVOTION, BUT I'M NOT THE GIRL YOU THINK I AM. LIFE HAS BEEN DIFFICULT AND IT'S CHANGED ME.
I DON'T CARE HOW MUCH YOU'VE CHANGED.
ANY VERSION OF YOU IS BETTER THAN THE MISERY WITHOUT YOU.
I'M DAMAGED GOODS, JACK. MY STORY IS OVER, BUT YOU STILL HAVE THE CHANCE TO LIVE A NORMAL LIFE. DON'T INSULT ME BY THROWING IT AWAY.
HWIST

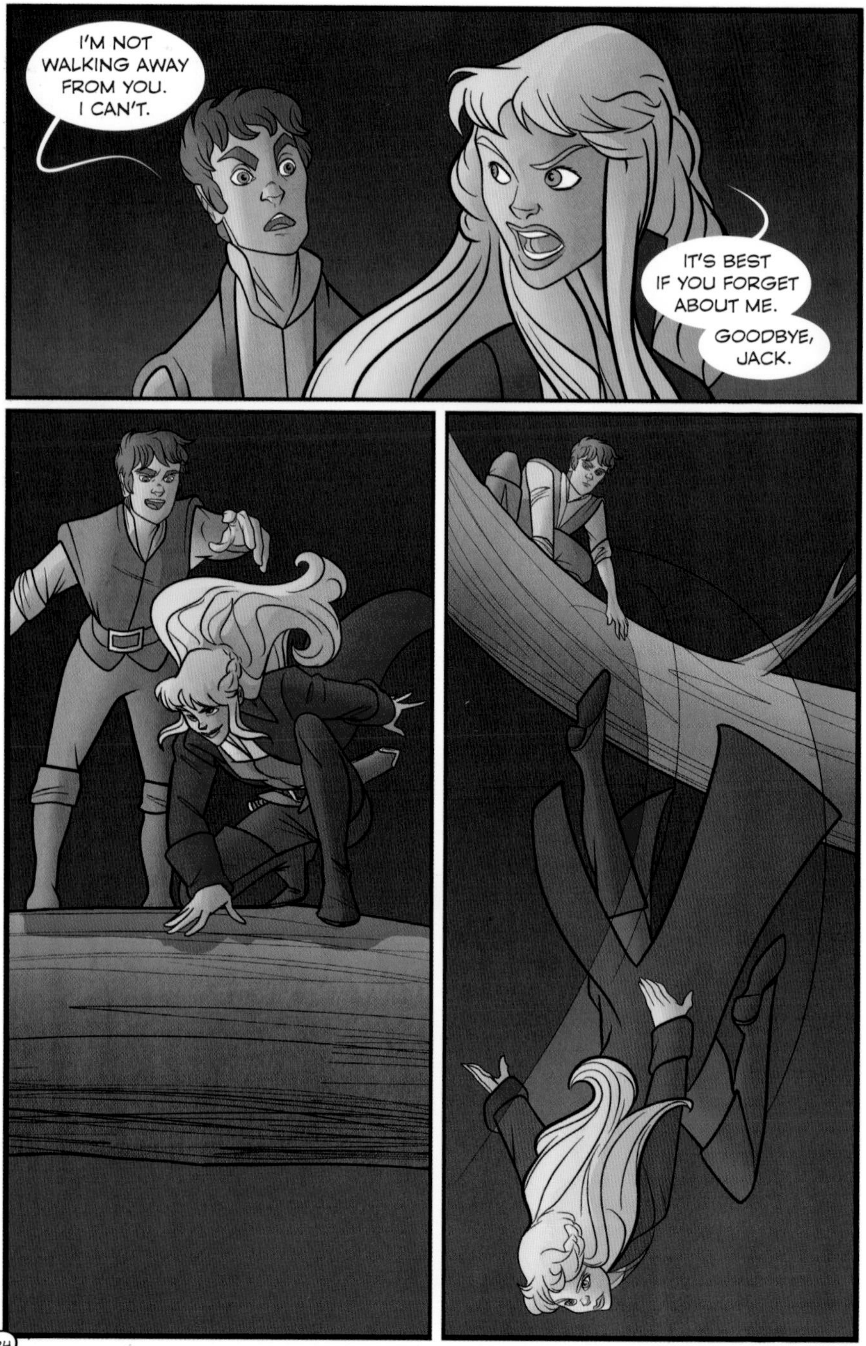
I'M NOT WALKING AWAY FROM YOU. I CAN'T.
IT'S BEST IF YOU FORGET ABOUT ME.
GOODBYE, JACK.

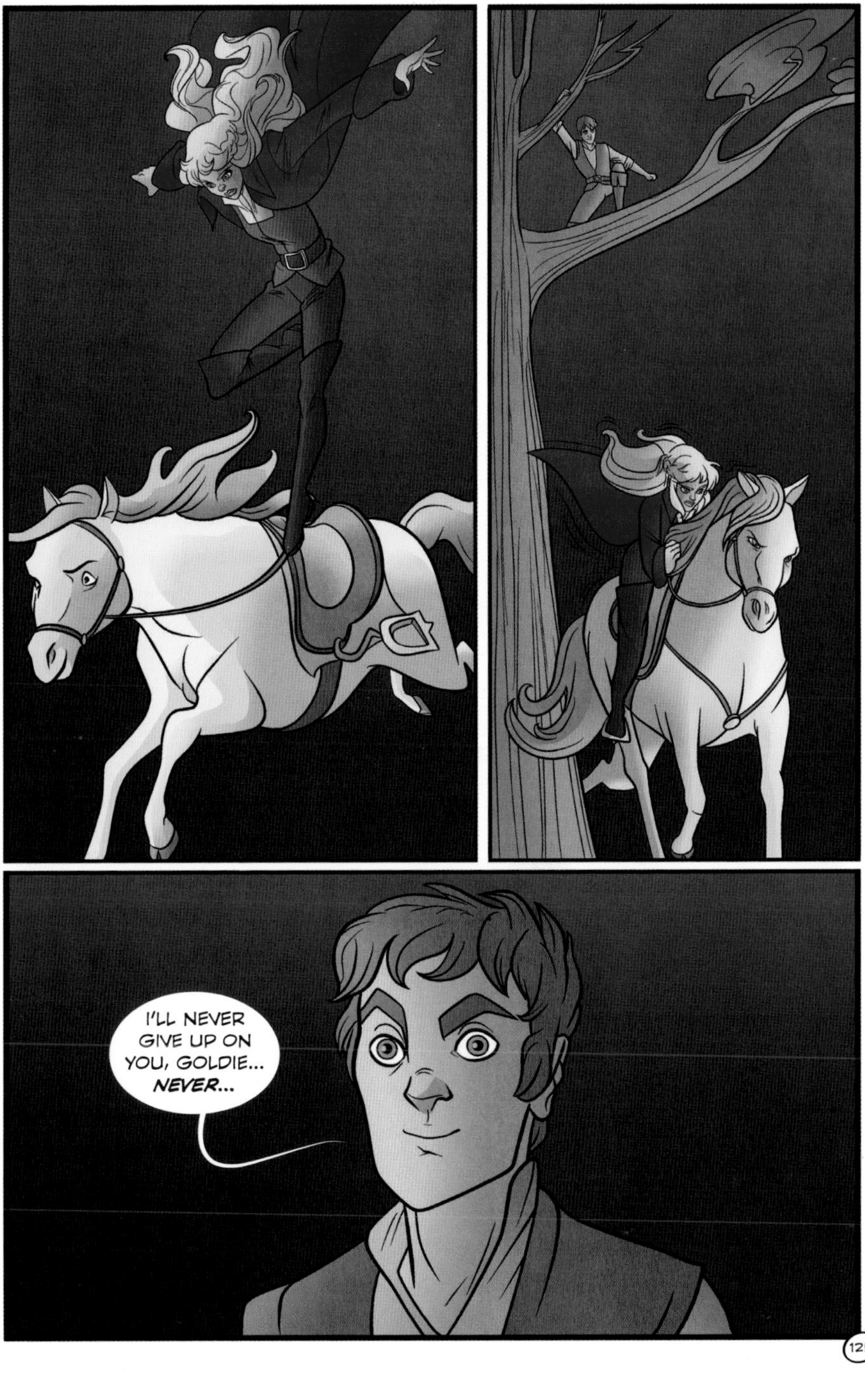
I'LL NEVER GIVE UP ON YOU, GOLDIE... NEVER...

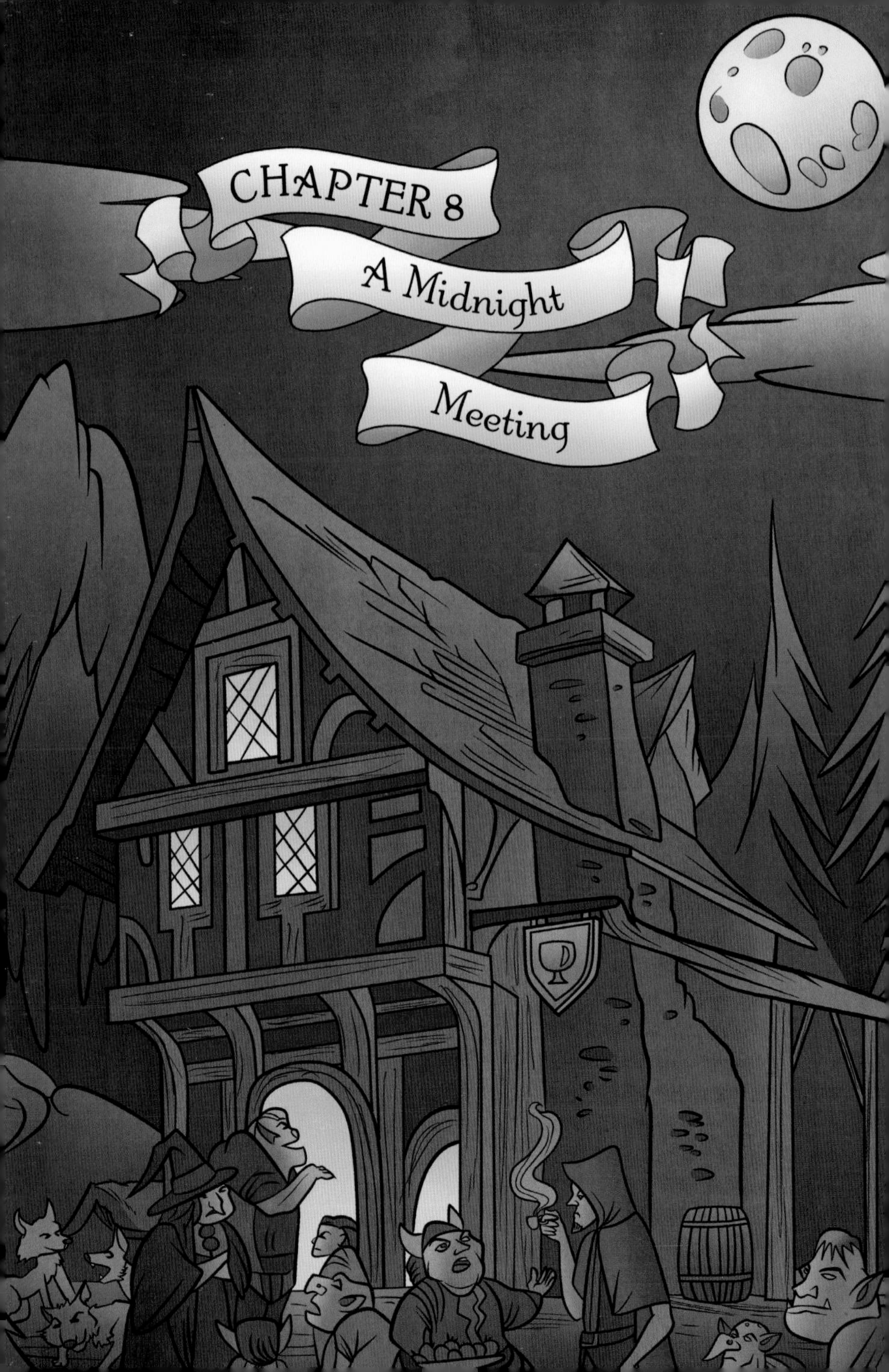
CHAPTER 8
A Midnight
Meeting

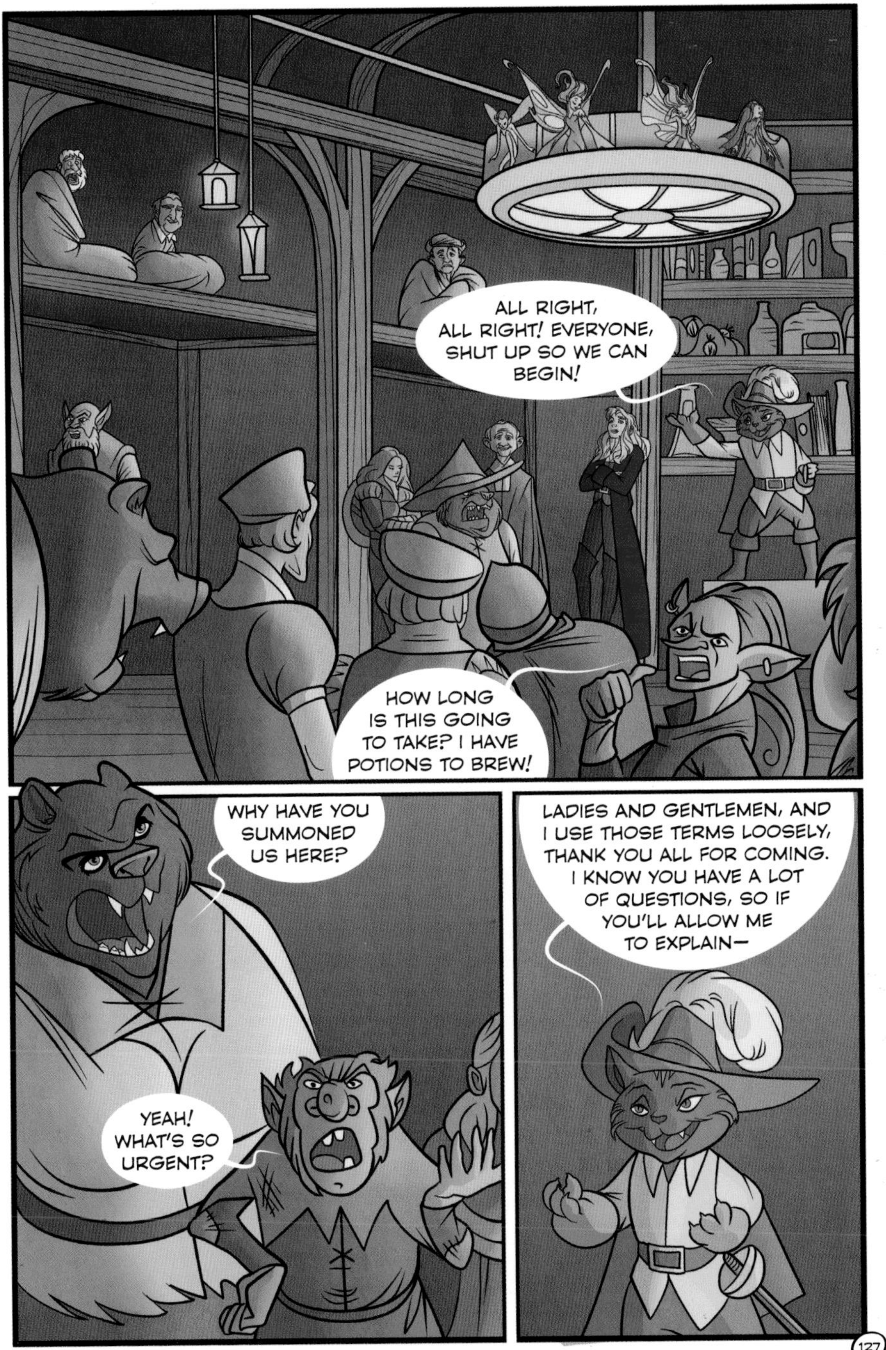
ALL RIGHT, ALL RIGHT! EVERYONE, SHUT UP SO WE CAN BEGIN!
HOW LONG IS THIS GOING TO TAKE? I HAVE POTIONS TO BREW!
WHY HAVE YOU SUMMONED US HERE?
YEAH! WHAT'S SO URGENT?
LADIES AND GENTLEMEN, AND I USE THOSE TERMS LOOSELY, THANK YOU ALL FOR COMING. I KNOW YOU HAVE A LOT OF QUESTIONS, SO IF YOU'LL ALLOW ME TO EXPLAIN—

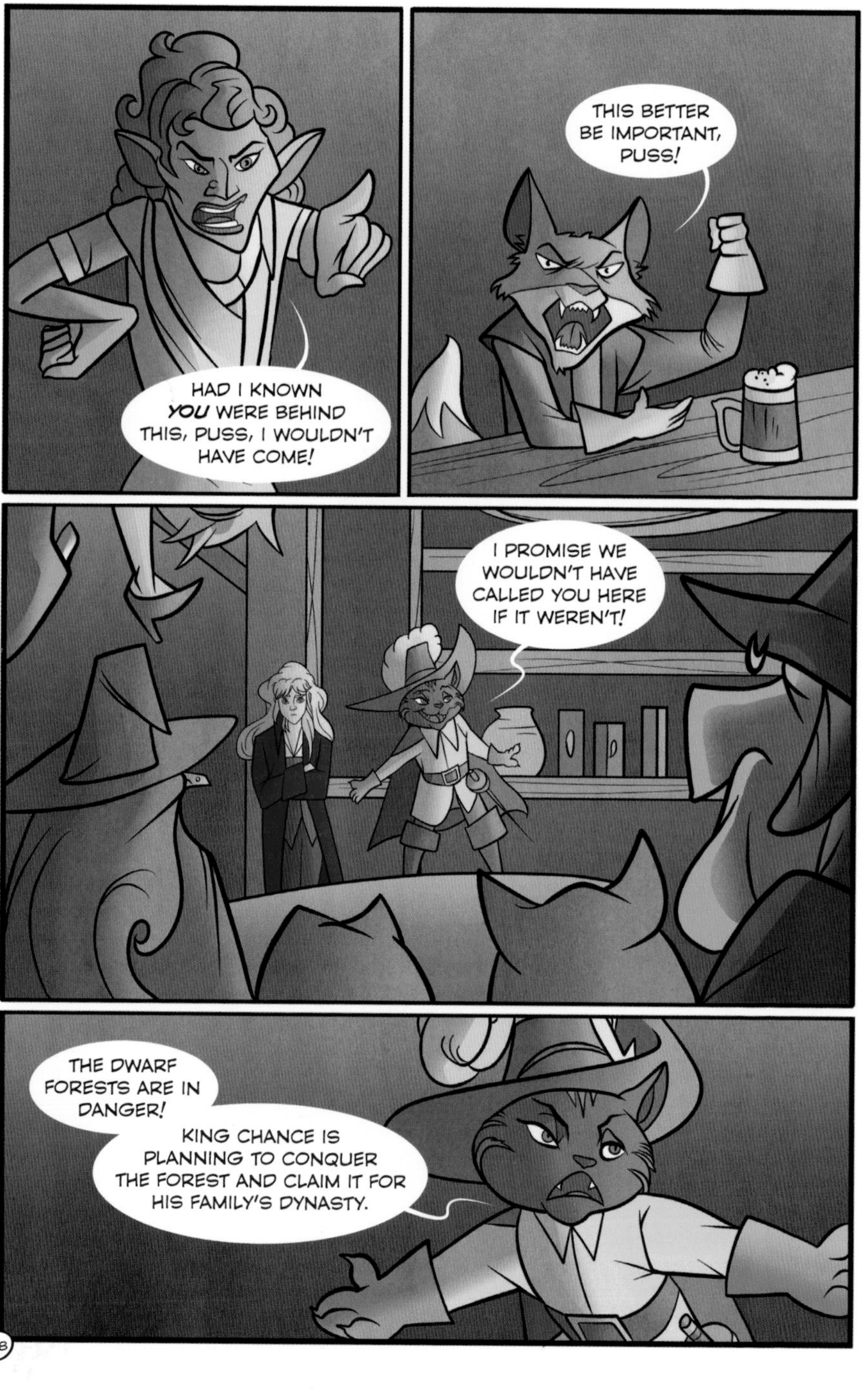

HAD I KNOWN *YOU* WERE BEHIND THIS, PUSS, I WOULDN'T HAVE COME!
THIS BETTER BE IMPORTANT, PUSS!
I PROMISE WE WOULDN'T HAVE CALLED YOU HERE IF IT WEREN'T!
THE DWARF FORESTS ARE IN DANGER!
KING CHANCE IS PLANNING TO CONQUER THE FOREST AND CLAIM IT FOR HIS FAMILY'S DYNASTY.

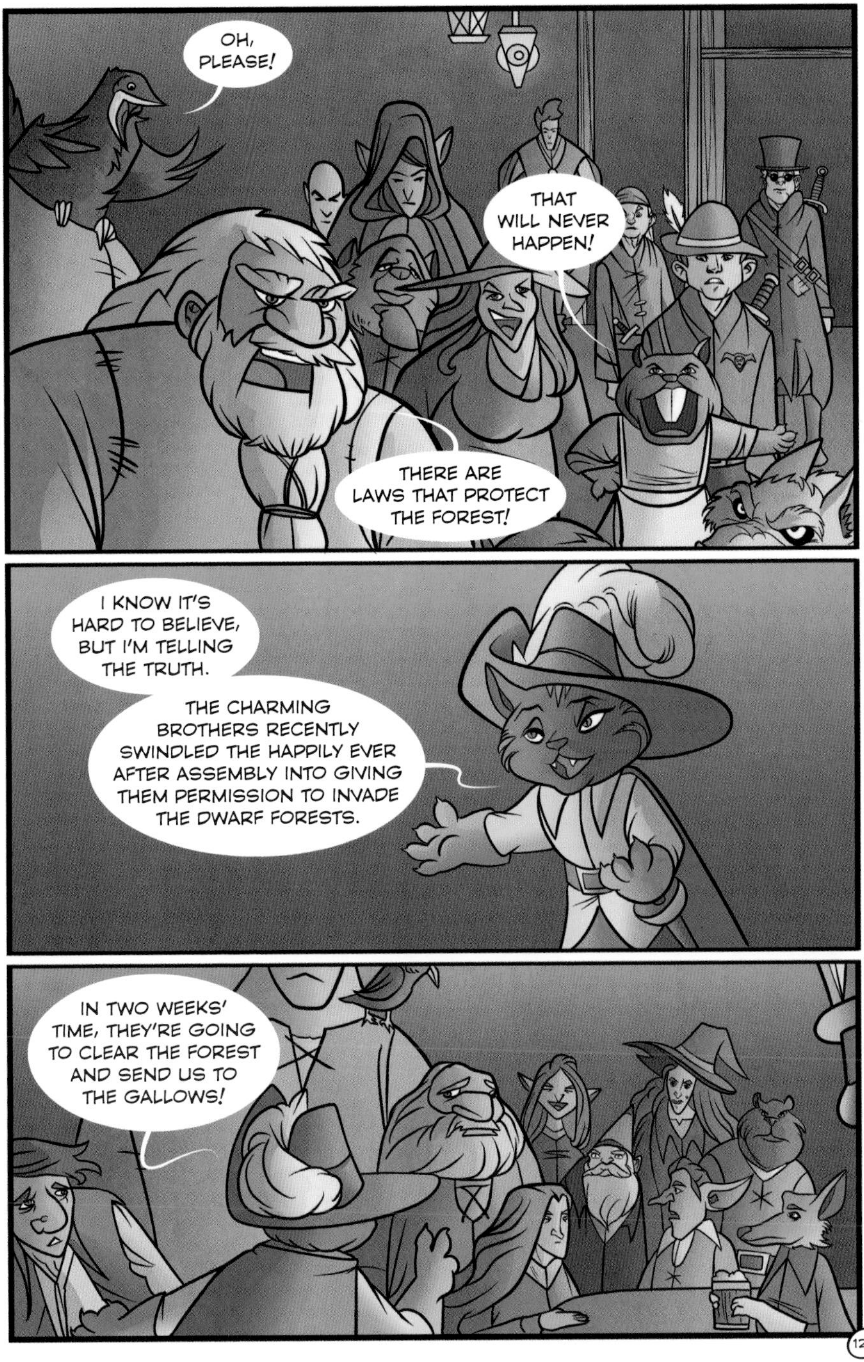
OH, PLEASE!
THAT WILL NEVER HAPPEN!
THERE ARE LAWS THAT PROTECT THE FOREST!
I KNOW IT'S HARD TO BELIEVE, BUT I'M TELLING THE TRUTH.
THE CHARMING BROTHERS RECENTLY SWINDLED THE HAPPILY EVER AFTER ASSEMBLY INTO GIVING THEM PERMISSION TO INVADE THE DWARF FORESTS.
IN TWO WEEKS' TIME, THEY'RE GOING TO CLEAR THE FOREST AND SEND US TO THE GALLOWS!

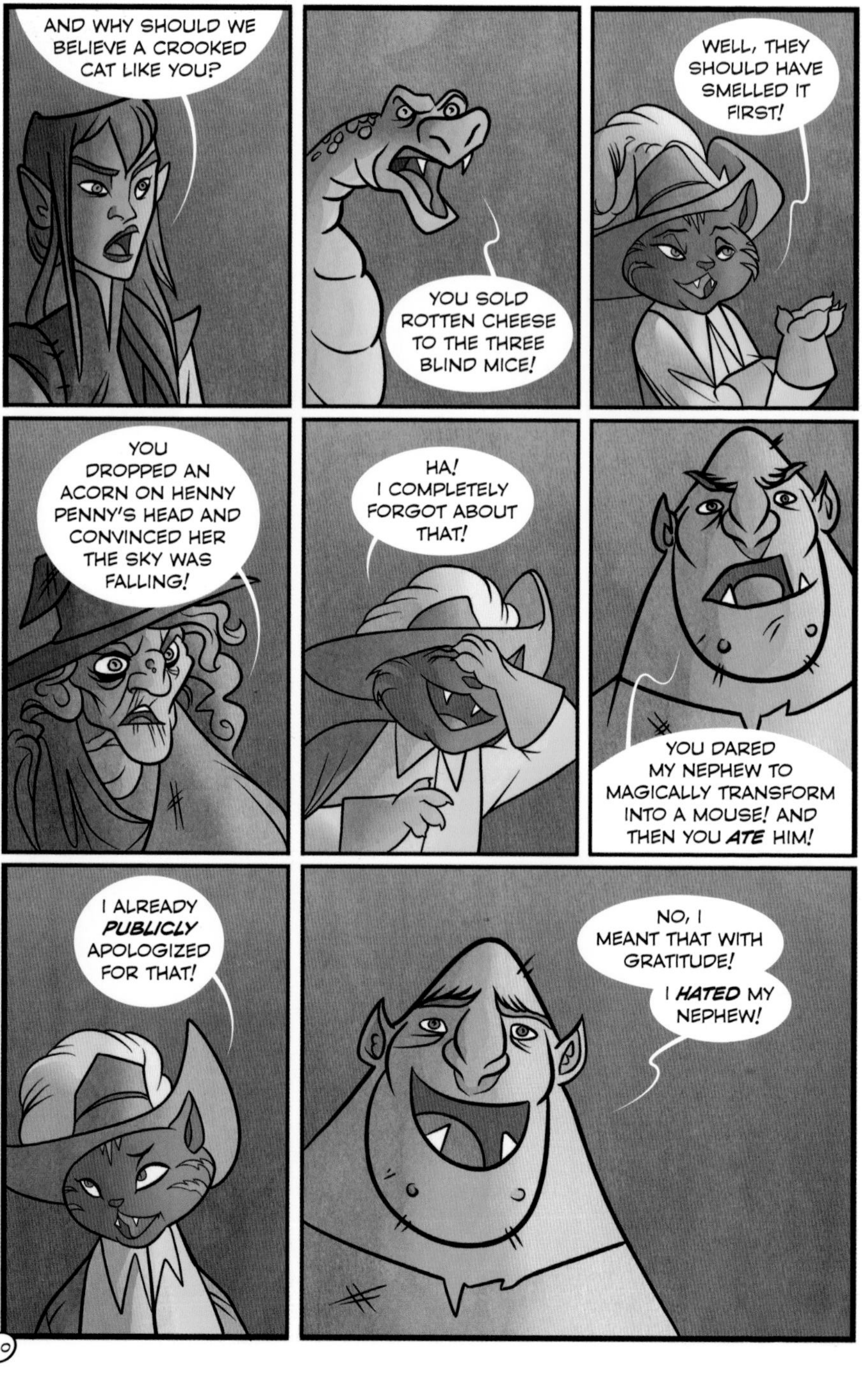
AND WHY SHOULD WE BELIEVE A CROOKED CAT LIKE YOU?
YOU SOLD ROTTEN CHEESE TO THE THREE BLIND MICE!
WELL, THEY SHOULD HAVE SMELLED IT FIRST!
YOU DROPPED AN ACORN ON HENNY PENNY'S HEAD AND CONVINCED HER THE SKY WAS FALLING!
HA! I COMPLETELY FORGOT ABOUT THAT!
YOU DARED MY NEPHEW TO MAGICALLY TRANSFORM INTO A MOUSE! AND THEN YOU ***ATE*** HIM!
I ALREADY ***PUBLICLY*** APOLOGIZED FOR THAT!
NO, I MEANT THAT WITH GRATITUDE!
I ***HATED*** MY NEPHEW!

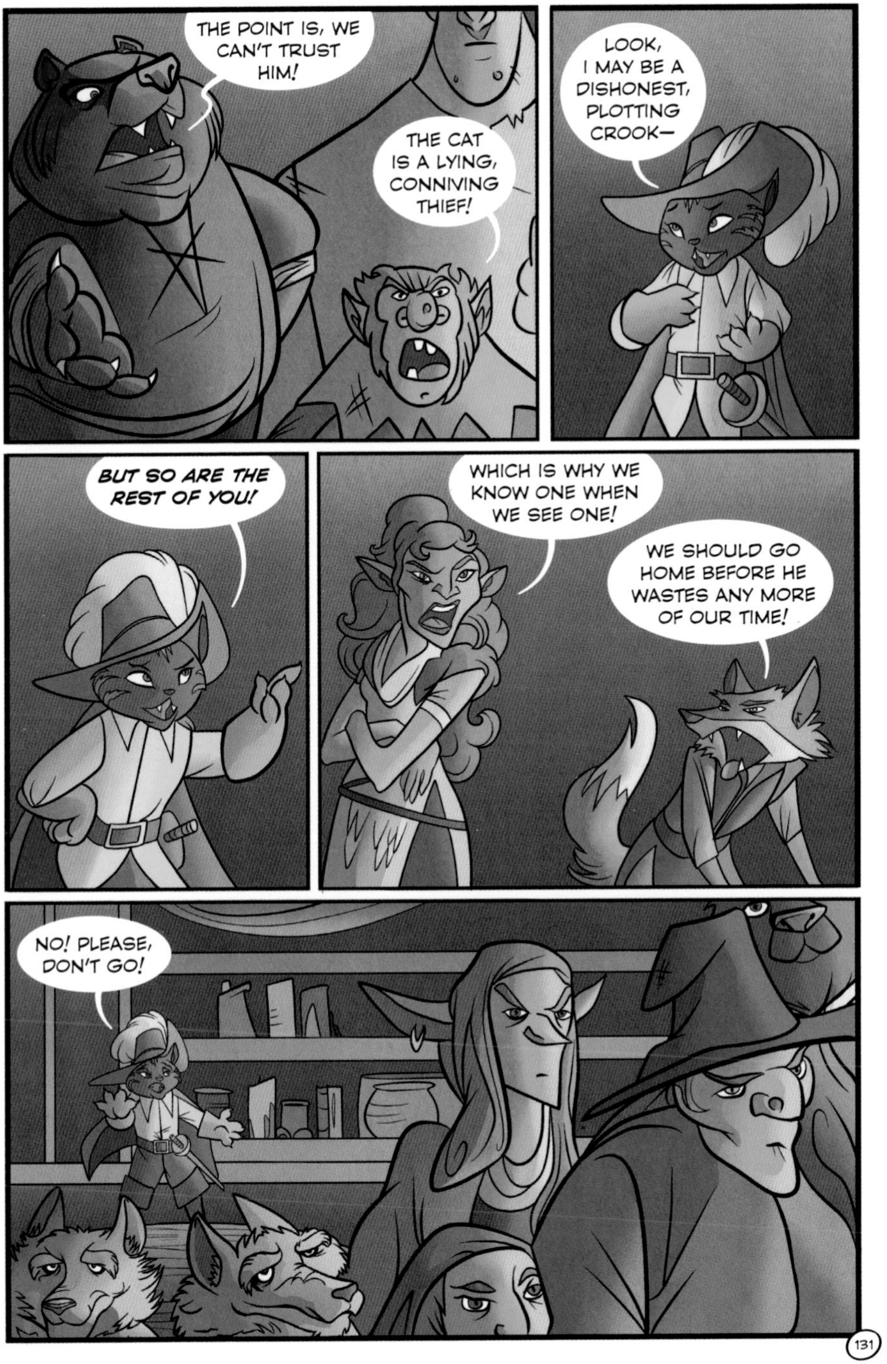
THE POINT IS, WE CAN'T TRUST HIM!
THE CAT IS A LYING, CONNIVING THIEF!
LOOK, I MAY BE A DISHONEST, PLOTTING CROOK—
BUT SO ARE THE REST OF YOU!
WHICH IS WHY WE KNOW ONE WHEN WE SEE ONE!
WE SHOULD GO HOME BEFORE HE WASTES ANY MORE OF OUR TIME!
NO! PLEASE, DON'T GO!

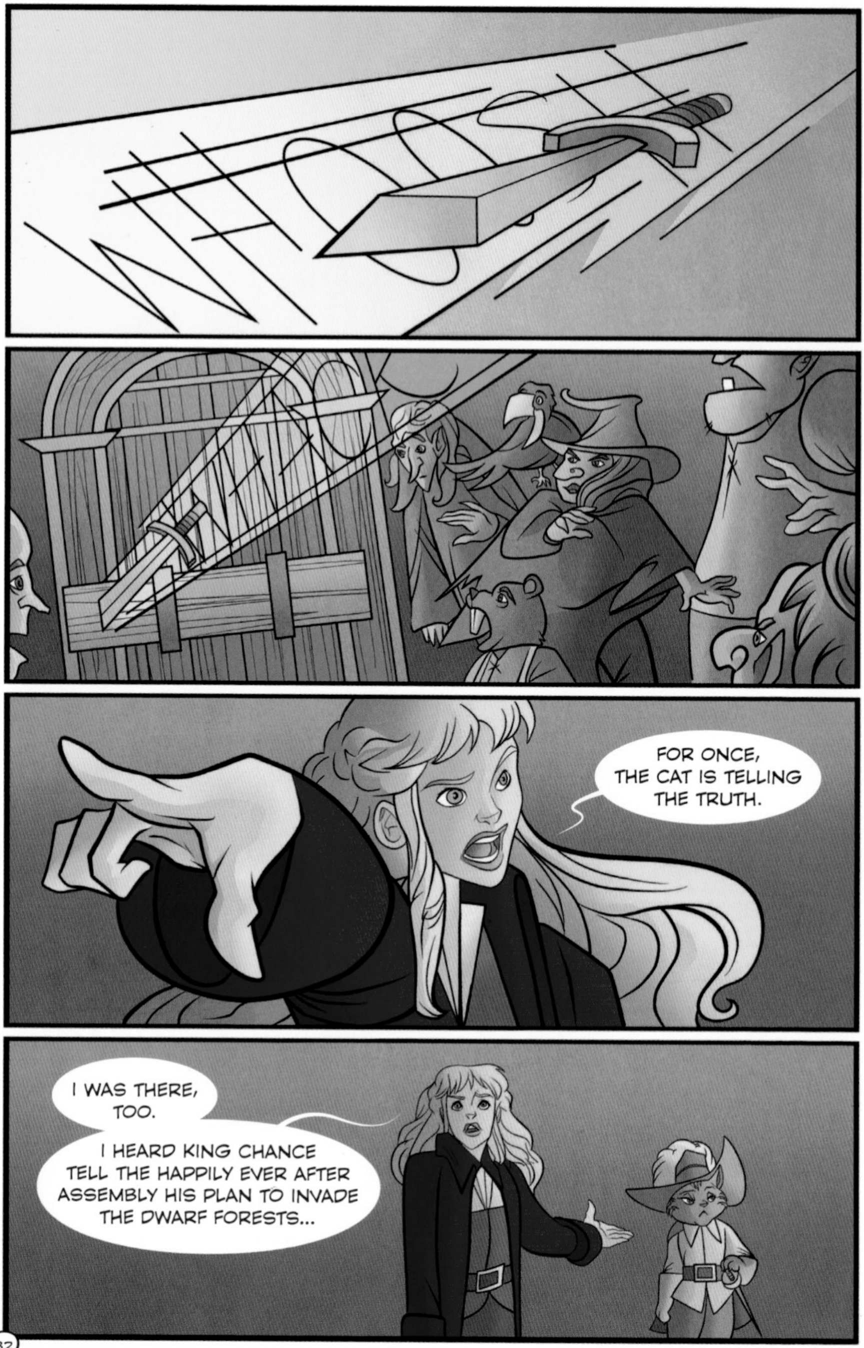
FOR ONCE, THE CAT IS TELLING THE TRUTH.
I WAS THERE, TOO.
I HEARD KING CHANCE TELL THE HAPPILY EVER AFTER ASSEMBLY HIS PLAN TO INVADE THE DWARF FORESTS...

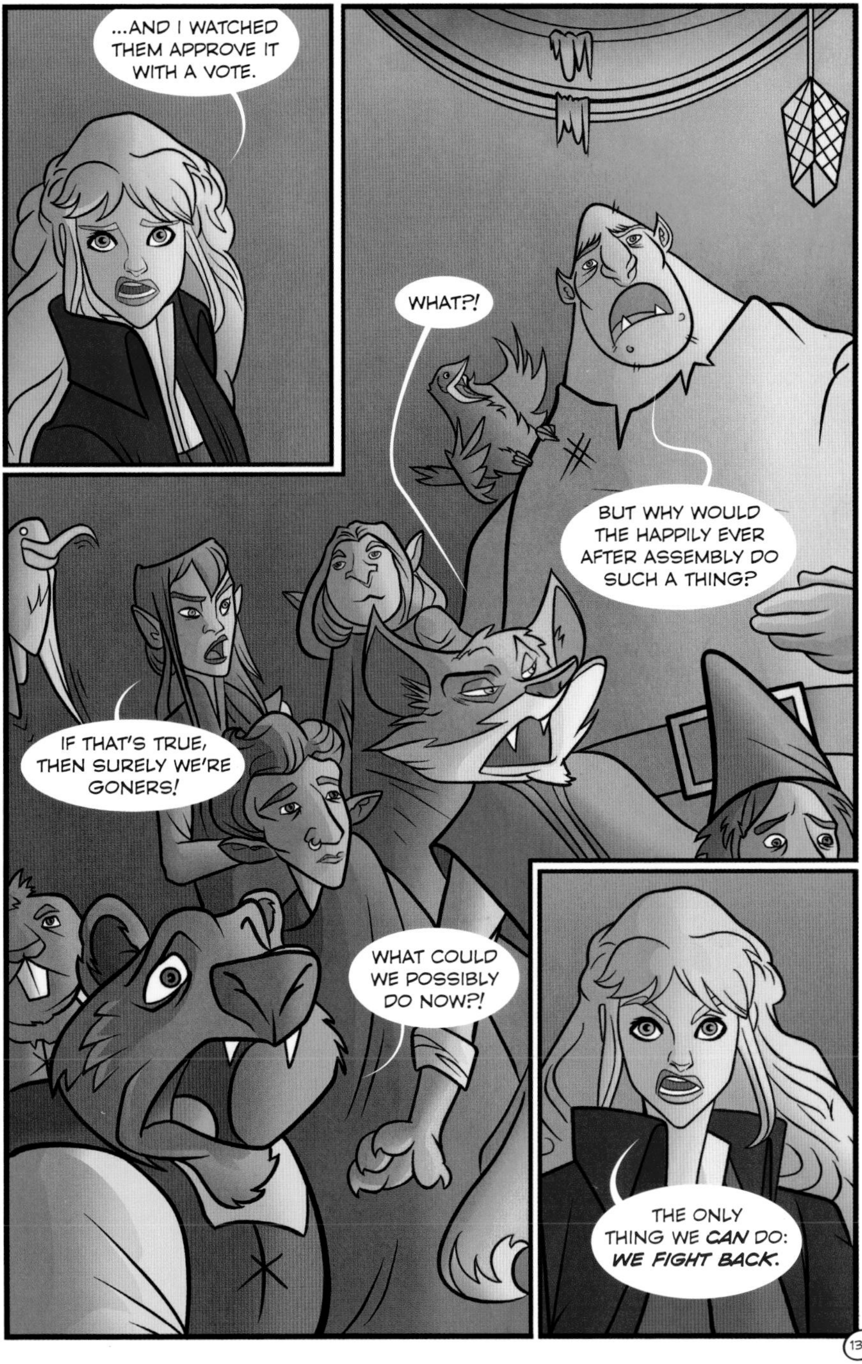
...AND I WATCHED THEM APPROVE IT WITH A VOTE.
WHAT?!
BUT WHY WOULD THE HAPPILY EVER AFTER ASSEMBLY DO SUCH A THING?
IF THAT'S TRUE, THEN SURELY WE'RE GONERS!
WHAT COULD WE POSSIBLY DO NOW?!
THE ONLY THING WE *CAN* DO: ***WE FIGHT BACK.***

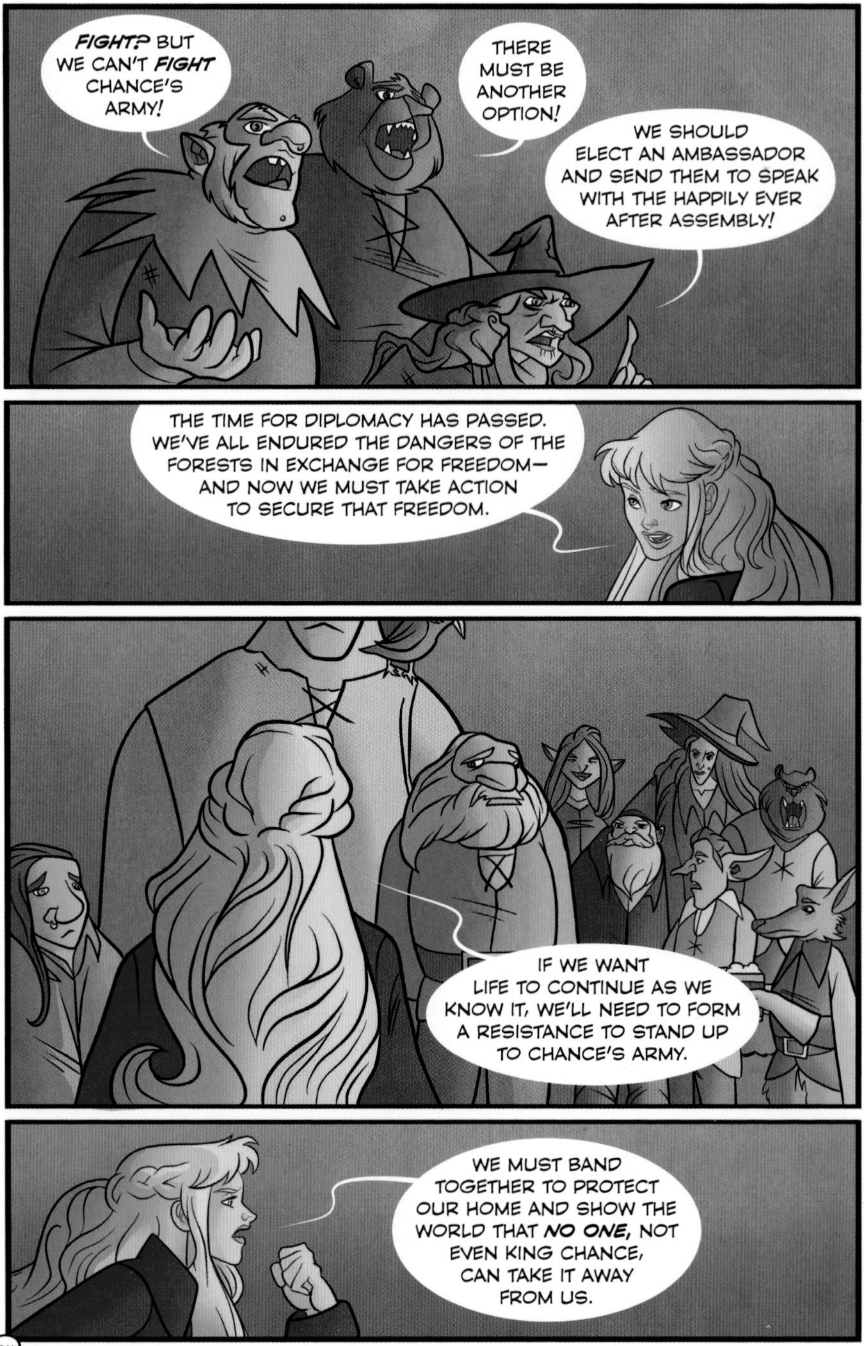
FIGHT? BUT WE CAN'T FIGHT CHANCE'S ARMY!
THERE MUST BE ANOTHER OPTION!
WE SHOULD ELECT AN AMBASSADOR AND SEND THEM TO SPEAK WITH THE HAPPILY EVER AFTER ASSEMBLY!
THE TIME FOR DIPLOMACY HAS PASSED. WE'VE ALL ENDURED THE DANGERS OF THE FORESTS IN EXCHANGE FOR FREEDOM— AND NOW WE MUST TAKE ACTION TO SECURE THAT FREEDOM.
IF WE WANT LIFE TO CONTINUE AS WE KNOW IT, WE'LL NEED TO FORM A RESISTANCE TO STAND UP TO CHANCE'S ARMY.
WE MUST BAND TOGETHER TO PROTECT OUR HOME AND SHOW THE WORLD THAT NO ONE, NOT EVEN KING CHANCE, CAN TAKE IT AWAY FROM US.

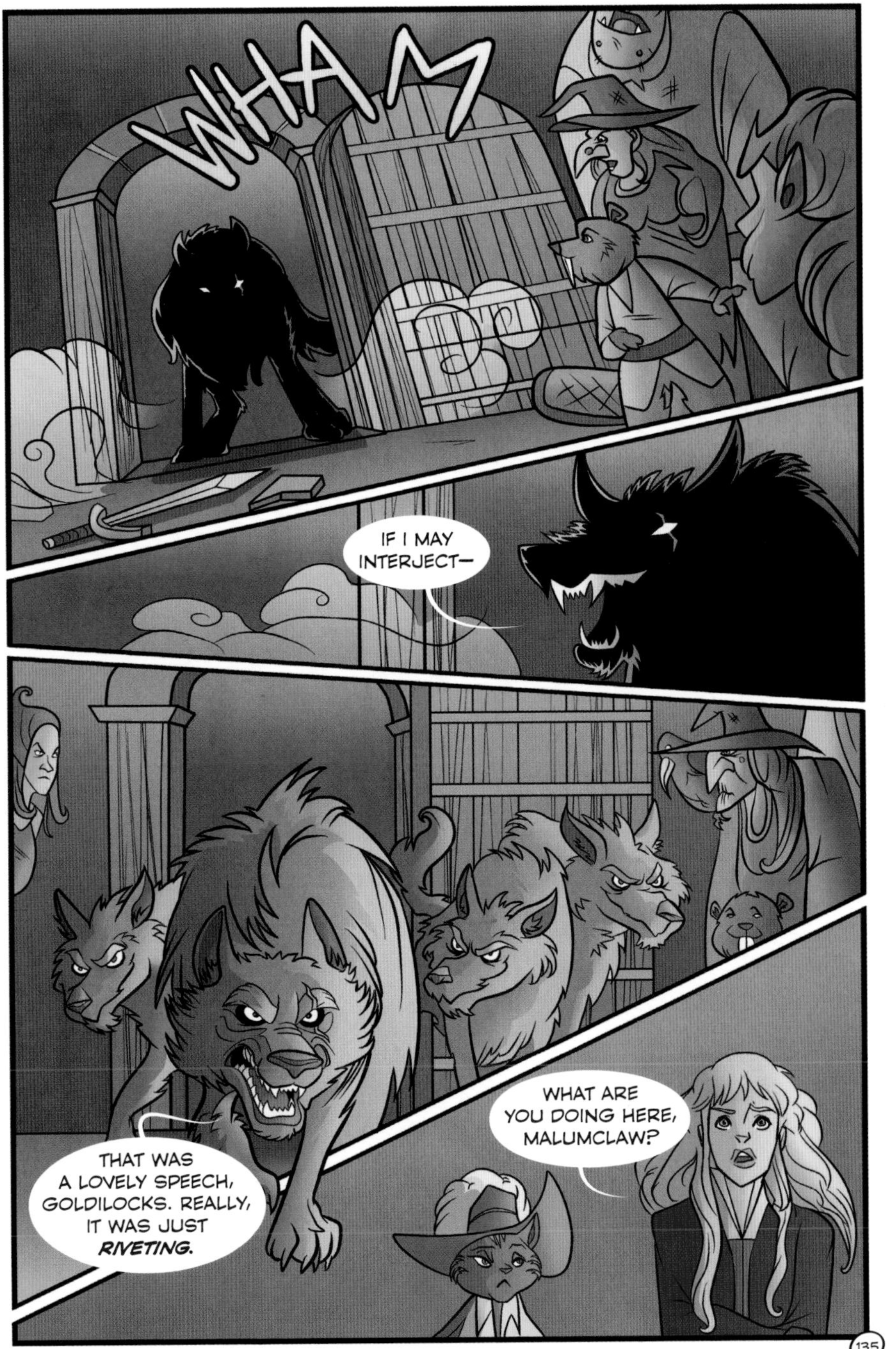
WHAM
IF I MAY INTERJECT—
THAT WAS A LOVELY SPEECH, GOLDILOCKS. REALLY, IT WAS JUST *RIVETING.*
WHAT ARE YOU DOING HERE, MALUMCLAW?

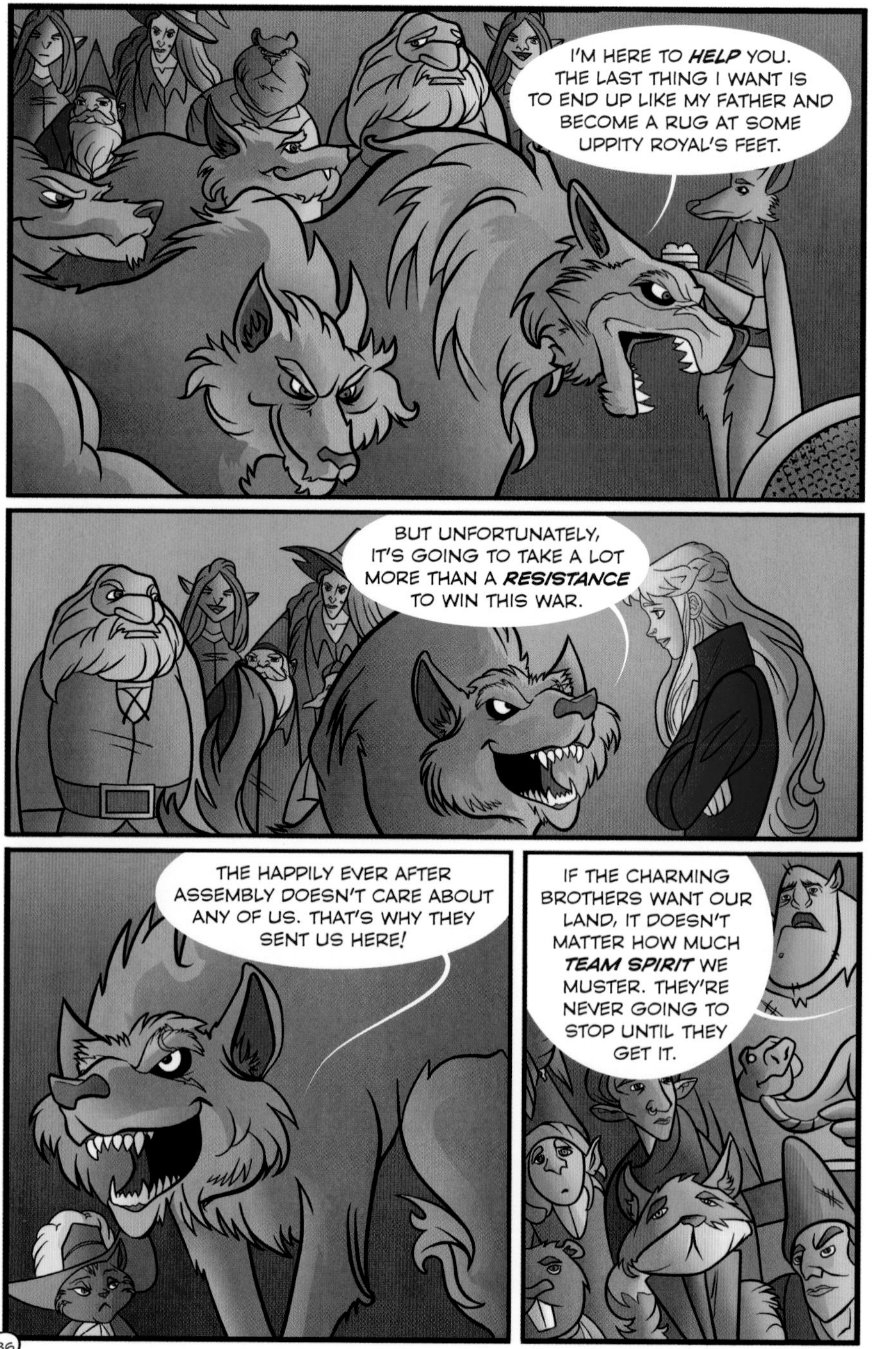
I'M HERE TO ***HELP*** YOU. THE LAST THING I WANT IS TO END UP LIKE MY FATHER AND BECOME A RUG AT SOME UPPITY ROYAL'S FEET.
BUT UNFORTUNATELY, IT'S GOING TO TAKE A LOT MORE THAN A ***RESISTANCE*** TO WIN THIS WAR.
THE HAPPILY EVER AFTER ASSEMBLY DOESN'T CARE ABOUT ANY OF US. THAT'S WHY THEY SENT US HERE!
IF THE CHARMING BROTHERS WANT OUR LAND, IT DOESN'T MATTER HOW MUCH ***TEAM SPIRIT*** WE MUSTER. THEY'RE NEVER GOING TO STOP UNTIL THEY GET IT.

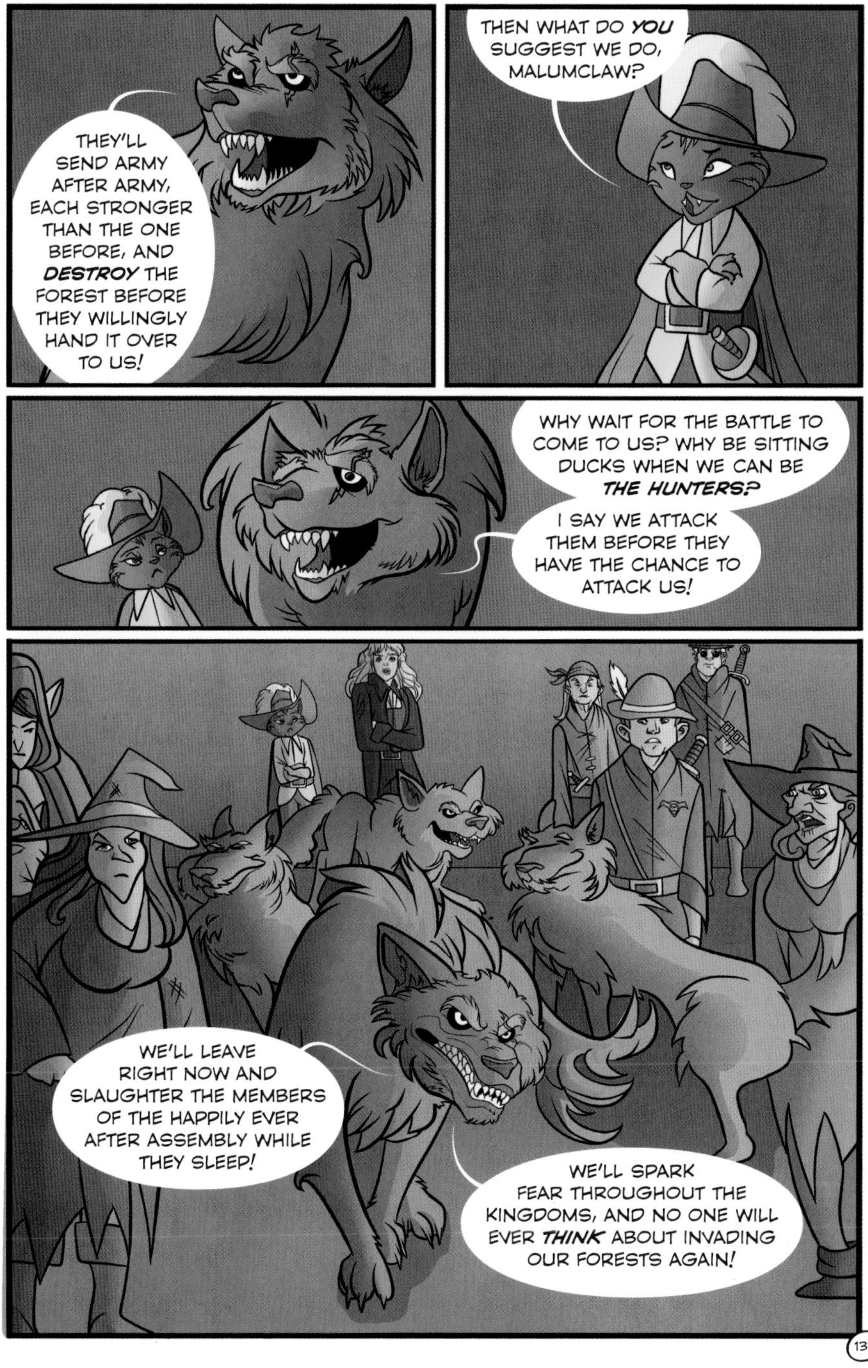
THEY'LL SEND ARMY AFTER ARMY, EACH STRONGER THAN THE ONE BEFORE, AND DESTROY THE FOREST BEFORE THEY WILLINGLY HAND IT OVER TO US!
THEN WHAT DO YOU SUGGEST WE DO, MALUMCLAW?
WHY WAIT FOR THE BATTLE TO COME TO US? WHY BE SITTING DUCKS WHEN WE CAN BE THE HUNTERS?
I SAY WE ATTACK THEM BEFORE THEY HAVE THE CHANCE TO ATTACK US!
WE'LL LEAVE RIGHT NOW AND SLAUGHTER THE MEMBERS OF THE HAPPILY EVER AFTER ASSEMBLY WHILE THEY SLEEP!
WE'LL SPARK FEAR THROUGHOUT THE KINGDOMS, AND NO ONE WILL EVER THINK ABOUT INVADING OUR FORESTS AGAIN!

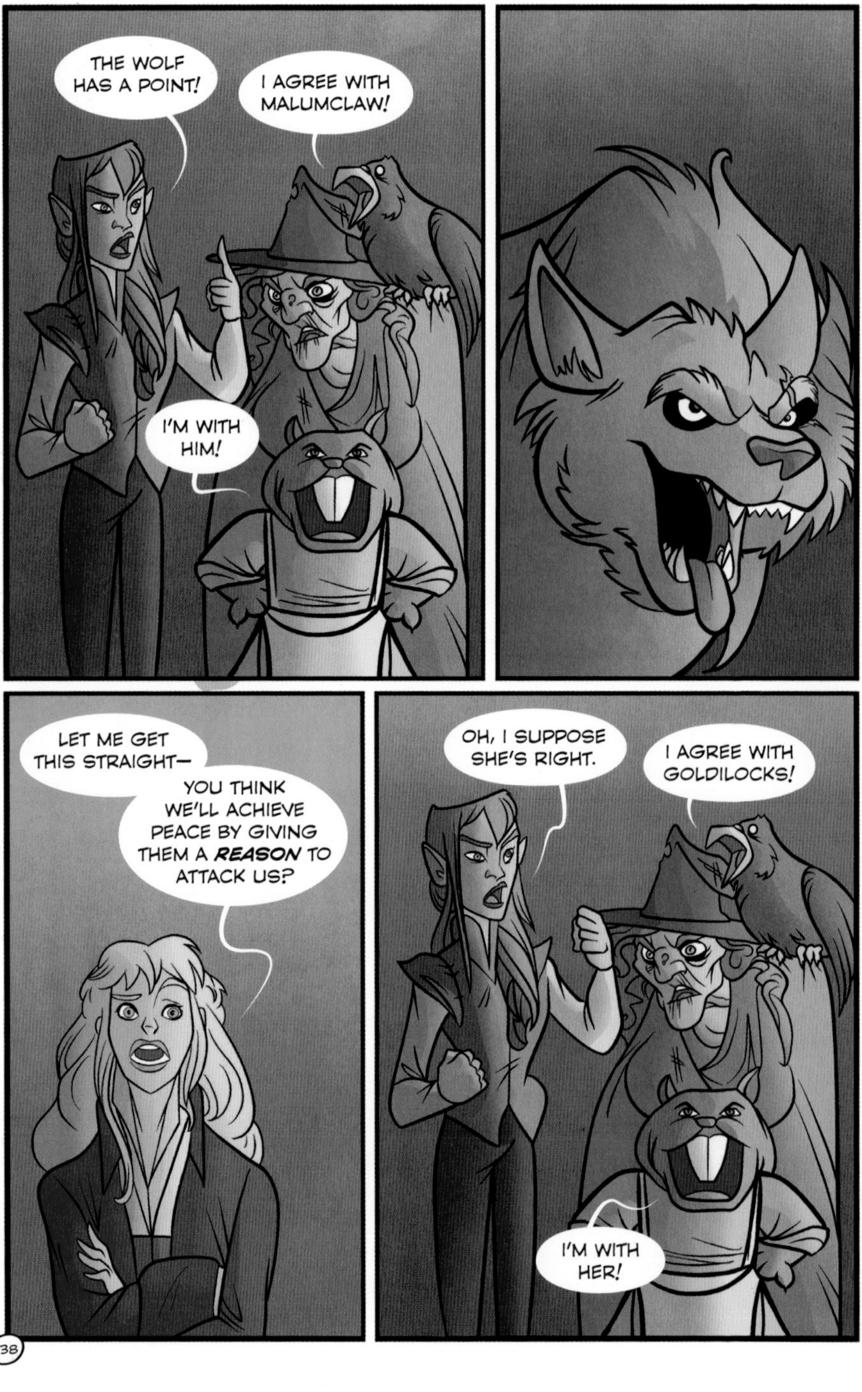
THE WOLF HAS A POINT!
I AGREE WITH MALUMCLAW!
I'M WITH HIM!
LET ME GET THIS STRAIGHT—
YOU THINK WE'LL ACHIEVE PEACE BY GIVING THEM A *REASON* TO ATTACK US?
OH, I SUPPOSE SHE'S RIGHT.
I AGREE WITH GOLDILOCKS!
I'M WITH HER!

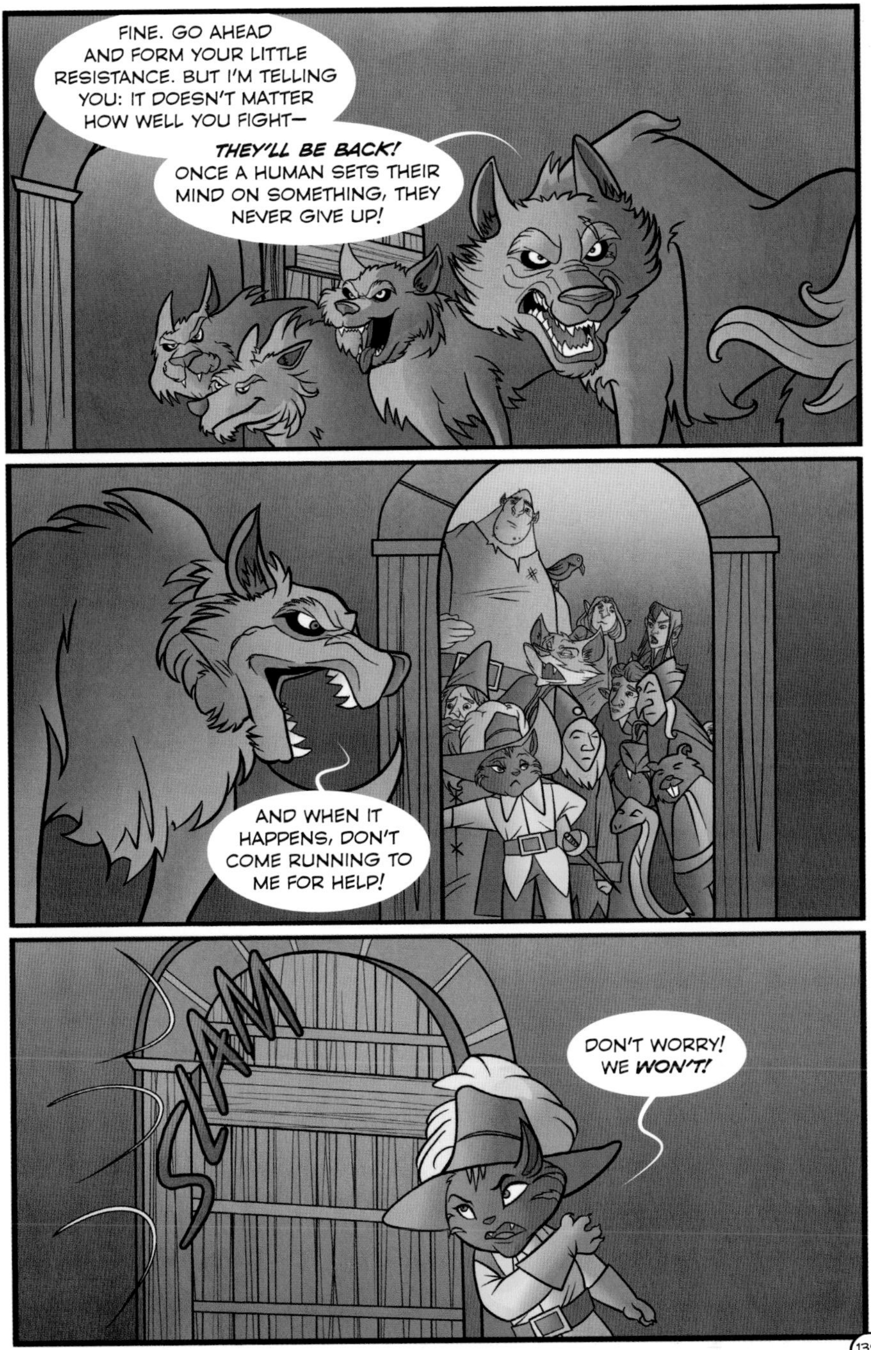
FINE. GO AHEAD AND FORM YOUR LITTLE RESISTANCE. BUT I'M TELLING YOU: IT DOESN'T MATTER HOW WELL YOU FIGHT—
THEY'LL BE BACK! ONCE A HUMAN SETS THEIR MIND ON SOMETHING, THEY NEVER GIVE UP!
AND WHEN IT HAPPENS, DON'T COME RUNNING TO ME FOR HELP!
SLAM
DON'T WORRY! WE ***WON'T!***

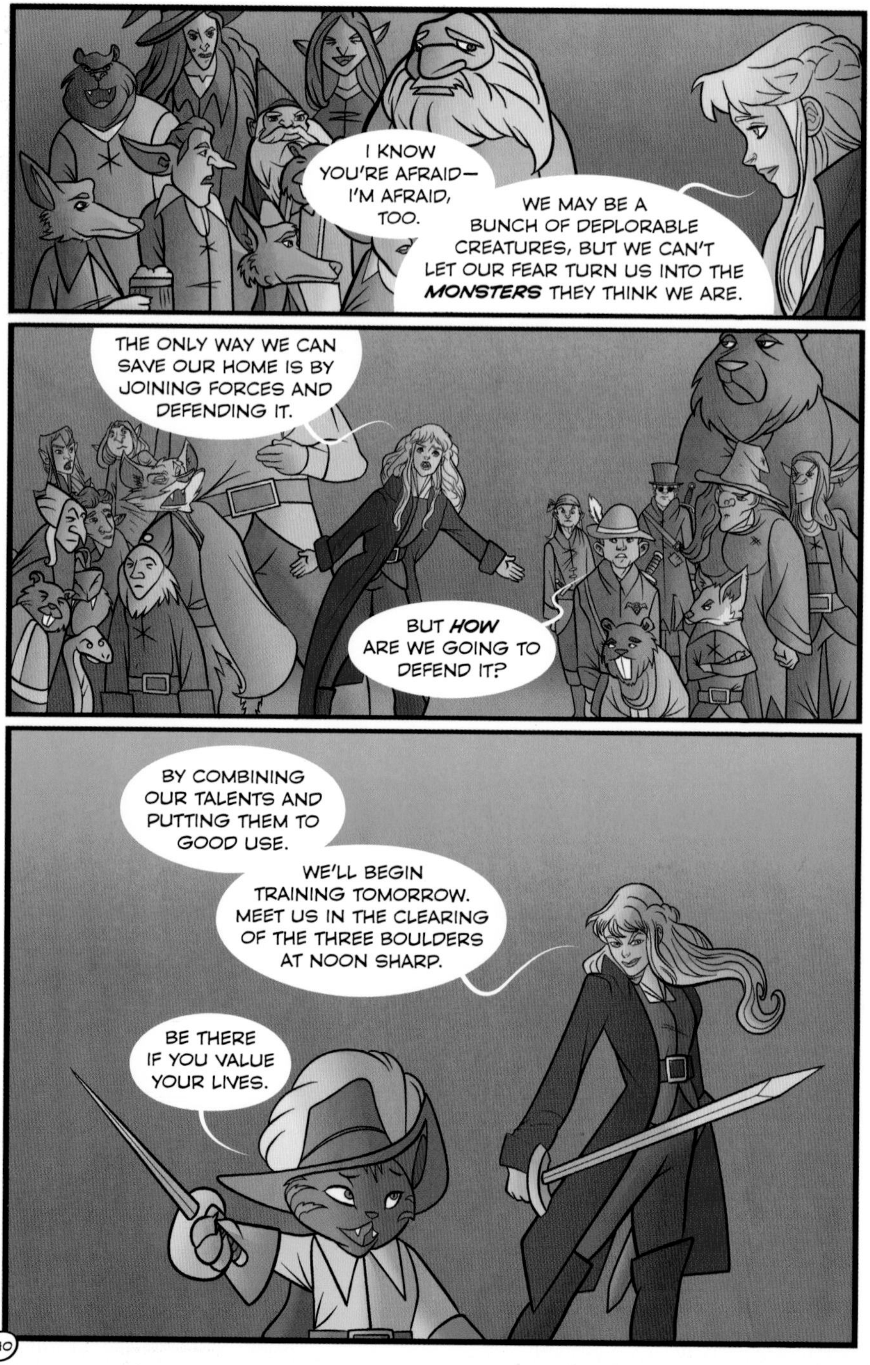
I KNOW YOU'RE AFRAID— I'M AFRAID, TOO.
WE MAY BE A BUNCH OF DEPLORABLE CREATURES, BUT WE CAN'T LET OUR FEAR TURN US INTO THE ***MONSTERS*** THEY THINK WE ARE.
THE ONLY WAY WE CAN SAVE OUR HOME IS BY JOINING FORCES AND DEFENDING IT.
BUT ***HOW*** ARE WE GOING TO DEFEND IT?
BY COMBINING OUR TALENTS AND PUTTING THEM TO GOOD USE.
WE'LL BEGIN TRAINING TOMORROW. MEET US IN THE CLEARING OF THE THREE BOULDERS AT NOON SHARP.
BE THERE IF YOU VALUE YOUR LIVES.

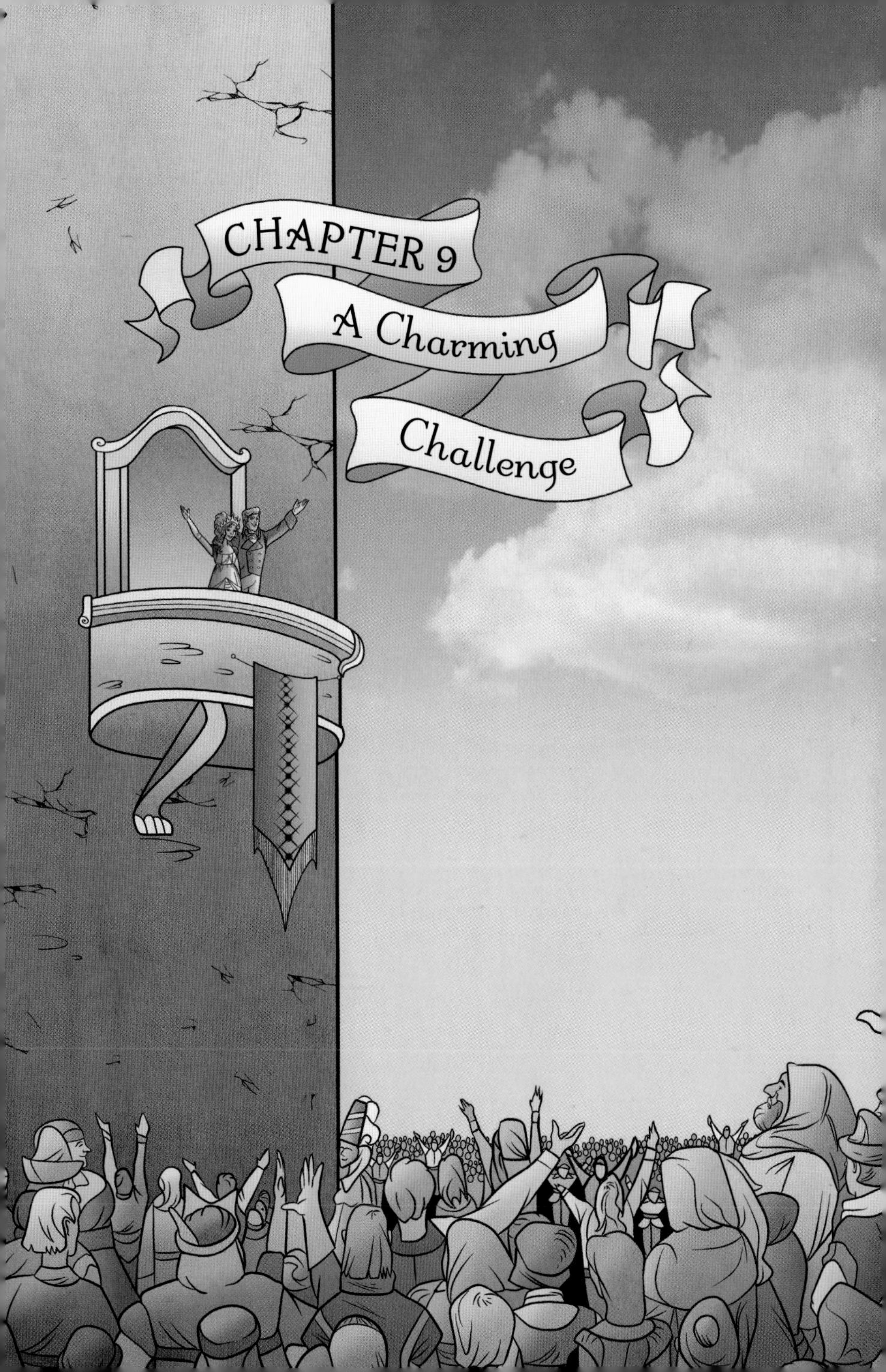
CHAPTER 9
A Charming
Challenge

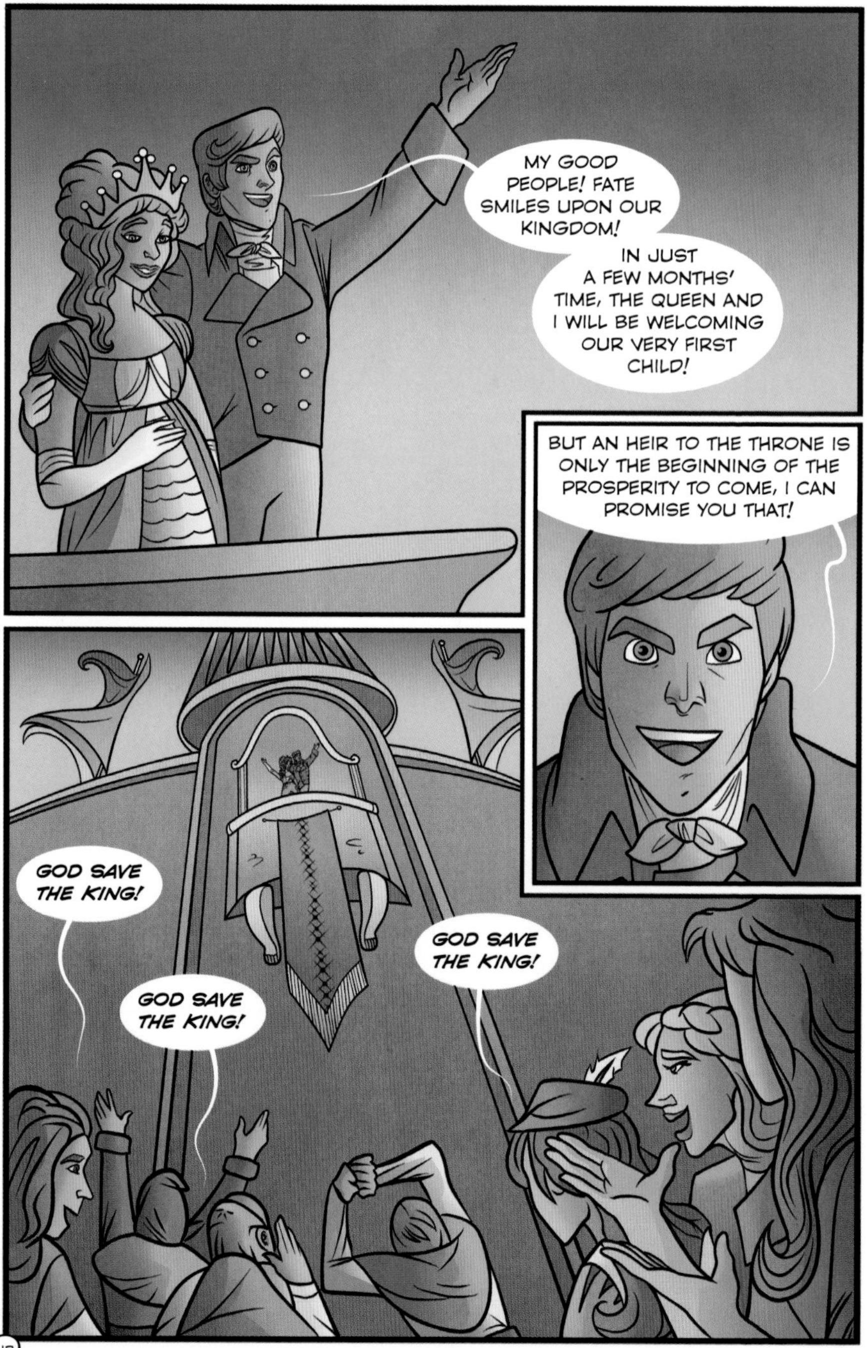
MY GOOD PEOPLE! FATE SMILES UPON OUR KINGDOM!
IN JUST A FEW MONTHS' TIME, THE QUEEN AND I WILL BE WELCOMING OUR VERY FIRST CHILD!
BUT AN HEIR TO THE THRONE IS ONLY THE BEGINNING OF THE PROSPERITY TO COME, I CAN PROMISE YOU THAT!
GOD SAVE THE KING!
GOD SAVE THE KING!
GOD SAVE THE KING!

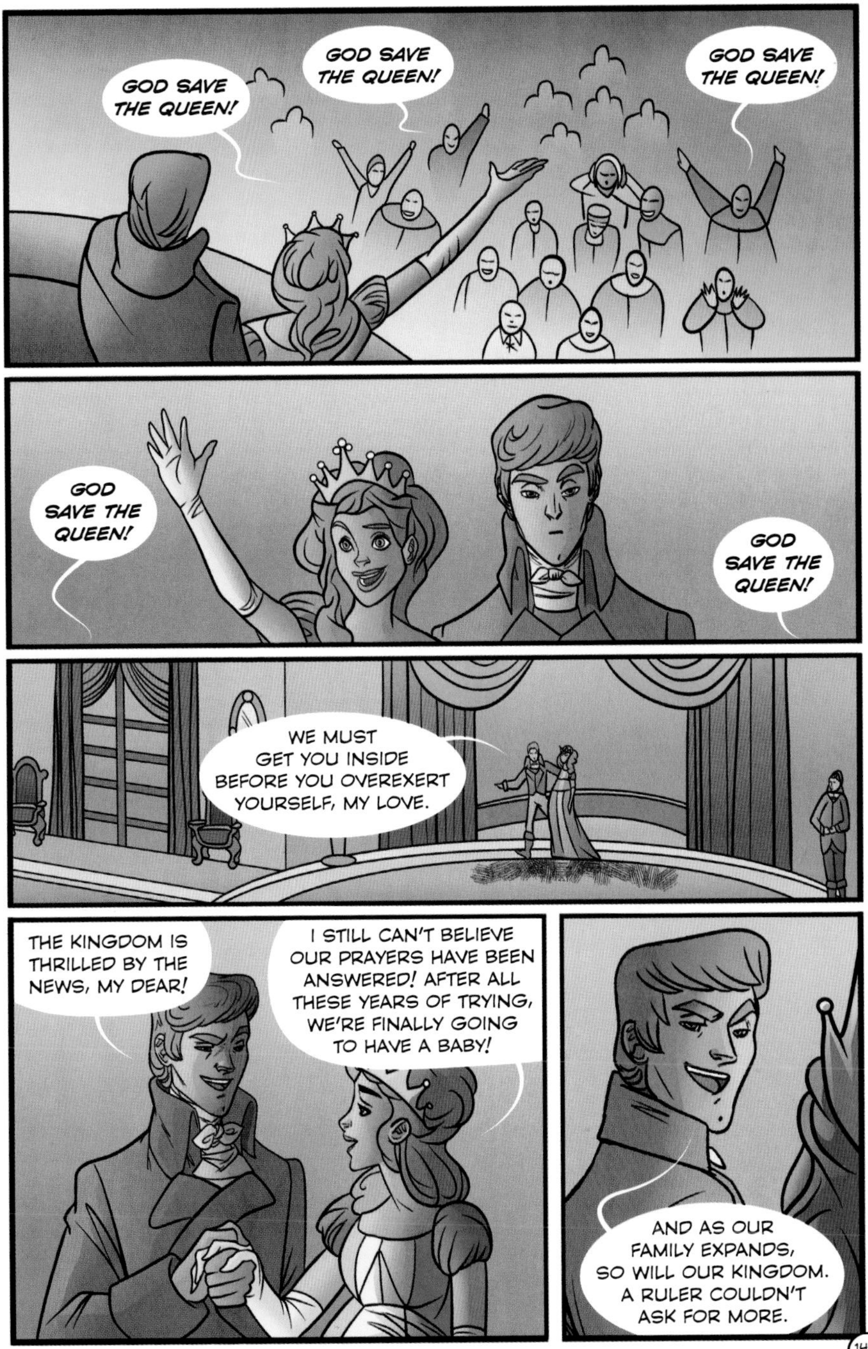
GOD SAVE THE QUEEN!
GOD SAVE THE QUEEN!
GOD SAVE THE QUEEN!
GOD SAVE THE QUEEN!
GOD SAVE THE QUEEN!
WE MUST GET YOU INSIDE BEFORE YOU OVEREXERT YOURSELF, MY LOVE.
THE KINGDOM IS THRILLED BY THE NEWS, MY DEAR!
I STILL CAN'T BELIEVE OUR PRAYERS HAVE BEEN ANSWERED! AFTER ALL THESE YEARS OF TRYING, WE'RE FINALLY GOING TO HAVE A BABY!
AND AS OUR FAMILY EXPANDS, SO WILL OUR KINGDOM. A RULER COULDN'T ASK FOR MORE.

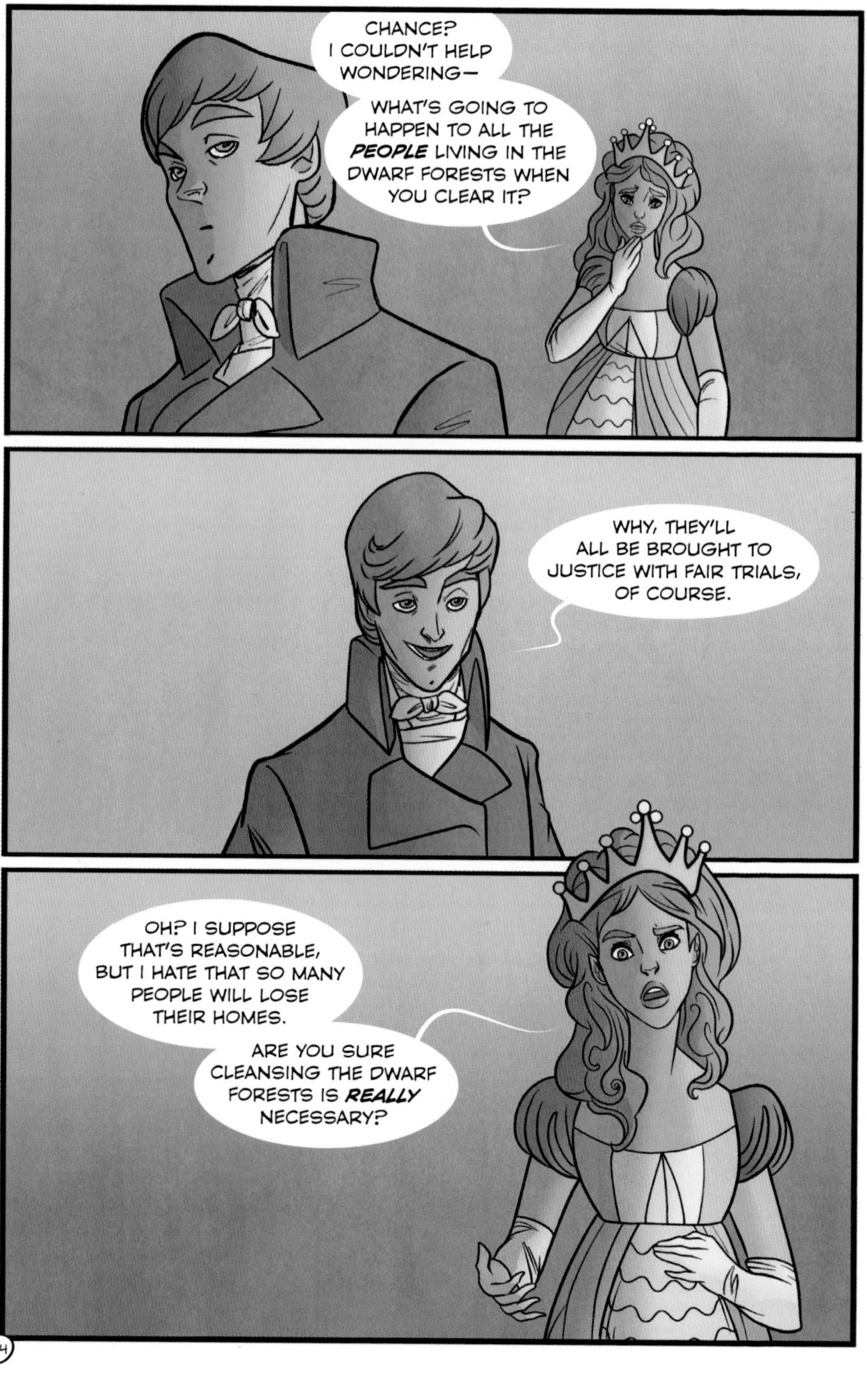
CHANCE? I COULDN'T HELP WONDERING—
WHAT'S GOING TO HAPPEN TO ALL THE *PEOPLE* LIVING IN THE DWARF FORESTS WHEN YOU CLEAR IT?
WHY, THEY'LL ALL BE BROUGHT TO JUSTICE WITH FAIR TRIALS, OF COURSE.
OH? I SUPPOSE THAT'S REASONABLE, BUT I HATE THAT SO MANY PEOPLE WILL LOSE THEIR HOMES.
ARE YOU SURE CLEANSING THE DWARF FORESTS IS *REALLY* NECESSARY?

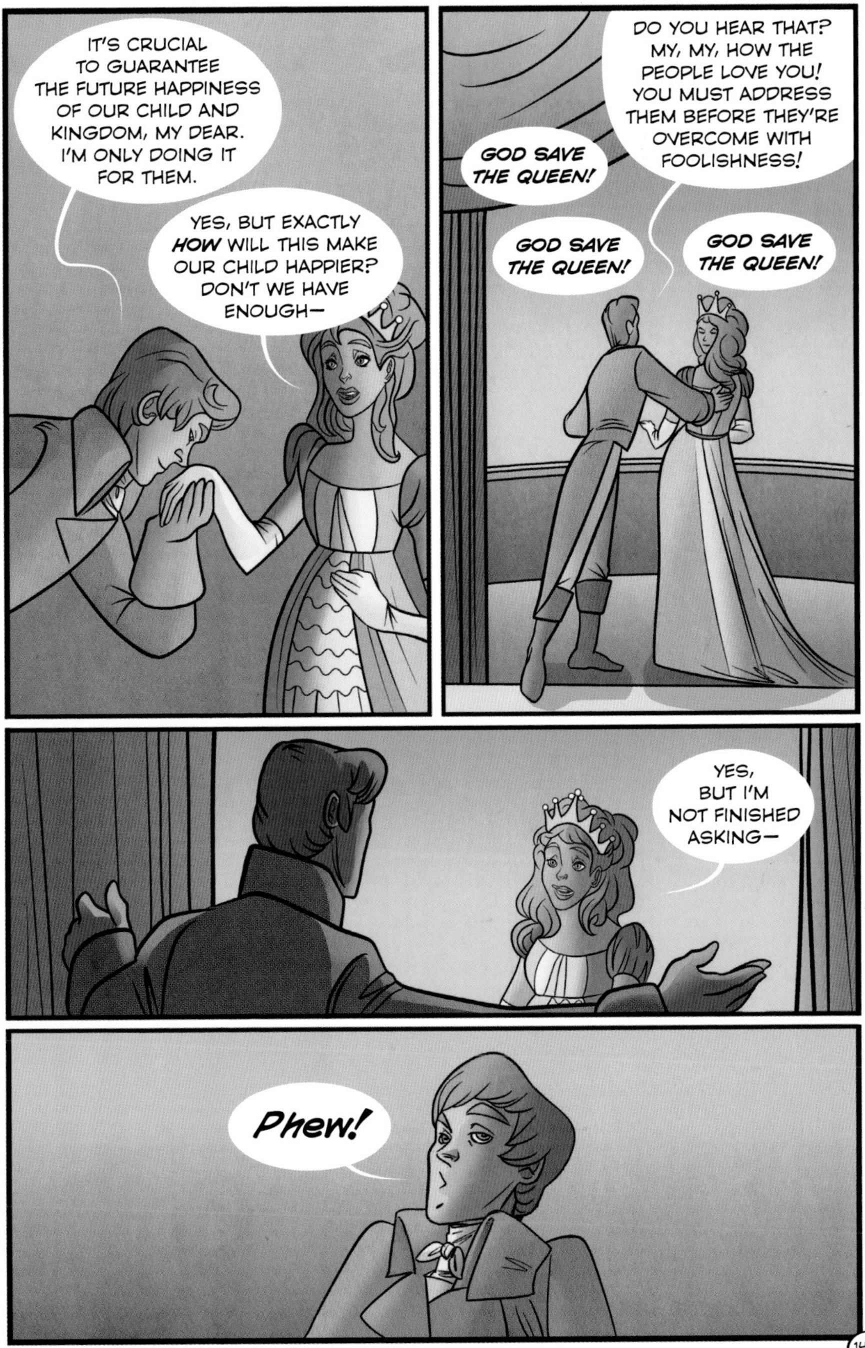

IT'S CRUCIAL TO GUARANTEE THE FUTURE HAPPINESS OF OUR CHILD AND KINGDOM, MY DEAR. I'M ONLY DOING IT FOR THEM.
YES, BUT EXACTLY **HOW** WILL THIS MAKE OUR CHILD HAPPIER? DON'T WE HAVE ENOUGH—
DO YOU HEAR THAT? MY, MY, HOW THE PEOPLE LOVE YOU! YOU MUST ADDRESS THEM BEFORE THEY'RE OVERCOME WITH FOOLISHNESS!
GOD SAVE THE QUEEN!
GOD SAVE THE QUEEN!
GOD SAVE THE QUEEN!
YES, BUT I'M NOT FINISHED ASKING—
Phew!

YOUR MAJESTY, A WORD, SIR?

YES? WHAT IS IT, GENERAL?

ONE OF MY MEN FOUND THIS PINNED TO A TREE IN THE DWARF FORESTS.

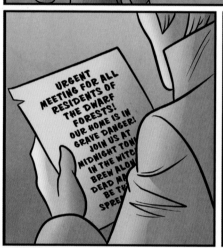

URGENT MEETING FOR ALL RESIDENTS OF THE DWARF FORESTS! OUR HOME IS IN GRAVE DANGER! JOIN US AT MIDNIGHT TON... IN THE WITC... BREW ALON... DEAD M... BE T... SPRE...

SHOULD WE BE CONCERNED?

THEY WOULD HAVE TO ASSEMBLE A VERY POWERFUL DEFENSE IN VERY LITTLE TIME TO STOP OUR ARMY, SIR. IT'S AN UNLIKELY TASK FOR A POPULATION OF DEGENERATES, BUT IT'S SOMETHING TO BE AWARE OF AS WE MOVE FORWARD.

STILL, UNDERESTIMATION IS A RISK I'M NOT WILLING TO TAKE. HOW LONG WOULD IT TAKE TO ASSEMBLE YOUR MEN FOR THE ATTACK?

THREE DAYS AT THE VERY LEAST, SIR.

GOOD. THEN MOVE UP THE INVASION, GENERAL. IN THREE DAYS, WE'LL TAKE THE DWARF FORESTS BY SURPRISE.

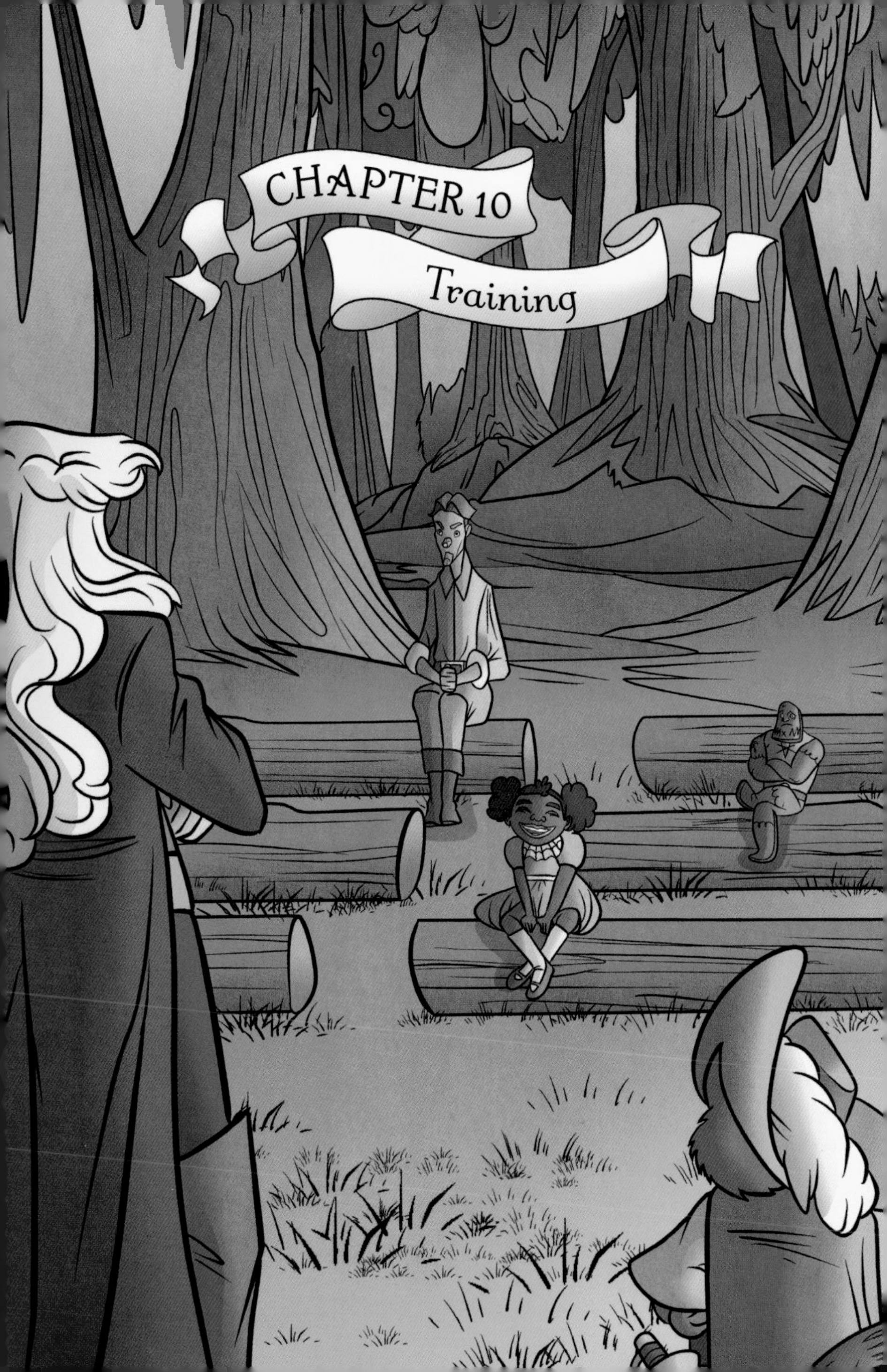
CHAPTER 10
Training

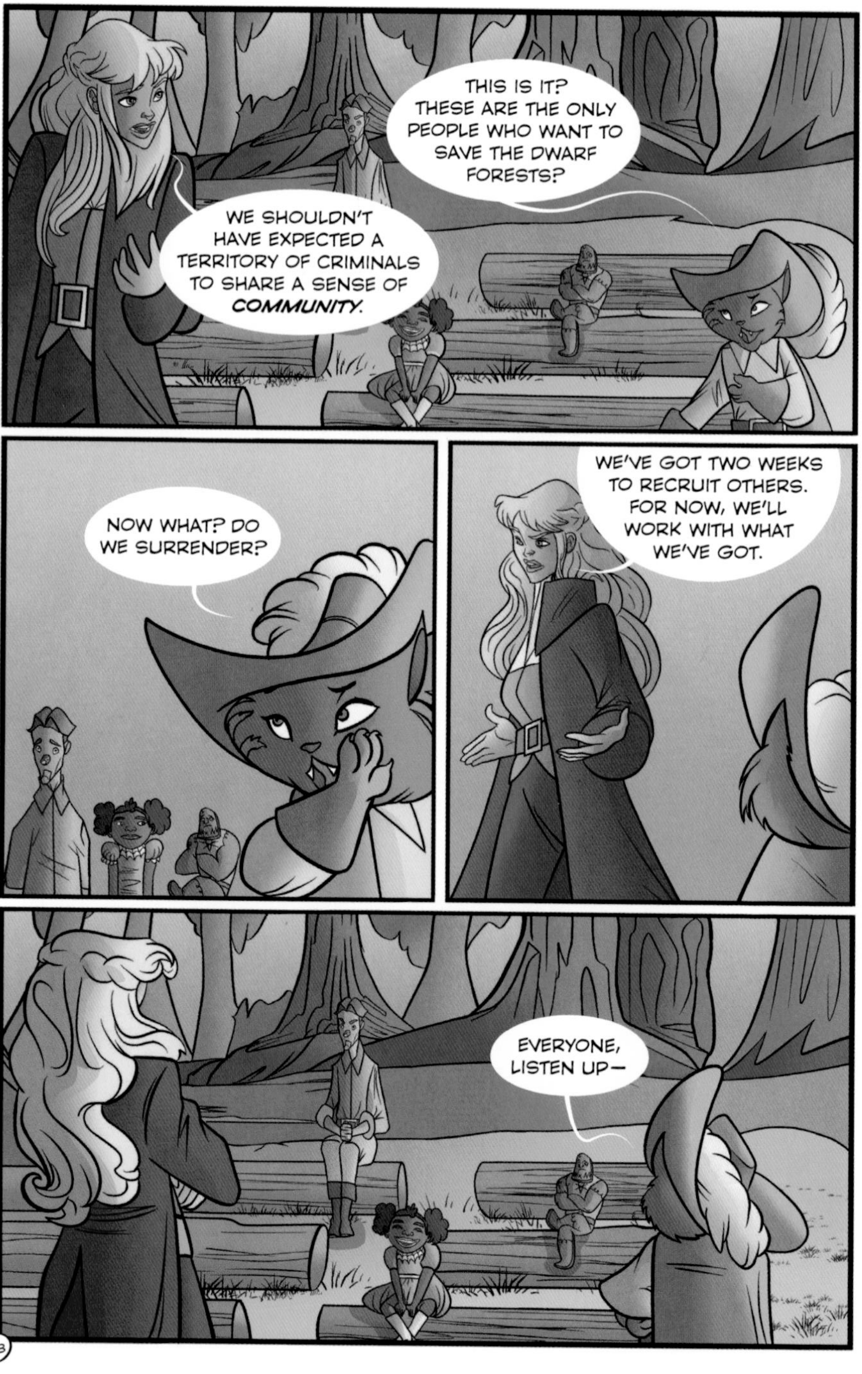
THIS IS IT? THESE ARE THE ONLY PEOPLE WHO WANT TO SAVE THE DWARF FORESTS?
WE SHOULDN'T HAVE EXPECTED A TERRITORY OF CRIMINALS TO SHARE A SENSE OF *COMMUNITY*.
NOW WHAT? DO WE SURRENDER?
WE'VE GOT TWO WEEKS TO RECRUIT OTHERS. FOR NOW, WE'LL WORK WITH WHAT WE'VE GOT.
EVERYONE, LISTEN UP—

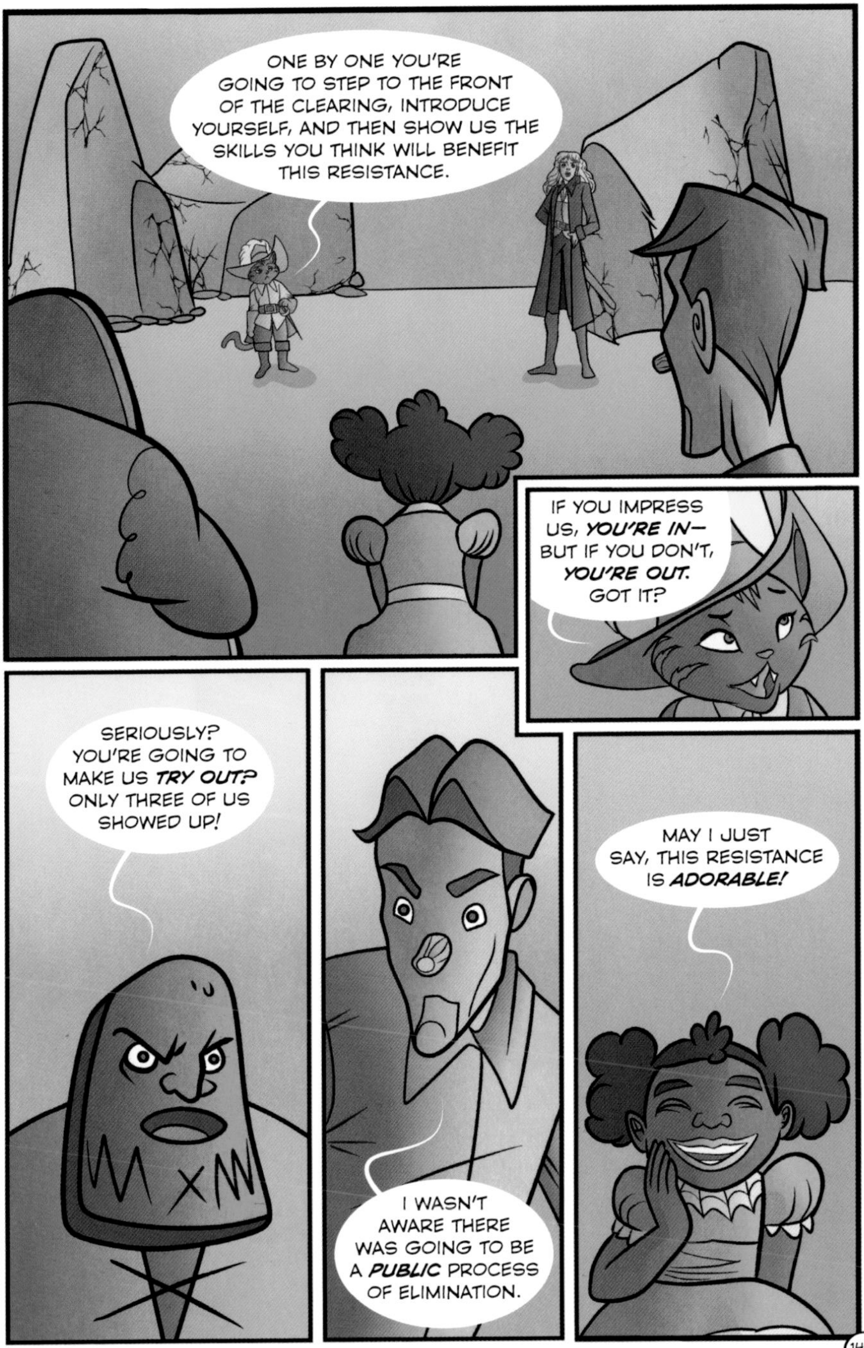
ONE BY ONE YOU'RE GOING TO STEP TO THE FRONT OF THE CLEARING, INTRODUCE YOURSELF, AND THEN SHOW US THE SKILLS YOU THINK WILL BENEFIT THIS RESISTANCE.
IF YOU IMPRESS US, *YOU'RE IN*—BUT IF YOU DON'T, *YOU'RE OUT.* GOT IT?
SERIOUSLY? YOU'RE GOING TO MAKE US *TRY OUT?* ONLY THREE OF US SHOWED UP!
I WASN'T AWARE THERE WAS GOING TO BE A *PUBLIC* PROCESS OF ELIMINATION.
MAY I JUST SAY, THIS RESISTANCE IS *ADORABLE!*

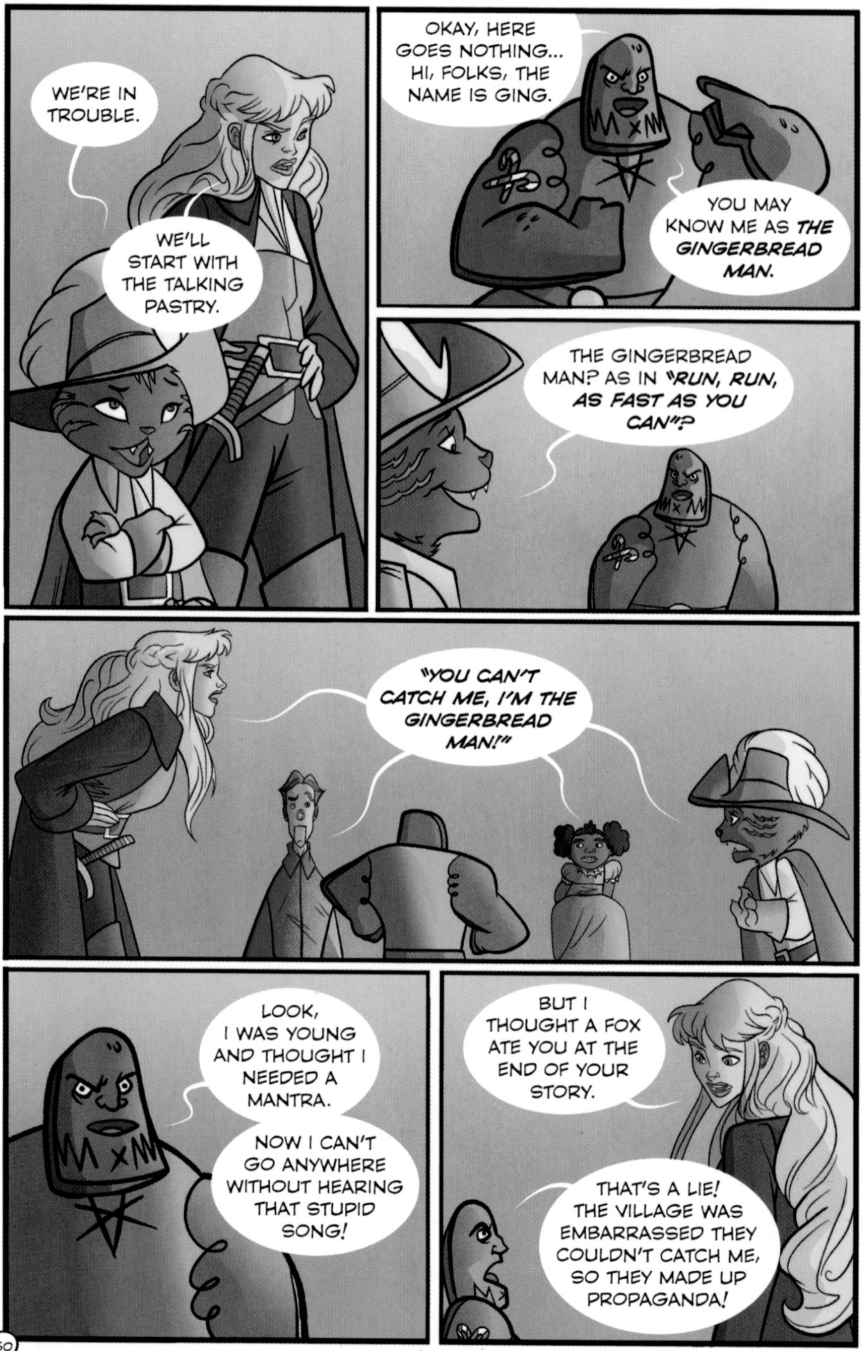

WE'RE IN TROUBLE.
WE'LL START WITH THE TALKING PASTRY.
OKAY, HERE GOES NOTHING... HI, FOLKS, THE NAME IS GING.
YOU MAY KNOW ME AS *THE GINGERBREAD MAN.*
THE GINGERBREAD MAN? AS IN *"RUN, RUN, AS FAST AS YOU CAN"?*
"YOU CAN'T CATCH ME, I'M THE GINGERBREAD MAN!"
LOOK, I WAS YOUNG AND THOUGHT I NEEDED A MANTRA.
NOW I CAN'T GO ANYWHERE WITHOUT HEARING THAT STUPID SONG!
BUT I THOUGHT A FOX ATE YOU AT THE END OF YOUR STORY.
THAT'S A LIE! THE VILLAGE WAS EMBARRASSED THEY COULDN'T CATCH ME, SO THEY MADE UP PROPAGANDA!

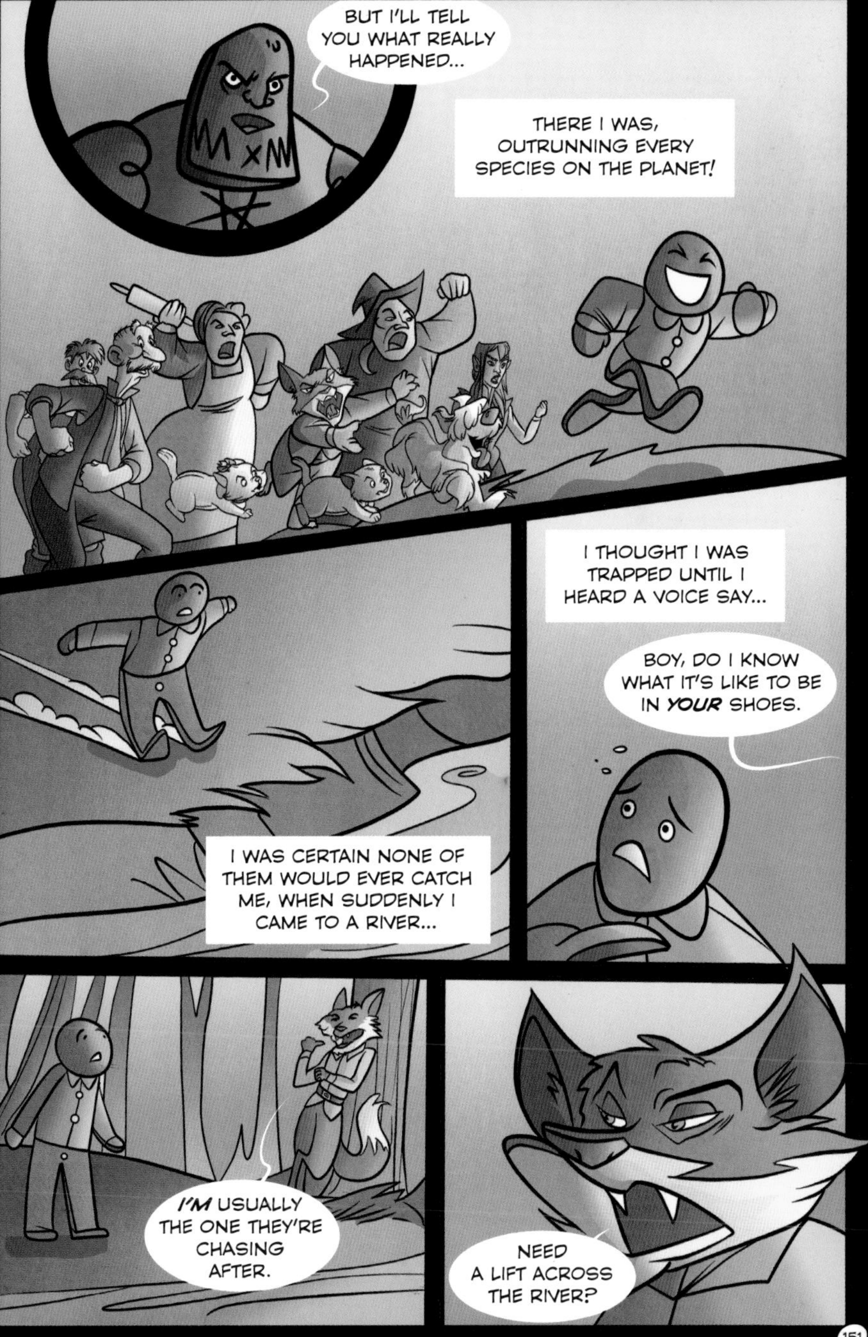
BUT I'LL TELL YOU WHAT REALLY HAPPENED...
THERE I WAS, OUTRUNNING EVERY SPECIES ON THE PLANET!
I WAS CERTAIN NONE OF THEM WOULD EVER CATCH ME, WHEN SUDDENLY I CAME TO A RIVER...
I THOUGHT I WAS TRAPPED UNTIL I HEARD A VOICE SAY...
BOY, DO I KNOW WHAT IT'S LIKE TO BE IN *YOUR* SHOES.
I'M USUALLY THE ONE THEY'RE CHASING AFTER.
NEED A LIFT ACROSS THE RIVER?

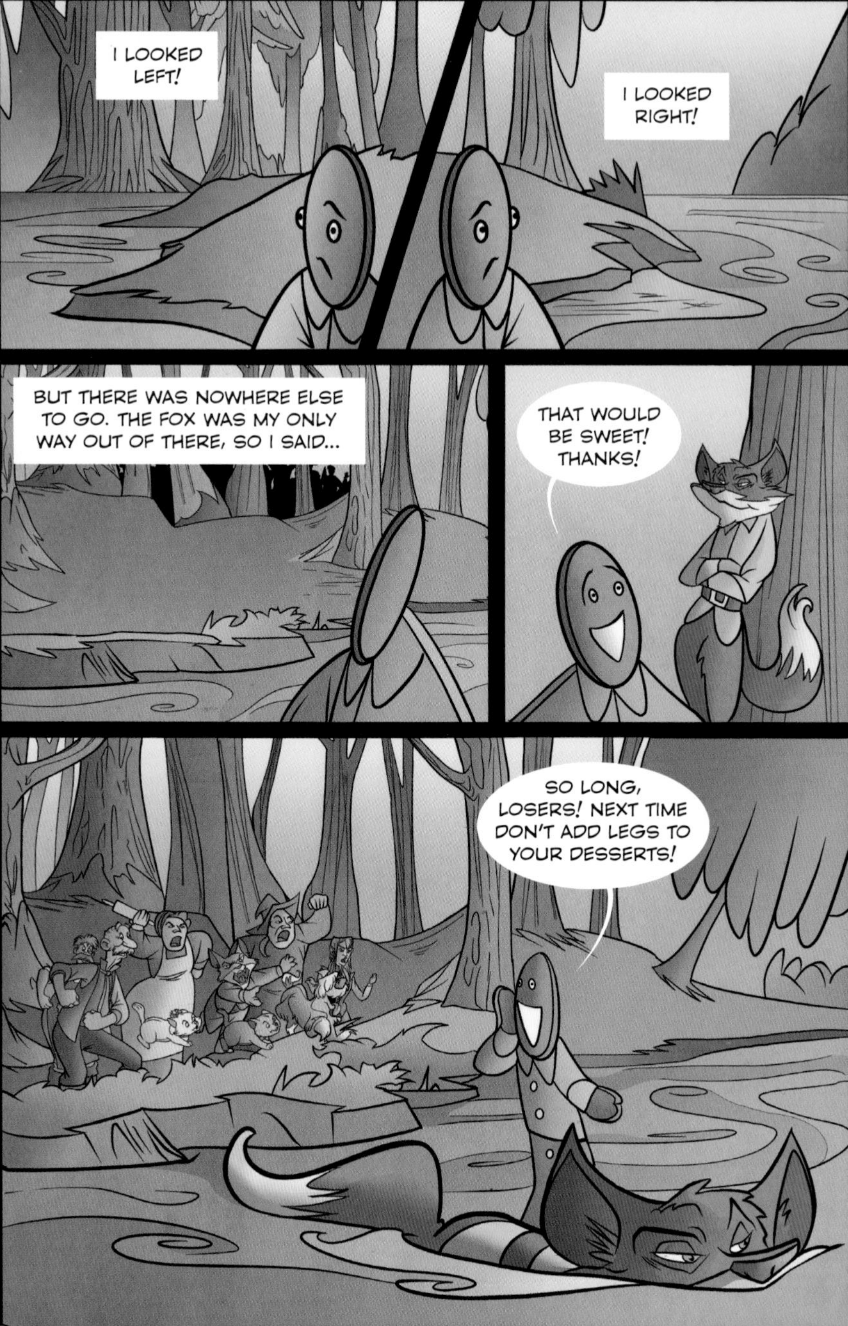
I LOOKED LEFT!
I LOOKED RIGHT!
BUT THERE WAS NOWHERE ELSE TO GO. THE FOX WAS MY ONLY WAY OUT OF THERE, SO I SAID...
THAT WOULD BE SWEET! THANKS!
SO LONG, LOSERS! NEXT TIME DON'T ADD LEGS TO YOUR DESSERTS!

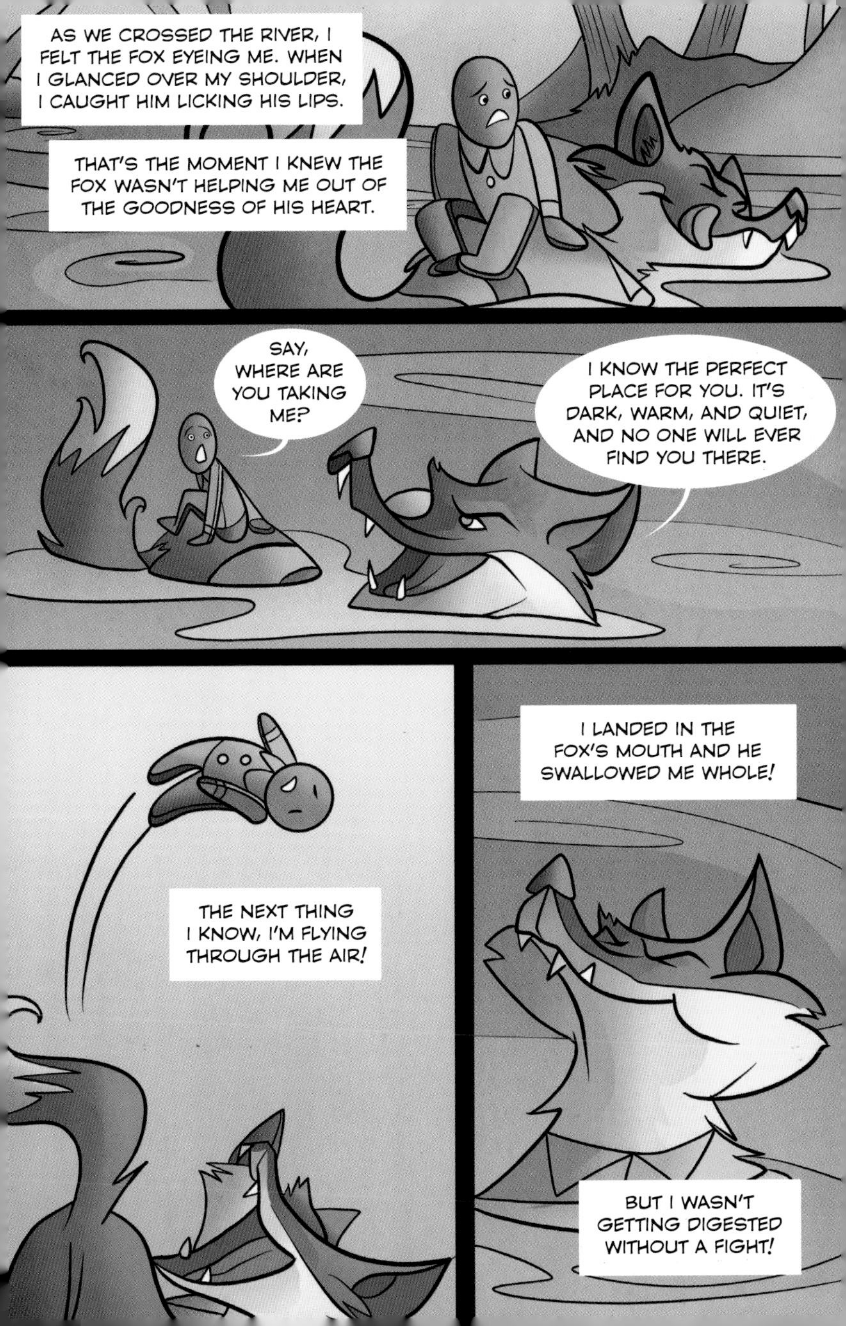
AS WE CROSSED THE RIVER, I FELT THE FOX EYEING ME. WHEN I GLANCED OVER MY SHOULDER, I CAUGHT HIM LICKING HIS LIPS.
THAT'S THE MOMENT I KNEW THE FOX WASN'T HELPING ME OUT OF THE GOODNESS OF HIS HEART.
SAY, WHERE ARE YOU TAKING ME?
I KNOW THE PERFECT PLACE FOR YOU. IT'S DARK, WARM, AND QUIET, AND NO ONE WILL EVER FIND YOU THERE.
THE NEXT THING I KNOW, I'M FLYING THROUGH THE AIR!
I LANDED IN THE FOX'S MOUTH AND HE SWALLOWED ME WHOLE!
BUT I WASN'T GETTING DIGESTED WITHOUT A FIGHT!

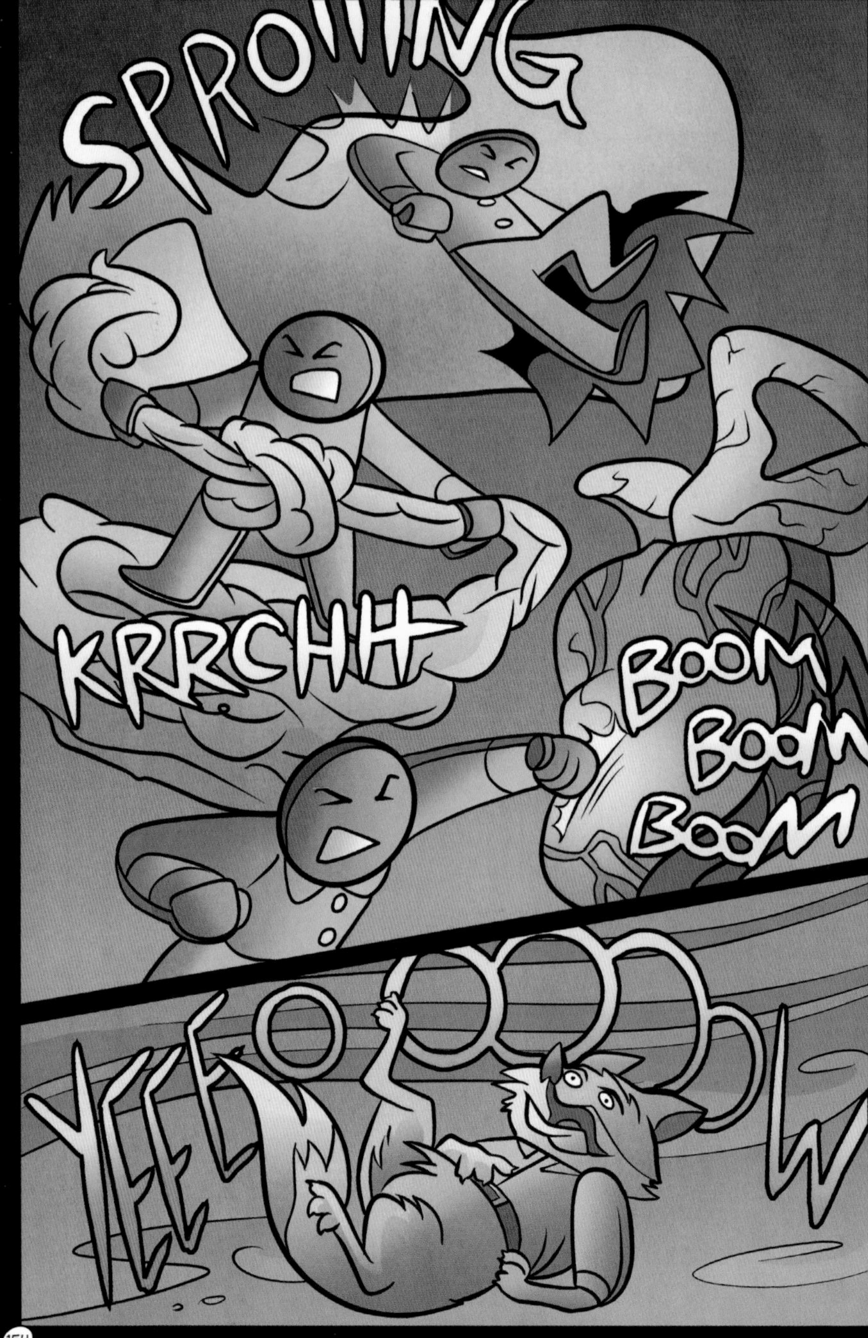
SPROIIING
KRRCHH
BOOM
BOOM
BOOM
YEEEOOOOOW

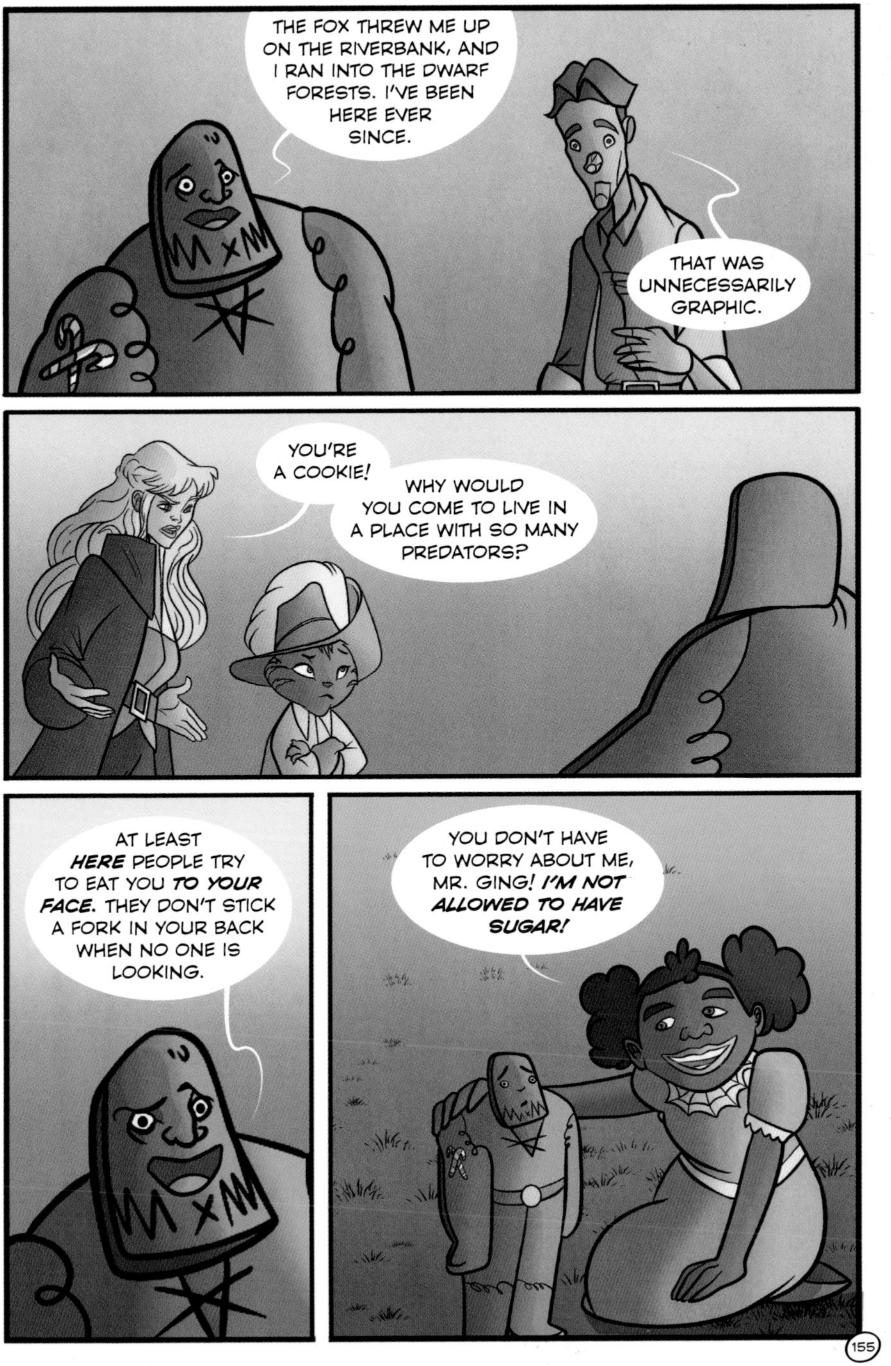
THE FOX THREW ME UP ON THE RIVERBANK, AND I RAN INTO THE DWARF FORESTS. I'VE BEEN HERE EVER SINCE.
THAT WAS UNNECESSARILY GRAPHIC.
YOU'RE A COOKIE!
WHY WOULD YOU COME TO LIVE IN A PLACE WITH SO MANY PREDATORS?
AT LEAST ***HERE*** PEOPLE TRY TO EAT YOU ***TO YOUR FACE.*** THEY DON'T STICK A FORK IN YOUR BACK WHEN NO ONE IS LOOKING.
YOU DON'T HAVE TO WORRY ABOUT ME, MR. GING! ***I'M NOT ALLOWED TO HAVE SUGAR!***

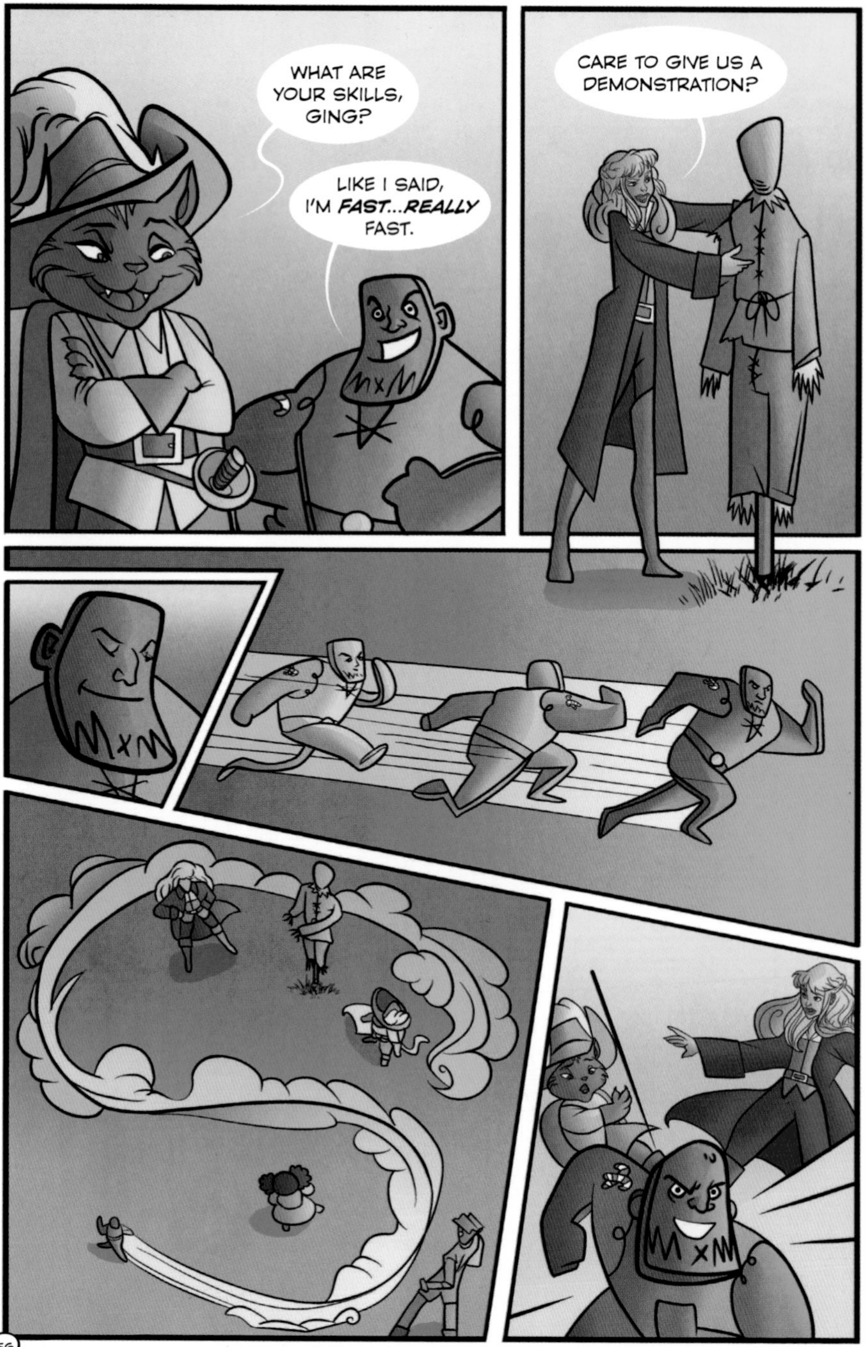
WHAT ARE YOUR SKILLS, GING?
LIKE I SAID, I'M ***FAST...REALLY*** FAST.
CARE TO GIVE US A DEMONSTRATION?

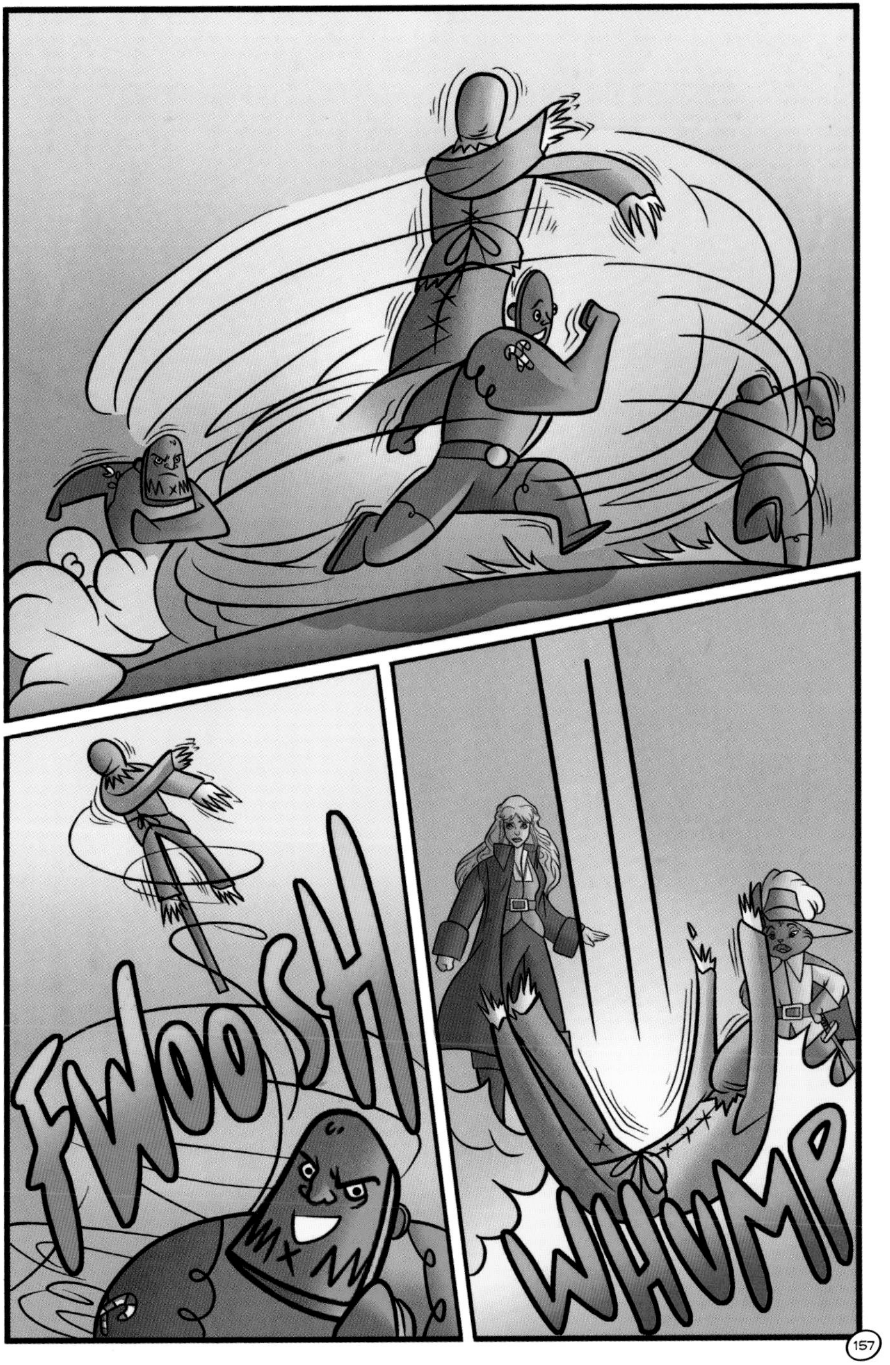
FWOOSH
WHUMP

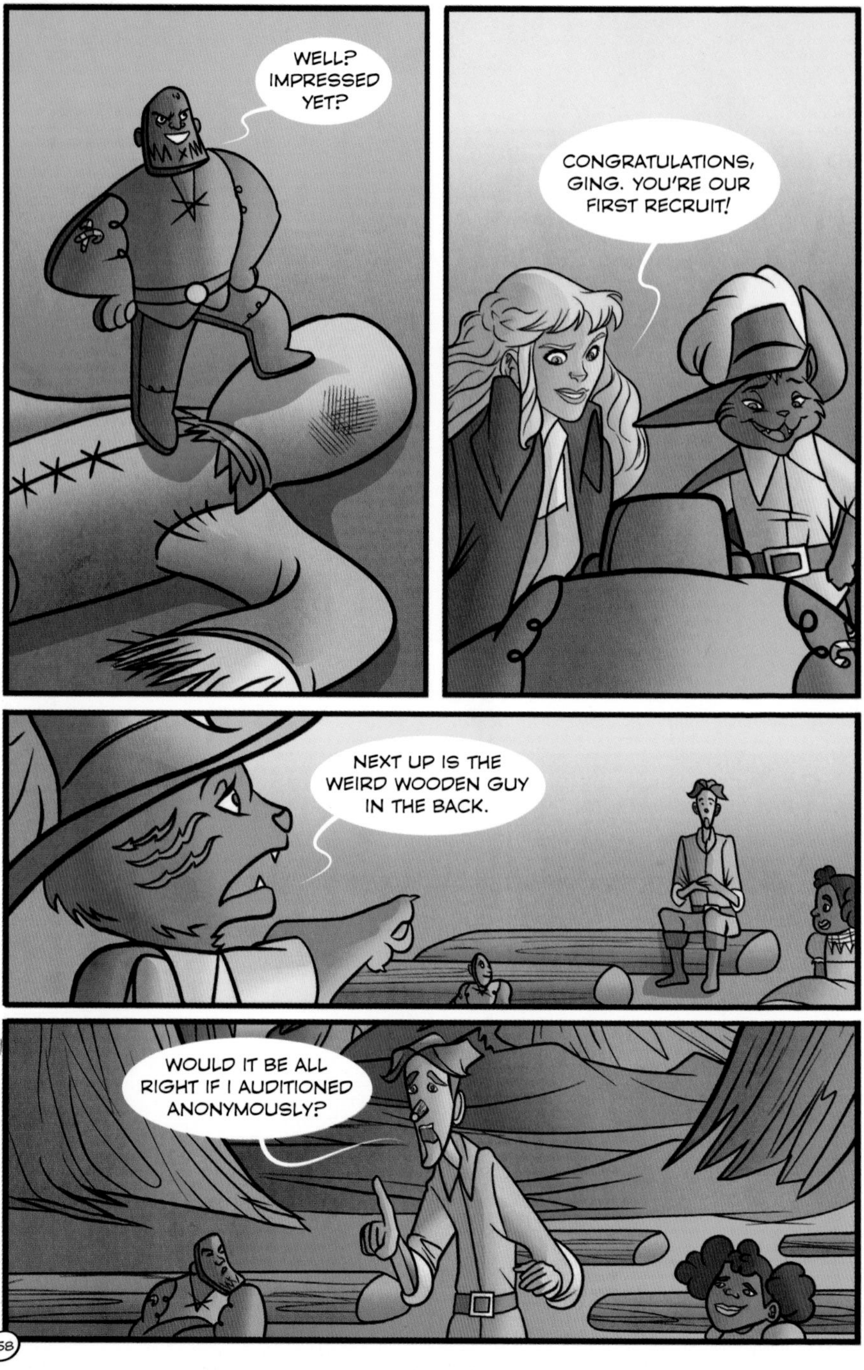
WELL? IMPRESSED YET?
CONGRATULATIONS, GING. YOU'RE OUR FIRST RECRUIT!
NEXT UP IS THE WEIRD WOODEN GUY IN THE BACK.
WOULD IT BE ALL RIGHT IF I AUDITIONED ANONYMOUSLY?

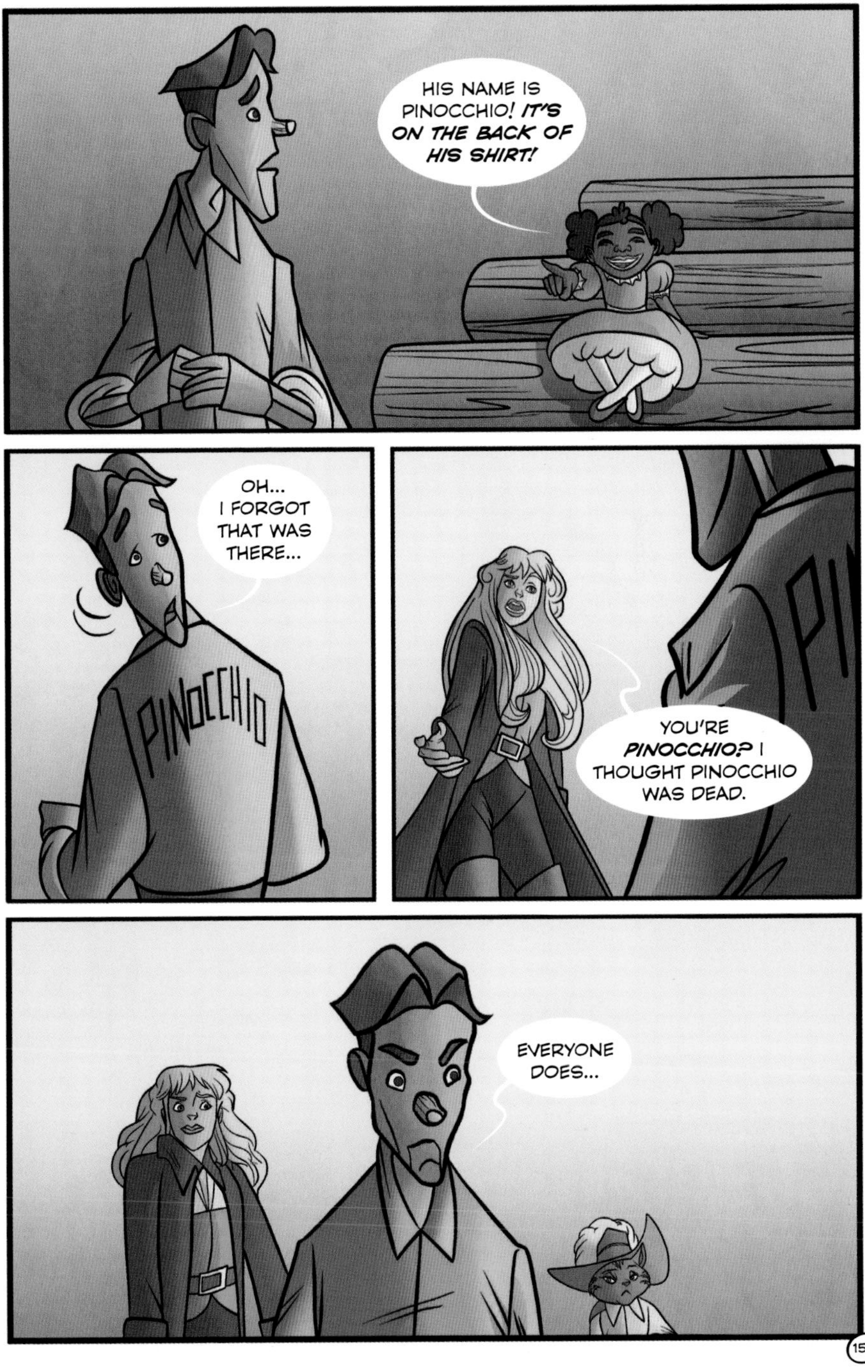
HIS NAME IS PINOCCHIO! *IT'S ON THE BACK OF HIS SHIRT!*
OH... I FORGOT THAT WAS THERE...
PINOCCHIO
YOU'RE *PINOCCHIO?* I THOUGHT PINOCCHIO WAS DEAD.
EVERYONE DOES...

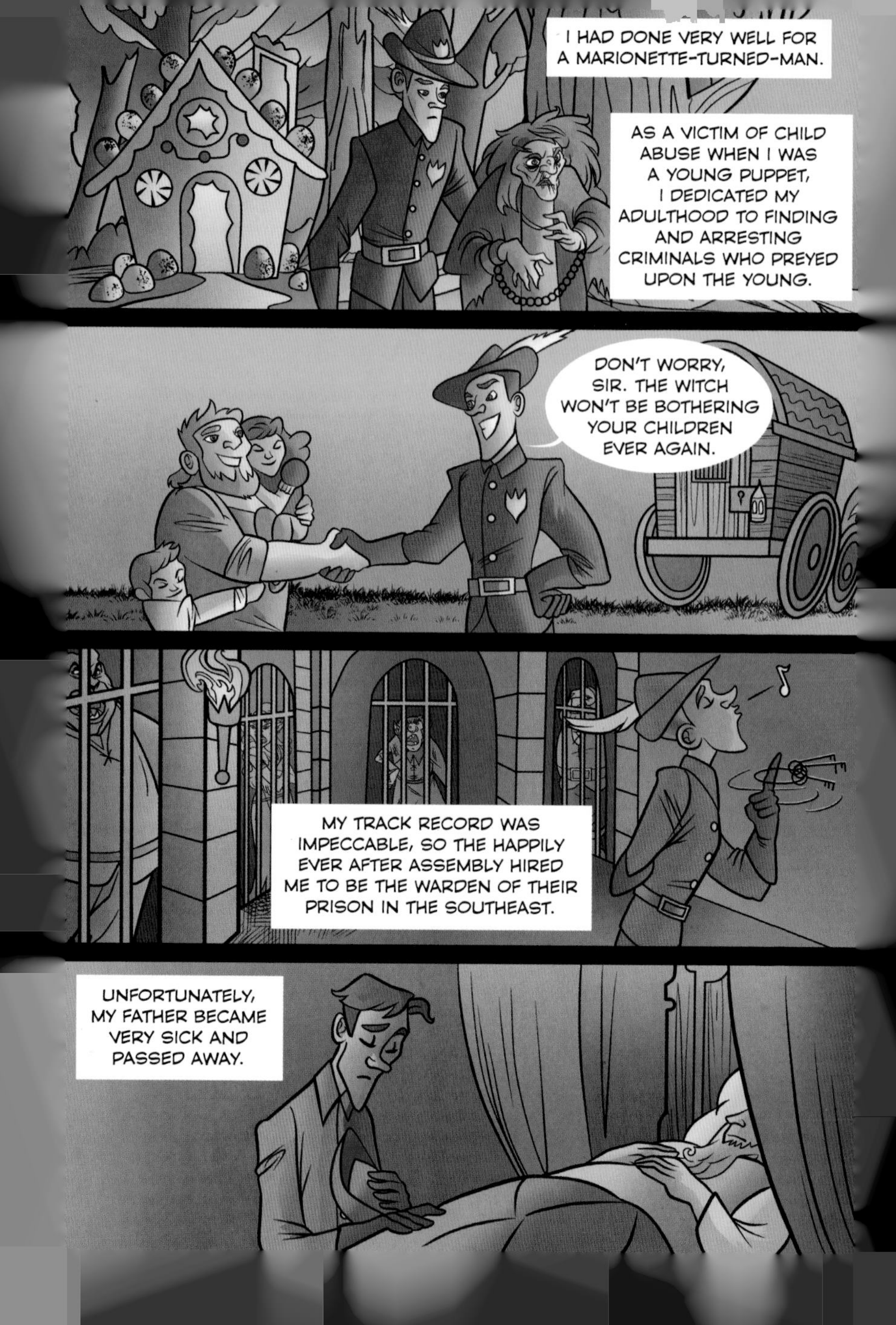
I HAD DONE VERY WELL FOR A MARIONETTE-TURNED-MAN.
AS A VICTIM OF CHILD ABUSE WHEN I WAS A YOUNG PUPPET, I DEDICATED MY ADULTHOOD TO FINDING AND ARRESTING CRIMINALS WHO PREYED UPON THE YOUNG.
DON'T WORRY, SIR. THE WITCH WON'T BE BOTHERING YOUR CHILDREN EVER AGAIN.
MY TRACK RECORD WAS IMPECCABLE, SO THE HAPPILY EVER AFTER ASSEMBLY HIRED ME TO BE THE WARDEN OF THEIR PRISON IN THE SOUTHEAST.
UNFORTUNATELY, MY FATHER BECAME VERY SICK AND PASSED AWAY.

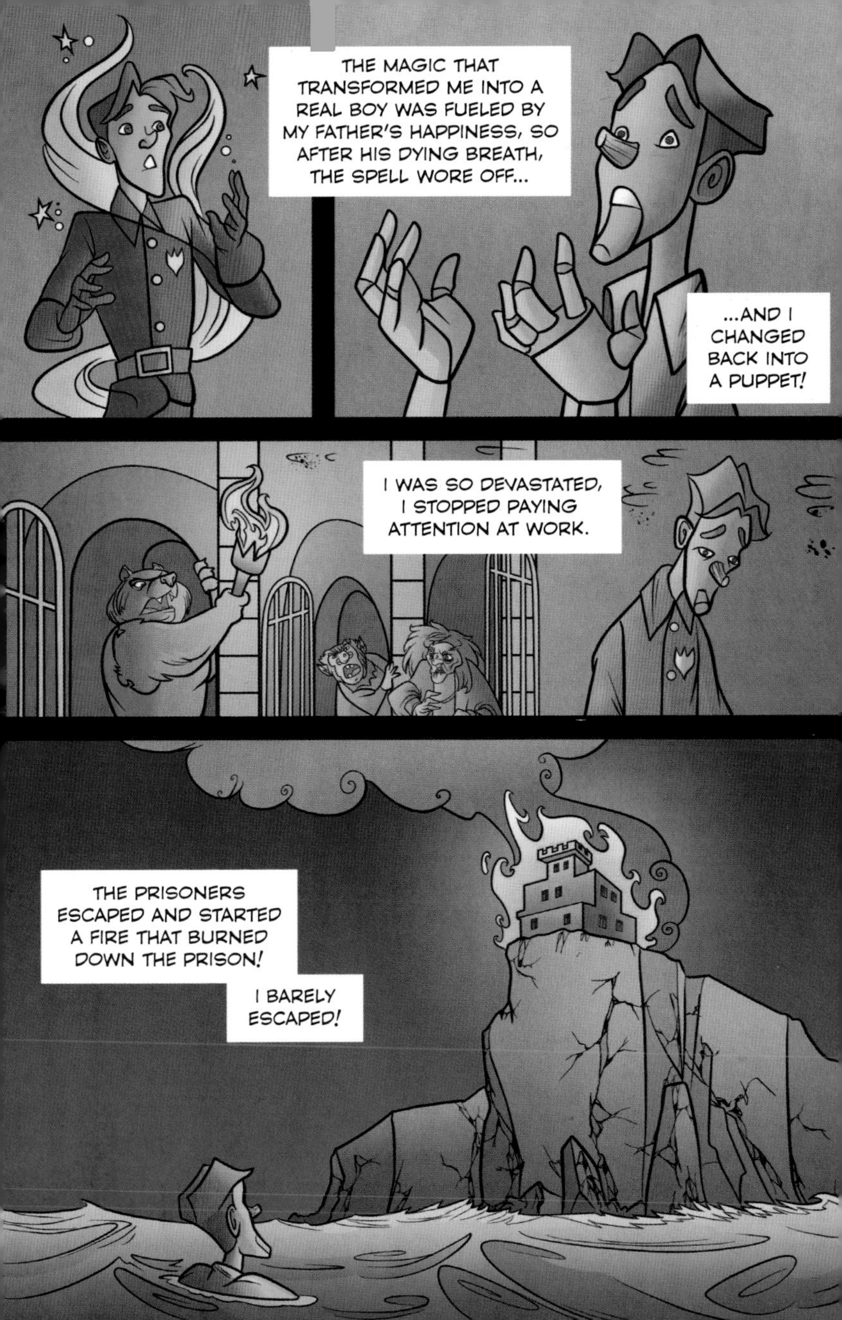
THE MAGIC THAT TRANSFORMED ME INTO A REAL BOY WAS FUELED BY MY FATHER'S HAPPINESS, SO AFTER HIS DYING BREATH, THE SPELL WORE OFF...
...AND I CHANGED BACK INTO A PUPPET!
I WAS SO DEVASTATED, I STOPPED PAYING ATTENTION AT WORK.
THE PRISONERS ESCAPED AND STARTED A FIRE THAT BURNED DOWN THE PRISON!
I BARELY ESCAPED!

EVERYONE ASSUMED I HAD PERISHED IN THE FIRE. THE HAPPILY EVER AFTER ASSEMBLY REBUILT THE PRISON AND NAMED IT PINOCCHIO PRISON IN MY HONOR.

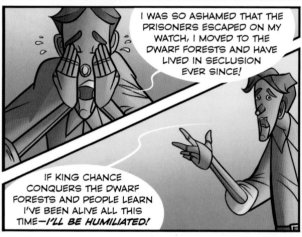

I WAS SO ASHAMED THAT THE PRISONERS ESCAPED ON MY WATCH, I MOVED TO THE DWARF FORESTS AND HAVE LIVED IN SECLUSION EVER SINCE!

IF KING CHANCE CONQUERS THE DWARF FORESTS AND PEOPLE LEARN I'VE BEEN ALIVE ALL THIS TIME—*I'LL BE HUMILIATED!*

AND HOW WILL *YOU* HELP US FIGHT?

I HAVE A FEW *TALENTS* THAT MAY COME IN HANDY.

THEN BY ALL MEANS, SHOW US.

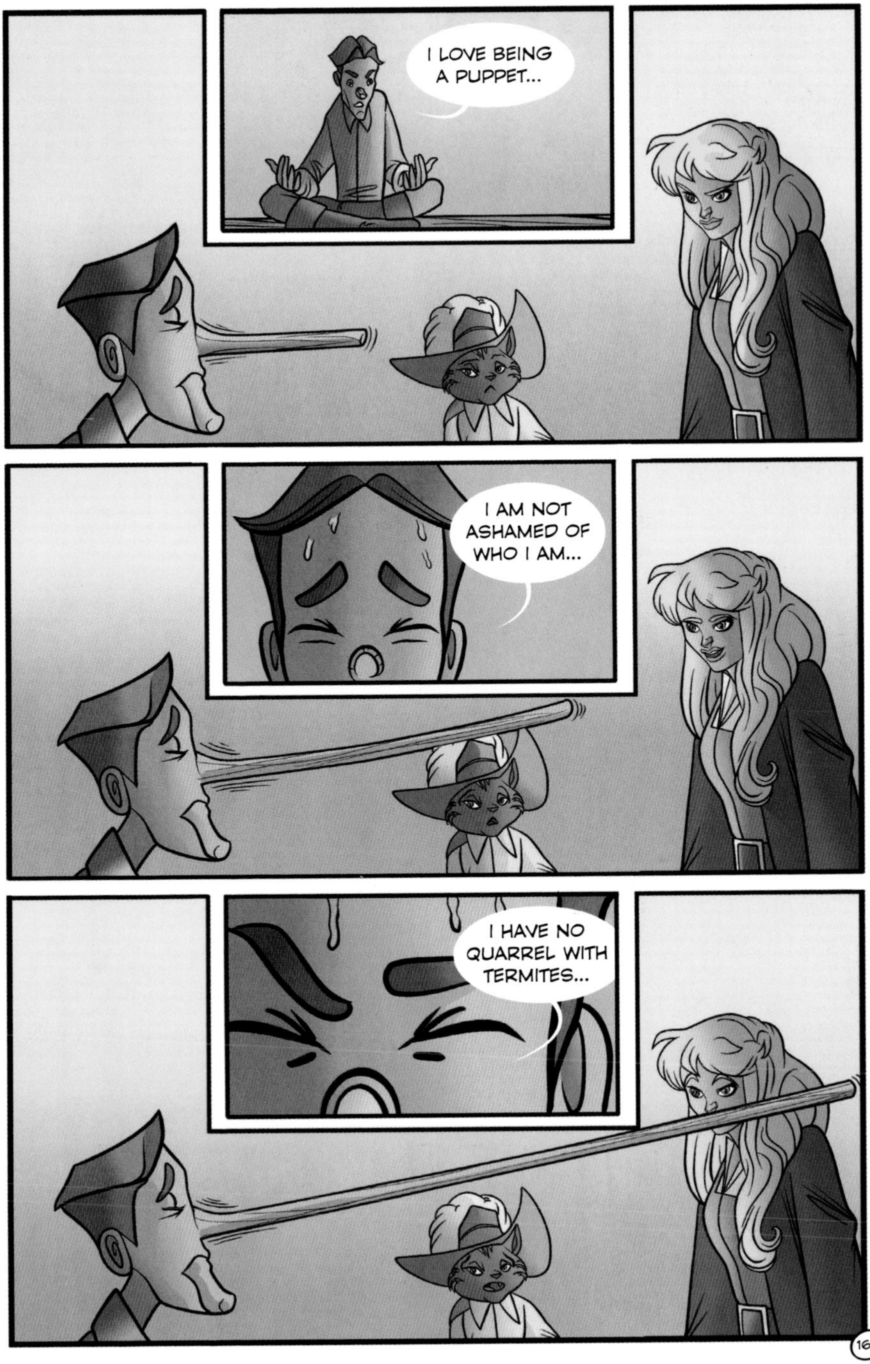
I LOVE BEING A PUPPET...
I AM NOT ASHAMED OF WHO I AM...
I HAVE NO QUARREL WITH TERMITES...

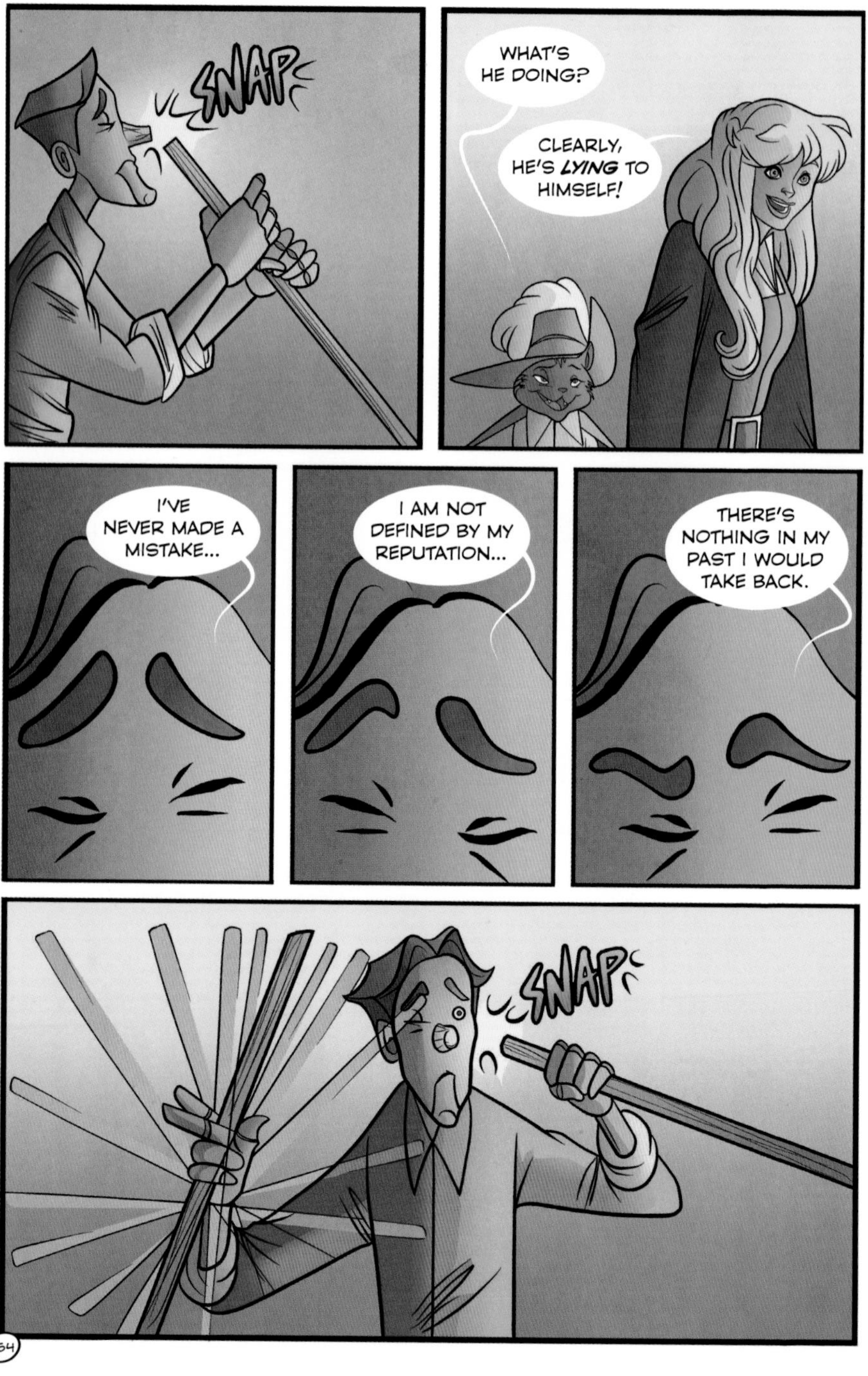
SNAP
WHAT'S HE DOING?
CLEARLY, HE'S *LYING* TO HIMSELF!
I'VE NEVER MADE A MISTAKE...
I AM NOT DEFINED BY MY REPUTATION...
THERE'S NOTHING IN MY PAST I WOULD TAKE BACK.
SNAP

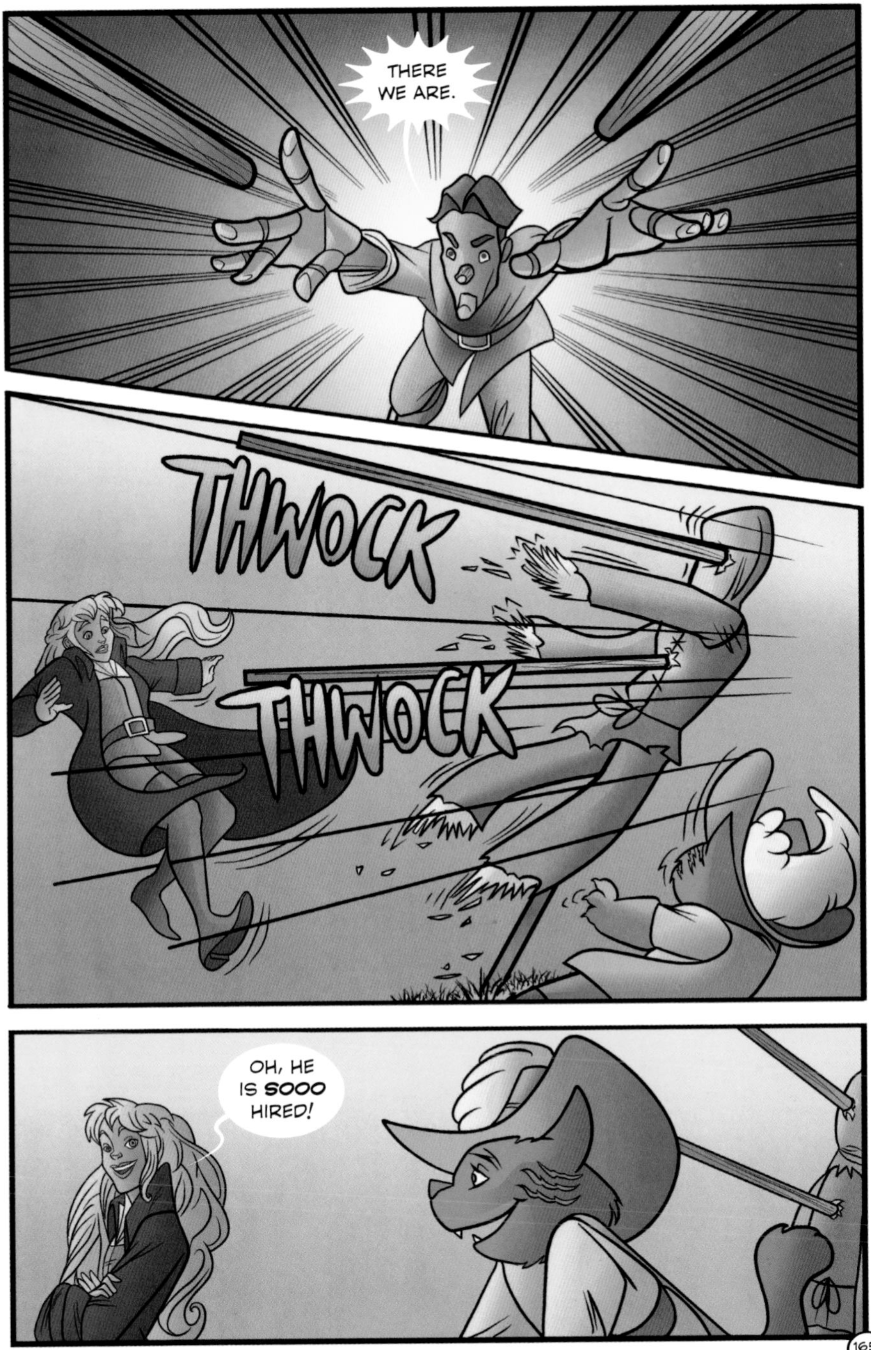
THERE WE ARE.
THWOCK
THWOCK
OH, HE IS **SOOO** HIRED!

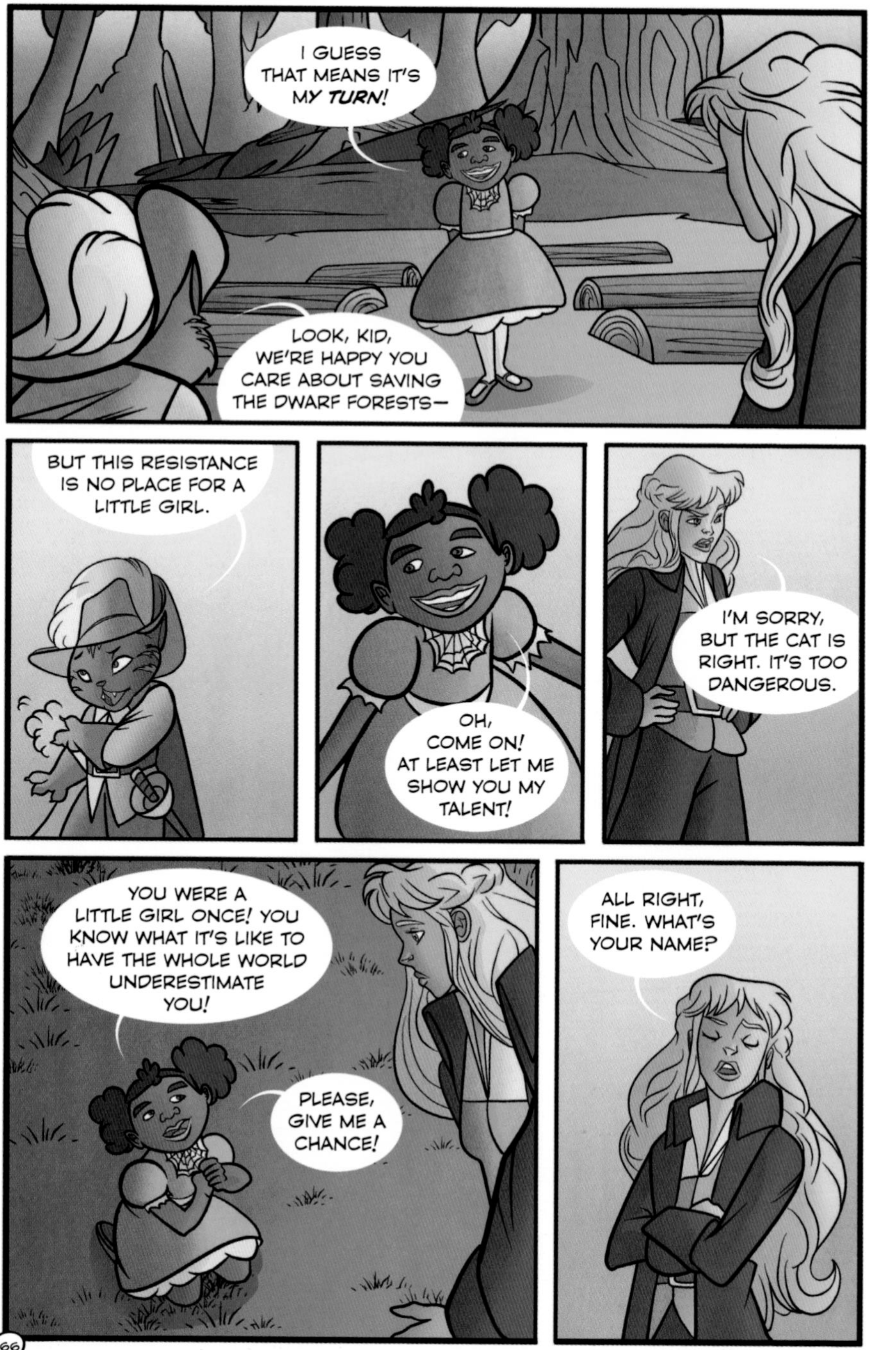
I GUESS THAT MEANS IT'S MY *TURN*!
LOOK, KID, WE'RE HAPPY YOU CARE ABOUT SAVING THE DWARF FORESTS—
BUT THIS RESISTANCE IS NO PLACE FOR A LITTLE GIRL.
OH, COME ON! AT LEAST LET ME SHOW YOU MY TALENT!
I'M SORRY, BUT THE CAT IS RIGHT. IT'S TOO DANGEROUS.
YOU WERE A LITTLE GIRL ONCE! YOU KNOW WHAT IT'S LIKE TO HAVE THE WHOLE WORLD UNDERESTIMATE YOU!
PLEASE, GIVE ME A CHANCE!
ALL RIGHT, FINE. WHAT'S YOUR NAME?

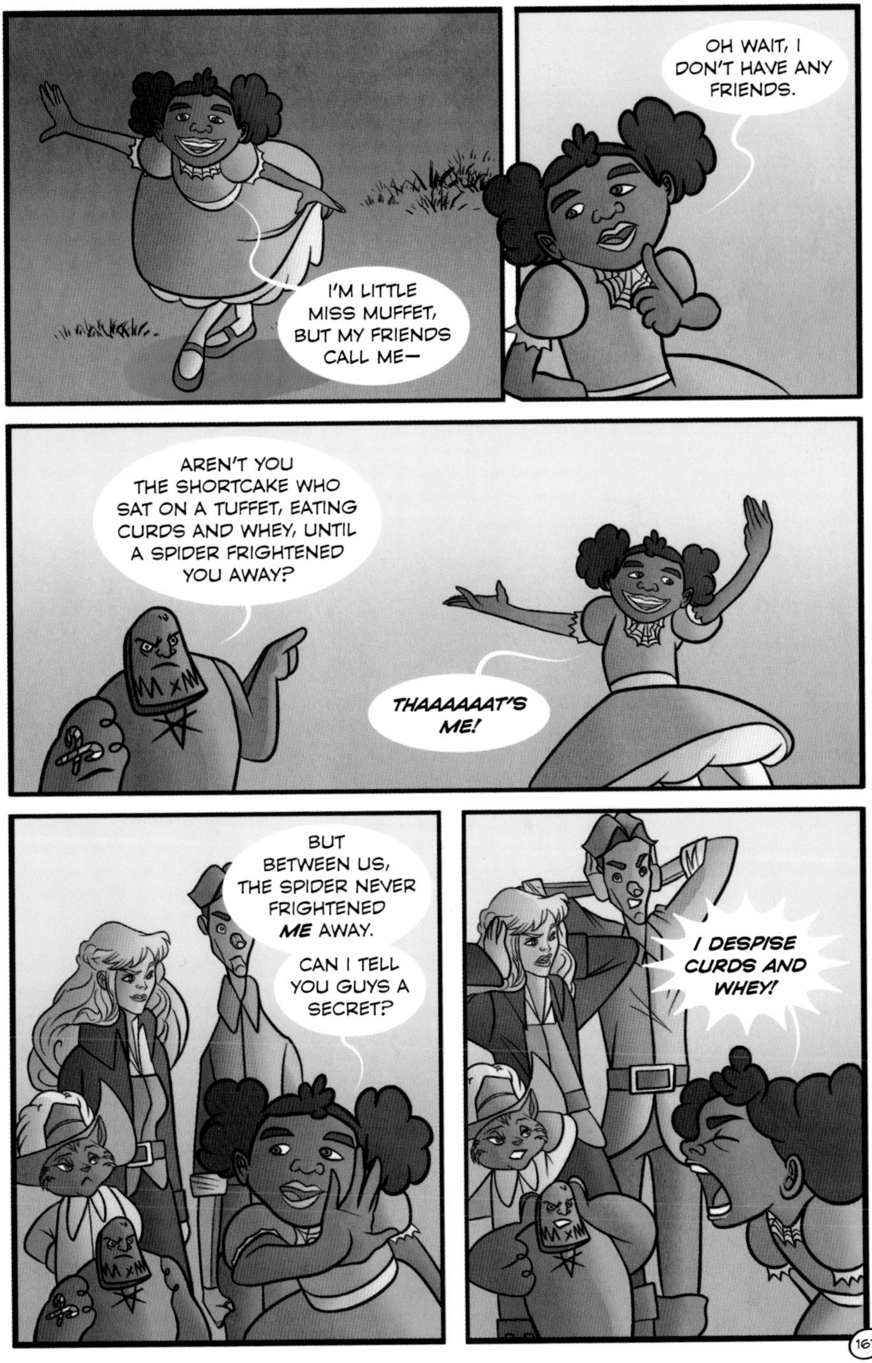
I'M LITTLE MISS MUFFET, BUT MY FRIENDS CALL ME—
OH WAIT, I DON'T HAVE ANY FRIENDS.
AREN'T YOU THE SHORTCAKE WHO SAT ON A TUFFET, EATING CURDS AND WHEY, UNTIL A SPIDER FRIGHTENED YOU AWAY?
THAAAAAAT'S ME!
BUT BETWEEN US, THE SPIDER NEVER FRIGHTENED ME AWAY.
CAN I TELL YOU GUYS A SECRET?
I DESPISE CURDS AND WHEY!

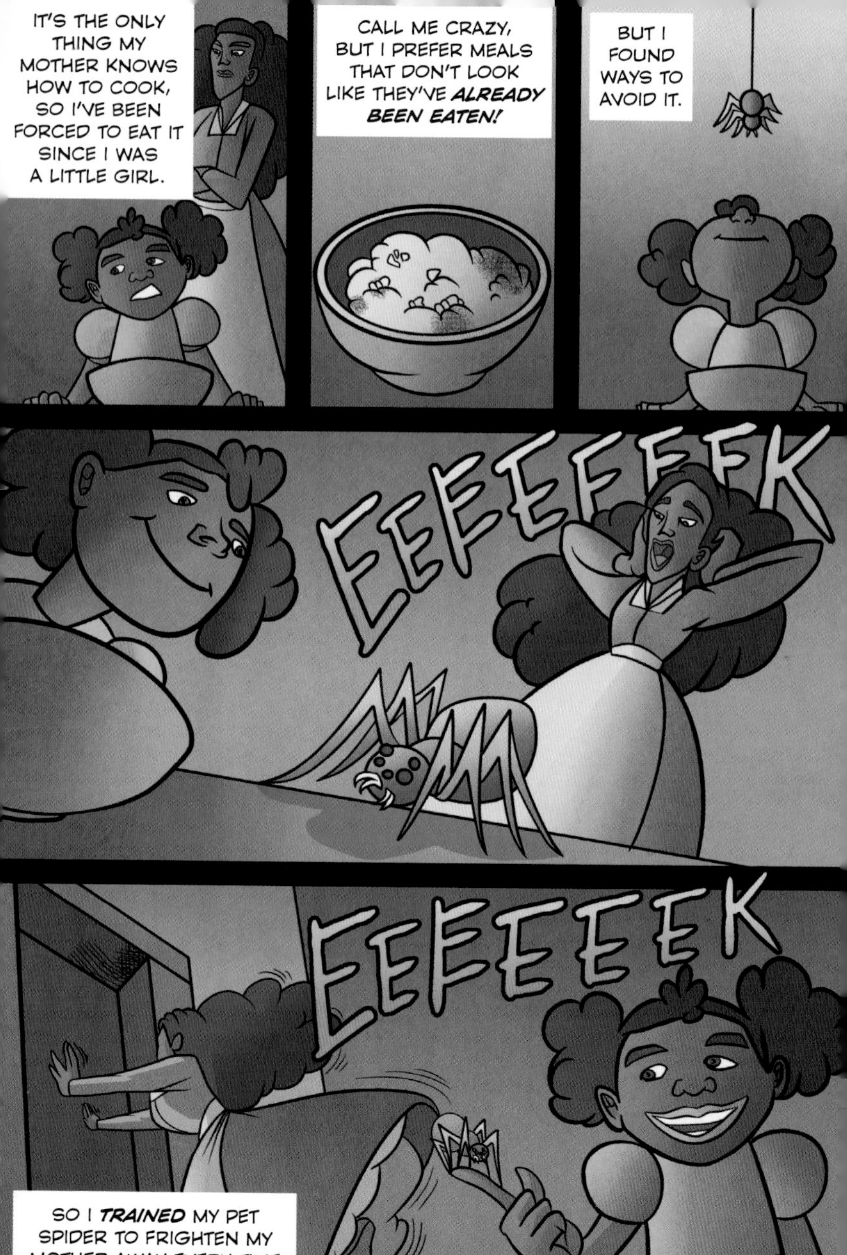
IT'S THE ONLY THING MY MOTHER KNOWS HOW TO COOK, SO I'VE BEEN FORCED TO EAT IT SINCE I WAS A LITTLE GIRL.
CALL ME CRAZY, BUT I PREFER MEALS THAT DON'T LOOK LIKE THEY'VE *ALREADY BEEN EATEN!*
BUT I FOUND WAYS TO AVOID IT.
EEEEEEEK
EEEEEEEK
SO I *TRAINED* MY PET SPIDER TO FRIGHTEN MY MOTHER AWAY EVERY TIME SHE MAKES ME EAT IT!

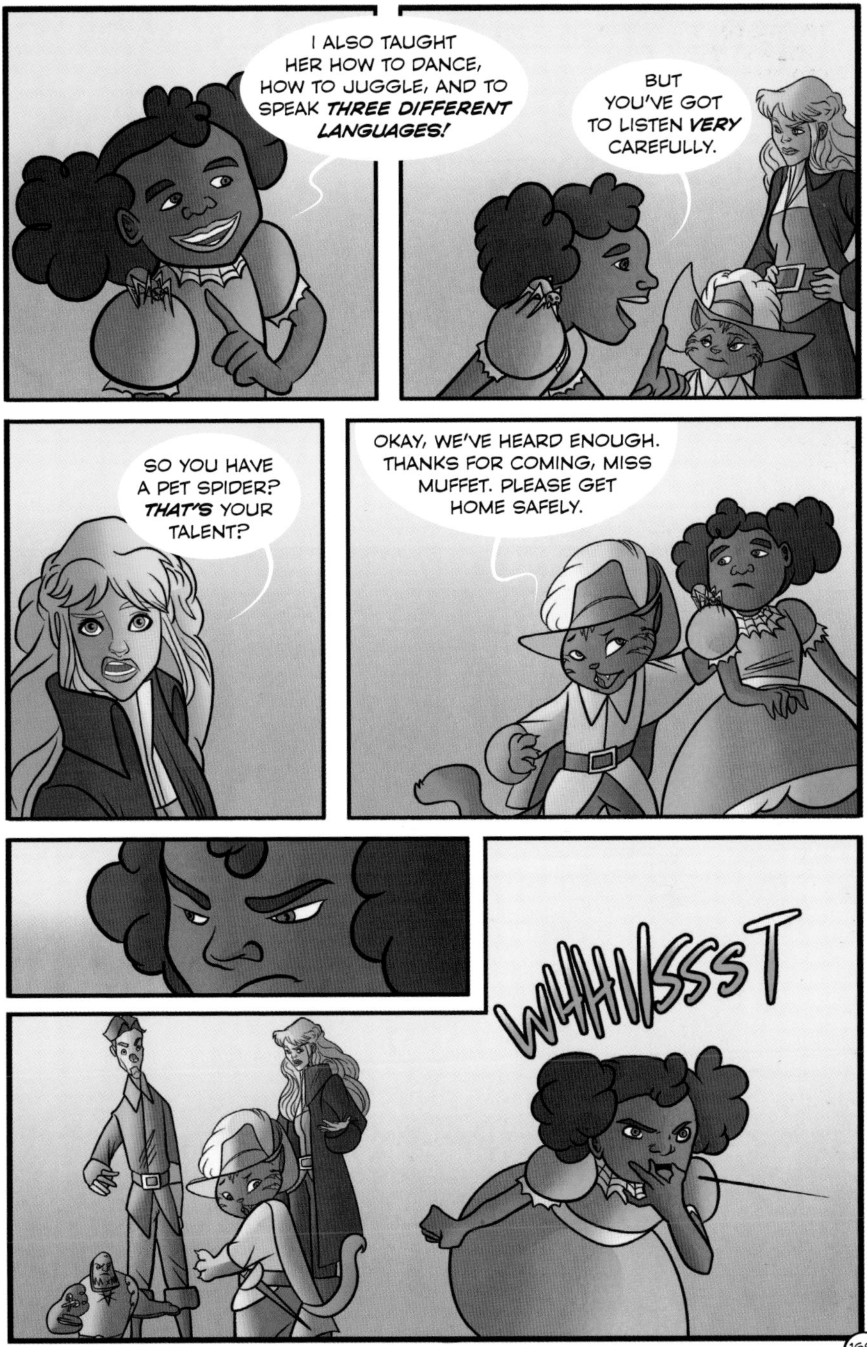
I ALSO TAUGHT HER HOW TO DANCE, HOW TO JUGGLE, AND TO SPEAK THREE DIFFERENT LANGUAGES!
BUT YOU'VE GOT TO LISTEN VERY CAREFULLY.
SO YOU HAVE A PET SPIDER? THAT'S YOUR TALENT?
OKAY, WE'VE HEARD ENOUGH. THANKS FOR COMING, MISS MUFFET. PLEASE GET HOME SAFELY.
WHHISSST

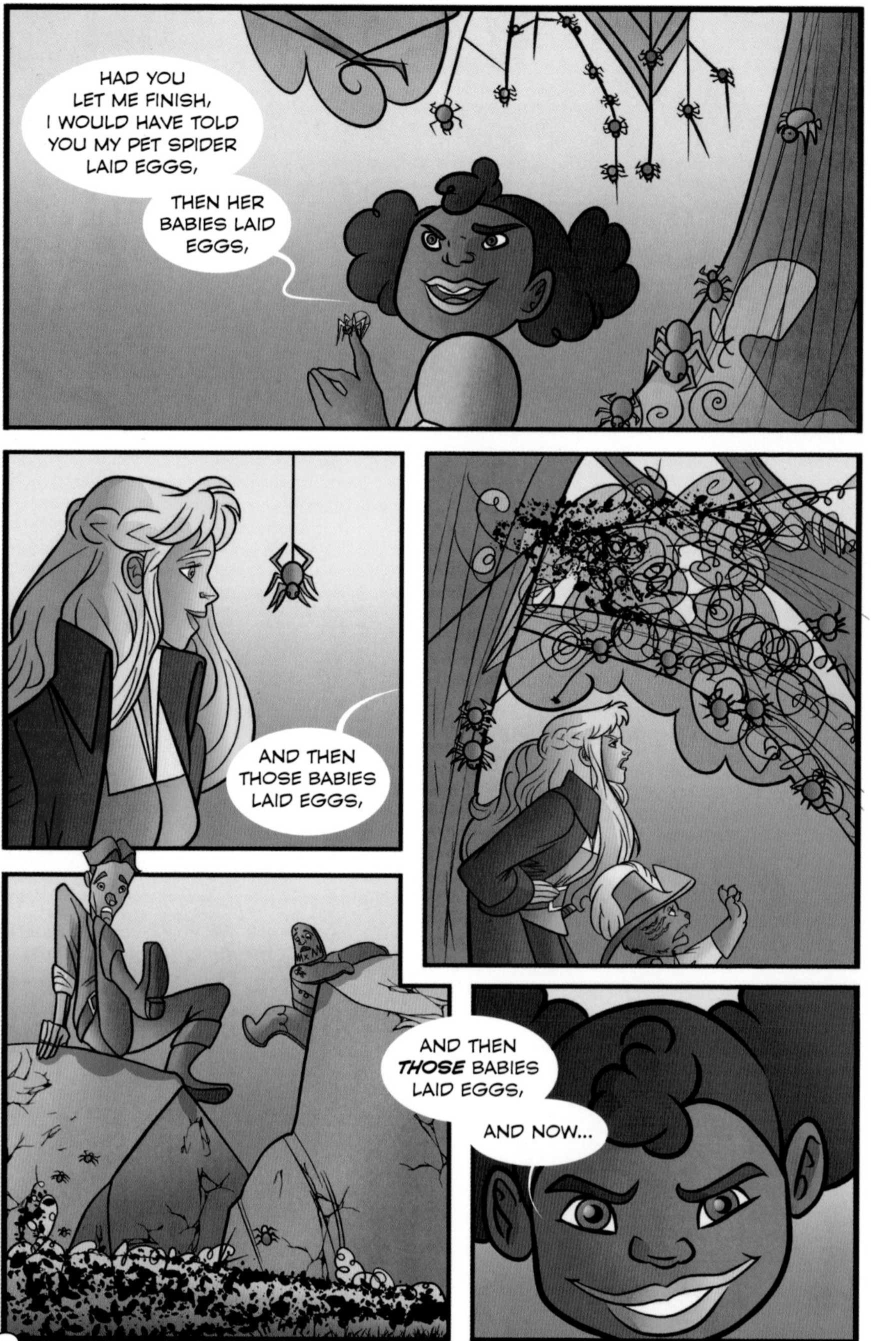
HAD YOU LET ME FINISH, I WOULD HAVE TOLD YOU MY PET SPIDER LAID EGGS,
THEN HER BABIES LAID EGGS,
AND THEN THOSE BABIES LAID EGGS,
AND THEN *THOSE* BABIES LAID EGGS,
AND NOW...

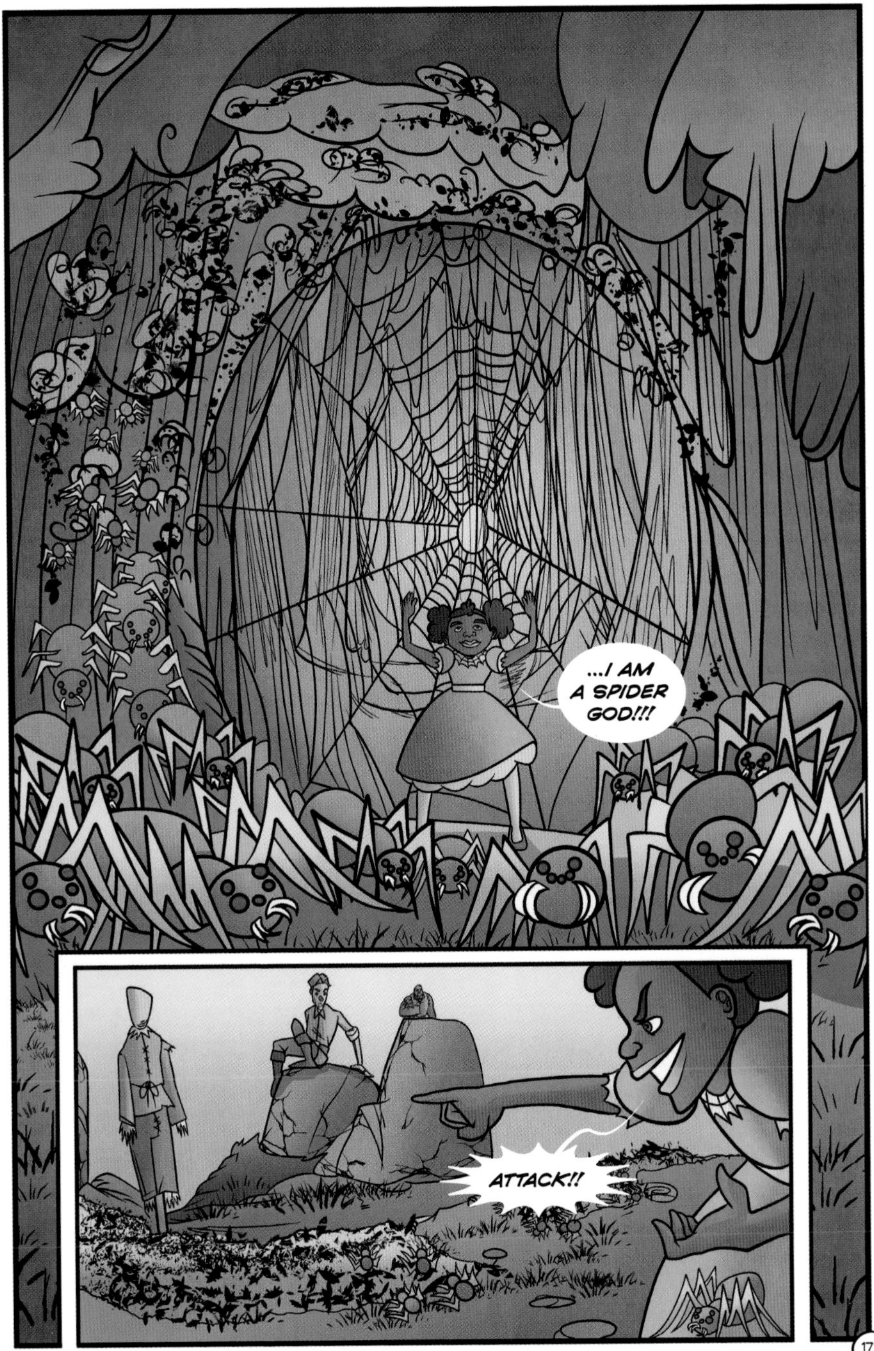
...I AM A SPIDER GOD!!!
ATTACK!!

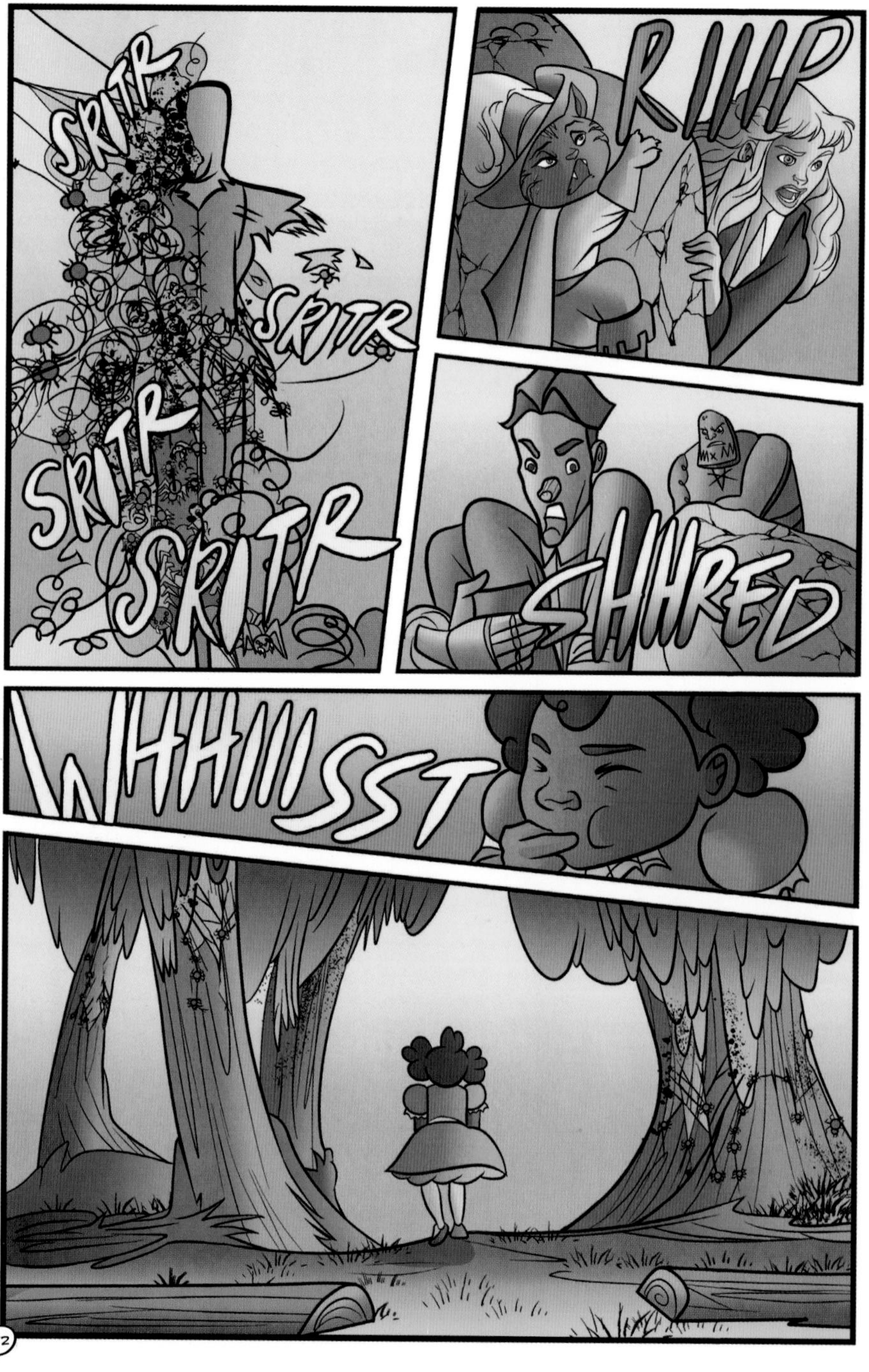
SRITR
SRITR
SRITR
SRITR
RIIIP
SHHRED
WHHIISST

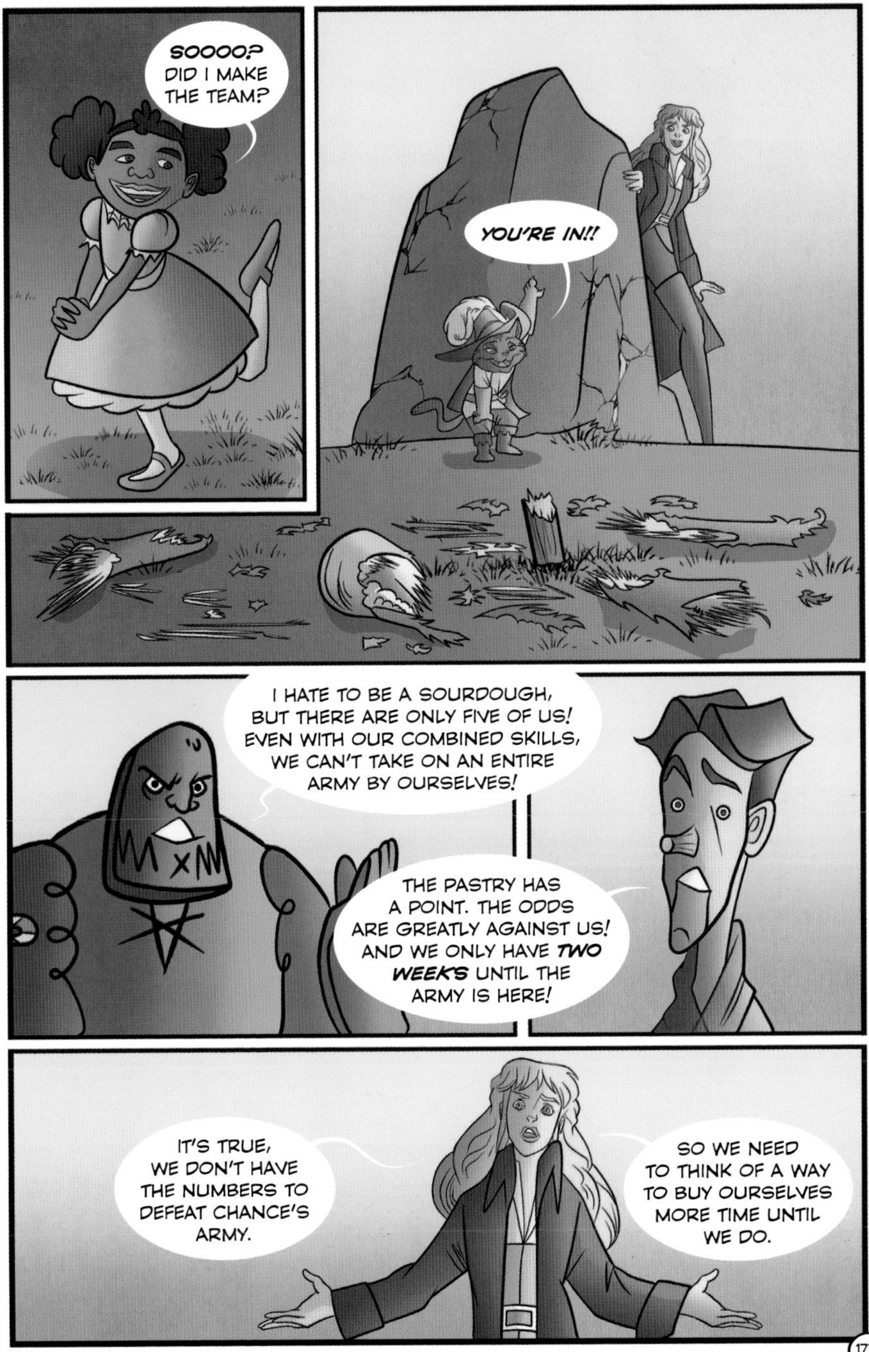
SOOOO?
DID I MAKE THE TEAM?
YOU'RE IN!!
I HATE TO BE A SOURDOUGH, BUT THERE ARE ONLY FIVE OF US! EVEN WITH OUR COMBINED SKILLS, WE CAN'T TAKE ON AN ENTIRE ARMY BY OURSELVES!
THE PASTRY HAS A POINT. THE ODDS ARE GREATLY AGAINST US! AND WE ONLY HAVE TWO WEEKS UNTIL THE ARMY IS HERE!
IT'S TRUE, WE DON'T HAVE THE NUMBERS TO DEFEAT CHANCE'S ARMY.
SO WE NEED TO THINK OF A WAY TO BUY OURSELVES MORE TIME UNTIL WE DO.

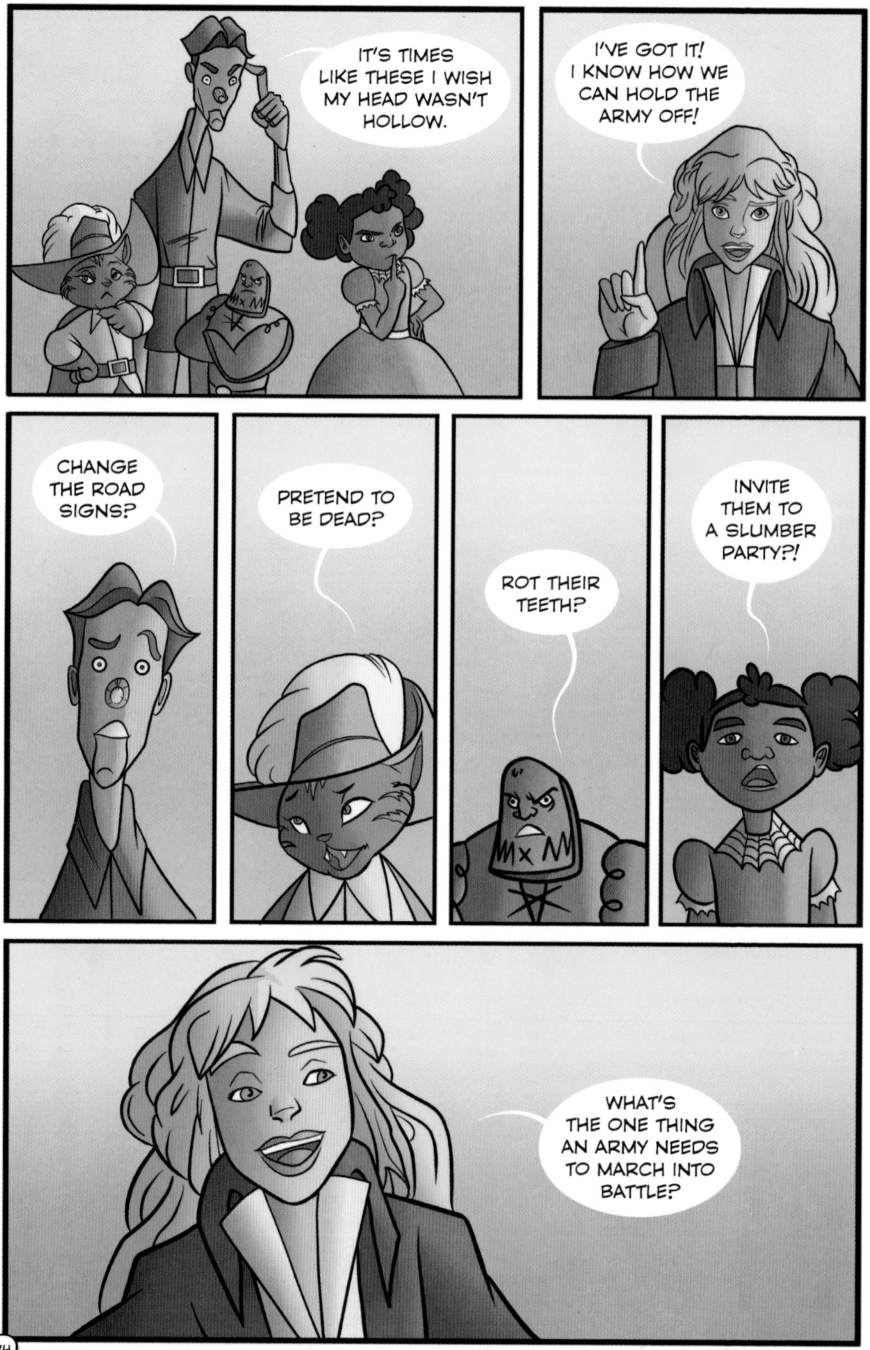
IT'S TIMES LIKE THESE I WISH MY HEAD WASN'T HOLLOW.
I'VE GOT IT! I KNOW HOW WE CAN HOLD THE ARMY OFF!
CHANGE THE ROAD SIGNS?
PRETEND TO BE DEAD?
ROT THEIR TEETH?
INVITE THEM TO A SLUMBER PARTY?!
WHAT'S THE ONE THING AN ARMY NEEDS TO MARCH INTO BATTLE?

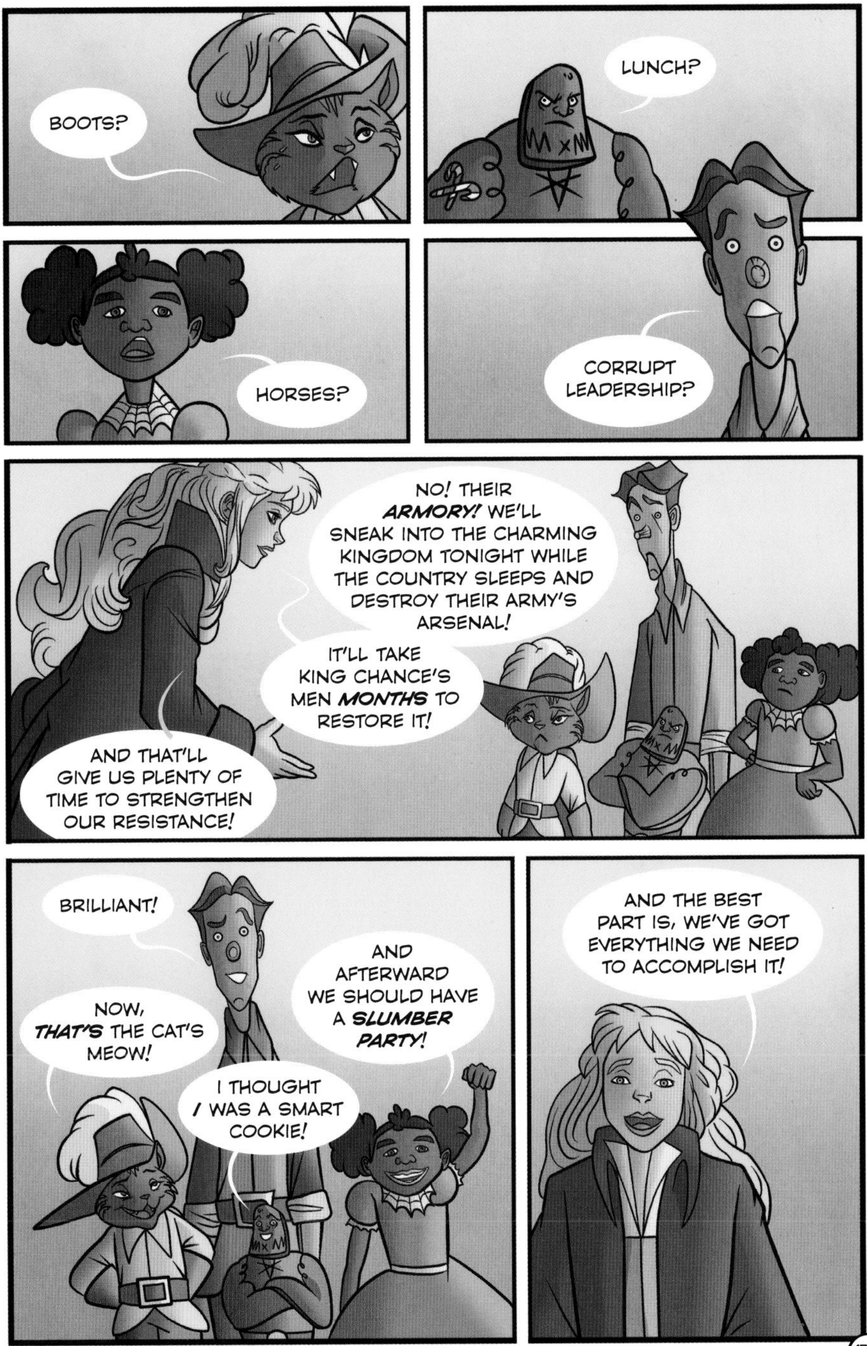
BOOTS?
LUNCH?
HORSES?
CORRUPT LEADERSHIP?
NO! THEIR *ARMORY!* WE'LL SNEAK INTO THE CHARMING KINGDOM TONIGHT WHILE THE COUNTRY SLEEPS AND DESTROY THEIR ARMY'S ARSENAL!
IT'LL TAKE KING CHANCE'S MEN *MONTHS* TO RESTORE IT!
AND THAT'LL GIVE US PLENTY OF TIME TO STRENGTHEN OUR RESISTANCE!
BRILLIANT!
NOW, *THAT'S* THE CAT'S MEOW!
AND AFTERWARD WE SHOULD HAVE A *SLUMBER PARTY!*
I THOUGHT *I* WAS A SMART COOKIE!
AND THE BEST PART IS, WE'VE GOT EVERYTHING WE NEED TO ACCOMPLISH IT!

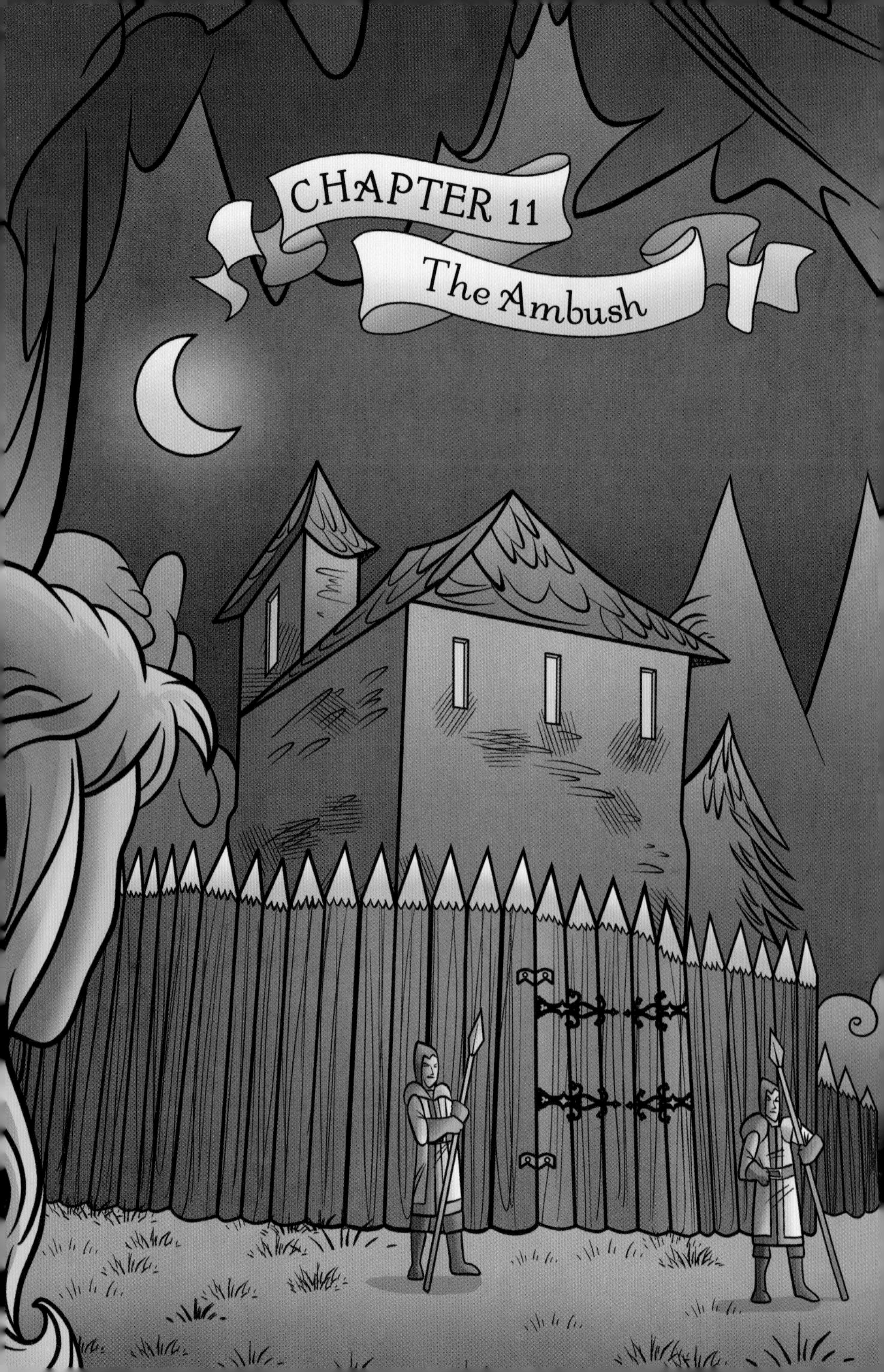
CHAPTER 11
The Ambush

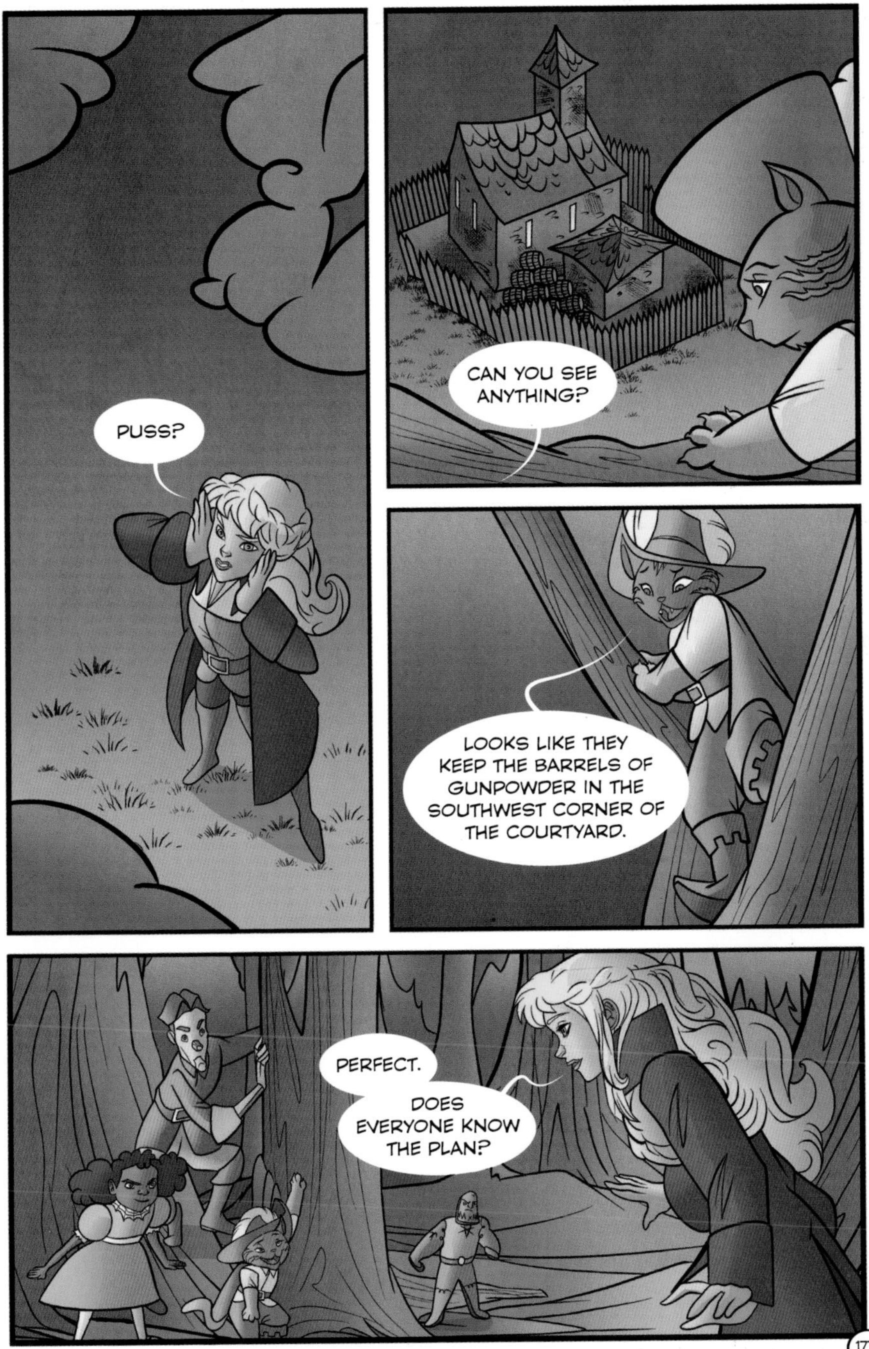
PUSS?
CAN YOU SEE ANYTHING?
LOOKS LIKE THEY KEEP THE BARRELS OF GUNPOWDER IN THE SOUTHWEST CORNER OF THE COURTYARD.
PERFECT.
DOES EVERYONE KNOW THE PLAN?

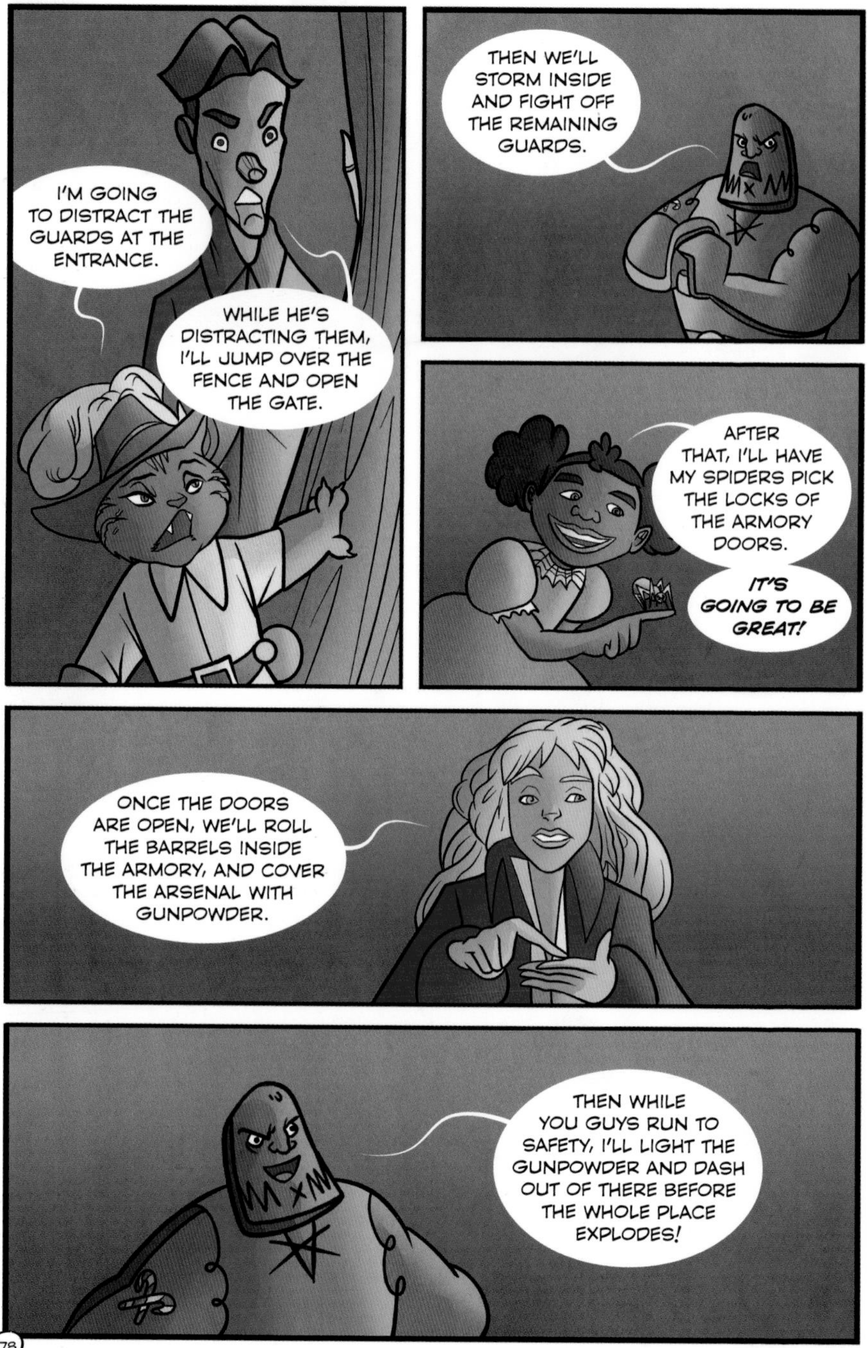
I'M GOING TO DISTRACT THE GUARDS AT THE ENTRANCE.
WHILE HE'S DISTRACTING THEM, I'LL JUMP OVER THE FENCE AND OPEN THE GATE.
THEN WE'LL STORM INSIDE AND FIGHT OFF THE REMAINING GUARDS.
AFTER THAT, I'LL HAVE MY SPIDERS PICK THE LOCKS OF THE ARMORY DOORS.
IT'S GOING TO BE GREAT!
ONCE THE DOORS ARE OPEN, WE'LL ROLL THE BARRELS INSIDE THE ARMORY, AND COVER THE ARSENAL WITH GUNPOWDER.
THEN WHILE YOU GUYS RUN TO SAFETY, I'LL LIGHT THE GUNPOWDER AND DASH OUT OF THERE BEFORE THE WHOLE PLACE EXPLODES!

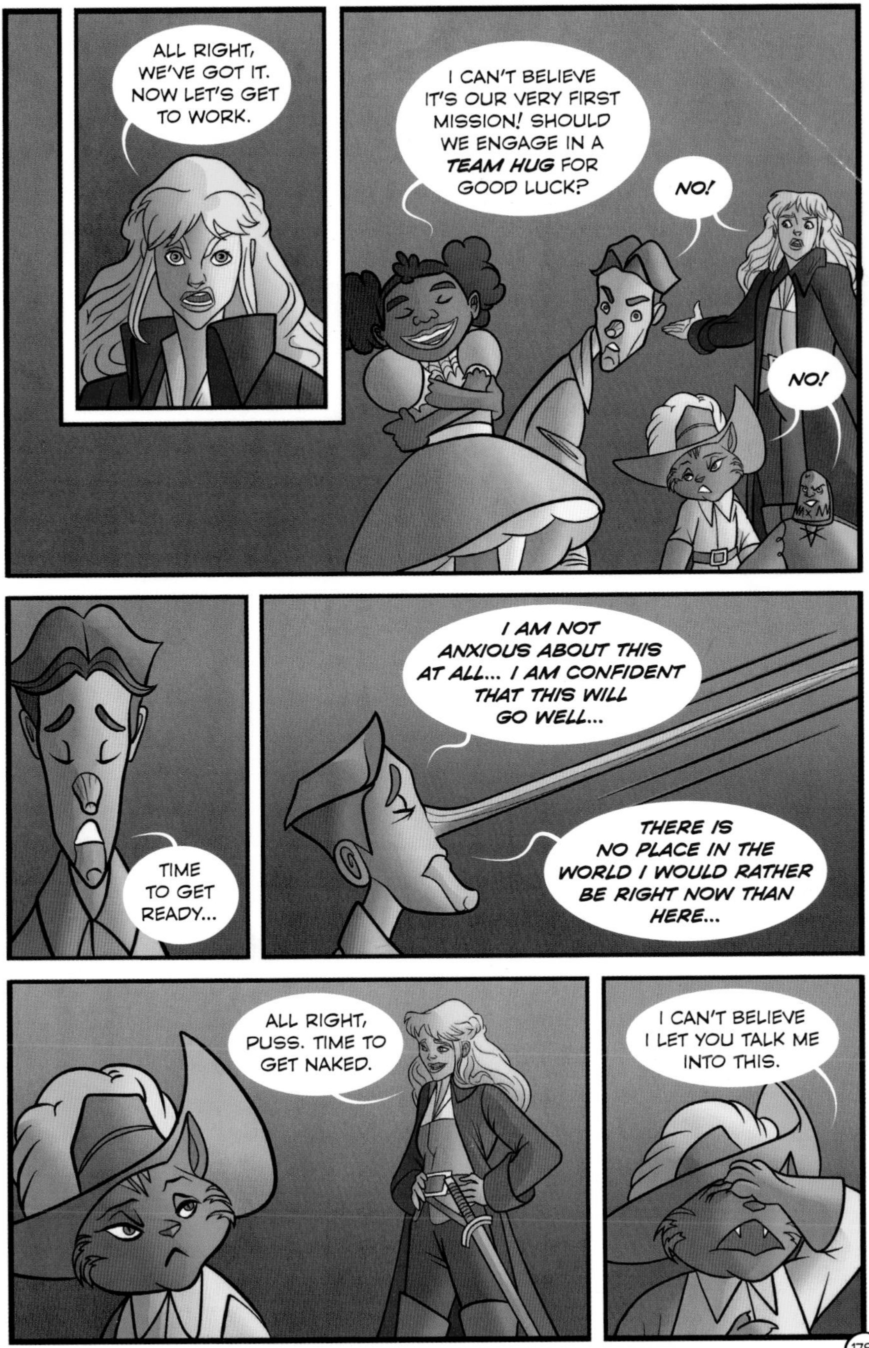
ALL RIGHT, WE'VE GOT IT. NOW LET'S GET TO WORK.
I CAN'T BELIEVE IT'S OUR VERY FIRST MISSION! SHOULD WE ENGAGE IN A TEAM HUG FOR GOOD LUCK?
NO!
NO!
TIME TO GET READY...
I AM NOT ANXIOUS ABOUT THIS AT ALL... I AM CONFIDENT THAT THIS WILL GO WELL...
THERE IS NO PLACE IN THE WORLD I WOULD RATHER BE RIGHT NOW THAN HERE...
ALL RIGHT, PUSS. TIME TO GET NAKED.
I CAN'T BELIEVE I LET YOU TALK ME INTO THIS.

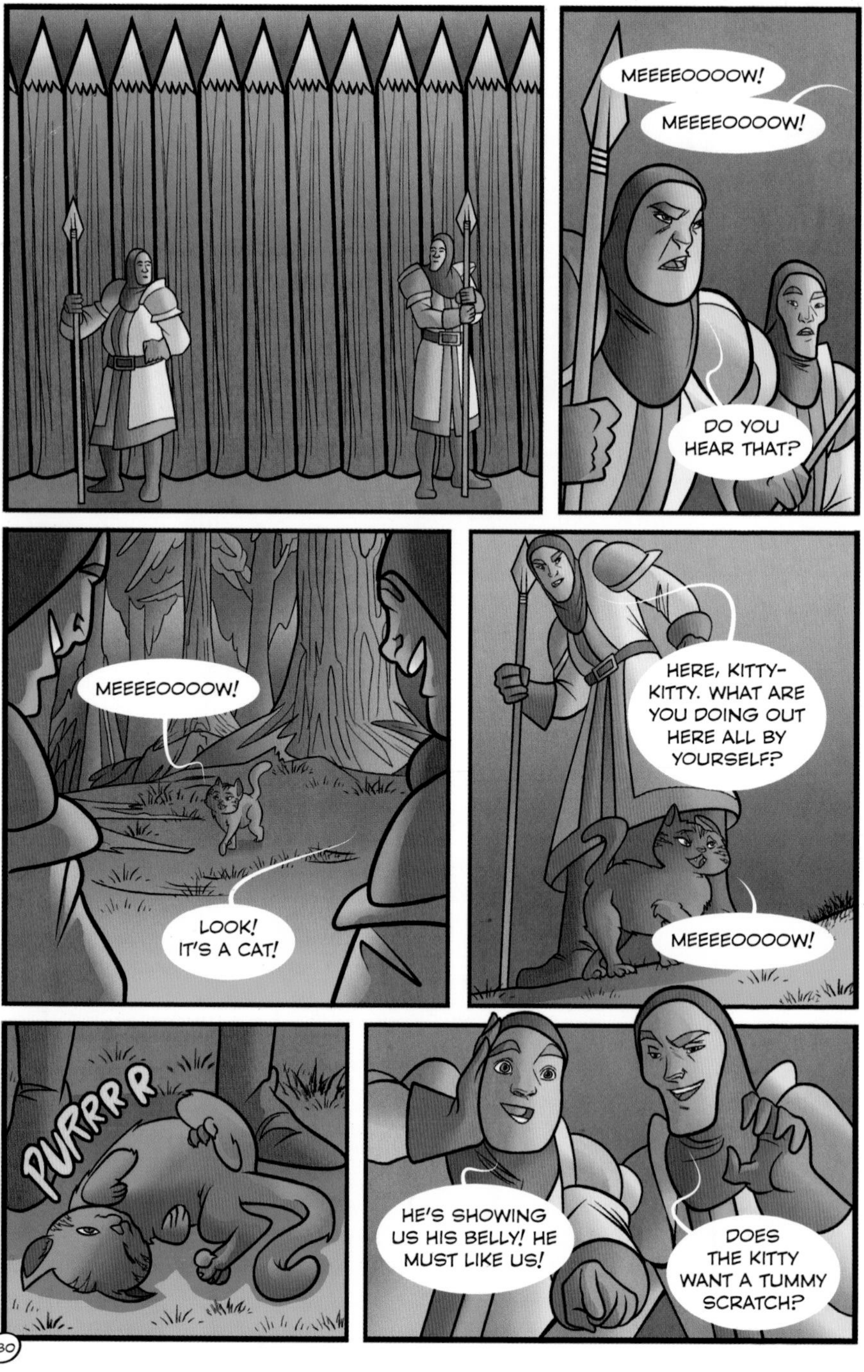
MEEEEOOOOW!
MEEEEOOOOW!
DO YOU HEAR THAT?
MEEEEOOOOW!
LOOK! IT'S A CAT!
HERE, KITTY-KITTY. WHAT ARE YOU DOING OUT HERE ALL BY YOURSELF?
MEEEEOOOOW!
PURRRR
HE'S SHOWING US HIS BELLY! HE MUST LIKE US!
DOES THE KITTY WANT A TUMMY SCRATCH?

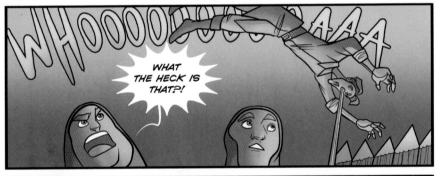

WHOOOOOOOAAAA

WHAT THE HECK IS THAT?!

SHNK SHNK

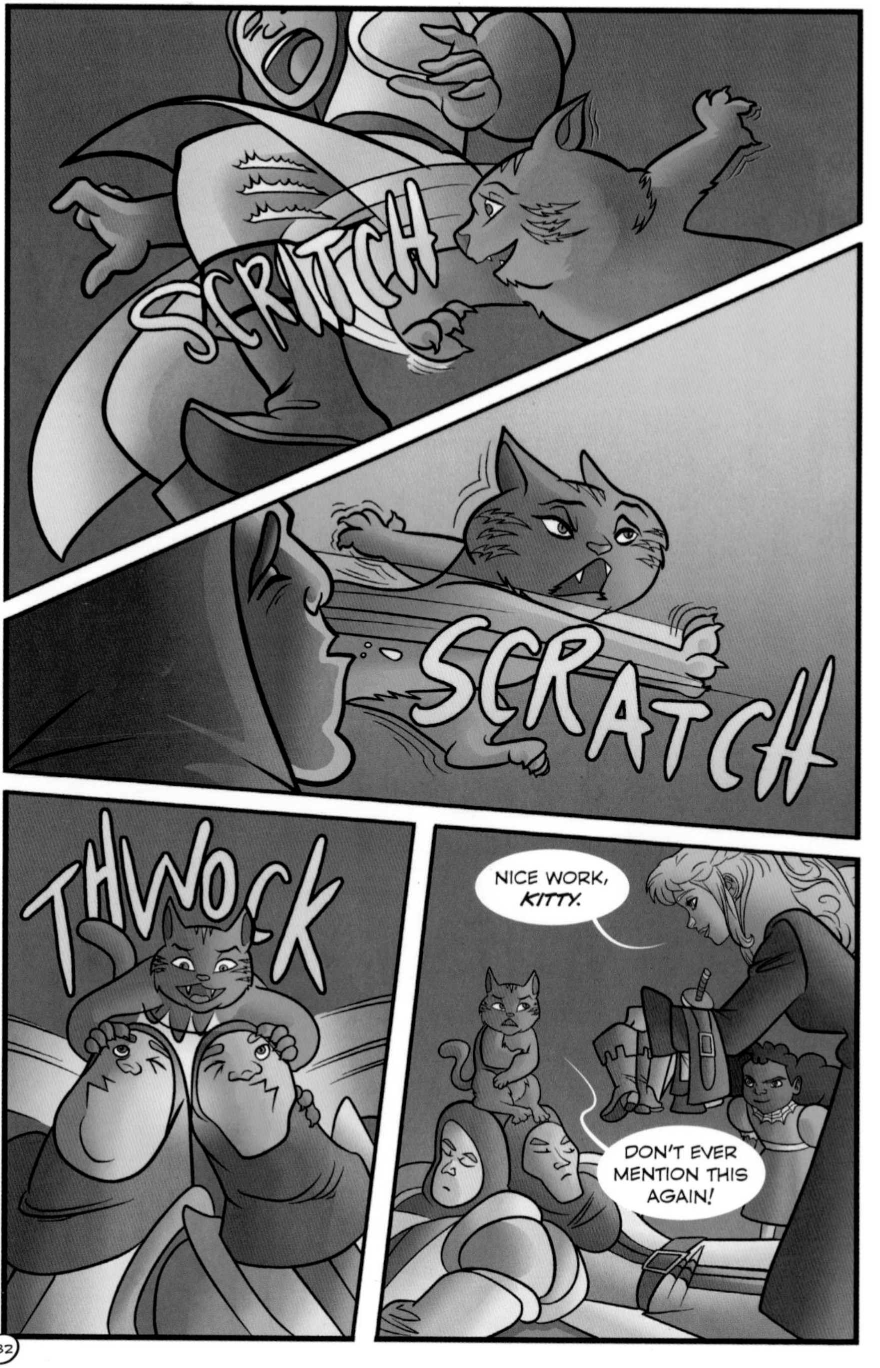
SCRITCH
SCRATCH
THWOCK
NICE WORK, *KITTY.*
DON'T EVER MENTION THIS AGAIN!

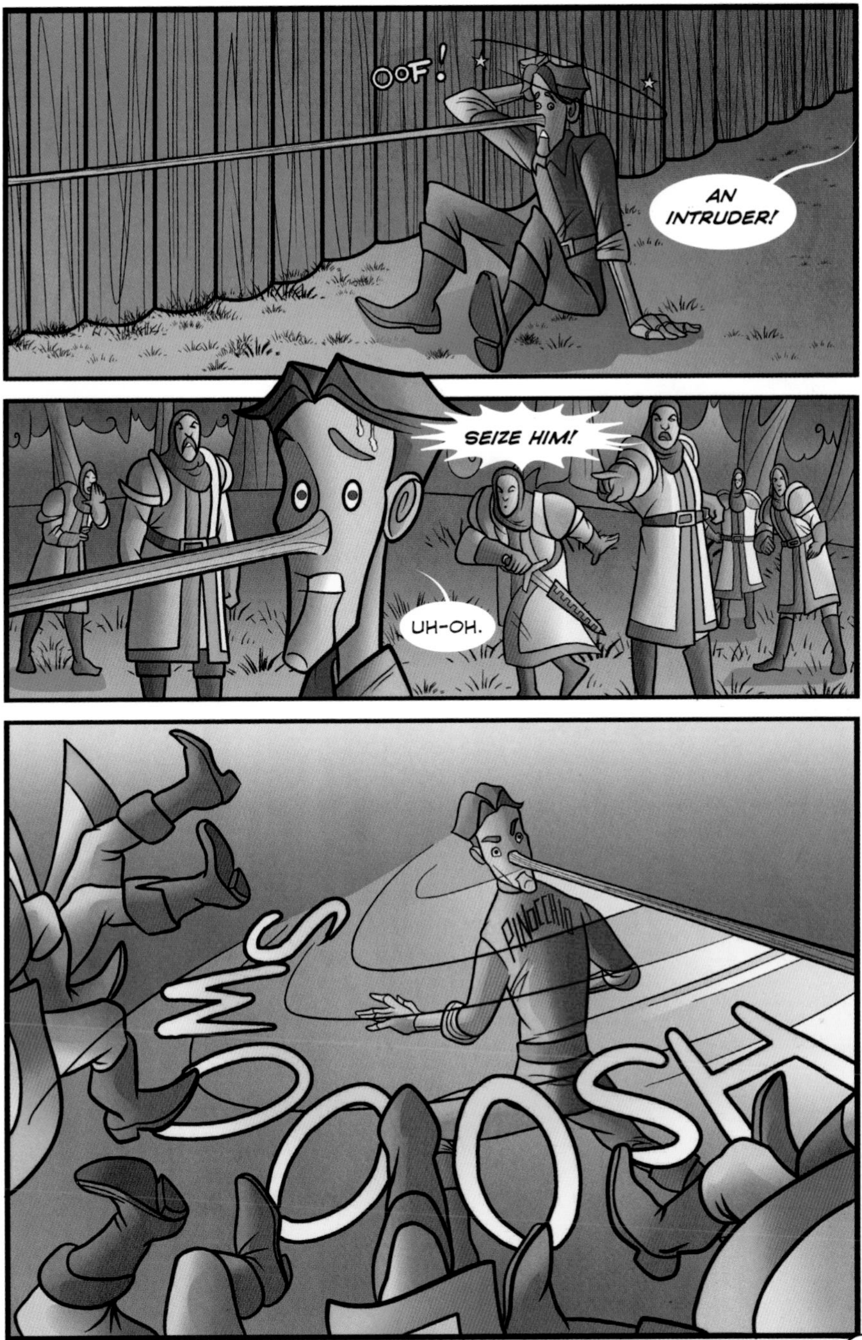
OOF!
AN INTRUDER!
SEIZE HIM!
UH-OH.
PINOCCHIO
SWOOSH

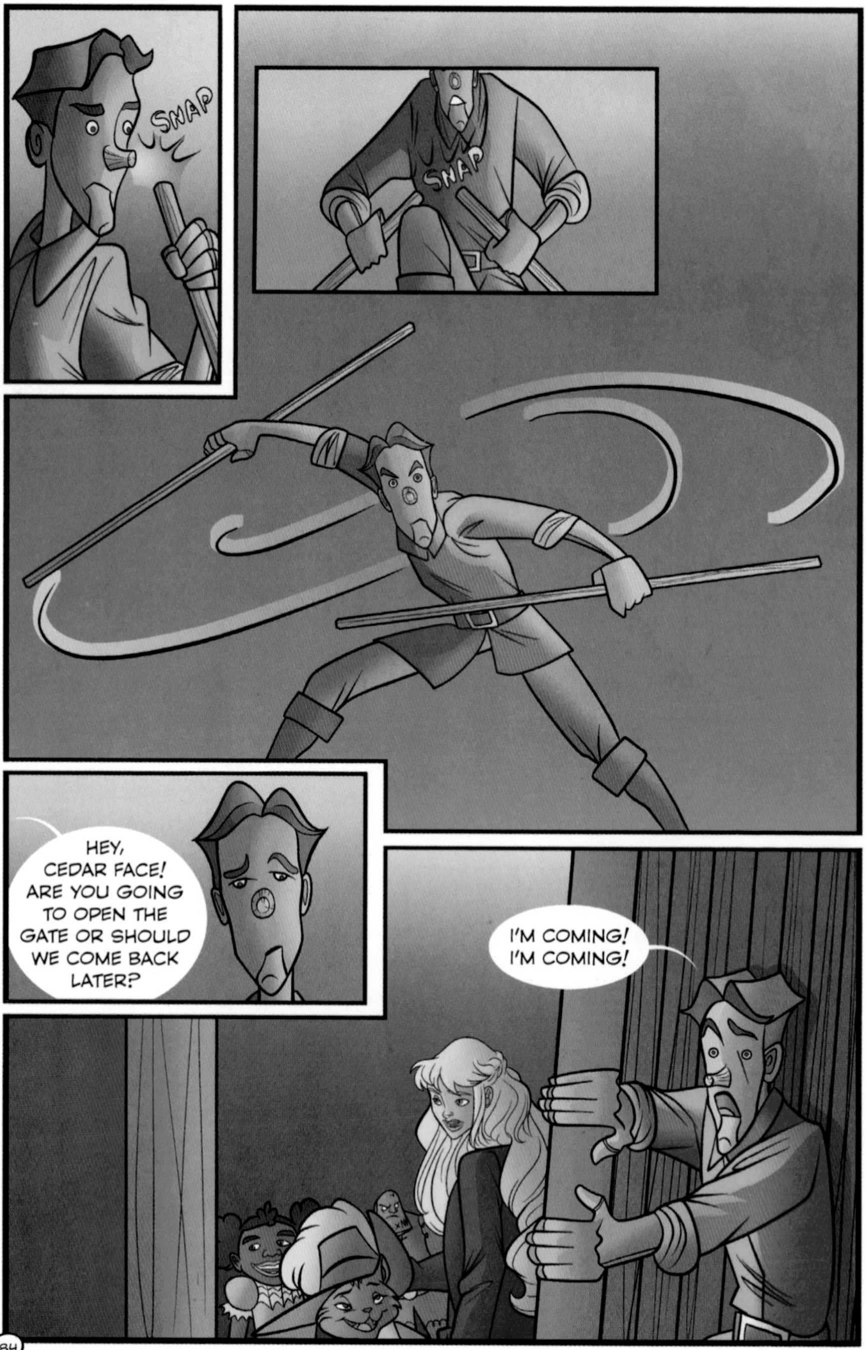
SNAP
SNAP
HEY, CEDAR FACE! ARE YOU GOING TO OPEN THE GATE OR SHOULD WE COME BACK LATER?
I'M COMING! I'M COMING!

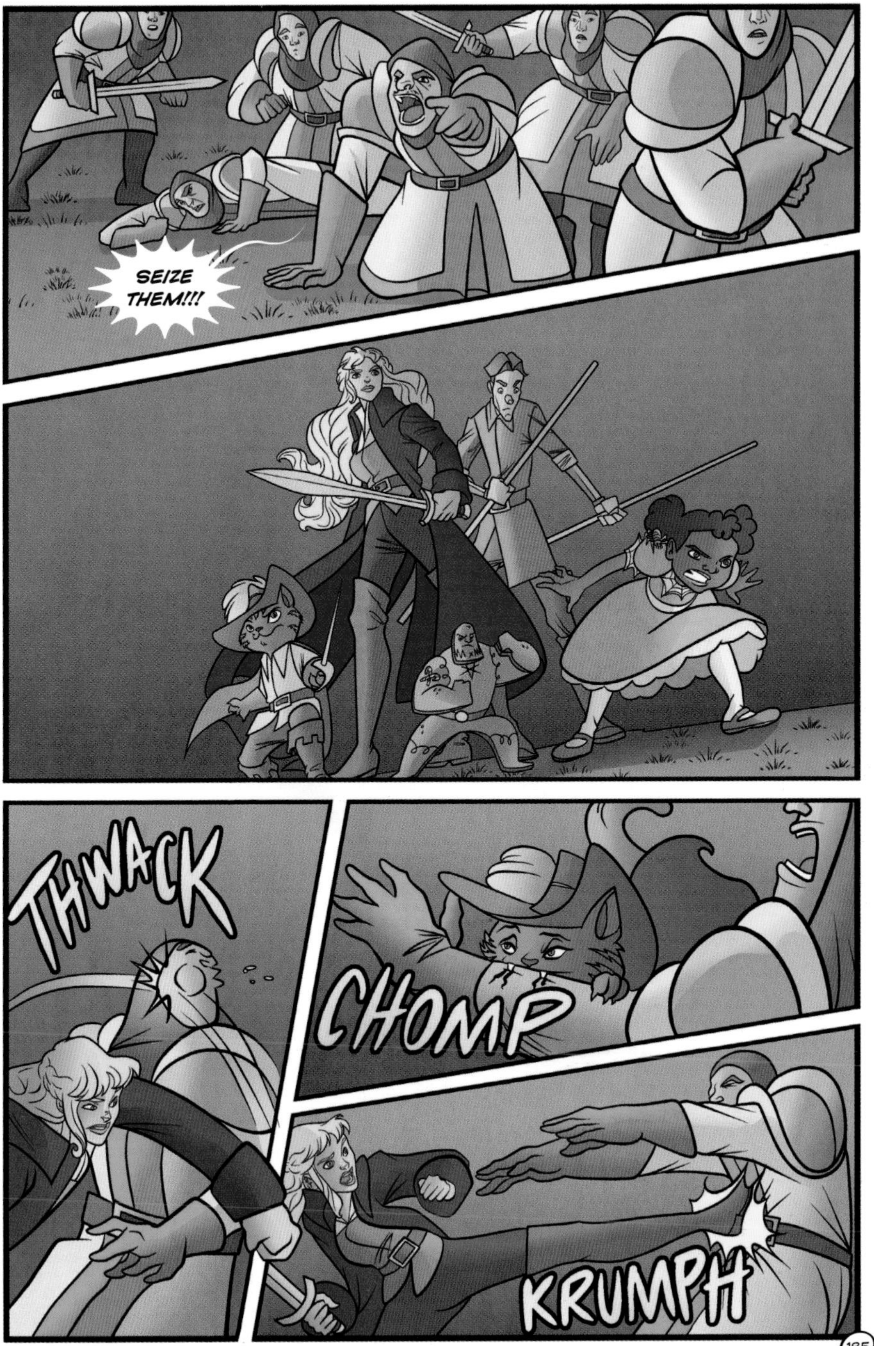
SEIZE THEM!!!
THWACK
CHOMP
KRUMPH

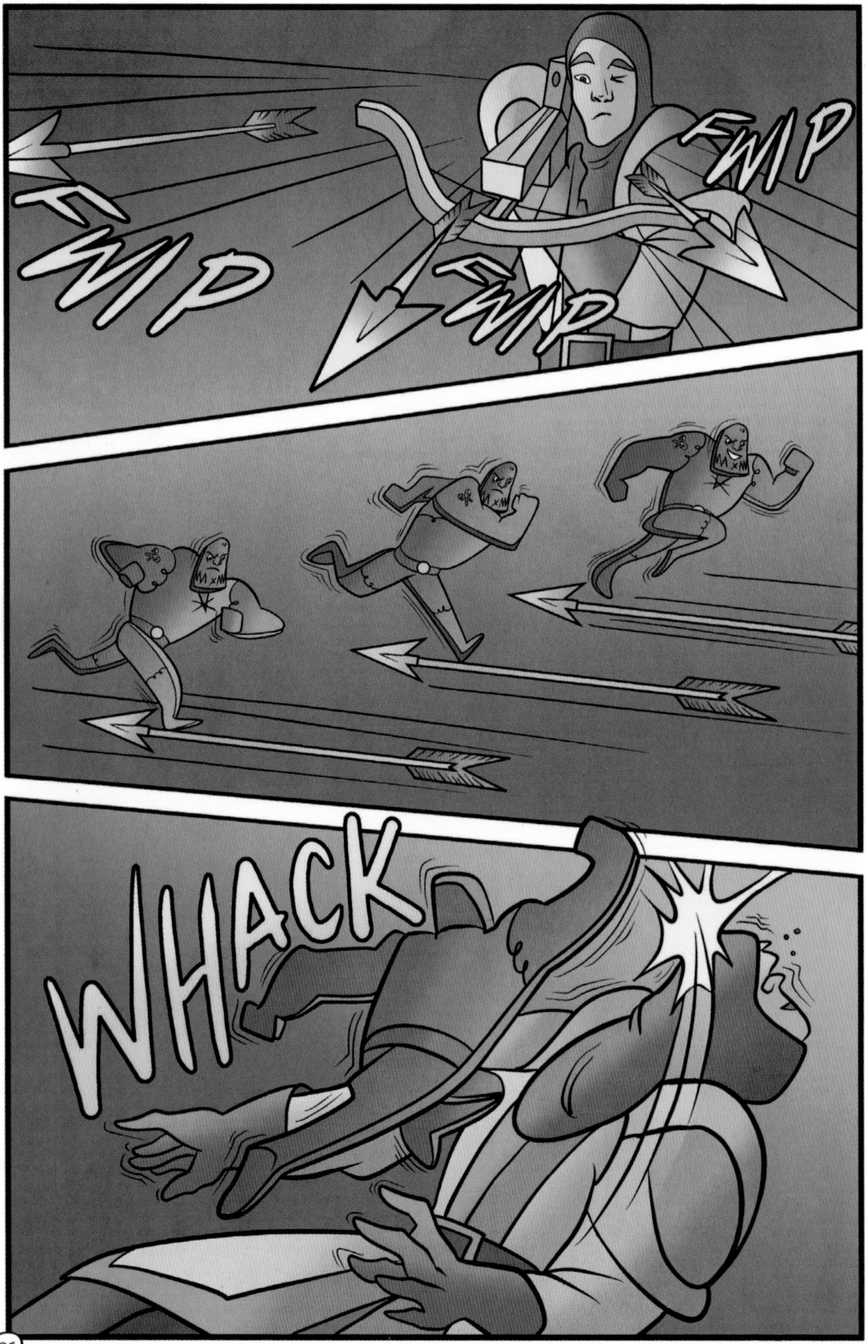
FWIP
FWIP
FWIP
WHACK

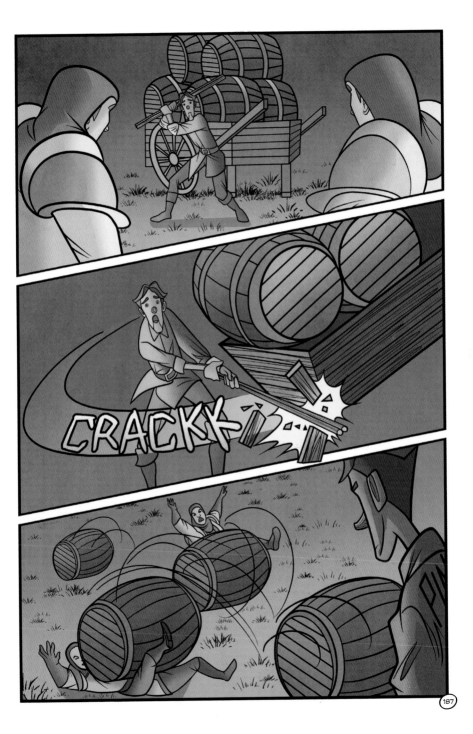

CRACKK

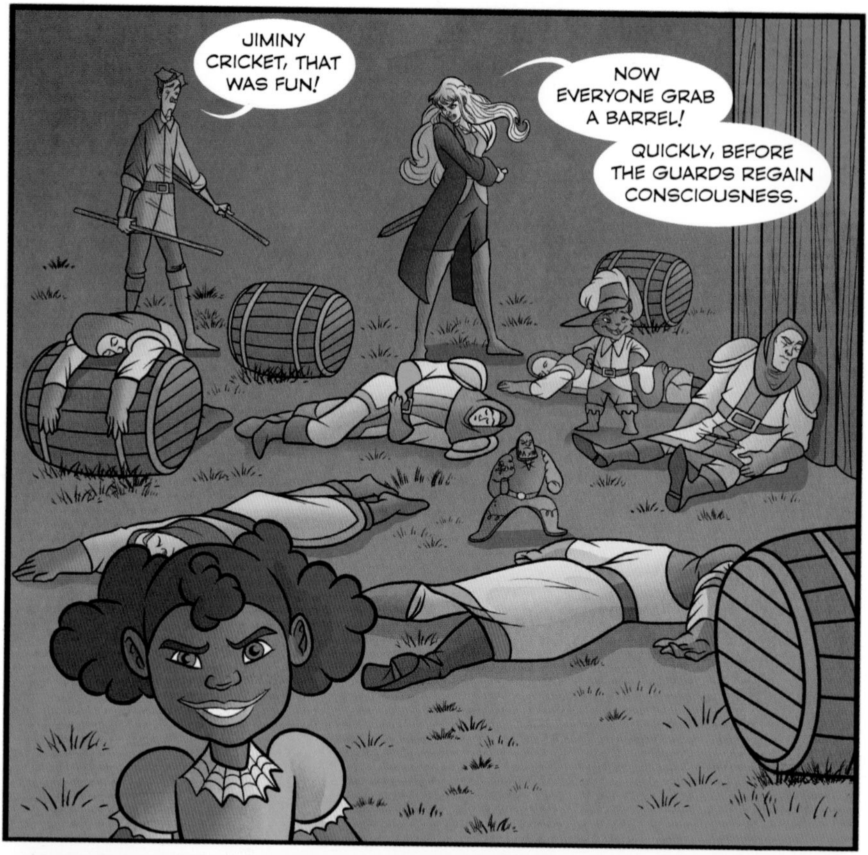
JIMINY CRICKET, THAT WAS FUN!
NOW EVERYONE GRAB A BARREL!
QUICKLY, BEFORE THE GUARDS REGAIN CONSCIOUSNESS.

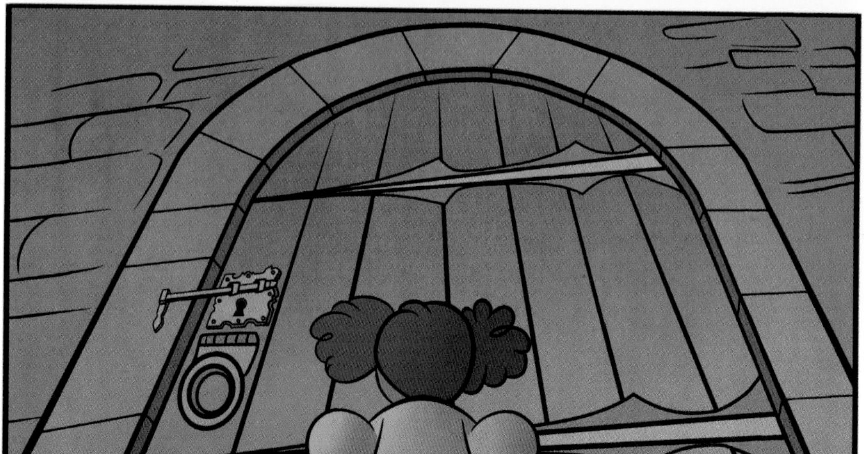

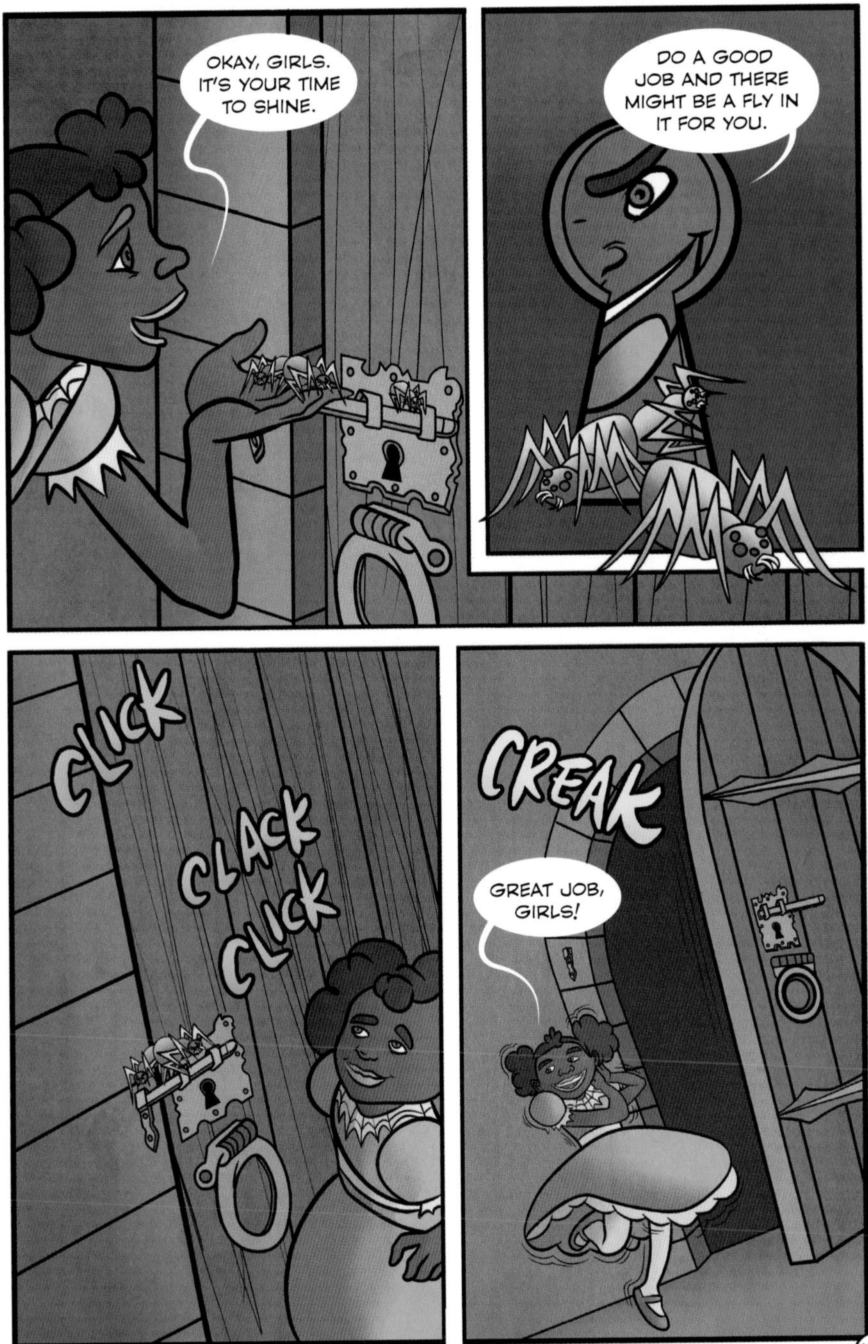
OKAY, GIRLS. IT'S YOUR TIME TO SHINE.
DO A GOOD JOB AND THERE MIGHT BE A FLY IN IT FOR YOU.
CLICK
CLACK
CLICK
CREAK
GREAT JOB, GIRLS!

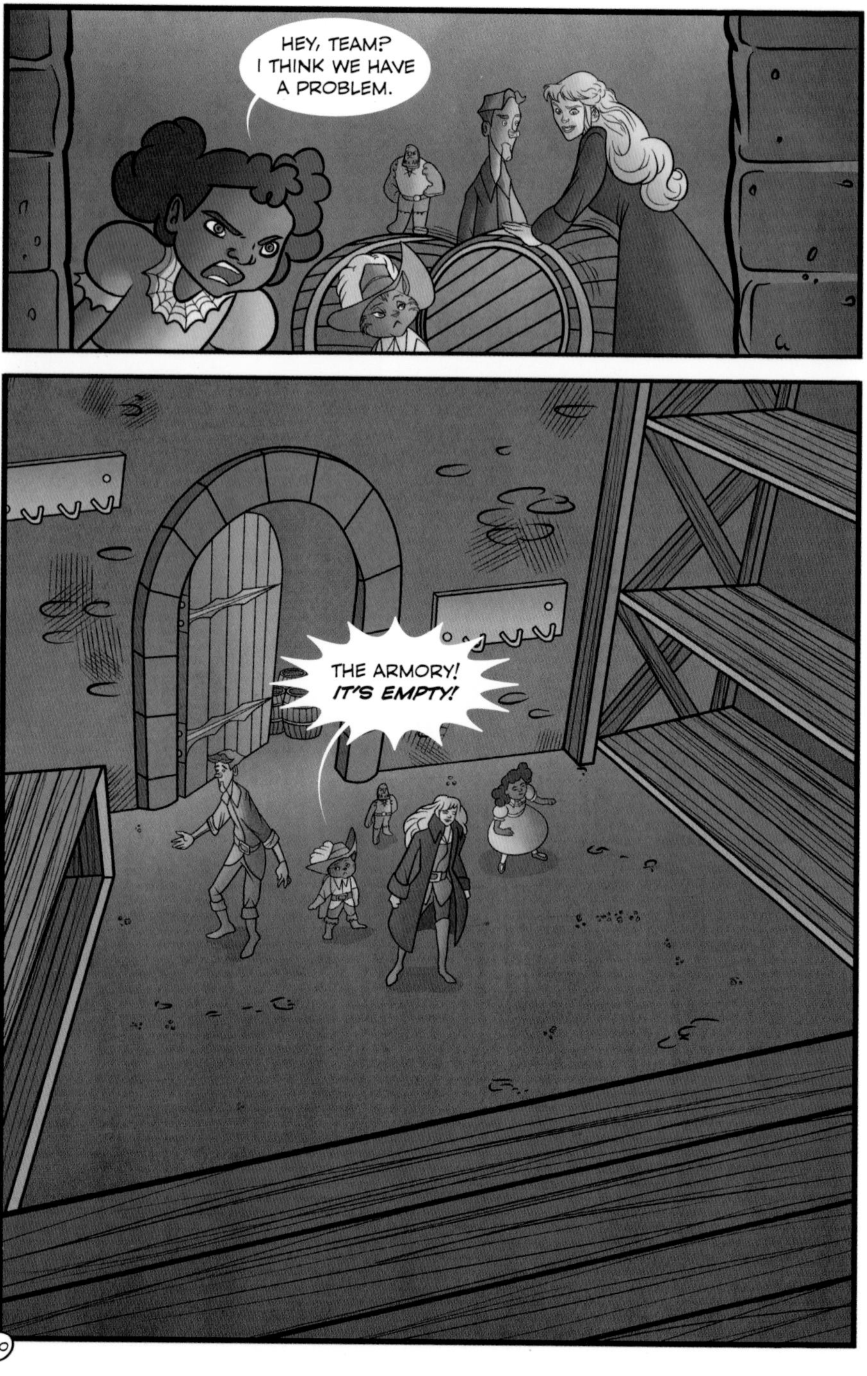
HEY, TEAM? I THINK WE HAVE A PROBLEM.
THE ARMORY! *IT'S EMPTY!*

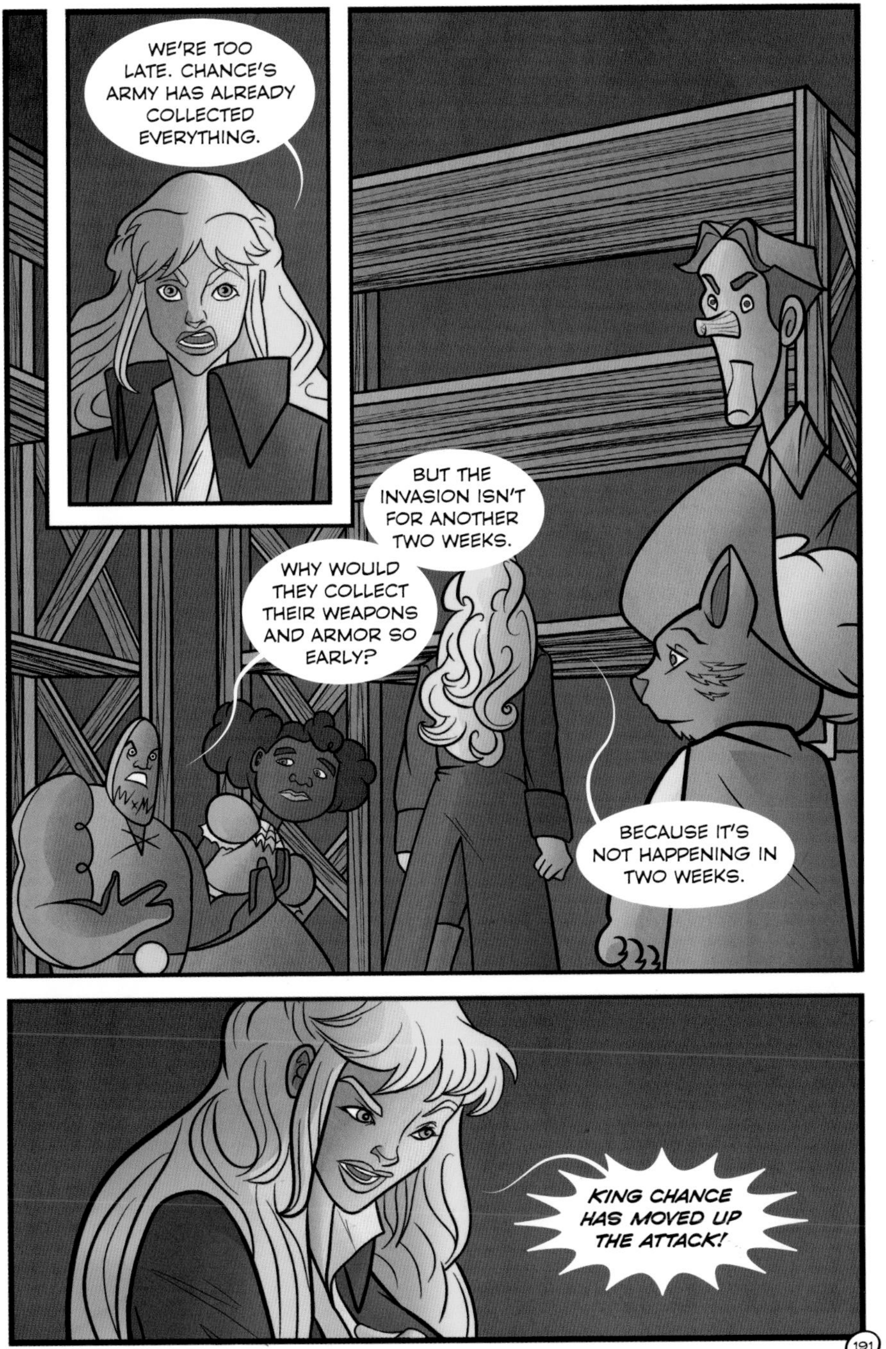
WE'RE TOO LATE. CHANCE'S ARMY HAS ALREADY COLLECTED EVERYTHING.
BUT THE INVASION ISN'T FOR ANOTHER TWO WEEKS.
WHY WOULD THEY COLLECT THEIR WEAPONS AND ARMOR SO EARLY?
BECAUSE IT'S NOT HAPPENING IN TWO WEEKS.
KING CHANCE HAS MOVED UP THE ATTACK!

CHAPTER 12

Dine and Dash

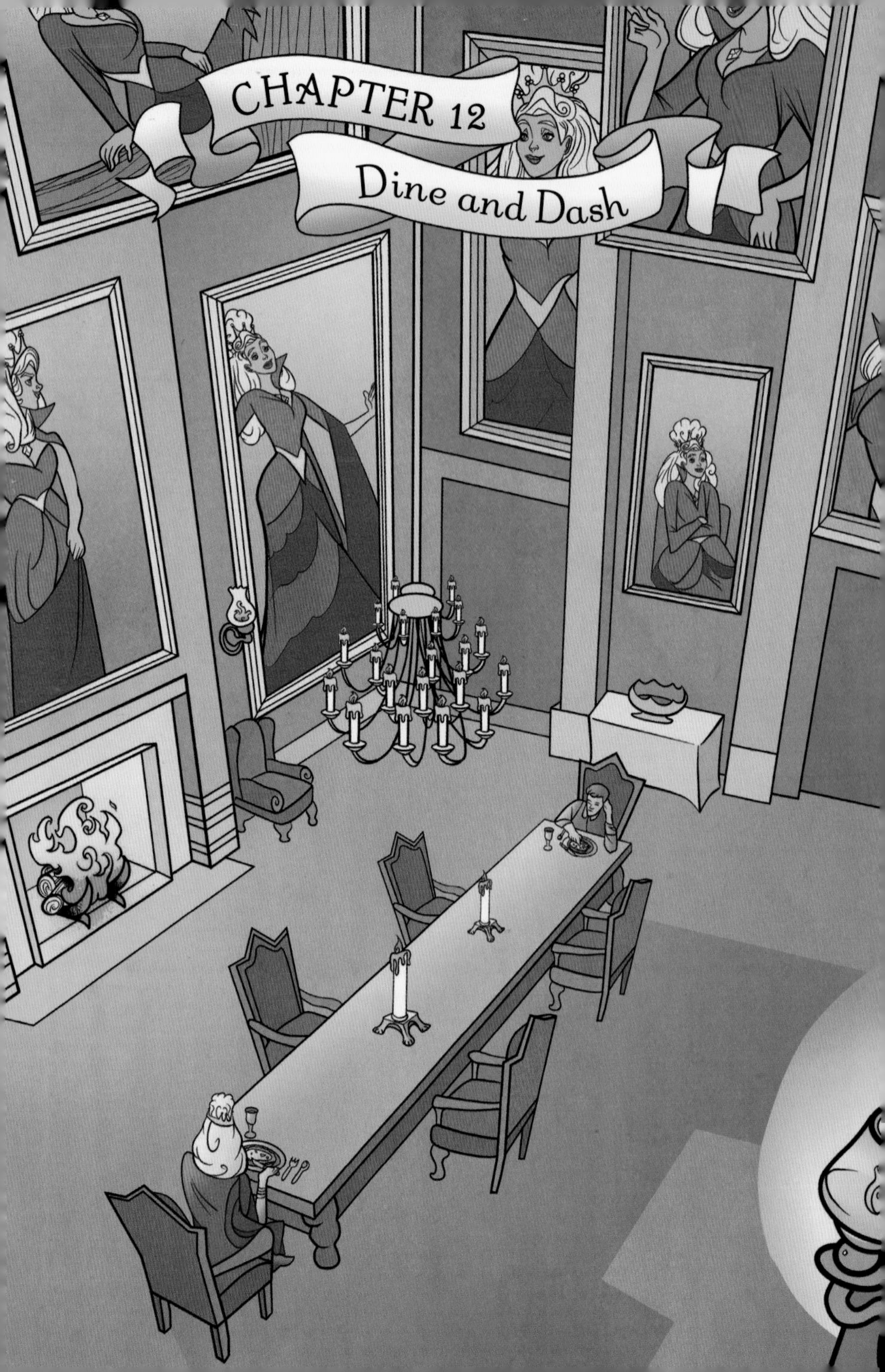

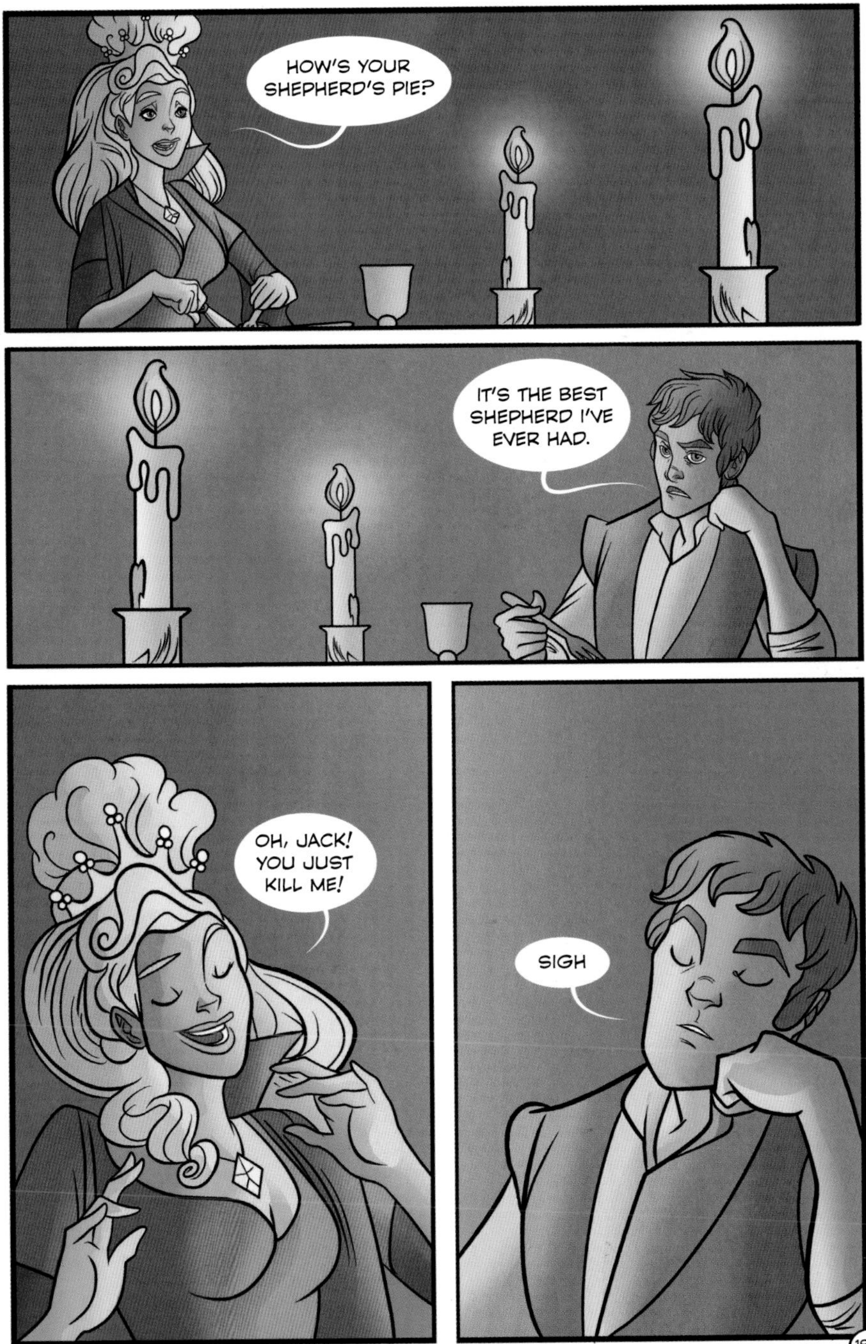
HOW'S YOUR SHEPHERD'S PIE?
IT'S THE BEST SHEPHERD I'VE EVER HAD.
OH, JACK! YOU JUST KILL ME!
SIGH

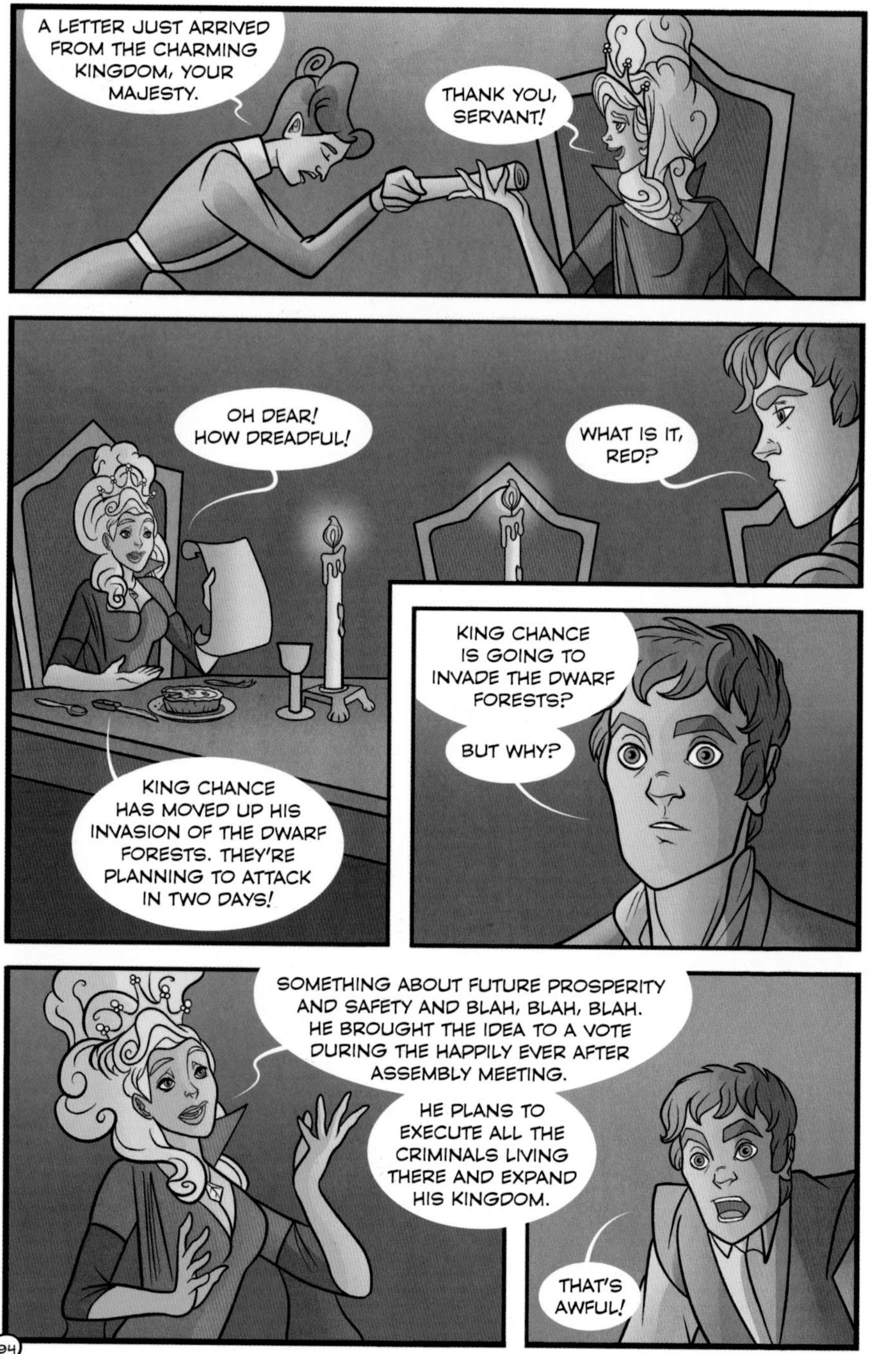
A LETTER JUST ARRIVED FROM THE CHARMING KINGDOM, YOUR MAJESTY.
THANK YOU, SERVANT!
OH DEAR! HOW DREADFUL!
WHAT IS IT, RED?
KING CHANCE HAS MOVED UP HIS INVASION OF THE DWARF FORESTS. THEY'RE PLANNING TO ATTACK IN TWO DAYS!
KING CHANCE IS GOING TO INVADE THE DWARF FORESTS?
BUT WHY?
SOMETHING ABOUT FUTURE PROSPERITY AND SAFETY AND BLAH, BLAH, BLAH. HE BROUGHT THE IDEA TO A VOTE DURING THE HAPPILY EVER AFTER ASSEMBLY MEETING.
HE PLANS TO EXECUTE ALL THE CRIMINALS LIVING THERE AND EXPAND HIS KINGDOM.
THAT'S AWFUL!

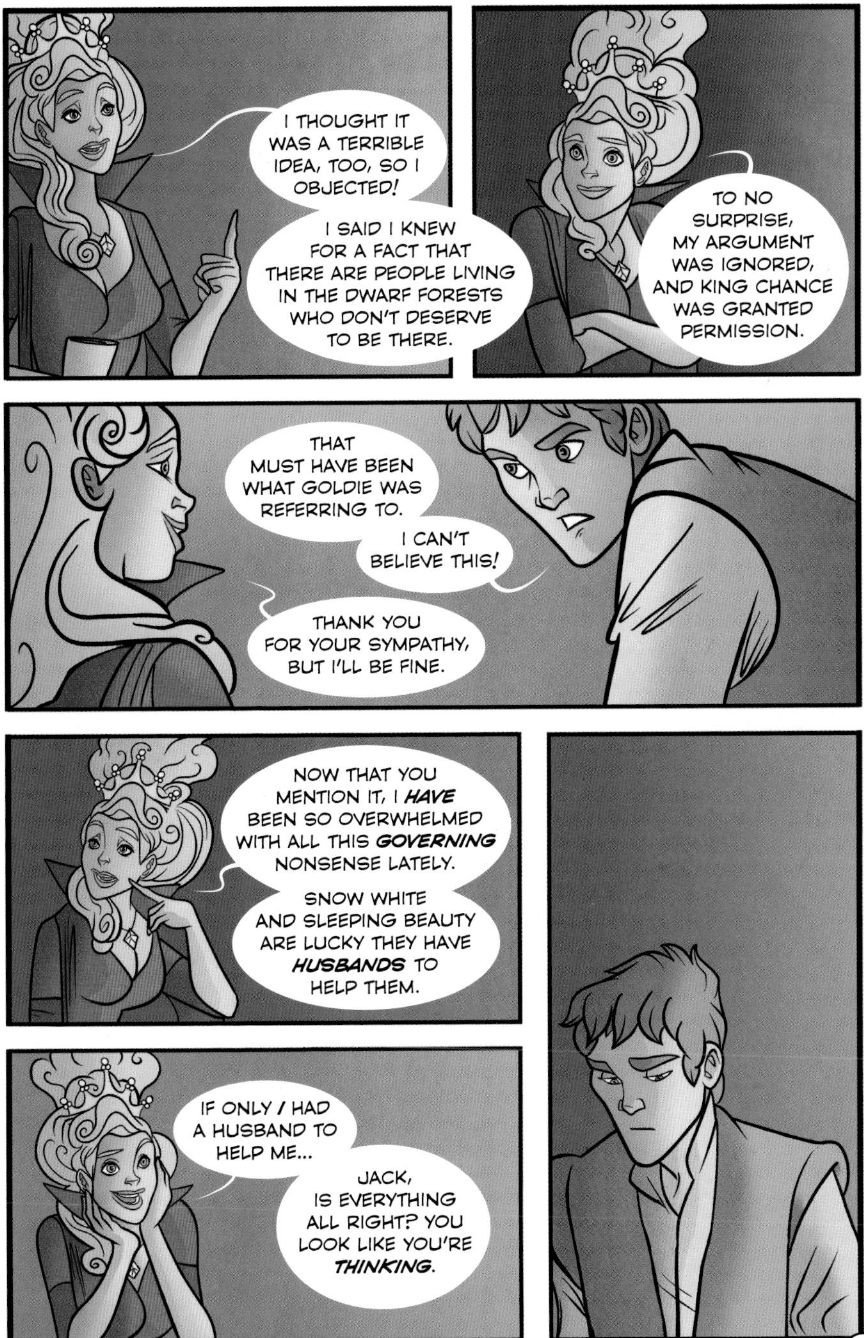
I THOUGHT IT WAS A TERRIBLE IDEA, TOO, SO I OBJECTED!
I SAID I KNEW FOR A FACT THAT THERE ARE PEOPLE LIVING IN THE DWARF FORESTS WHO DON'T DESERVE TO BE THERE.
TO NO SURPRISE, MY ARGUMENT WAS IGNORED, AND KING CHANCE WAS GRANTED PERMISSION.
THAT MUST HAVE BEEN WHAT GOLDIE WAS REFERRING TO.
I CAN'T BELIEVE THIS!
THANK YOU FOR YOUR SYMPATHY, BUT I'LL BE FINE.
NOW THAT YOU MENTION IT, I *HAVE* BEEN SO OVERWHELMED WITH ALL THIS *GOVERNING* NONSENSE LATELY.
SNOW WHITE AND SLEEPING BEAUTY ARE LUCKY THEY HAVE *HUSBANDS* TO HELP THEM.
IF ONLY *I* HAD A HUSBAND TO HELP ME...
JACK, IS EVERYTHING ALL RIGHT? YOU LOOK LIKE YOU'RE *THINKING*.

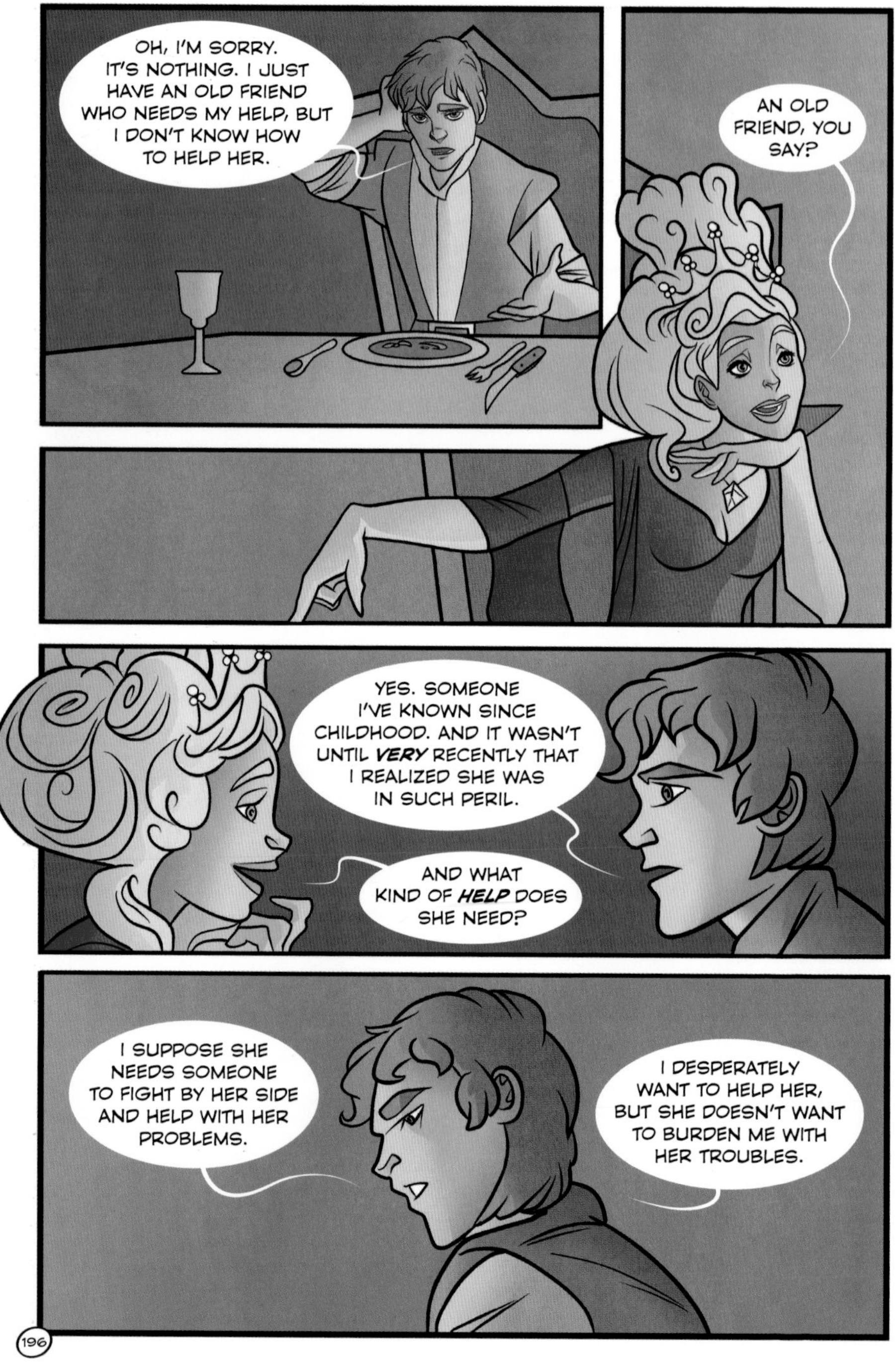
OH, I'M SORRY. IT'S NOTHING. I JUST HAVE AN OLD FRIEND WHO NEEDS MY HELP, BUT I DON'T KNOW HOW TO HELP HER.
AN OLD FRIEND, YOU SAY?
YES. SOMEONE I'VE KNOWN SINCE CHILDHOOD. AND IT WASN'T UNTIL *VERY* RECENTLY THAT I REALIZED SHE WAS IN SUCH PERIL.
AND WHAT KIND OF *HELP* DOES SHE NEED?
I SUPPOSE SHE NEEDS SOMEONE TO FIGHT BY HER SIDE AND HELP WITH HER PROBLEMS.
I DESPERATELY WANT TO HELP HER, BUT SHE DOESN'T WANT TO BURDEN ME WITH HER TROUBLES.

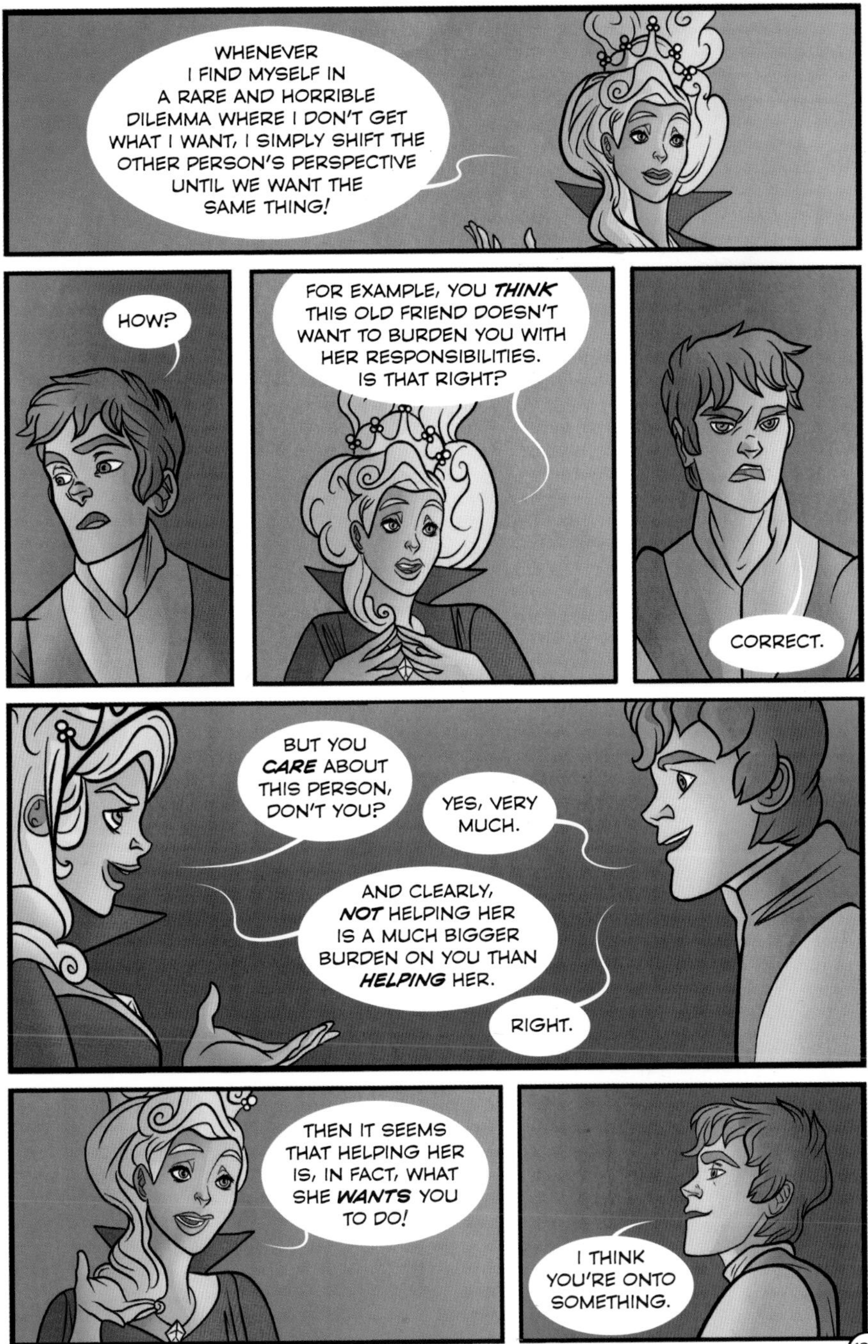
WHENEVER I FIND MYSELF IN A RARE AND HORRIBLE DILEMMA WHERE I DON'T GET WHAT I WANT, I SIMPLY SHIFT THE OTHER PERSON'S PERSPECTIVE UNTIL WE WANT THE SAME THING!
HOW?
FOR EXAMPLE, YOU ***THINK*** THIS OLD FRIEND DOESN'T WANT TO BURDEN YOU WITH HER RESPONSIBILITIES. IS THAT RIGHT?
CORRECT.
BUT YOU ***CARE*** ABOUT THIS PERSON, DON'T YOU?
YES, VERY MUCH.
AND CLEARLY, ***NOT*** HELPING HER IS A MUCH BIGGER BURDEN ON YOU THAN ***HELPING*** HER.
RIGHT.
THEN IT SEEMS THAT HELPING HER IS, IN FACT, WHAT SHE ***WANTS*** YOU TO DO!
I THINK YOU'RE ONTO SOMETHING.

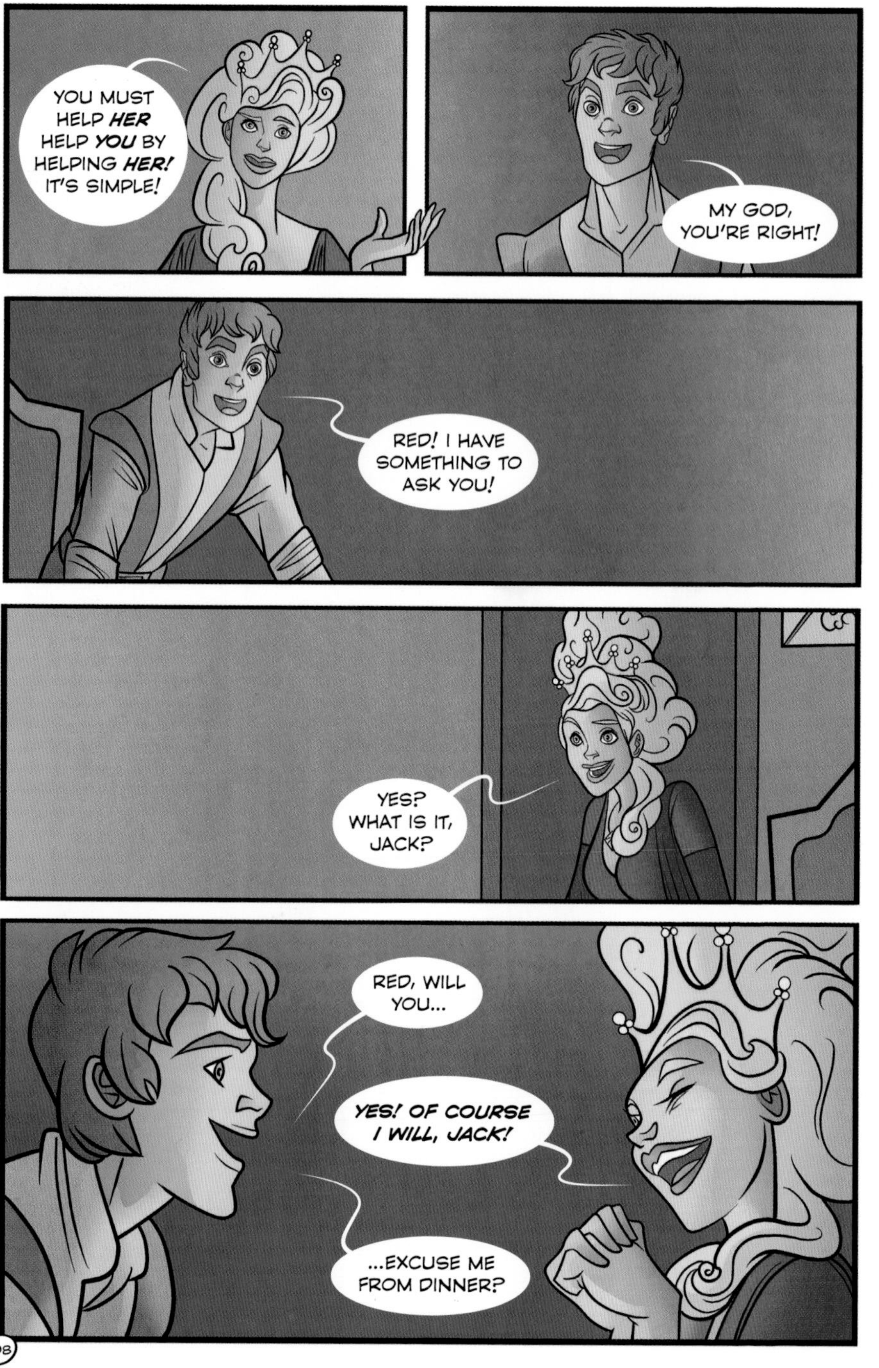
YOU MUST HELP ***HER*** HELP ***YOU*** BY HELPING ***HER!*** IT'S SIMPLE!
MY GOD, YOU'RE RIGHT!
RED! I HAVE SOMETHING TO ASK YOU!
YES? WHAT IS IT, JACK?
RED, WILL YOU...
YES! OF COURSE I WILL, JACK!
...EXCUSE ME FROM DINNER?

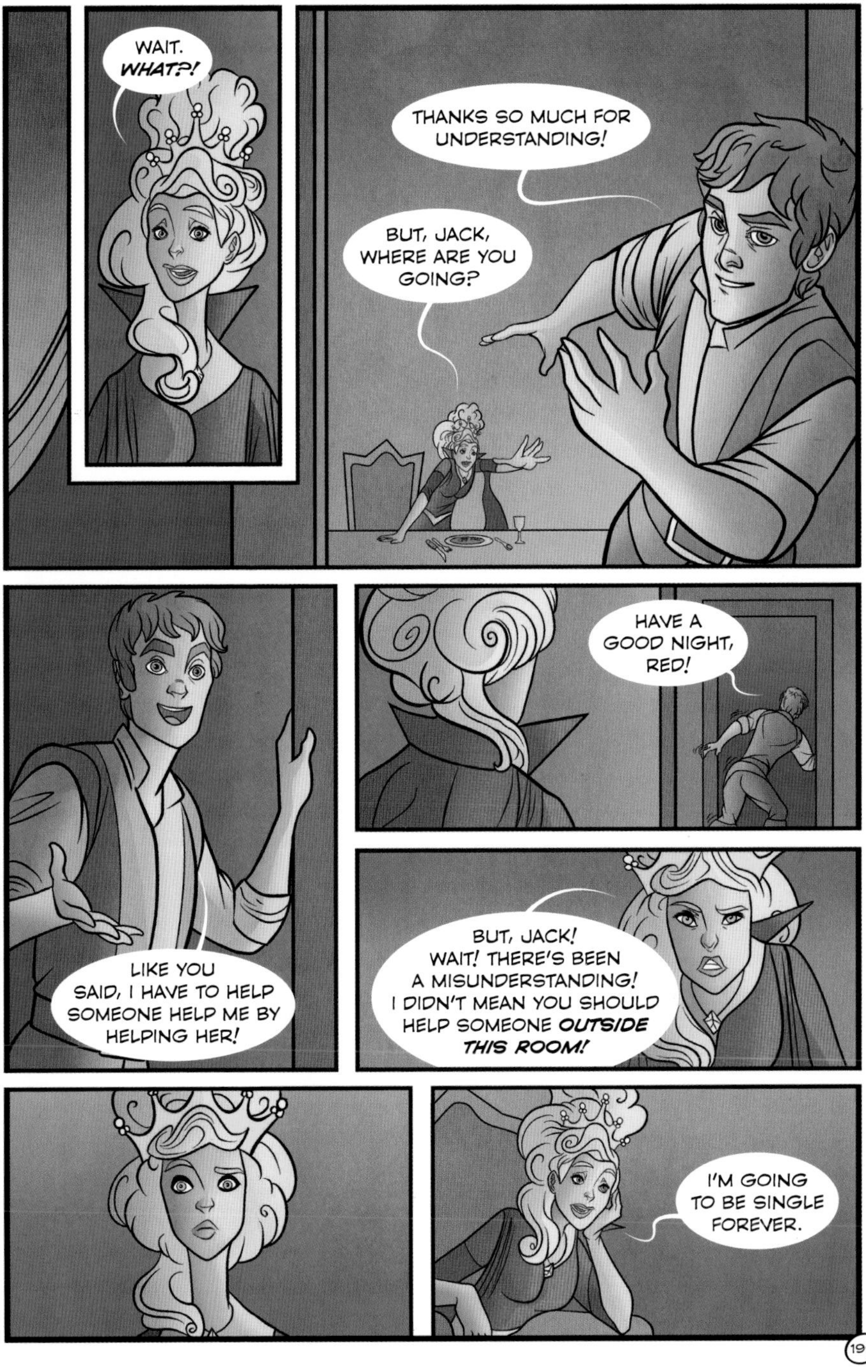
WAIT. *WHAT?!*
THANKS SO MUCH FOR UNDERSTANDING!
BUT, JACK, WHERE ARE YOU GOING?
LIKE YOU SAID, I HAVE TO HELP SOMEONE HELP ME BY HELPING HER!
HAVE A GOOD NIGHT, RED!
BUT, JACK! WAIT! THERE'S BEEN A MISUNDERSTANDING! I DIDN'T MEAN YOU SHOULD HELP SOMEONE *OUTSIDE THIS ROOM!*
I'M GOING TO BE SINGLE FOREVER.

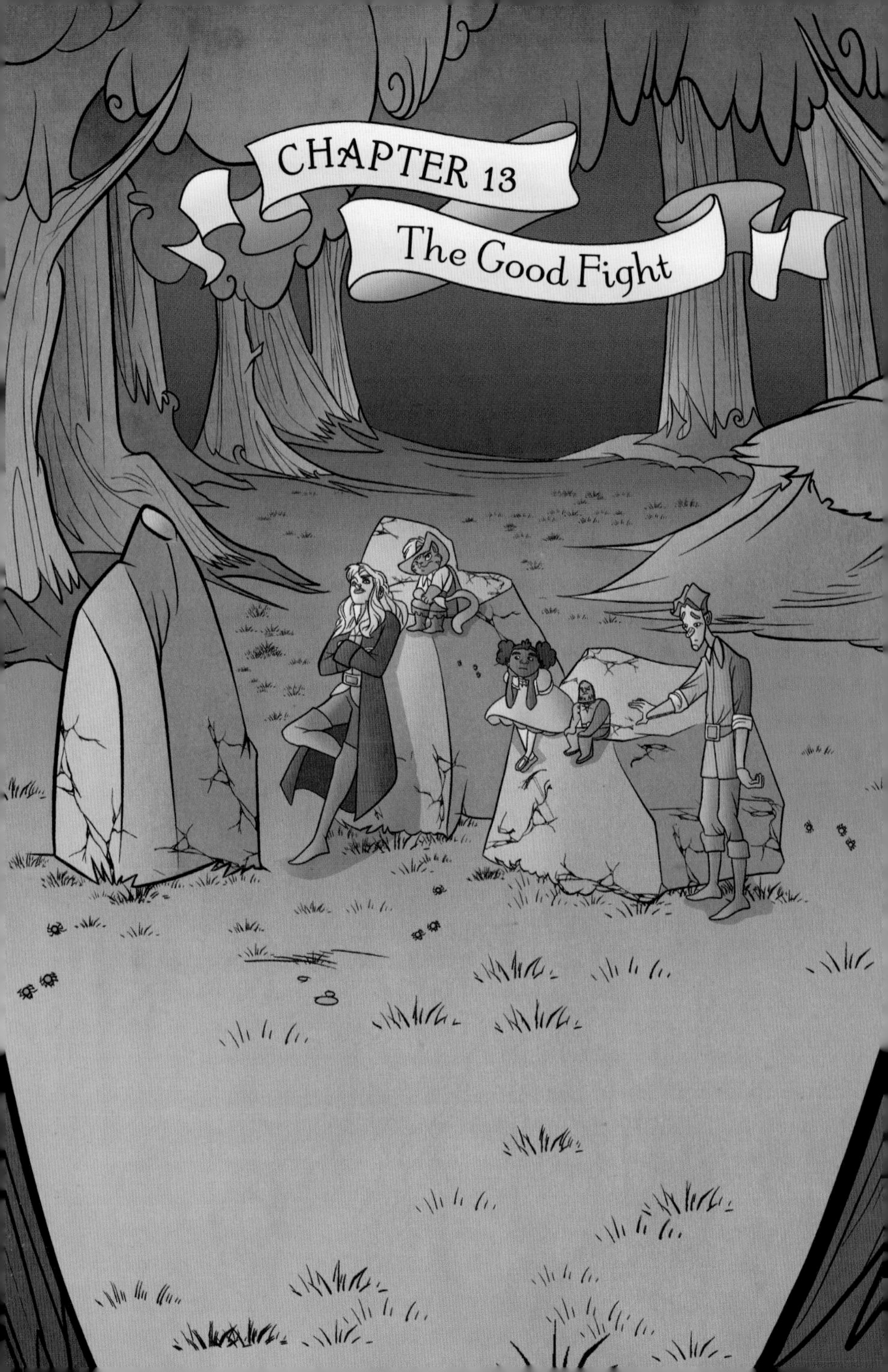
CHAPTER 13
The Good Fight

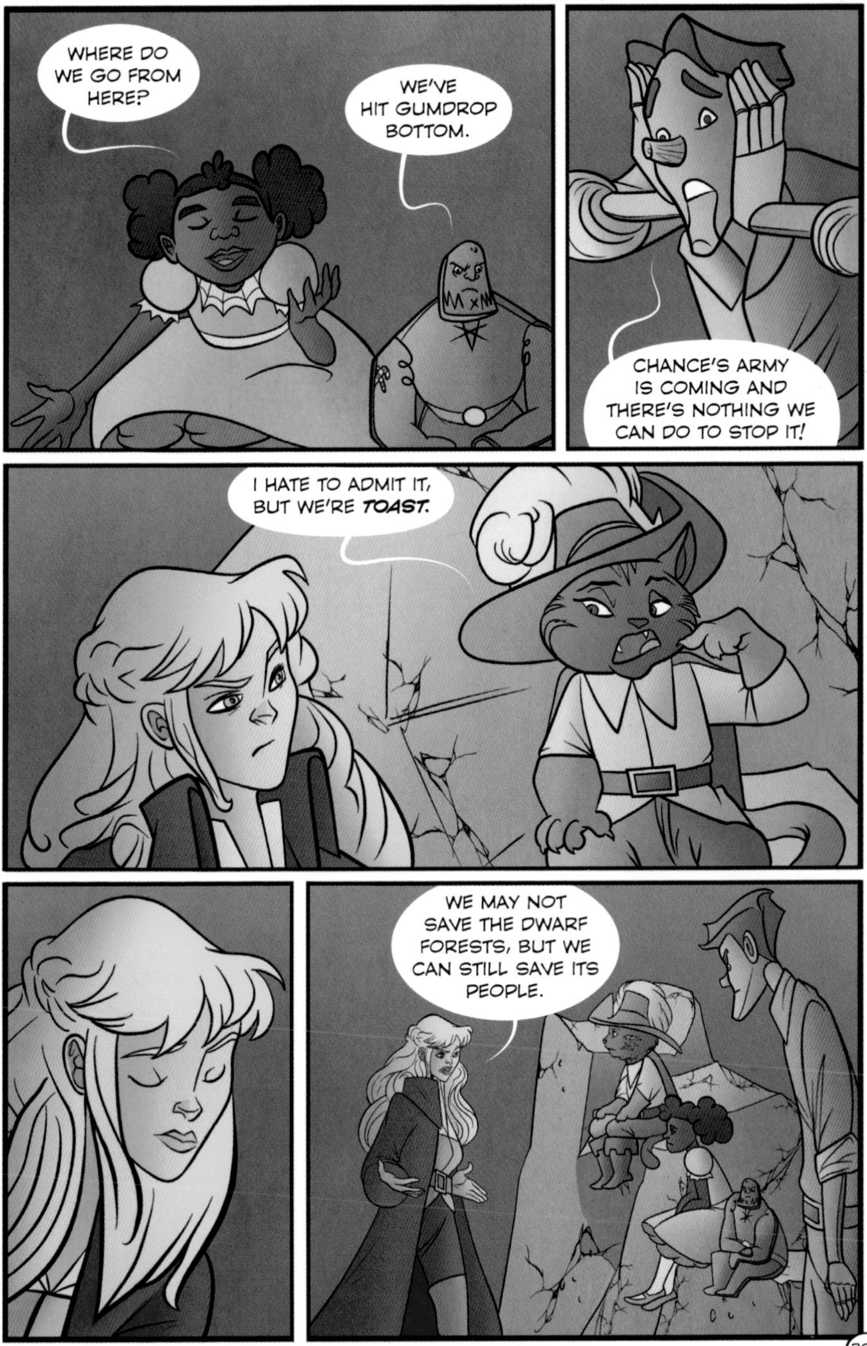
WHERE DO WE GO FROM HERE?
WE'VE HIT GUMDROP BOTTOM.
CHANCE'S ARMY IS COMING AND THERE'S NOTHING WE CAN DO TO STOP IT!
I HATE TO ADMIT IT, BUT WE'RE *TOAST.*
WE MAY NOT SAVE THE DWARF FORESTS, BUT WE CAN STILL SAVE ITS PEOPLE.

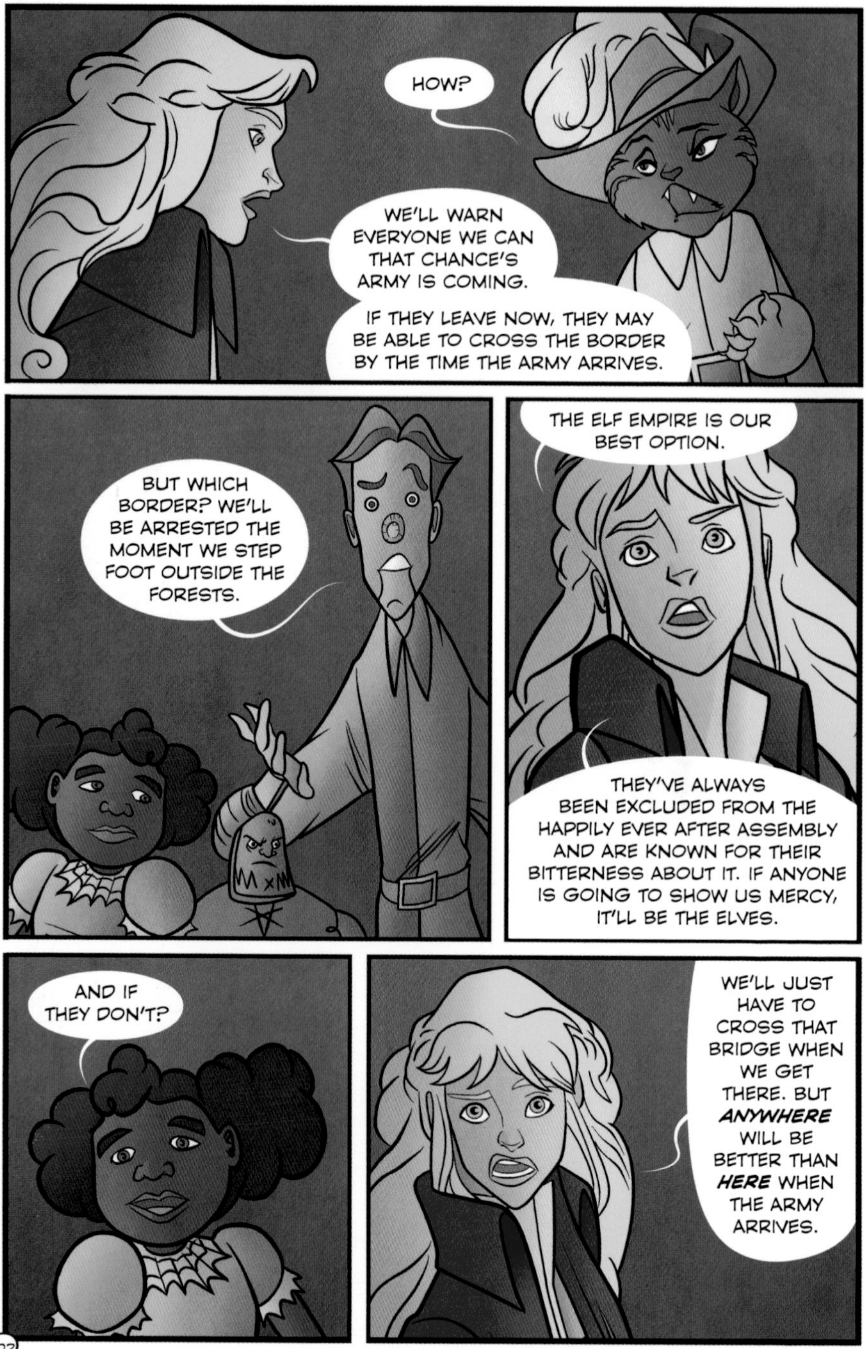
HOW?
WE'LL WARN EVERYONE WE CAN THAT CHANCE'S ARMY IS COMING.
IF THEY LEAVE NOW, THEY MAY BE ABLE TO CROSS THE BORDER BY THE TIME THE ARMY ARRIVES.
BUT WHICH BORDER? WE'LL BE ARRESTED THE MOMENT WE STEP FOOT OUTSIDE THE FORESTS.
THE ELF EMPIRE IS OUR BEST OPTION.
THEY'VE ALWAYS BEEN EXCLUDED FROM THE HAPPILY EVER AFTER ASSEMBLY AND ARE KNOWN FOR THEIR BITTERNESS ABOUT IT. IF ANYONE IS GOING TO SHOW US MERCY, IT'LL BE THE ELVES.
AND IF THEY DON'T?
WE'LL JUST HAVE TO CROSS THAT BRIDGE WHEN WE GET THERE. BUT ***ANYWHERE*** WILL BE BETTER THAN ***HERE*** WHEN THE ARMY ARRIVES.

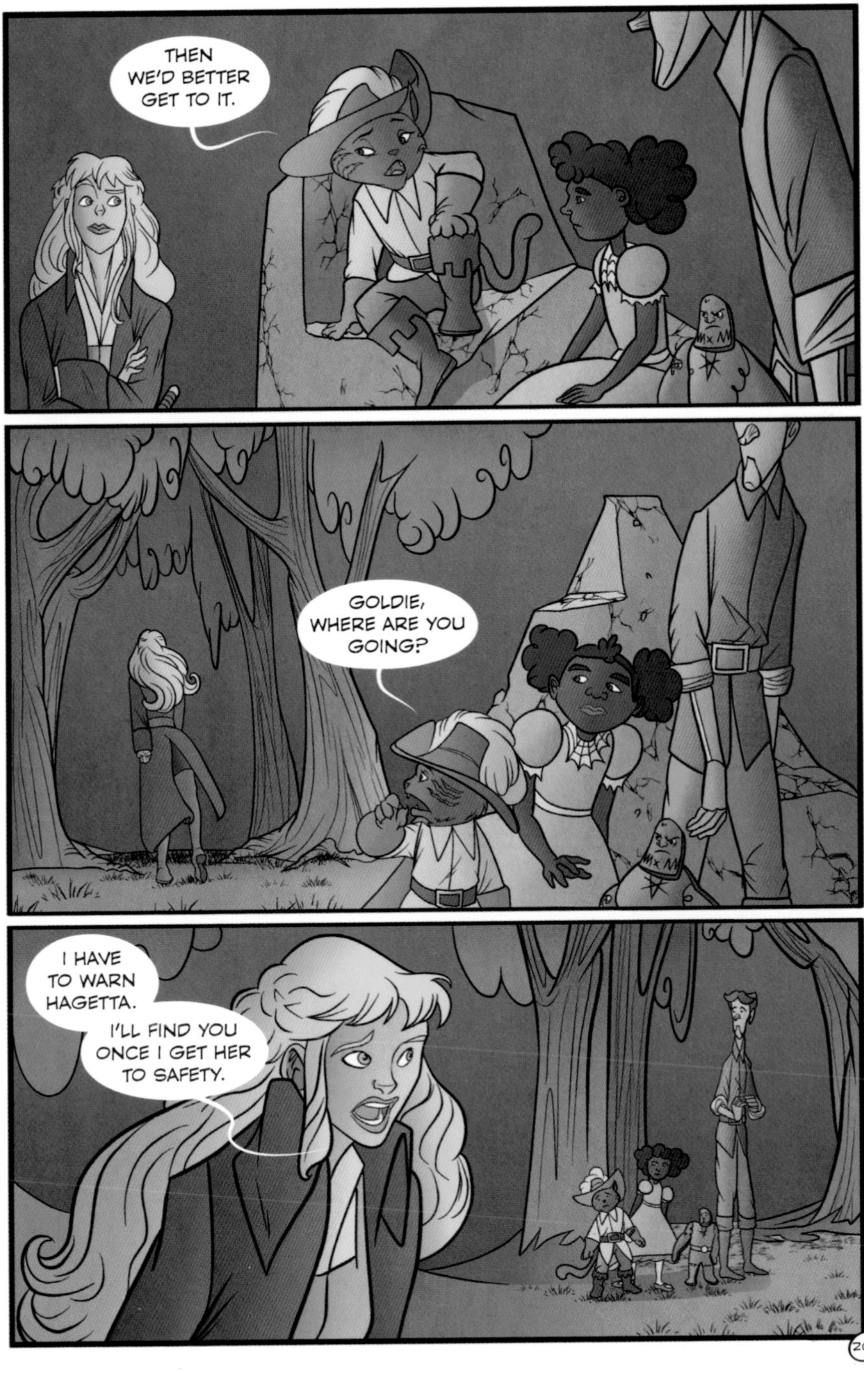
THEN WE'D BETTER GET TO IT.
GOLDIE, WHERE ARE YOU GOING?
I HAVE TO WARN HAGETTA.
I'LL FIND YOU ONCE I GET HER TO SAFETY.

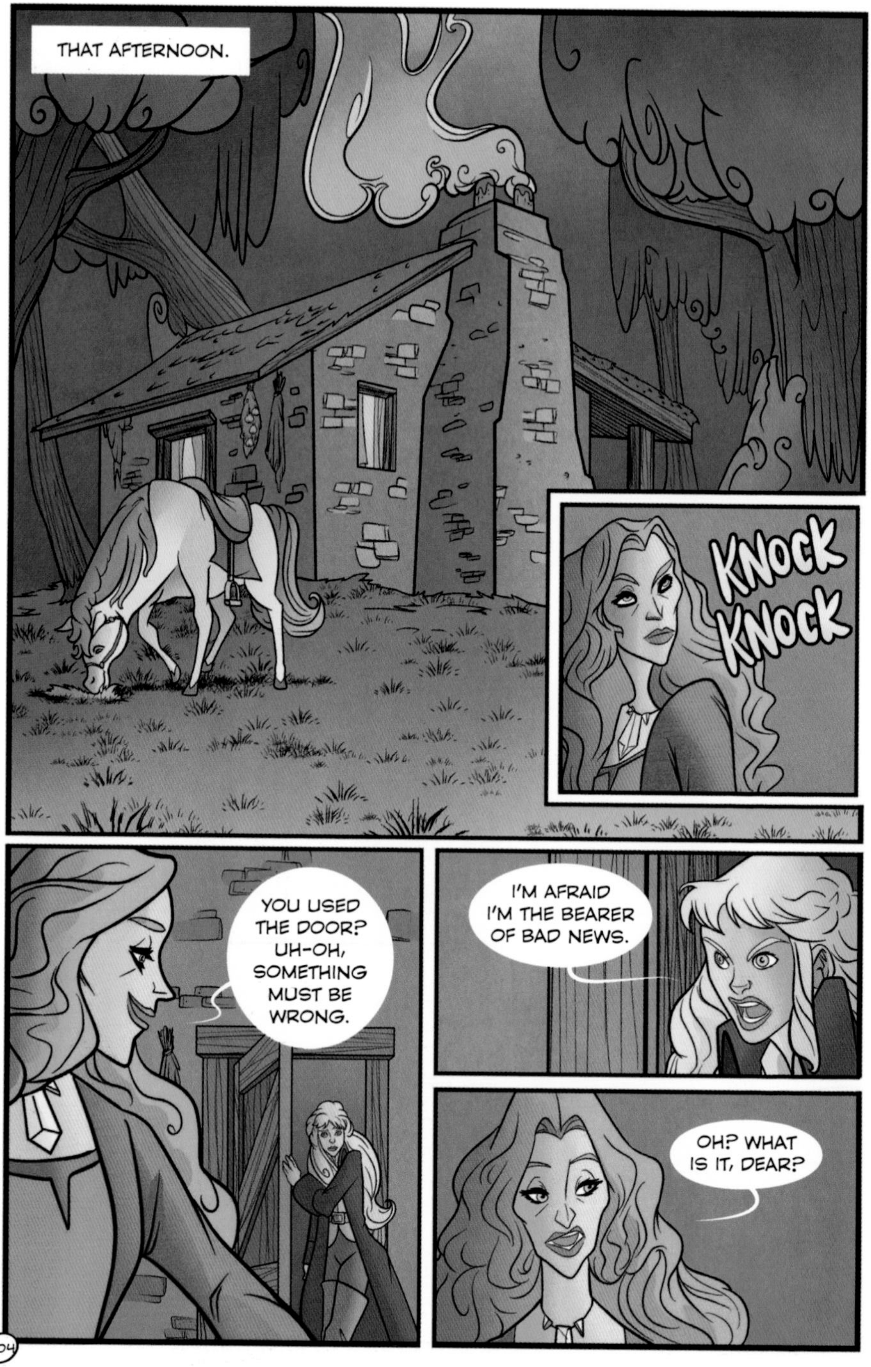
THAT AFTERNOON.
KNOCK KNOCK
YOU USED THE DOOR? UH-OH, SOMETHING MUST BE WRONG.
I'M AFRAID I'M THE BEARER OF BAD NEWS.
OH? WHAT IS IT, DEAR?

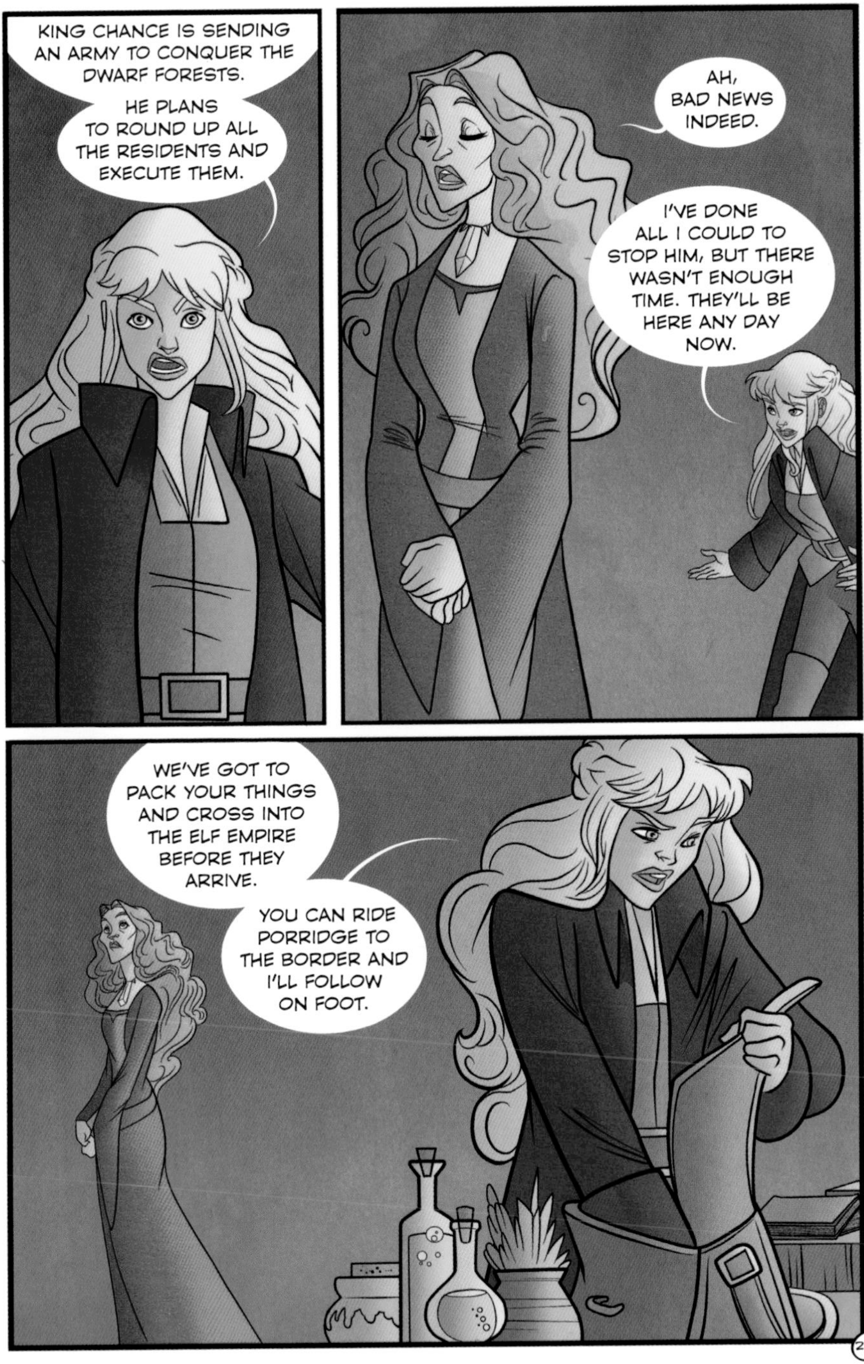
KING CHANCE IS SENDING AN ARMY TO CONQUER THE DWARF FORESTS.
HE PLANS TO ROUND UP ALL THE RESIDENTS AND EXECUTE THEM.
AH, BAD NEWS INDEED.
I'VE DONE ALL I COULD TO STOP HIM, BUT THERE WASN'T ENOUGH TIME. THEY'LL BE HERE ANY DAY NOW.
WE'VE GOT TO PACK YOUR THINGS AND CROSS INTO THE ELF EMPIRE BEFORE THEY ARRIVE.
YOU CAN RIDE PORRIDGE TO THE BORDER AND I'LL FOLLOW ON FOOT.

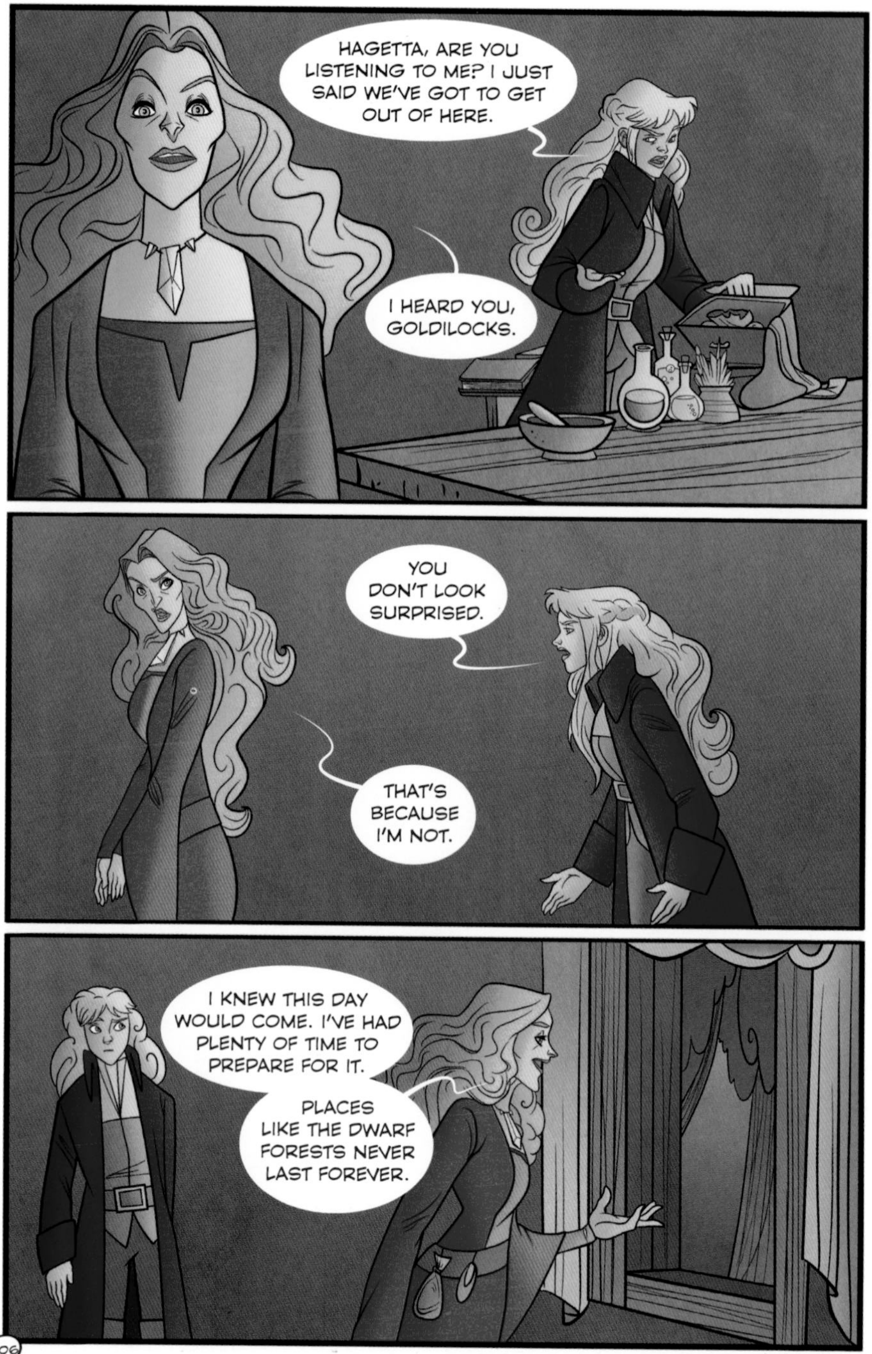
HAGETTA, ARE YOU LISTENING TO ME? I JUST SAID WE'VE GOT TO GET OUT OF HERE.
I HEARD YOU, GOLDILOCKS.
YOU DON'T LOOK SURPRISED.
THAT'S BECAUSE I'M NOT.
I KNEW THIS DAY WOULD COME. I'VE HAD PLENTY OF TIME TO PREPARE FOR IT.
PLACES LIKE THE DWARF FORESTS NEVER LAST FOREVER.

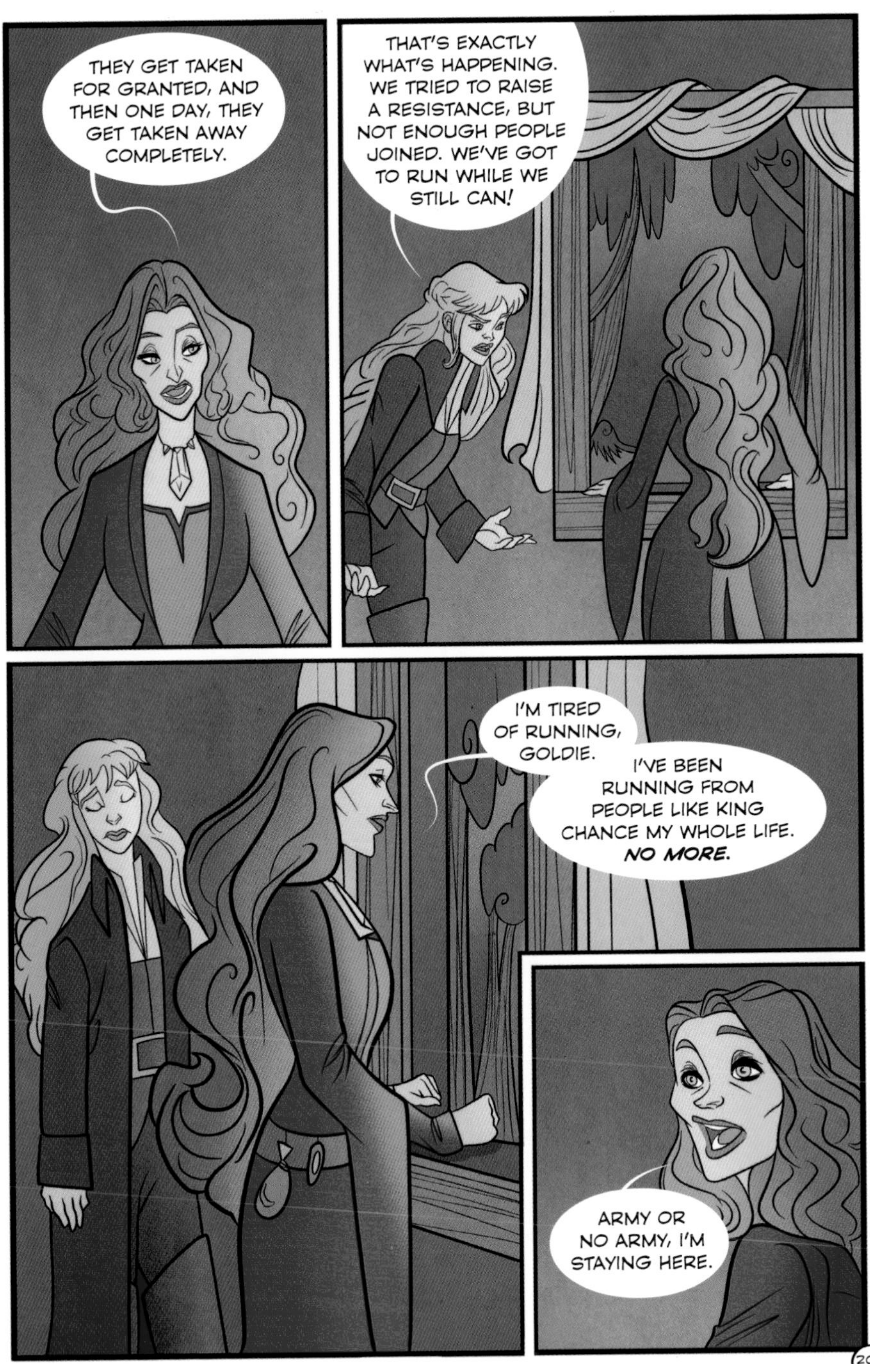
THEY GET TAKEN FOR GRANTED, AND THEN ONE DAY, THEY GET TAKEN AWAY COMPLETELY.
THAT'S EXACTLY WHAT'S HAPPENING. WE TRIED TO RAISE A RESISTANCE, BUT NOT ENOUGH PEOPLE JOINED. WE'VE GOT TO RUN WHILE WE STILL CAN!
I'M TIRED OF RUNNING, GOLDIE.
I'VE BEEN RUNNING FROM PEOPLE LIKE KING CHANCE MY WHOLE LIFE. ***NO MORE.***
ARMY OR NO ARMY, I'M STAYING HERE.

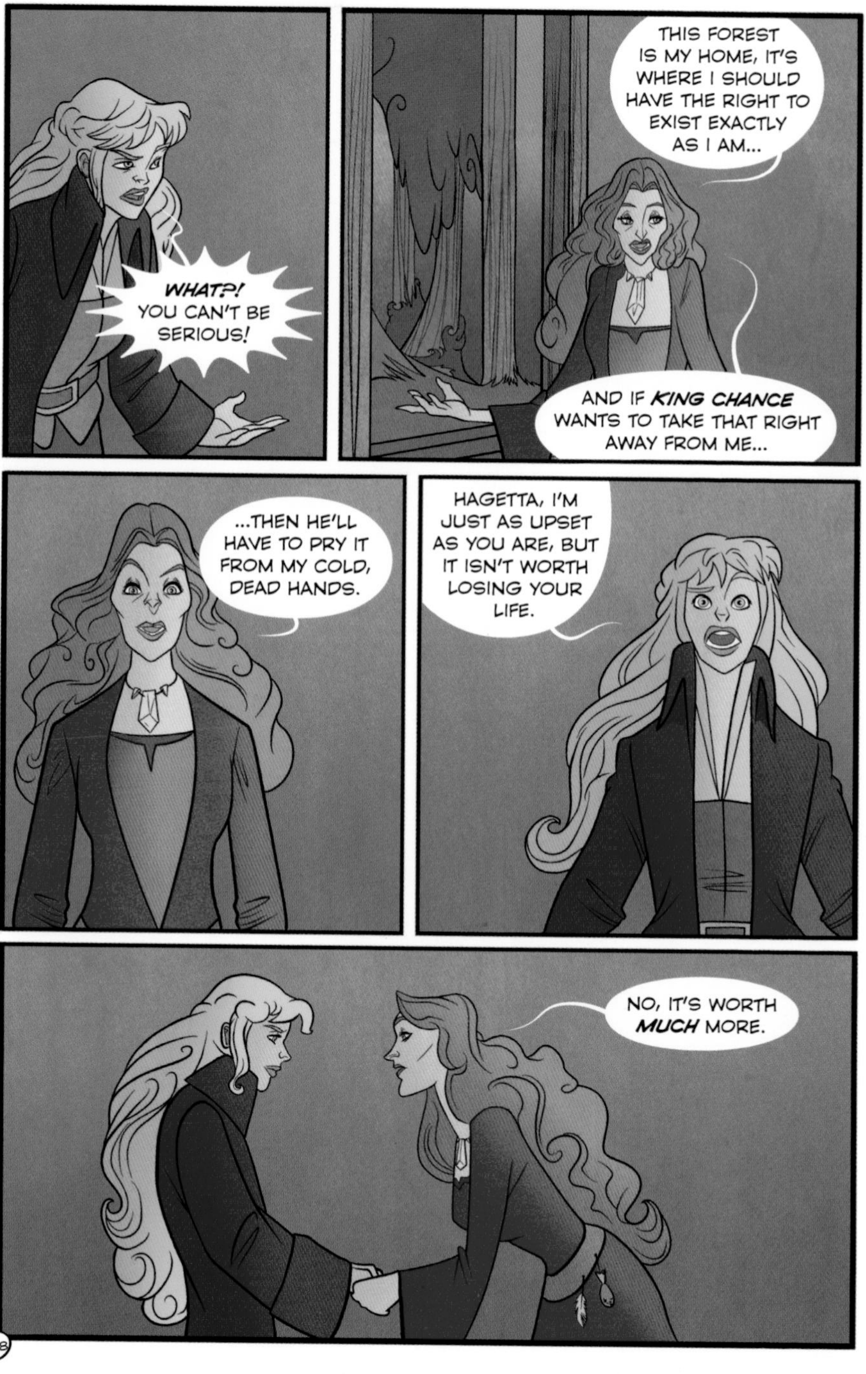
WHAT?! YOU CAN'T BE SERIOUS!
THIS FOREST IS MY HOME, IT'S WHERE I SHOULD HAVE THE RIGHT TO EXIST EXACTLY AS I AM...
AND IF KING CHANCE WANTS TO TAKE THAT RIGHT AWAY FROM ME...
...THEN HE'LL HAVE TO PRY IT FROM MY COLD, DEAD HANDS.
HAGETTA, I'M JUST AS UPSET AS YOU ARE, BUT IT ISN'T WORTH LOSING YOUR LIFE.
NO, IT'S WORTH MUCH MORE.

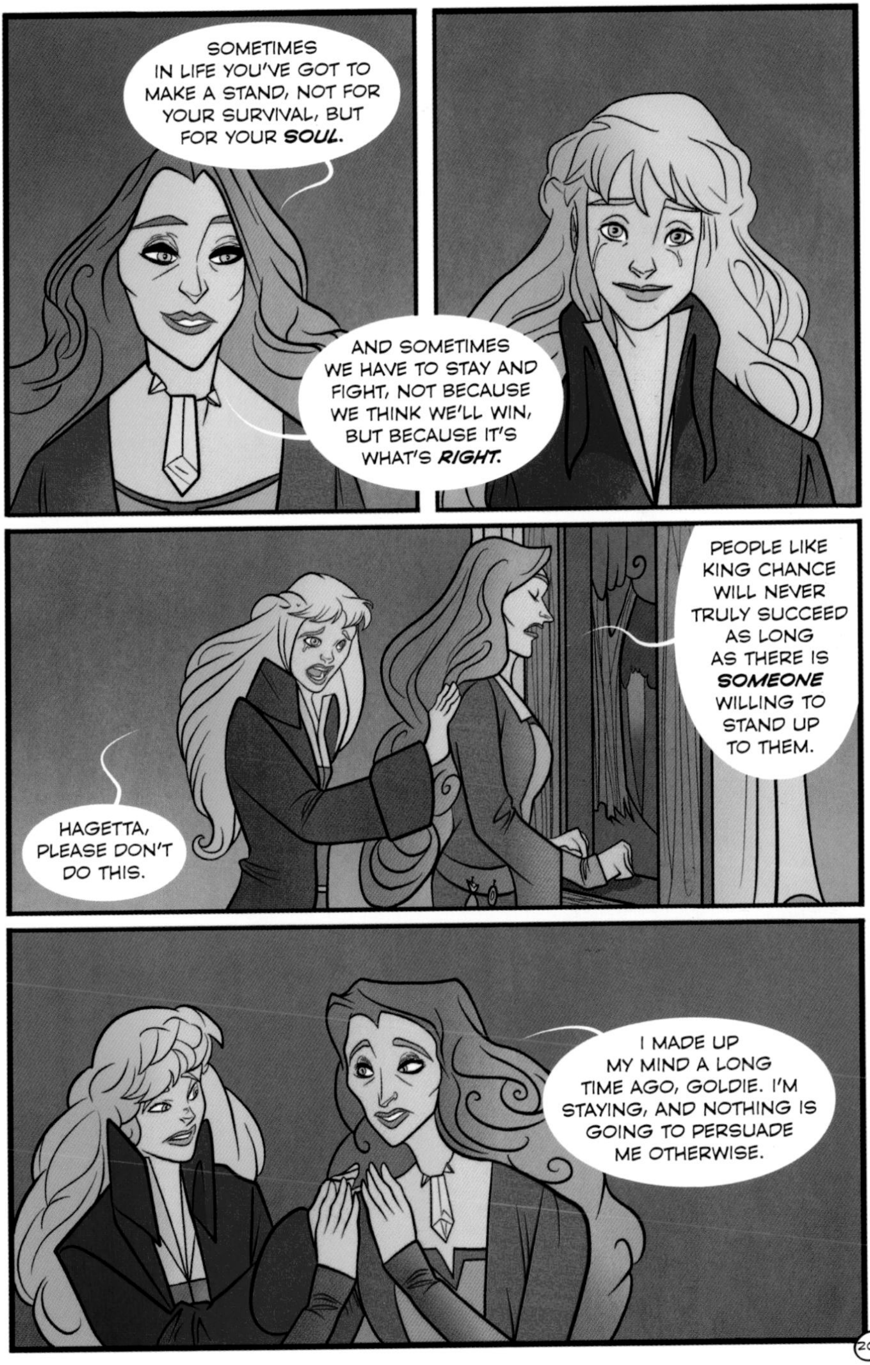
SOMETIMES IN LIFE YOU'VE GOT TO MAKE A STAND, NOT FOR YOUR SURVIVAL, BUT FOR YOUR **SOUL.**
AND SOMETIMES WE HAVE TO STAY AND FIGHT, NOT BECAUSE WE THINK WE'LL WIN, BUT BECAUSE IT'S WHAT'S **RIGHT.**
PEOPLE LIKE KING CHANCE WILL NEVER TRULY SUCCEED AS LONG AS THERE IS **SOMEONE** WILLING TO STAND UP TO THEM.
HAGETTA, PLEASE DON'T DO THIS.
I MADE UP MY MIND A LONG TIME AGO, GOLDIE. I'M STAYING, AND NOTHING IS GOING TO PERSUADE ME OTHERWISE.

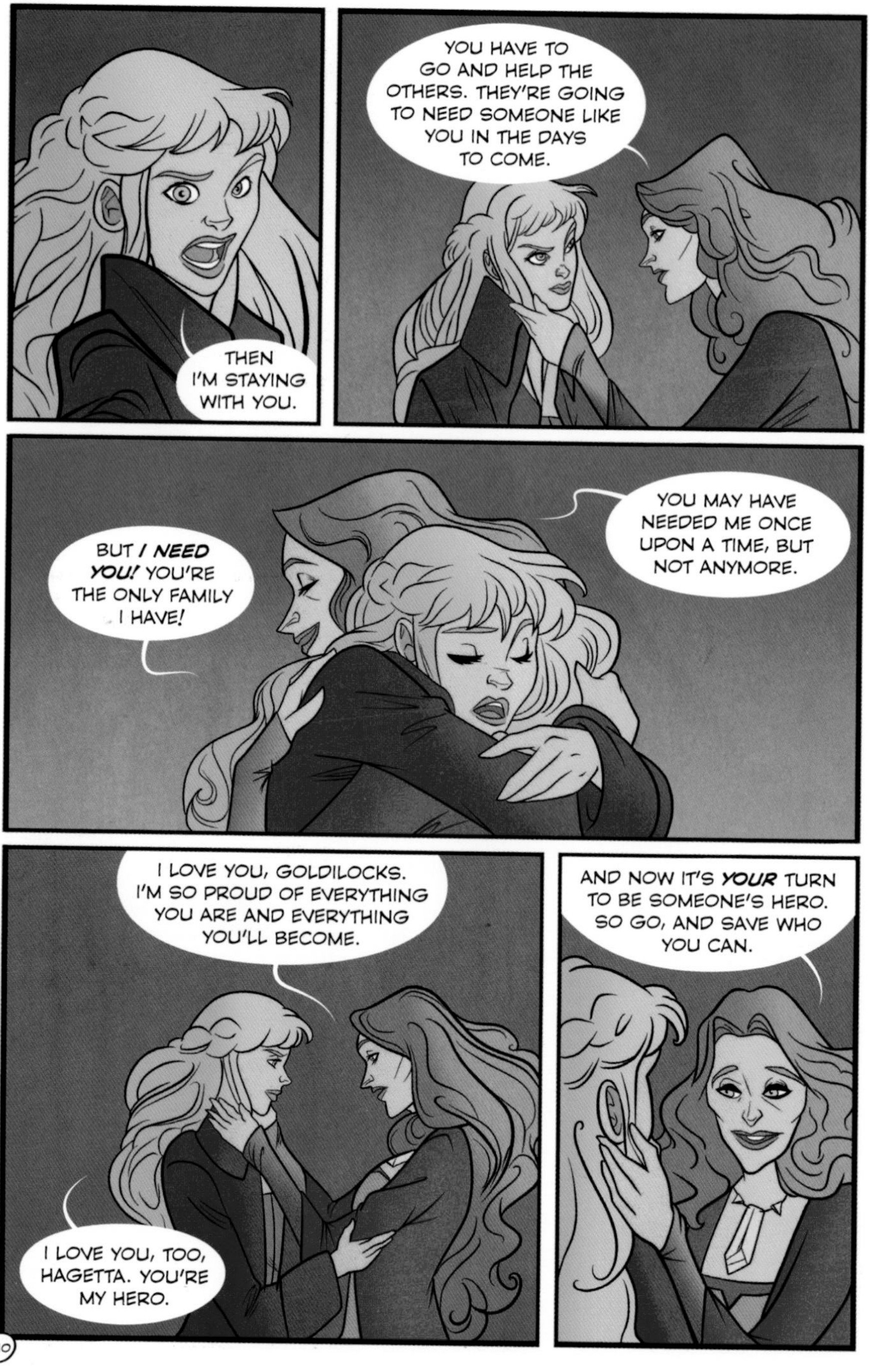
THEN I'M STAYING WITH YOU.
YOU HAVE TO GO AND HELP THE OTHERS. THEY'RE GOING TO NEED SOMEONE LIKE YOU IN THE DAYS TO COME.
BUT ***I NEED YOU!*** YOU'RE THE ONLY FAMILY I HAVE!
YOU MAY HAVE NEEDED ME ONCE UPON A TIME, BUT NOT ANYMORE.
I LOVE YOU, GOLDILOCKS. I'M SO PROUD OF EVERYTHING YOU ARE AND EVERYTHING YOU'LL BECOME.
I LOVE YOU, TOO, HAGETTA. YOU'RE MY HERO.
AND NOW IT'S ***YOUR*** TURN TO BE SOMEONE'S HERO. SO GO, AND SAVE WHO YOU CAN.

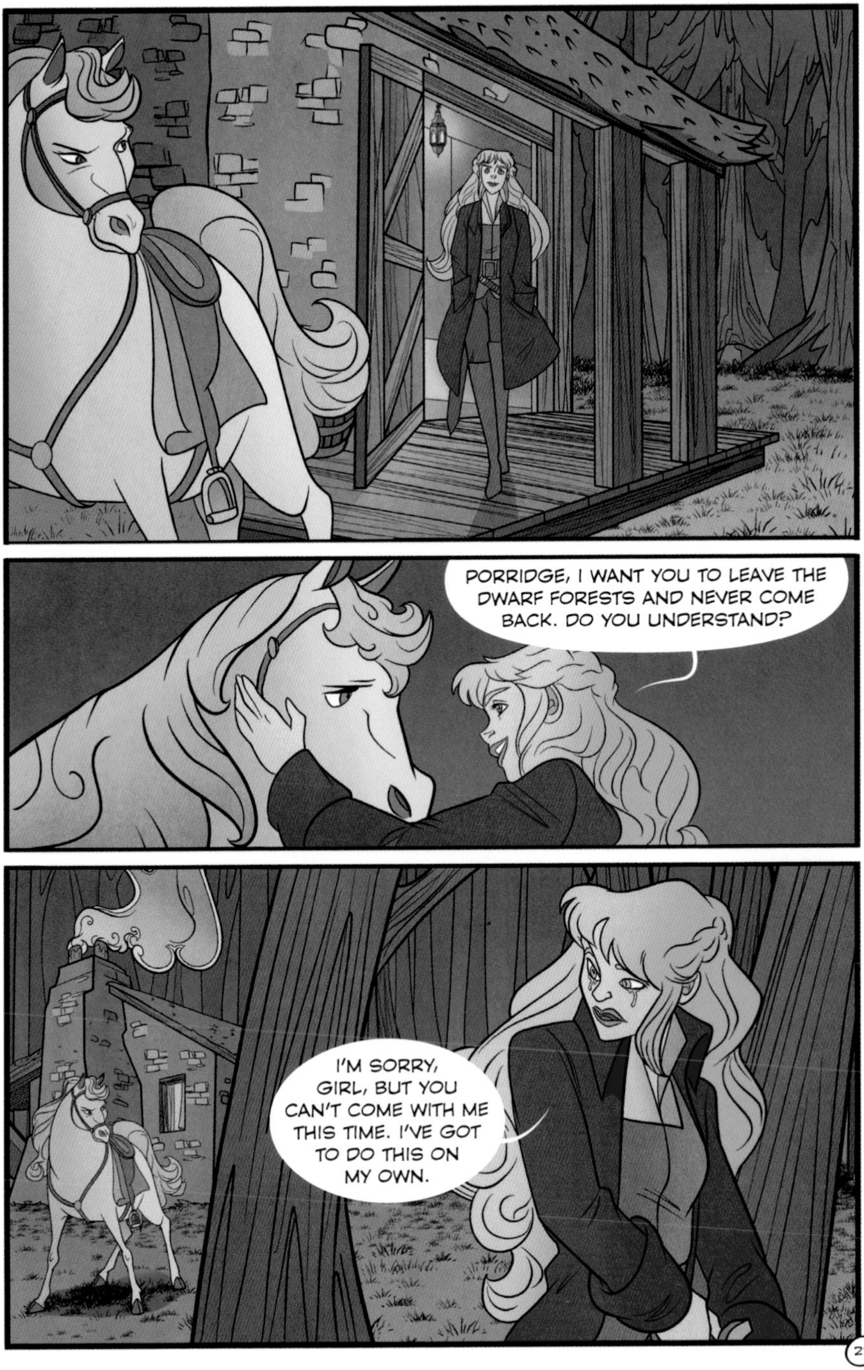
PORRIDGE, I WANT YOU TO LEAVE THE DWARF FORESTS AND NEVER COME BACK. DO YOU UNDERSTAND?
I'M SORRY, GIRL, BUT YOU CAN'T COME WITH ME THIS TIME. I'VE GOT TO DO THIS ON MY OWN.

CHAPTER 14
The Evacuation

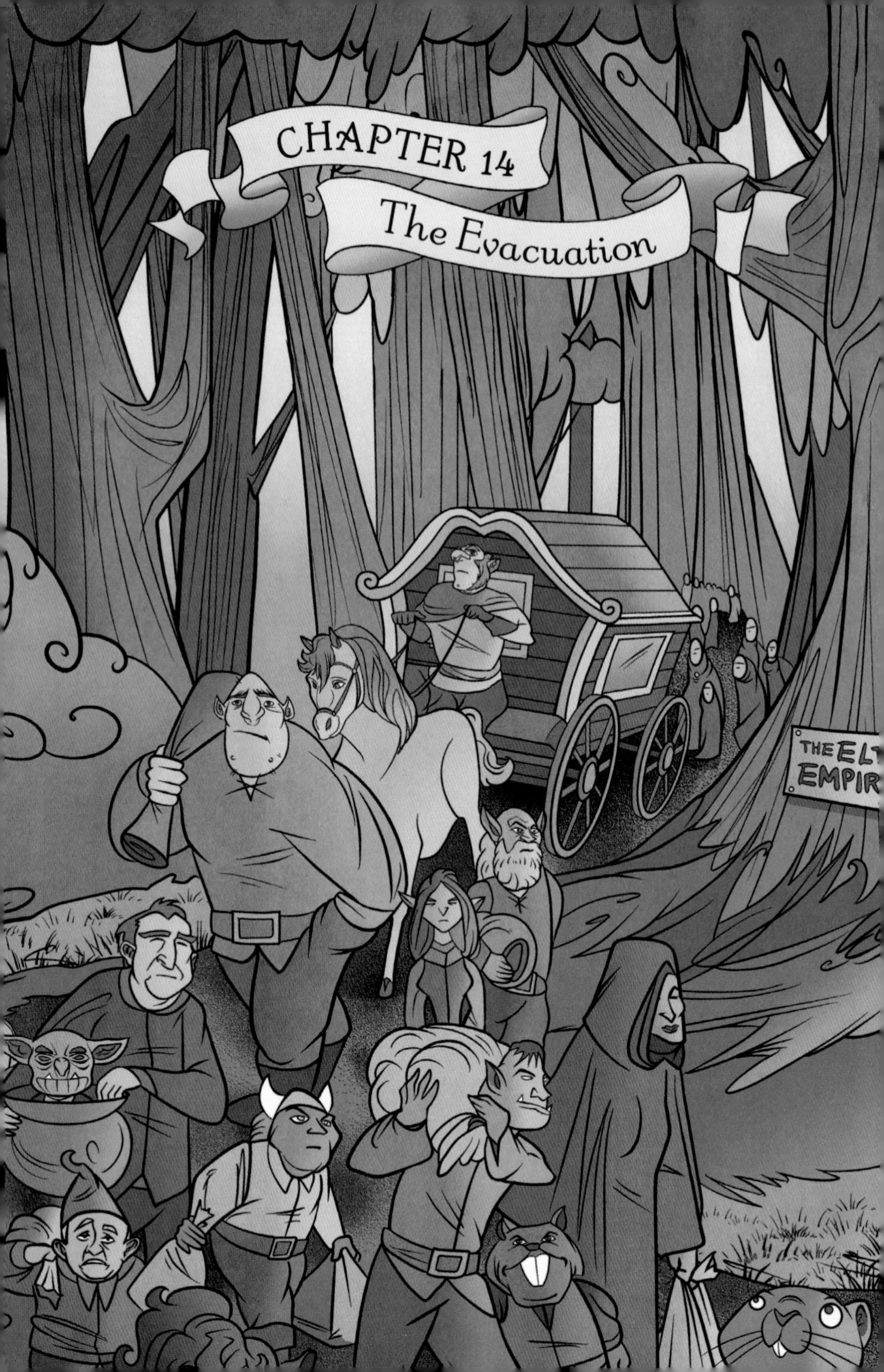

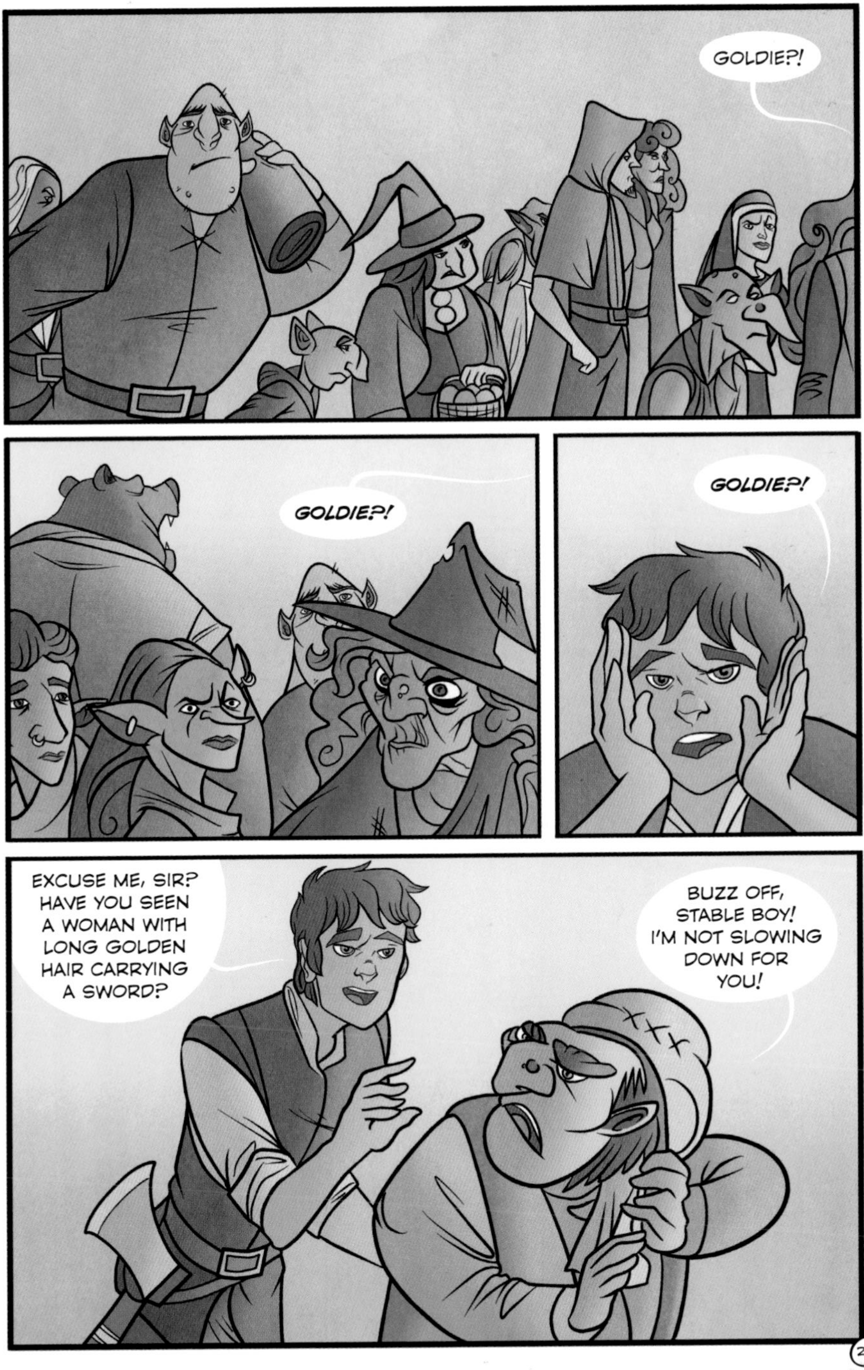
GOLDIE?!
GOLDIE?!
GOLDIE?!
EXCUSE ME, SIR? HAVE YOU SEEN A WOMAN WITH LONG GOLDEN HAIR CARRYING A SWORD?
BUZZ OFF, STABLE BOY! I'M NOT SLOWING DOWN FOR YOU!

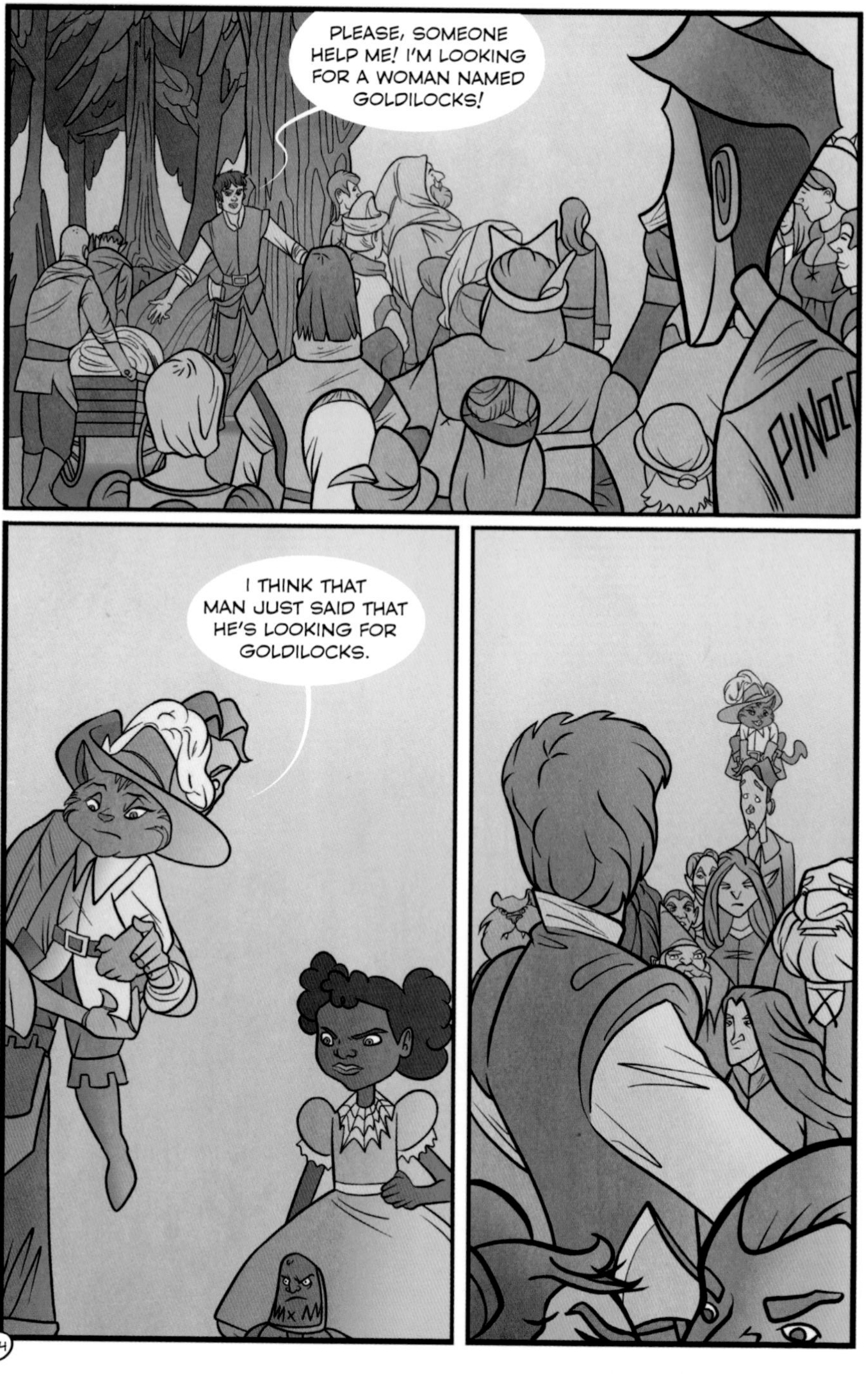
PLEASE, SOMEONE HELP ME! I'M LOOKING FOR A WOMAN NAMED GOLDILOCKS!
PINOC
I THINK THAT MAN JUST SAID THAT HE'S LOOKING FOR GOLDILOCKS.

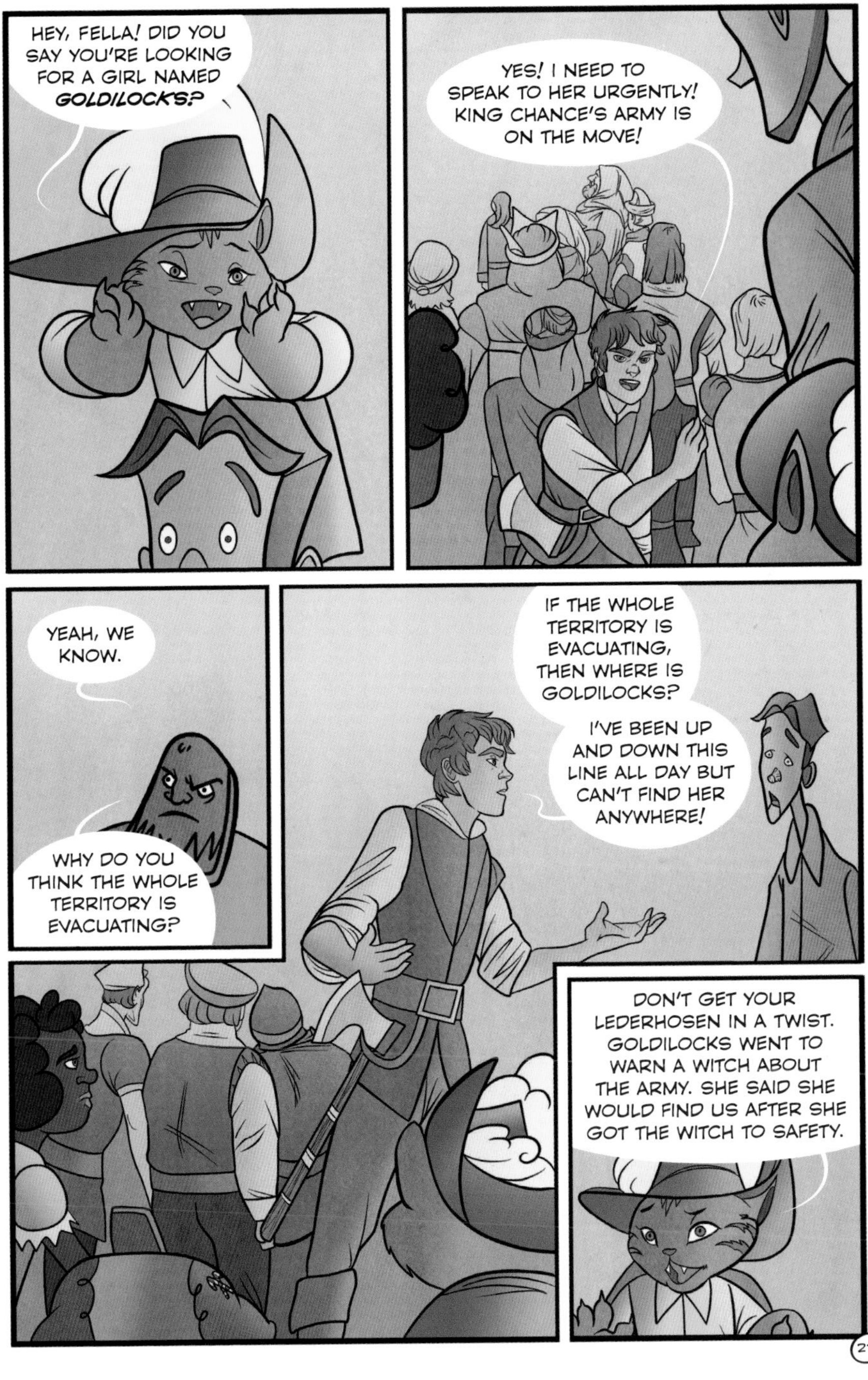
HEY, FELLA! DID YOU SAY YOU'RE LOOKING FOR A GIRL NAMED GOLDILOCKS?
YES! I NEED TO SPEAK TO HER URGENTLY! KING CHANCE'S ARMY IS ON THE MOVE!
YEAH, WE KNOW.
WHY DO YOU THINK THE WHOLE TERRITORY IS EVACUATING?
IF THE WHOLE TERRITORY IS EVACUATING, THEN WHERE IS GOLDILOCKS?
I'VE BEEN UP AND DOWN THIS LINE ALL DAY BUT CAN'T FIND HER ANYWHERE!
DON'T GET YOUR LEDERHOSEN IN A TWIST. GOLDILOCKS WENT TO WARN A WITCH ABOUT THE ARMY. SHE SAID SHE WOULD FIND US AFTER SHE GOT THE WITCH TO SAFETY.

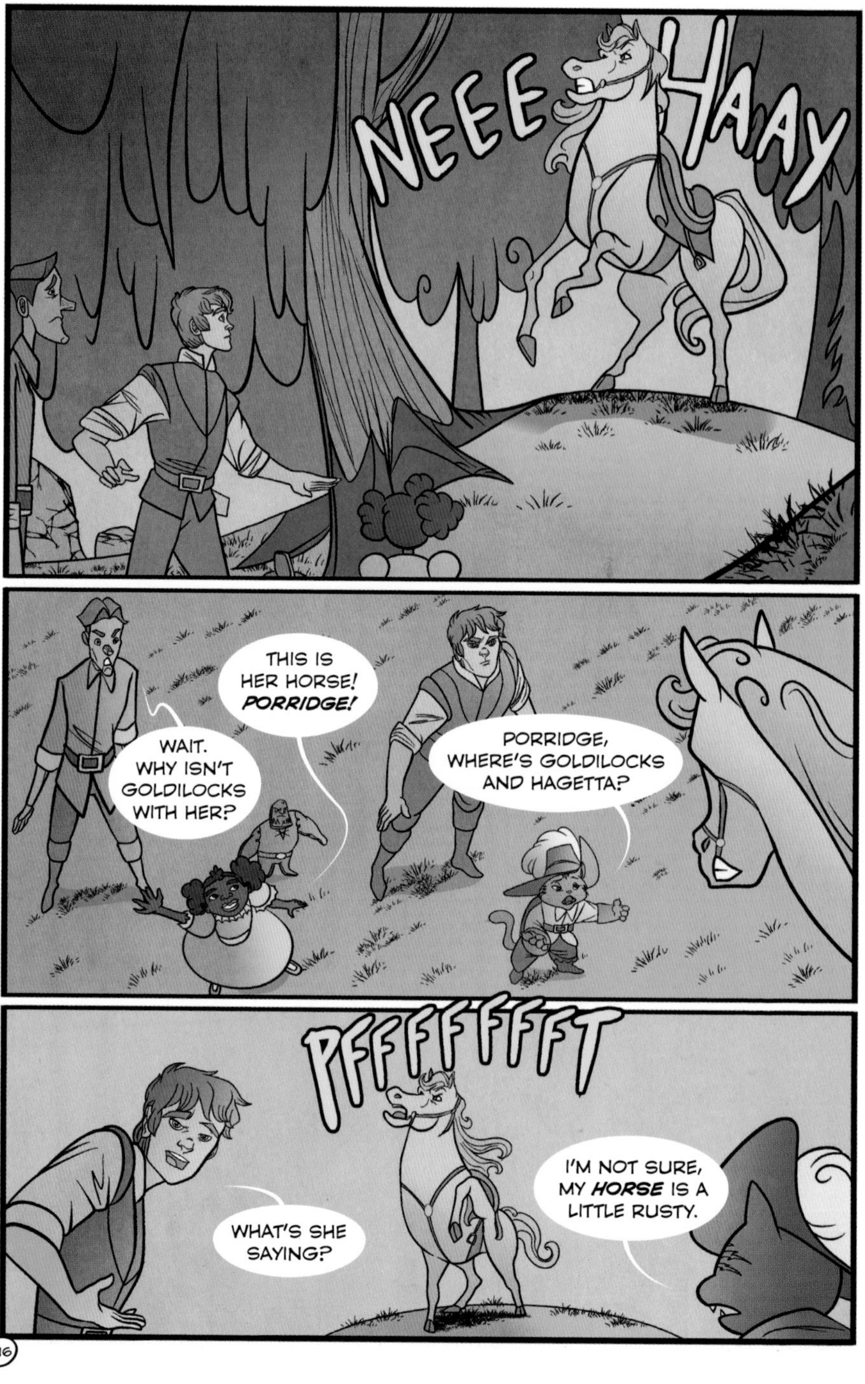
NEEEHAAY
THIS IS HER HORSE! ***PORRIDGE!***
WAIT. WHY ISN'T GOLDILOCKS WITH HER?
PORRIDGE, WHERE'S GOLDILOCKS AND HAGETTA?
PFFFFFFFT
WHAT'S SHE SAYING?
I'M NOT SURE, MY ***HORSE*** IS A LITTLE RUSTY.

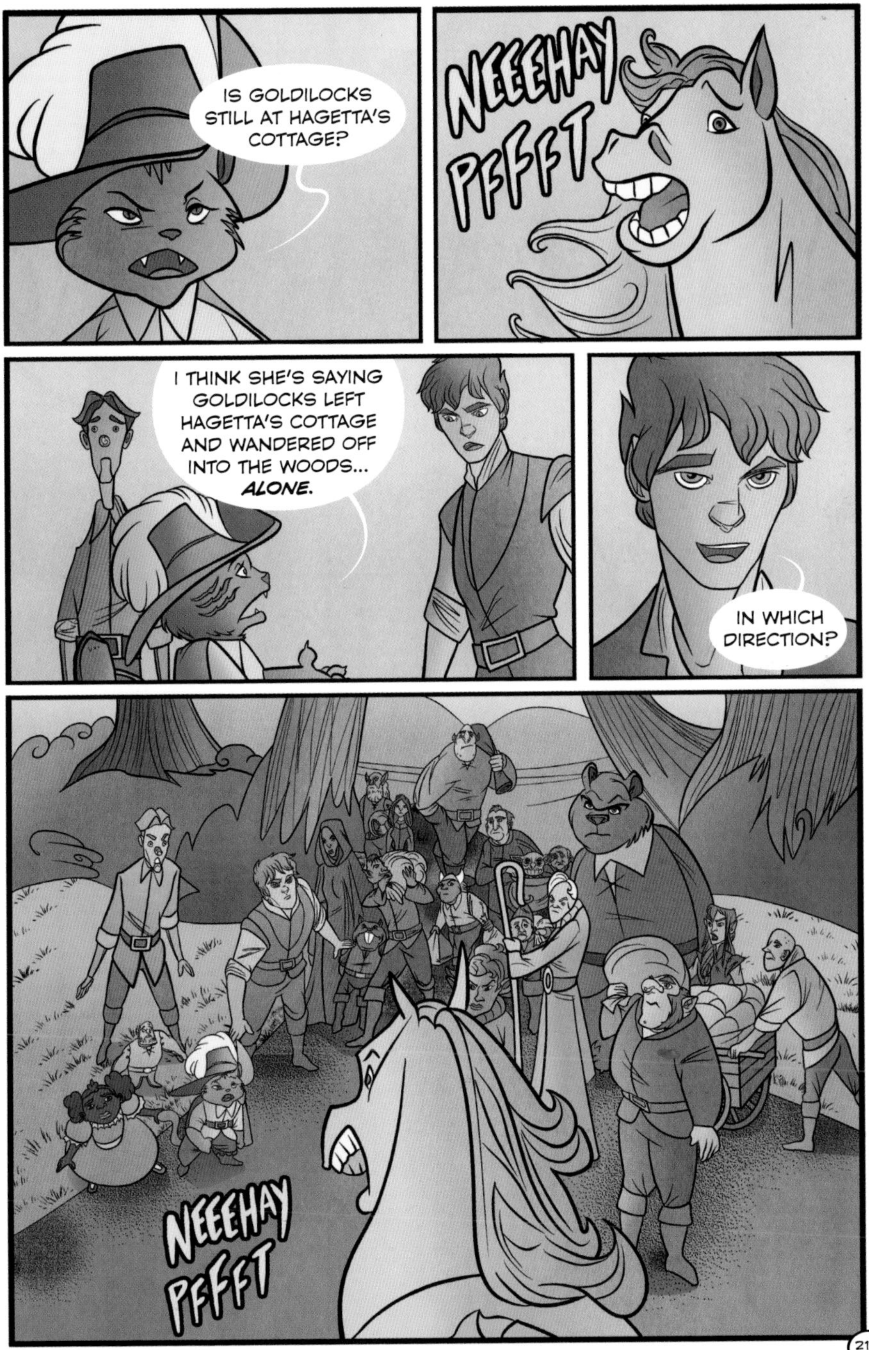
IS GOLDILOCKS STILL AT HAGETTA'S COTTAGE?
NEEEHAY PFFFT
I THINK SHE'S SAYING GOLDILOCKS LEFT HAGETTA'S COTTAGE AND WANDERED OFF INTO THE WOODS... *ALONE*.
IN WHICH DIRECTION?
NEEEHAY PFFFT

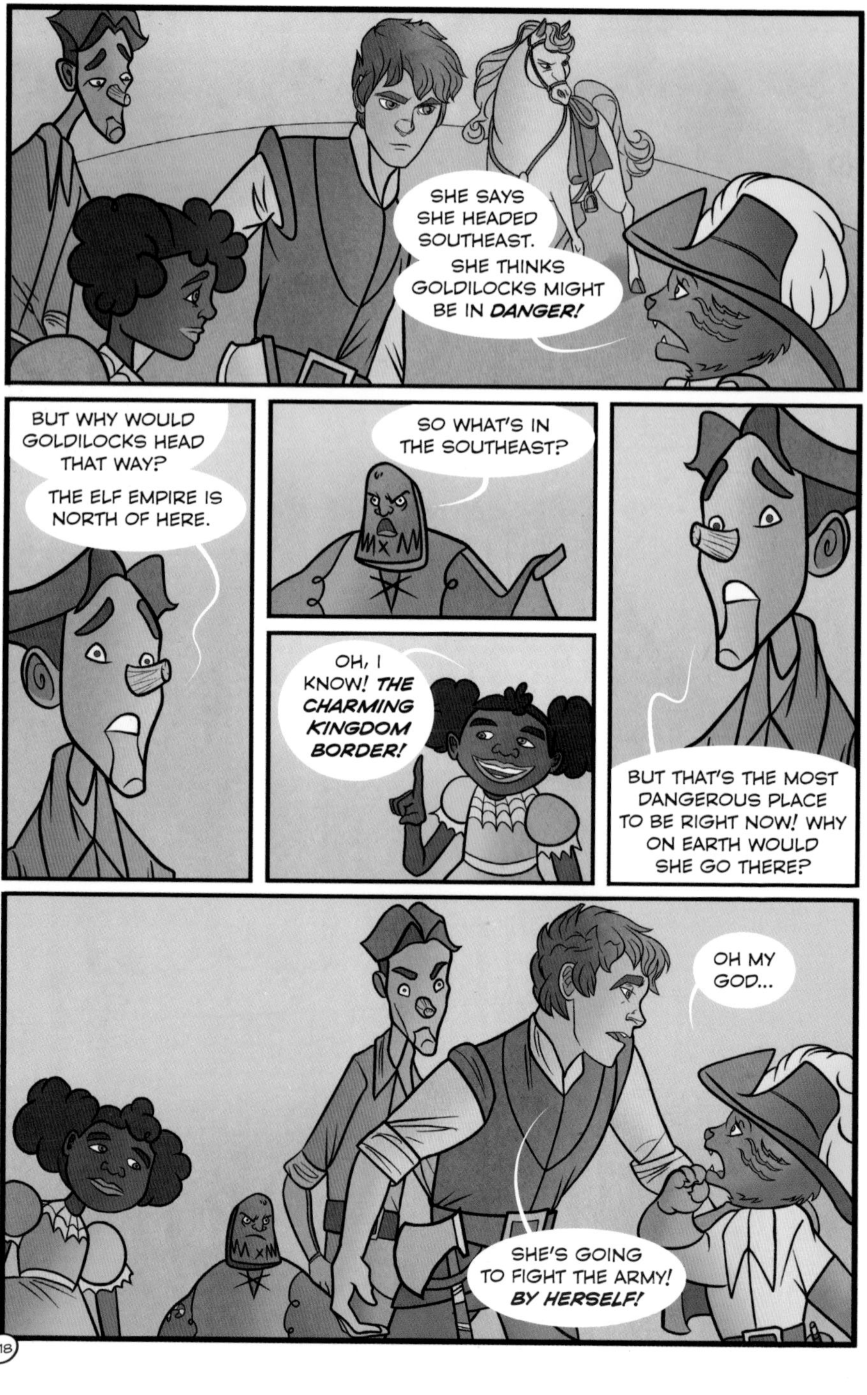
SHE SAYS SHE HEADED SOUTHEAST.
SHE THINKS GOLDILOCKS MIGHT BE IN *DANGER!*
BUT WHY WOULD GOLDILOCKS HEAD THAT WAY?
THE ELF EMPIRE IS NORTH OF HERE.
SO WHAT'S IN THE SOUTHEAST?
OH, I KNOW! ***THE CHARMING KINGDOM BORDER!***
BUT THAT'S THE MOST DANGEROUS PLACE TO BE RIGHT NOW! WHY ON EARTH WOULD SHE GO THERE?
OH MY GOD...
SHE'S GOING TO FIGHT THE ARMY! ***BY HERSELF!***

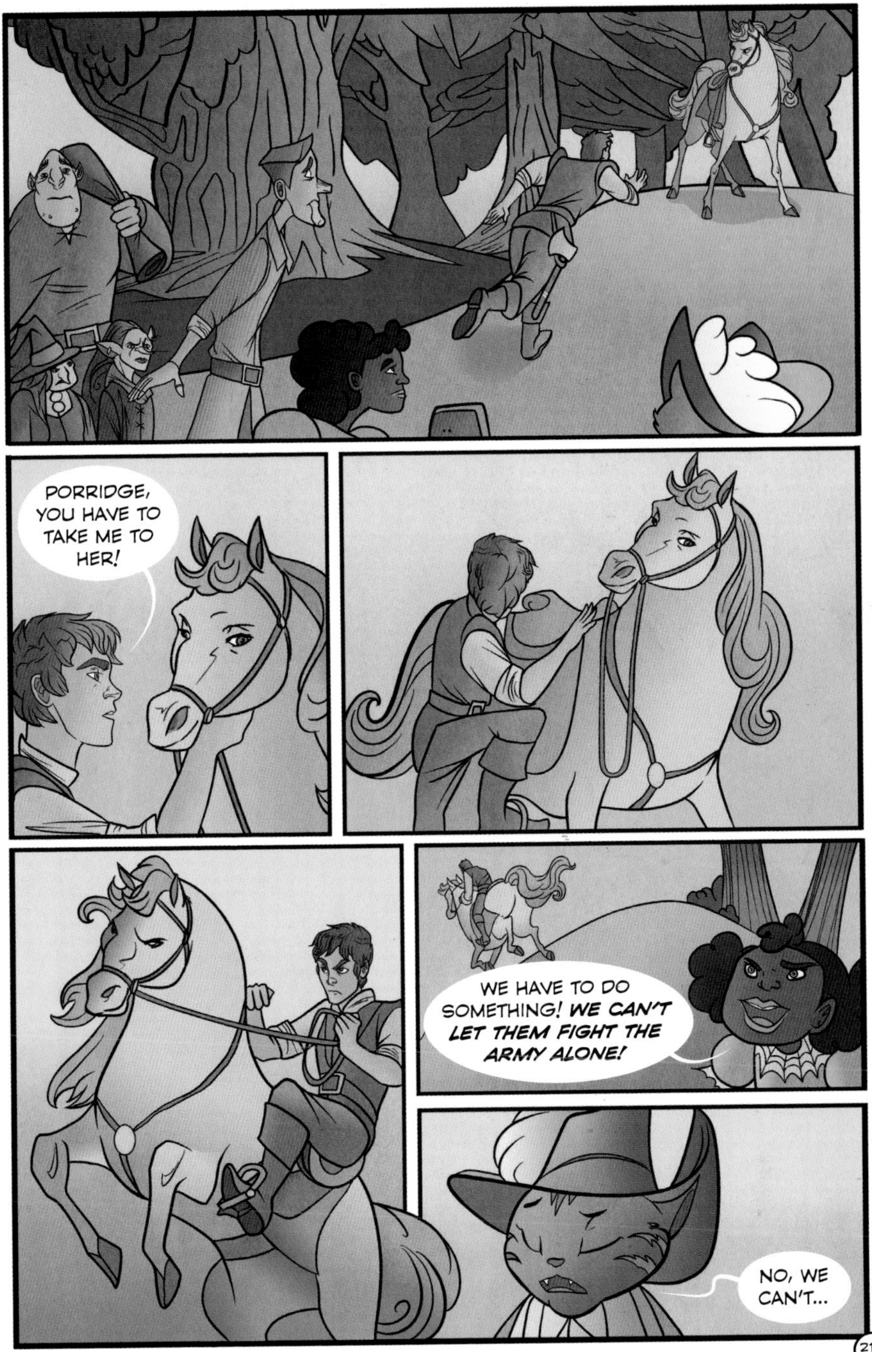
PORRIDGE, YOU HAVE TO TAKE ME TO HER!
WE HAVE TO DO SOMETHING! WE CAN'T LET THEM FIGHT THE ARMY ALONE!
NO, WE CAN'T...

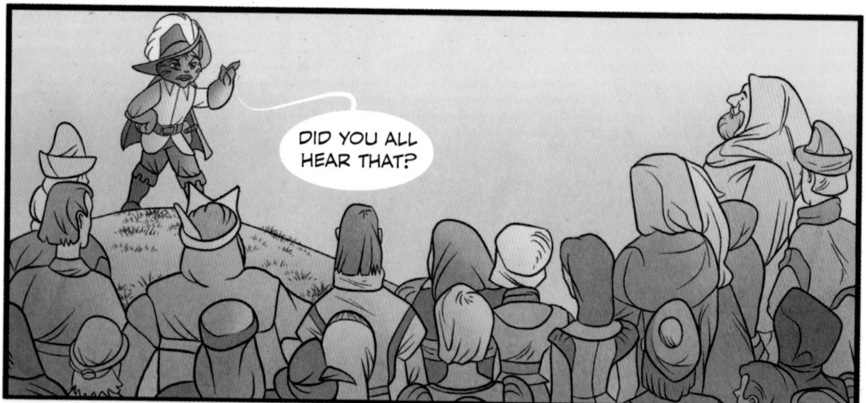
DID YOU ALL HEAR THAT?

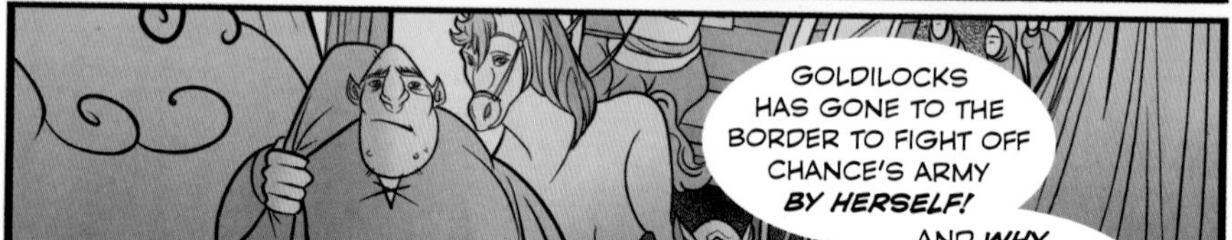
GOLDILOCKS HAS GONE TO THE BORDER TO FIGHT OFF CHANCE'S ARMY ***BY HERSELF!***
AND ***WHY,*** YOU ASK? BECAUSE THE REST OF YOU WERE TOO COWARDLY TO STAND UP FOR YOURSELVES!

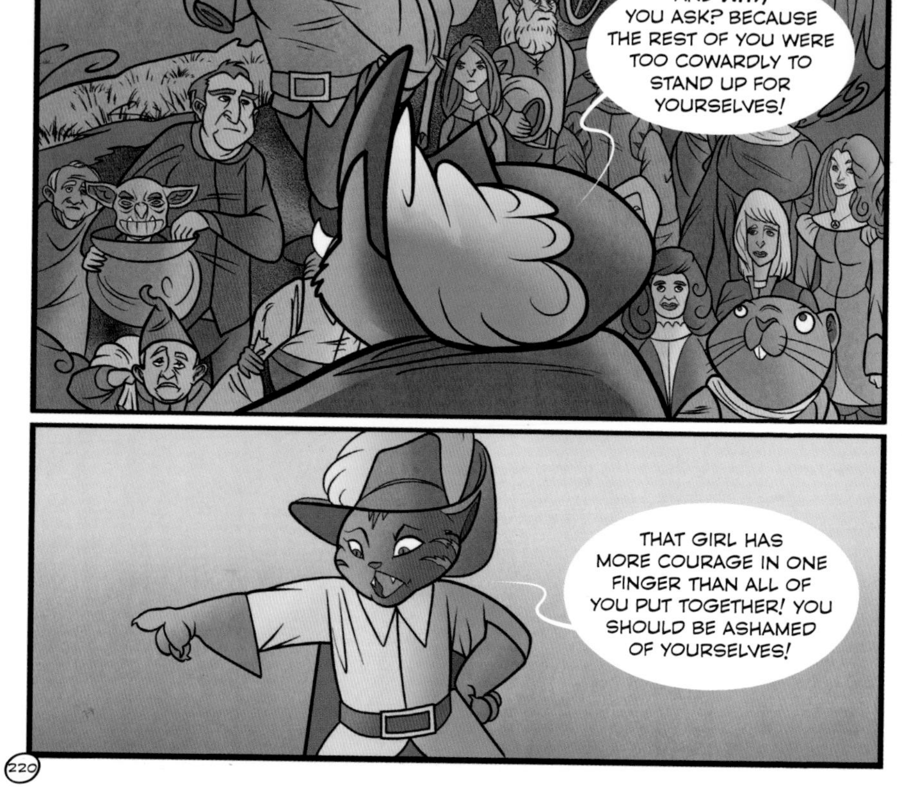
THAT GIRL HAS MORE COURAGE IN ONE FINGER THAN ALL OF YOU PUT TOGETHER! YOU SHOULD BE ASHAMED OF YOURSELVES!

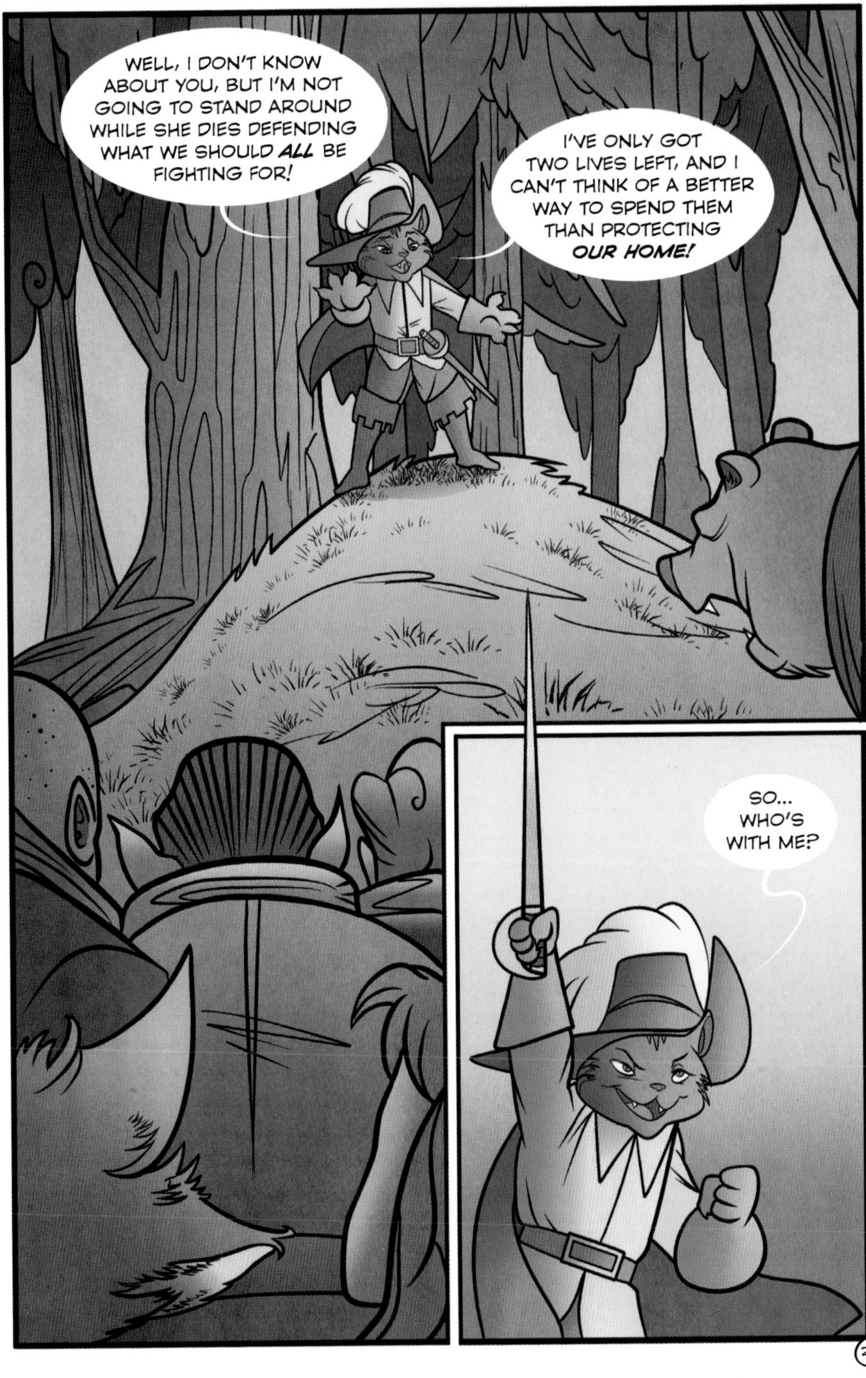
WELL, I DON'T KNOW ABOUT YOU, BUT I'M NOT GOING TO STAND AROUND WHILE SHE DIES DEFENDING WHAT WE SHOULD ***ALL*** BE FIGHTING FOR!
I'VE ONLY GOT TWO LIVES LEFT, AND I CAN'T THINK OF A BETTER WAY TO SPEND THEM THAN PROTECTING ***OUR HOME!***
SO... WHO'S WITH ME?

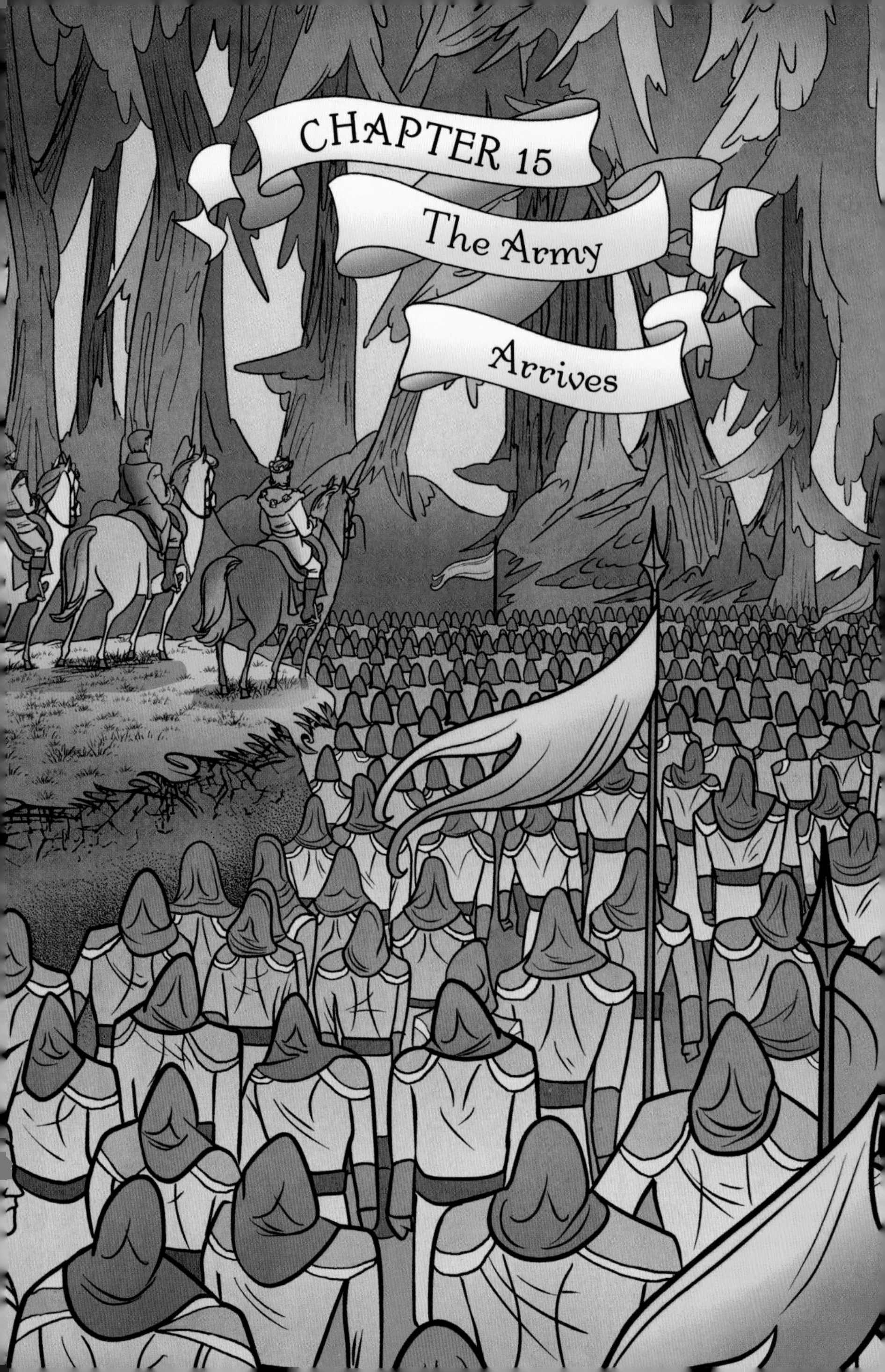
CHAPTER 15
The Army
Arrives

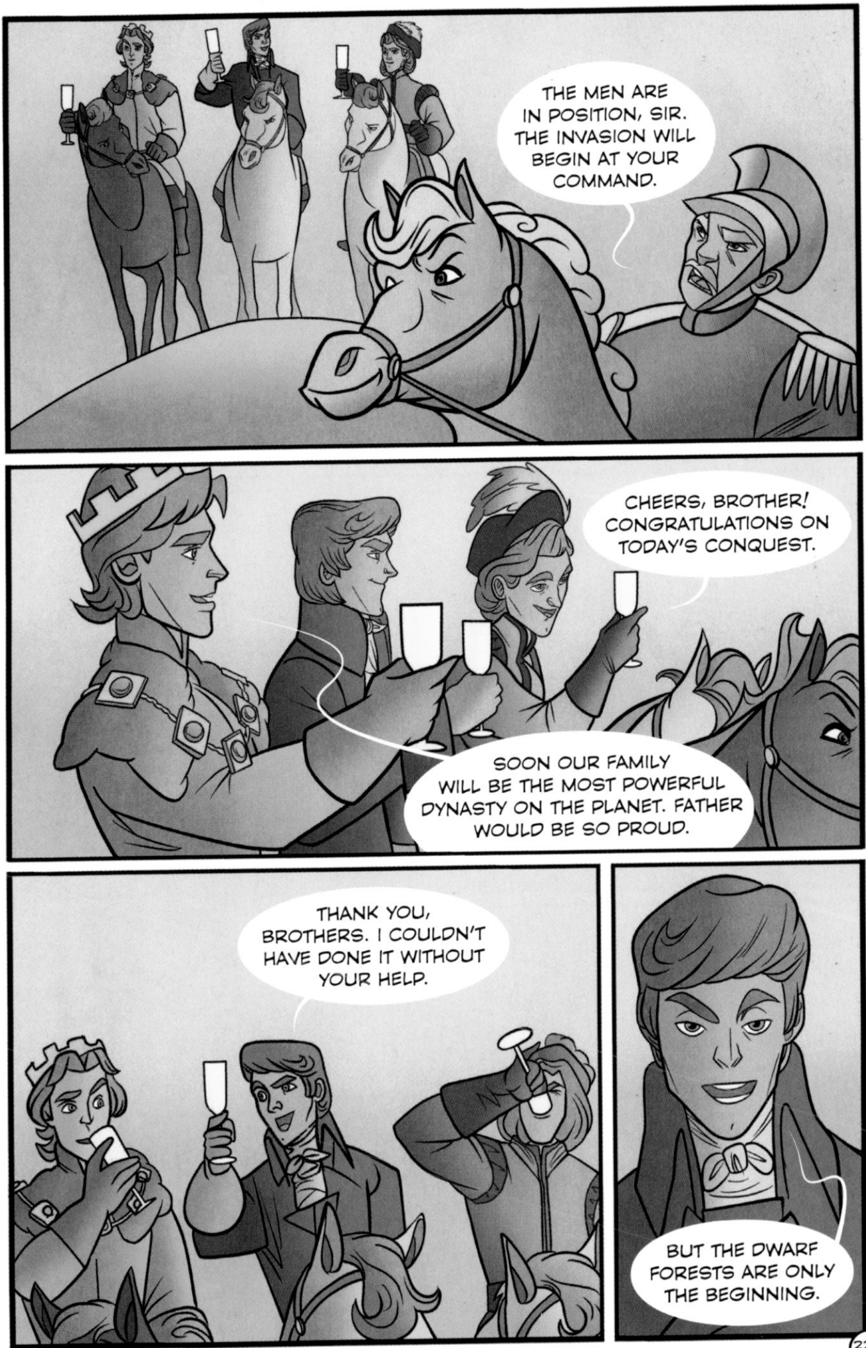
THE MEN ARE IN POSITION, SIR. THE INVASION WILL BEGIN AT YOUR COMMAND.
CHEERS, BROTHER! CONGRATULATIONS ON TODAY'S CONQUEST.
SOON OUR FAMILY WILL BE THE MOST POWERFUL DYNASTY ON THE PLANET. FATHER WOULD BE SO PROUD.
THANK YOU, BROTHERS. I COULDN'T HAVE DONE IT WITHOUT YOUR HELP.
BUT THE DWARF FORESTS ARE ONLY THE BEGINNING.

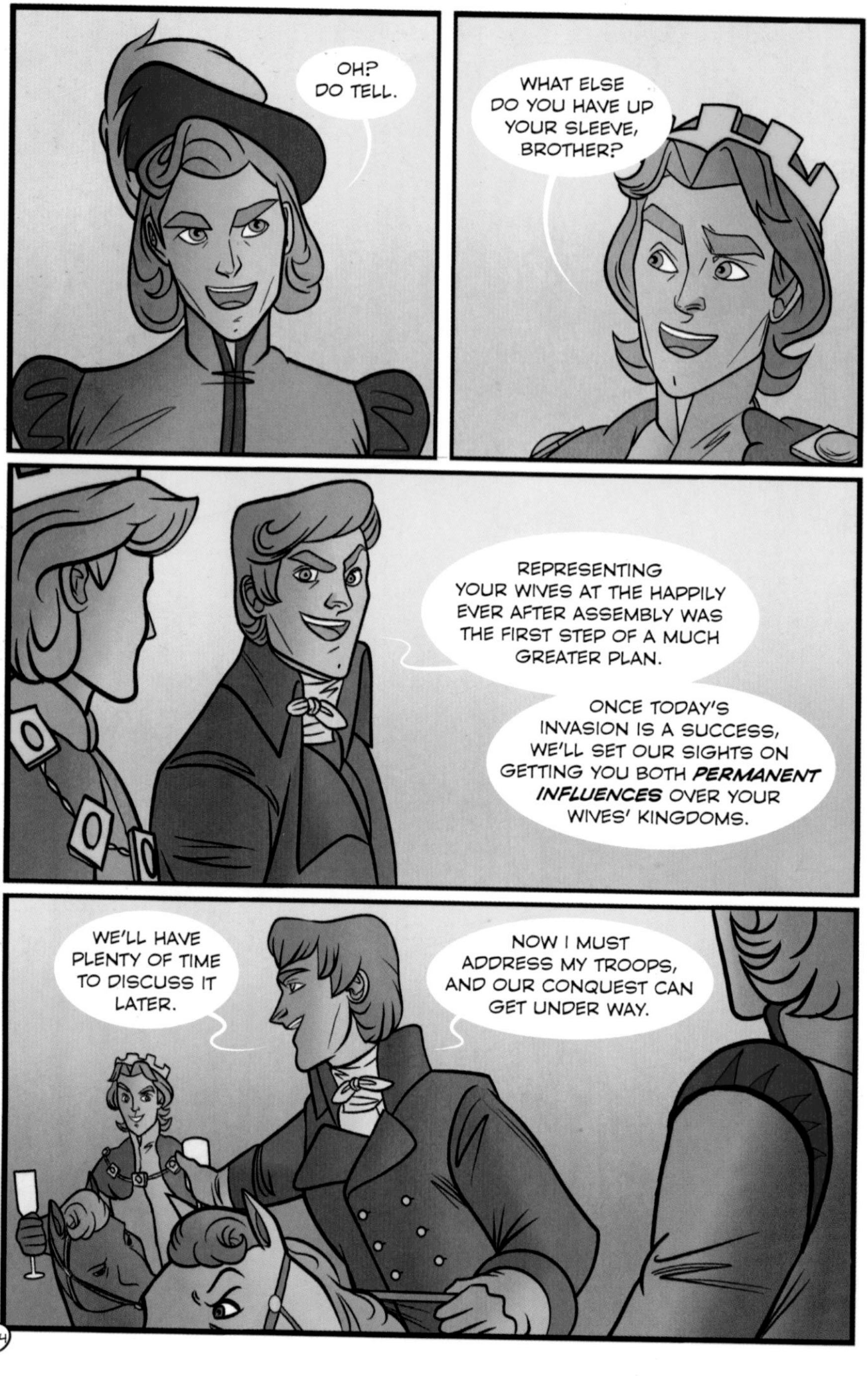
OH?
DO TELL.
WHAT ELSE DO YOU HAVE UP YOUR SLEEVE, BROTHER?
REPRESENTING YOUR WIVES AT THE HAPPILY EVER AFTER ASSEMBLY WAS THE FIRST STEP OF A MUCH GREATER PLAN.
ONCE TODAY'S INVASION IS A SUCCESS, WE'LL SET OUR SIGHTS ON GETTING YOU BOTH ***PERMANENT INFLUENCES*** OVER YOUR WIVES' KINGDOMS.
WE'LL HAVE PLENTY OF TIME TO DISCUSS IT LATER.
NOW I MUST ADDRESS MY TROOPS, AND OUR CONQUEST CAN GET UNDER WAY.

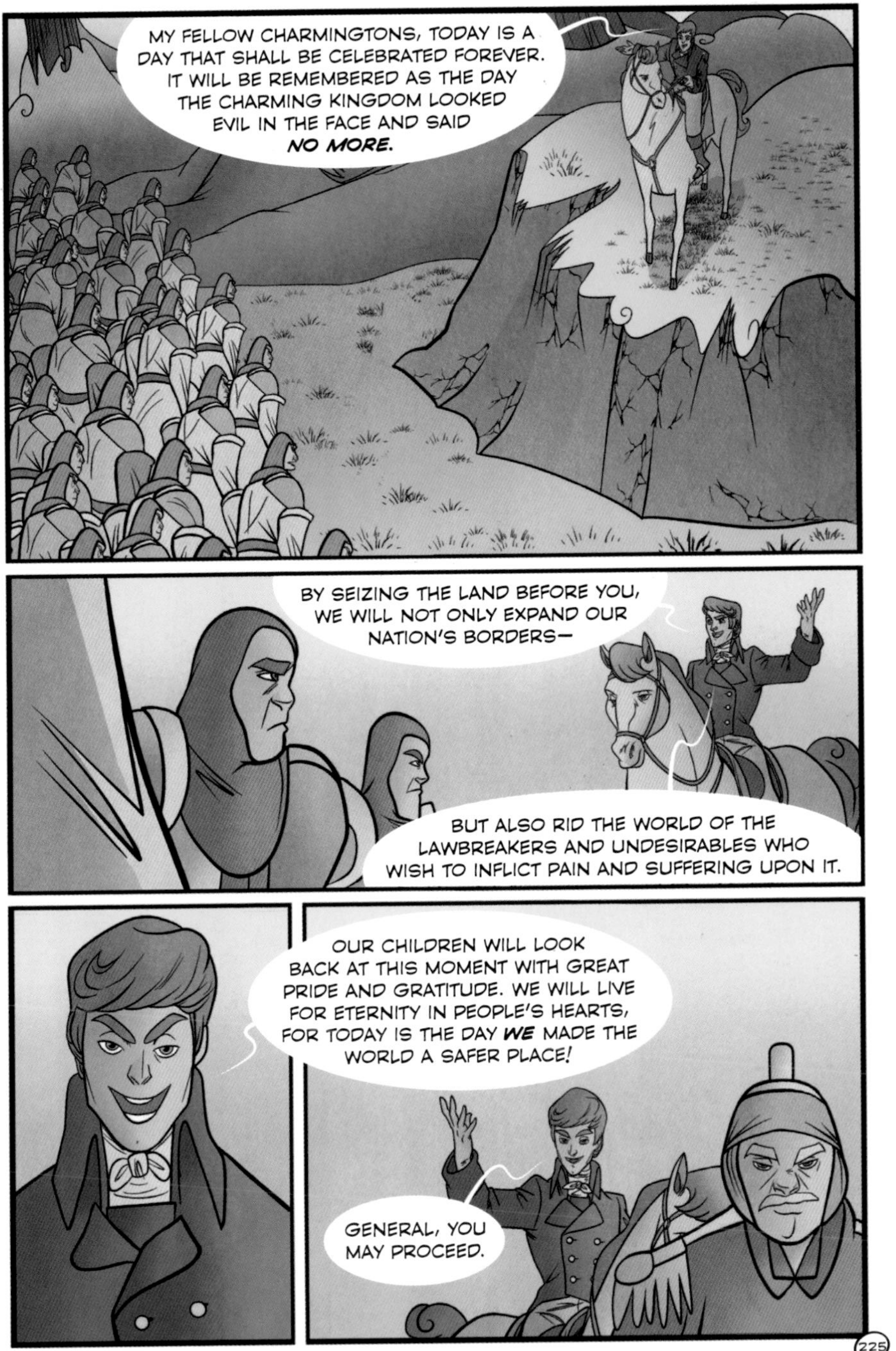
MY FELLOW CHARMINGTONS, TODAY IS A DAY THAT SHALL BE CELEBRATED FOREVER. IT WILL BE REMEMBERED AS THE DAY THE CHARMING KINGDOM LOOKED EVIL IN THE FACE AND SAID ***NO MORE.***
BY SEIZING THE LAND BEFORE YOU, WE WILL NOT ONLY EXPAND OUR NATION'S BORDERS—
BUT ALSO RID THE WORLD OF THE LAWBREAKERS AND UNDESIRABLES WHO WISH TO INFLICT PAIN AND SUFFERING UPON IT.
OUR CHILDREN WILL LOOK BACK AT THIS MOMENT WITH GREAT PRIDE AND GRATITUDE. WE WILL LIVE FOR ETERNITY IN PEOPLE'S HEARTS, FOR TODAY IS THE DAY ***WE*** MADE THE WORLD A SAFER PLACE!
GENERAL, YOU MAY PROCEED.

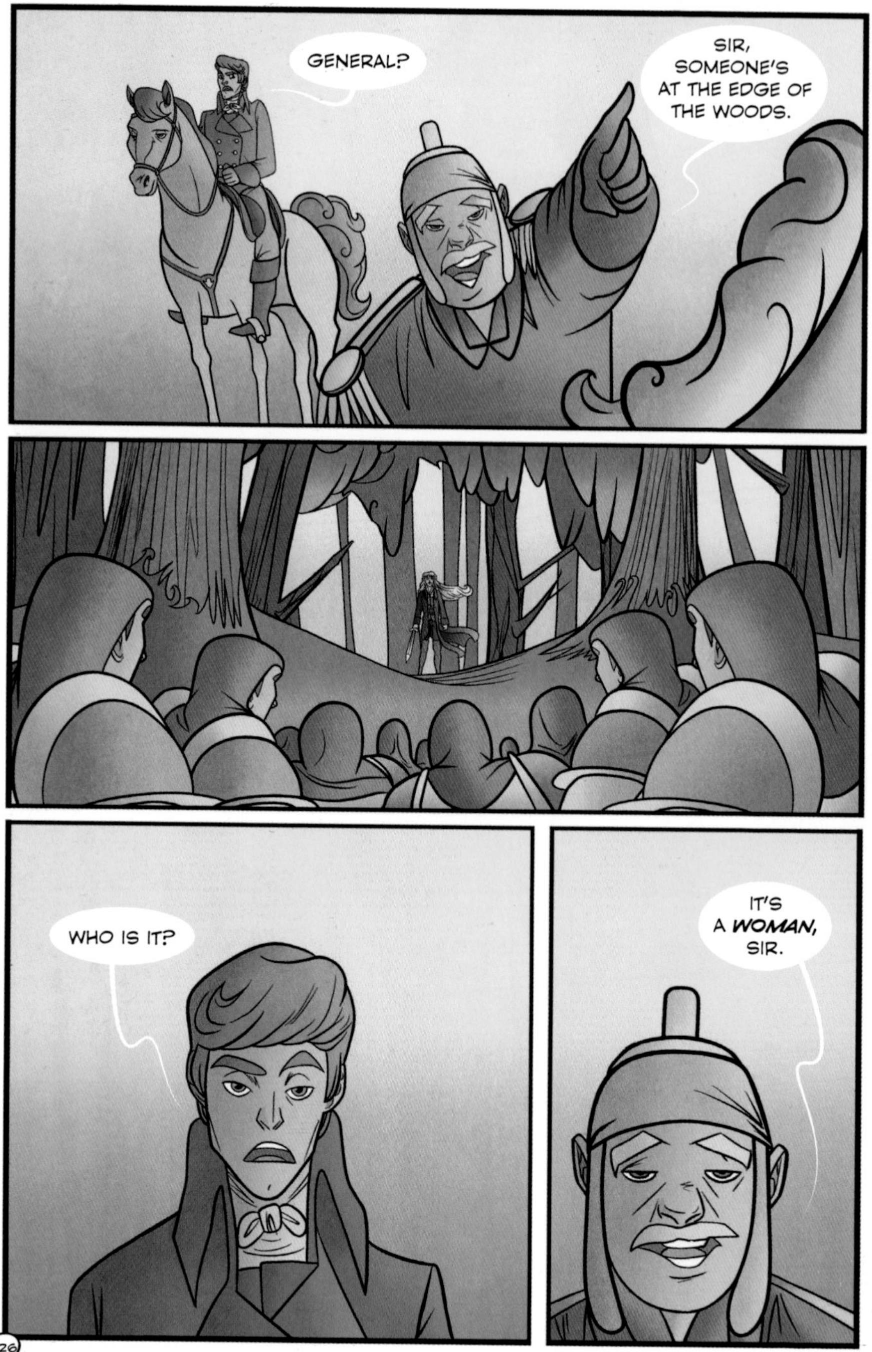
GENERAL?
SIR, SOMEONE'S AT THE EDGE OF THE WOODS.
WHO IS IT?
IT'S A *WOMAN,* SIR.

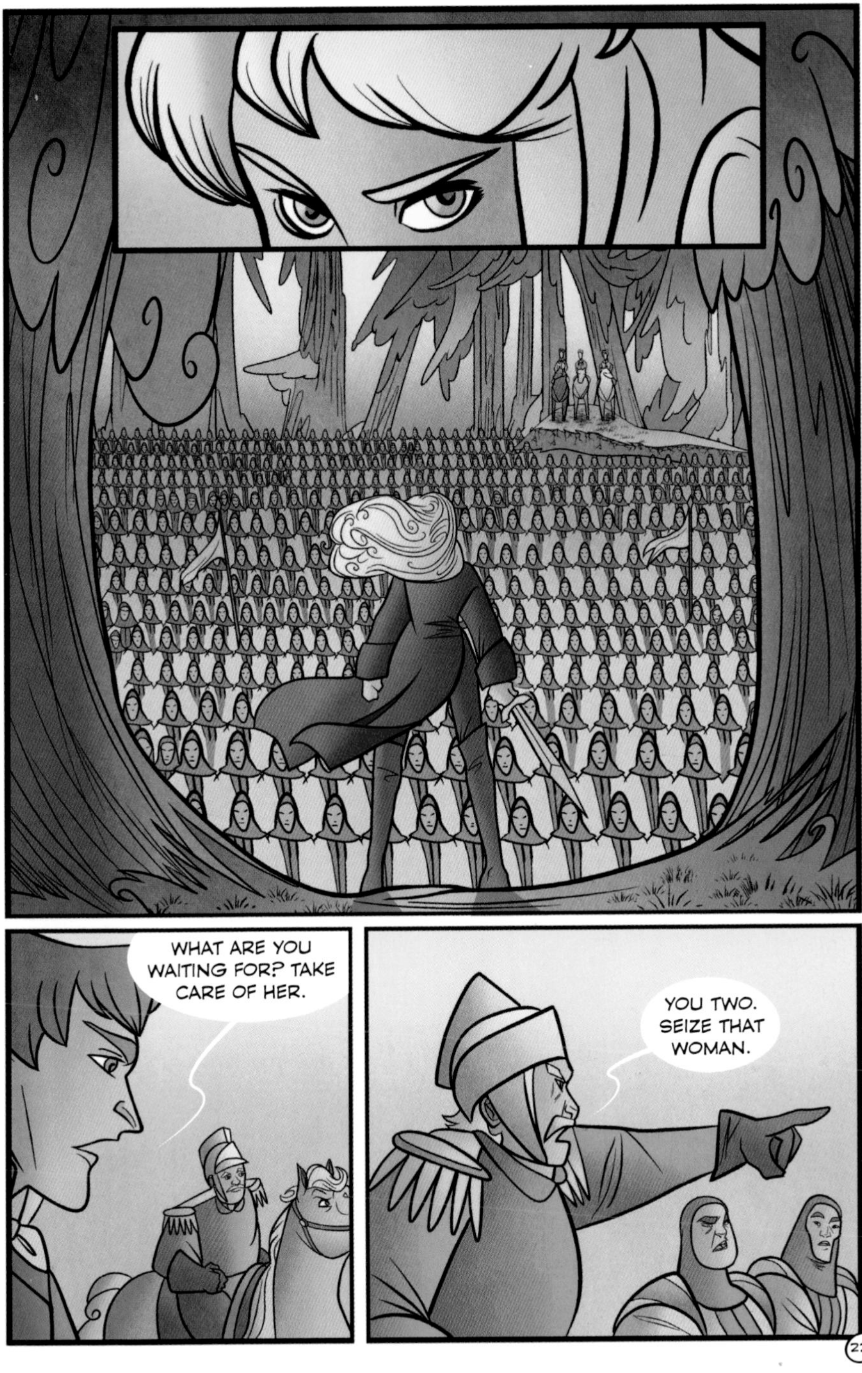
WHAT ARE YOU WAITING FOR? TAKE CARE OF HER.
YOU TWO. SEIZE THAT WOMAN.

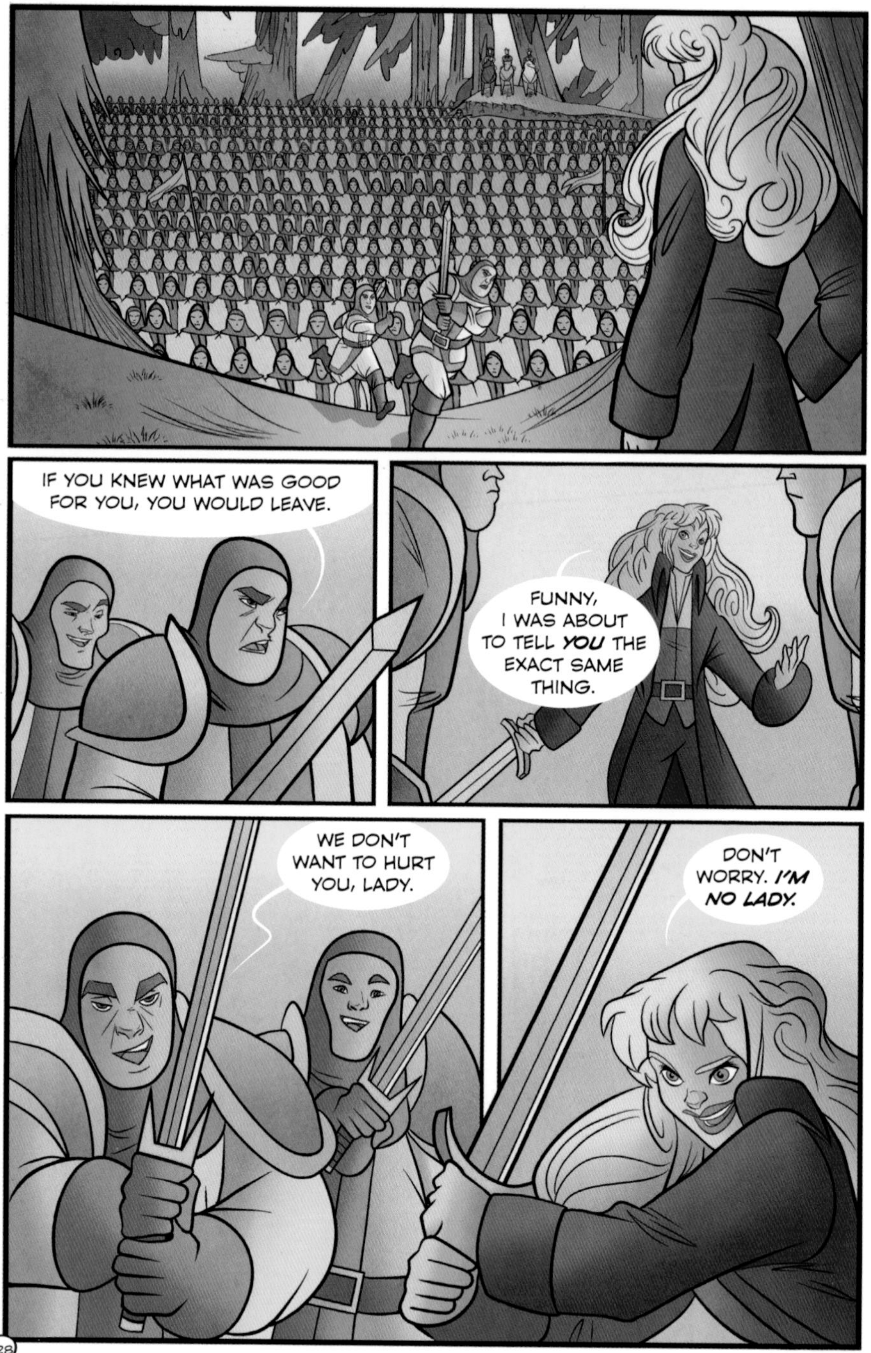
IF YOU KNEW WHAT WAS GOOD FOR YOU, YOU WOULD LEAVE.
FUNNY, I WAS ABOUT TO TELL *YOU* THE EXACT SAME THING.
WE DON'T WANT TO HURT YOU, LADY.
DON'T WORRY. *I'M NO LADY.*

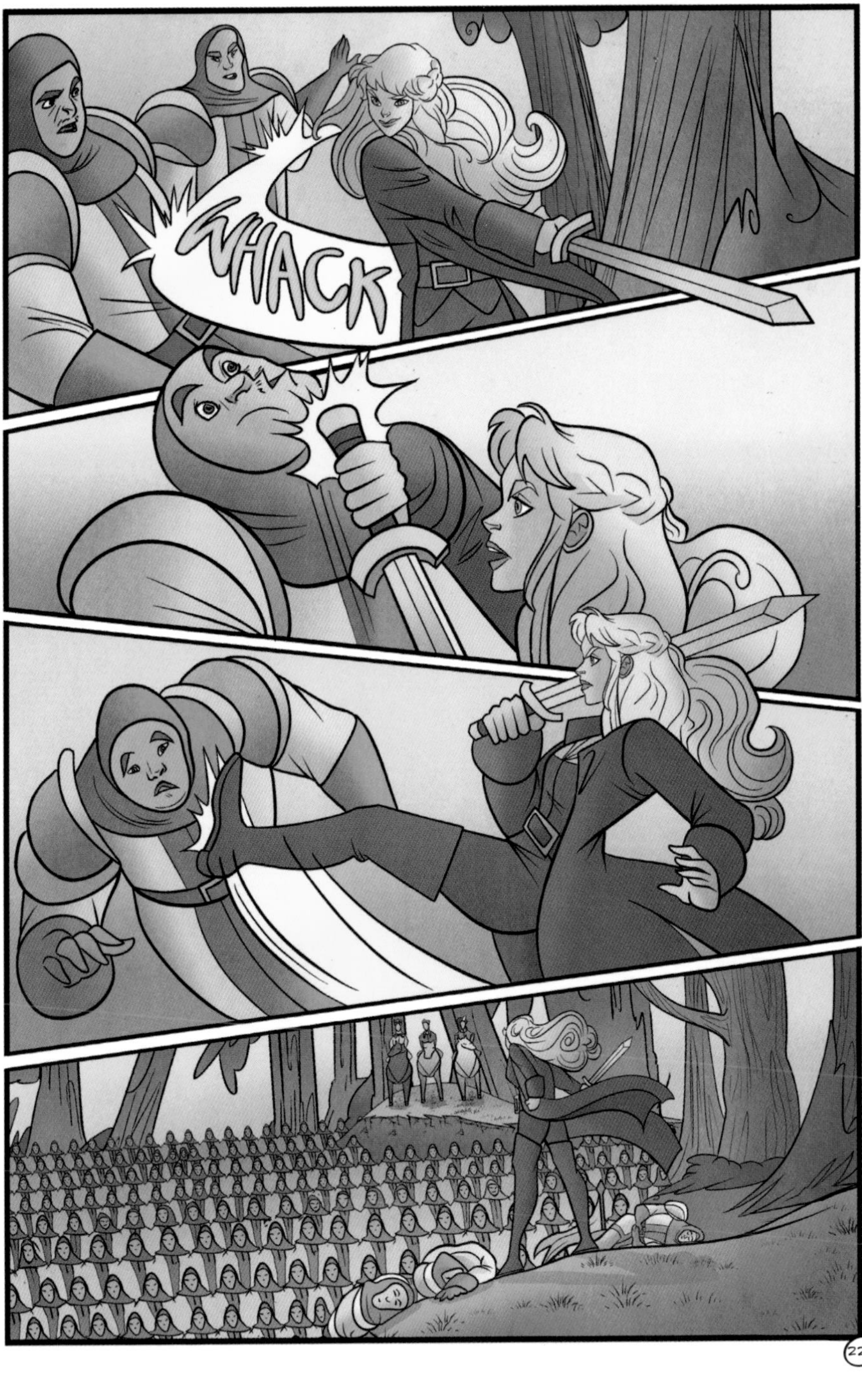
WHACK

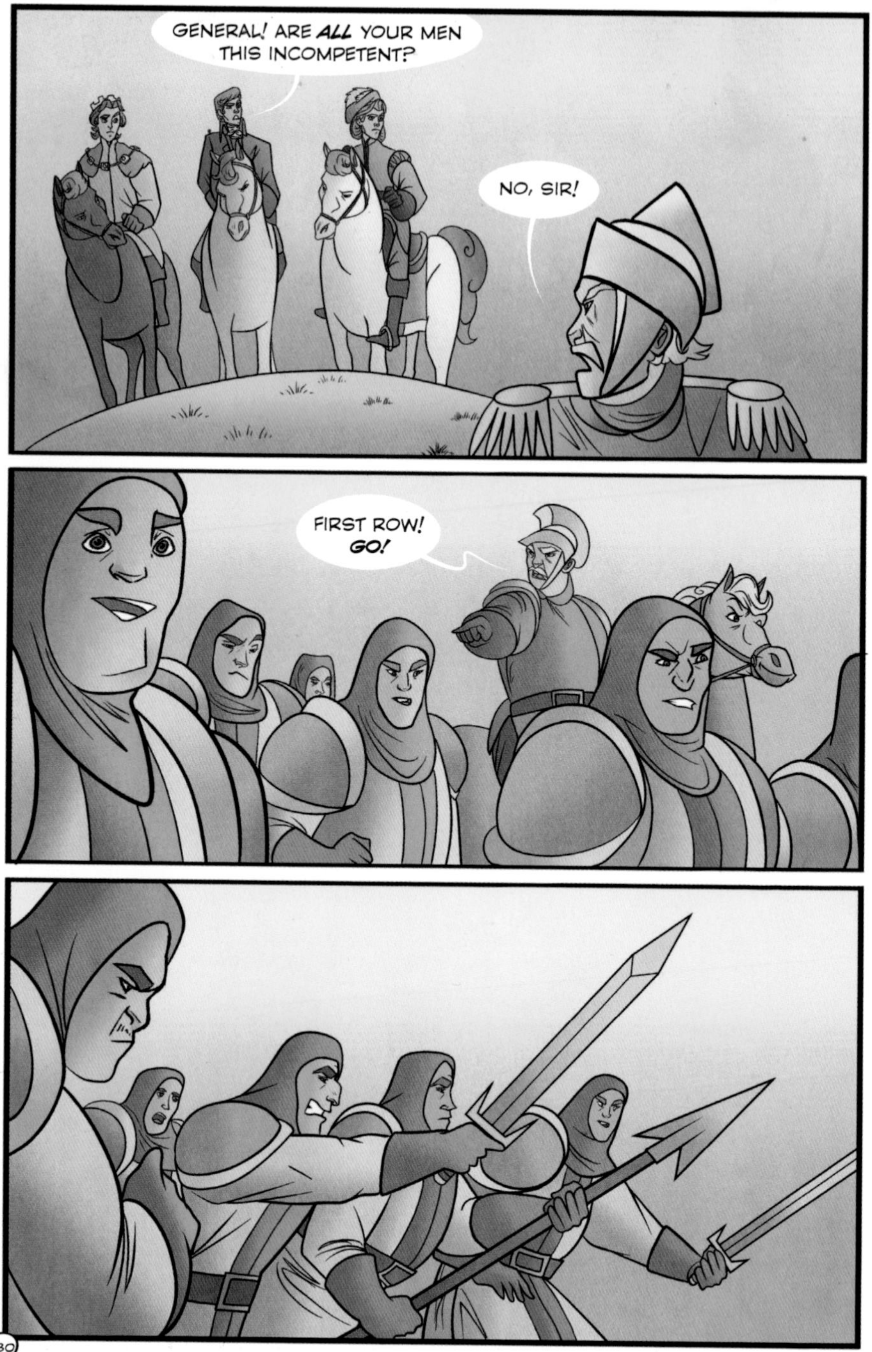
GENERAL! ARE ALL YOUR MEN THIS INCOMPETENT?
NO, SIR!
FIRST ROW! GO!

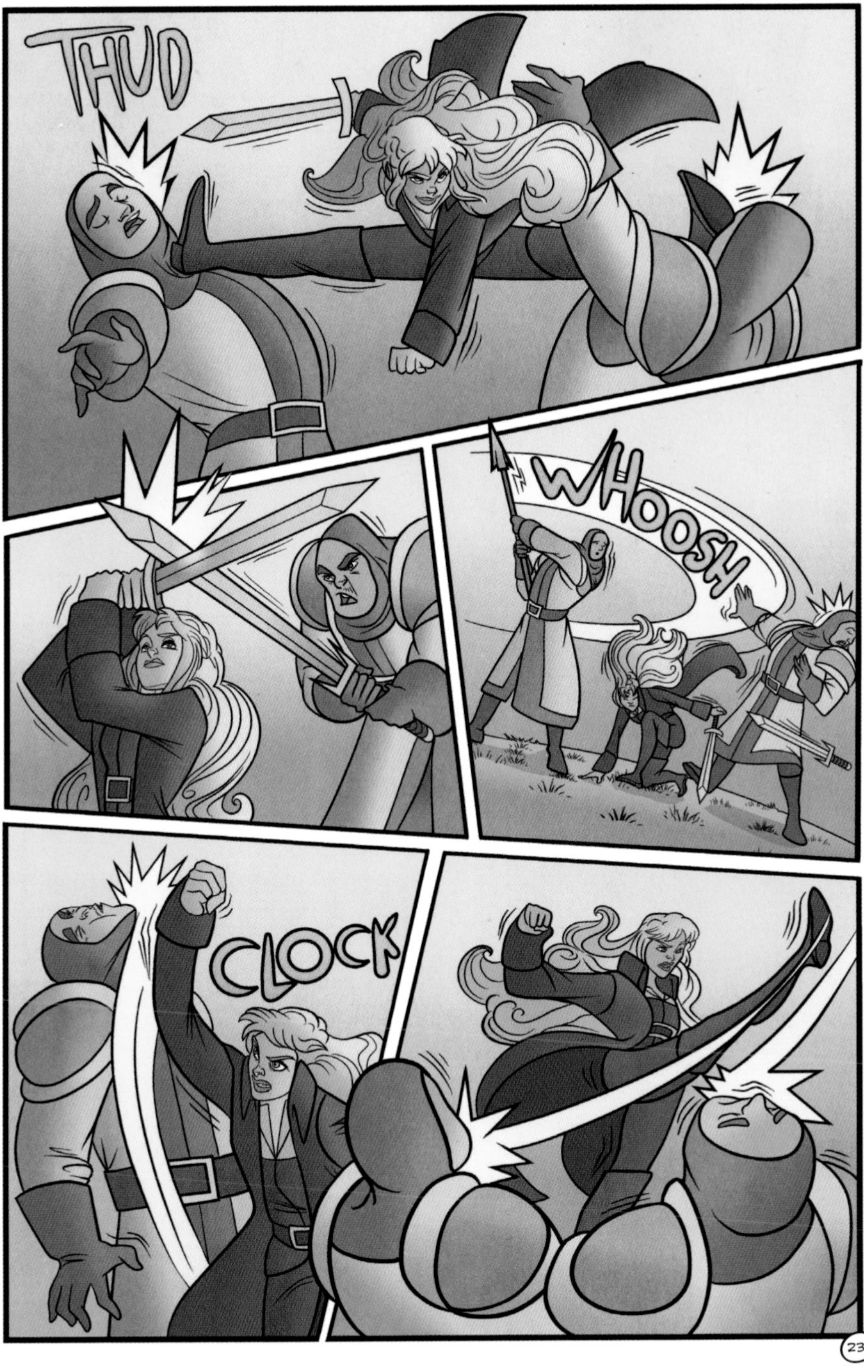
THUD
WHOOSH
CLOCK

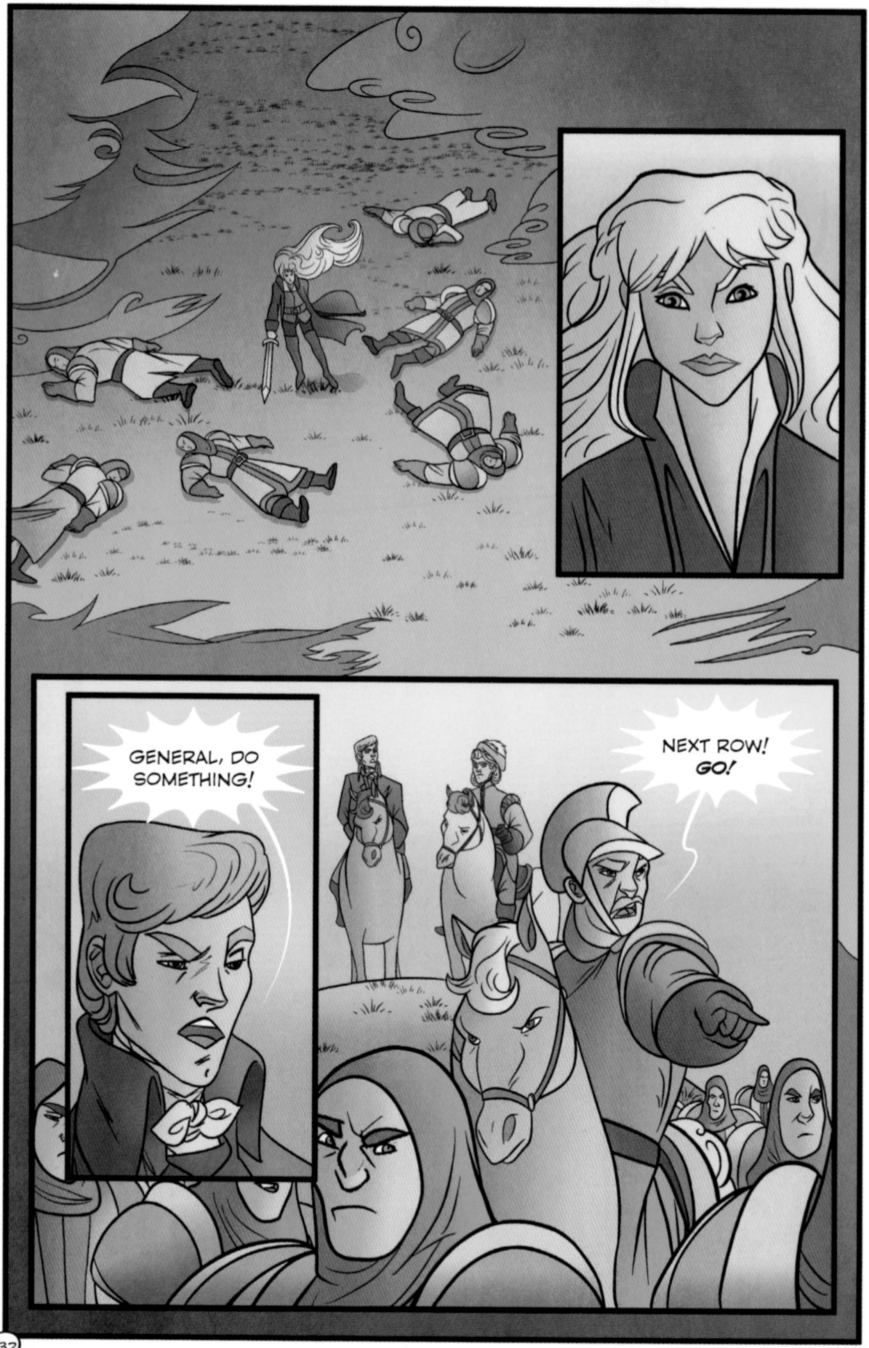
GENERAL, DO SOMETHING!
NEXT ROW! *GO!*

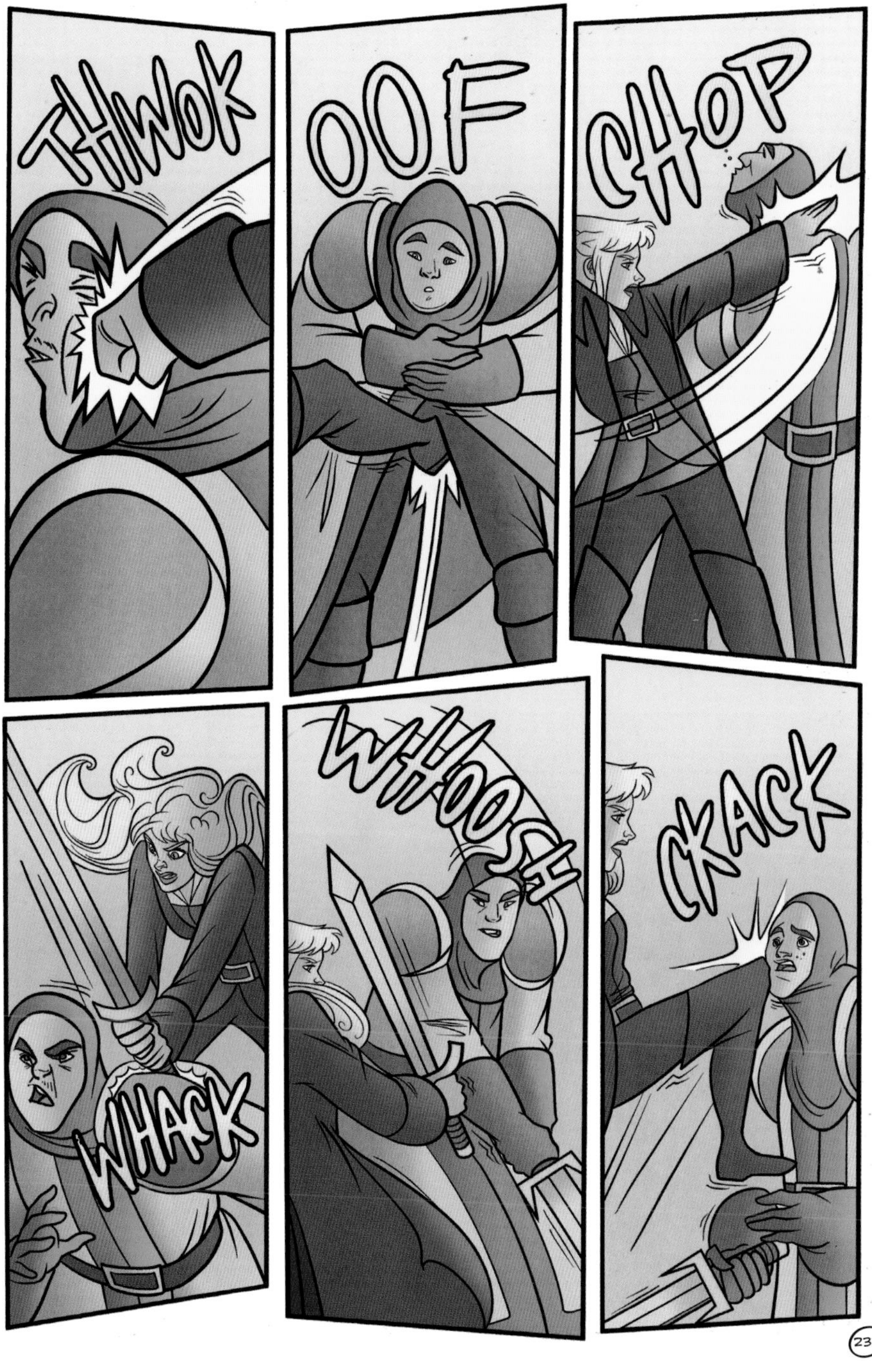
THWOK
OOF
CHOP
WHACK
WHOOSH
CRACK

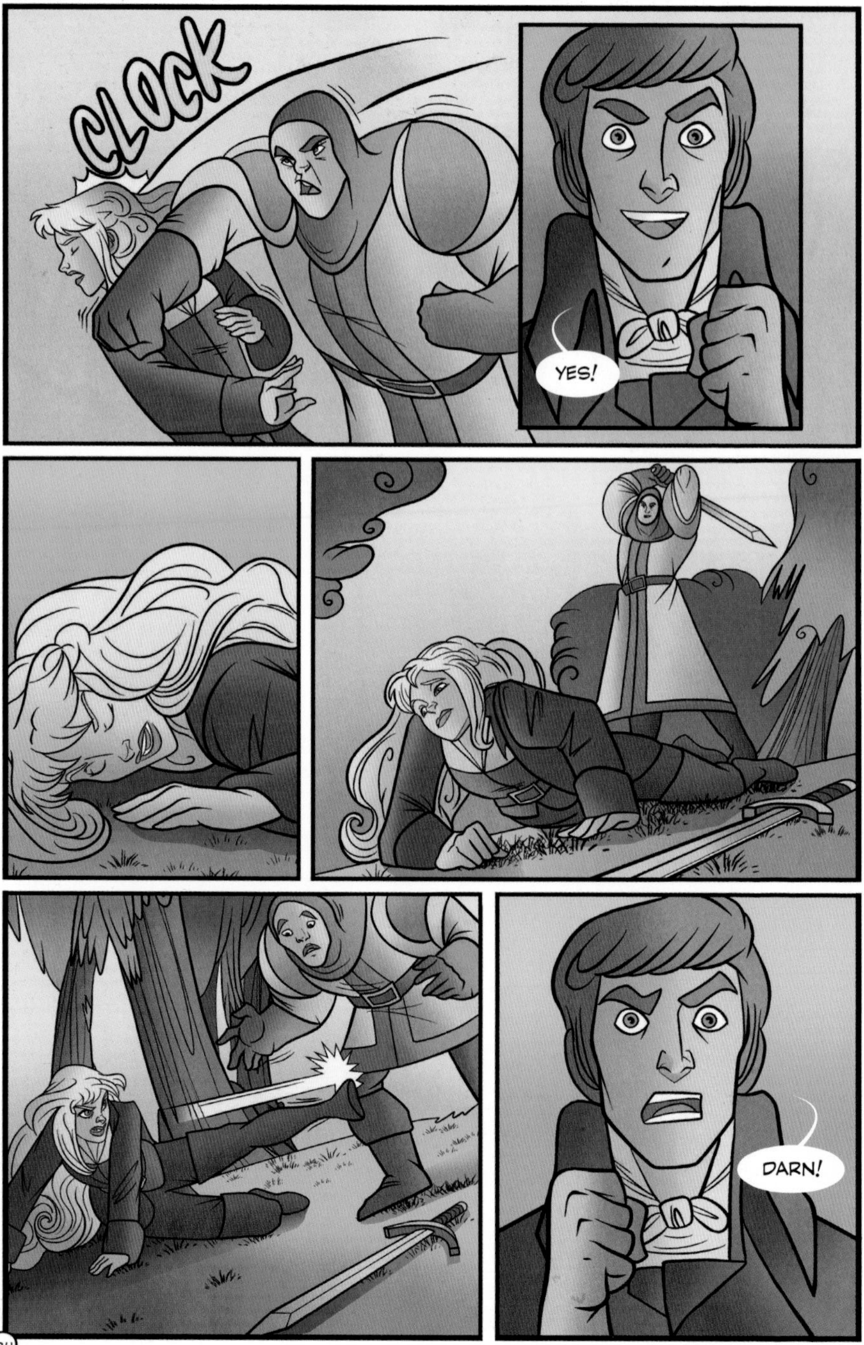
CLOCK
YES!
DARN!

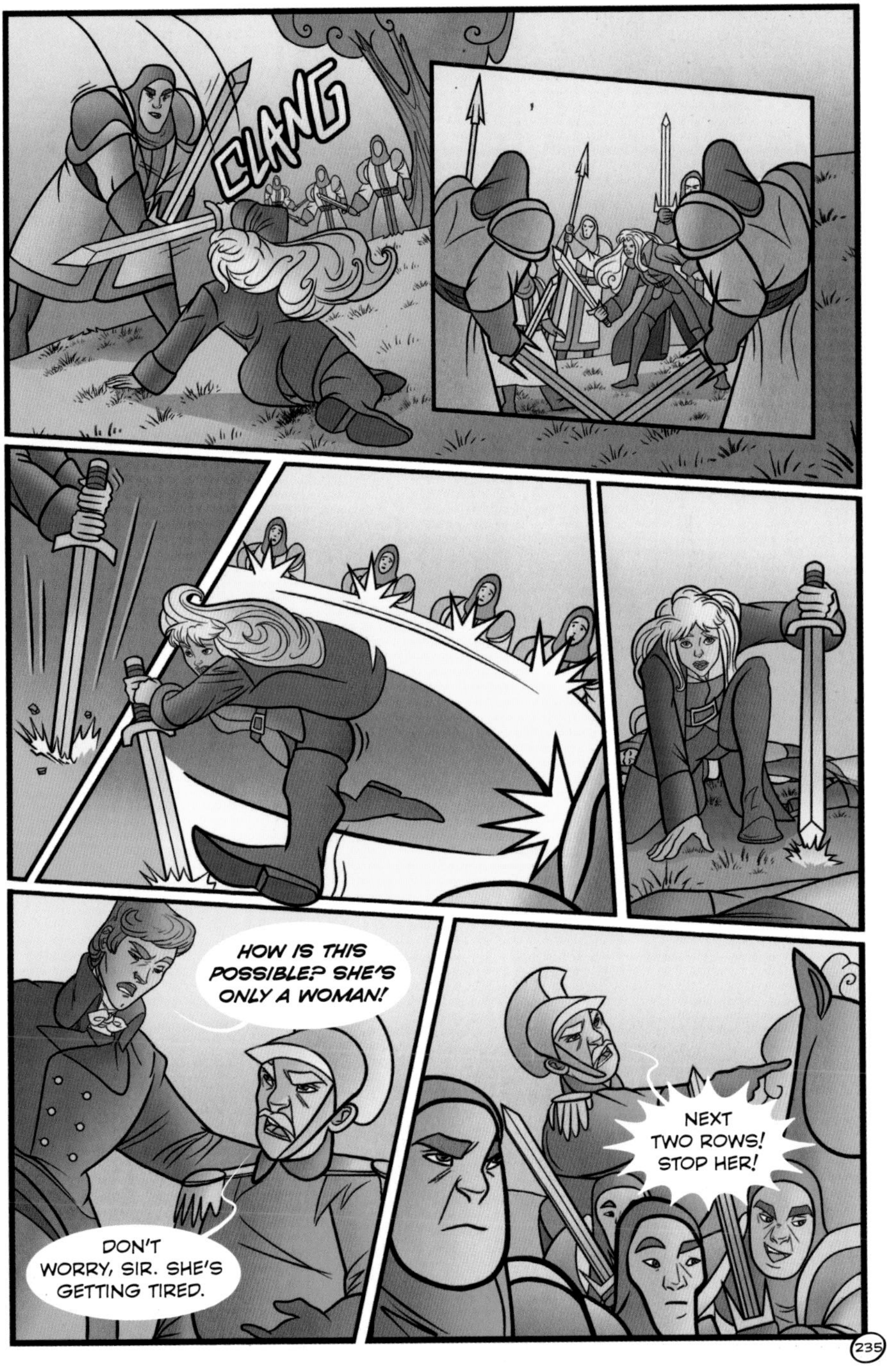
CLANG
HOW IS THIS POSSIBLE? SHE'S ONLY A WOMAN!
DON'T WORRY, SIR. SHE'S GETTING TIRED.
NEXT TWO ROWS! STOP HER!

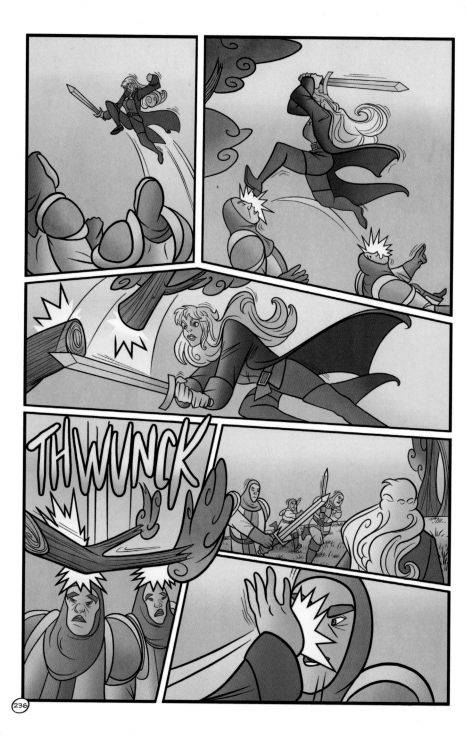

THWUNCK

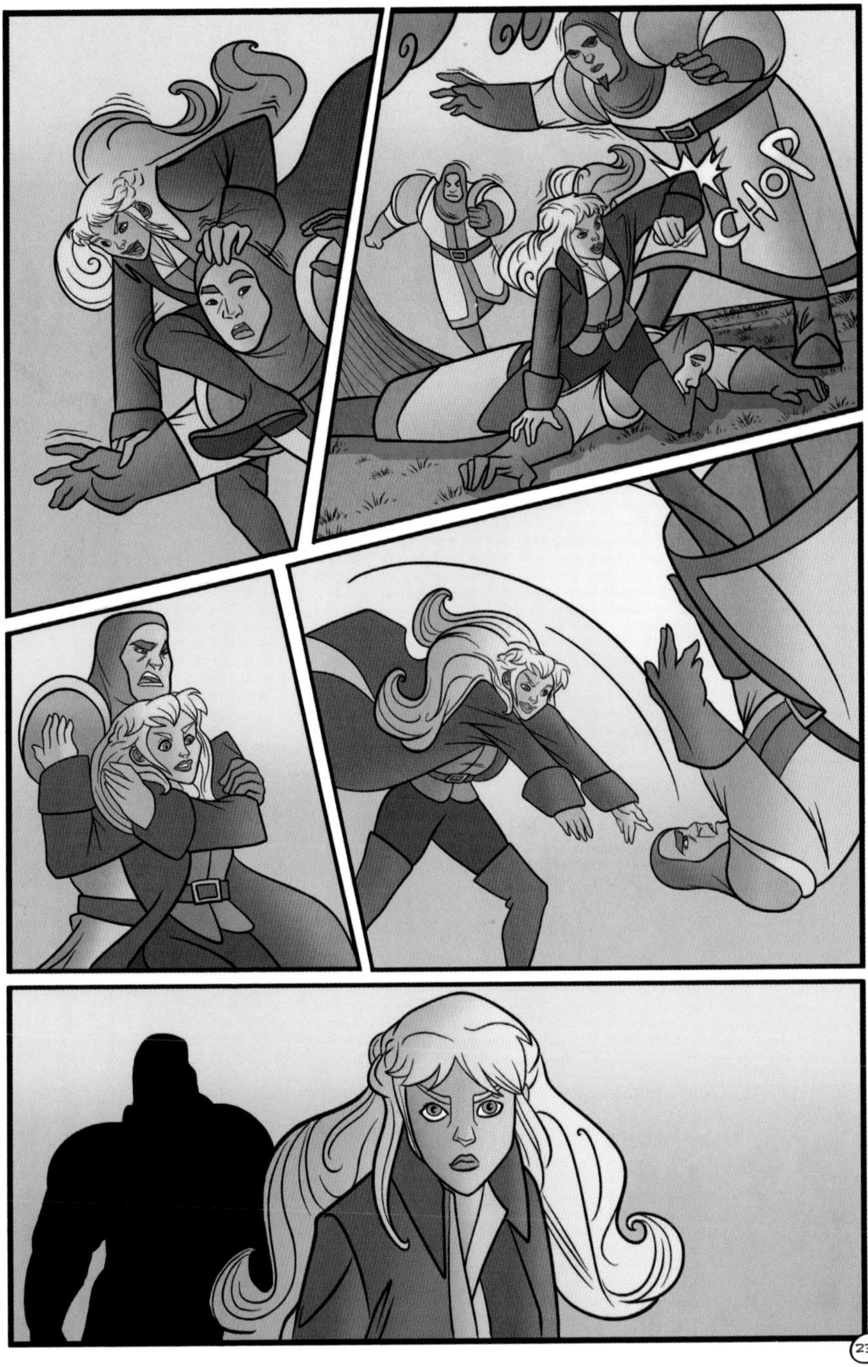
CHOP

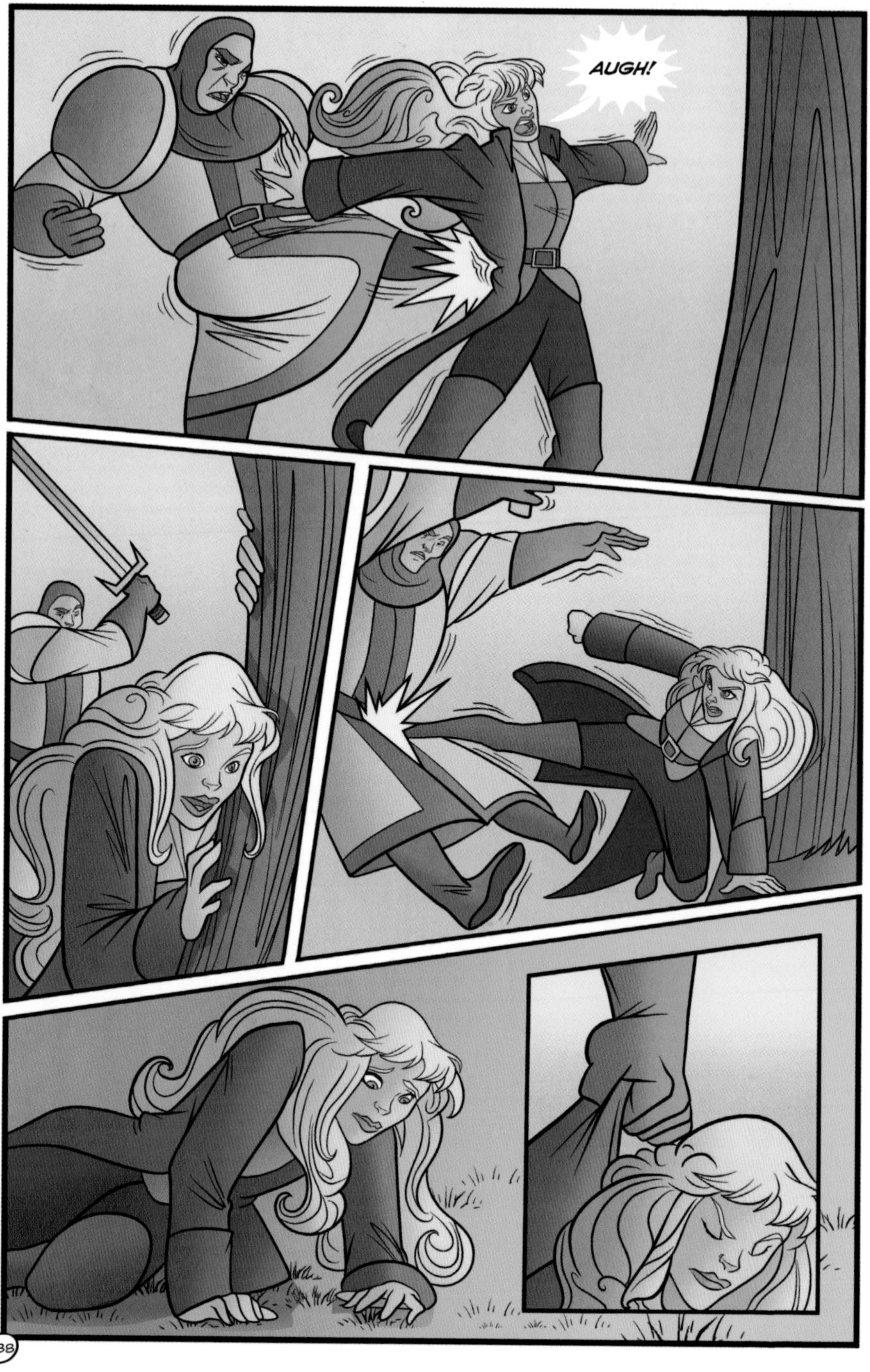
AUGH!

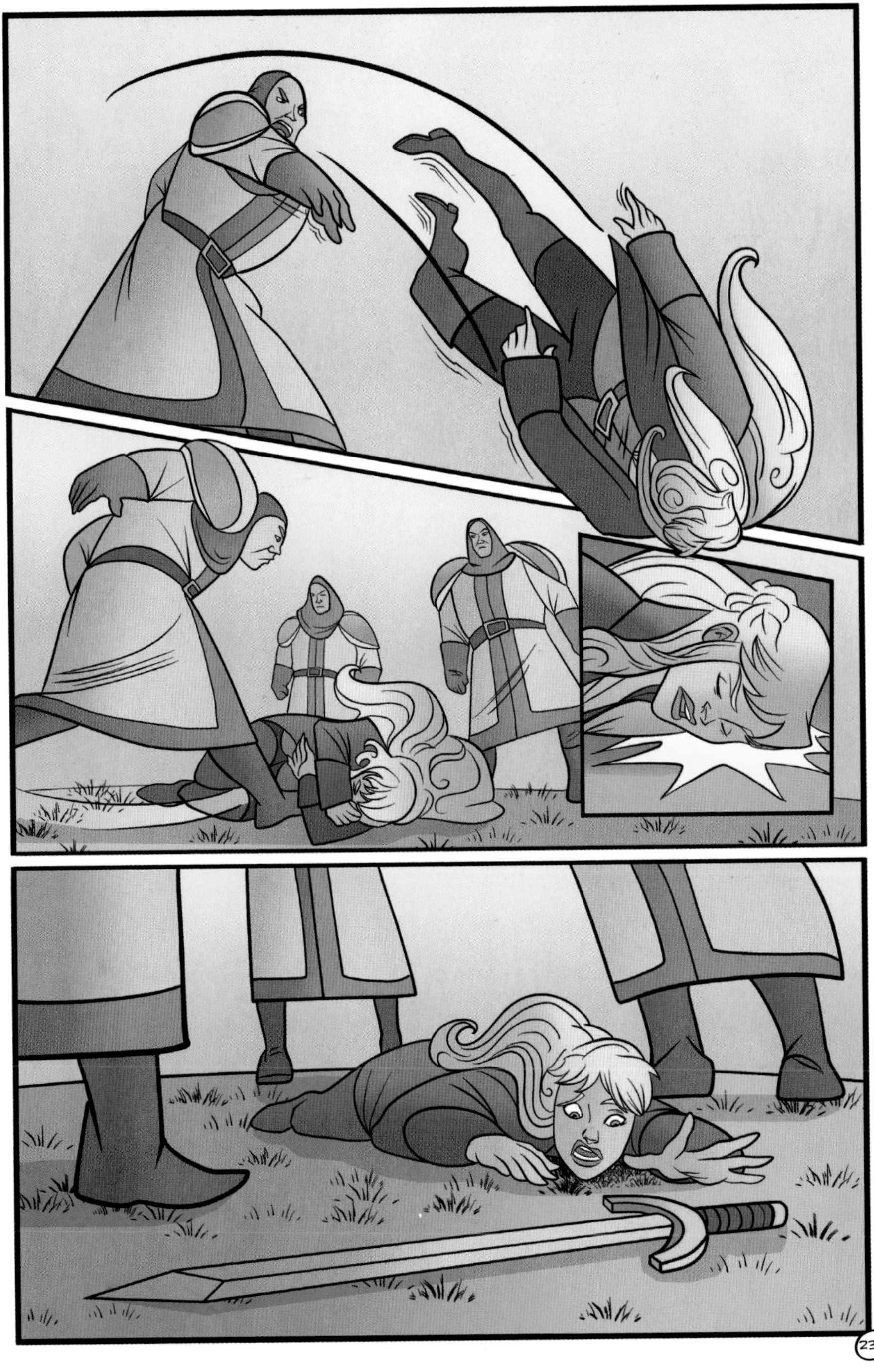

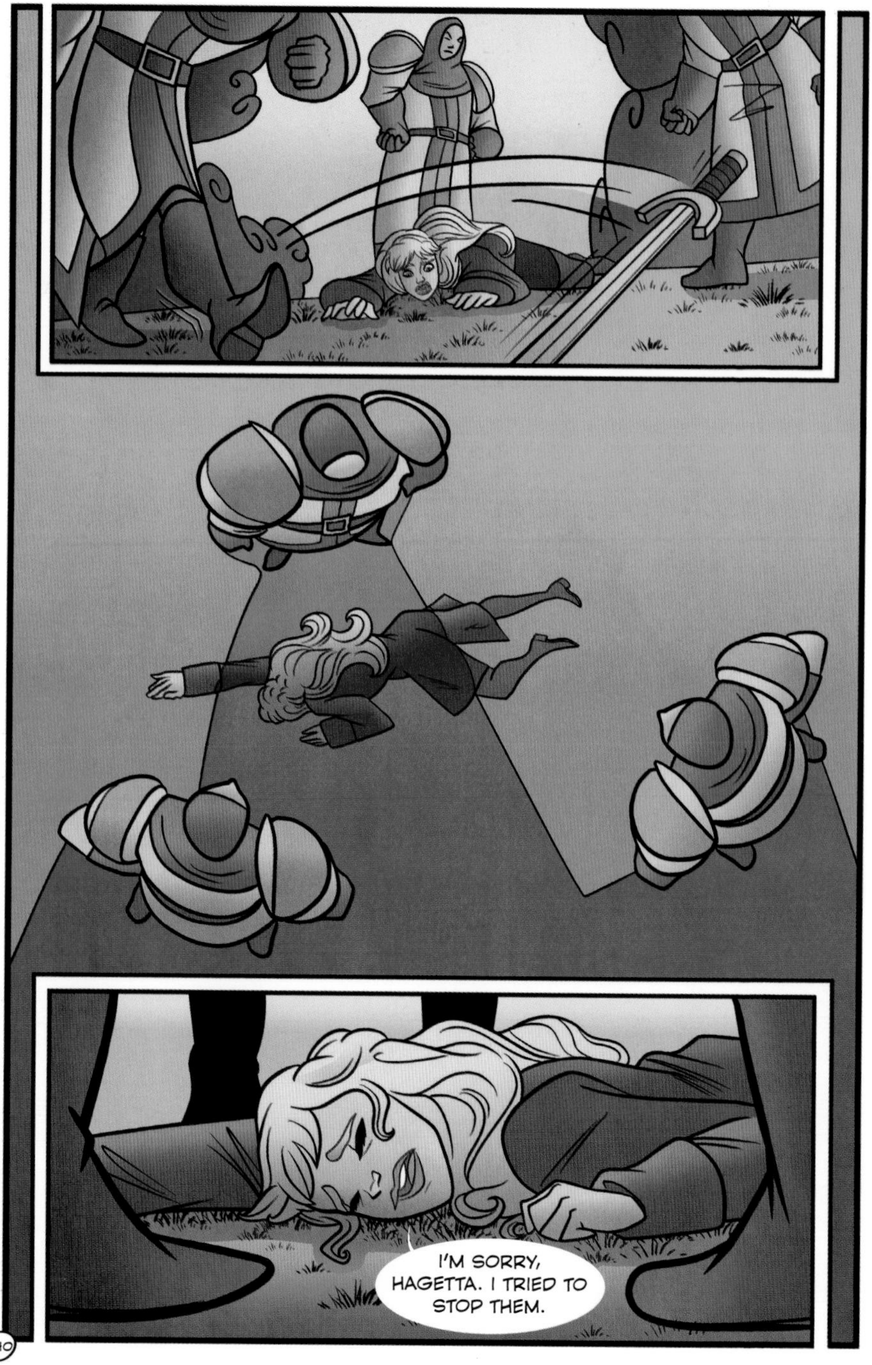
I'M SORRY, HAGETTA. I TRIED TO STOP THEM.

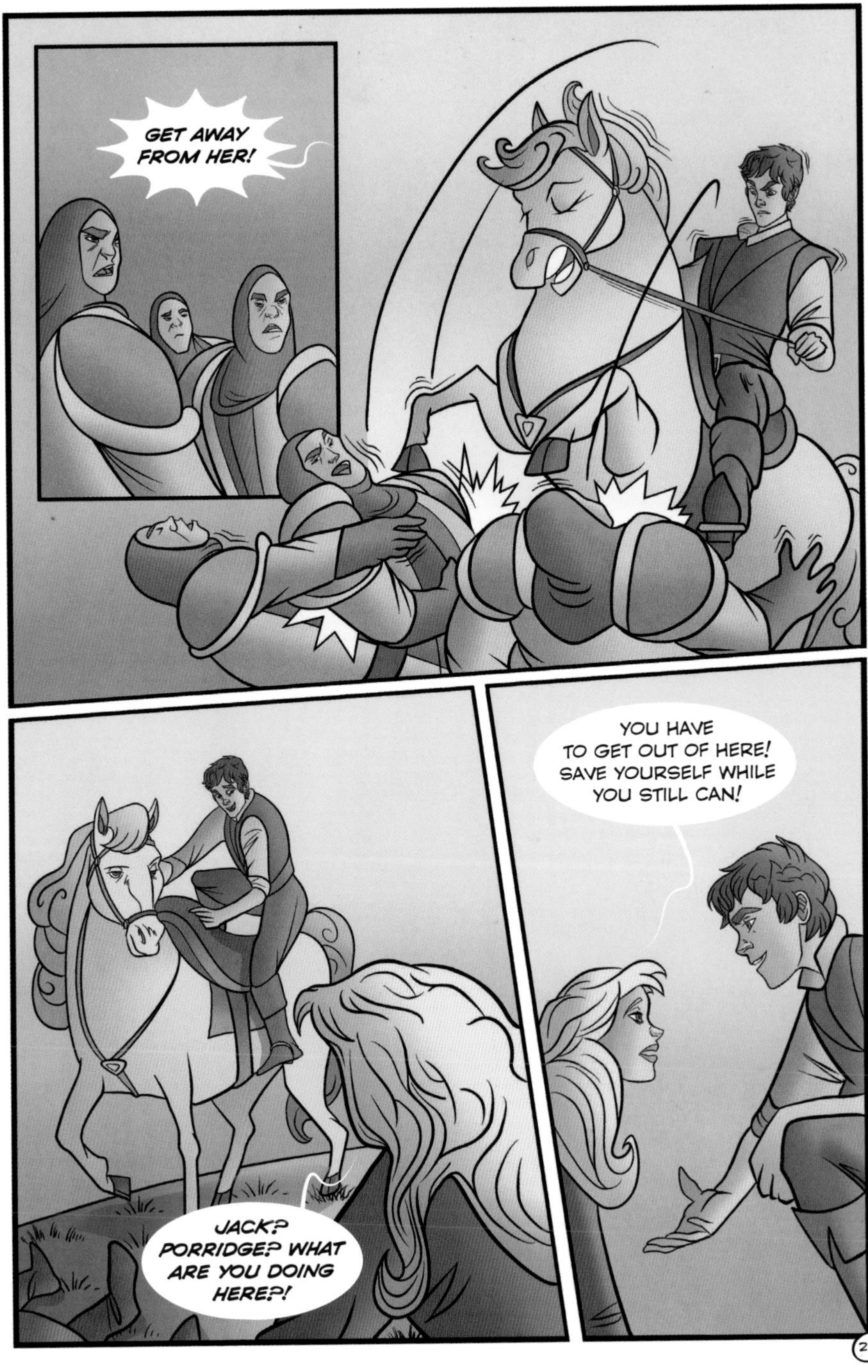
GET AWAY FROM HER!
JACK? PORRIDGE? WHAT ARE YOU DOING HERE?!
YOU HAVE TO GET OUT OF HERE! SAVE YOURSELF WHILE YOU STILL CAN!

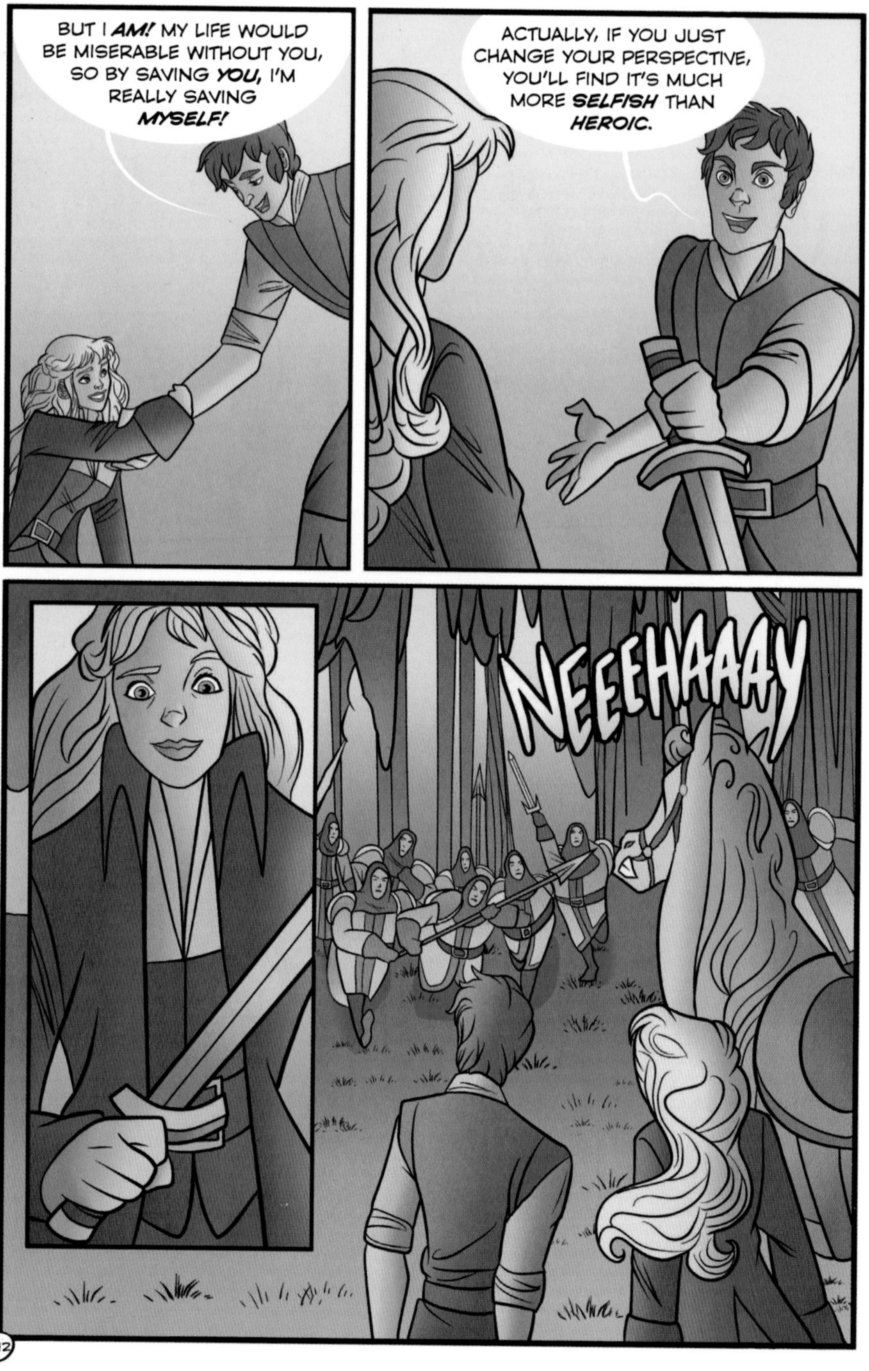
BUT I AM! MY LIFE WOULD BE MISERABLE WITHOUT YOU, SO BY SAVING YOU, I'M REALLY SAVING MYSELF!
ACTUALLY, IF YOU JUST CHANGE YOUR PERSPECTIVE, YOU'LL FIND IT'S MUCH MORE SELFISH THAN HEROIC.
NEEEHAAAY

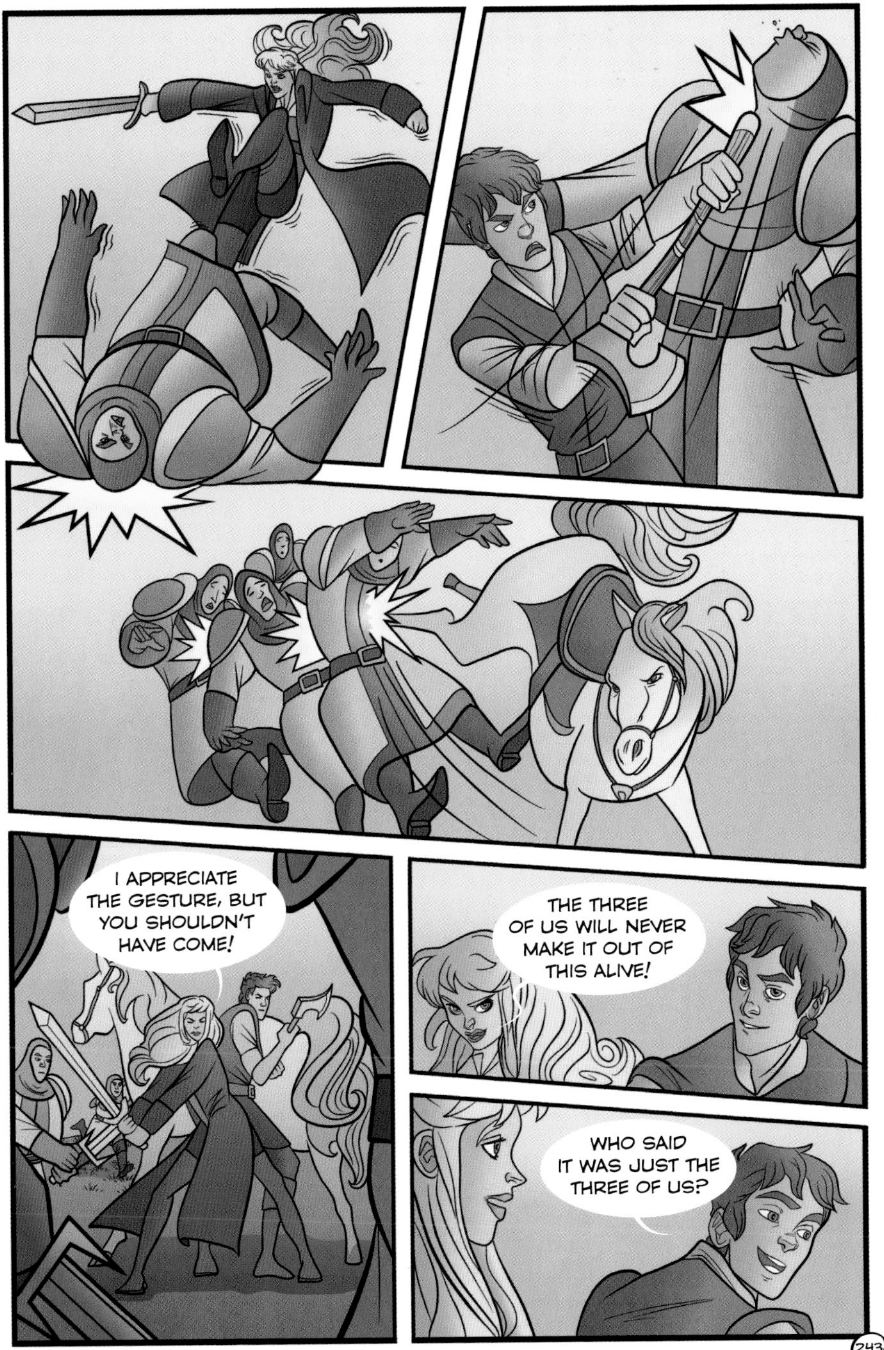

I APPRECIATE THE GESTURE, BUT YOU SHOULDN'T HAVE COME!
THE THREE OF US WILL NEVER MAKE IT OUT OF THIS ALIVE!
WHO SAID IT WAS JUST THE THREE OF US?

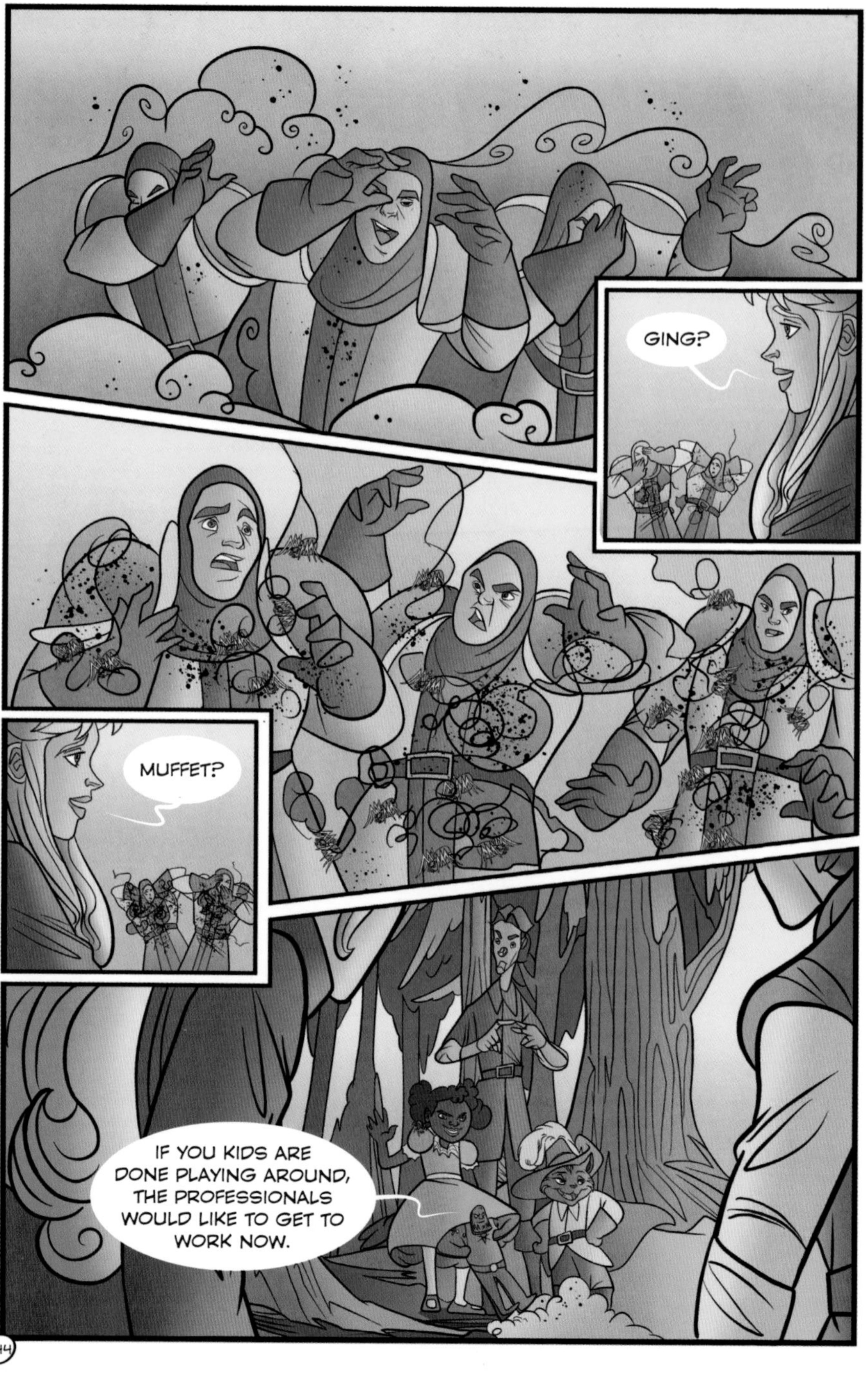
GING?
MUFFET?
IF YOU KIDS ARE DONE PLAYING AROUND, THE PROFESSIONALS WOULD LIKE TO GET TO WORK NOW.

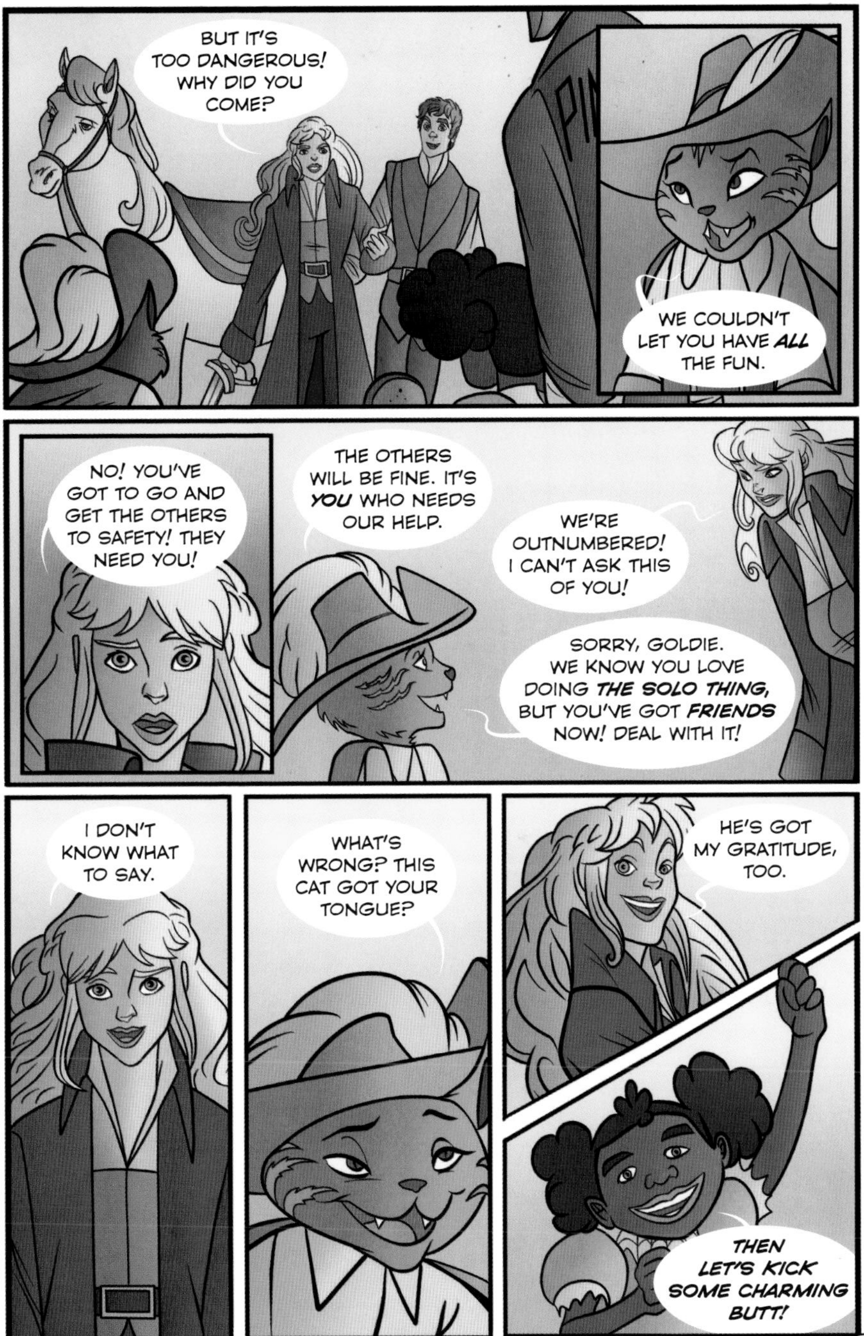
BUT IT'S TOO DANGEROUS! WHY DID YOU COME?
WE COULDN'T LET YOU HAVE ALL THE FUN.
NO! YOU'VE GOT TO GO AND GET THE OTHERS TO SAFETY! THEY NEED YOU!
THE OTHERS WILL BE FINE. IT'S YOU WHO NEEDS OUR HELP.
WE'RE OUTNUMBERED! I CAN'T ASK THIS OF YOU!
SORRY, GOLDIE. WE KNOW YOU LOVE DOING THE SOLO THING, BUT YOU'VE GOT FRIENDS NOW! DEAL WITH IT!
I DON'T KNOW WHAT TO SAY.
WHAT'S WRONG? THIS CAT GOT YOUR TONGUE?
HE'S GOT MY GRATITUDE, TOO.
THEN LET'S KICK SOME CHARMING BUTT!

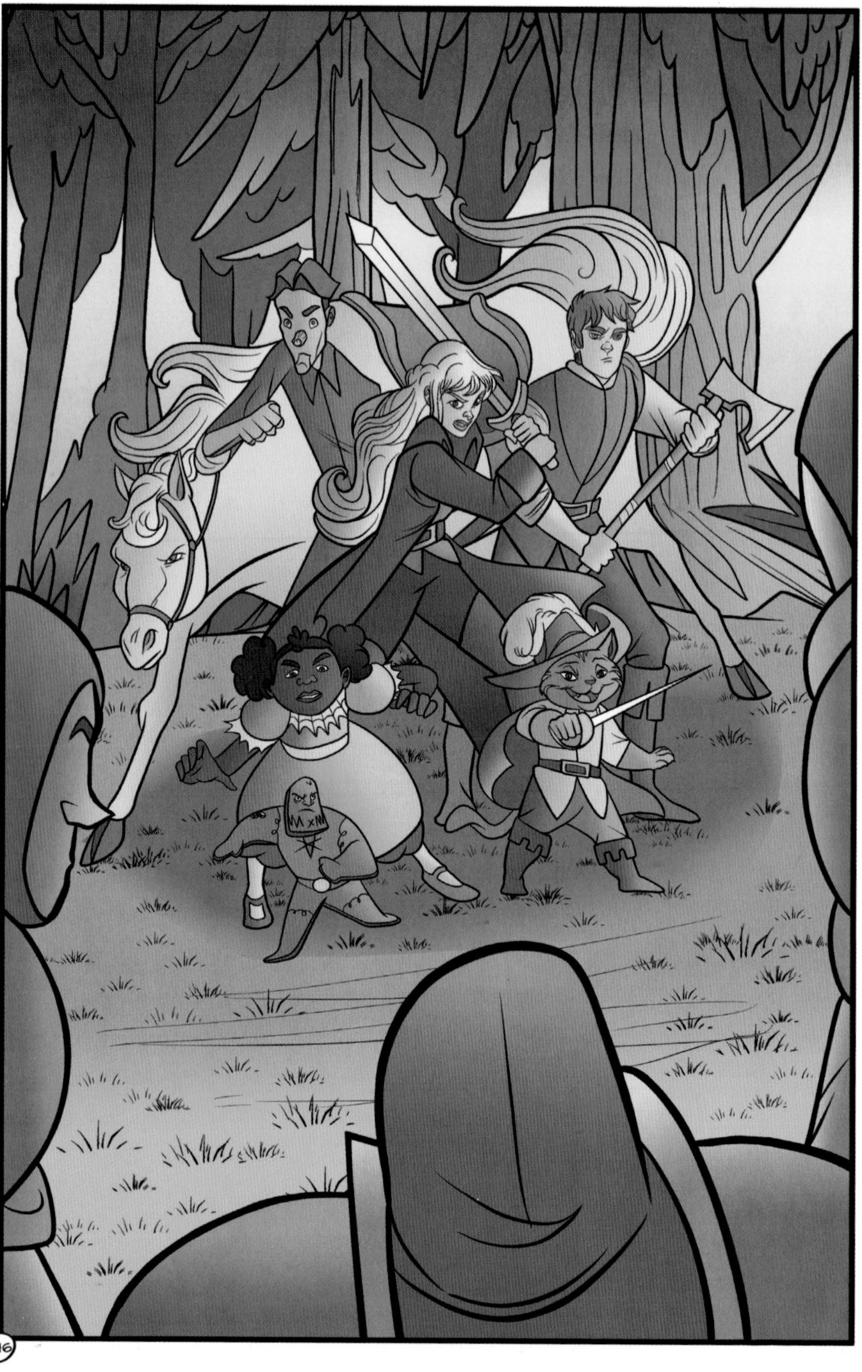

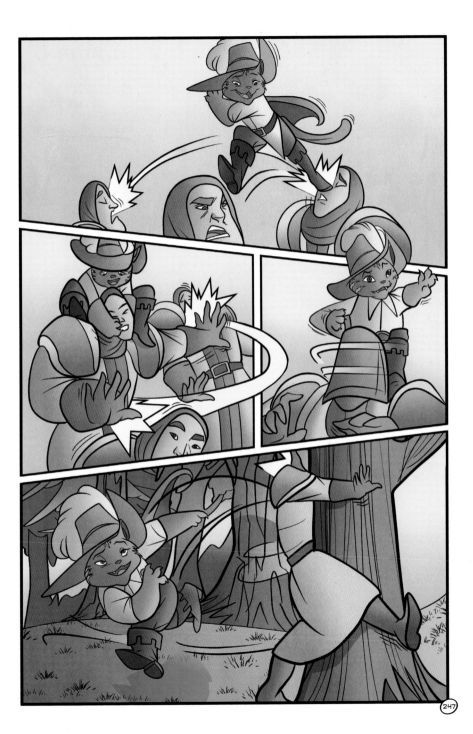

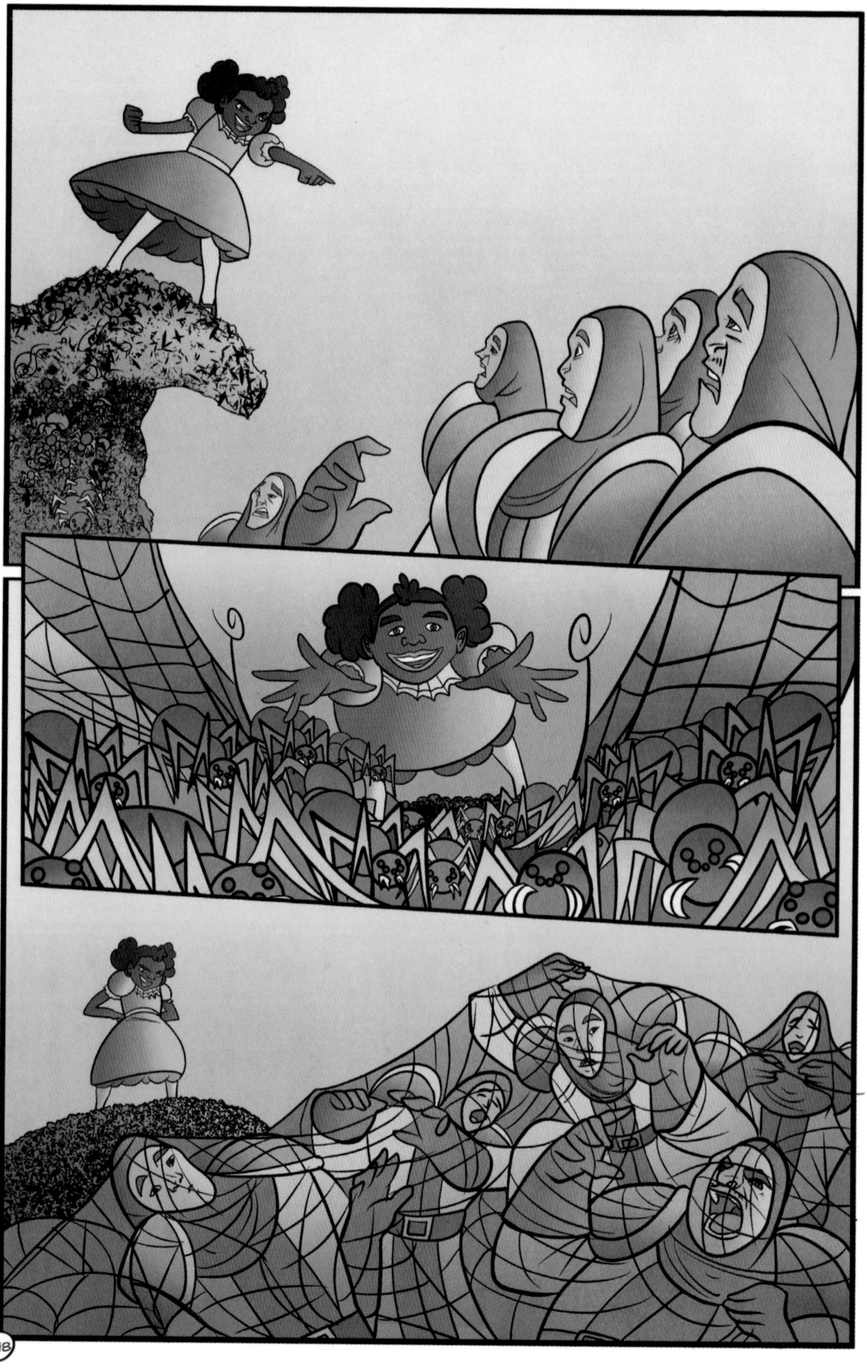

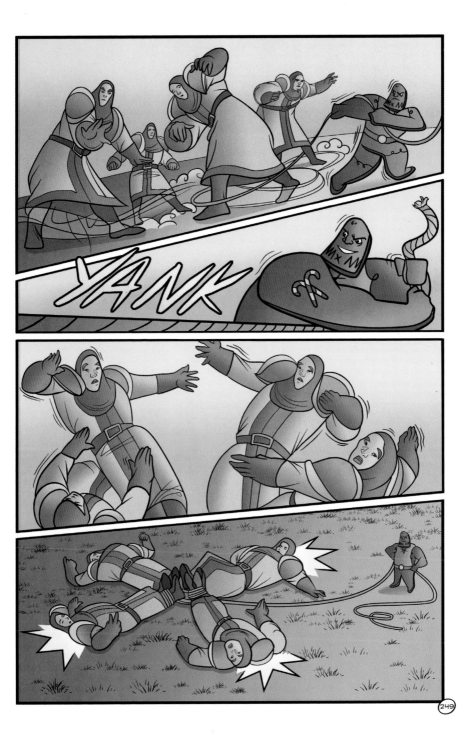

YANK

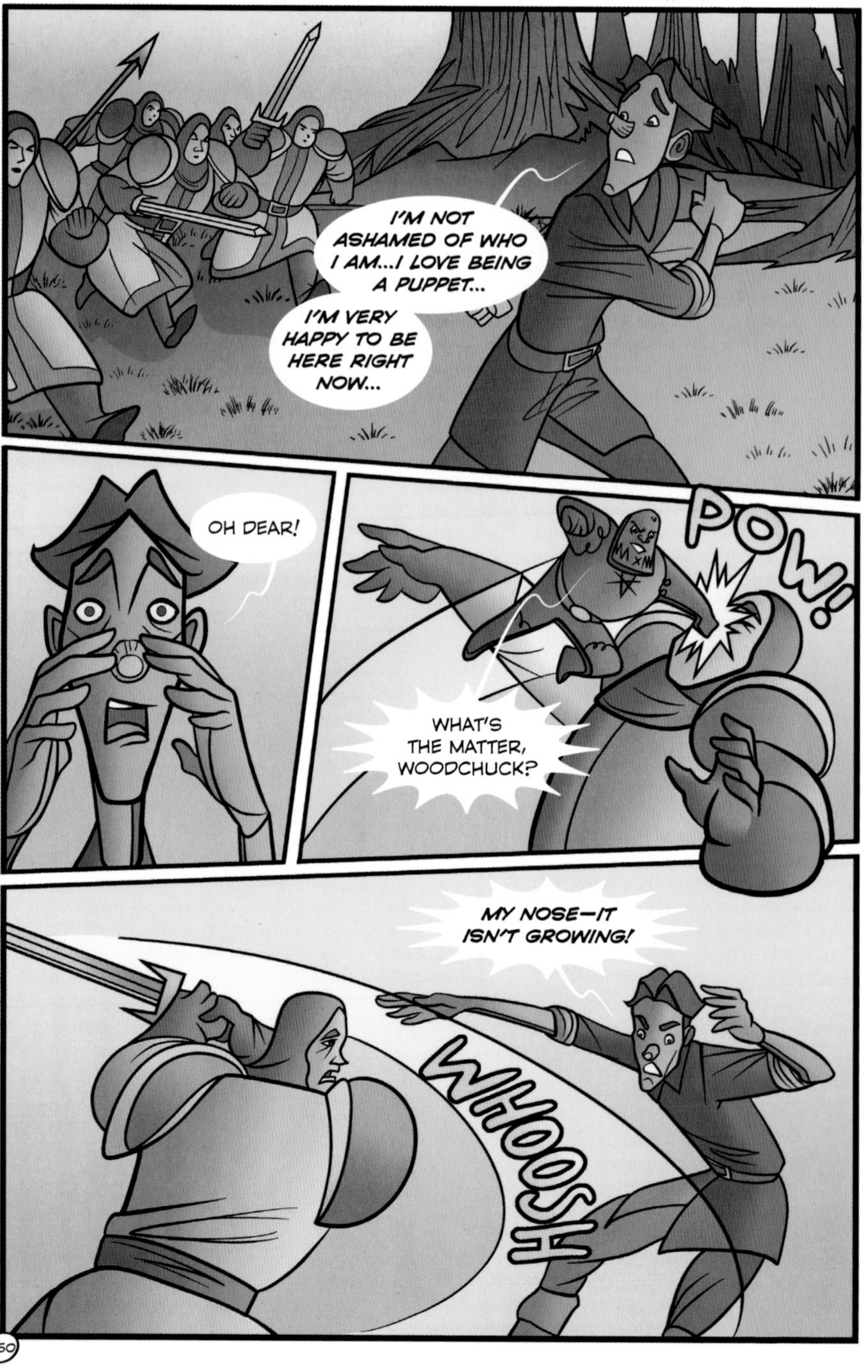
I'M NOT ASHAMED OF WHO I AM...I LOVE BEING A PUPPET...
I'M VERY HAPPY TO BE HERE RIGHT NOW...
OH DEAR!
POW!
WHAT'S THE MATTER, WOODCHUCK?
MY NOSE—IT ISN'T GROWING!
WHOOSH

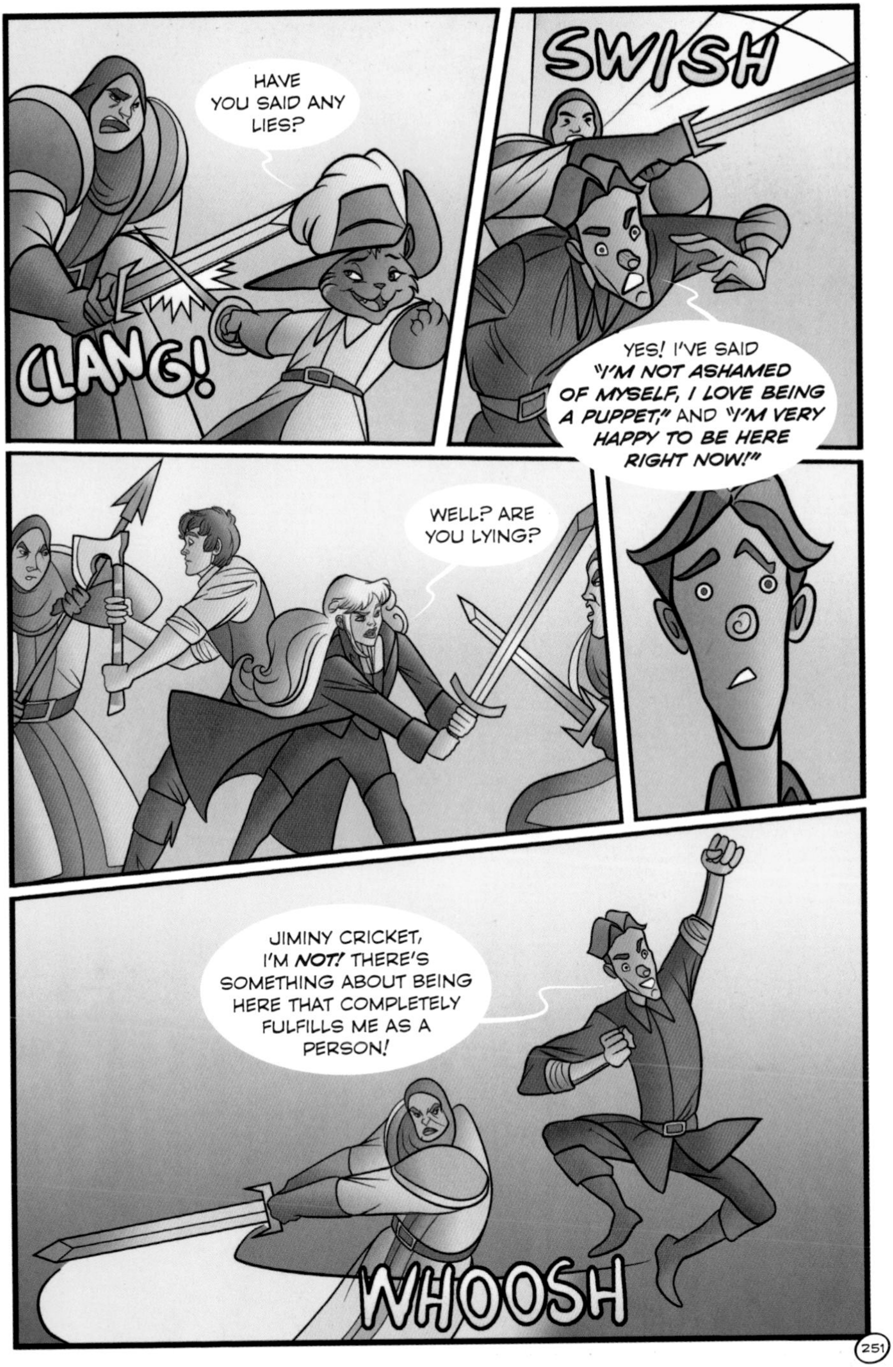
HAVE YOU SAID ANY LIES?
CLANG!
SWISH
YES! I'VE SAID *"I'M NOT ASHAMED OF MYSELF, I LOVE BEING A PUPPET,"* AND *"I'M VERY HAPPY TO BE HERE RIGHT NOW!"*
WELL? ARE YOU LYING?
JIMINY CRICKET, I'M ***NOT!*** THERE'S SOMETHING ABOUT BEING HERE THAT COMPLETELY FULFILLS ME AS A PERSON!
WHOOSH

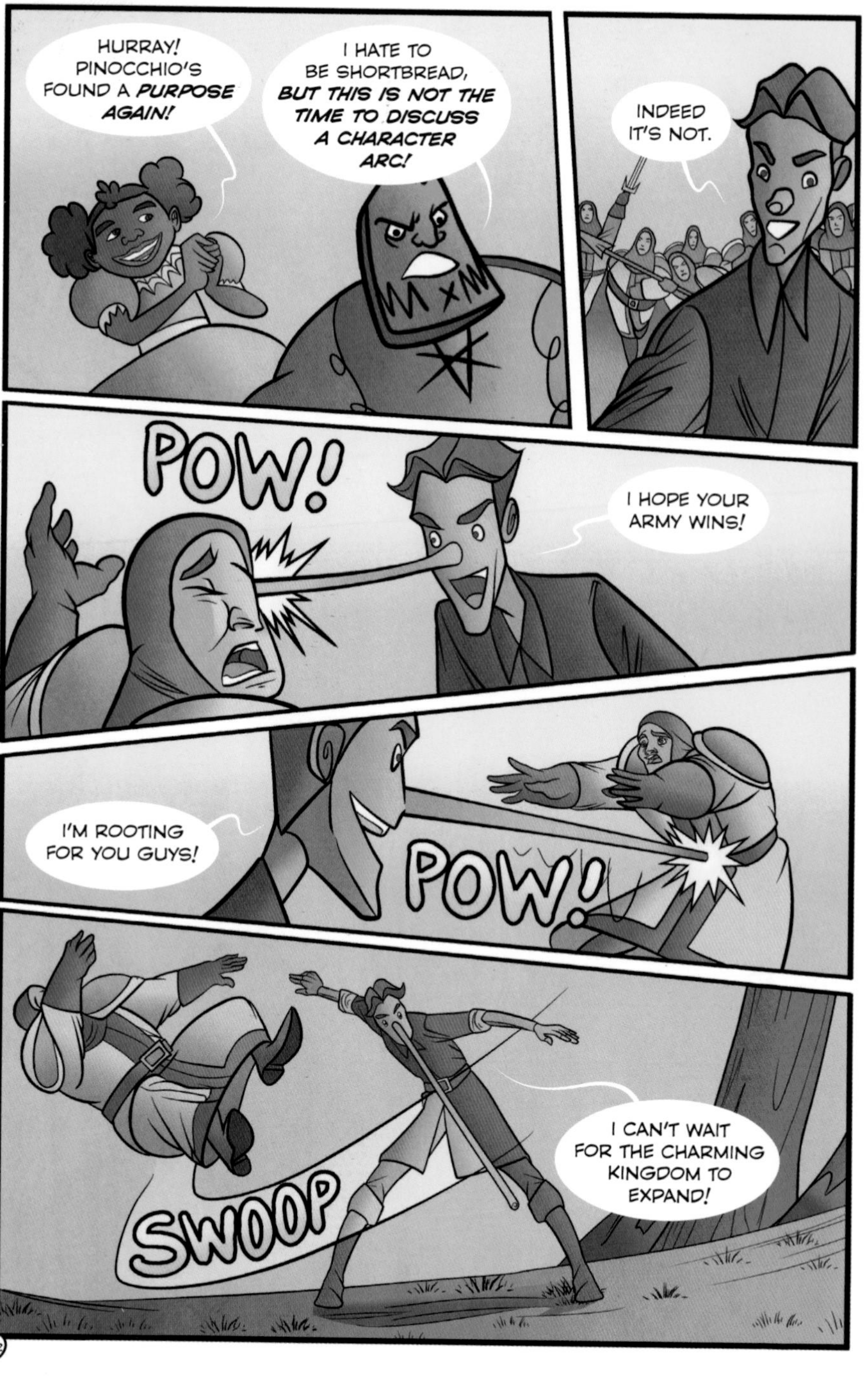
HURRAY! PINOCCHIO'S FOUND A *PURPOSE* AGAIN!
I HATE TO BE SHORTBREAD, ***BUT THIS IS NOT THE TIME TO DISCUSS A CHARACTER ARC!***
INDEED IT'S NOT.
POW!
I HOPE YOUR ARMY WINS!
I'M ROOTING FOR YOU GUYS!
POW!
SWOOP
I CAN'T WAIT FOR THE CHARMING KINGDOM TO EXPAND!

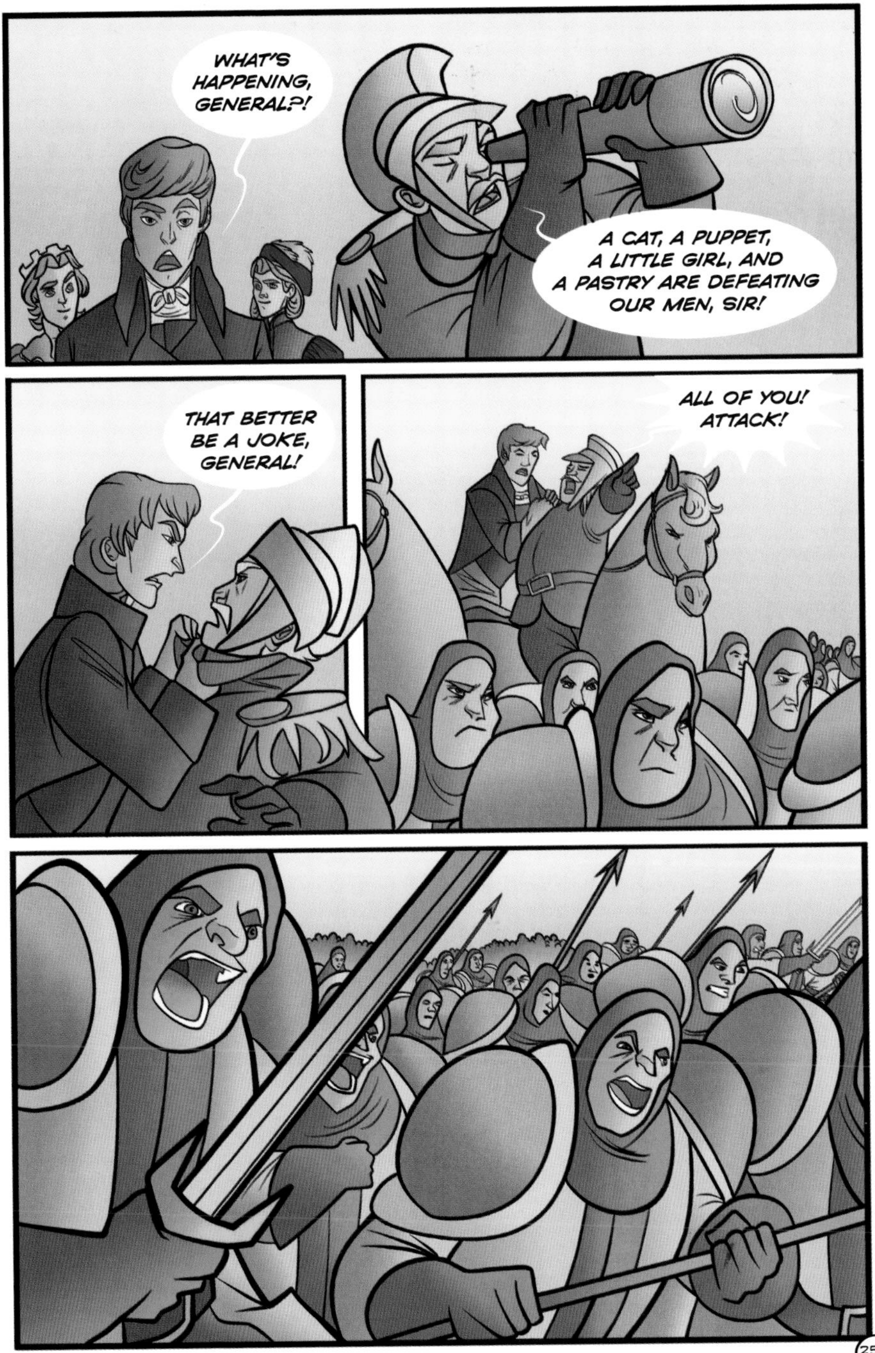
WHAT'S HAPPENING, GENERAL?!
A CAT, A PUPPET, A LITTLE GIRL, AND A PASTRY ARE DEFEATING OUR MEN, SIR!
THAT BETTER BE A JOKE, GENERAL!
ALL OF YOU! ATTACK!

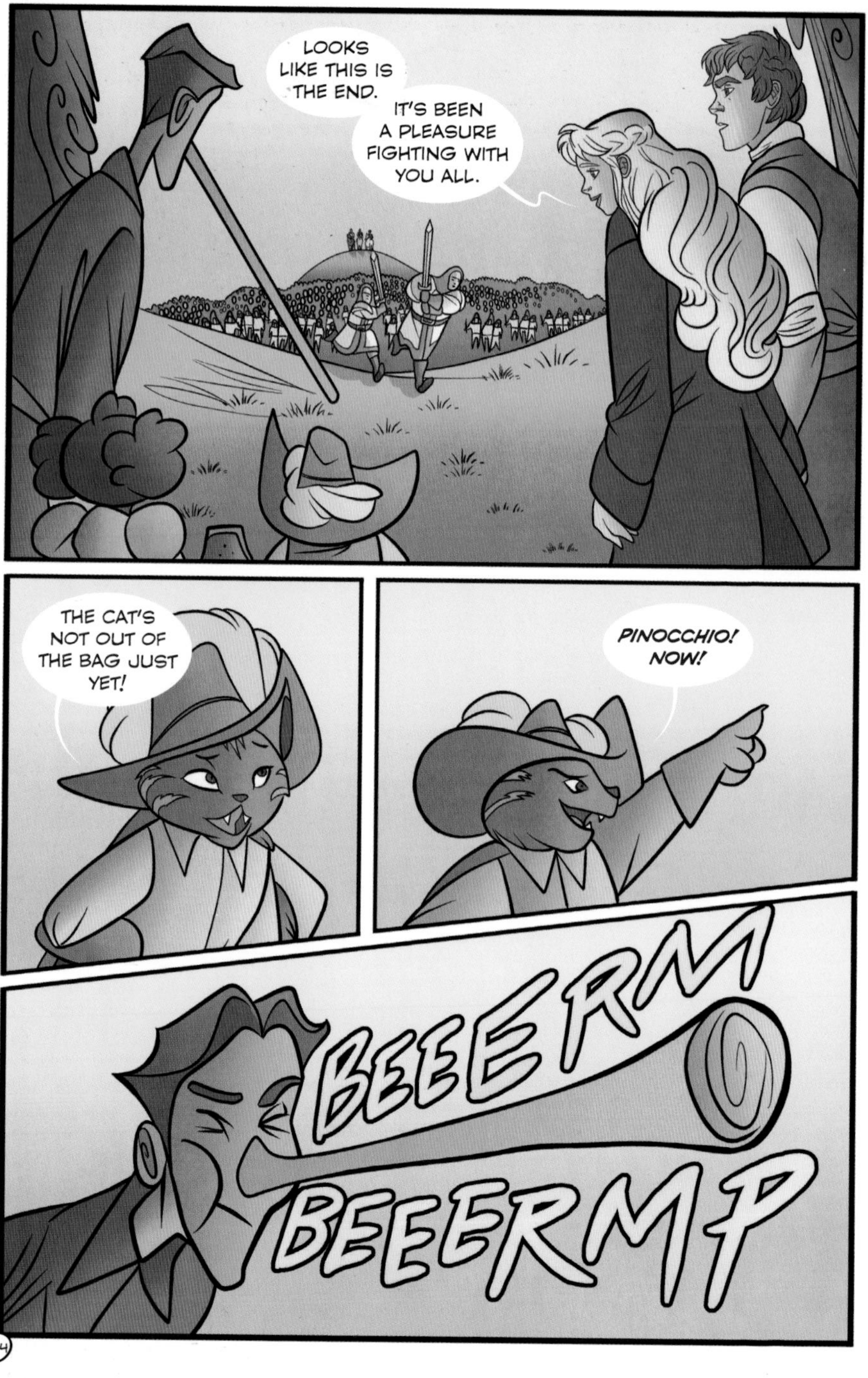
LOOKS LIKE THIS IS THE END.
IT'S BEEN A PLEASURE FIGHTING WITH YOU ALL.
THE CAT'S NOT OUT OF THE BAG JUST YET!
PINOCCHIO! NOW!
BEEERM
BEEERMP

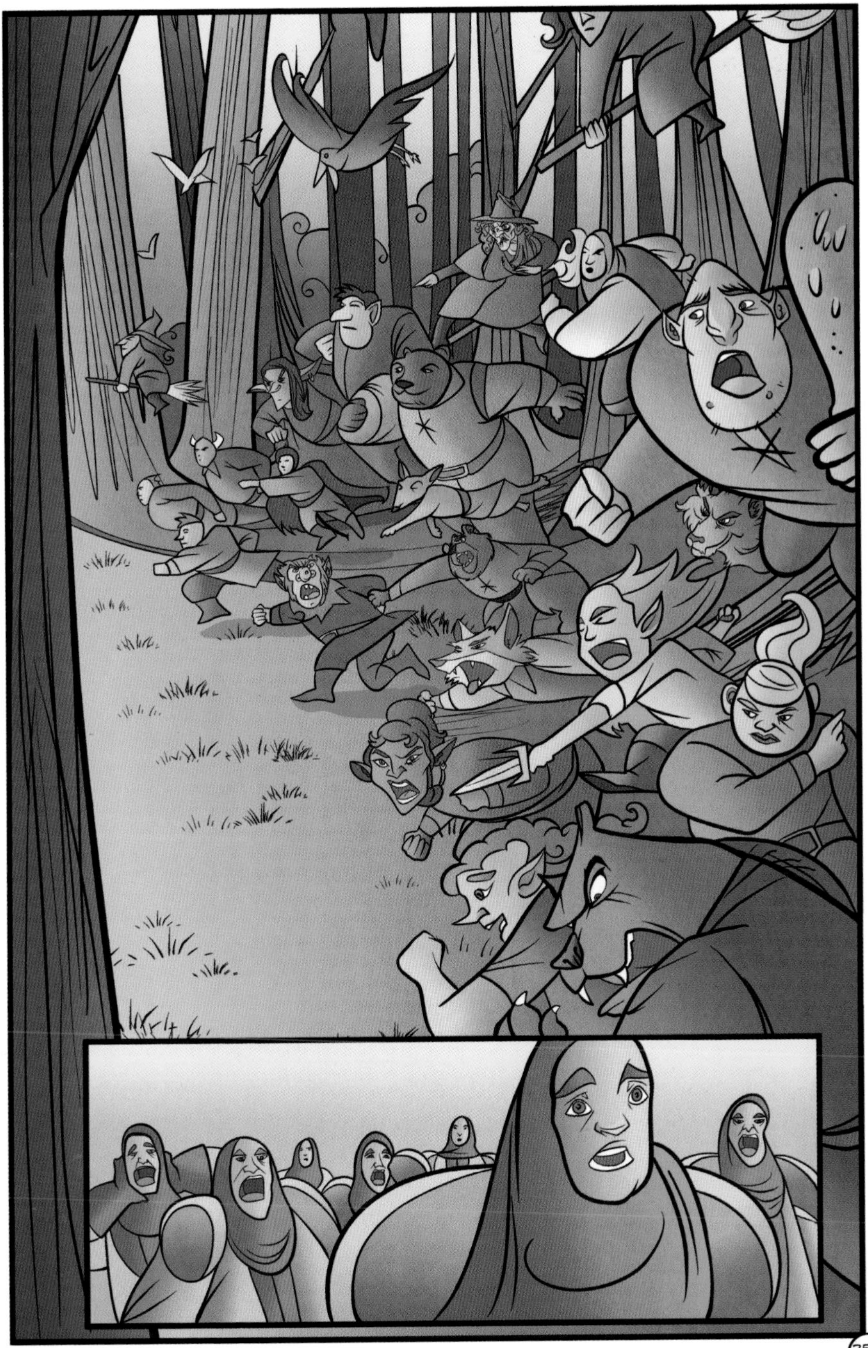

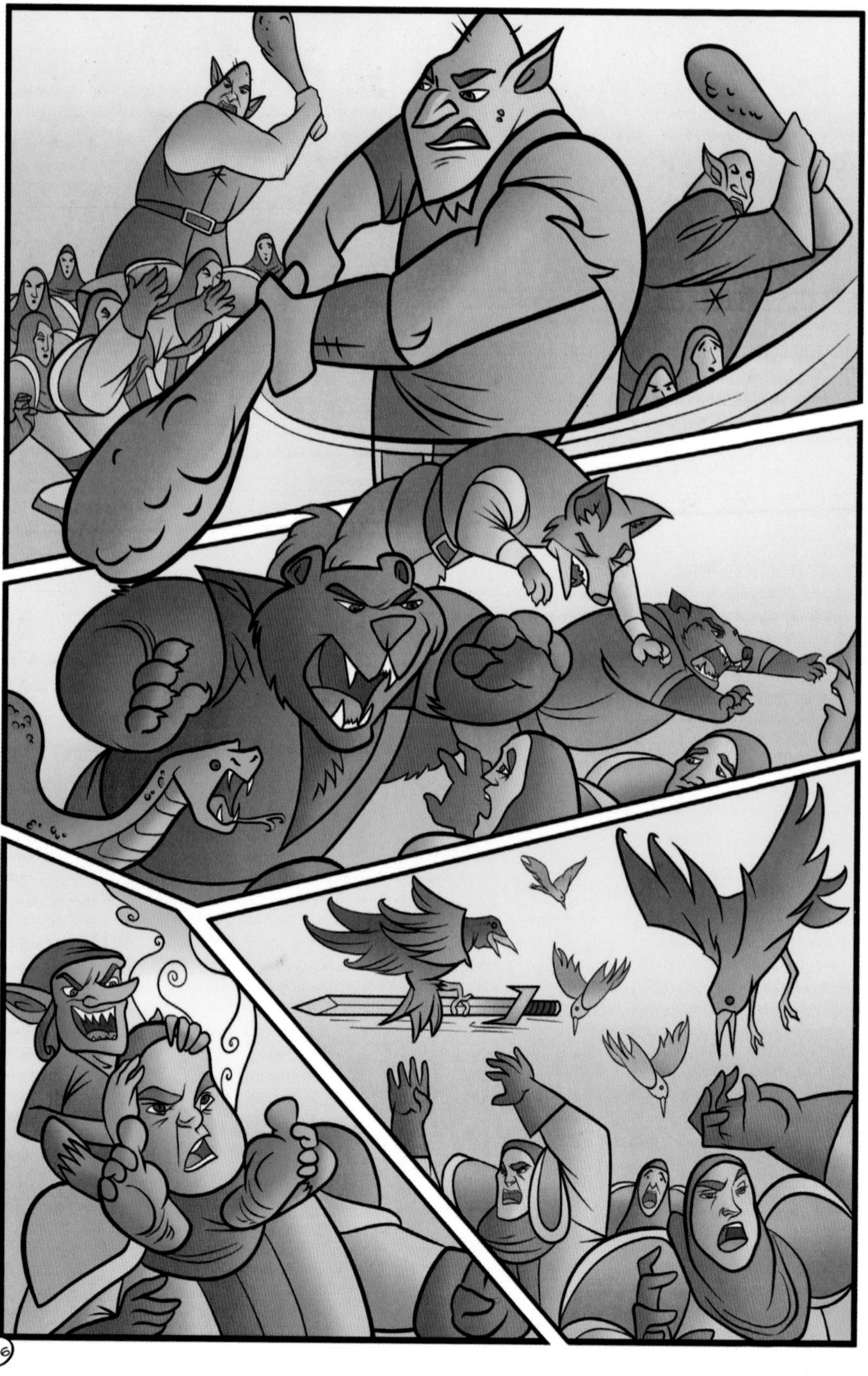

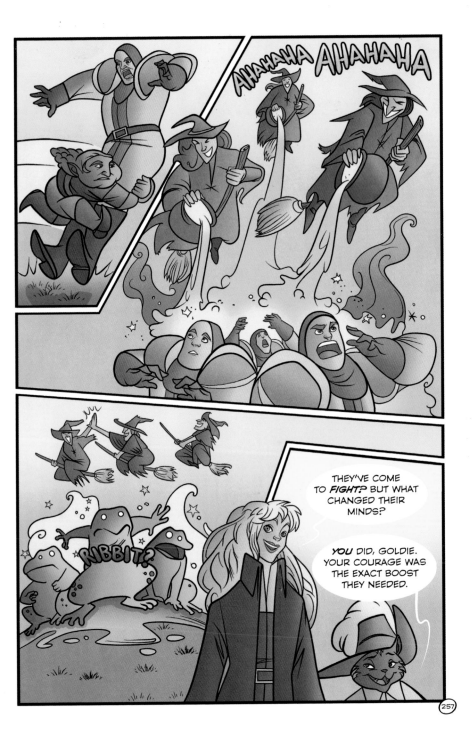

AHAHAHA AHAHAHA

THEY'VE COME TO *FIGHT?* BUT WHAT CHANGED THEIR MINDS?

YOU DID, GOLDIE. YOUR COURAGE WAS THE EXACT BOOST THEY NEEDED.

RIBBIT?

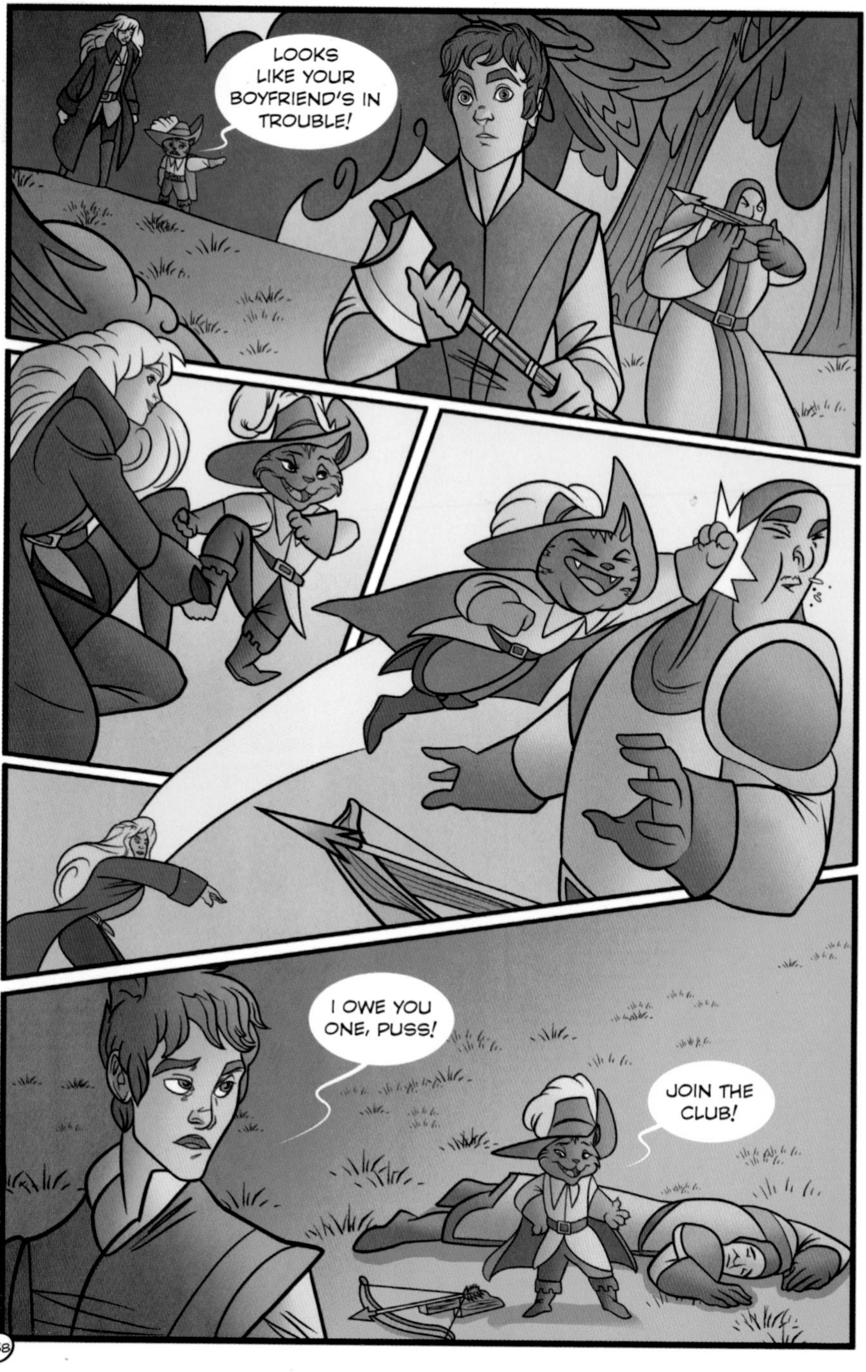
LOOKS LIKE YOUR BOYFRIEND'S IN TROUBLE!
I OWE YOU ONE, PUSS!
JOIN THE CLUB!

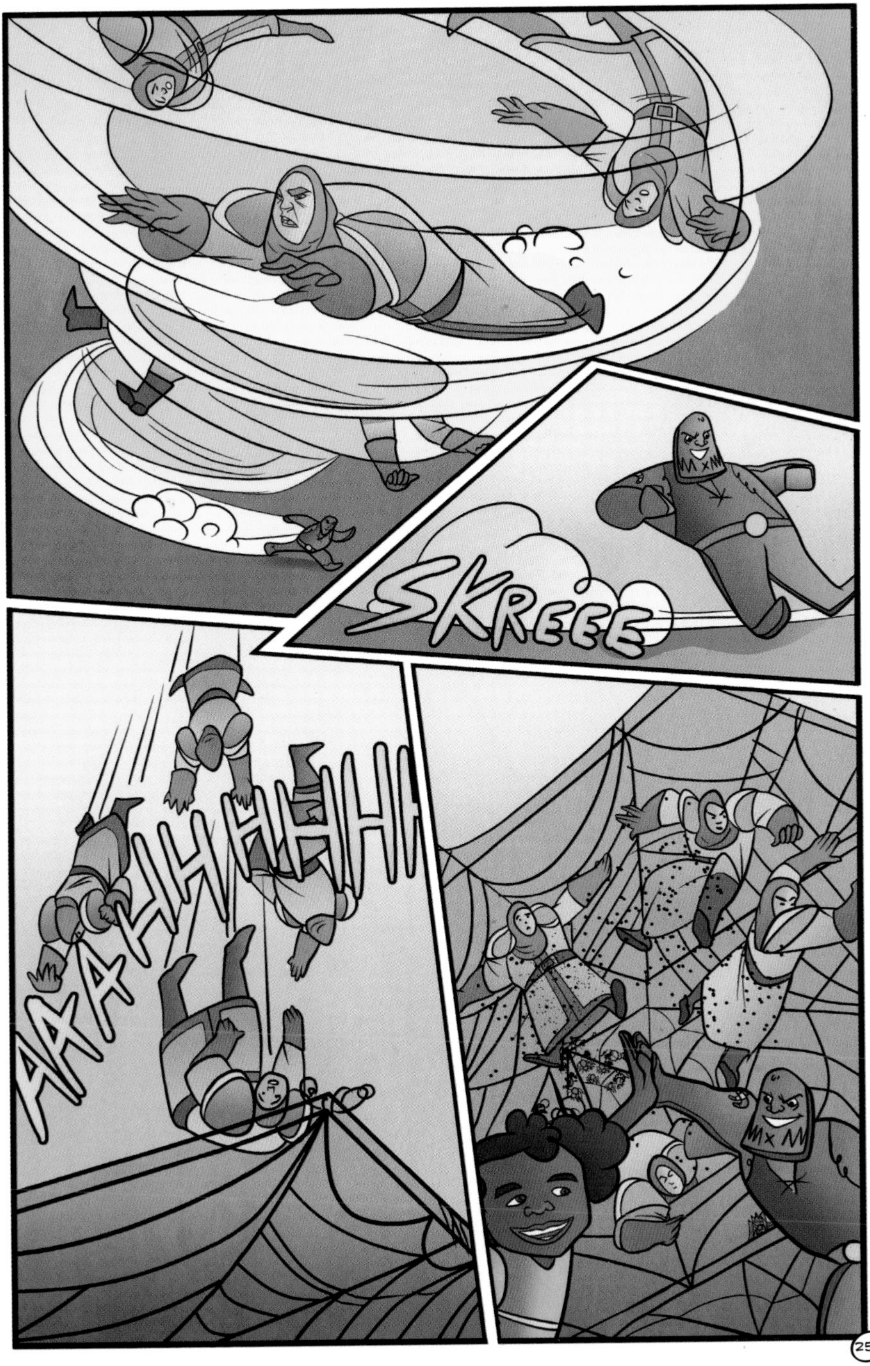
SKREEE
AAAHHHHHHH

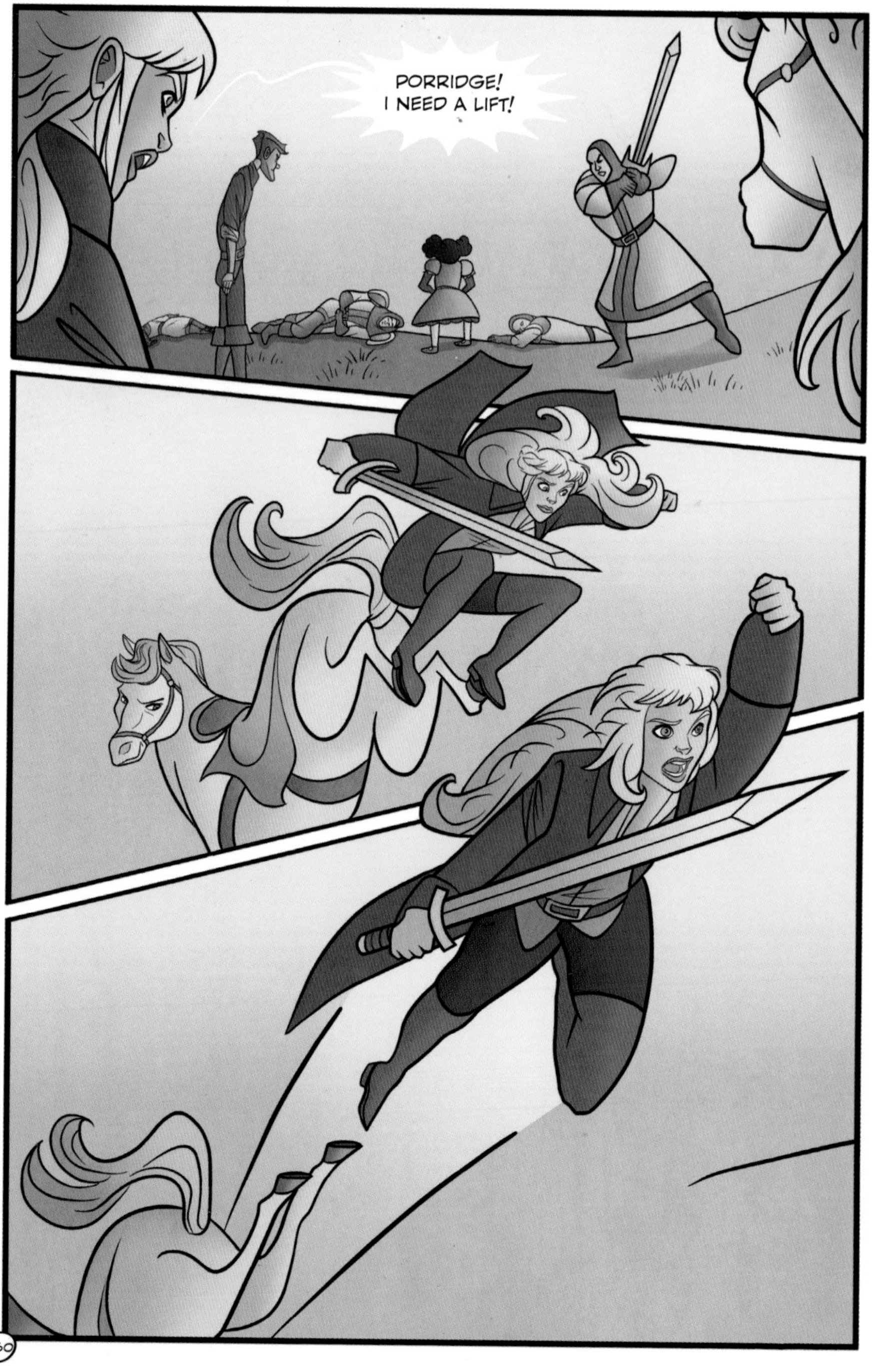
PORRIDGE!
I NEED A LIFT!

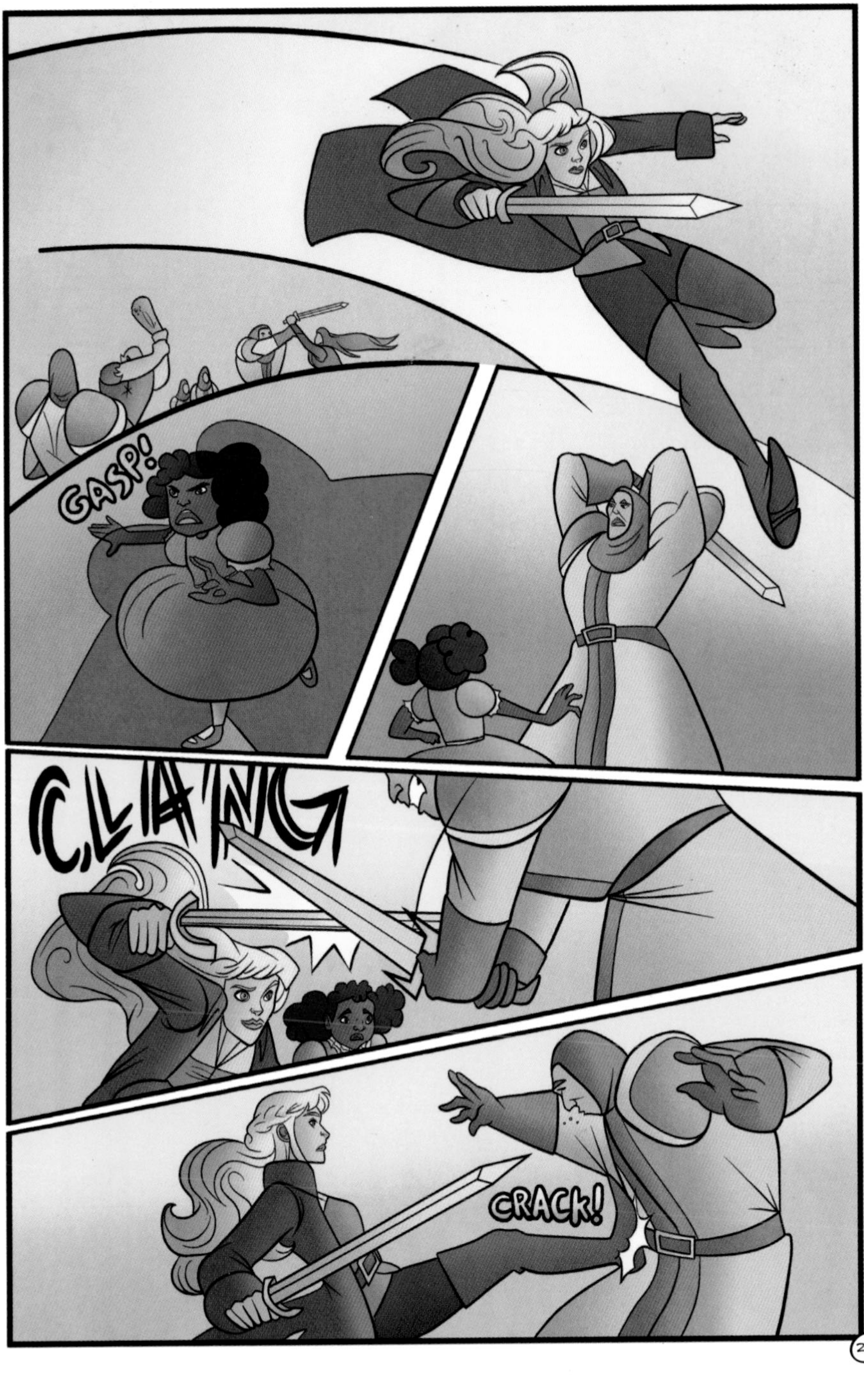
GASP!
CLANG
CRACK!

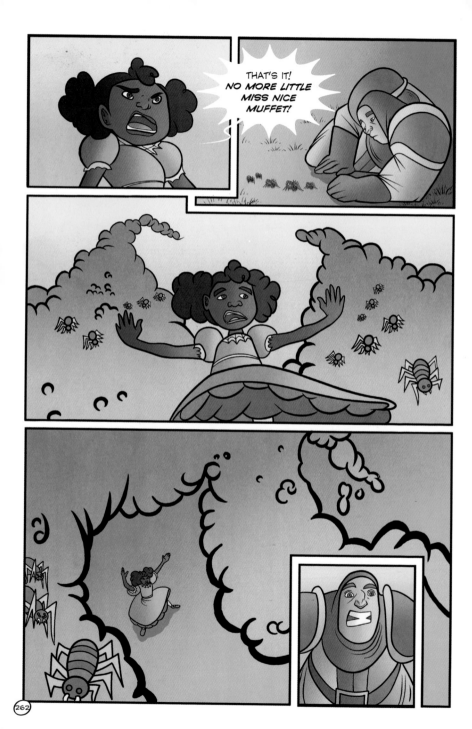

THAT'S IT! NO MORE LITTLE MISS NICE MUFFET!

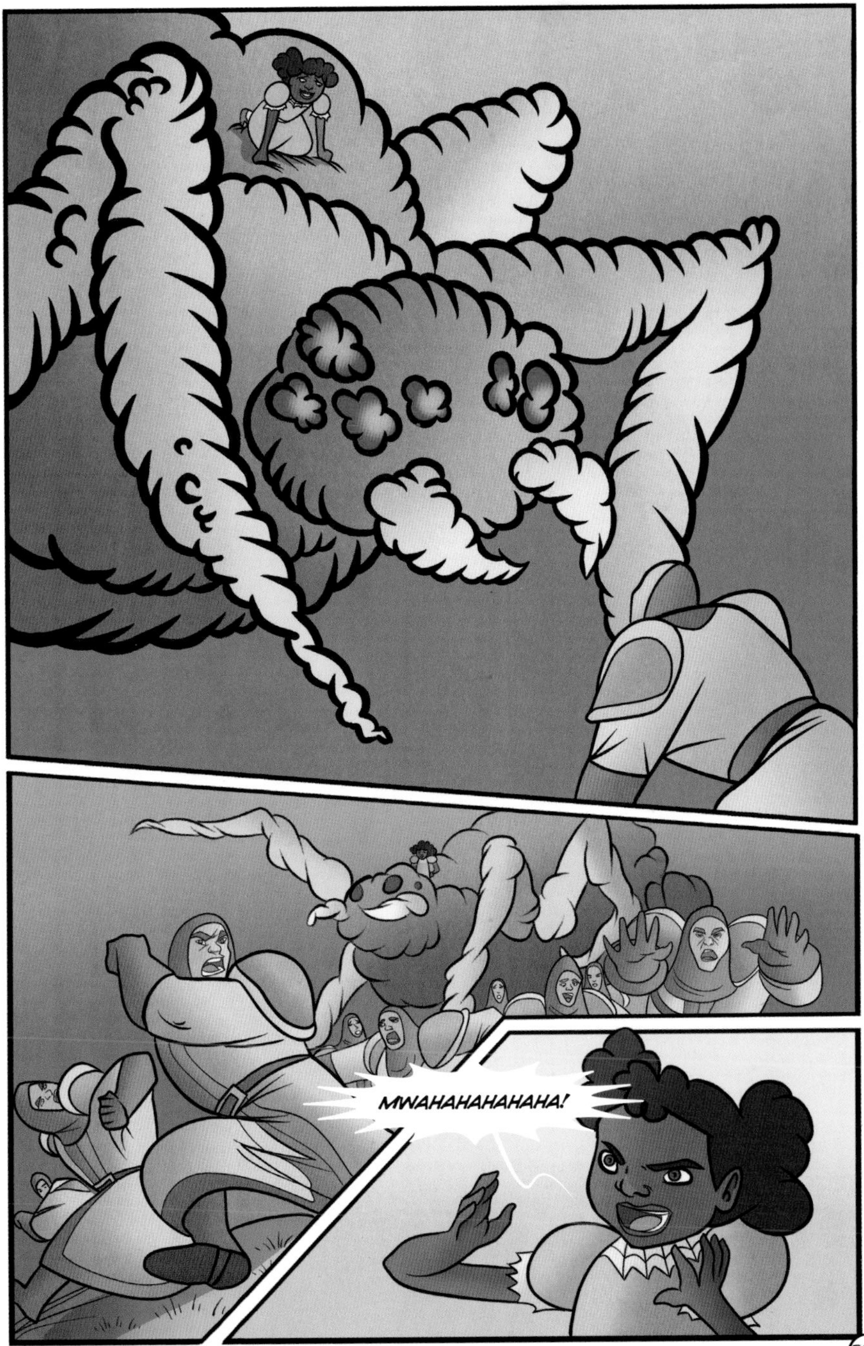
MWAHAHAHAHAHA!

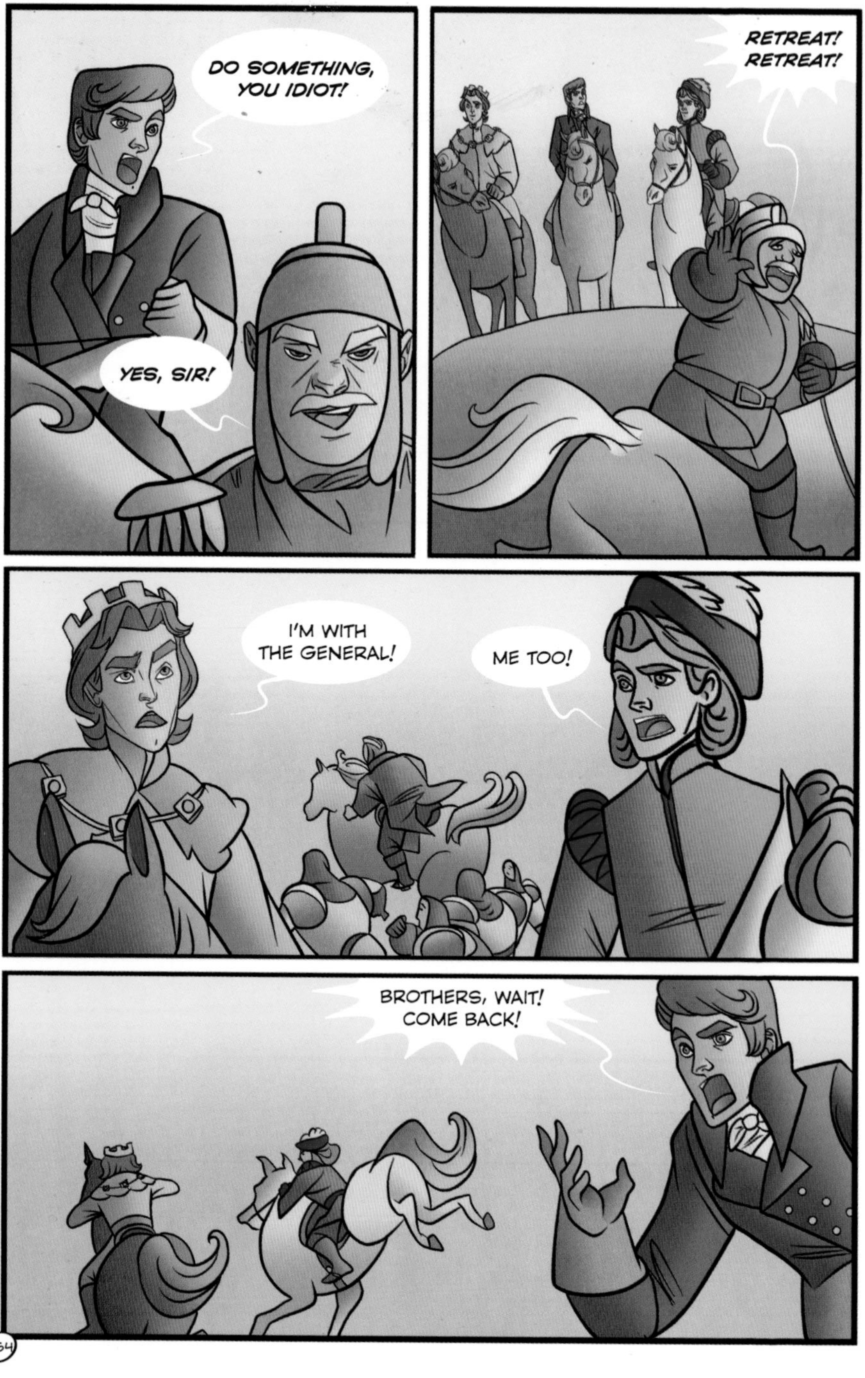
DO SOMETHING, YOU IDIOT!
YES, SIR!
RETREAT! RETREAT!
I'M WITH THE GENERAL!
ME TOO!
BROTHERS, WAIT! COME BACK!

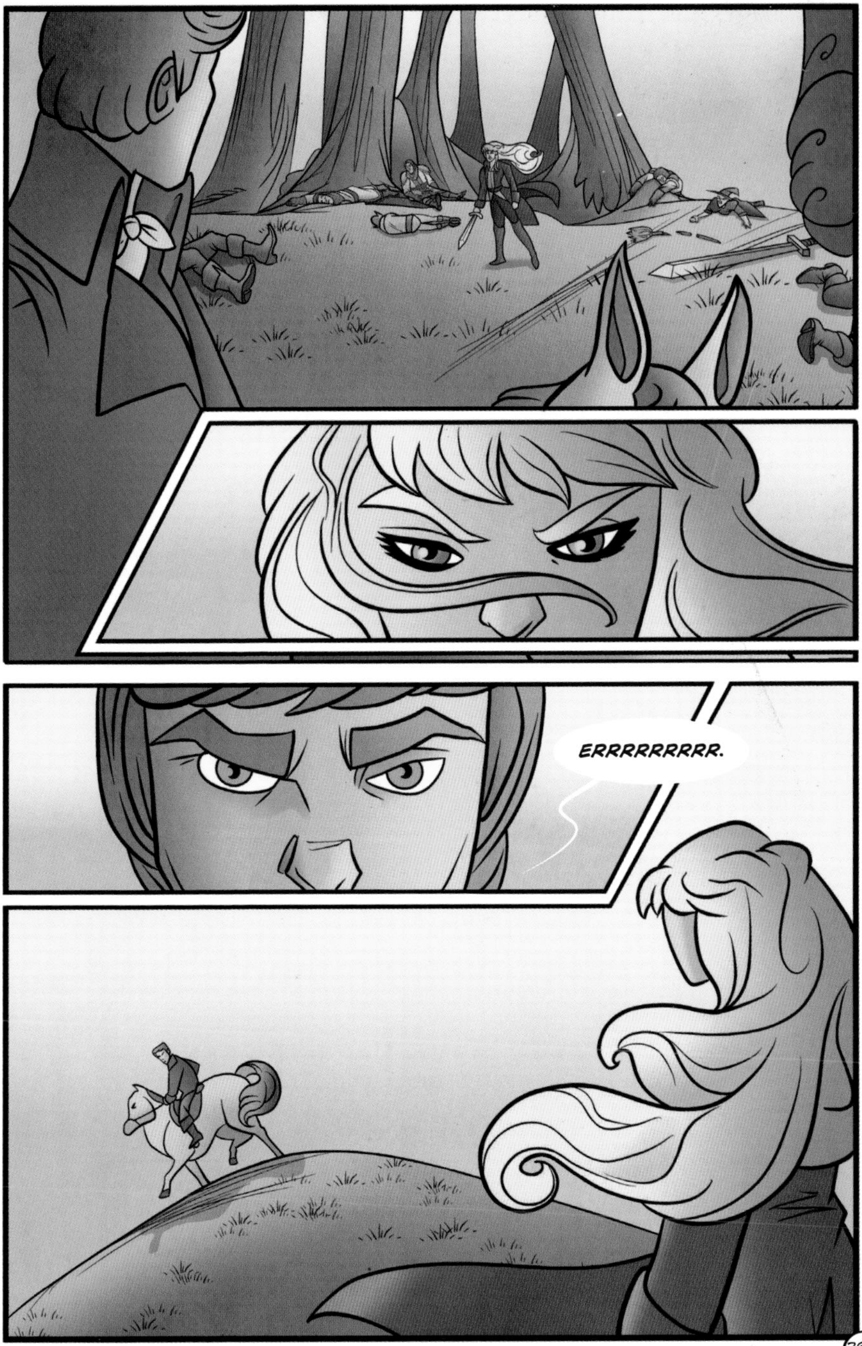
ERRRRRRRRR.

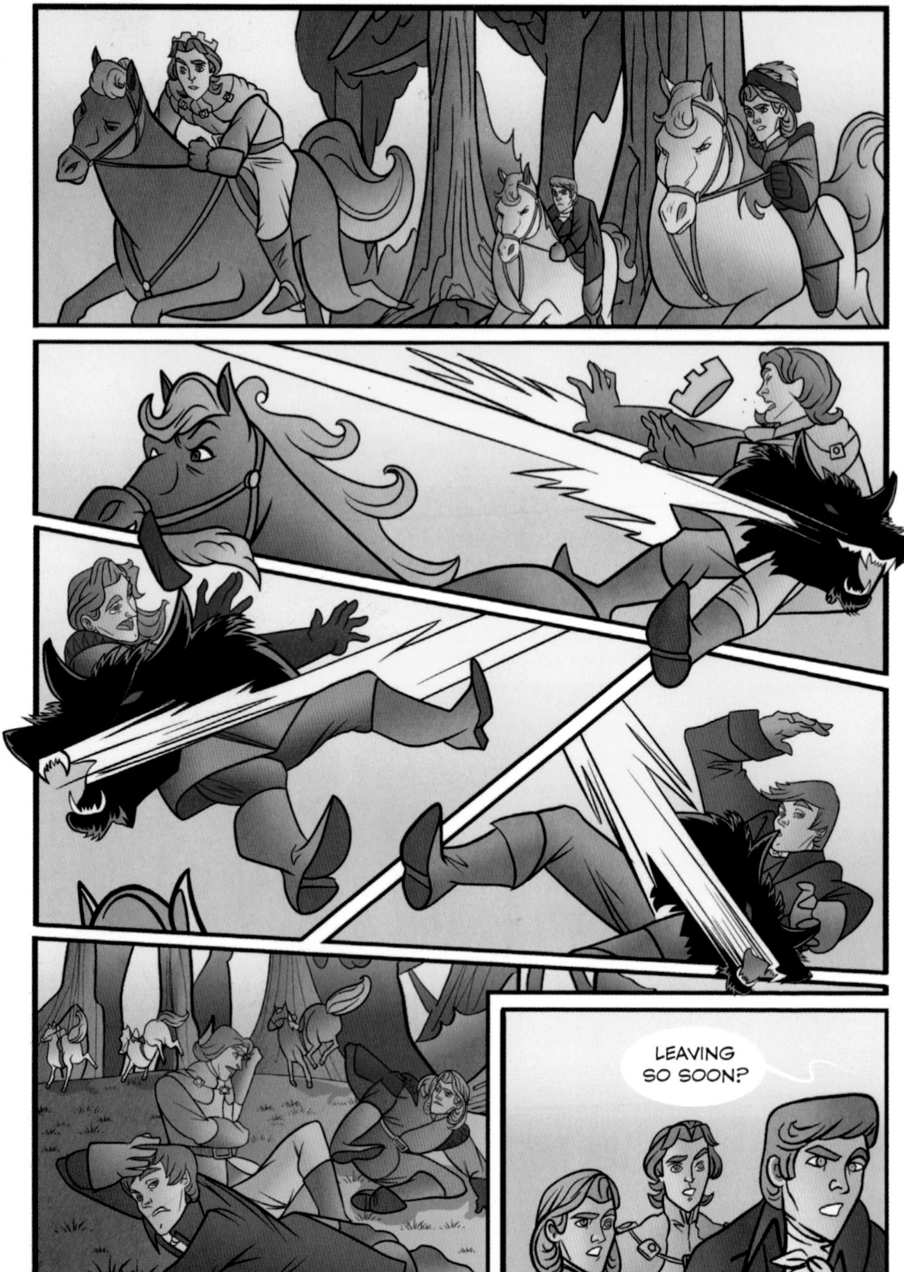
LEAVING
SO SOON?

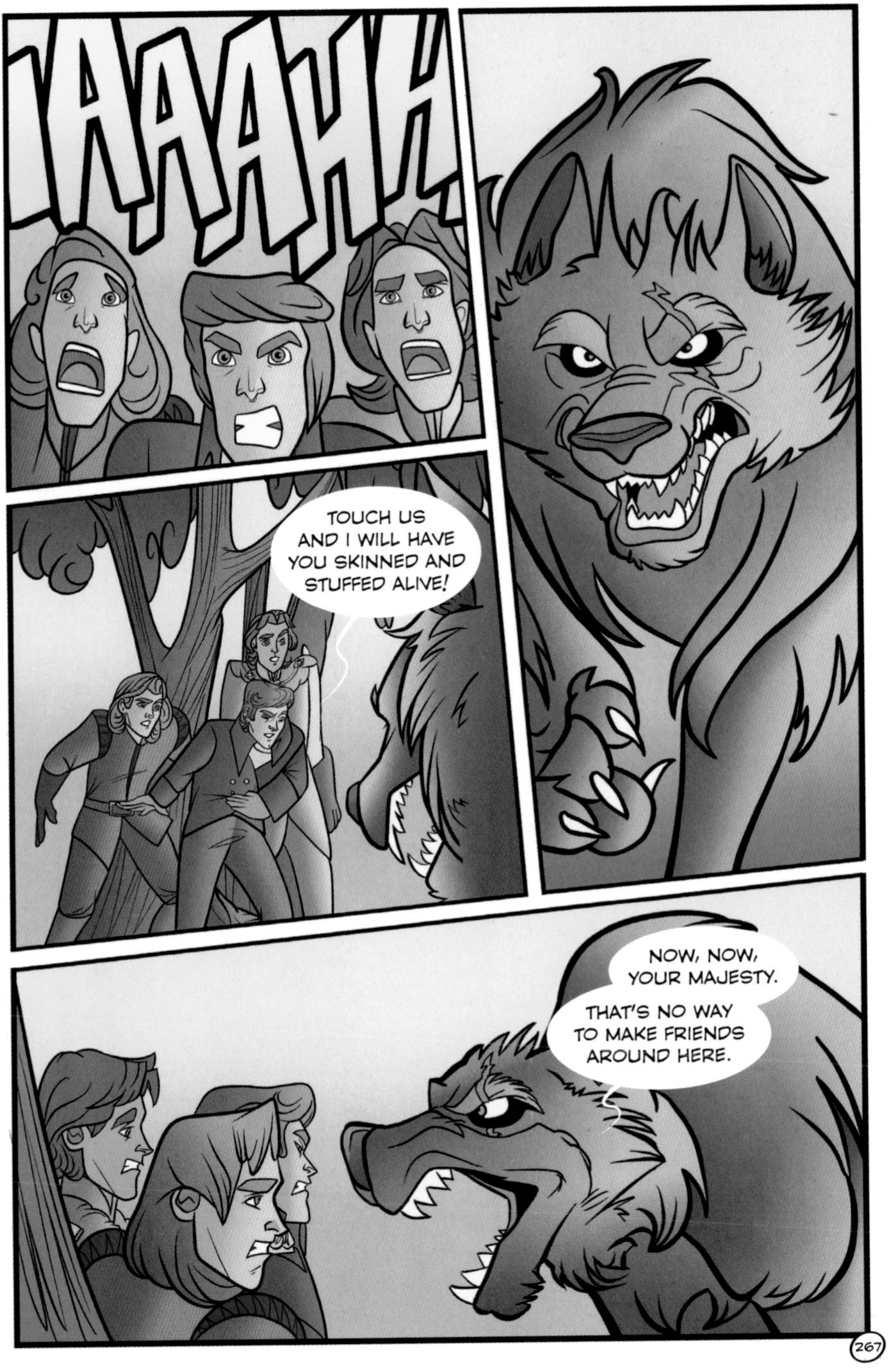
AAAH!
TOUCH US AND I WILL HAVE YOU SKINNED AND STUFFED ALIVE!
NOW, NOW, YOUR MAJESTY.
THAT'S NO WAY TO MAKE FRIENDS AROUND HERE.

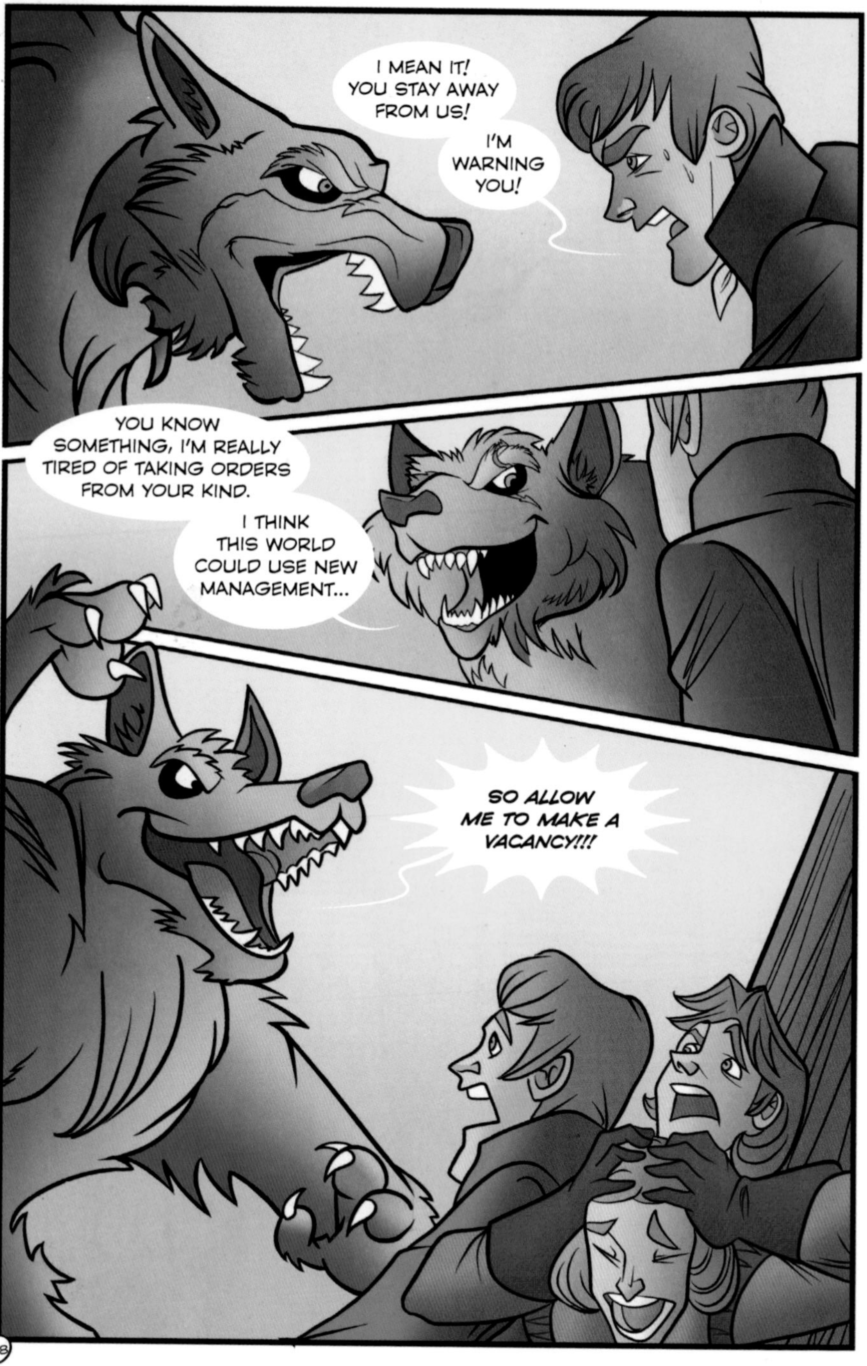
I MEAN IT! YOU STAY AWAY FROM US!
I'M WARNING YOU!
YOU KNOW SOMETHING, I'M REALLY TIRED OF TAKING ORDERS FROM YOUR KIND.
I THINK THIS WORLD COULD USE NEW MANAGEMENT...
SO ALLOW ME TO MAKE A VACANCY!!!

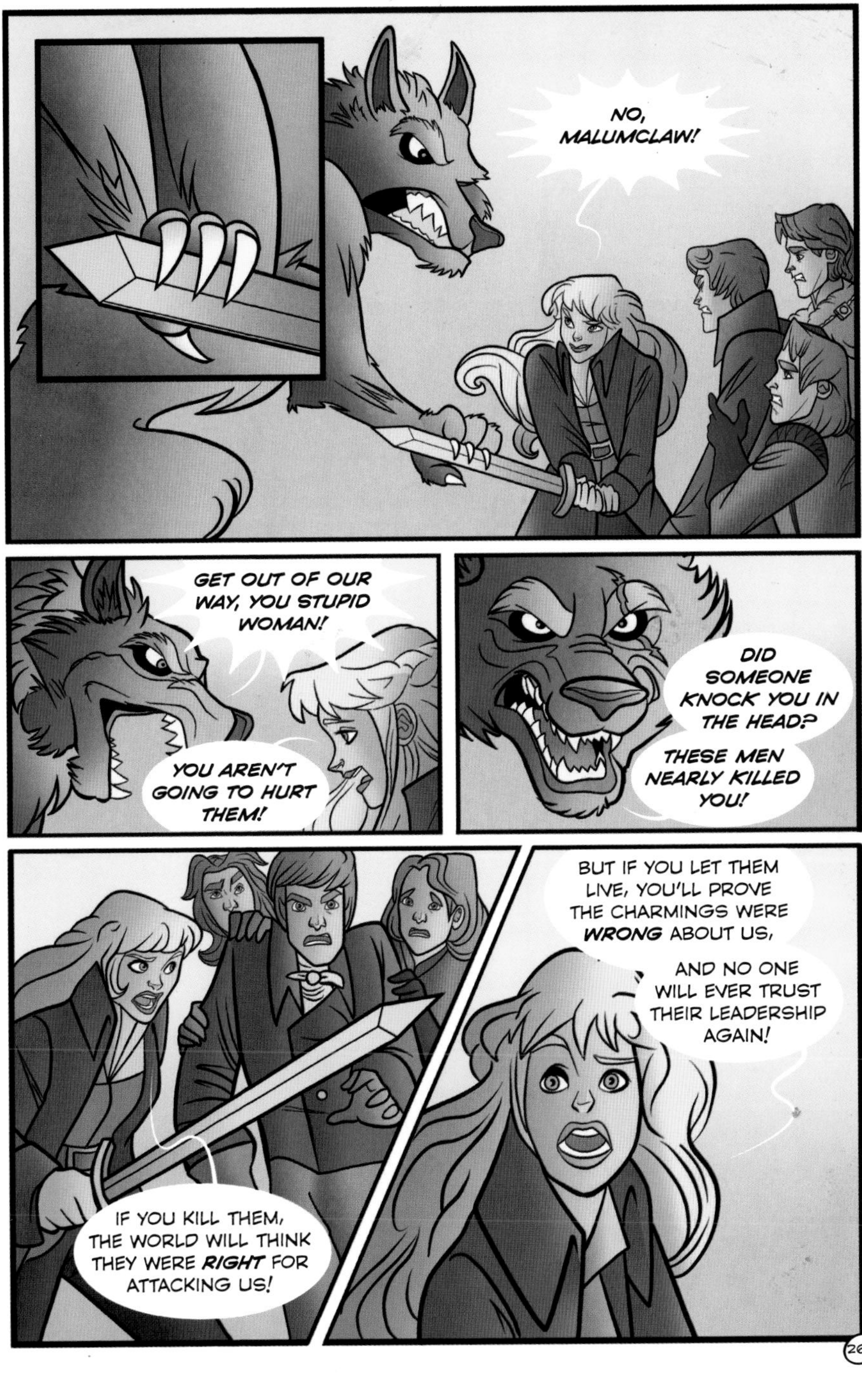
NO, MALUMCLAW!
GET OUT OF OUR WAY, YOU STUPID WOMAN!
YOU AREN'T GOING TO HURT THEM!
DID SOMEONE KNOCK YOU IN THE HEAD?
THESE MEN NEARLY KILLED YOU!
IF YOU KILL THEM, THE WORLD WILL THINK THEY WERE RIGHT FOR ATTACKING US!
BUT IF YOU LET THEM LIVE, YOU'LL PROVE THE CHARMINGS WERE WRONG ABOUT US,
AND NO ONE WILL EVER TRUST THEIR LEADERSHIP AGAIN!

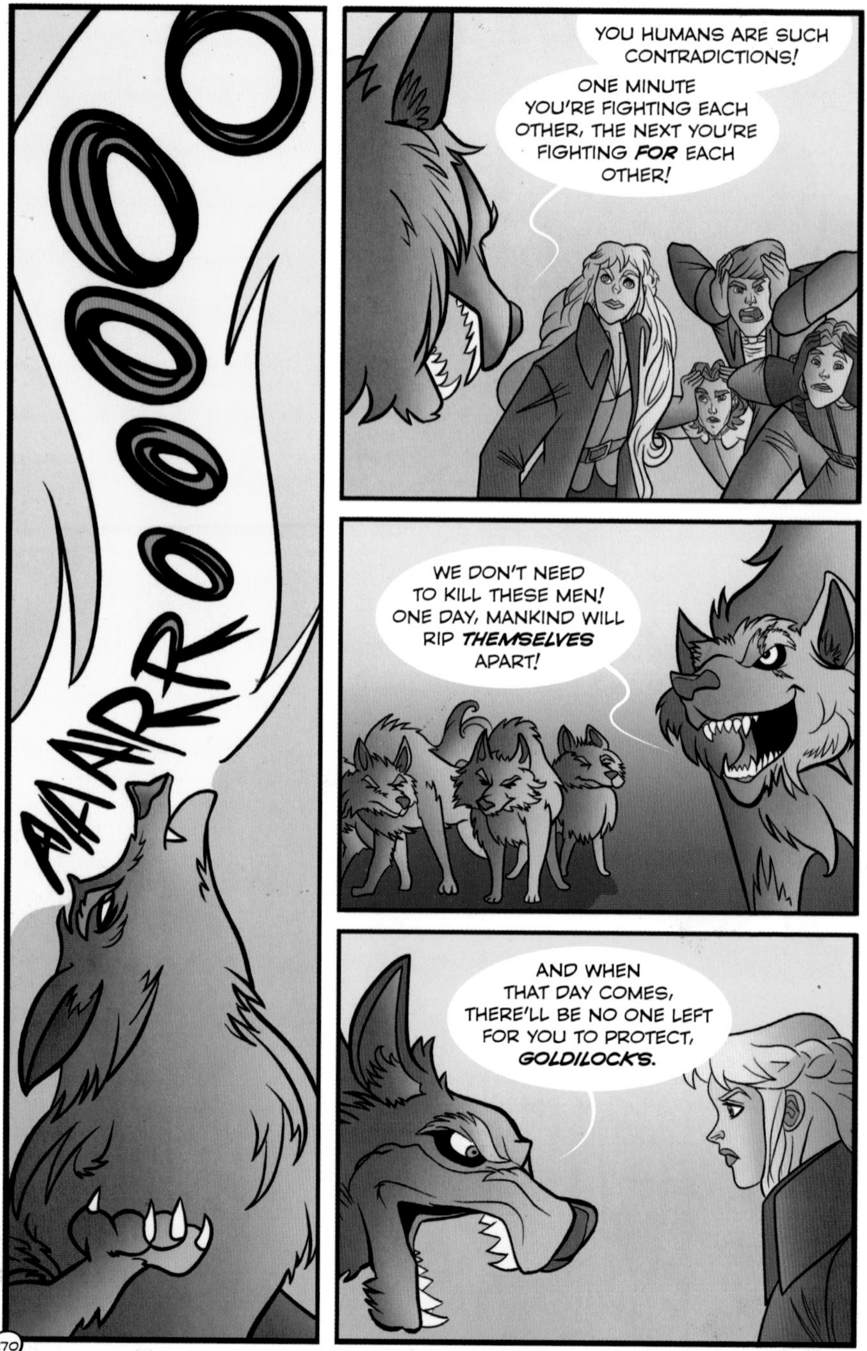
AAARROOOOOO
YOU HUMANS ARE SUCH CONTRADICTIONS!
ONE MINUTE YOU'RE FIGHTING EACH OTHER, THE NEXT YOU'RE FIGHTING *FOR* EACH OTHER!
WE DON'T NEED TO KILL THESE MEN! ONE DAY, MANKIND WILL RIP *THEMSELVES* APART!
AND WHEN THAT DAY COMES, THERE'LL BE NO ONE LEFT FOR YOU TO PROTECT, *GOLDILOCKS*.

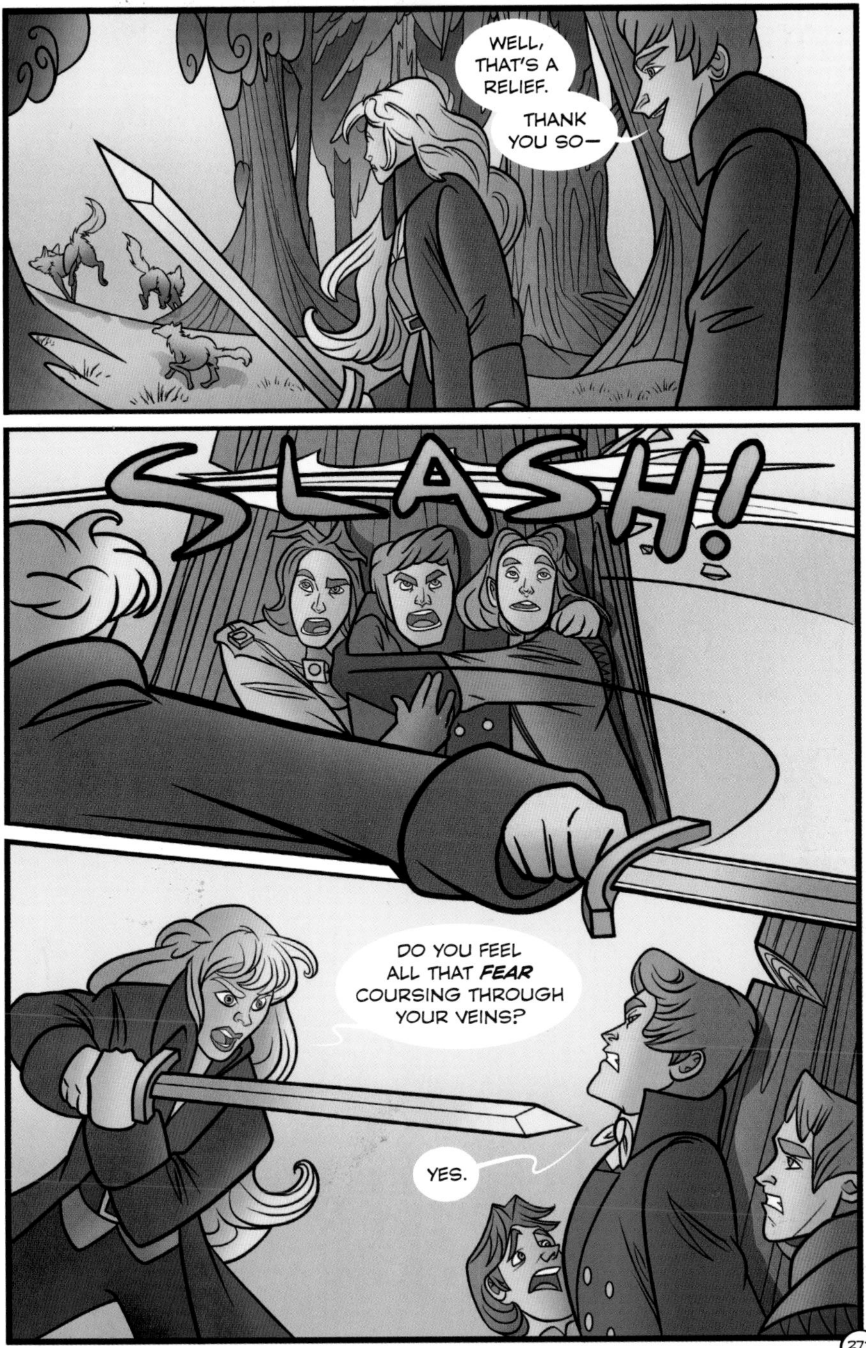
WELL, THAT'S A RELIEF.
THANK YOU SO—
SLASH!
DO YOU FEEL ALL THAT ***FEAR*** COURSING THROUGH YOUR VEINS?
YES.

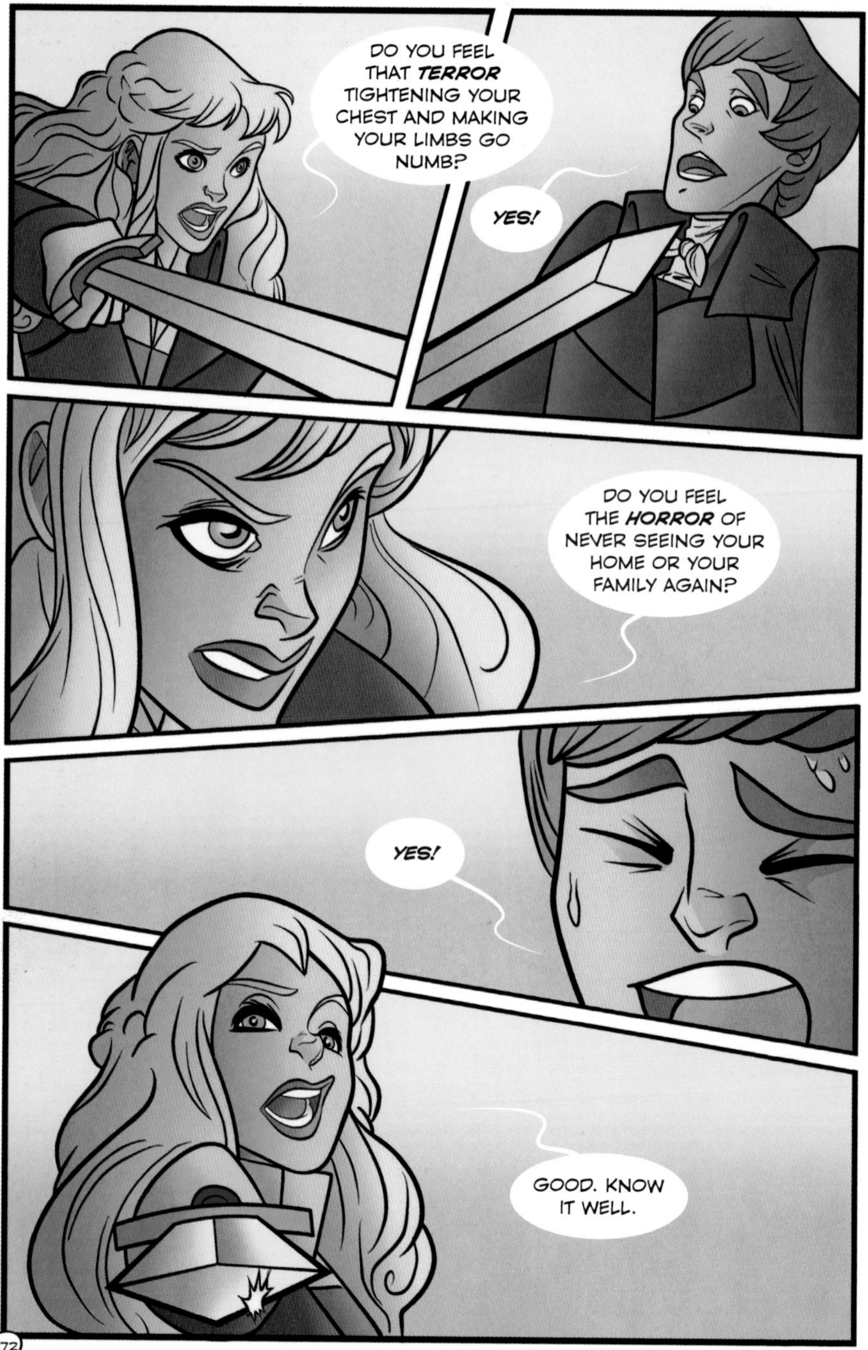
DO YOU FEEL THAT TERROR TIGHTENING YOUR CHEST AND MAKING YOUR LIMBS GO NUMB?
YES!
DO YOU FEEL THE HORROR OF NEVER SEEING YOUR HOME OR YOUR FAMILY AGAIN?
YES!
GOOD. KNOW IT WELL.

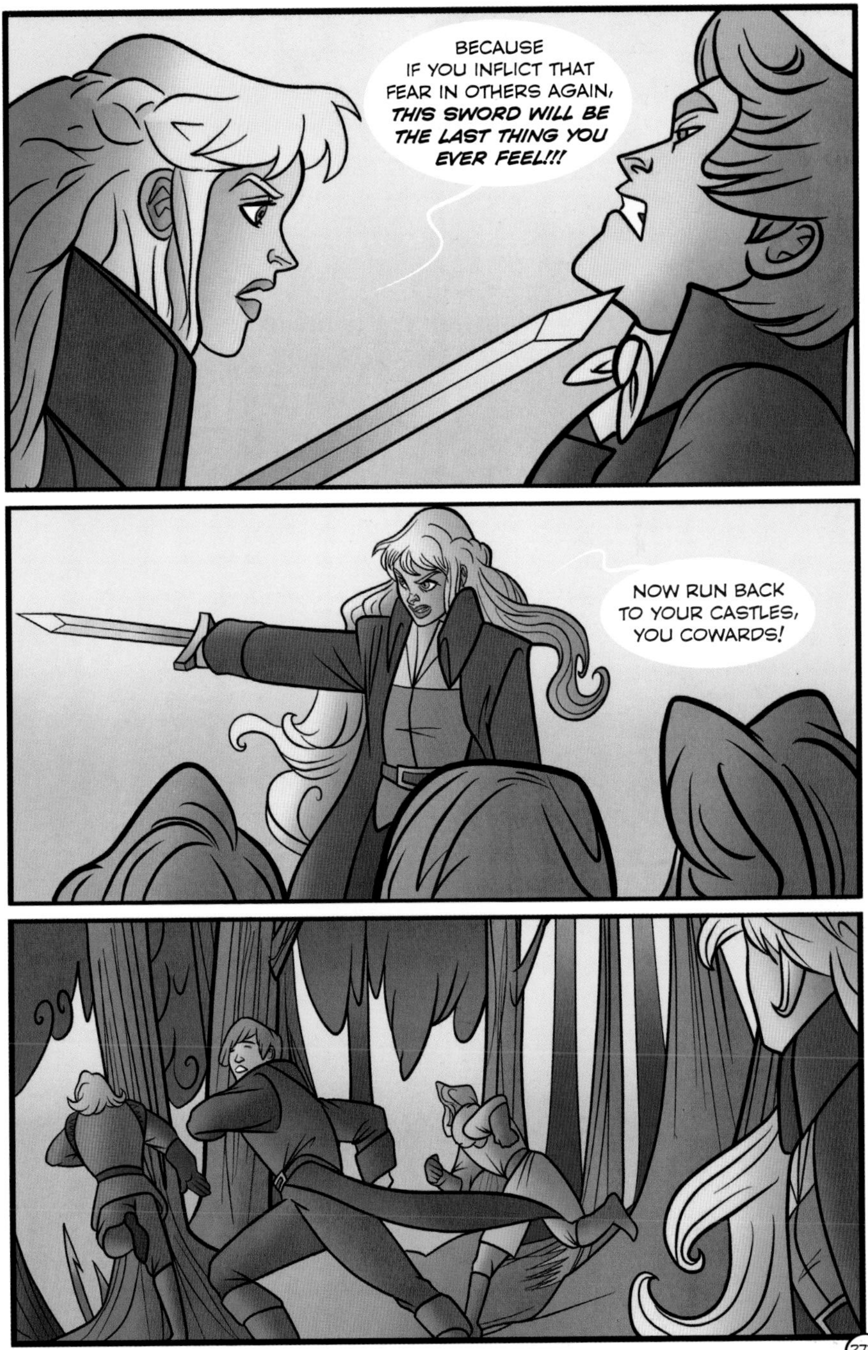
BECAUSE IF YOU INFLICT THAT FEAR IN OTHERS AGAIN, ***THIS SWORD WILL BE THE LAST THING YOU EVER FEEL!!!***
NOW RUN BACK TO YOUR CASTLES, YOU COWARDS!

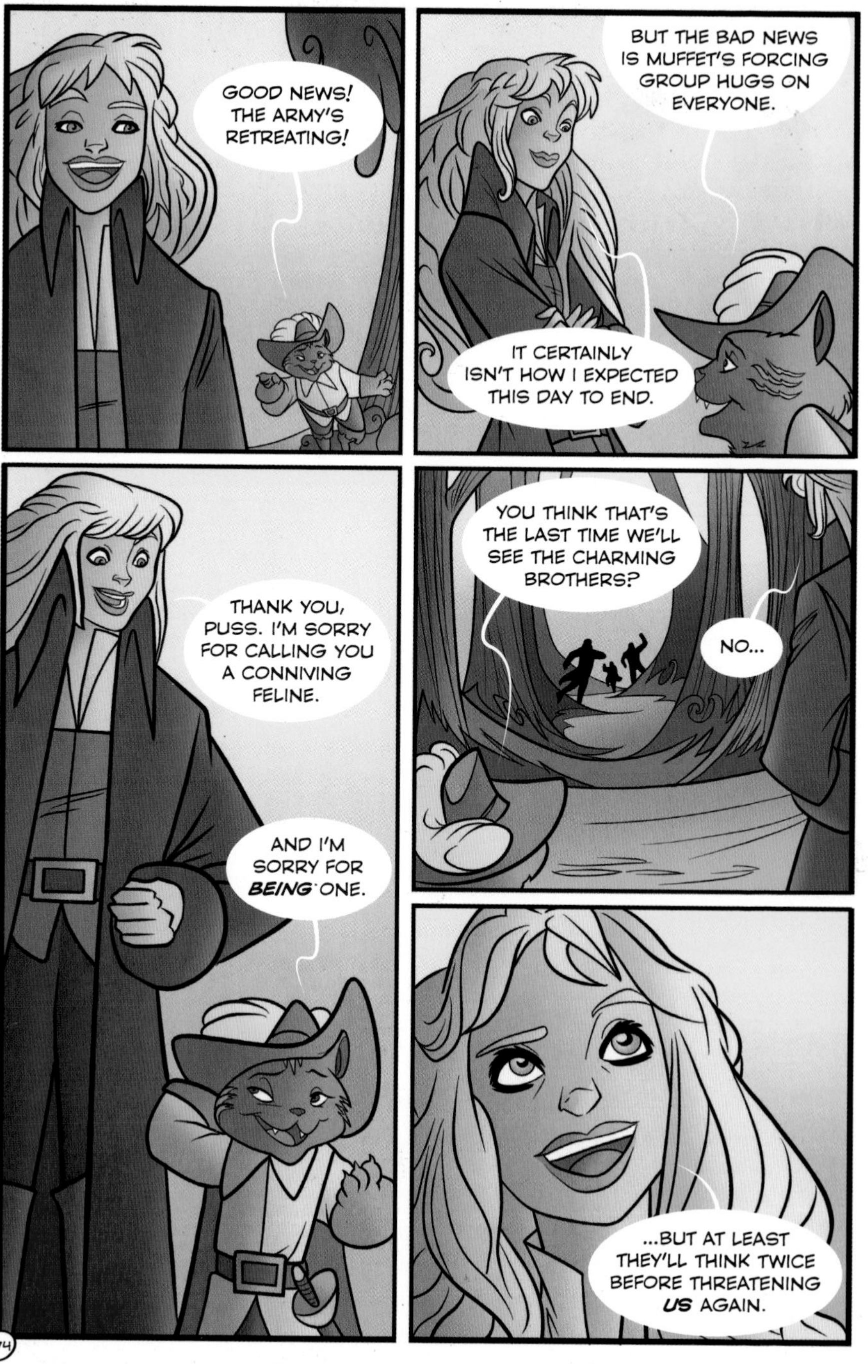
GOOD NEWS! THE ARMY'S RETREATING!
BUT THE BAD NEWS IS MUFFET'S FORCING GROUP HUGS ON EVERYONE.
IT CERTAINLY ISN'T HOW I EXPECTED THIS DAY TO END.
THANK YOU, PUSS. I'M SORRY FOR CALLING YOU A CONNIVING FELINE.
AND I'M SORRY FOR *BEING* ONE.
YOU THINK THAT'S THE LAST TIME WE'LL SEE THE CHARMING BROTHERS?
NO...
...BUT AT LEAST THEY'LL THINK TWICE BEFORE THREATENING *US* AGAIN.

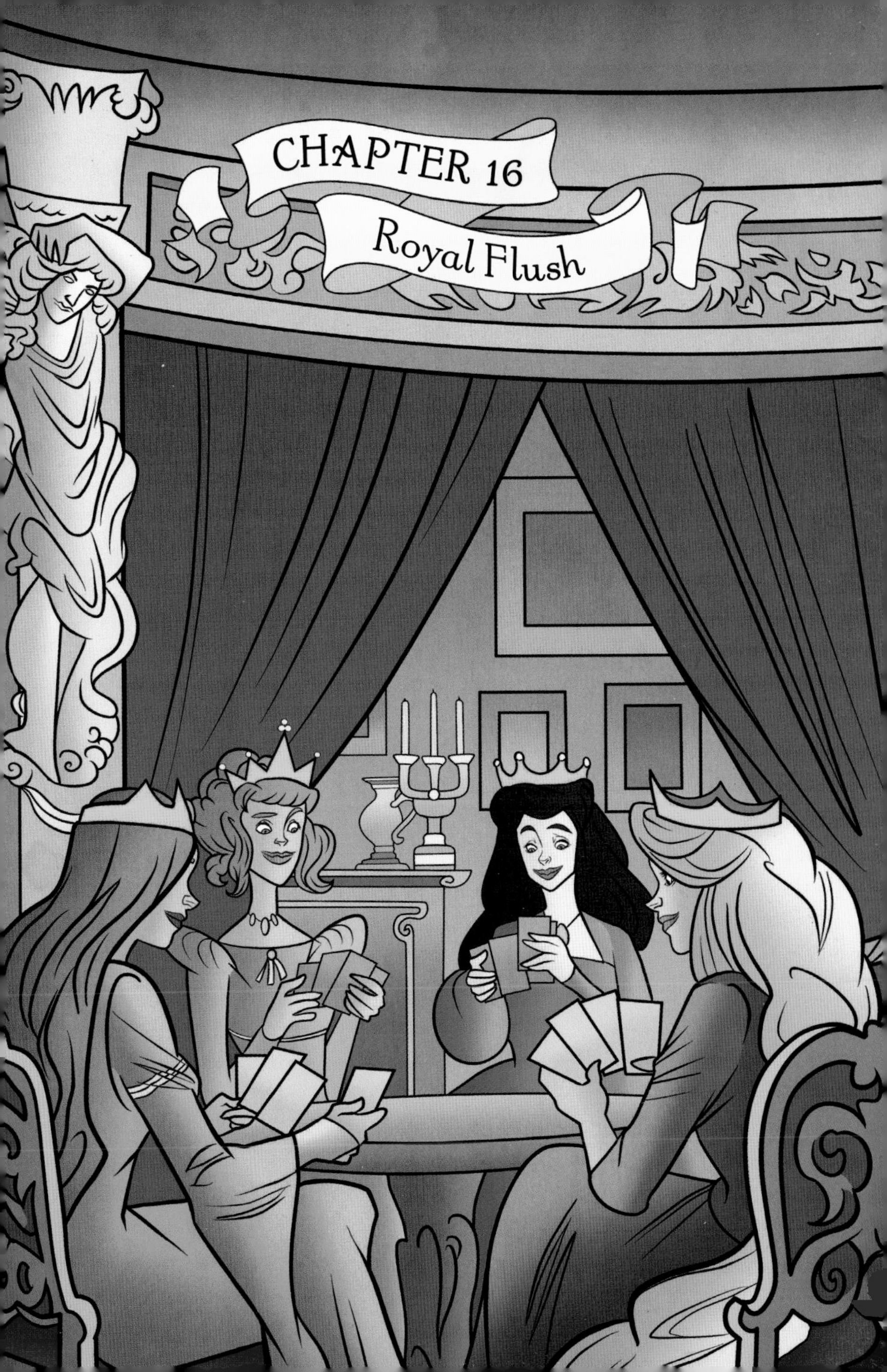
CHAPTER 16
Royal Flush

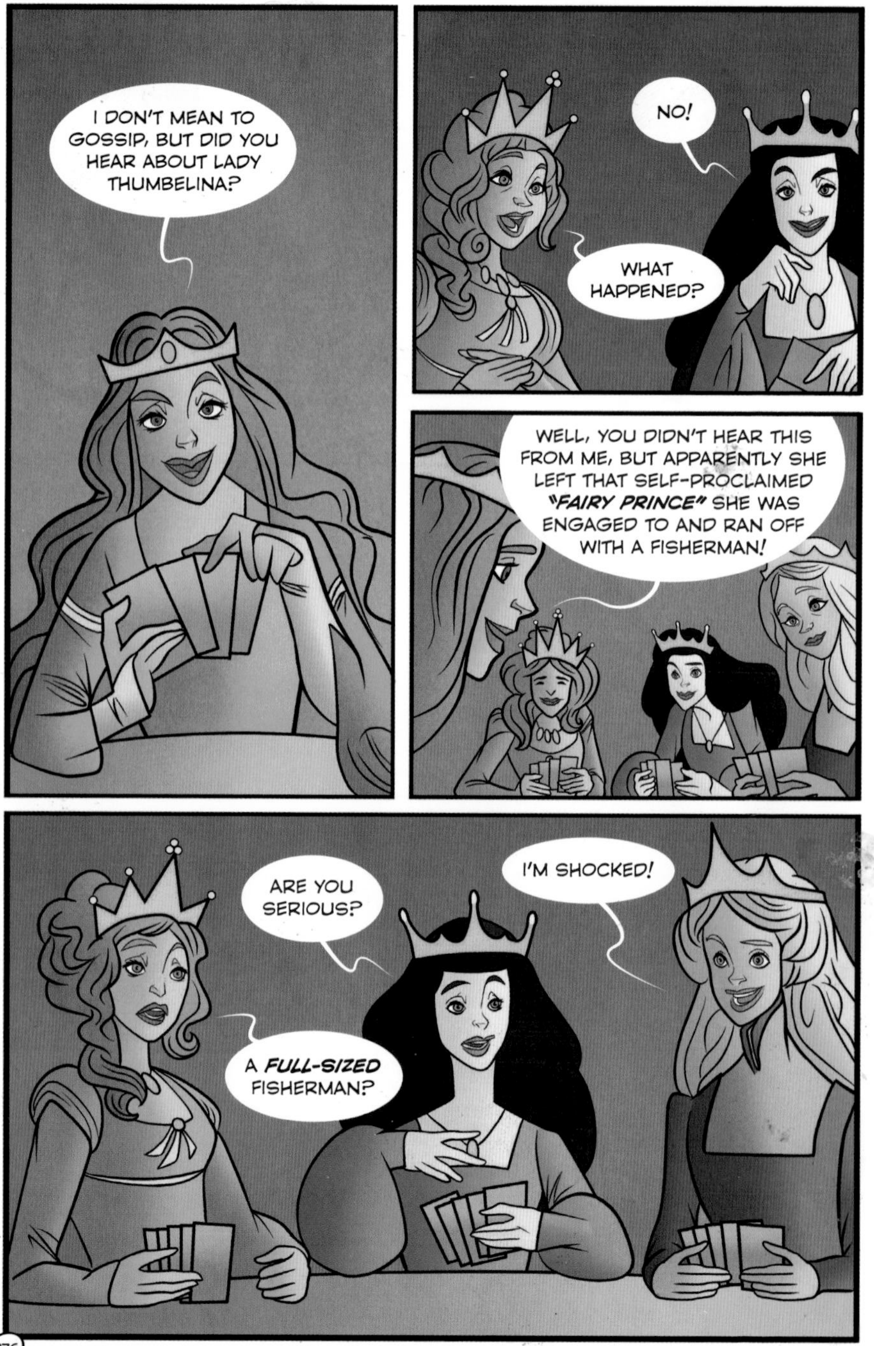
I DON'T MEAN TO GOSSIP, BUT DID YOU HEAR ABOUT LADY THUMBELINA?
NO!
WHAT HAPPENED?
WELL, YOU DIDN'T HEAR THIS FROM ME, BUT APPARENTLY SHE LEFT THAT SELF-PROCLAIMED *"FAIRY PRINCE"* SHE WAS ENGAGED TO AND RAN OFF WITH A FISHERMAN!
ARE YOU SERIOUS?
I'M SHOCKED!
A ***FULL-SIZED*** FISHERMAN?

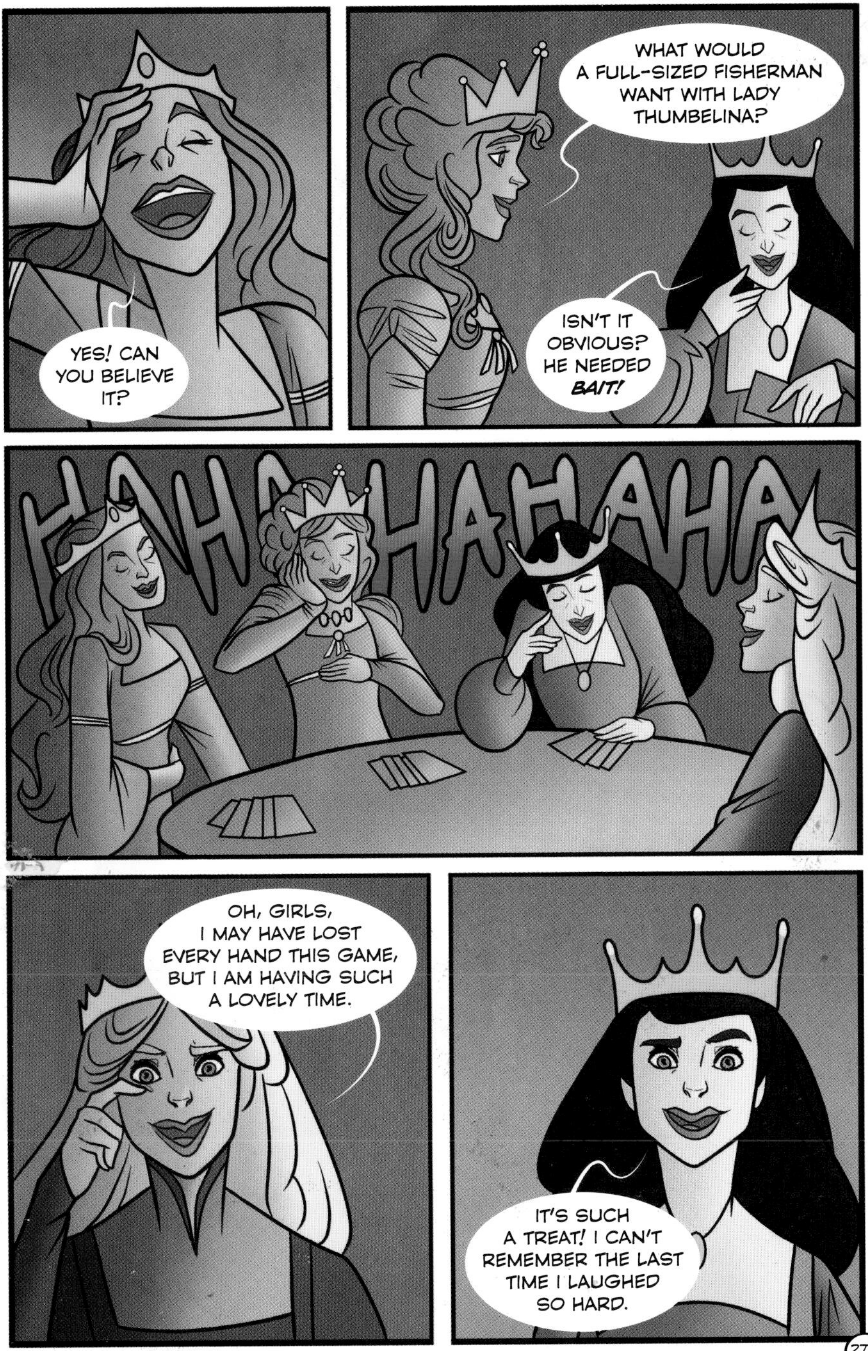
YES! CAN YOU BELIEVE IT?
WHAT WOULD A FULL-SIZED FISHERMAN WANT WITH LADY THUMBELINA?
ISN'T IT OBVIOUS? HE NEEDED *BAIT!*
HAHAHAHAHAHA
OH, GIRLS, I MAY HAVE LOST EVERY HAND THIS GAME, BUT I AM HAVING SUCH A LOVELY TIME.
IT'S SUCH A TREAT! I CAN'T REMEMBER THE LAST TIME I LAUGHED SO HARD.

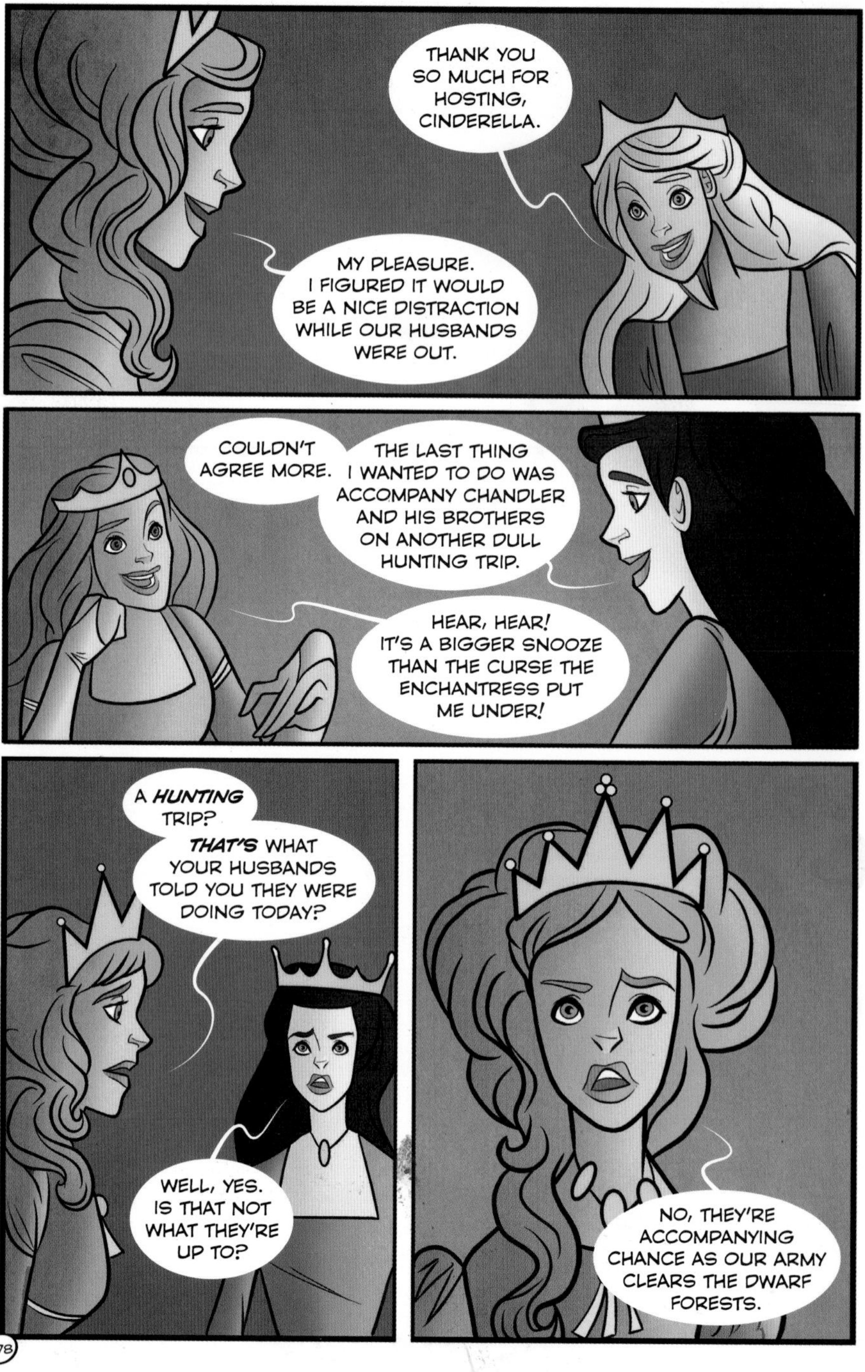

THANK YOU SO MUCH FOR HOSTING, CINDERELLA.
MY PLEASURE. I FIGURED IT WOULD BE A NICE DISTRACTION WHILE OUR HUSBANDS WERE OUT.
COULDN'T AGREE MORE.
THE LAST THING I WANTED TO DO WAS ACCOMPANY CHANDLER AND HIS BROTHERS ON ANOTHER DULL HUNTING TRIP.
HEAR, HEAR! IT'S A BIGGER SNOOZE THAN THE CURSE THE ENCHANTRESS PUT ME UNDER!
A *HUNTING* TRIP?
THAT'S WHAT YOUR HUSBANDS TOLD YOU THEY WERE DOING TODAY?
WELL, YES. IS THAT NOT WHAT THEY'RE UP TO?
NO, THEY'RE ACCOMPANYING CHANCE AS OUR ARMY CLEARS THE DWARF FORESTS.

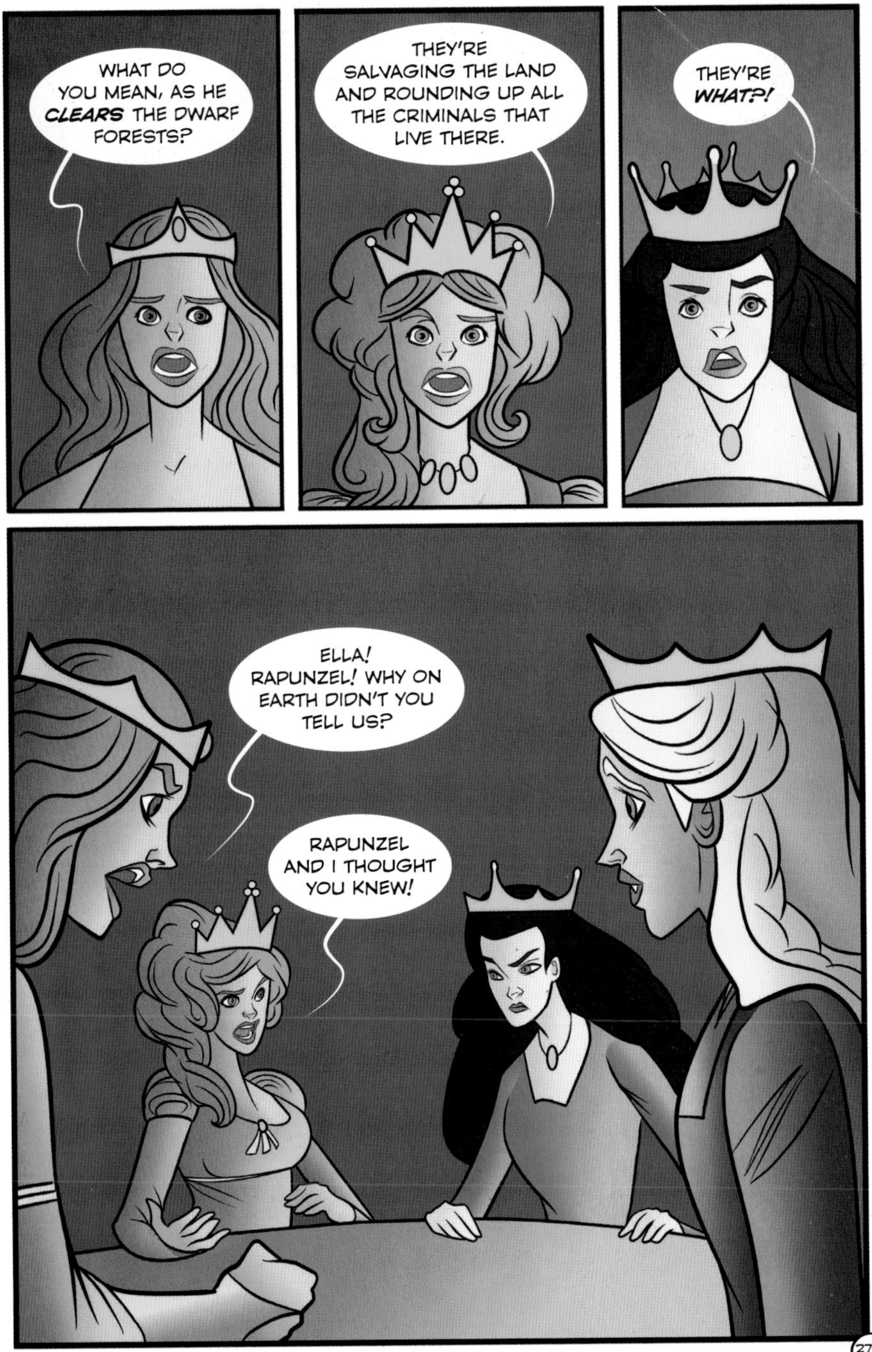
WHAT DO YOU MEAN, AS HE **CLEARS** THE DWARF FORESTS?
THEY'RE SALVAGING THE LAND AND ROUNDING UP ALL THE CRIMINALS THAT LIVE THERE.
THEY'RE **WHAT?!**
ELLA! RAPUNZEL! WHY ON EARTH DIDN'T YOU TELL US?
RAPUNZEL AND I THOUGHT YOU KNEW!

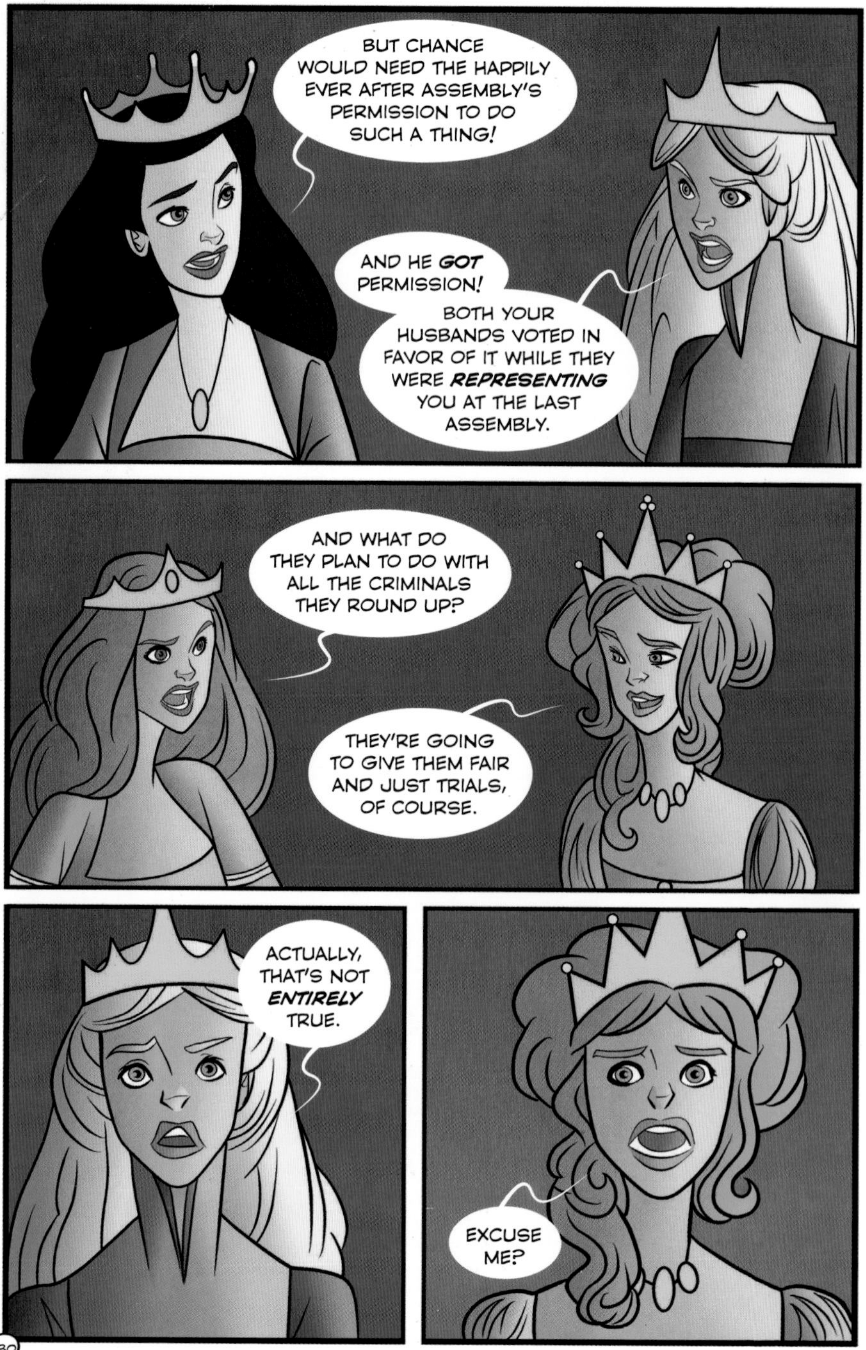
BUT CHANCE WOULD NEED THE HAPPILY EVER AFTER ASSEMBLY'S PERMISSION TO DO SUCH A THING!
AND HE GOT PERMISSION!
BOTH YOUR HUSBANDS VOTED IN FAVOR OF IT WHILE THEY WERE REPRESENTING YOU AT THE LAST ASSEMBLY.
AND WHAT DO THEY PLAN TO DO WITH ALL THE CRIMINALS THEY ROUND UP?
THEY'RE GOING TO GIVE THEM FAIR AND JUST TRIALS, OF COURSE.
ACTUALLY, THAT'S NOT ENTIRELY TRUE.
EXCUSE ME?

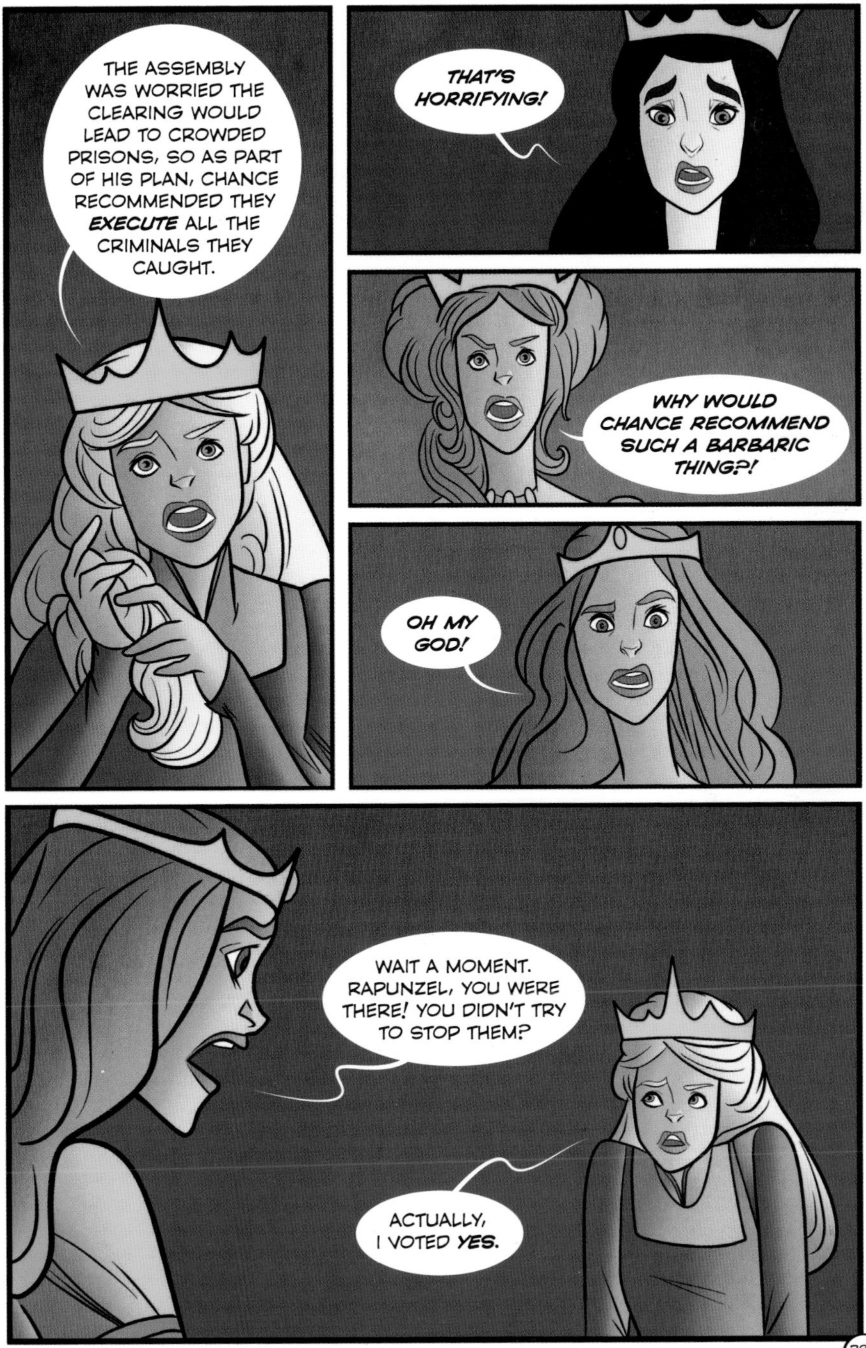
THE ASSEMBLY WAS WORRIED THE CLEARING WOULD LEAD TO CROWDED PRISONS, SO AS PART OF HIS PLAN, CHANCE RECOMMENDED THEY EXECUTE ALL THE CRIMINALS THEY CAUGHT.
THAT'S HORRIFYING!
WHY WOULD CHANCE RECOMMEND SUCH A BARBARIC THING?!
OH MY GOD!
WAIT A MOMENT. RAPUNZEL, YOU WERE THERE! YOU DIDN'T TRY TO STOP THEM?
ACTUALLY, I VOTED YES.

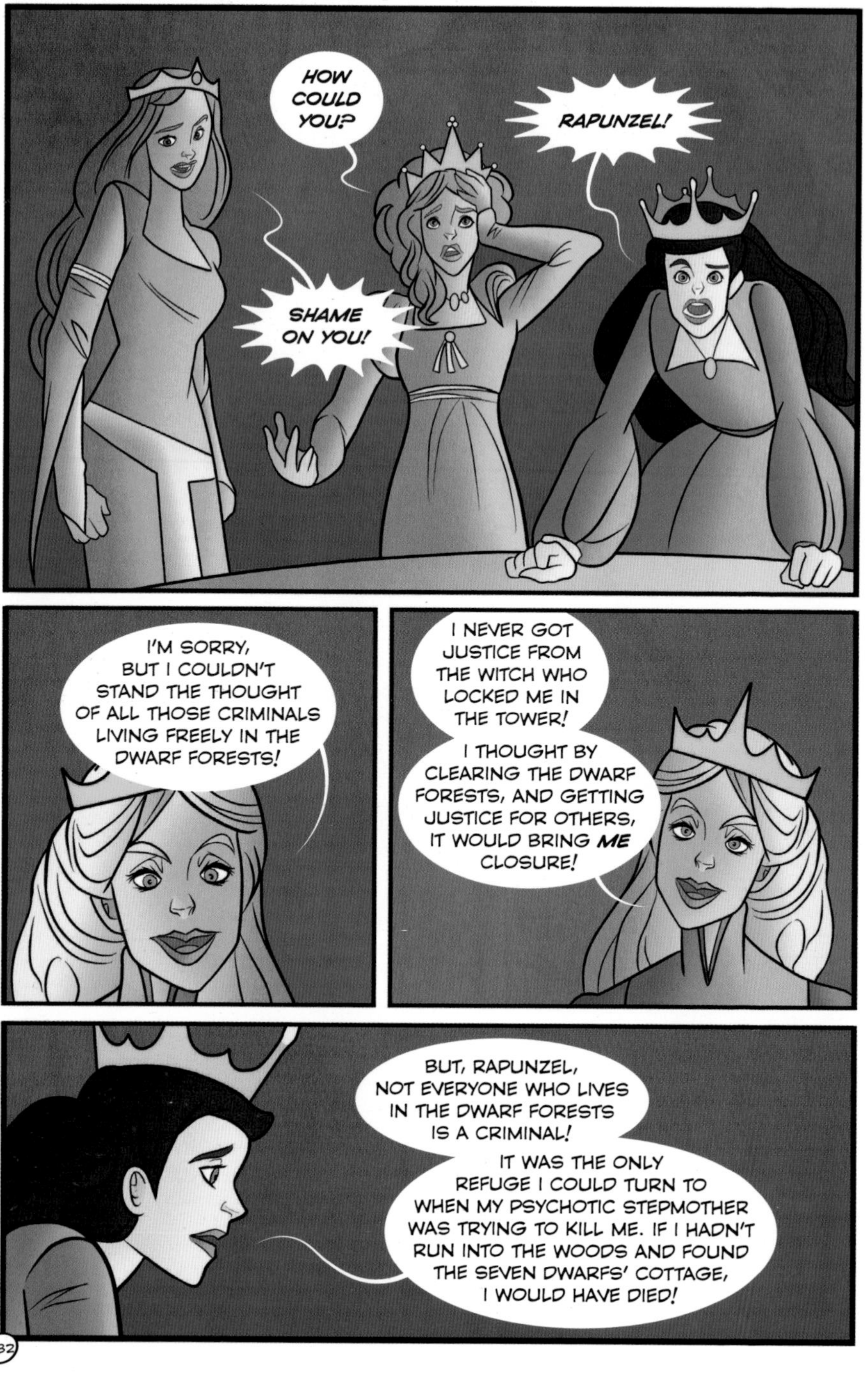
HOW COULD YOU?
RAPUNZEL!
SHAME ON YOU!
I'M SORRY, BUT I COULDN'T STAND THE THOUGHT OF ALL THOSE CRIMINALS LIVING FREELY IN THE DWARF FORESTS!
I NEVER GOT JUSTICE FROM THE WITCH WHO LOCKED ME IN THE TOWER!
I THOUGHT BY CLEARING THE DWARF FORESTS, AND GETTING JUSTICE FOR OTHERS, IT WOULD BRING ***ME*** CLOSURE!
BUT, RAPUNZEL, NOT EVERYONE WHO LIVES IN THE DWARF FORESTS IS A CRIMINAL!
IT WAS THE ONLY REFUGE I COULD TURN TO WHEN MY PSYCHOTIC STEPMOTHER WAS TRYING TO KILL ME. IF I HADN'T RUN INTO THE WOODS AND FOUND THE SEVEN DWARFS' COTTAGE, I WOULD HAVE DIED!

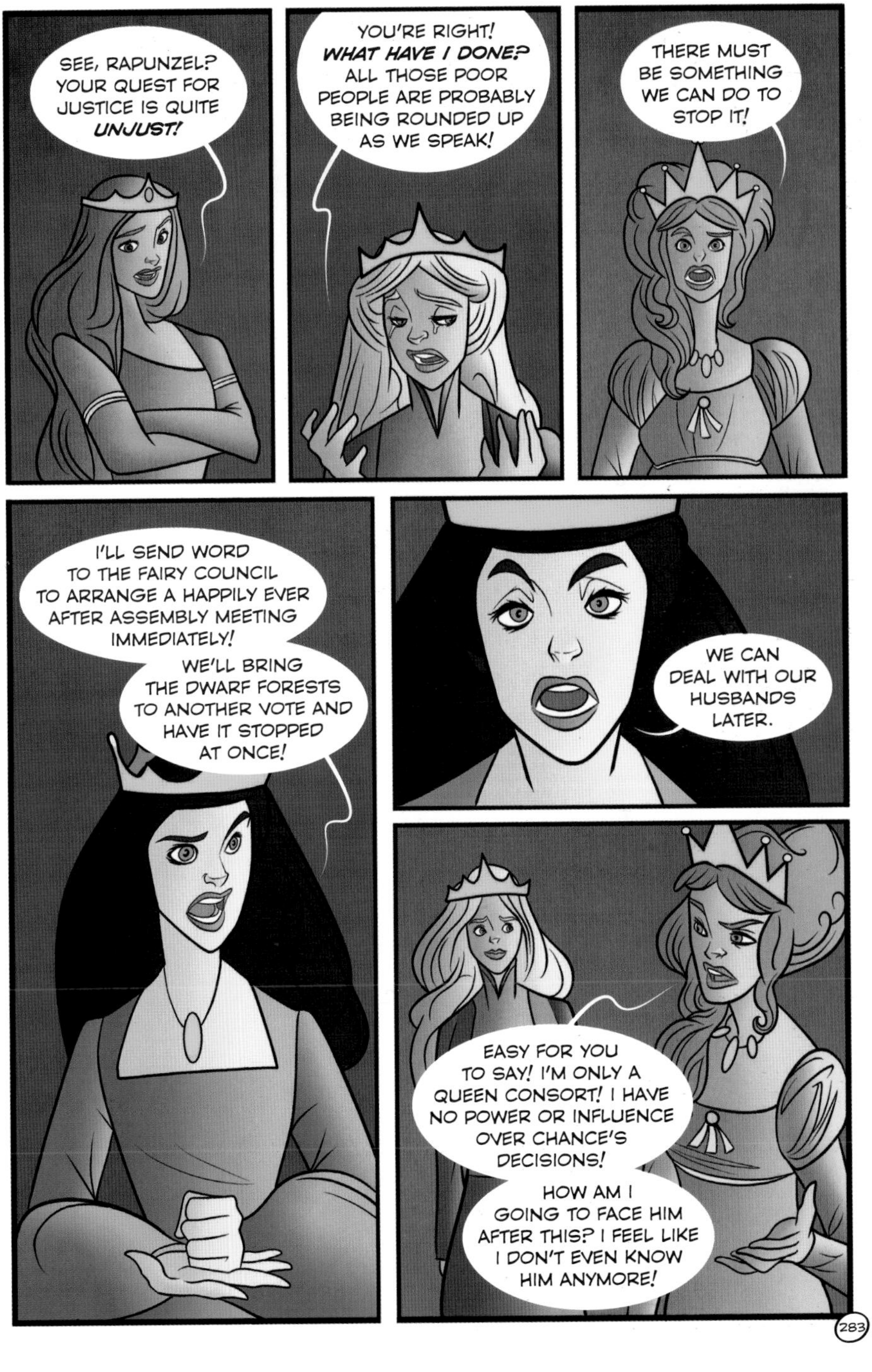
SEE, RAPUNZEL? YOUR QUEST FOR JUSTICE IS QUITE *UNJUST!*
YOU'RE RIGHT! ***WHAT HAVE I DONE?*** ALL THOSE POOR PEOPLE ARE PROBABLY BEING ROUNDED UP AS WE SPEAK!
THERE MUST BE SOMETHING WE CAN DO TO STOP IT!
I'LL SEND WORD TO THE FAIRY COUNCIL TO ARRANGE A HAPPILY EVER AFTER ASSEMBLY MEETING IMMEDIATELY!
WE'LL BRING THE DWARF FORESTS TO ANOTHER VOTE AND HAVE IT STOPPED AT ONCE!
WE CAN DEAL WITH OUR HUSBANDS LATER.
EASY FOR YOU TO SAY! I'M ONLY A QUEEN CONSORT! I HAVE NO POWER OR INFLUENCE OVER CHANCE'S DECISIONS!
HOW AM I GOING TO FACE HIM AFTER THIS? I FEEL LIKE I DON'T EVEN KNOW HIM ANYMORE!

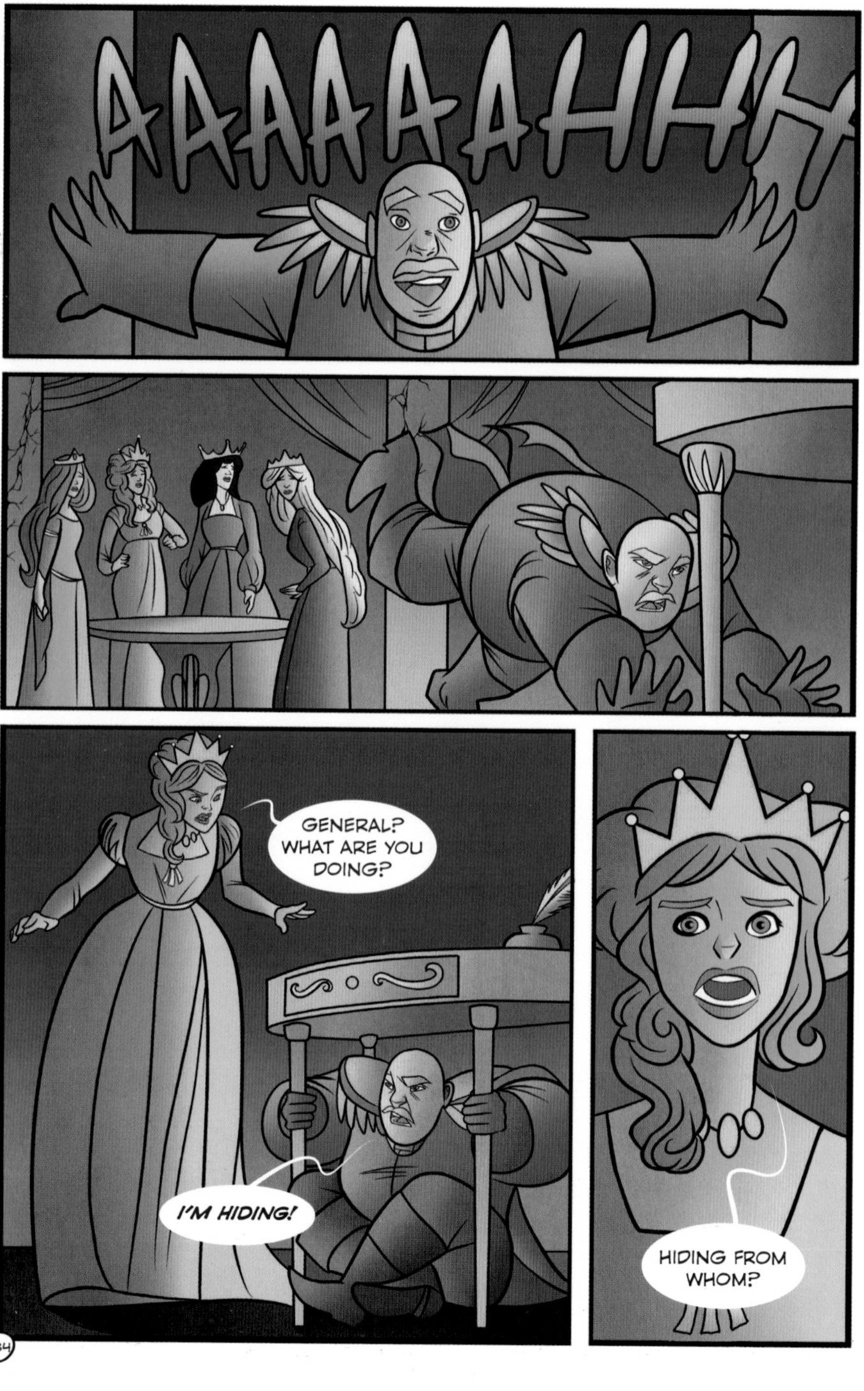
AAAAAAHHHH
GENERAL? WHAT ARE YOU DOING?
I'M HIDING!
HIDING FROM WHOM?

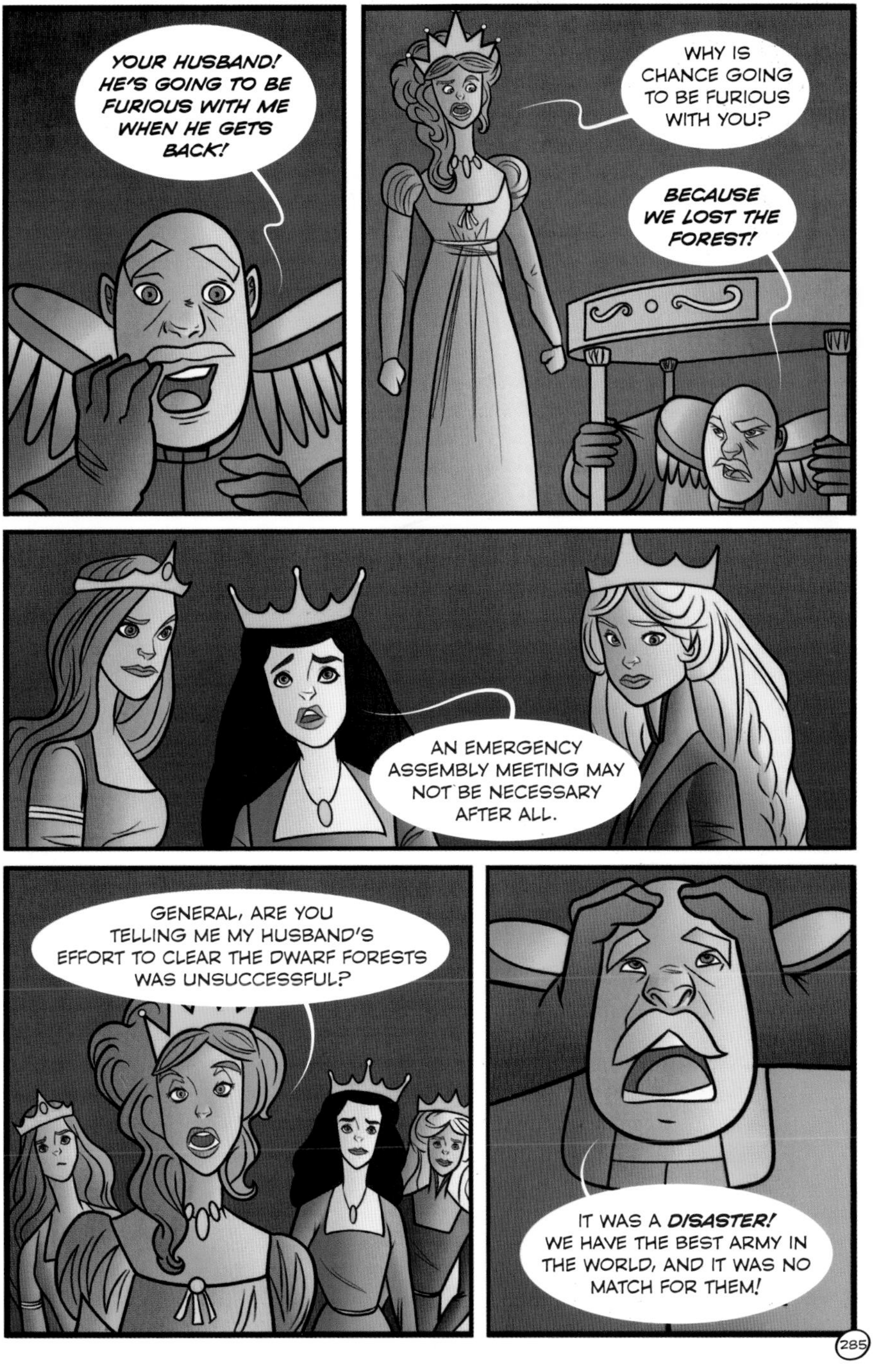
YOUR HUSBAND! HE'S GOING TO BE FURIOUS WITH ME WHEN HE GETS BACK!
WHY IS CHANCE GOING TO BE FURIOUS WITH YOU?
BECAUSE WE LOST THE FOREST!
AN EMERGENCY ASSEMBLY MEETING MAY NOT BE NECESSARY AFTER ALL.
GENERAL, ARE YOU TELLING ME MY HUSBAND'S EFFORT TO CLEAR THE DWARF FORESTS WAS UNSUCCESSFUL?
IT WAS A DISASTER! WE HAVE THE BEST ARMY IN THE WORLD, AND IT WAS NO MATCH FOR THEM!

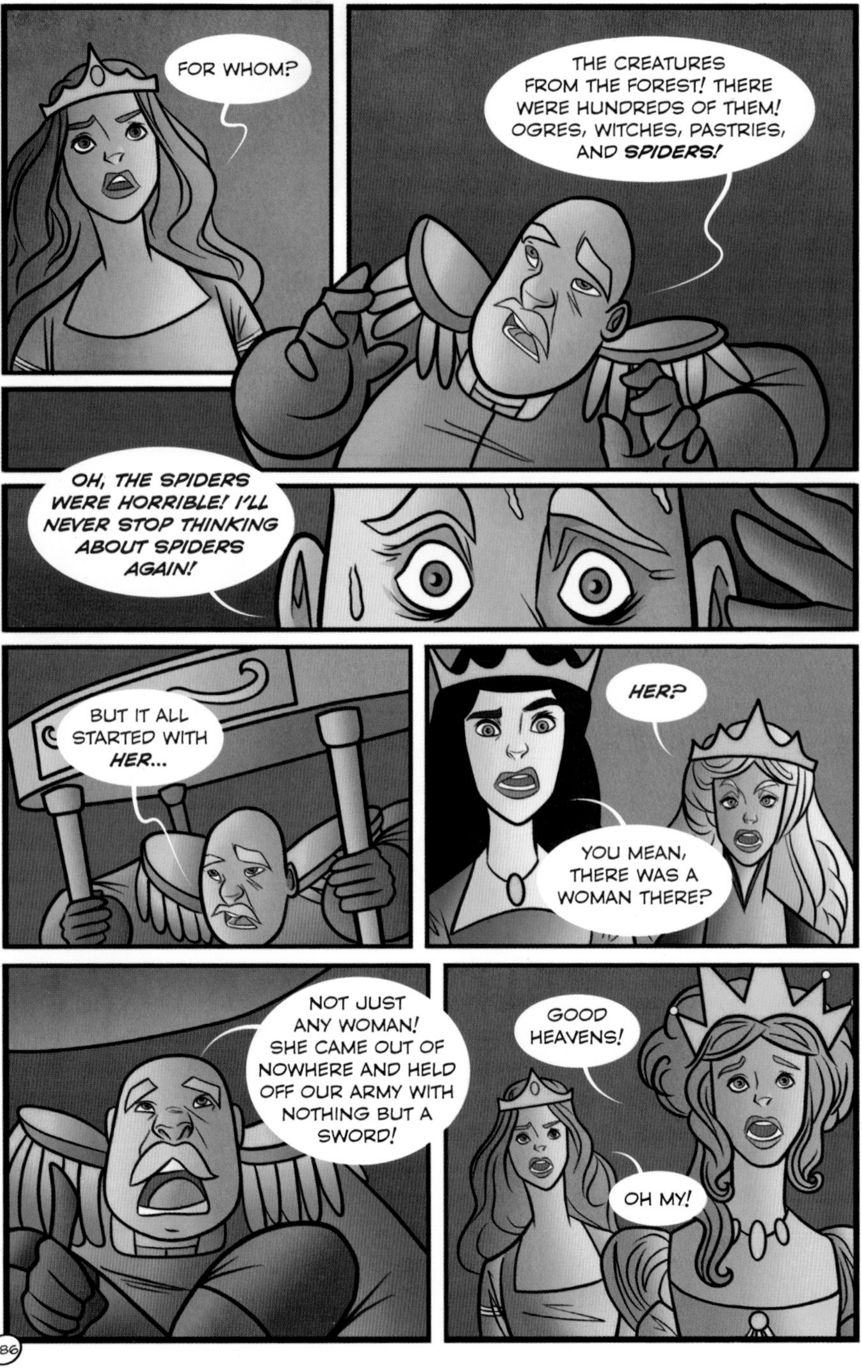
FOR WHOM?
THE CREATURES FROM THE FOREST! THERE WERE HUNDREDS OF THEM! OGRES, WITCHES, PASTRIES, AND SPIDERS!
OH, THE SPIDERS WERE HORRIBLE! I'LL NEVER STOP THINKING ABOUT SPIDERS AGAIN!
BUT IT ALL STARTED WITH HER...
HER?
YOU MEAN, THERE WAS A WOMAN THERE?
NOT JUST ANY WOMAN! SHE CAME OUT OF NOWHERE AND HELD OFF OUR ARMY WITH NOTHING BUT A SWORD!
GOOD HEAVENS!
OH MY!

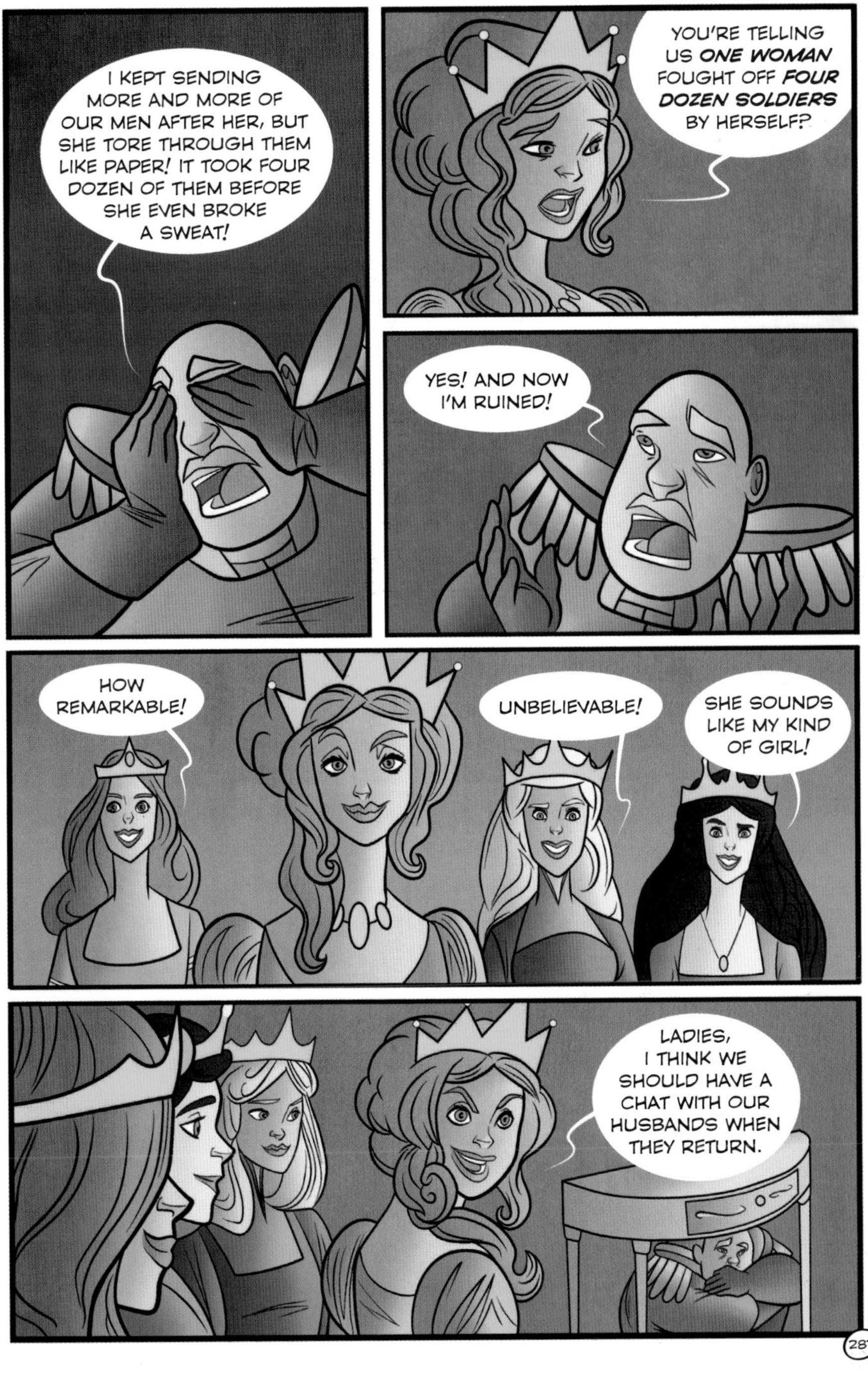
I KEPT SENDING MORE AND MORE OF OUR MEN AFTER HER, BUT SHE TORE THROUGH THEM LIKE PAPER! IT TOOK FOUR DOZEN OF THEM BEFORE SHE EVEN BROKE A SWEAT!
YOU'RE TELLING US **ONE WOMAN** FOUGHT OFF **FOUR DOZEN SOLDIERS** BY HERSELF?
YES! AND NOW I'M RUINED!
HOW REMARKABLE!
UNBELIEVABLE!
SHE SOUNDS LIKE MY KIND OF GIRL!
LADIES, I THINK WE SHOULD HAVE A CHAT WITH OUR HUSBANDS WHEN THEY RETURN.

CHAPTER 17

Just Beginning

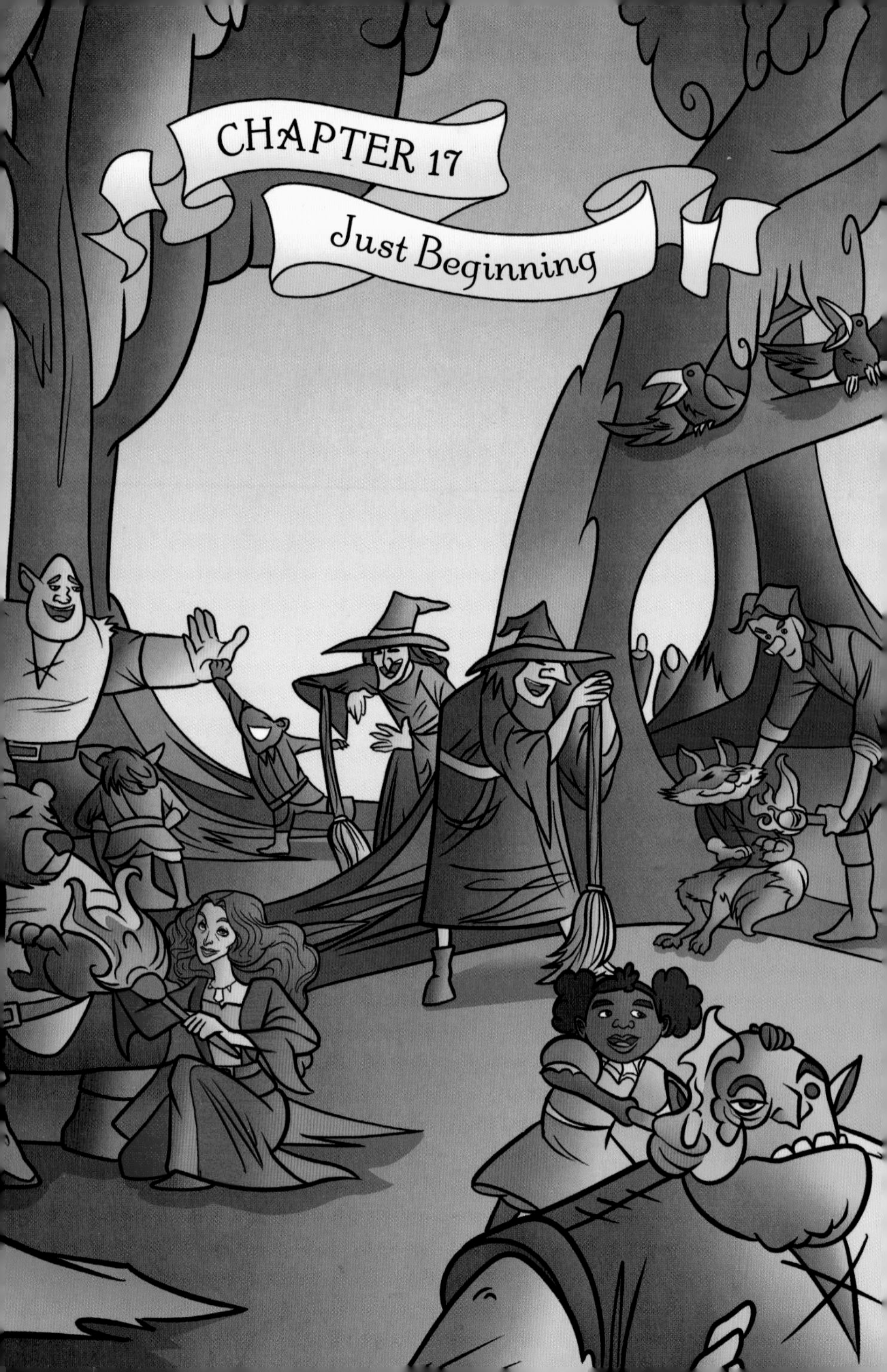

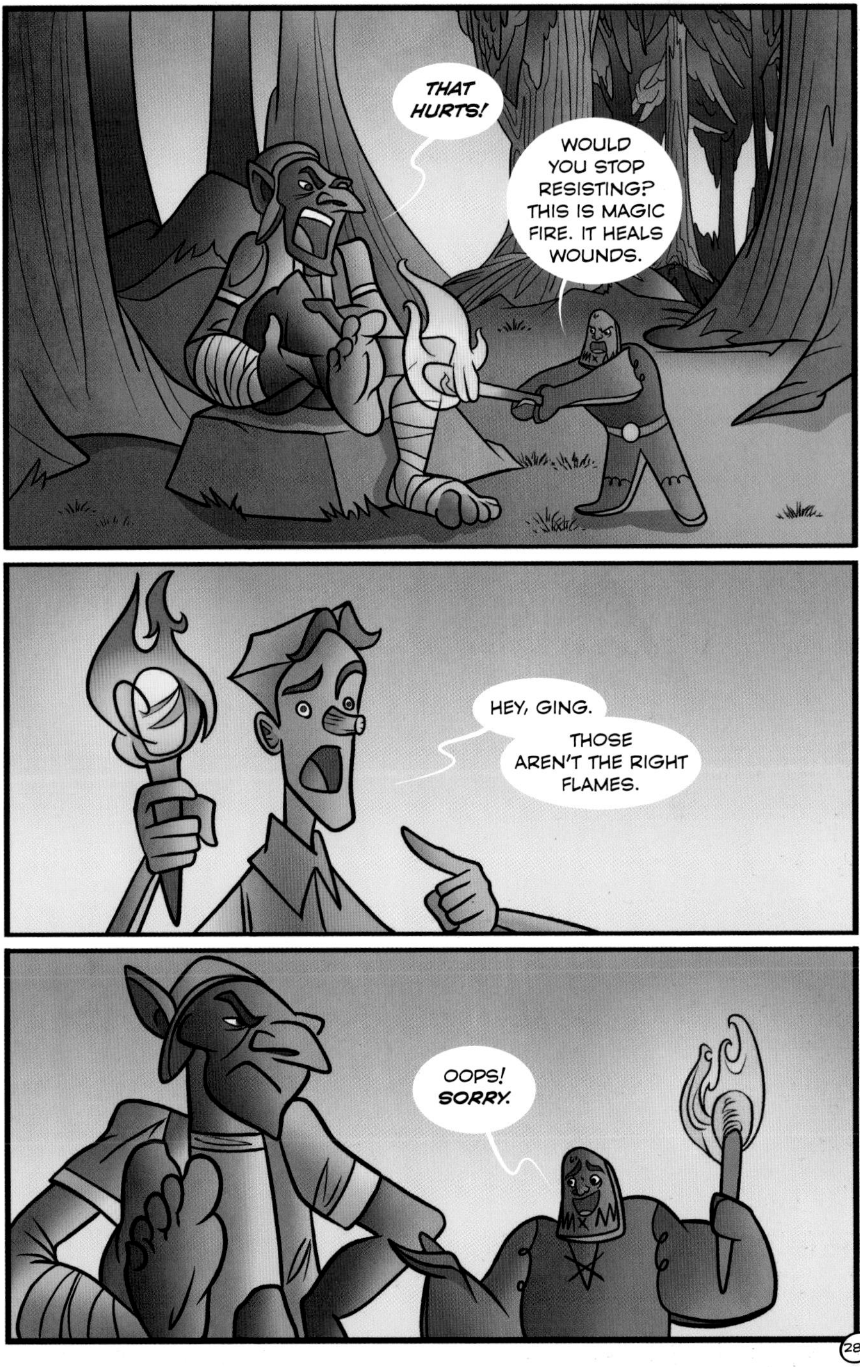
THAT HURTS!
WOULD YOU STOP RESISTING? THIS IS MAGIC FIRE. IT HEALS WOUNDS.
HEY, GING.
THOSE AREN'T THE RIGHT FLAMES.
OOPS! SORRY.

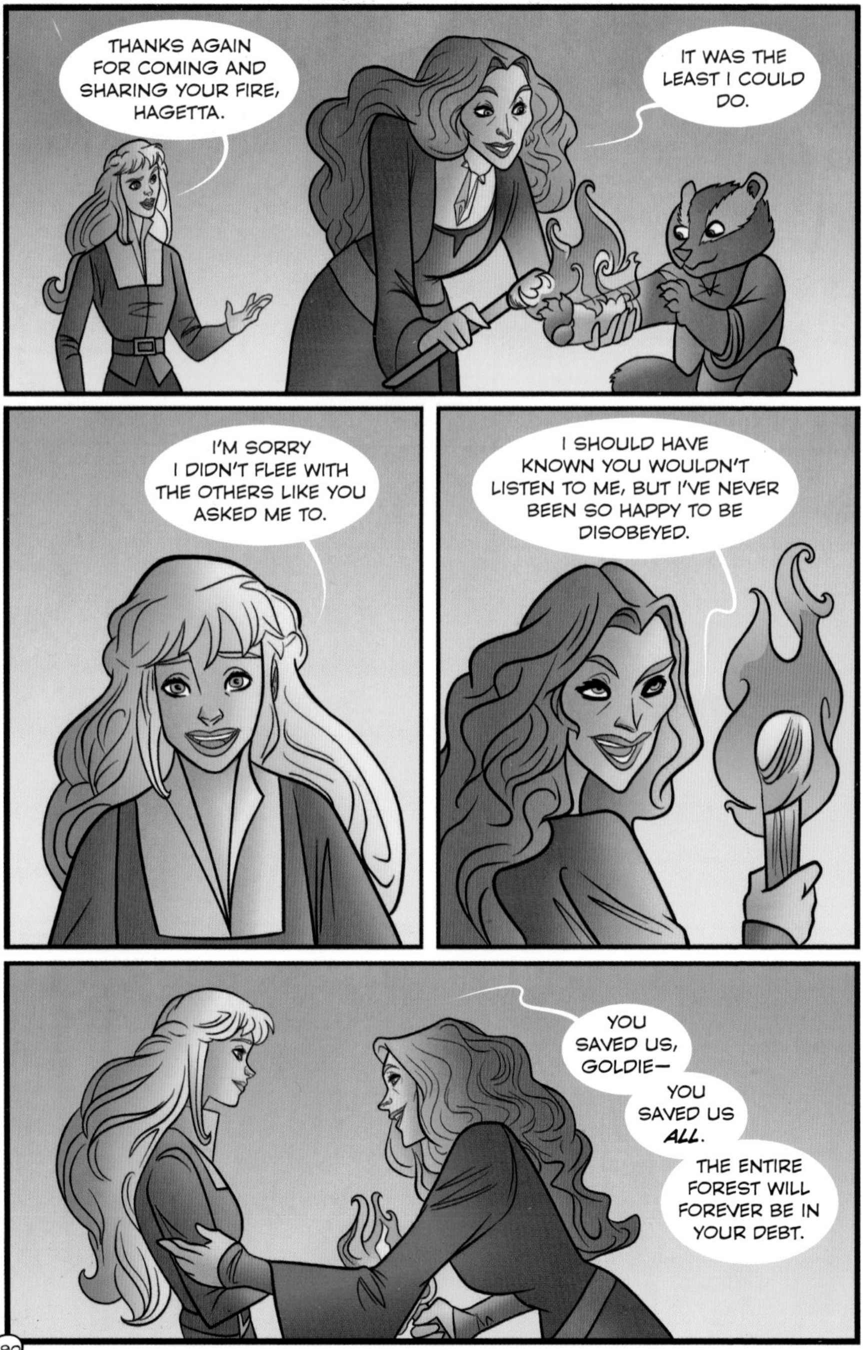
THANKS AGAIN FOR COMING AND SHARING YOUR FIRE, HAGETTA.
IT WAS THE LEAST I COULD DO.
I'M SORRY I DIDN'T FLEE WITH THE OTHERS LIKE YOU ASKED ME TO.
I SHOULD HAVE KNOWN YOU WOULDN'T LISTEN TO ME, BUT I'VE NEVER BEEN SO HAPPY TO BE DISOBEYED.
YOU SAVED US, GOLDIE—
YOU SAVED US ALL.
THE ENTIRE FOREST WILL FOREVER BE IN YOUR DEBT.

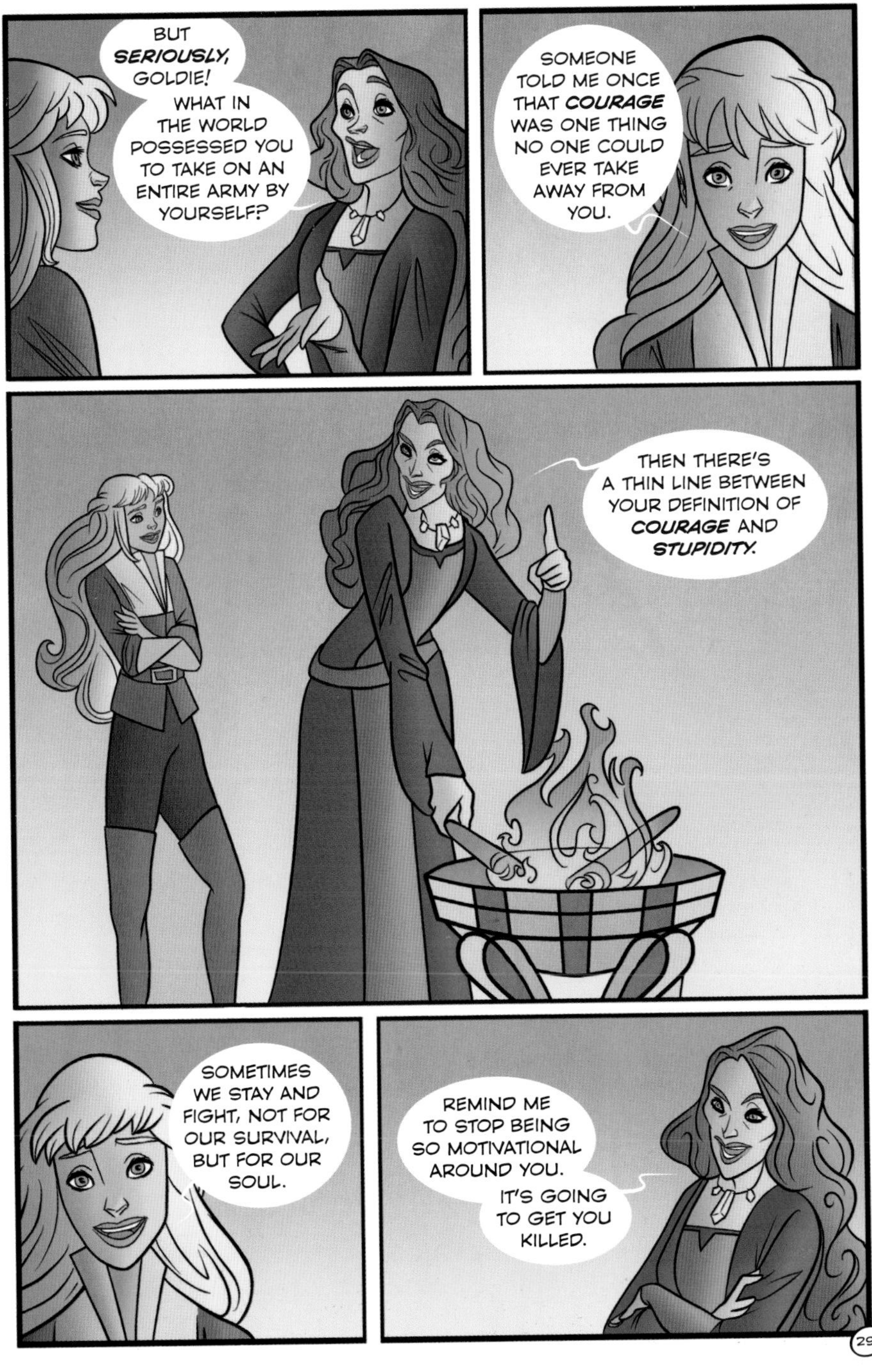
BUT SERIOUSLY, GOLDIE!
WHAT IN THE WORLD POSSESSED YOU TO TAKE ON AN ENTIRE ARMY BY YOURSELF?
SOMEONE TOLD ME ONCE THAT COURAGE WAS ONE THING NO ONE COULD EVER TAKE AWAY FROM YOU.
THEN THERE'S A THIN LINE BETWEEN YOUR DEFINITION OF COURAGE AND STUPIDITY.
SOMETIMES WE STAY AND FIGHT, NOT FOR OUR SURVIVAL, BUT FOR OUR SOUL.
REMIND ME TO STOP BEING SO MOTIVATIONAL AROUND YOU.
IT'S GOING TO GET YOU KILLED.

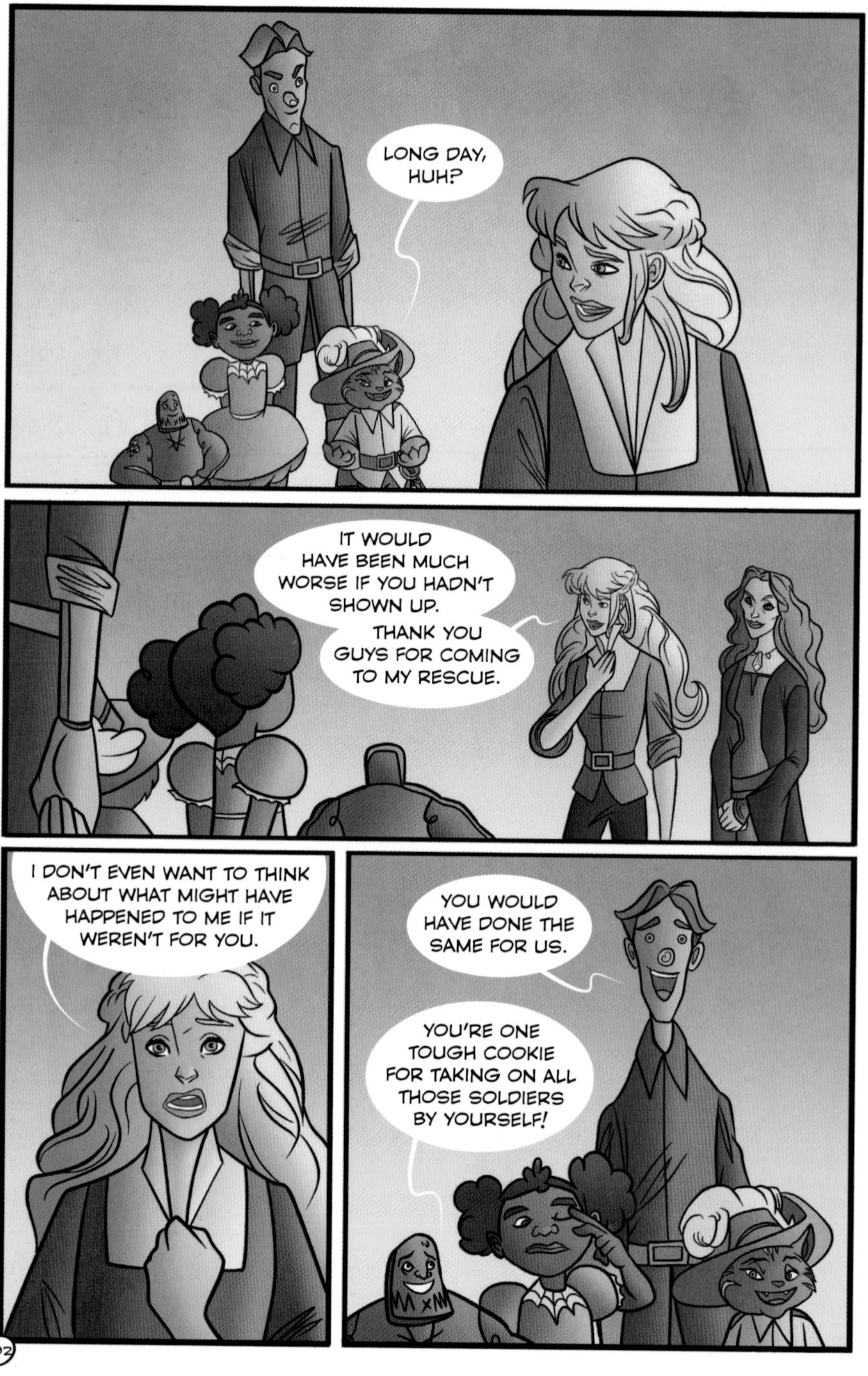
LONG DAY, HUH?
IT WOULD HAVE BEEN MUCH WORSE IF YOU HADN'T SHOWN UP.
THANK YOU GUYS FOR COMING TO MY RESCUE.
I DON'T EVEN WANT TO THINK ABOUT WHAT MIGHT HAVE HAPPENED TO ME IF IT WEREN'T FOR YOU.
YOU WOULD HAVE DONE THE SAME FOR US.
YOU'RE ONE TOUGH COOKIE FOR TAKING ON ALL THOSE SOLDIERS BY YOURSELF!

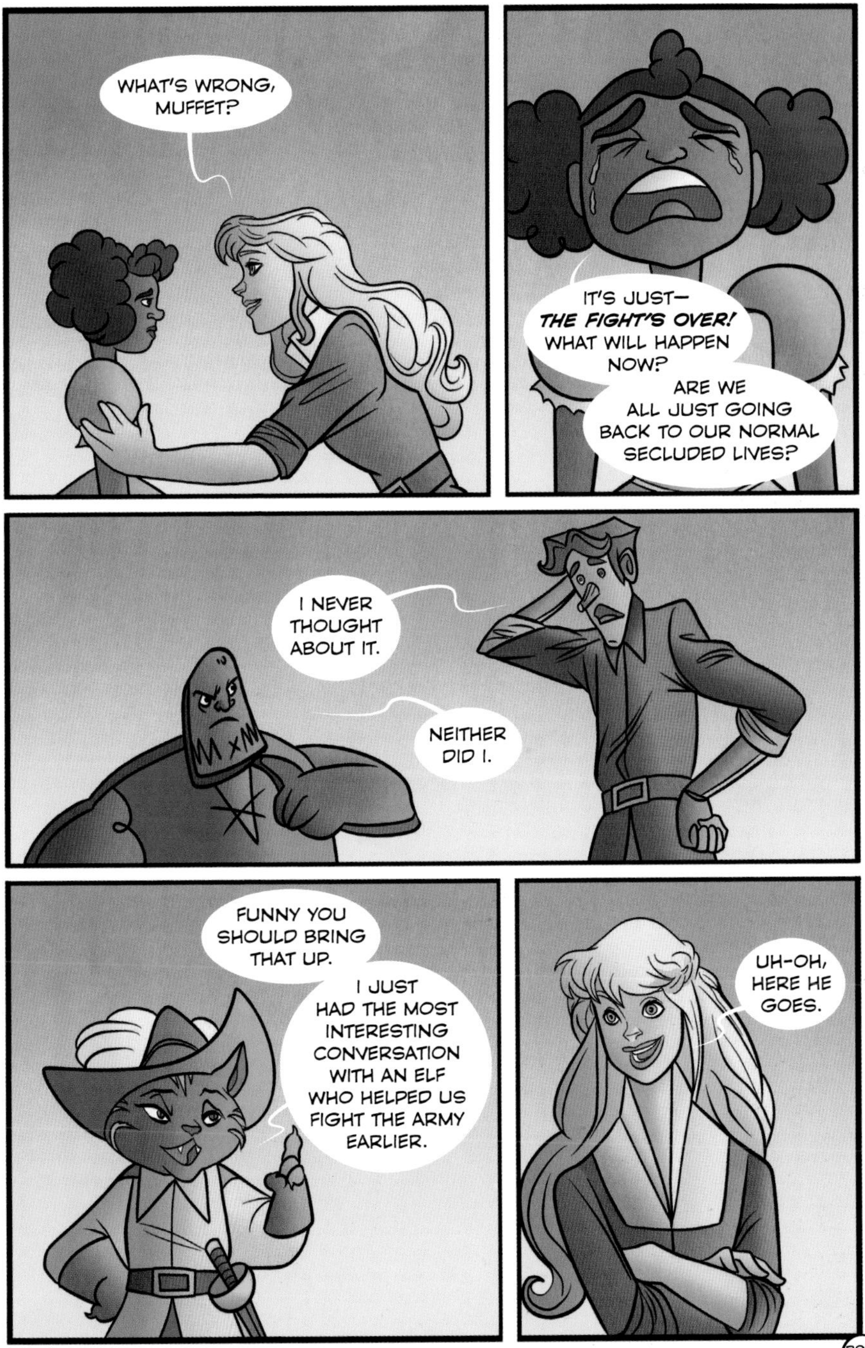
WHAT'S WRONG, MUFFET?
IT'S JUST— THE FIGHT'S OVER! WHAT WILL HAPPEN NOW?
ARE WE ALL JUST GOING BACK TO OUR NORMAL SECLUDED LIVES?
I NEVER THOUGHT ABOUT IT.
NEITHER DID I.
FUNNY YOU SHOULD BRING THAT UP.
I JUST HAD THE MOST INTERESTING CONVERSATION WITH AN ELF WHO HELPED US FIGHT THE ARMY EARLIER.
UH-OH, HERE HE GOES.

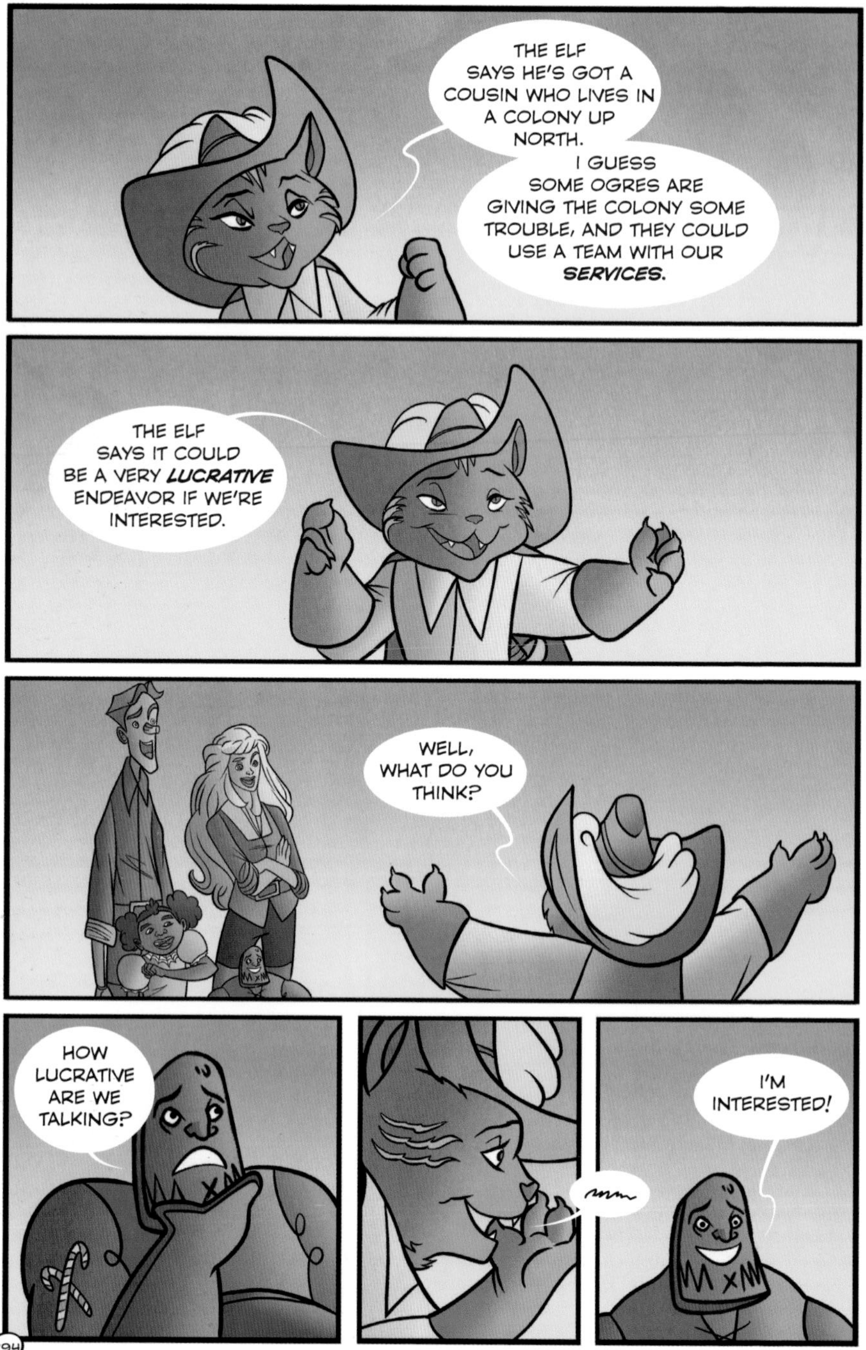
THE ELF SAYS HE'S GOT A COUSIN WHO LIVES IN A COLONY UP NORTH.
I GUESS SOME OGRES ARE GIVING THE COLONY SOME TROUBLE, AND THEY COULD USE A TEAM WITH OUR *SERVICES.*
THE ELF SAYS IT COULD BE A VERY *LUCRATIVE* ENDEAVOR IF WE'RE INTERESTED.
WELL, WHAT DO YOU THINK?
HOW LUCRATIVE ARE WE TALKING?
mmm
I'M INTERESTED!

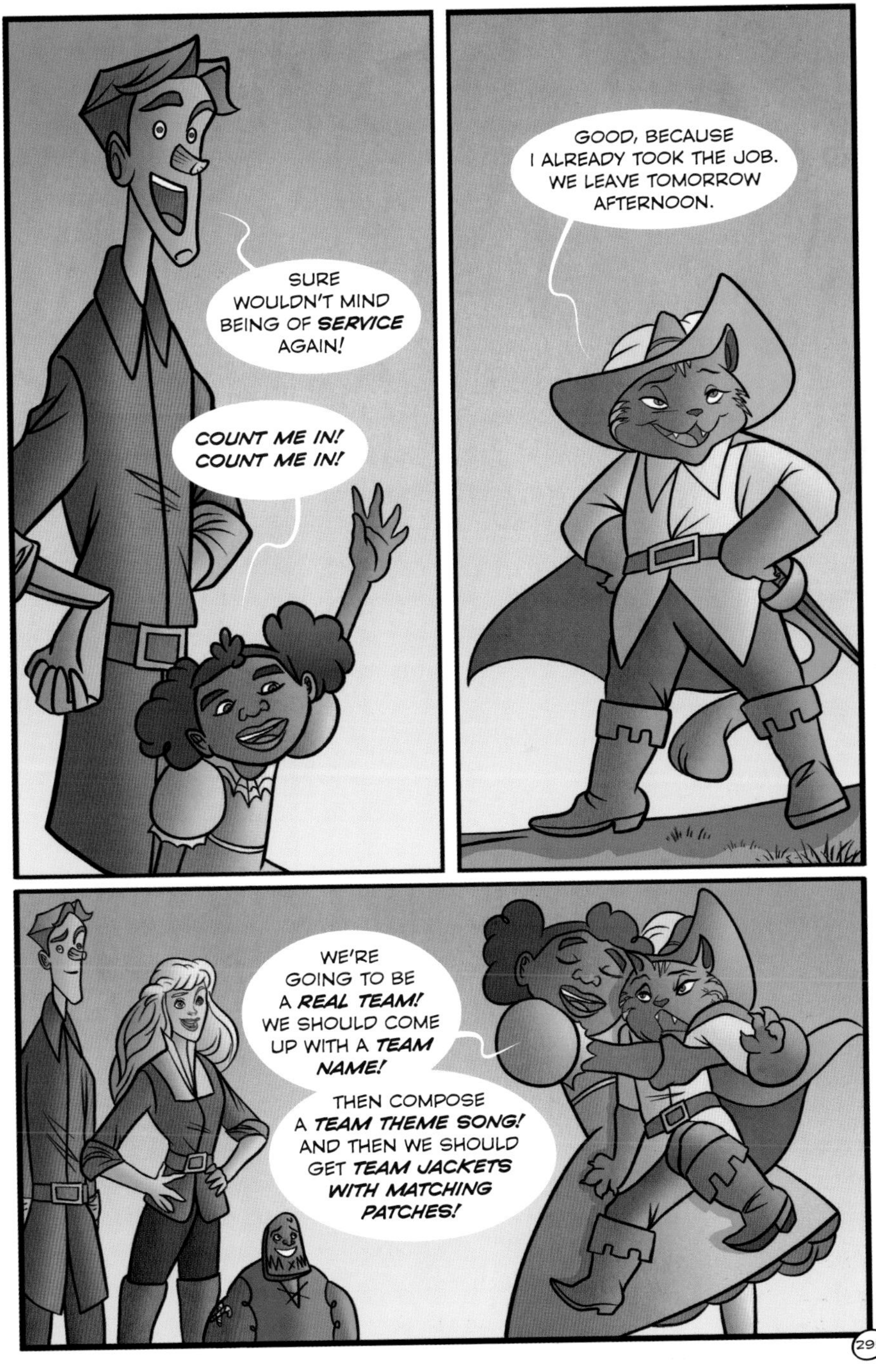
SURE WOULDN'T MIND BEING OF *SERVICE* AGAIN!
COUNT ME IN! COUNT ME IN!
GOOD, BECAUSE I ALREADY TOOK THE JOB. WE LEAVE TOMORROW AFTERNOON.
WE'RE GOING TO BE A *REAL TEAM!* WE SHOULD COME UP WITH A *TEAM NAME!*
THEN COMPOSE A *TEAM THEME SONG!* AND THEN WE SHOULD GET *TEAM JACKETS WITH MATCHING PATCHES!*

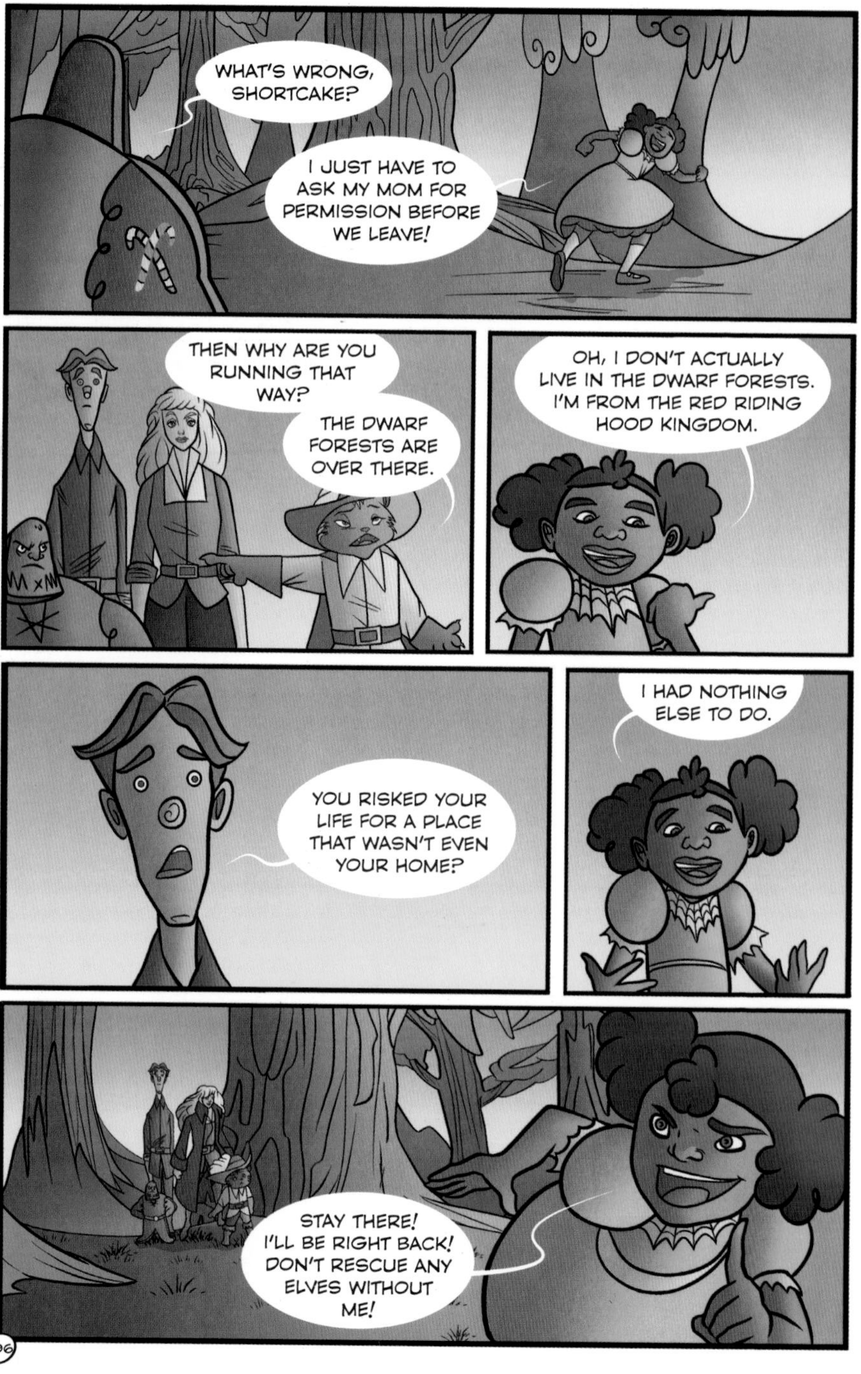
WHAT'S WRONG, SHORTCAKE?
I JUST HAVE TO ASK MY MOM FOR PERMISSION BEFORE WE LEAVE!
THEN WHY ARE YOU RUNNING THAT WAY?
THE DWARF FORESTS ARE OVER THERE.
OH, I DON'T ACTUALLY LIVE IN THE DWARF FORESTS. I'M FROM THE RED RIDING HOOD KINGDOM.
YOU RISKED YOUR LIFE FOR A PLACE THAT WASN'T EVEN YOUR HOME?
I HAD NOTHING ELSE TO DO.
STAY THERE! I'LL BE RIGHT BACK! DON'T RESCUE ANY ELVES WITHOUT ME!

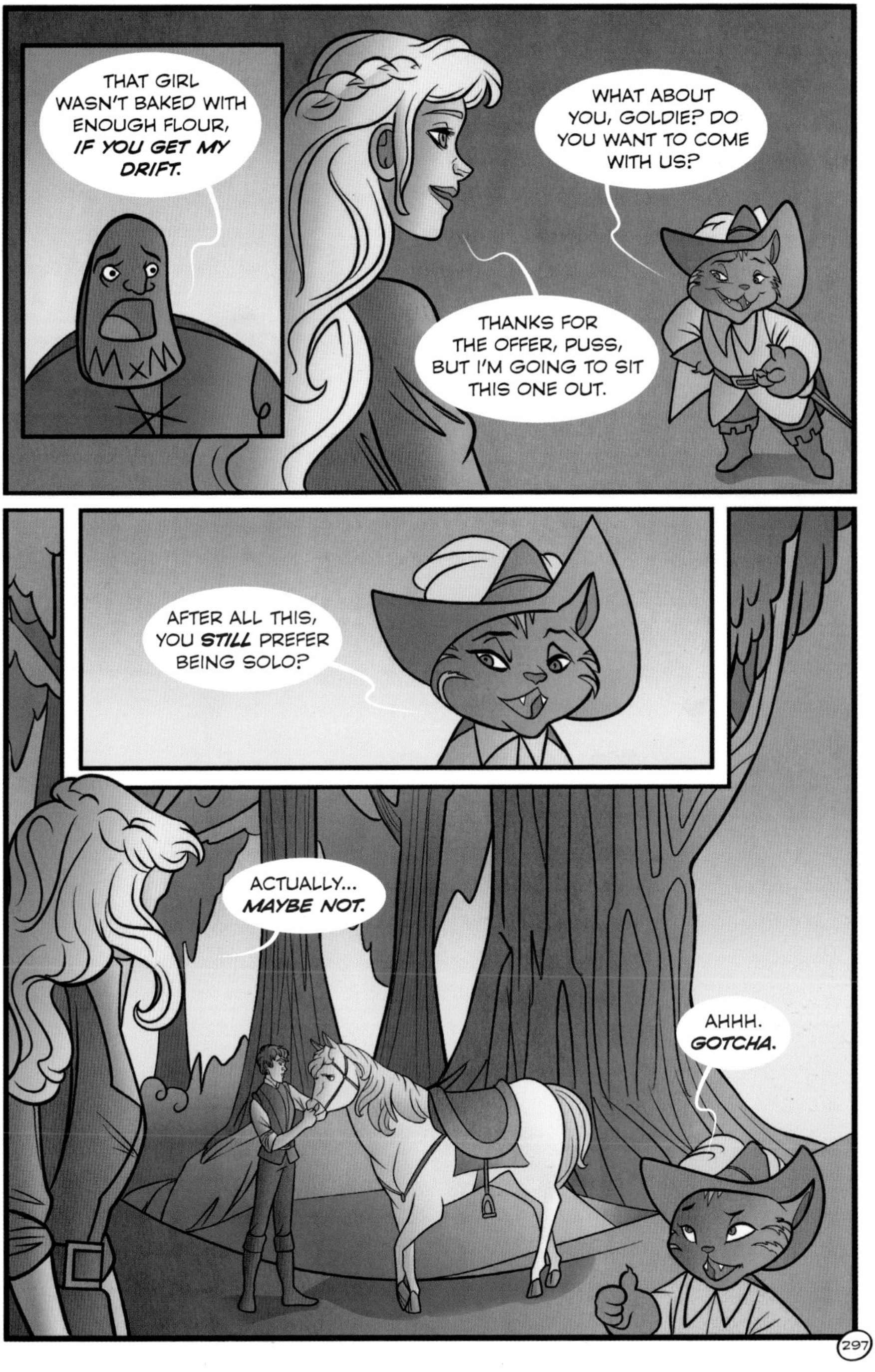
THAT GIRL WASN'T BAKED WITH ENOUGH FLOUR, *IF YOU GET MY DRIFT.*
WHAT ABOUT YOU, GOLDIE? DO YOU WANT TO COME WITH US?
THANKS FOR THE OFFER, PUSS, BUT I'M GOING TO SIT THIS ONE OUT.
AFTER ALL THIS, YOU *STILL* PREFER BEING SOLO?
ACTUALLY... *MAYBE NOT.*
AHHH. *GOTCHA.*

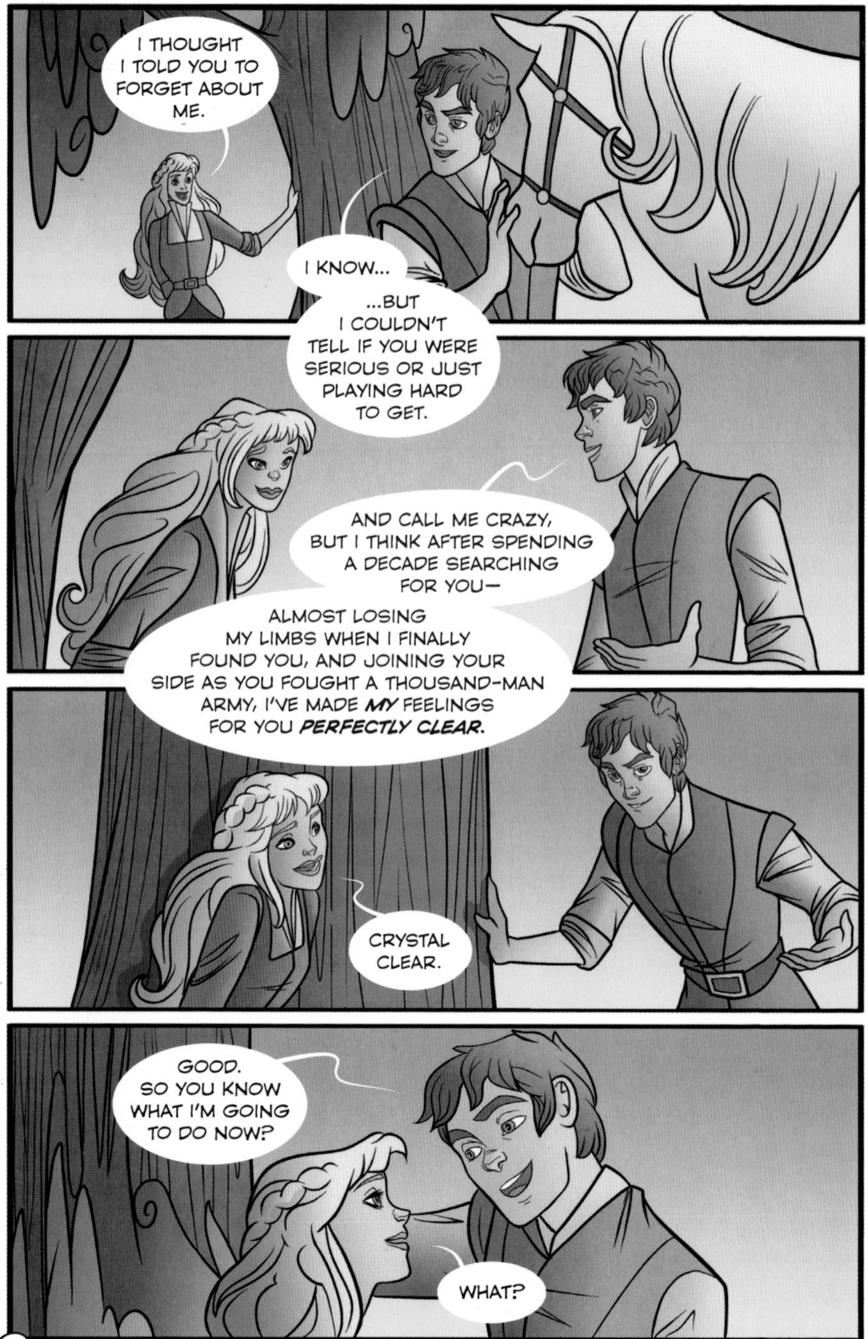

I THOUGHT I TOLD YOU TO FORGET ABOUT ME.
I KNOW...
...BUT I COULDN'T TELL IF YOU WERE SERIOUS OR JUST PLAYING HARD TO GET.
AND CALL ME CRAZY, BUT I THINK AFTER SPENDING A DECADE SEARCHING FOR YOU—
ALMOST LOSING MY LIMBS WHEN I FINALLY FOUND YOU, AND JOINING YOUR SIDE AS YOU FOUGHT A THOUSAND-MAN ARMY, I'VE MADE *MY* FEELINGS FOR YOU ***PERFECTLY CLEAR.***
CRYSTAL CLEAR.
GOOD. SO YOU KNOW WHAT I'M GOING TO DO NOW?
WHAT?

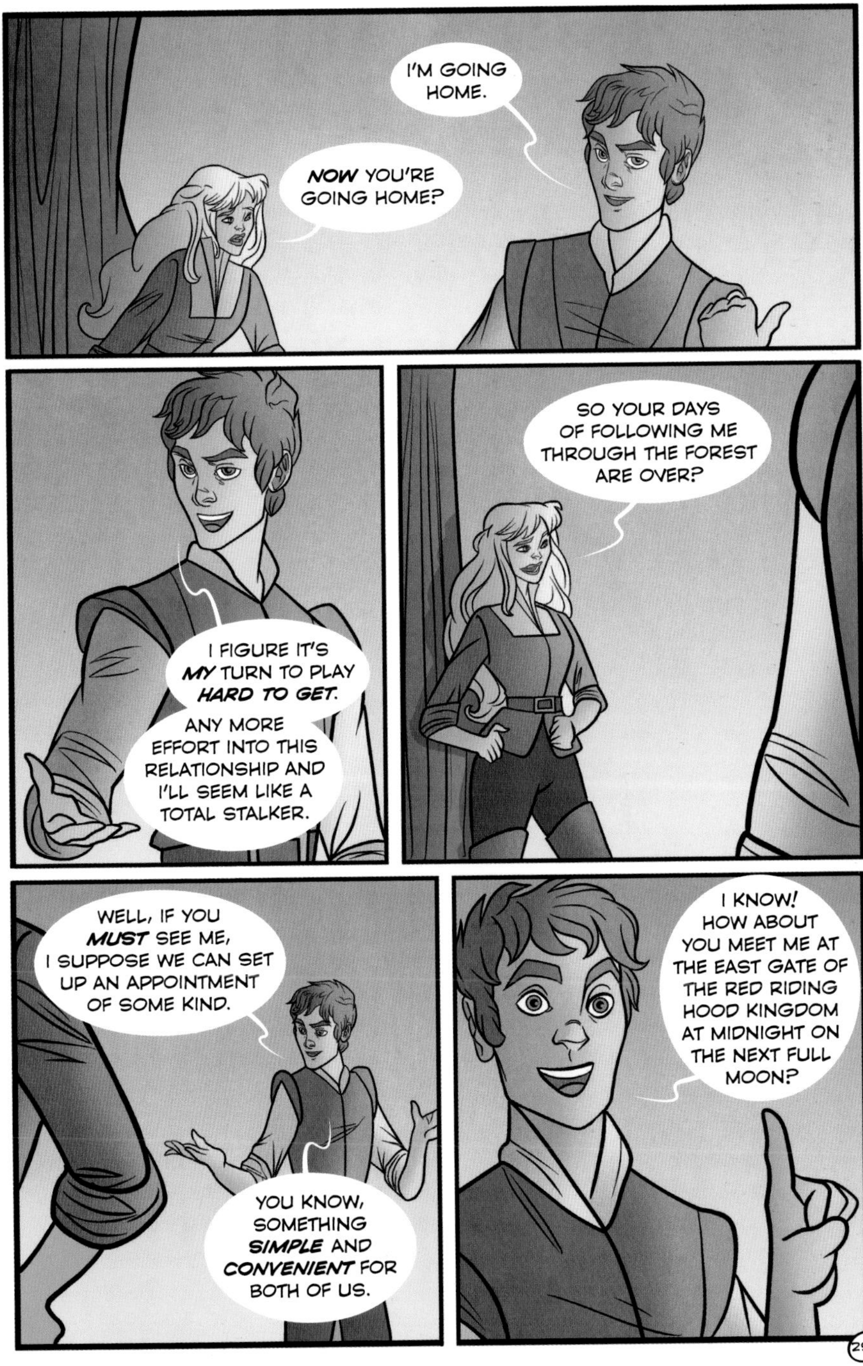
I'M GOING HOME.
NOW YOU'RE GOING HOME?
SO YOUR DAYS OF FOLLOWING ME THROUGH THE FOREST ARE OVER?
I FIGURE IT'S MY TURN TO PLAY HARD TO GET.
ANY MORE EFFORT INTO THIS RELATIONSHIP AND I'LL SEEM LIKE A TOTAL STALKER.
WELL, IF YOU MUST SEE ME, I SUPPOSE WE CAN SET UP AN APPOINTMENT OF SOME KIND.
YOU KNOW, SOMETHING SIMPLE AND CONVENIENT FOR BOTH OF US.
I KNOW! HOW ABOUT YOU MEET ME AT THE EAST GATE OF THE RED RIDING HOOD KINGDOM AT MIDNIGHT ON THE NEXT FULL MOON?

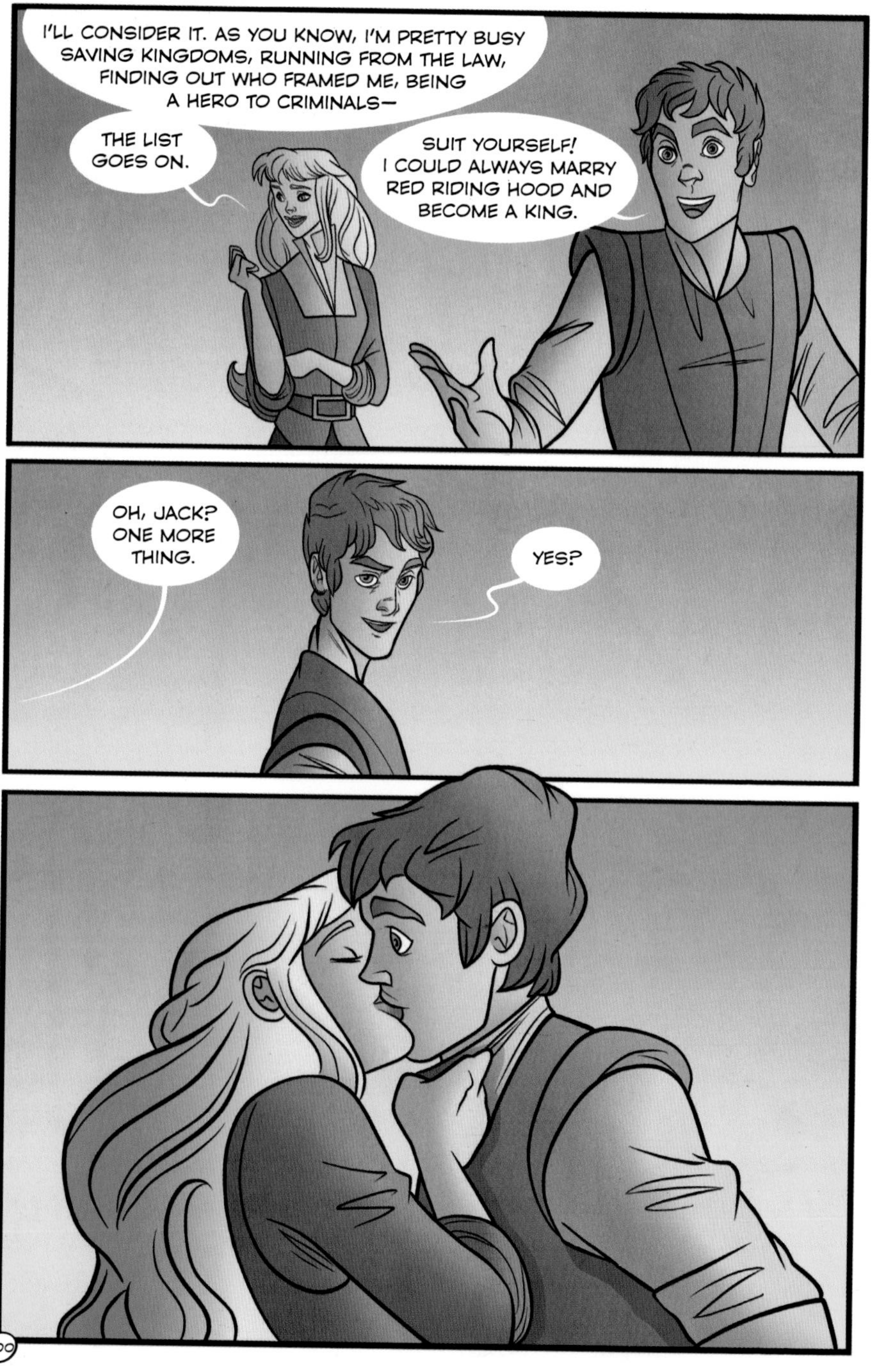
I'LL CONSIDER IT. AS YOU KNOW, I'M PRETTY BUSY SAVING KINGDOMS, RUNNING FROM THE LAW, FINDING OUT WHO FRAMED ME, BEING A HERO TO CRIMINALS—
THE LIST GOES ON.
SUIT YOURSELF! I COULD ALWAYS MARRY RED RIDING HOOD AND BECOME A KING.
OH, JACK? ONE MORE THING.
YES?

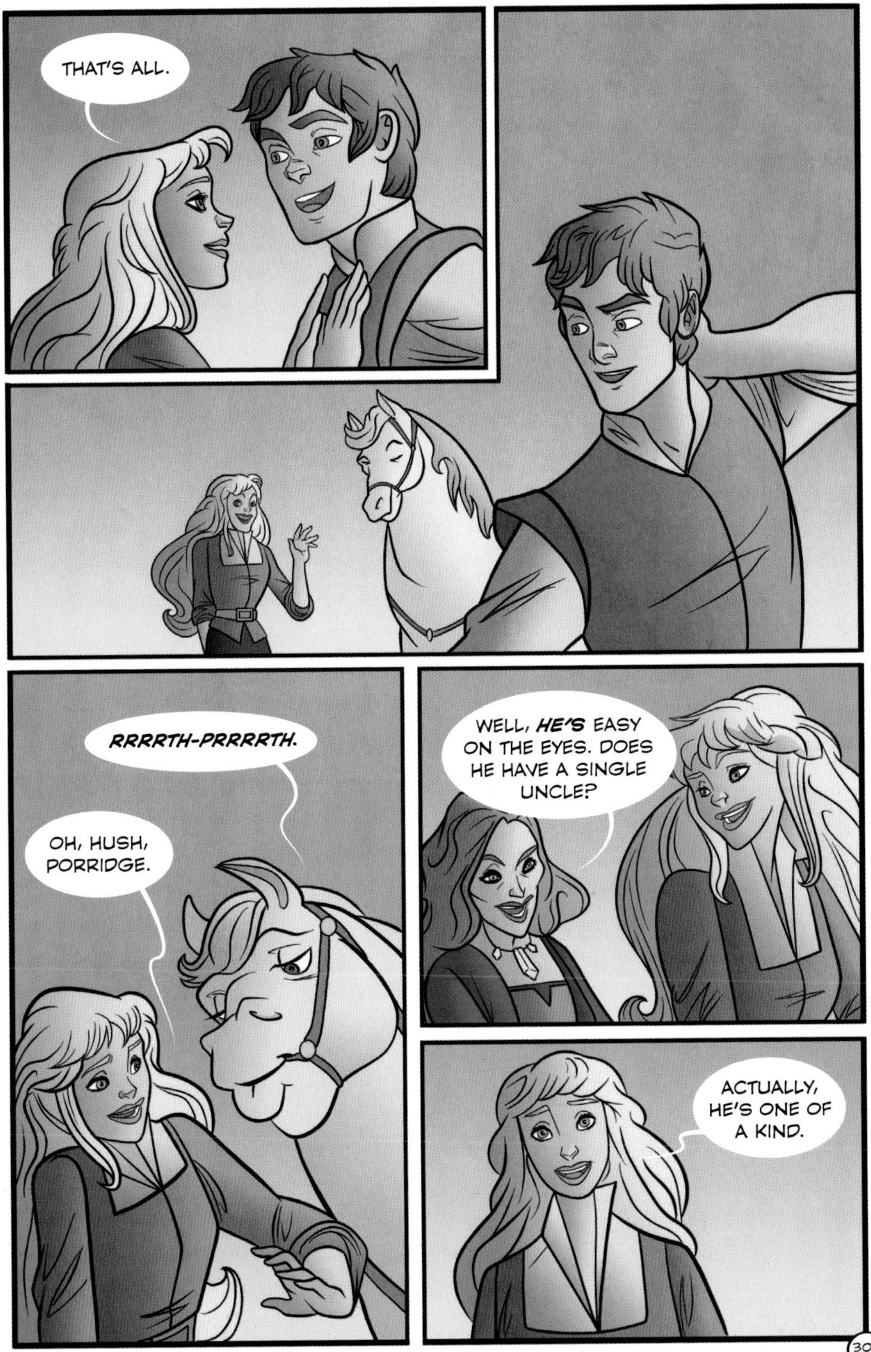
THAT'S ALL.
RRRRTH-PRRRRTH.
OH, HUSH, PORRIDGE.
WELL, ***HE'S*** EASY ON THE EYES. DOES HE HAVE A SINGLE UNCLE?
ACTUALLY, HE'S ONE OF A KIND.

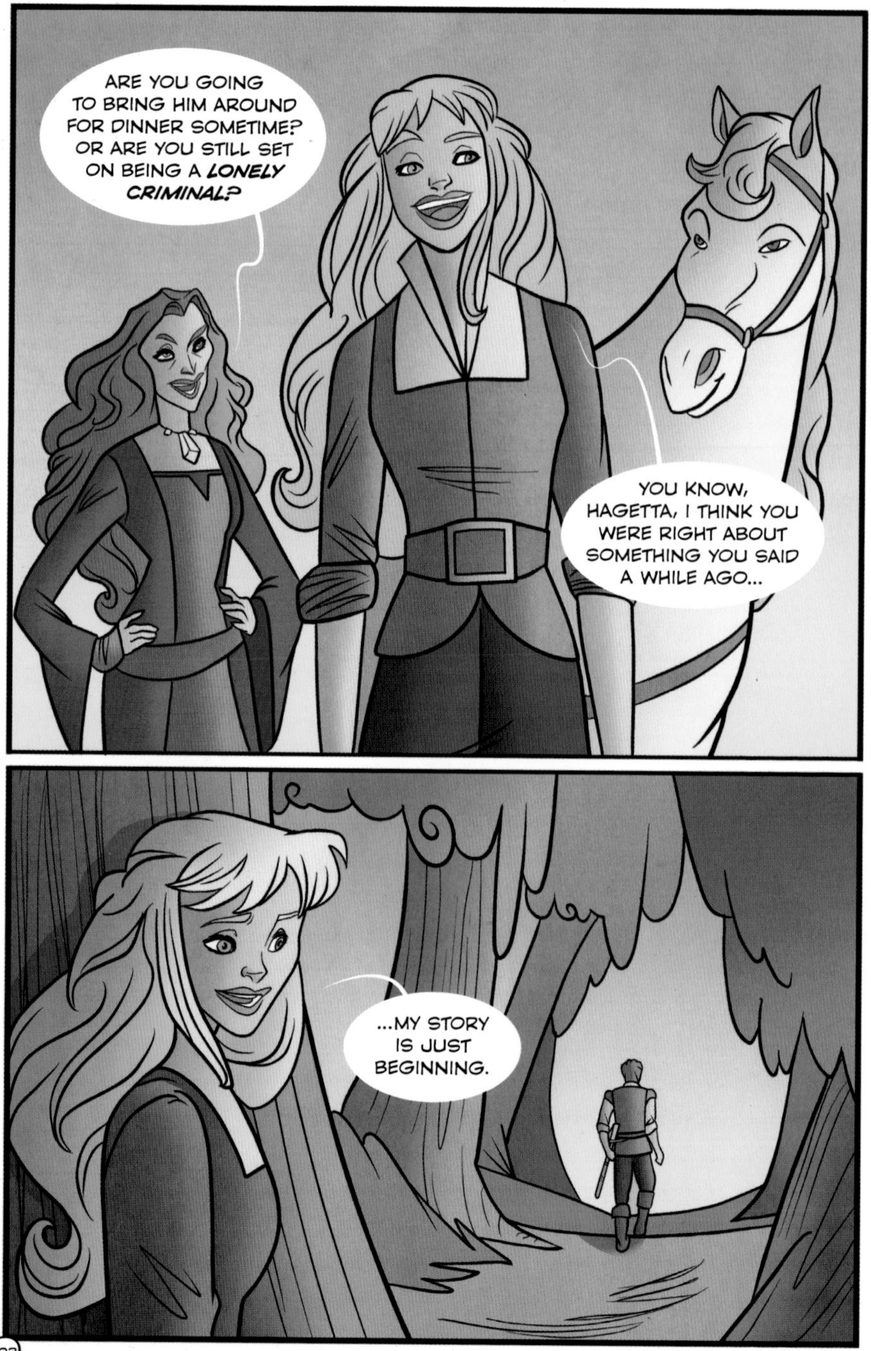
ARE YOU GOING TO BRING HIM AROUND FOR DINNER SOMETIME? OR ARE YOU STILL SET ON BEING A *LONELY CRIMINAL?*
YOU KNOW, HAGETTA, I THINK YOU WERE RIGHT ABOUT SOMETHING YOU SAID A WHILE AGO...
...MY STORY IS JUST BEGINNING.

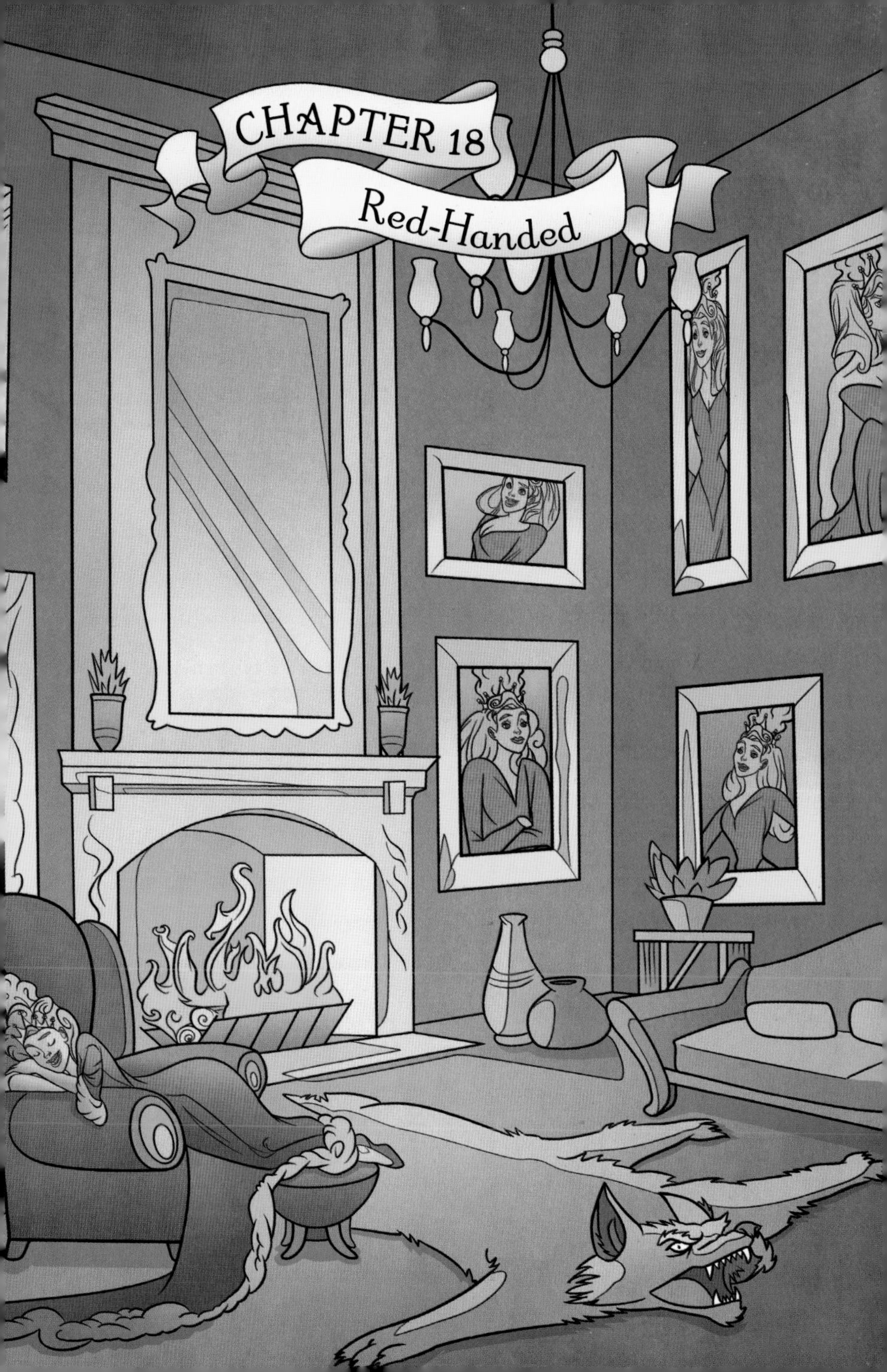
CHAPTER 18
Red-Handed

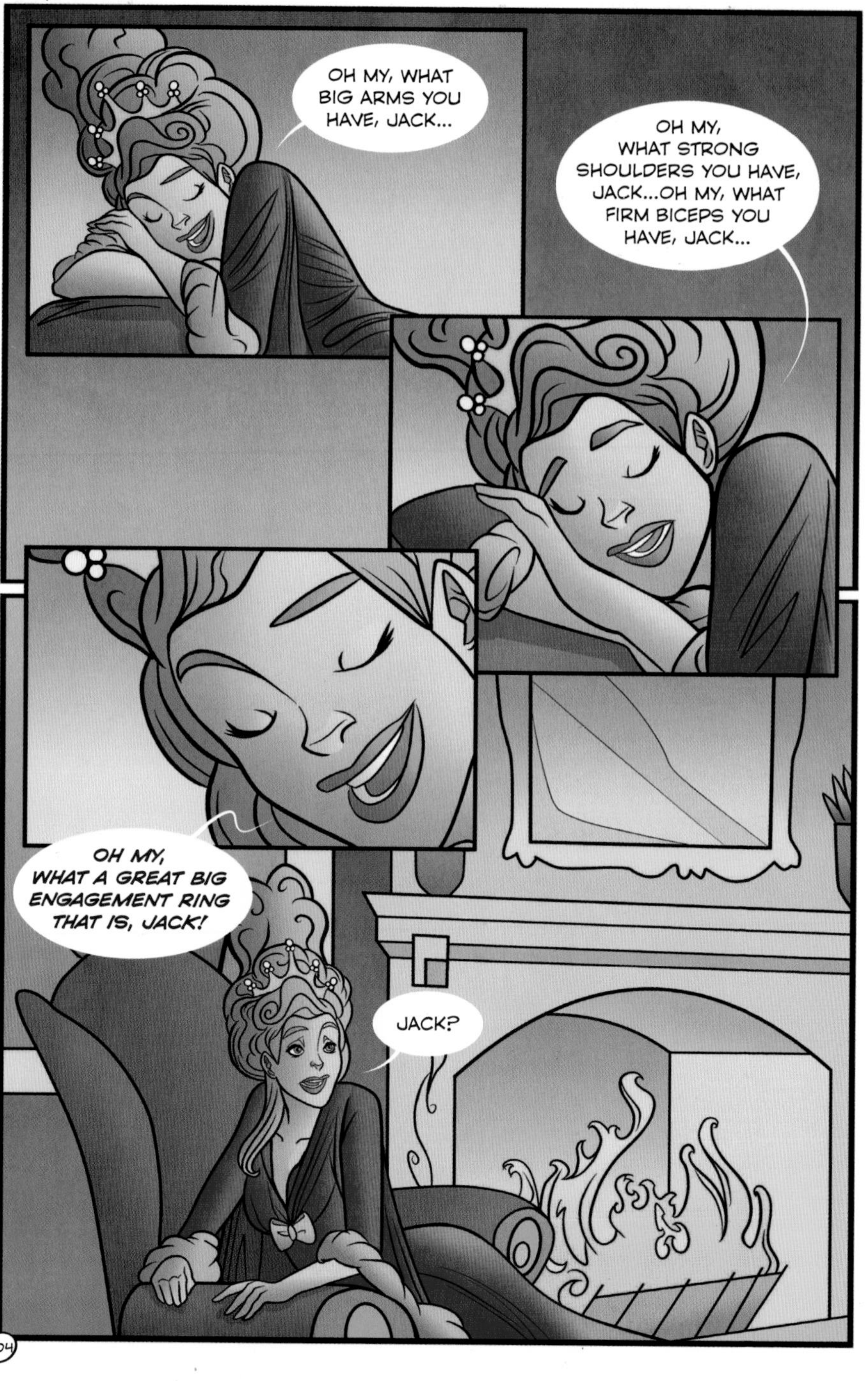
OH MY, WHAT BIG ARMS YOU HAVE, JACK...
OH MY, WHAT STRONG SHOULDERS YOU HAVE, JACK...OH MY, WHAT FIRM BICEPS YOU HAVE, JACK...
OH MY, WHAT A GREAT BIG ENGAGEMENT RING THAT IS, JACK!
JACK?

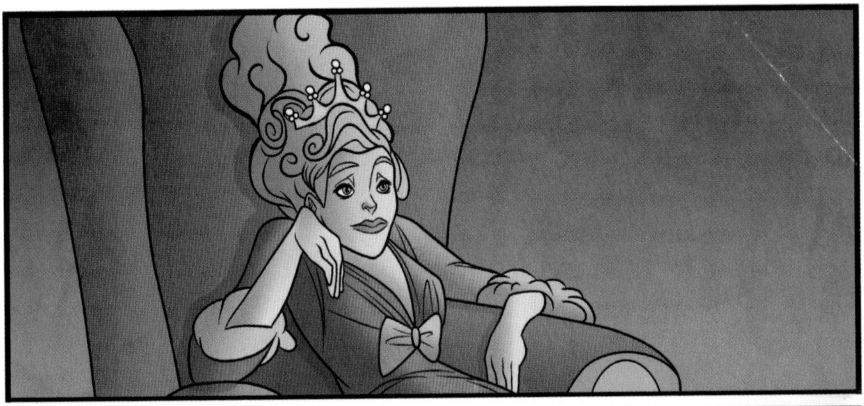

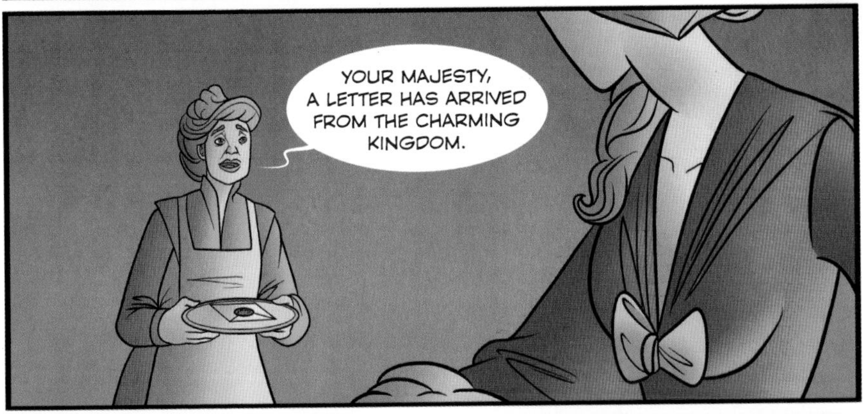
YOUR MAJESTY,
A LETTER HAS ARRIVED
FROM THE CHARMING
KINGDOM.

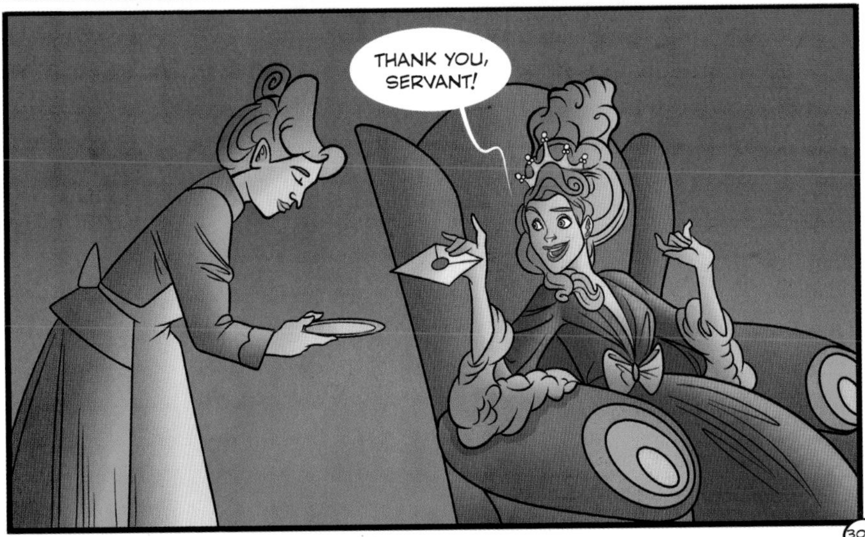
THANK YOU,
SERVANT!

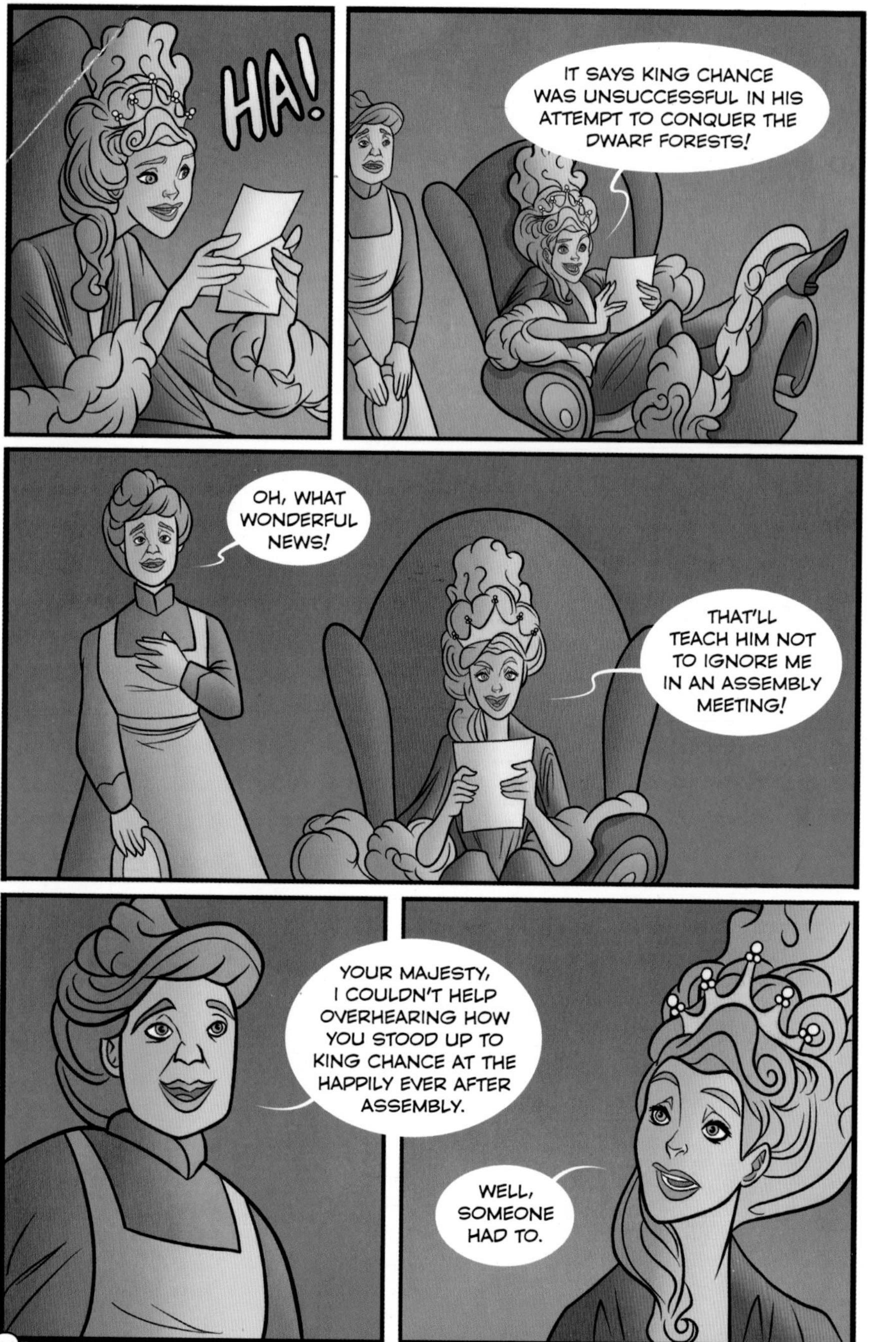
HA!
IT SAYS KING CHANCE WAS UNSUCCESSFUL IN HIS ATTEMPT TO CONQUER THE DWARF FORESTS!
OH, WHAT WONDERFUL NEWS!
THAT'LL TEACH HIM NOT TO IGNORE ME IN AN ASSEMBLY MEETING!
YOUR MAJESTY, I COULDN'T HELP OVERHEARING HOW YOU STOOD UP TO KING CHANCE AT THE HAPPILY EVER AFTER ASSEMBLY.
WELL, SOMEONE HAD TO.

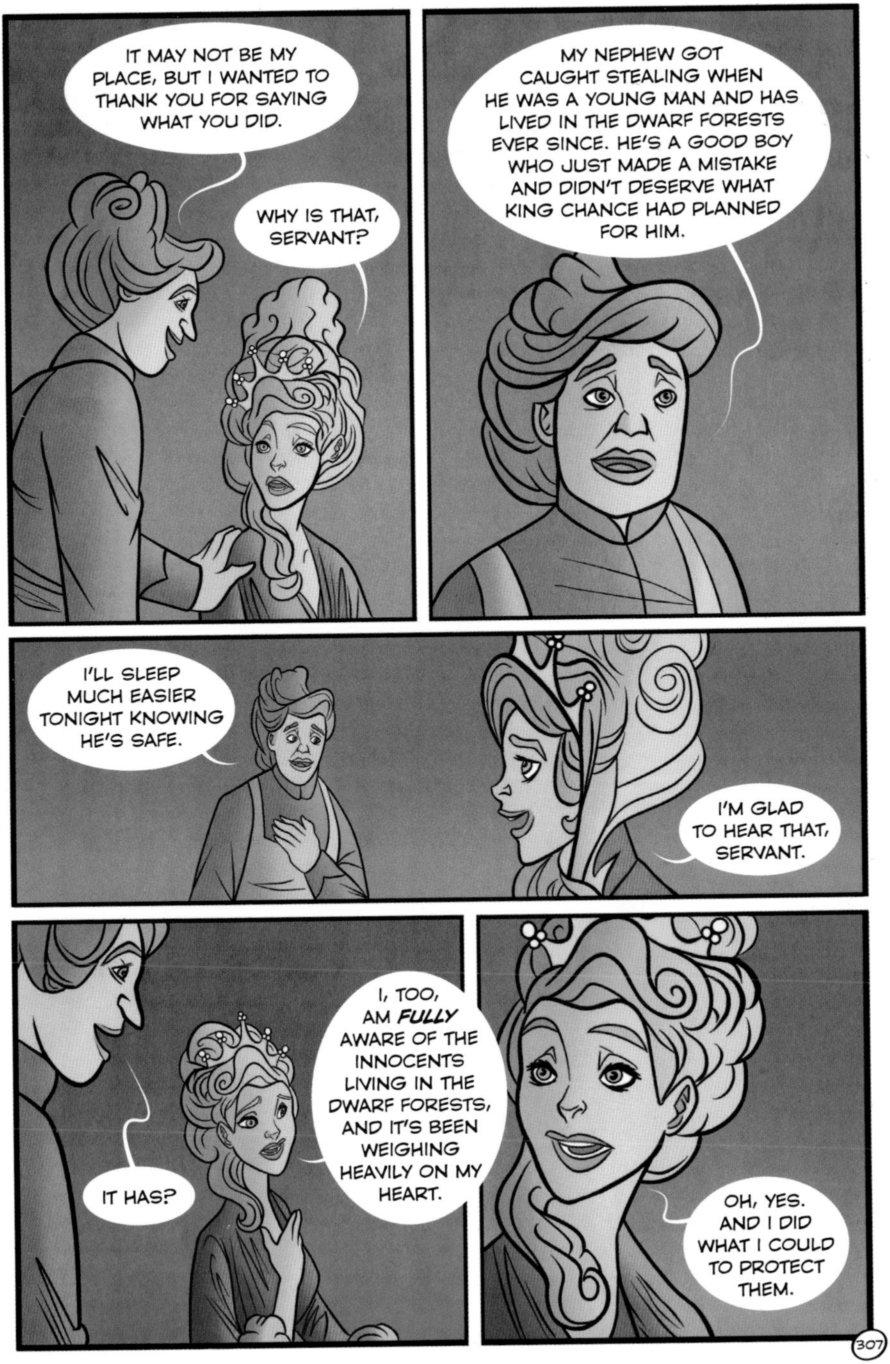
IT MAY NOT BE MY PLACE, BUT I WANTED TO THANK YOU FOR SAYING WHAT YOU DID.
WHY IS THAT, SERVANT?
MY NEPHEW GOT CAUGHT STEALING WHEN HE WAS A YOUNG MAN AND HAS LIVED IN THE DWARF FORESTS EVER SINCE. HE'S A GOOD BOY WHO JUST MADE A MISTAKE AND DIDN'T DESERVE WHAT KING CHANCE HAD PLANNED FOR HIM.
I'LL SLEEP MUCH EASIER TONIGHT KNOWING HE'S SAFE.
I'M GLAD TO HEAR THAT, SERVANT.
IT HAS?
I, TOO, AM ***FULLY*** AWARE OF THE INNOCENTS LIVING IN THE DWARF FORESTS, AND IT'S BEEN WEIGHING HEAVILY ON MY HEART.
OH, YES. AND I DID WHAT I COULD TO PROTECT THEM.

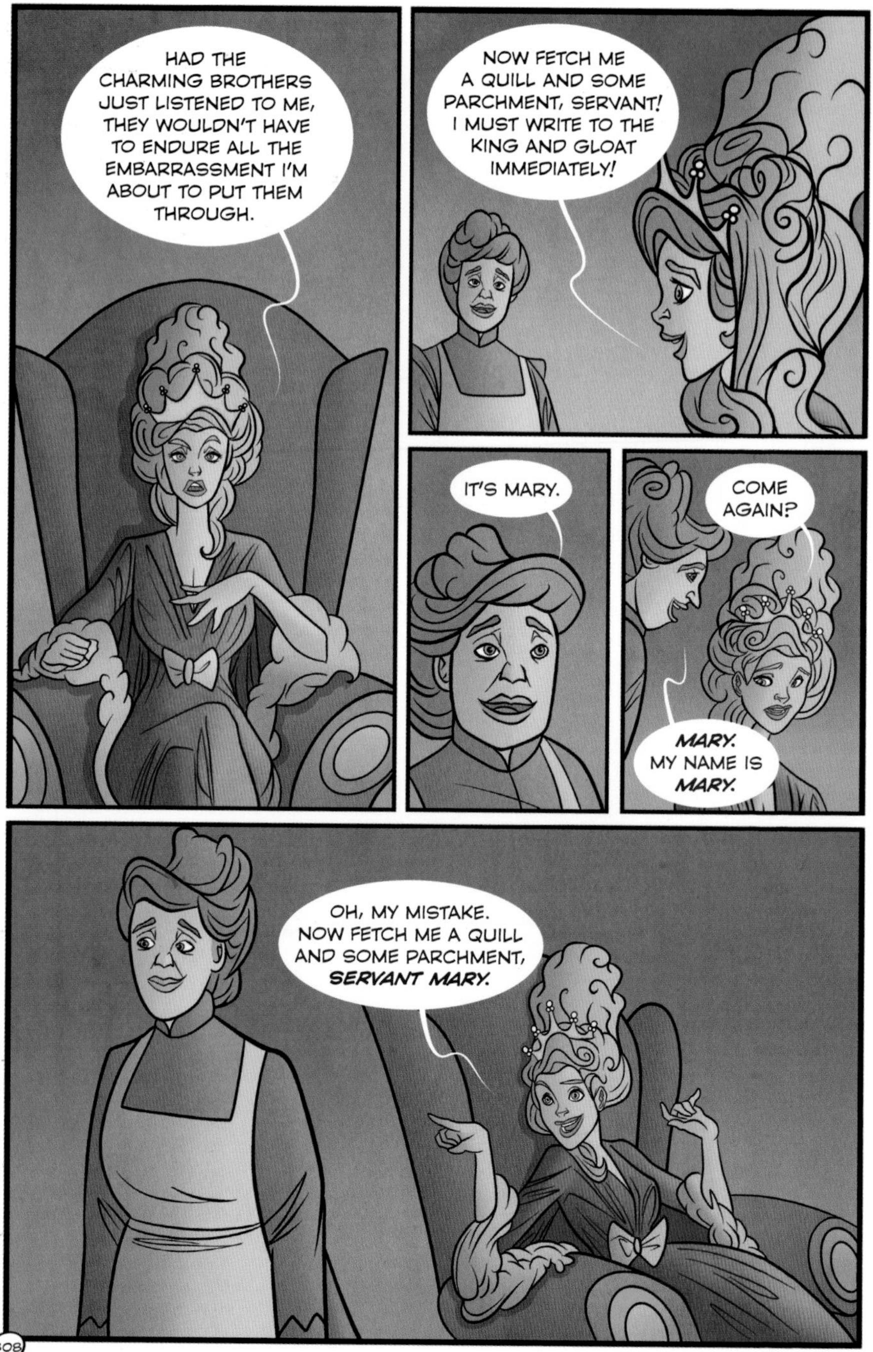
HAD THE CHARMING BROTHERS JUST LISTENED TO ME, THEY WOULDN'T HAVE TO ENDURE ALL THE EMBARRASSMENT I'M ABOUT TO PUT THEM THROUGH.
NOW FETCH ME A QUILL AND SOME PARCHMENT, SERVANT! I MUST WRITE TO THE KING AND GLOAT IMMEDIATELY!
IT'S MARY.
COME AGAIN?
MARY. MY NAME IS *MARY.*
OH, MY MISTAKE. NOW FETCH ME A QUILL AND SOME PARCHMENT, ***SERVANT MARY.***

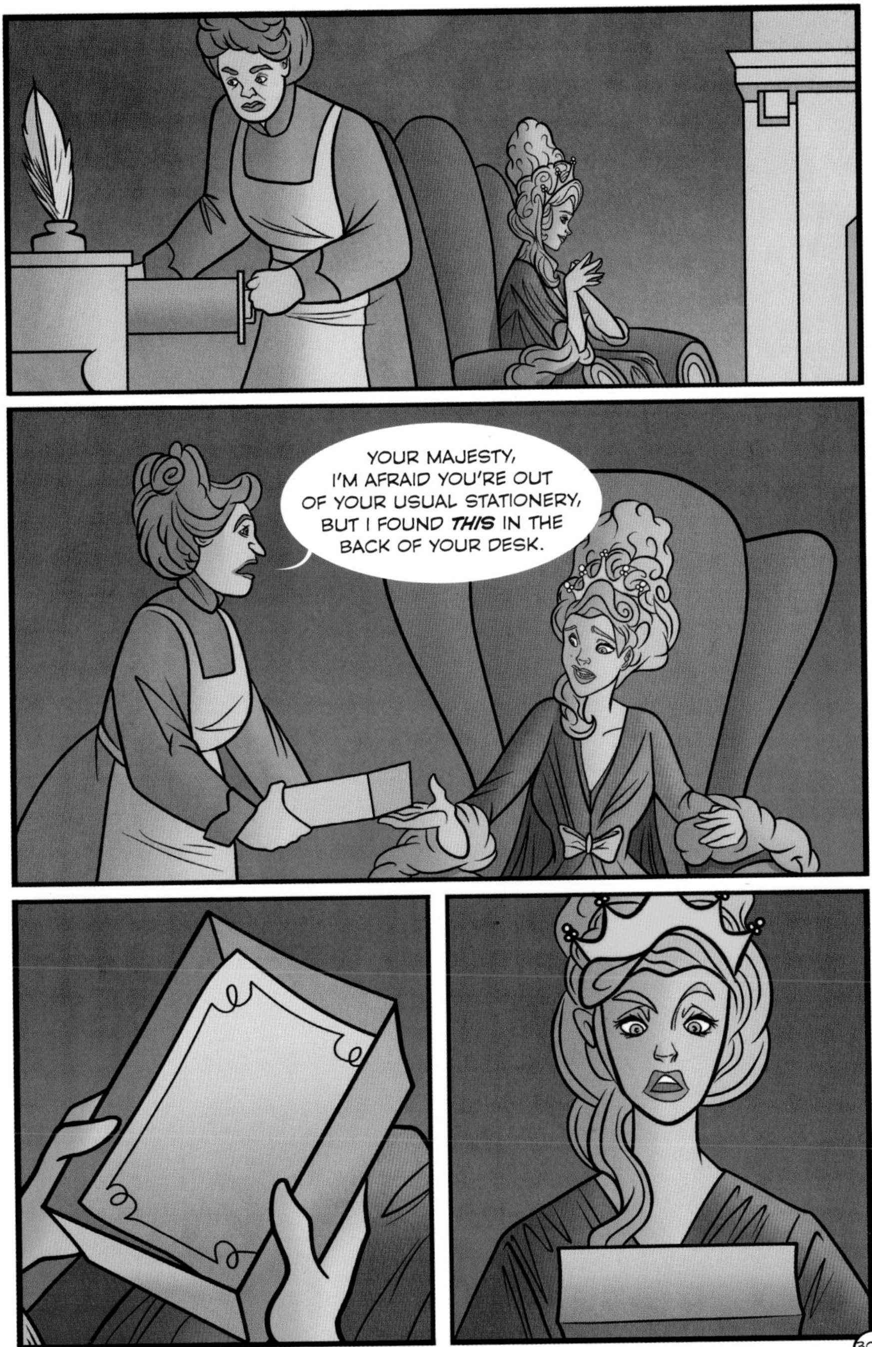
YOUR MAJESTY, I'M AFRAID YOU'RE OUT OF YOUR USUAL STATIONERY, BUT I FOUND *THIS* IN THE BACK OF YOUR DESK.

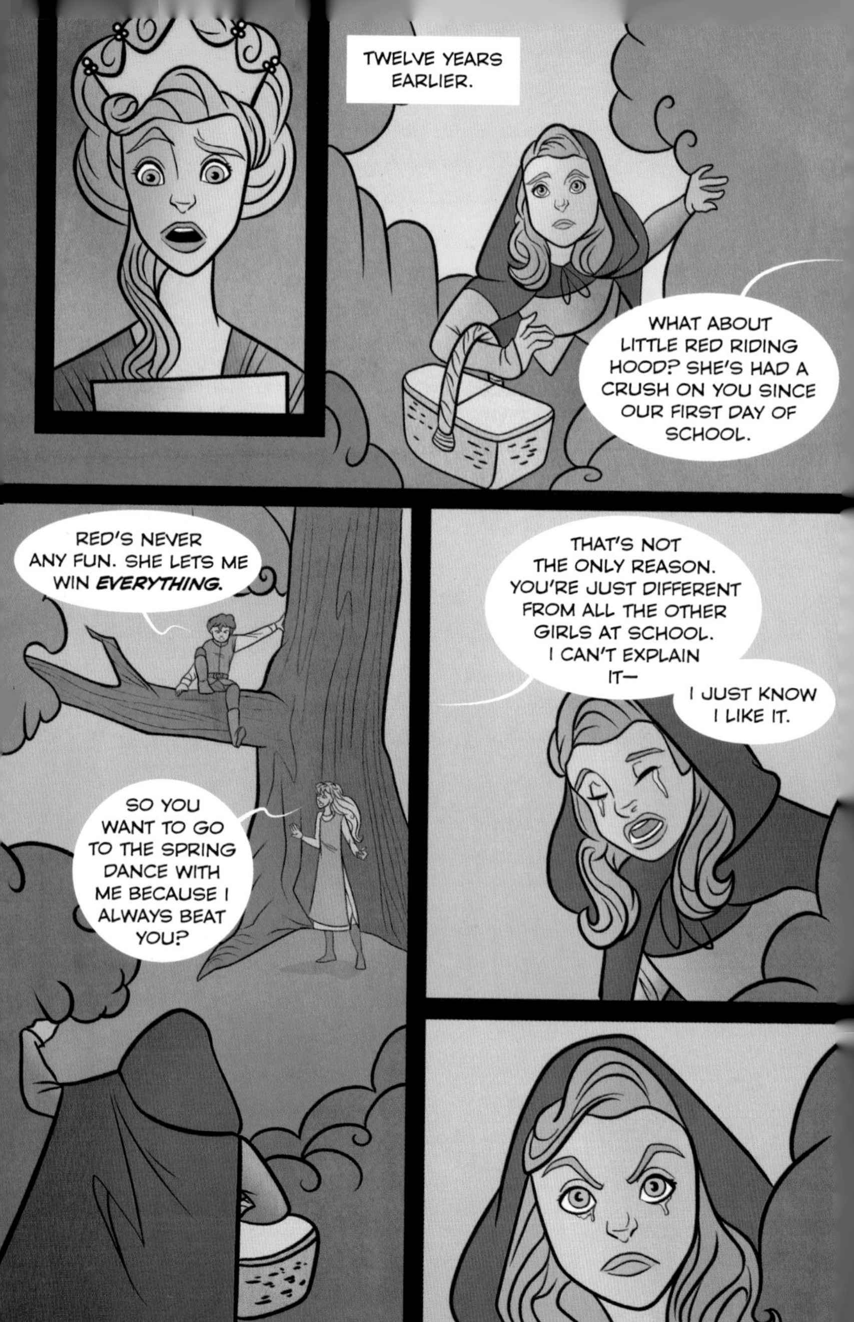
TWELVE YEARS EARLIER.
WHAT ABOUT LITTLE RED RIDING HOOD? SHE'S HAD A CRUSH ON YOU SINCE OUR FIRST DAY OF SCHOOL.
RED'S NEVER ANY FUN. SHE LETS ME WIN *EVERYTHING*.
SO YOU WANT TO GO TO THE SPRING DANCE WITH ME BECAUSE I ALWAYS BEAT YOU?
THAT'S NOT THE ONLY REASON. YOU'RE JUST DIFFERENT FROM ALL THE OTHER GIRLS AT SCHOOL. I CAN'T EXPLAIN IT—
I JUST KNOW I LIKE IT.

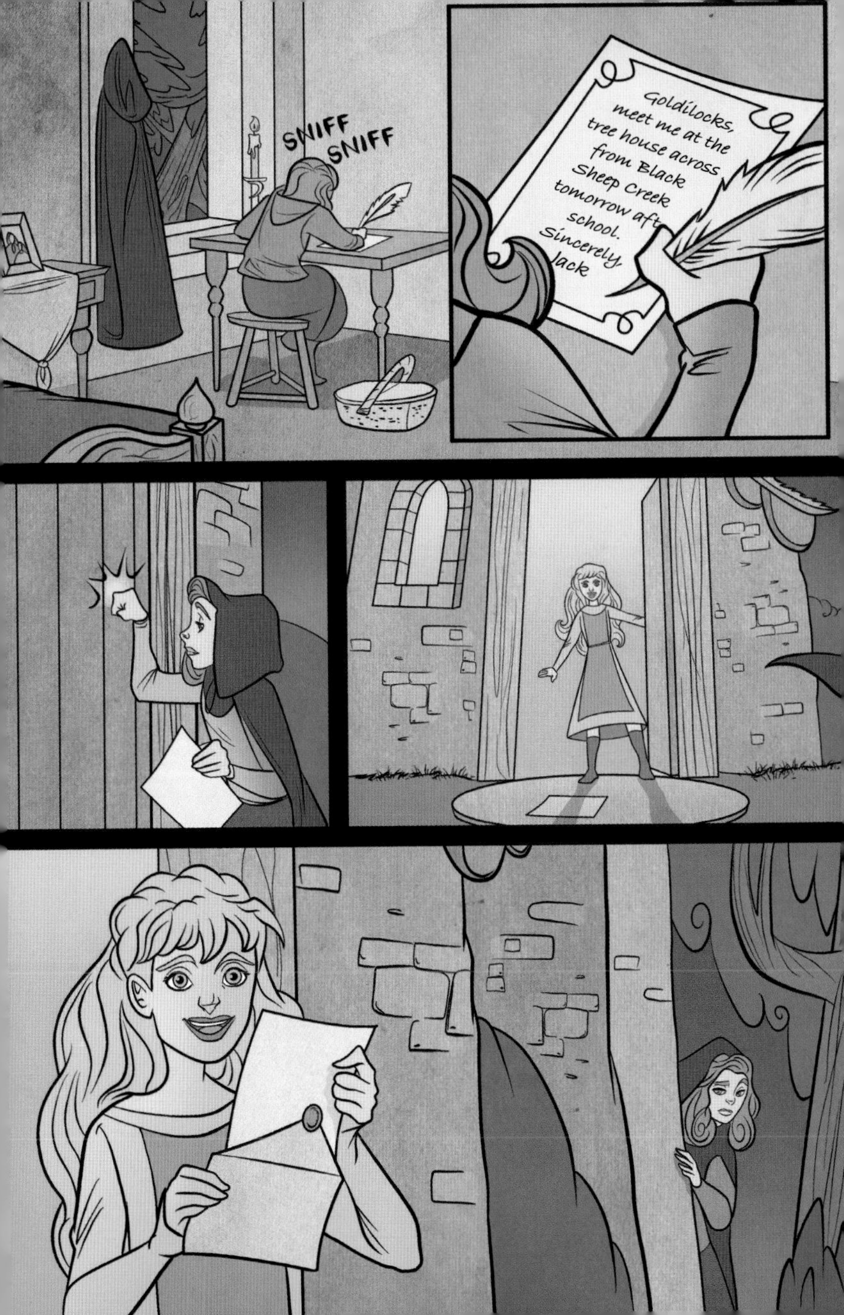
SNIFF
SNIFF
Goldilocks,
meet me at the
tree house across
from Black
Sheep Creek
tomorrow aft
school.
Sincerely,
Jack

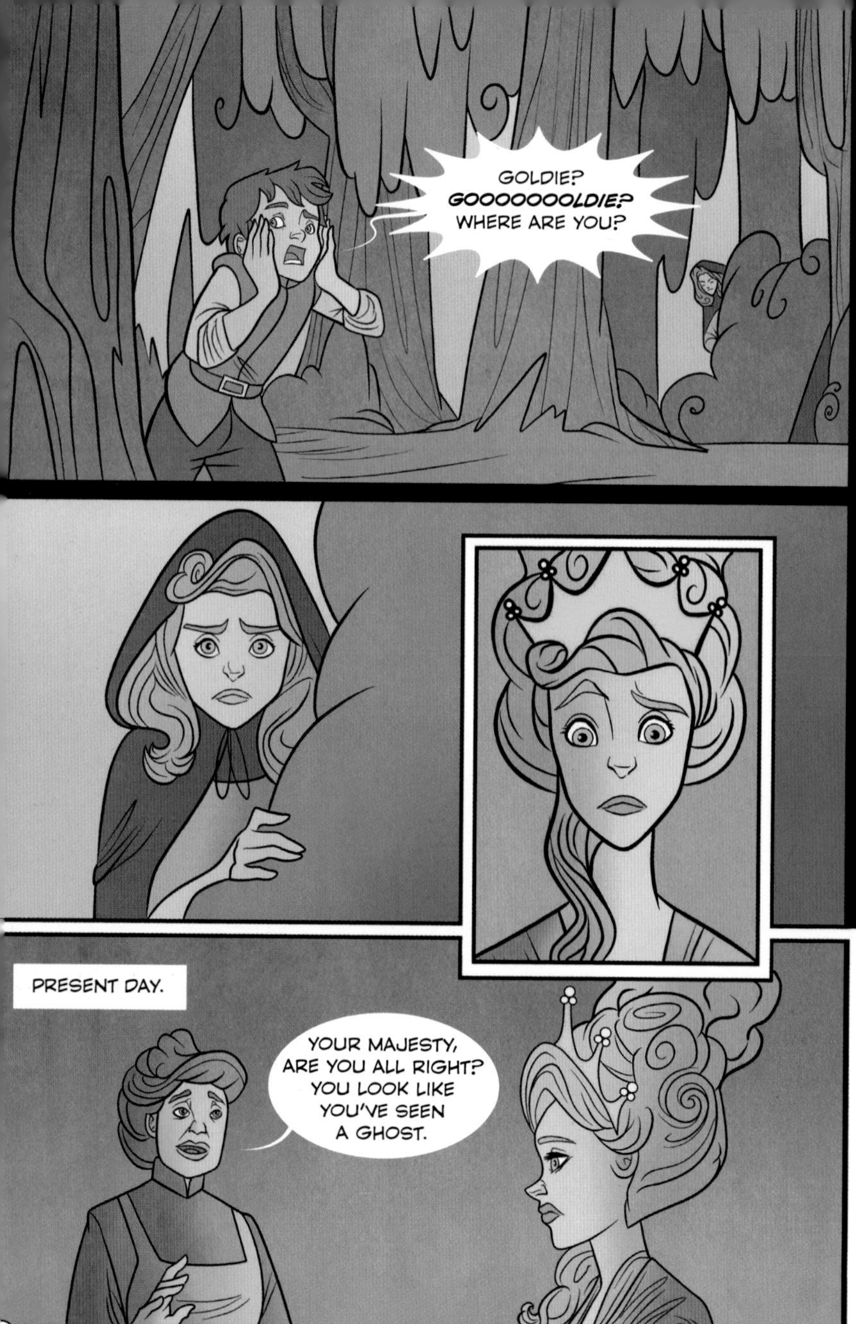
GOLDIE? GOOOOOOOLDIE? WHERE ARE YOU?
PRESENT DAY.
YOUR MAJESTY, ARE YOU ALL RIGHT? YOU LOOK LIKE YOU'VE SEEN A GHOST.

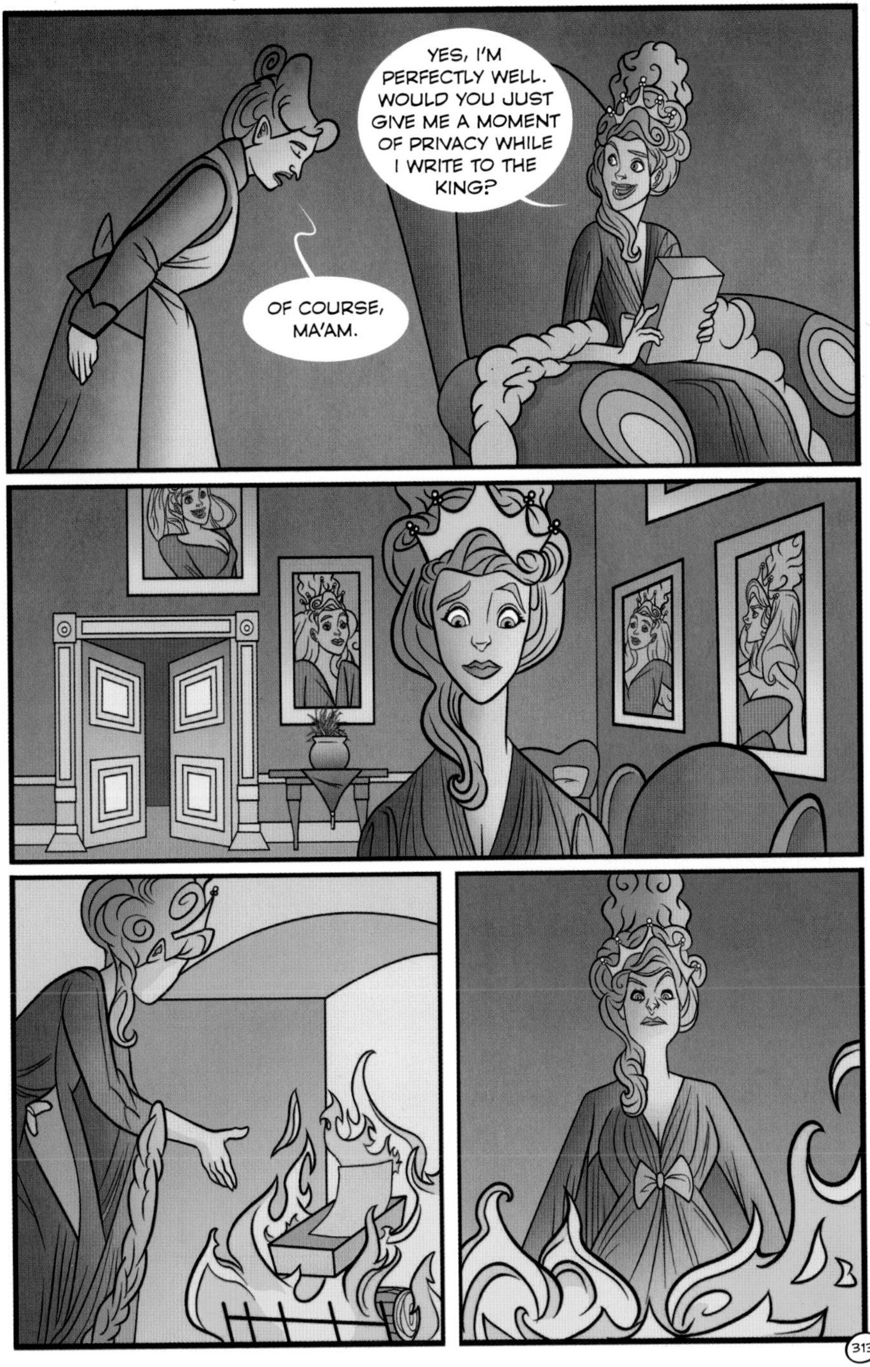
YES, I'M PERFECTLY WELL. WOULD YOU JUST GIVE ME A MOMENT OF PRIVACY WHILE I WRITE TO THE KING?
OF COURSE, MA'AM.

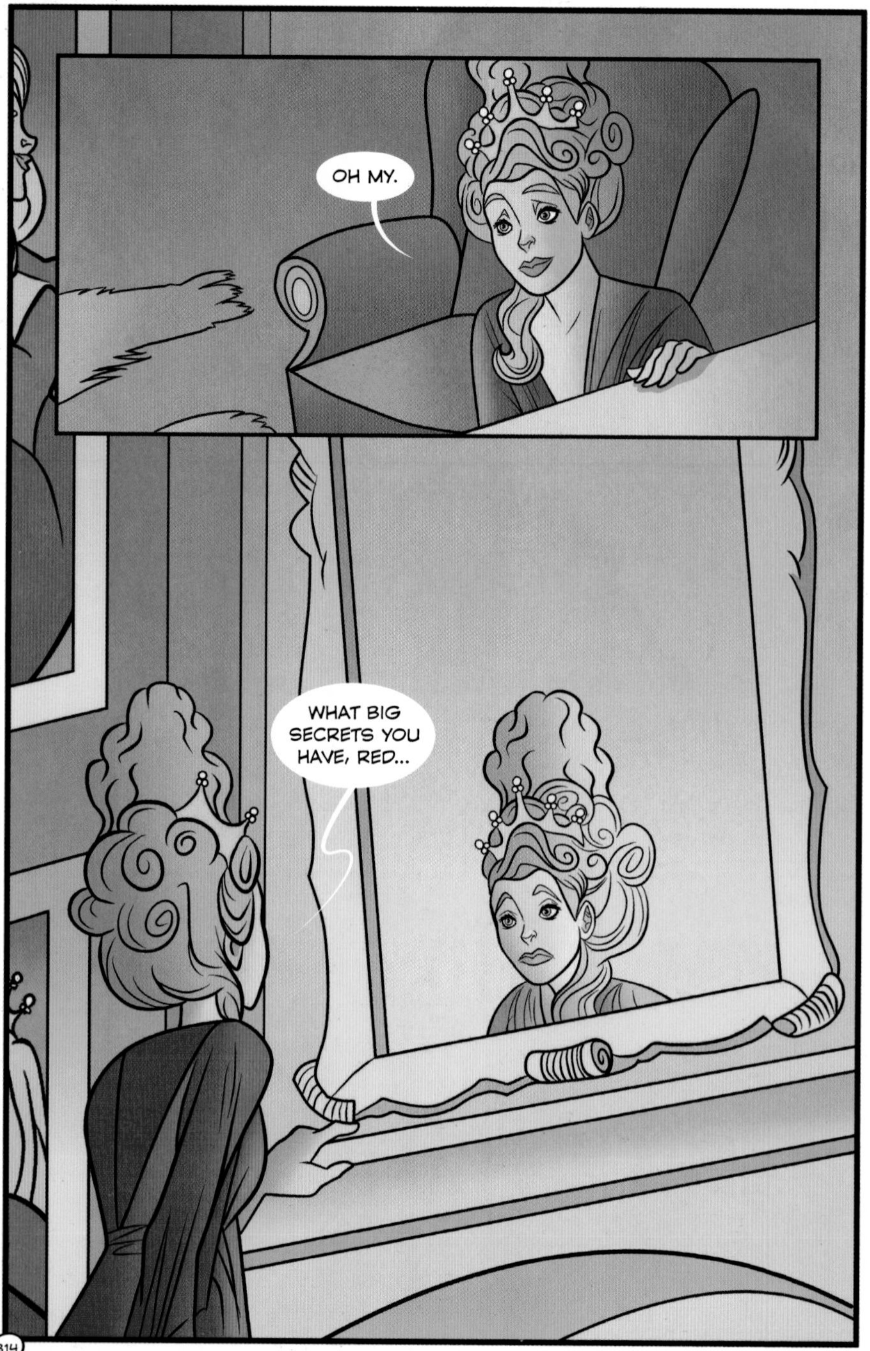
OH MY.
WHAT BIG SECRETS YOU HAVE, RED...

CHAPTER 19

Dead or Alive

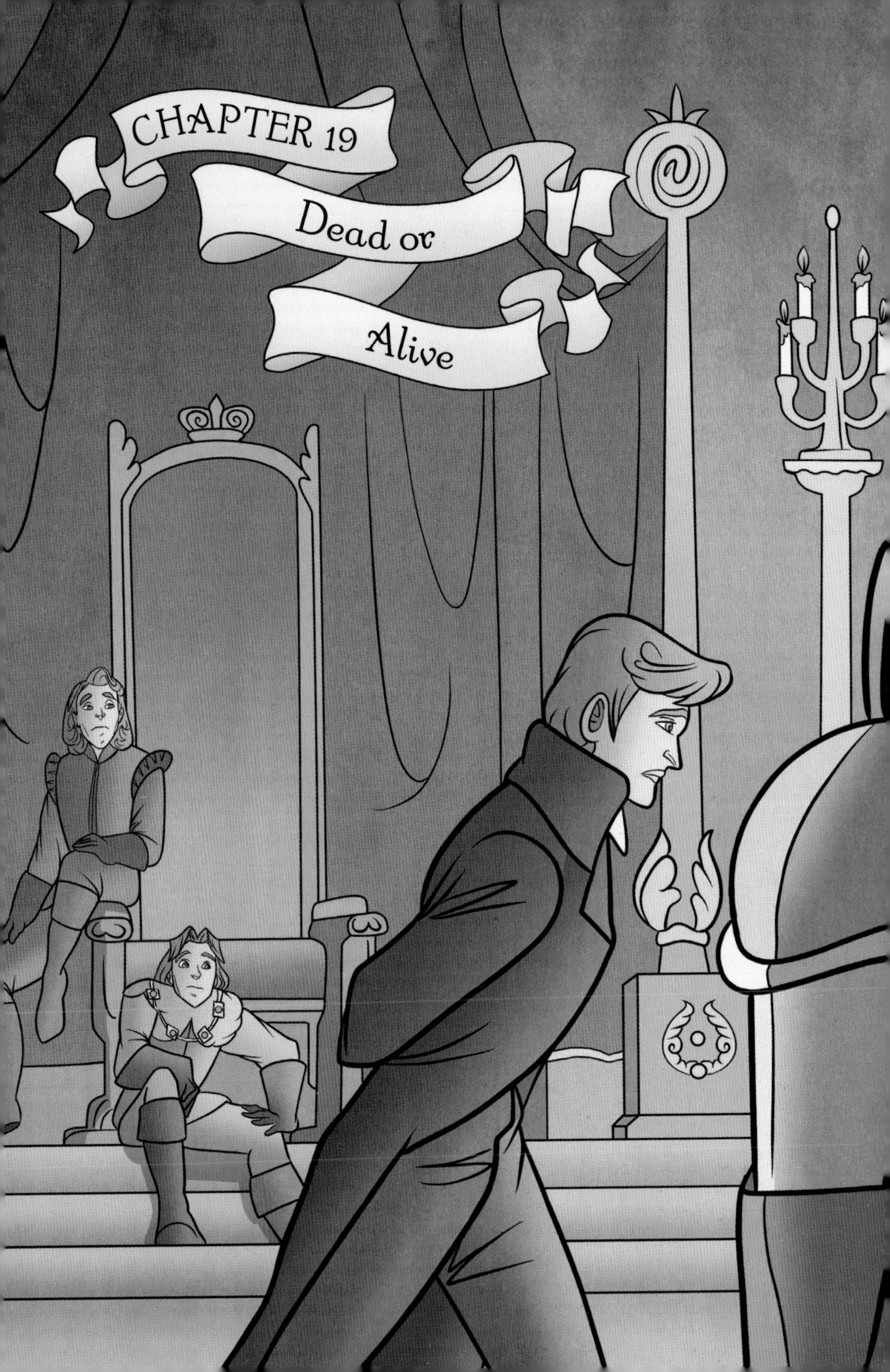

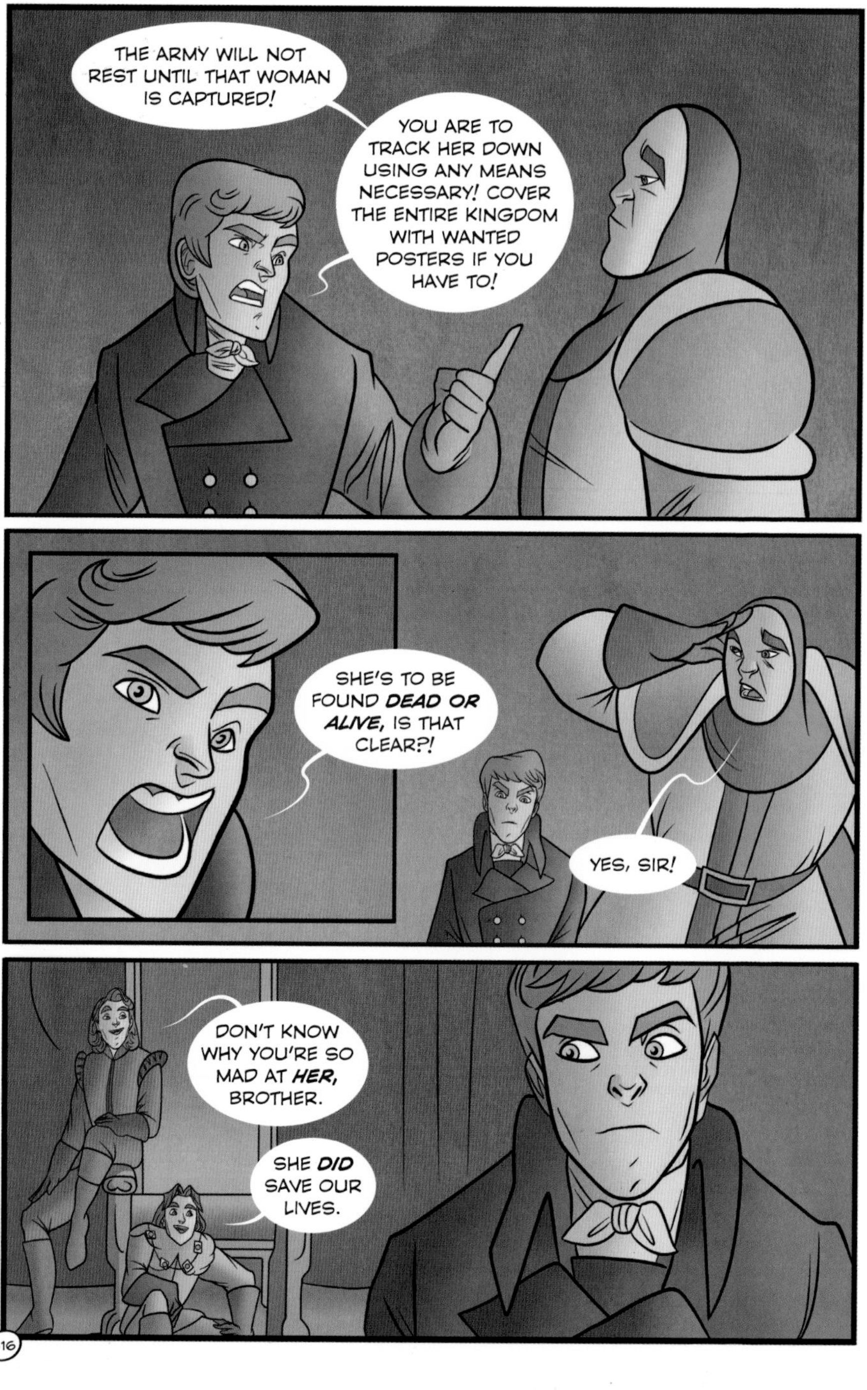
THE ARMY WILL NOT REST UNTIL THAT WOMAN IS CAPTURED!
YOU ARE TO TRACK HER DOWN USING ANY MEANS NECESSARY! COVER THE ENTIRE KINGDOM WITH WANTED POSTERS IF YOU HAVE TO!
SHE'S TO BE FOUND DEAD OR ALIVE, IS THAT CLEAR?!
YES, SIR!
DON'T KNOW WHY YOU'RE SO MAD AT HER, BROTHER.
SHE DID SAVE OUR LIVES.

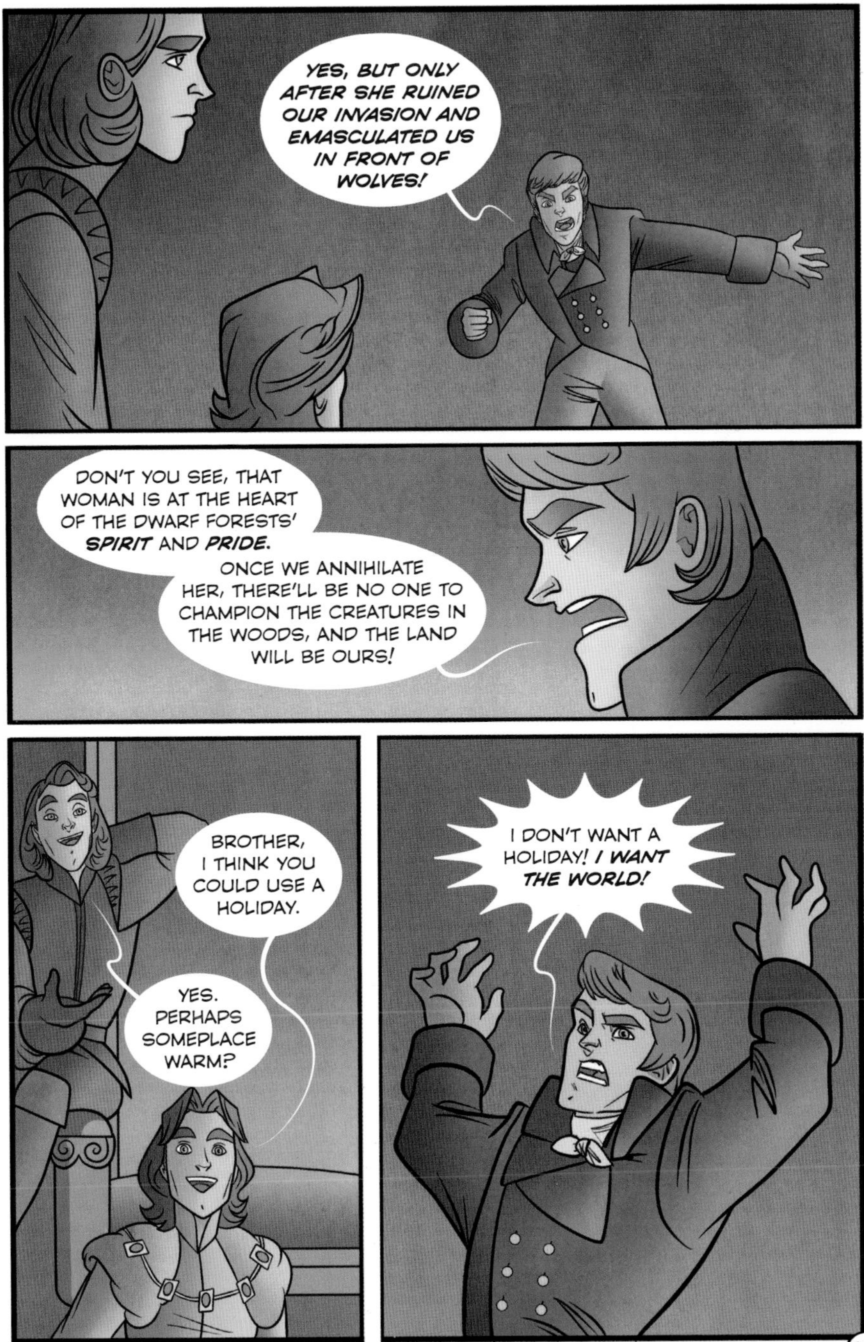
YES, BUT ONLY AFTER SHE RUINED OUR INVASION AND EMASCULATED US IN FRONT OF WOLVES!
DON'T YOU SEE, THAT WOMAN IS AT THE HEART OF THE DWARF FORESTS' SPIRIT AND PRIDE.
ONCE WE ANNIHILATE HER, THERE'LL BE NO ONE TO CHAMPION THE CREATURES IN THE WOODS, AND THE LAND WILL BE OURS!
BROTHER, I THINK YOU COULD USE A HOLIDAY.
YES. PERHAPS SOMEPLACE WARM?
I DON'T WANT A HOLIDAY! I WANT THE WORLD!

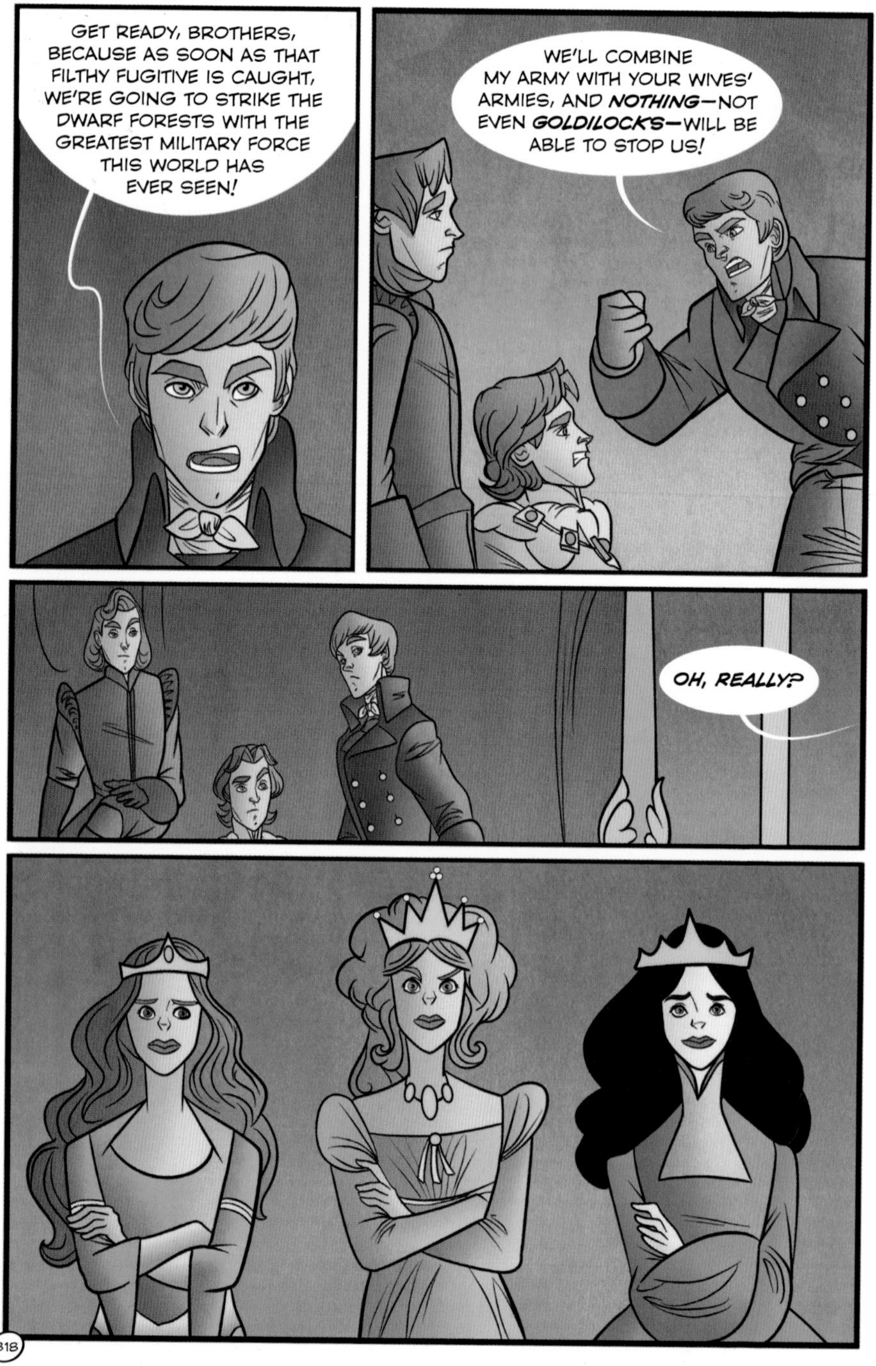
GET READY, BROTHERS, BECAUSE AS SOON AS THAT FILTHY FUGITIVE IS CAUGHT, WE'RE GOING TO STRIKE THE DWARF FORESTS WITH THE GREATEST MILITARY FORCE THIS WORLD HAS EVER SEEN!
WE'LL COMBINE MY ARMY WITH YOUR WIVES' ARMIES, AND *NOTHING*—NOT EVEN *GOLDILOCKS*—WILL BE ABLE TO STOP US!
OH, REALLY?

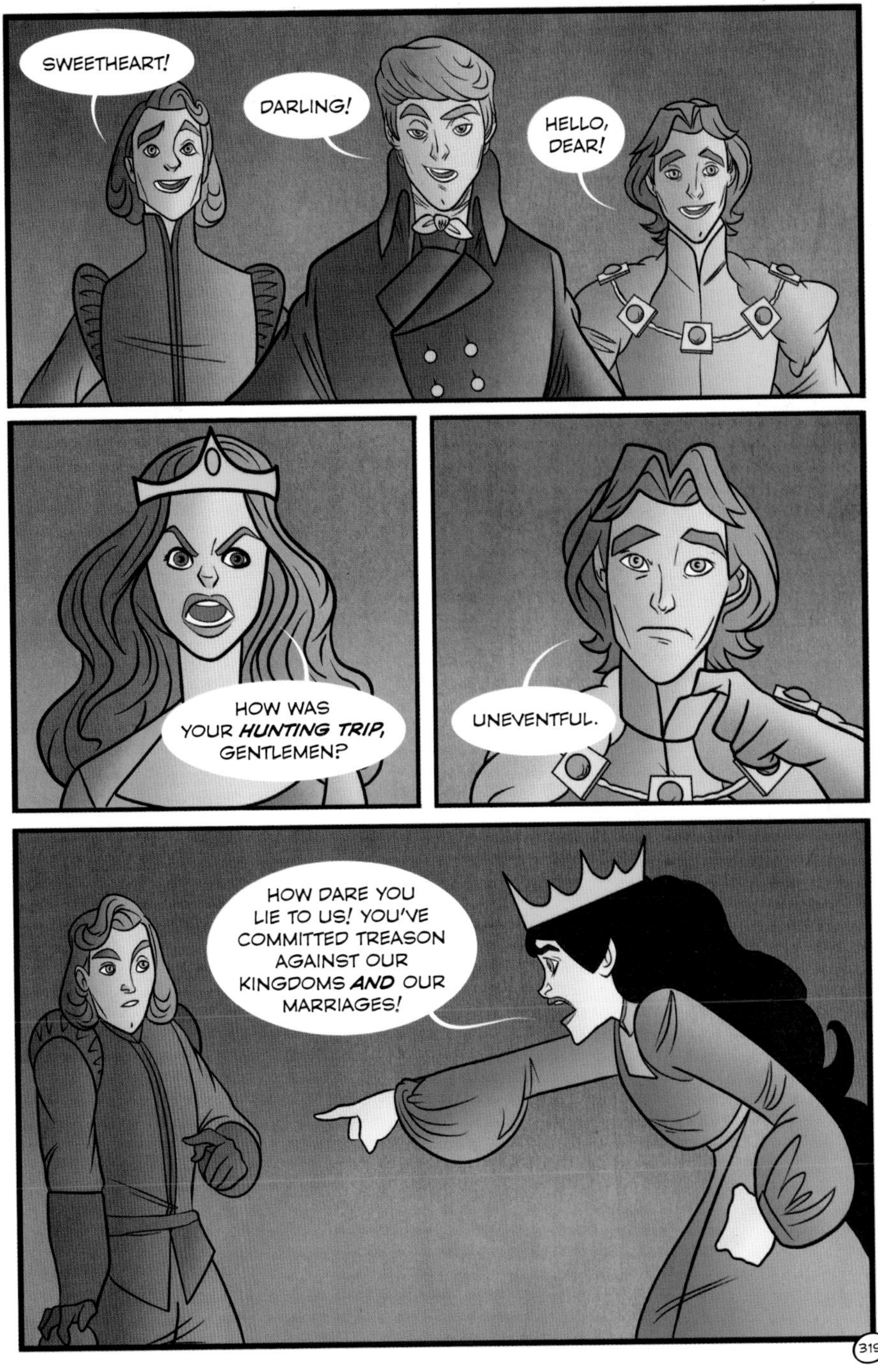
SWEETHEART!
DARLING!
HELLO, DEAR!
HOW WAS YOUR HUNTING TRIP, GENTLEMEN?
UNEVENTFUL.
HOW DARE YOU LIE TO US! YOU'VE COMMITTED TREASON AGAINST OUR KINGDOMS AND OUR MARRIAGES!

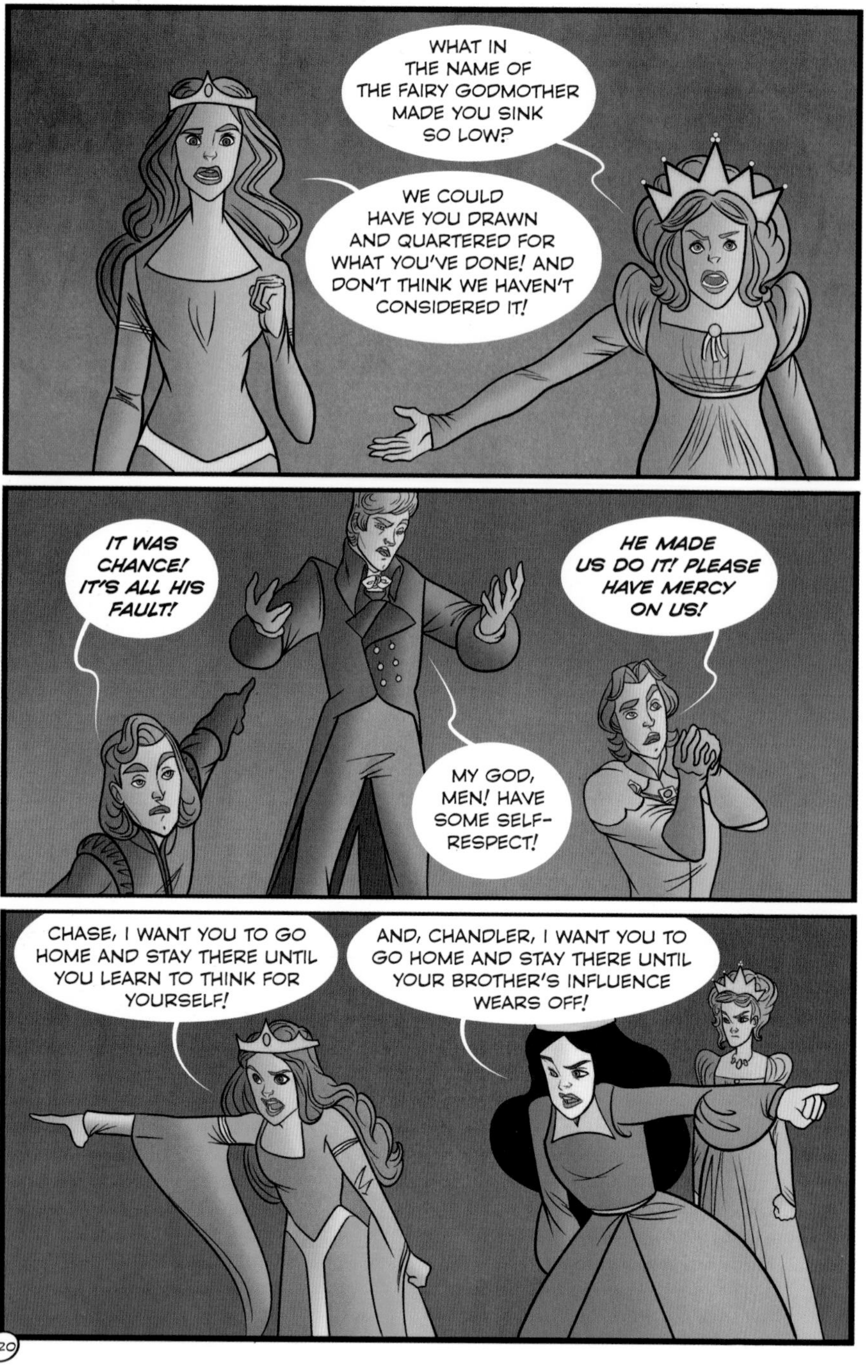
WHAT IN THE NAME OF THE FAIRY GODMOTHER MADE YOU SINK SO LOW?
WE COULD HAVE YOU DRAWN AND QUARTERED FOR WHAT YOU'VE DONE! AND DON'T THINK WE HAVEN'T CONSIDERED IT!
IT WAS CHANCE! IT'S ALL HIS FAULT!
HE MADE US DO IT! PLEASE HAVE MERCY ON US!
MY GOD, MEN! HAVE SOME SELF-RESPECT!
CHASE, I WANT YOU TO GO HOME AND STAY THERE UNTIL YOU LEARN TO THINK FOR YOURSELF!
AND, CHANDLER, I WANT YOU TO GO HOME AND STAY THERE UNTIL YOUR BROTHER'S INFLUENCE WEARS OFF!

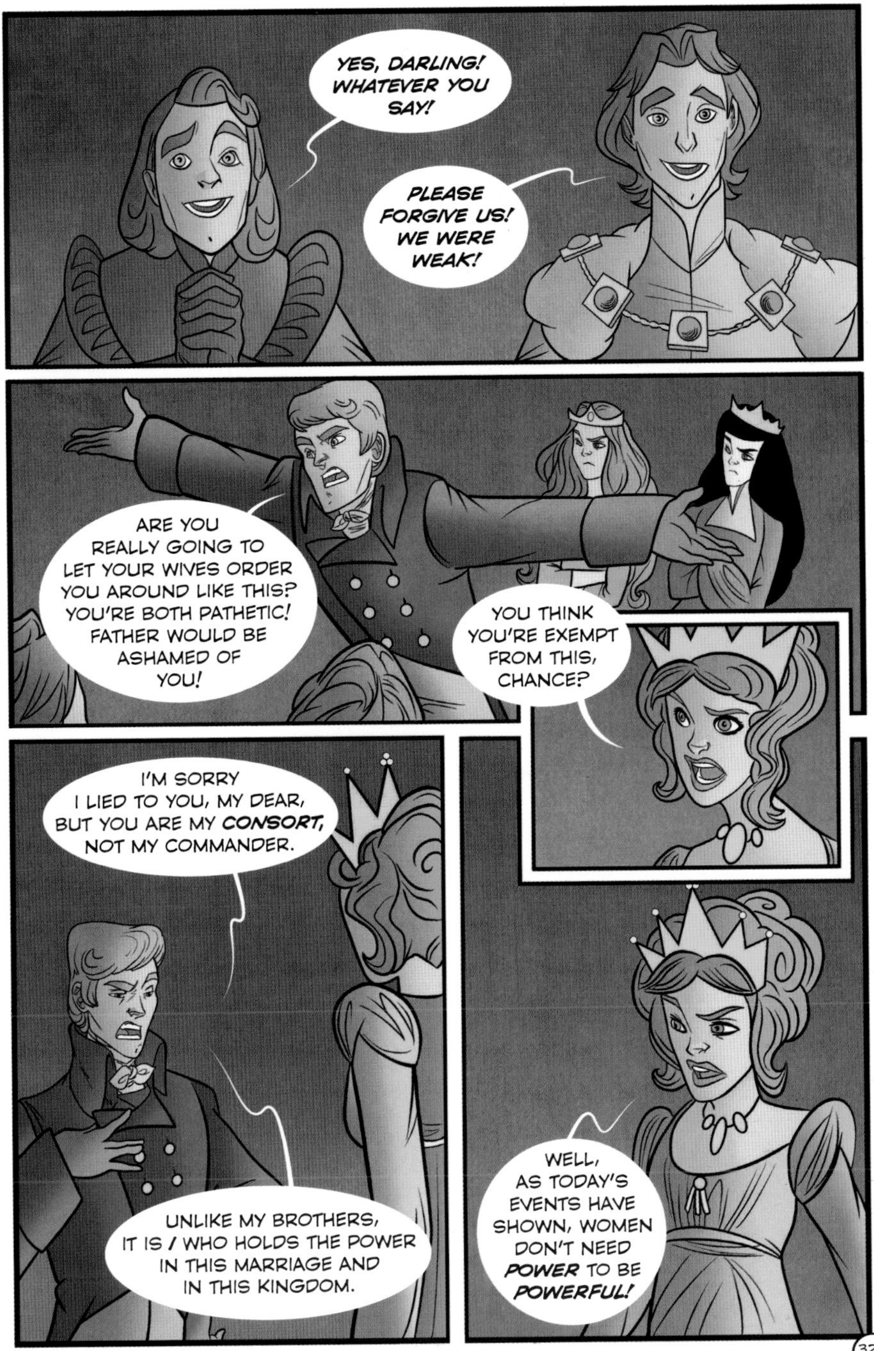
YES, DARLING! WHATEVER YOU SAY!
PLEASE FORGIVE US! WE WERE WEAK!
ARE YOU REALLY GOING TO LET YOUR WIVES ORDER YOU AROUND LIKE THIS? YOU'RE BOTH PATHETIC! FATHER WOULD BE ASHAMED OF YOU!
YOU THINK YOU'RE EXEMPT FROM THIS, CHANCE?
I'M SORRY I LIED TO YOU, MY DEAR, BUT YOU ARE MY CONSORT, NOT MY COMMANDER.
UNLIKE MY BROTHERS, IT IS I WHO HOLDS THE POWER IN THIS MARRIAGE AND IN THIS KINGDOM.
WELL, AS TODAY'S EVENTS HAVE SHOWN, WOMEN DON'T NEED POWER TO BE POWERFUL!

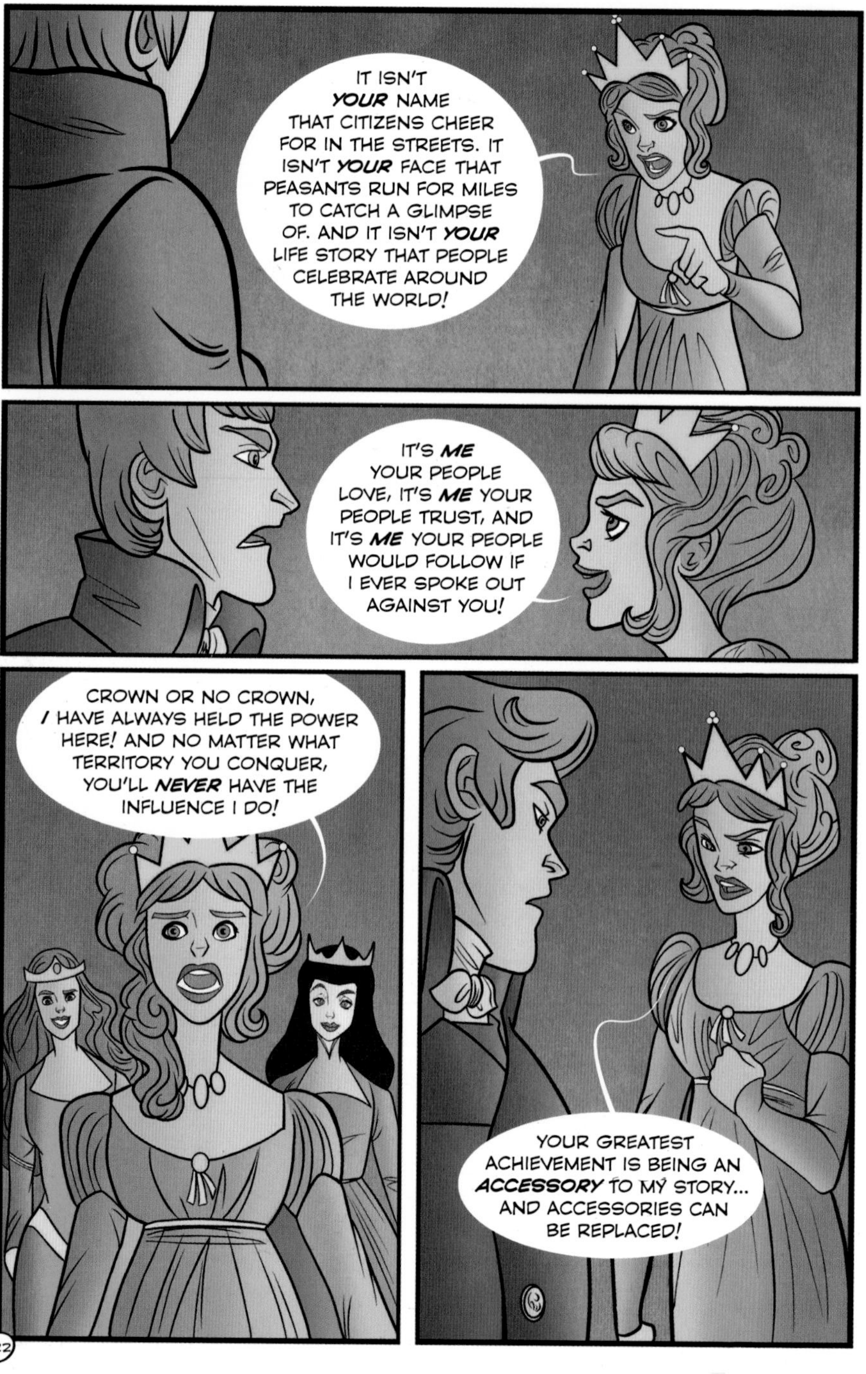
IT ISN'T YOUR NAME THAT CITIZENS CHEER FOR IN THE STREETS. IT ISN'T YOUR FACE THAT PEASANTS RUN FOR MILES TO CATCH A GLIMPSE OF. AND IT ISN'T YOUR LIFE STORY THAT PEOPLE CELEBRATE AROUND THE WORLD!
IT'S ME YOUR PEOPLE LOVE, IT'S ME YOUR PEOPLE TRUST, AND IT'S ME YOUR PEOPLE WOULD FOLLOW IF I EVER SPOKE OUT AGAINST YOU!
CROWN OR NO CROWN, I HAVE ALWAYS HELD THE POWER HERE! AND NO MATTER WHAT TERRITORY YOU CONQUER, YOU'LL NEVER HAVE THE INFLUENCE I DO!
YOUR GREATEST ACHIEVEMENT IS BEING AN ACCESSORY TO MY STORY... AND ACCESSORIES CAN BE REPLACED!

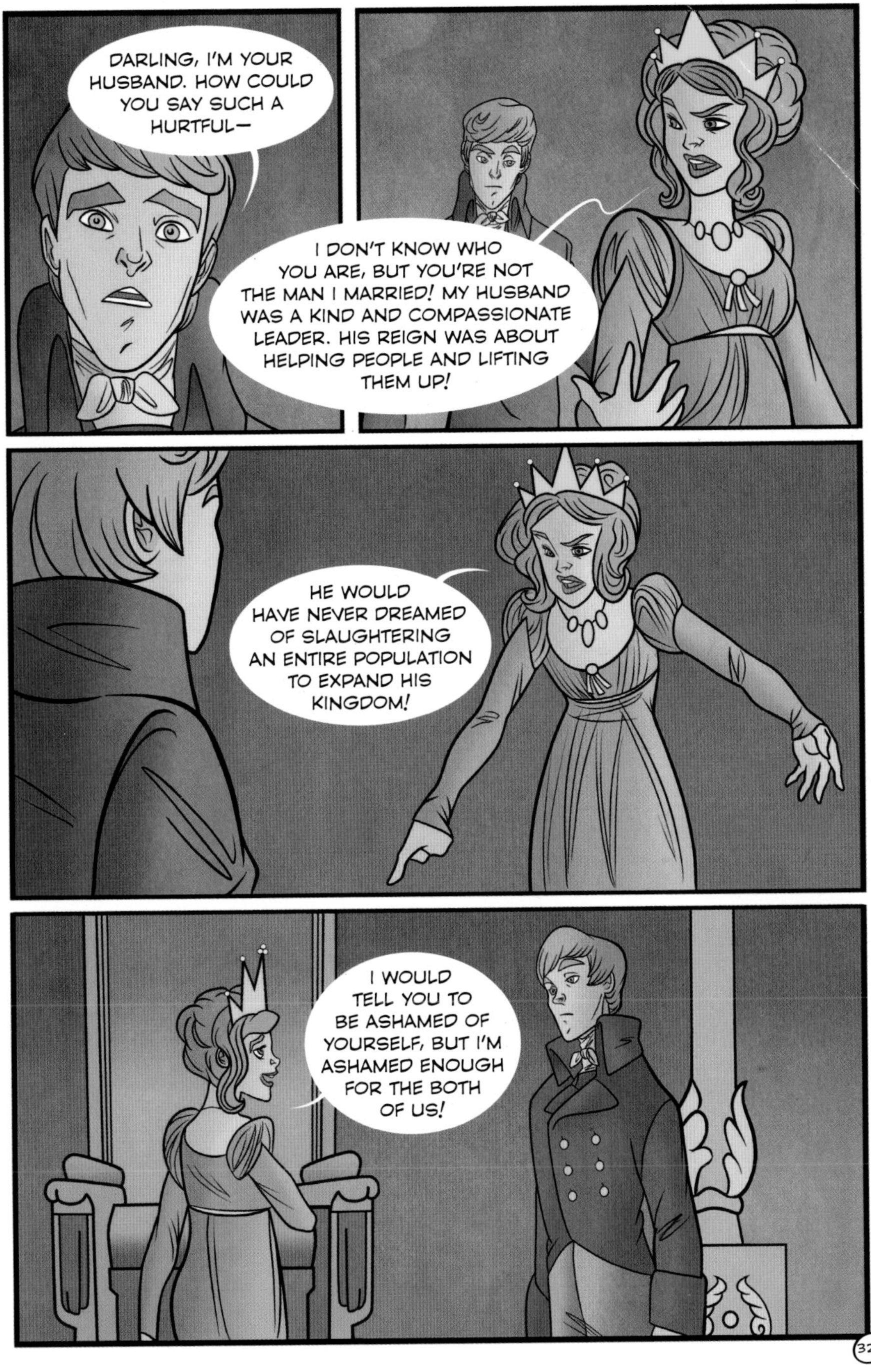
DARLING, I'M YOUR HUSBAND. HOW COULD YOU SAY SUCH A HURTFUL—
I DON'T KNOW WHO YOU ARE, BUT YOU'RE NOT THE MAN I MARRIED! MY HUSBAND WAS A KIND AND COMPASSIONATE LEADER. HIS REIGN WAS ABOUT HELPING PEOPLE AND LIFTING THEM UP!
HE WOULD HAVE NEVER DREAMED OF SLAUGHTERING AN ENTIRE POPULATION TO EXPAND HIS KINGDOM!
I WOULD TELL YOU TO BE ASHAMED OF YOURSELF, BUT I'M ASHAMED ENOUGH FOR THE BOTH OF US!

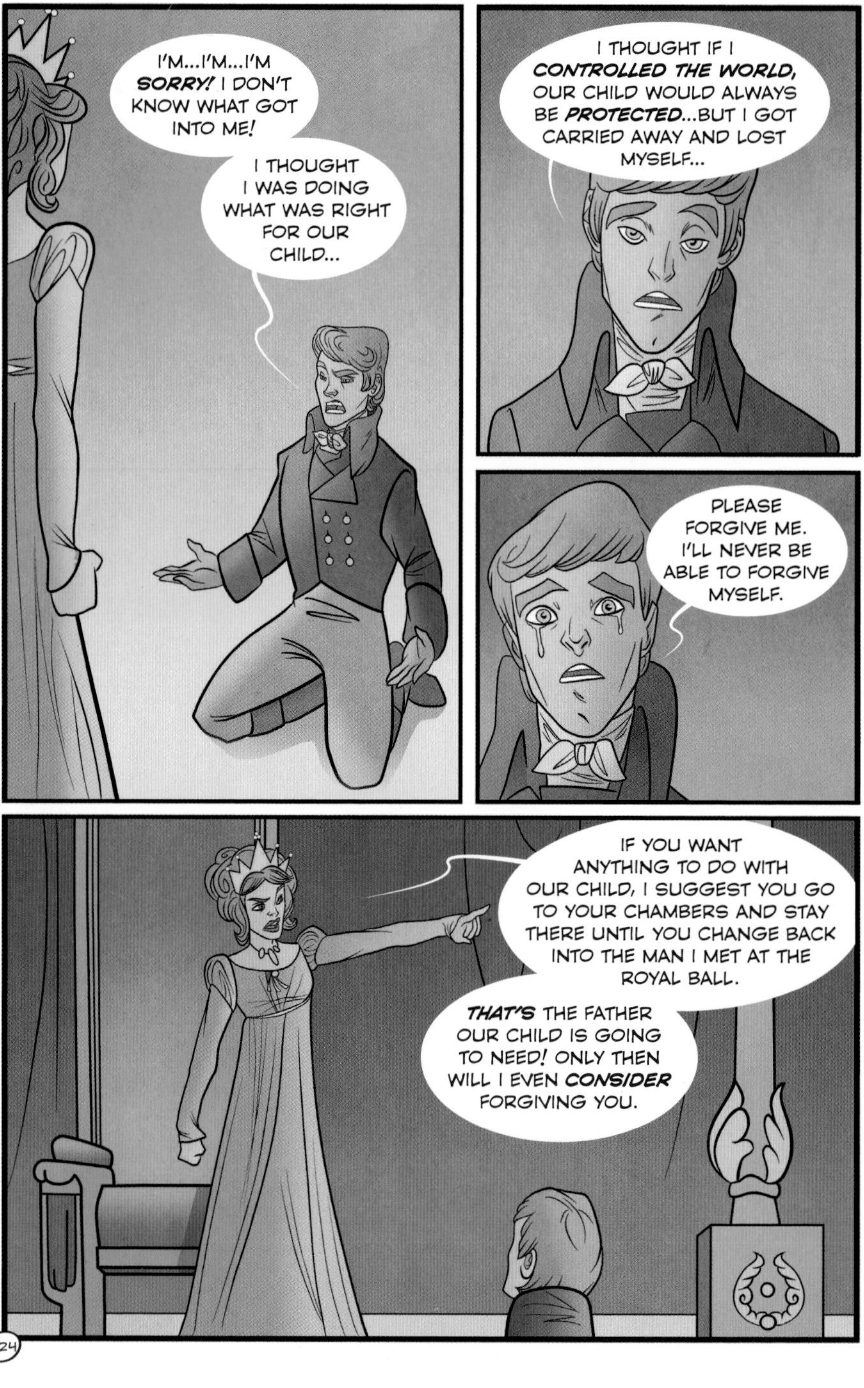
I'M...I'M...I'M SORRY! I DON'T KNOW WHAT GOT INTO ME!
I THOUGHT I WAS DOING WHAT WAS RIGHT FOR OUR CHILD...
I THOUGHT IF I CONTROLLED THE WORLD, OUR CHILD WOULD ALWAYS BE PROTECTED...BUT I GOT CARRIED AWAY AND LOST MYSELF...
PLEASE FORGIVE ME. I'LL NEVER BE ABLE TO FORGIVE MYSELF.
IF YOU WANT ANYTHING TO DO WITH OUR CHILD, I SUGGEST YOU GO TO YOUR CHAMBERS AND STAY THERE UNTIL YOU CHANGE BACK INTO THE MAN I MET AT THE ROYAL BALL.
THAT'S THE FATHER OUR CHILD IS GOING TO NEED! ONLY THEN WILL I EVEN CONSIDER FORGIVING YOU.

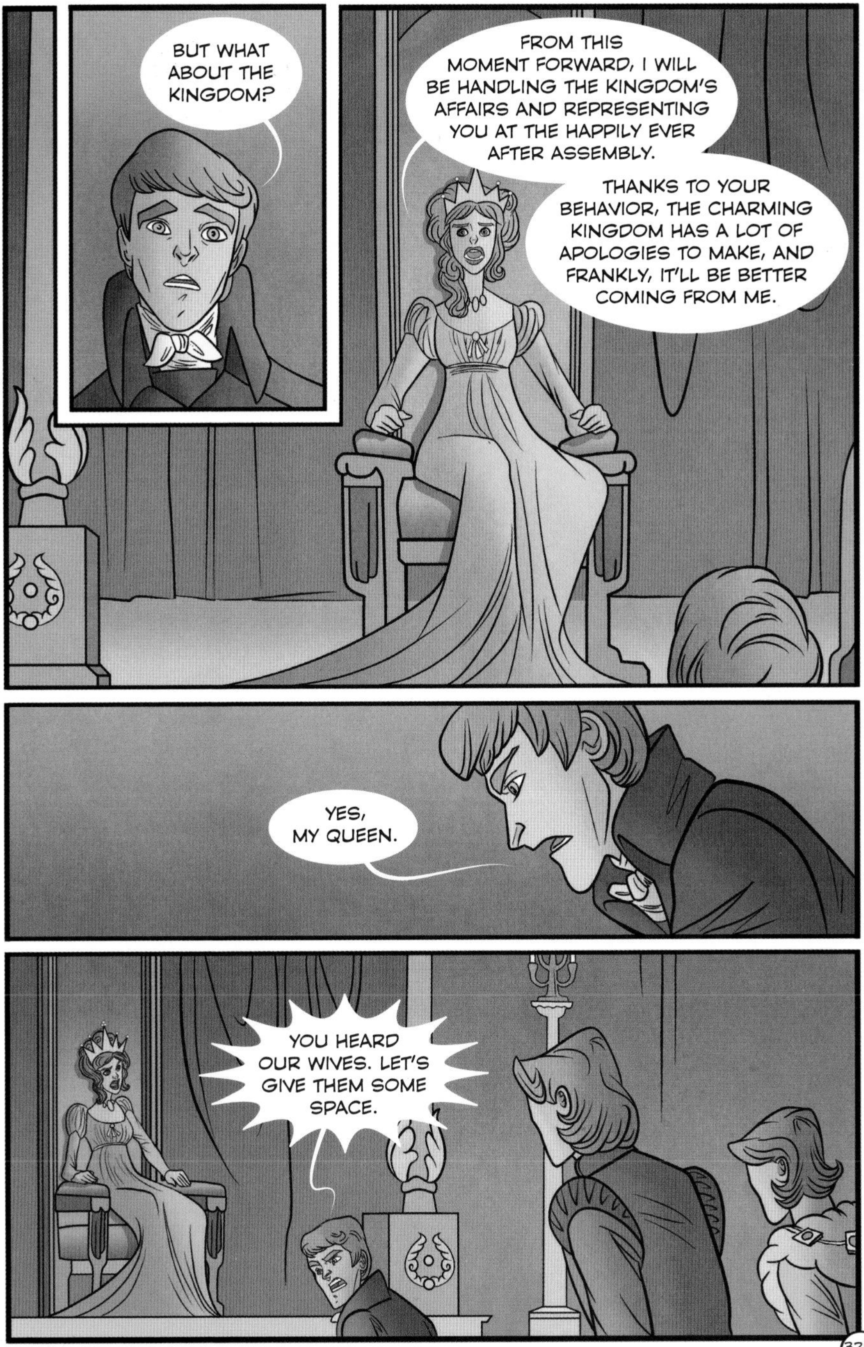
BUT WHAT ABOUT THE KINGDOM?
FROM THIS MOMENT FORWARD, I WILL BE HANDLING THE KINGDOM'S AFFAIRS AND REPRESENTING YOU AT THE HAPPILY EVER AFTER ASSEMBLY.
THANKS TO YOUR BEHAVIOR, THE CHARMING KINGDOM HAS A LOT OF APOLOGIES TO MAKE, AND FRANKLY, IT'LL BE BETTER COMING FROM ME.
YES, MY QUEEN.
YOU HEARD OUR WIVES. LET'S GIVE THEM SOME SPACE.

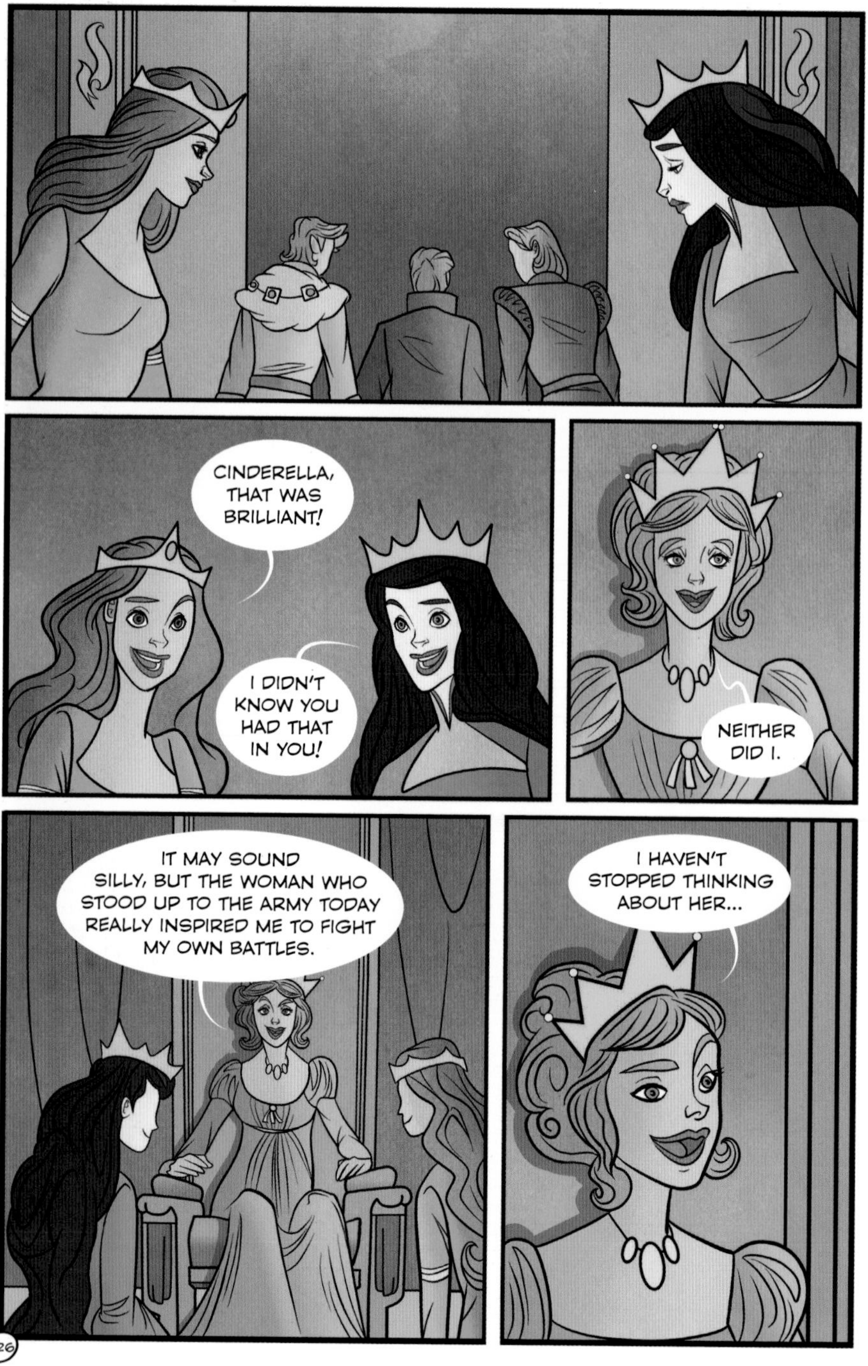
CINDERELLA, THAT WAS BRILLIANT!
I DIDN'T KNOW YOU HAD THAT IN YOU!
NEITHER DID I.
IT MAY SOUND SILLY, BUT THE WOMAN WHO STOOD UP TO THE ARMY TODAY REALLY INSPIRED ME TO FIGHT MY OWN BATTLES.
I HAVEN'T STOPPED THINKING ABOUT HER...

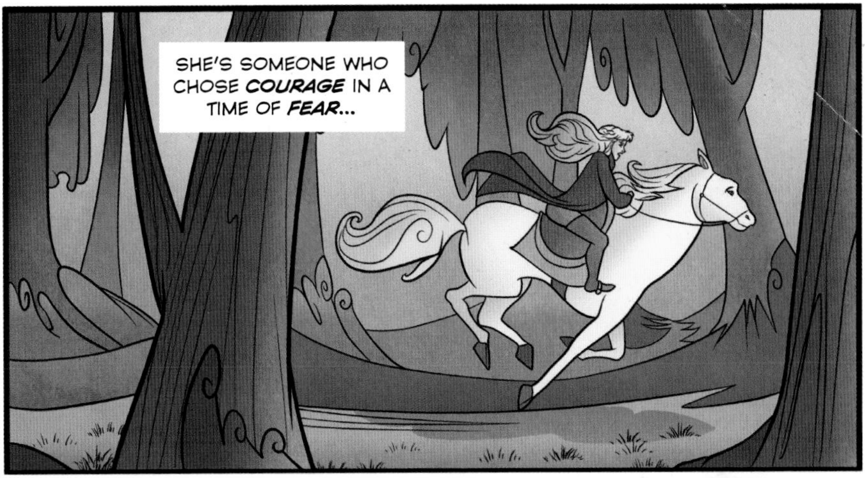
SHE'S SOMEONE WHO CHOSE *COURAGE* IN A TIME OF *FEAR*...

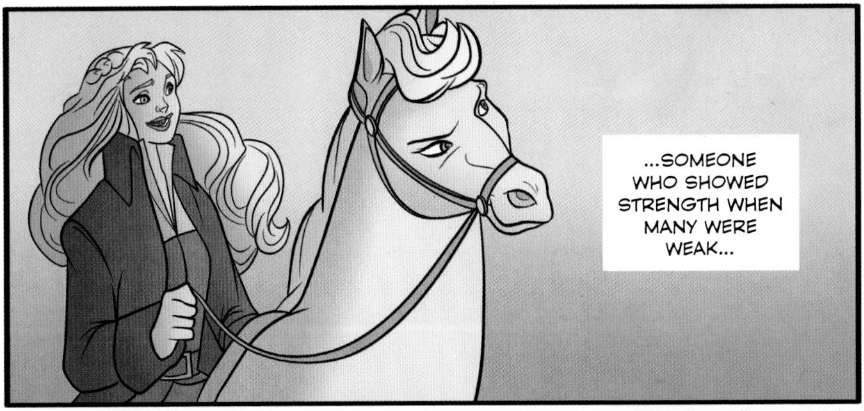
...SOMEONE WHO SHOWED STRENGTH WHEN MANY WERE WEAK...

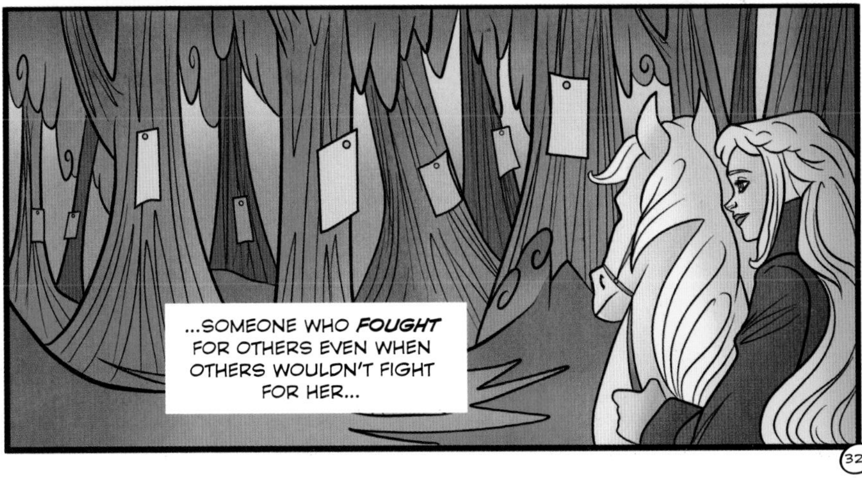
...SOMEONE WHO *FOUGHT* FOR OTHERS EVEN WHEN OTHERS WOULDN'T FIGHT FOR HER...

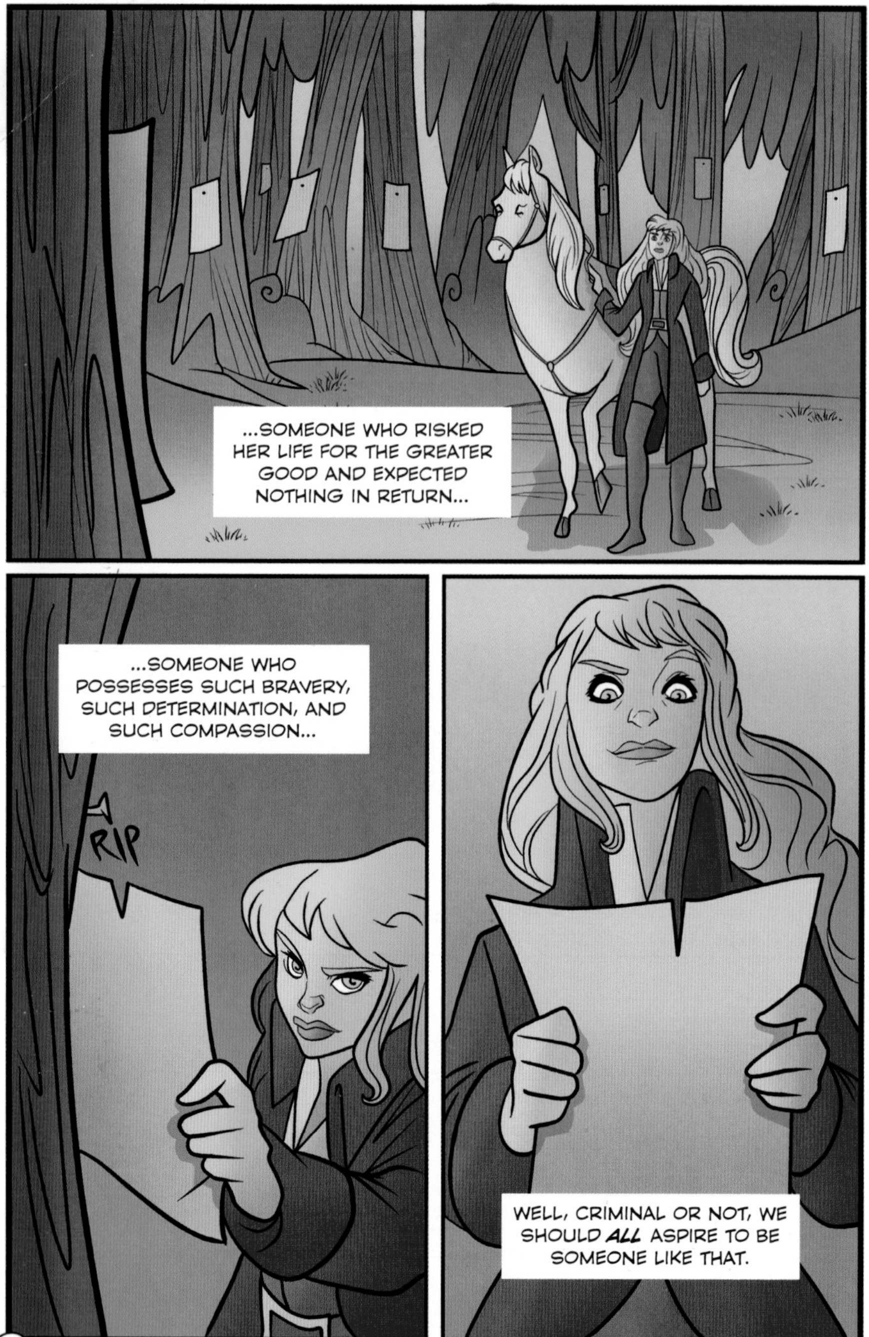
...SOMEONE WHO RISKED HER LIFE FOR THE GREATER GOOD AND EXPECTED NOTHING IN RETURN...
...SOMEONE WHO POSSESSES SUCH BRAVERY, SUCH DETERMINATION, AND SUCH COMPASSION...
RIP
WELL, CRIMINAL OR NOT, WE SHOULD ***ALL*** ASPIRE TO BE SOMEONE LIKE THAT.